THE GREEN TABLE

LANGUAGE OF DANCE SERIES

EDITOR
Ann Hutchinson Guest
Director, Language of Dance Centre
London, UK

ASSOCIATE EDITOR
Ray Cook
Associate Professor, Vassar College
Poughkeepsie, New York

THE GREEN TABLE
A Dance of Death in Eight Scenes

BOOK AND CHOREOGRAPHY BY
KURT JOOSS

MUSIC BY
F.A. COHEN

TEXT WRITTEN AND COMPILED BY
ANNA MARKARD

LABANOTATION BY
GRETCHEN SCHUMACHER

EDITED BY
ANN HUTCHINSON GUEST

Routledge
New York and London

Published in 2003 by
Routledge
29 West 35th Street
New York, NY 10001
www.routledge-ny.com

Published in Great Britain by
Routledge
11 New Fetter Lane
London EC4P 4EE
www.routledge.co.uk

Routledge is an imprint of the Taylor & Francis Group.

Printed in the United States of America on acid-free paper.

Permission for photographs in Part 1 given by: Renger-Patzch (page viii); McMillan (page x). In Part 2 permissions given by Jooss Archive (page 2); Renoldi (page 6); Shirali (page 6); BBC Hulton Picture Library (page 28); van Leeuwen (page 42); Jooss Archive (page 76); Anthony (page 76); For a full list of photographers in the section "Selected Photographs from *The Green Table*" please see pages 67-69 of Part 2.

10 9 8 7 6 5 4 3 2 1

ISBN 0-415-94255-1

Cataloging-in-Publication Data is available form the Library of Congress

CONTENTS

CONTENTS (continued)

INTRODUCTION TO THE SERIES

The *Language of Dance Series* aims to expand the literature of dance through publication of key works that cover a range of dance styles and dance periods.

A language is spoken, written and read. Those intimately involved in the study and performance of dance will have experienced the language of dance in its 'spoken' form, i.e. when it is danced. During the years spent in mastering dance, the component parts are discovered and become part of one's dance language. Through its written form these component parts, the 'building blocks' common to all forms of dance become clear, as well as how these blocks are used. The study of the Language of Dance incorporates these basic elements and the way they are put together to produce choreographic sentences. How the movement sequences are performed, the manner of "uttering" them, rests on the individual's interpretation.

Through careful selection of appropriate movement description, these gems of dance heritage have been translated into Labanotation, the highly developed method of analyzing and recording movement.

In the *Language of Dance Series*, understanding of the material is enriched through study and performance notes which provide an aid in exploring the movement sequences and bringing the choreography to life. Whenever possible there is included historical background to place the work in context, and additional information of value to researchers and dance scholars.

Dr. Ann Hutchinson Guest, Editor

(Renger-Patzsch)

Kurt Jooss 1932

FOREWORD

The Green Table is, without doubt, one of the great dance masterpieces of this century; Kurt Jooss's choreography with its telling simplicity and powerful imagery brilliantly illustrates the futility of war as political argument erupts, resulting in hostilities. Each ensuing scene is brought to its devastating conclusion as Death claims his victims. Nothing has been achieved as the manipulators of world affairs re-appear and resume their never ending arguments. On and on and on.... A powerful work with a message as true today as when it was created in 1932.

This now famous dance drama has certainly stood the test of time with countless performances by a wide range of companies during the past 65 years. However, without the meticulous attention to detail it has always received from Jooss and his colleagues, in particular his wife Aino Siimola, and now from his daughter Anna Markard, its fame and popularity would surely never have been so great. Obviously this sort of dedicated family supervision cannot go on forever so it is gratifying to know that steps are being taken to ensure that there will be experts available to supervise future productions and watch over the existing ones. Together with all the information contained in this new publication which incorporates a wealth of background material, the music score and the Labanotation score, the accurate reproduction of *The Green Table* is assured for future generations.

We all know that human memory is fallible - just witness the different versions of ballets, both classical and contemporary, that now exist as a result of being handed down from dancer to dancer and teacher to teacher - different timing, different stress on a particular step have often led to a disastrous change in the choreography. Now, of course, with the advent of movement notation we have complete and accurate records of many of the dance works created in this century and on which future productions can be based. Although most dance creations, including *The Green Table*, will always need a producer to breathe life into the final rehearsals, it is quite astounding to discover how much can be recreated from the score alone.

In my experience, having danced many roles in *The Green Table*, I have learned that this work depends largely for its success on the understanding of the dynamics of each character's movements rather than personal interpretation. This demands rigorous adherence to the choreography, musical phrasing and the use of the body as an instrument of expression, regardless of whether one is playing the central role of Death or an exhausted whore in the background of the sleazy brothel scene. The intensities, depth of feeling and concentration that is also required makes this ballet one of the most satisfying and moving works in which I have ever been privileged to appear.

We owe an enormous debt of gratitude to Ann Hutchinson Guest and all those who have worked so tirelessly with her on the compilation of this extremely important publication. This will ensure that Kurt Jooss's masterpiece *The Green Table* can be accurately performed in the future and keep its place as one of the great works of our dance heritage.

Peter Wright, May 1997

(McMillan)

Ann Hutchinson Guest, Kurt Jooss, New York, c. 1965

ACKNOWLEDGEMENTS

My greatest debt of gratitude goes to Ann Hutchinson Guest, my friend and colleague, who throughout the final stages of this publication, and no matter what the obstacles, has been steadfast and enthusiastic maintaining that "if I believe in a project I just keep going and somehow in the end things fall into place".

In the 80's Odette Blum, was the driving force and also instrumental in obtaining a grant from Ohio State University, thus enabling the testing, checking and correcting of the score. But first, during the 70's the new score had to be produced - this, funded by the Dance Notation Bureau, was subsequently undertaken by Muriel Topaz with Charlotte Wile and finally re-written by Gretchen Schumacher. This score is an admirable achievement by all concerned and I have been the happy witness!

My thanks also go to: Jane Marriett, Irene Politis, JoAnn Latus and Roma Dispirito for contributing their expert skills to the progress and completion of this project. Spreading pages of the score around her on the floor, Clare Lidbury checked and queried what she saw in rehearsals and greatly helped with proof reading. Above all my admiration and special thanks go to Jane Dulieu who has been the coordinator, weaving together the multiple threads relating to the physical production of these volumes. Claudia Jeschke and Suzanne K. Walther have kindly donated their articles thereby enriching our publication. Many photographers generously waived their fees thus making the wide selection of photographs possible. The rehearsal music has been meticulously edited and re-written by Jonathan Still.

I am endebted and most grateful to the following for their grants and contributions:
Dance Notation Bureau, New York
Department of Research and Graduate Studies, Ohio State University
Department of Dance and Seed Grant Program, Ohio State University
Elmgrant Trust, Dartington Hall, Totnes
Jooss Estate, Hamburg
Language of Dance Centre, London
Carina Ari Memorial Foundation, Stockholm

A lovely, most welcome surprise was a contribution from the estate of Jack Emerson Skinner. Jack, whom I remember well, joined Ballets Jooss during the war as a pacifist conscientious objector. On the Company's British tours with CEMA (Council for the Encouragement of Music and the Arts), one of his roles was the Old Soldier in *The Green Table* and it is most fitting that a contribution to this book has been made in his memory.

Hermann, my husband, has been a critical sounding board, he also influenced the layout and "look" of these volumes and has given me support and confidence throughout. My thanks and appreciation to all for their active involvement, support and belief in this demanding project.

Anna Markard

THE GREEN TABLE

Part 1

The Labanotation Score

LABANOTATION GLOSSARY

Keys for Score

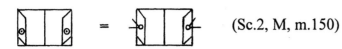 (Sc.2, M, m.150)

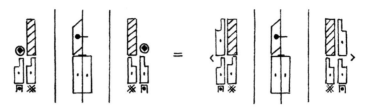 Hold according to the standard system of reference. (Sc.2, G, m.122)

For example:

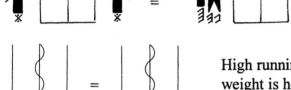

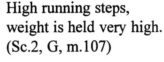

Hands down, palms touching side seam of pants (side of pelvis). (Sc.3, P, m.74)

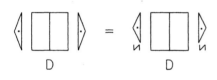

High running steps, weight is held very high. (Sc.2, G, m.107)

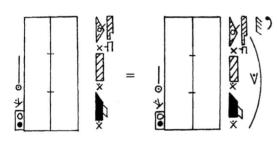

When Death's arms are notated without a pre-sign, it is understood that the extremities are at the periphery of the kinesphere, i.e. they are straight, not in the neutral state (ⱴ). (Sc.2, D, m.5)

Items specific to Scenes 1 and 8 - The Gentlemen in Black

This and similar movements begin with central initiation which flows to the periphery, ending with a clear emphasis on the hand. (Sc.1, b, m.13)

All high levels are on full ball unless otherwise specified. (Sc.1, m.14)

All retained contacts are done with a straight knee unless otherwise specified. (Sc.1,e, m.16)

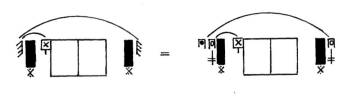   Left hand contacts waist at back, right hand contacts left hand. (Sc.1, a,b, m.22)

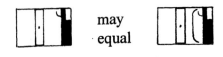   All leg gestures under the table may take weight as needed to facilitate the movement. (Sc.1, a,c,e,d, m.19)

    Lowering of center of gravity. (Sc.1, b, m.54-56)

    Hands are approximately level with mid-chest. (Sc.1, g, m.29)

Table

In the Table Scenes (Sc.1 and Sc.8), all ⅜ grasps are on edge of table, also ⇑ ⇑ supports, elsewhere the floor is understood.

When the hand is contacting the table the thumb is hooked under the edge of the table, palms are flat on top of the table.

(Sc.1, a,c,e,d, m.17)   (Sc.1, b, starting position)

    Supporting weight on table. (Sc.1, a, m.93)

    When a body part is indicated to be touching the table, the level of the supporting legs will be either middle or low according to what is necessary. (Sc.1, a, m.27)

Generally when the dancer is near the table their hips or thighs should be touching the table.

    Front of pelvis touches front edge of table. (Sc.1, m.73)

floor   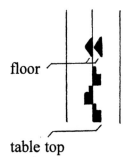   After a support is indicated to be on the table, supporting on the table continues until an indication for support on the floor is written. (Sc.1, k, m.94,95)

table top

Entrances and Exits

1. Generally, entrances are unemphasized.
2. The specific number of exit steps, where notated, are to be performed as written.

Orientation

Face line of direction. (Sc.2, B, m.152)

Face focal point. (Sc.1, m.61)

• = z   Torso turns to face focal point. (Sc.3, B, m.5)

Turn right or left to face focal point. (Sc.1, h,j,g,f, m.61)

Rise at start of right or left turn to end facing the focal point. (Sc.6, U,R,K,N, m.97)

Rise at start of turn right or left to end with back to the focal point. (Sc.6, A,Y,Z,X, m.97)

Track Pins

Track pins are signs which indicate relationship to the center lines of the body. Track pins are used when more specificity is required for a limb. They may be used with sagittal, lateral and diagonal movements.

The basic symbol for showing tracks is: ǂ   (Sc.1, j, m.15)

Sagittal Tracks for the Arms:
There are five sagittal tracks for the arms.
They are:

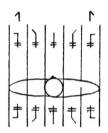

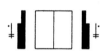 Hands are on the center line (touching is not assumed). (Sc.1, a,c,e,d, m.20)

 The extremity of the limb will be in the track which lies in front of the opposite shoulder. (Sc.1, k, m.45)

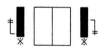 The extremity of the left limb will be in the track which lies behind the right shoulder. The extremity of the right limb will be in the track which lies in front of the left shoulder. (Sc.3, D, m.53)

 The extremity of the limbs will be in the intermediate track toward the opposite arm.(Sc.1, a, m.13)

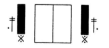 Hands on center line behind back. (Sc.1, k, m.96)

 Arm in left intermediate track behind back. (Sc.3, b, m.7)

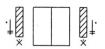 Extremities next to center line, i.e. with a slight space between them. (Sc.2, D, m.8)

Dynamic signs and usages

⚐ Accent without sound. (Sc.1, e, m.13)   ⚑ Accent with sound. (Sc.1, f, m.17)

Large accent signs when placed all the way out on right refer to the whole movement.

The whole movement is accented
without sound. (Sc.1, m.38)

The whole movement is accented
with sound. (Sc.2, D, m.21)

In a staccato action the accent is placed beside the action, exactly in relation to the beat and of
the same size as the action, e.g. Sc.2, D, m.29.
When an accent sign is placed at the beginning or end of a symbol or series of symbols it will
indicate dynamic phrasing: impactive: e.g. Sc.2, D, m.21 (series of symbols), Sc.2, D, m.26
(one symbol), impulsive: Sc.3, P, m.98.
An accent sign placed beside a foot hook or contact bow on a movement symbol will indicate
timing of accent according to the general timing convention for touches e.g. Sc.7, D, m.96, i.e.
touch where the symbol begins.
An accent will indicate exact timing in relation to the beat, e.g. Sc.1, j, m.30.
Additional qualities, besides suddeness, should be in context.

Death's boots will create sound even when not specially indicated.

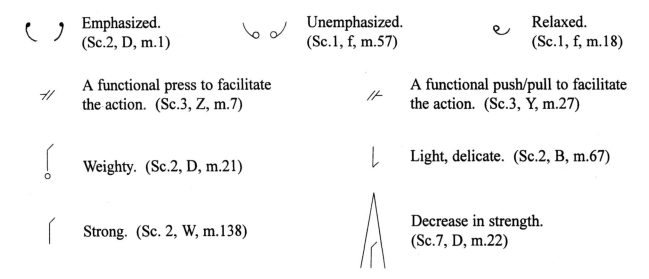

| | Emphasized. (Sc.2, D, m.1) | | Unemphasized. (Sc.1, f, m.57) | | Relaxed. (Sc.1, f, m.18) |

A functional press to facilitate the action. (Sc.3, Z, m.7)

A functional push/pull to facilitate the action. (Sc.3, Y, m.27)

Weighty. (Sc.2, D, m.21)

Light, delicate. (Sc.2, B, m.67)

Strong. (Sc. 2, W, m.138)

Decrease in strength. (Sc.7, D, m.22)

The use of single effort elements has been made with the understanding that the performer
exphasizes each in the dynamic context of the phrase. It is not intended to suggest that it is the
only quality to be performed.

Strong and sudden. (Sc.2, D, m.17)   Light and sustained. (Sc.5, W, m.28,29)   Strong and bound. (Sc.3, P, m.78)

Strong and direct.
(Sc.2, D, m.24)

Light and bound.
(Sc.7, B, m.68)

Impactive phrase: becoming increasingly strong and fast concluding with an impact. (Sc.2, D, m.17)

Becoming increasingly light and bound. (Sc.7, B, m.68)

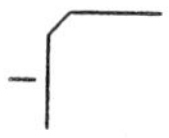

Strong, direct and sustained. (Sc.4, P, m.45)

Strong, direct and sudden. (Sc.5, W, m.65)

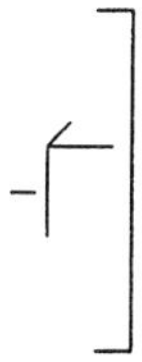

Bound flow, sustained and strong qualities are maintained. (Sc.2, D, m.16)

Phrasing bow. A dynamic or choreographic entity. (Sc.2, B, m.73)

Phrasing bow. Impulsive, energy diminishing from a greater to a lesser intensity. (Sc.3, P, m.92)

Body Parts

Buttocks.
(Sc.6, U,R,K,N m.97)

Lower buttocks.
(Sc.6, P, m.60)

Mouth.
(Sc.1, j, m.30)

Open mouth as if yelling.
(Sc.1, j, m.30)

Look at dancer X.
(Sc.2, B, m.83)

Look at dancer G's ankles.
(Sc.4, P, m.46)

Look at the back of dancer G's head. (Sc.4, P, m.46)

Look at Dancer "O".
(Sc.2, W, m.124)

Right eye.
(Sc.4, P, m.42)

Left eye.
(Sc.3, Z,X,A, m.54)

Top of the head.
(Sc.1, a, m.27)

Right side high of the head. (Sc.1, a, m.27)

Front of neck.
(Sc.5, Z, m.94)

Left side of neck.
(Sc.1, e, m.41)

Under the left shoulder.
(Sc.3, Z, m.5)

Heart.
(Sc.1, e, m.16)

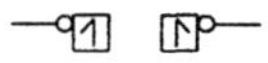

Upper edge of shoulders.
(Sc.2, D, m.19)

Back of the knuckles.
(Sc.5, A,X,Y, m.129)

Clenched tight fist.
(Sc.1, h,g, m.45)

Relaxed fist.
(Sc.1, g, f, m.14)

Backward sagittal spread of the fingers. (Sc.3, P, m.90)

Lateral spread of the hand. (Sc.2, O, m.129)

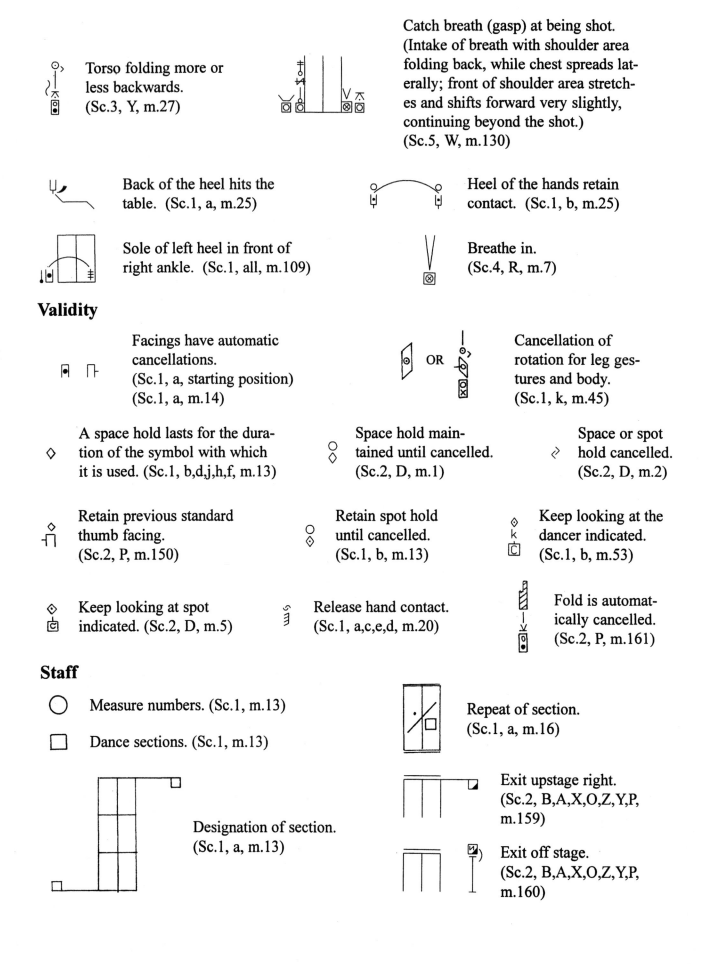

Torso folding more or less backwards. (Sc.3, Y, m.27)

Catch breath (gasp) at being shot. (Intake of breath with shoulder area folding back, while chest spreads laterally; front of shoulder area stretches and shifts forward very slightly, continuing beyond the shot.) (Sc.5, W, m.130)

Back of the heel hits the table. (Sc.1, a, m.25)

Heel of the hands retain contact. (Sc.1, b, m.25)

Sole of left heel in front of right ankle. (Sc.1, all, m.109)

Breathe in. (Sc.4, R, m.7)

Validity

Facings have automatic cancellations. (Sc.1, a, starting position) (Sc.1, a, m.14)

Cancellation of rotation for leg gestures and body. (Sc.1, k, m.45)

A space hold lasts for the duration of the symbol with which it is used. (Sc.1, b,d,j,h,f, m.13)

Space hold maintained until cancelled. (Sc.2, D, m.1)

Space or spot hold cancelled. (Sc.2, D, m.2)

Retain previous standard thumb facing. (Sc.2, P, m.150)

Retain spot hold until cancelled. (Sc.1, b, m.13)

Keep looking at the dancer indicated. (Sc.1, b, m.53)

Keep looking at spot indicated. (Sc.2, D, m.5)

Release hand contact. (Sc.1, a,c,e,d, m.20)

Fold is automatically cancelled. (Sc.2, P, m.161)

Staff

Measure numbers. (Sc.1, m.13)

Dance sections. (Sc.1, m.13)

Repeat of section. (Sc.1, a, m.16)

Designation of section. (Sc.1, a, m.13)

Exit upstage right. (Sc.2, B,A,X,O,Z,Y,P, m.159)

Exit off stage. (Sc.2, B,A,X,O,Z,Y,P, m.160)

 Pathway for a group of men. (Sc.2, m.148,149)

 Pathway for a group (any gender). (Sc.2, m.26,27)

 On floor plan. Dancer D takes a long time to cover this distance. (Sc.2, D, m.142-144)

Sectional Repeats

Scene 1 - The Gentlemen in Black

P   Opening pose. (Sc.1, a, m.16)

G   Gentlemen repeat. (Sc.1, m.13-28)

Scene 2 - The Dance of Death and Farewells

A   Death's solo. (Sc.2, D, m.1-15)

B   Death's solo. (Sc.2, D, 17-32)

S   Stamp (Death). (Sc.2, D, m.57)

F ⇑   Feet and Flag bounces. (Sc.2, B, m.77-80)

F   Bounces (feet only). (Sc.2, B, m.107)

M   March. (Sc.2, A, m.81)

Scene 3 - The Battle

C   Conflict. (Sc.3, m.2-7)

Scene 5 - The Partisan

D   Death walk. (Sc.5, D, m.106,107)

Scene 6 - The Brothel

R   Rocking. (Sc.6, L,U, m.1-4)

↓W   ↓W   Waltz. (Sc.6, m.98,99)

Props

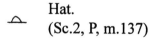 Hat. (Sc.2, P, m.137)

B   Belt. (Sc.5, W, m.10)

Pistol. (Sc.1, m.101)

Jacket pocket. (Sc.8, m.5)

Flag

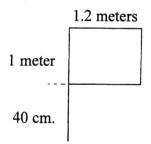
1.2 meters
1 meter
40 cm.

⊐   Flag. (Sc.2, B, m.60)

F   Pre-sign used to indicate direction of flag. (Sc.2, B, m.62)

If ⊙ is written for F, the flag continues the line of the arm or lower arm. The wrist will bend or rotate to achieve the direction for the flag. (Sc.2, B, m.66)

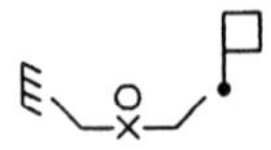

(Sc.2, B, m.60)    (Sc.2, B, m.107)

Below staff reminder to continue grasping flag.

Below the staff. Reminder of where flag is.
(Sc.3, Y, starting position)

The cloth.
(Sc.2, B, m.63)

The flag makes noise.
(Sc.2, B, m.63)

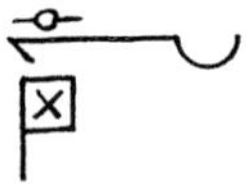

Flag over person.
(Sc.3, Y, m.27)

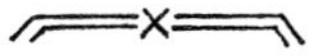

Sliding support on flag pole.
(Sc.2, B, m.63)

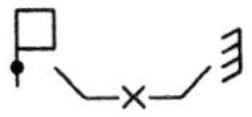

Placement of the dot indicates the point at which the flag is held.
(Sc.2, B, m.101)

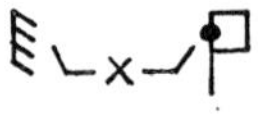

Pole held without gathering cloth.
(Sc.2, B, m.101)

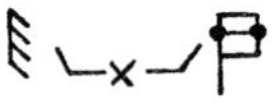

Gathered cloth held with pole.
(Sc.2, B, m.68)

Scarf

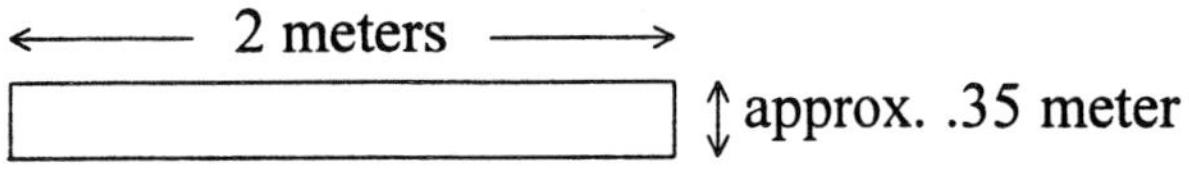

←——— 2 meters ———→

↕ approx. .35 meter

Wool crepe scarf
(Sc.5, W, m.5)

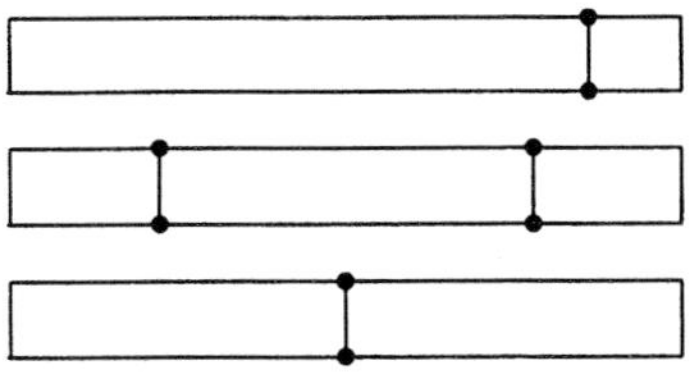

Where scarf is held by hands.
(Sc. 5, W, m.1)

Timing

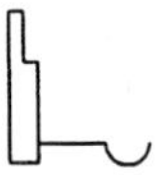

(Sc.2, Y, m.109)    (Sc.3, A, m.2) 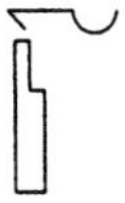   (Sc.1, c, m.56)

Addressing has time significance for gestures.

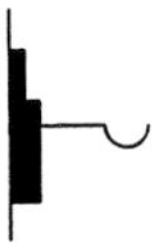

Addressing has no time significance for steps.

(Sc.2, G, m.108)

Freedom in timing (old sign).
(Sc.2, B, m.83)

Freedom in timing within overall duration.
(Sc.5, W, m.130,131)

Duration of travel-ing is ad lib.
(Sc.2, D, m.97-102)

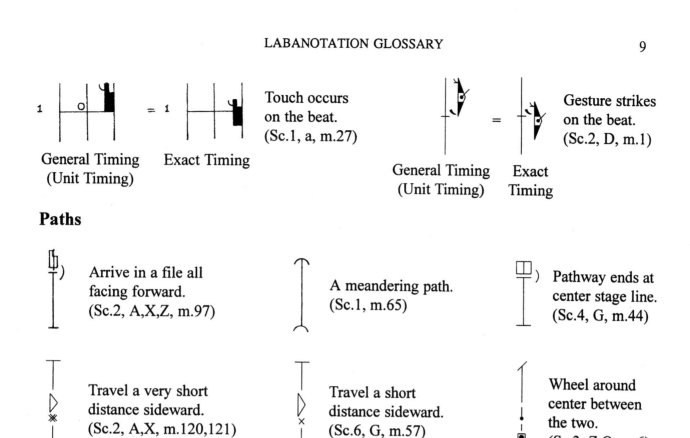

General Timing
(Unit Timing)   Exact Timing

Touch occurs
on the beat.
(Sc.1, a, m.27)

General Timing
(Unit Timing)   Exact Timing

Gesture strikes
on the beat.
(Sc.2, D, m.1)

Paths

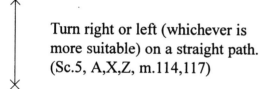

Arrive in a file all
facing forward.
(Sc.2, A,X,Z, m.97)

A meandering path.
(Sc.1, m.65)

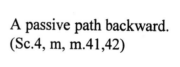

Pathway ends at
center stage line.
(Sc.4, G, m.44)

Travel a very short
distance sideward.
(Sc.2, A,X, m.120,121)

Travel a short
distance sideward.
(Sc.6, G, m.57)

Wheel around
center between
the two.
(Sc.3, Z,O, m.6)

Turn right or left (whichever is
more suitable) on a straight path.
(Sc.5, A,X,Z, m.114,117)

A passive path backward.
(Sc.4, m, m.41,42)

Miscellaneous

A real Labanotation "contraction", full
rounding of the spine, including the back
movement of the pelvis. Reader should be
careful to distinguish between ✕ and ⋎ .
(Sc.3, P, m.73)

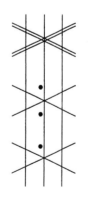

Whole body
closing gradually.
(Sc.7, P, m.85)

A rounding of the torso while the
shoulders are allowed to go slightly
forward of the hips. (Sc.3, p, m.96)

A black diamond inside a direction
symbol indicates that the movement is
performed on an undeviating path, the
direction judged from front at the end
of the turn. (Sc.1, k,j,h,g,f, m.23)

Curl up as you somersault
backwards (overall flexion).
(Sc.3, A, m.4)

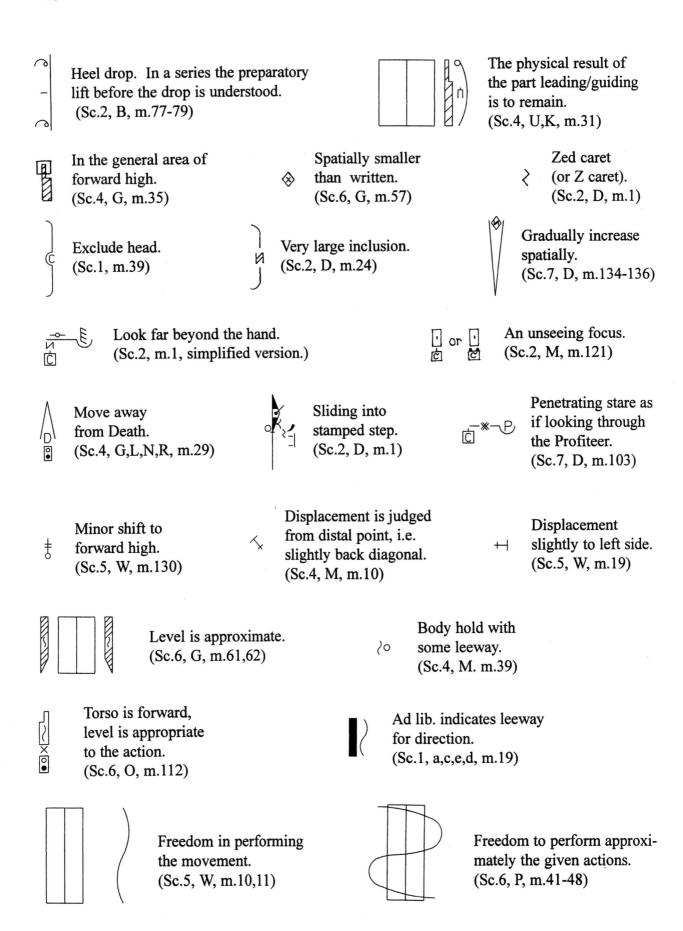

Heel drop. In a series the preparatory lift before the drop is understood. (Sc.2, B, m.77-79)

The physical result of the part leading/guiding is to remain. (Sc.4, U,K, m.31)

In the general area of forward high. (Sc.4, G, m.35)

Spatially smaller than written. (Sc.6, G, m.57)

Zed caret (or Z caret). (Sc.2, D, m.1)

Exclude head. (Sc.1, m.39)

Very large inclusion. (Sc.2, D, m.24)

Gradually increase spatially. (Sc.7, D, m.134-136)

Look far beyond the hand. (Sc.2, m.1, simplified version.)

An unseeing focus. (Sc.2, M, m.121)

Move away from Death. (Sc.4, G,L,N,R, m.29)

Sliding into stamped step. (Sc.2, D, m.1)

Penetrating stare as if looking through the Profiteer. (Sc.7, D, m.103)

Minor shift to forward high. (Sc.5, W, m.130)

Displacement is judged from distal point, i.e. slightly back diagonal. (Sc.4, M, m.10)

Displacement slightly to left side. (Sc.5, W, m.19)

Level is approximate. (Sc.6, G, m.61,62)

Body hold with some leeway. (Sc.4, M. m.39)

Torso is forward, level is appropriate to the action. (Sc.6, O, m.112)

Ad lib. indicates leeway for direction. (Sc.1, a,c,e,d, m.19)

Freedom in performing the movement. (Sc.5, W, m.10,11)

Freedom to perform approximately the given actions. (Sc.6, P, m.41-48)

BREAKDOWN OF CHOREOGRAPHIC CONTENT

	Dance Score Page (Part 1)	Measure	Music Score Page (Part 2)
Scene 1:			
The Gentlemen in Black	16		89
Tango	16	11	89
First Argument	26	29	90
Sways	26	35	90
Second Argument	28	45	90
Lobby	34	53	90
Dispute	41	61	91
Angry Steps	42	65	91
Révérence	44	69	91
Busy Steps	44	71	91
Reprise	46	77	92
Last Argument	46	93	92
Passés	51	101	93
Shot	51	109	93
Scene 2:			
The Dance of Death and Farewells	53		94
Death's Solo ('A' Section)	53	1	94
'B' Section	55	17	94
Reprise 'A'	56	33	96
Death Stands	57	49	97
Standard Bearer	57	61	97
1st Soldier	61	77	98
2nd Soldier	62	81	99
3rd Soldier	63	85	99
First Drill	65	93	99
Duet	68	106	100
Trio	75	122	101
Profiteer	81	137	102
Second Drill	82	138	102
Circle March	86	146	102
Diagonal	93	154	103

	Dance Score Page (Part 1)	Measure	Music Score Page (Part 2)
Scene 5: (continued)			
First Run	176	60	118
Climax	176	68	118
Second Soldiers' Crossing	178	86	119
Second Run	179	92	119
Kill	180	94	119
Death Walks	183	106	120
Scene 6:			
The Brothel	192		122
First Duet	200	33	123
Balancés	206	57	124
Second Duet	208	65	124
Third Duet	212	81	124
Profiteer Claps	215	96	125
Fourth Duet	221	113	125
Spiral	224	137	126
Kiss	226	151	126
Diagonal with Death	227	157	127
Death and Girl	229	169	127
Military Waltz	229	173	127
Circle	231	183	127
Threading	232	191	128
Cradle	233	199	128
Scene 7:			
The Aftermath	235		129
Walk Begins	238	12	129
Procession	239	22	130
Clock Step	241	28	130
Mowing Down	244	36	131
Standard Bearer	245	43	132
Death Reaches Out	246	47	132
Runs	248	55	132
Last Struggle	249	59	133

	Dance Score Page (Part 1)	Measure	Music Score Page (Part 2)

THE CHOREOGRAPHIC SCORE

OF

THE GREEN TABLE

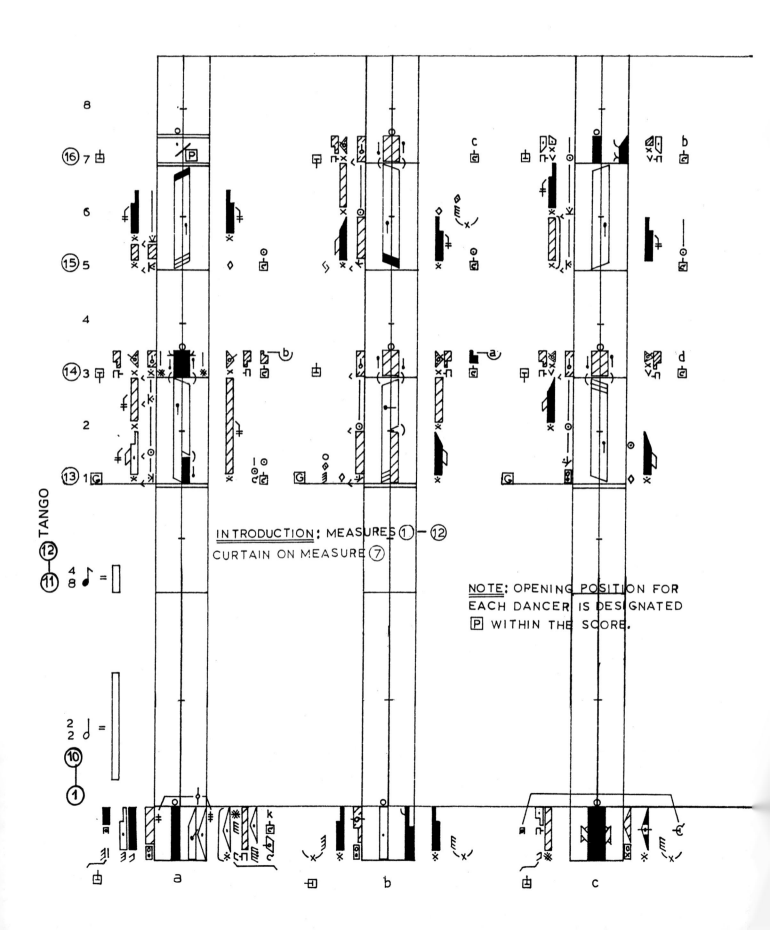

INTRODUCTION: MEASURES ①–⑫

CURTAIN ON MEASURE ⑦

NOTE: OPENING POSITION FOR
EACH DANCER IS DESIGNATED
P WITHIN THE SCORE.

TANGO

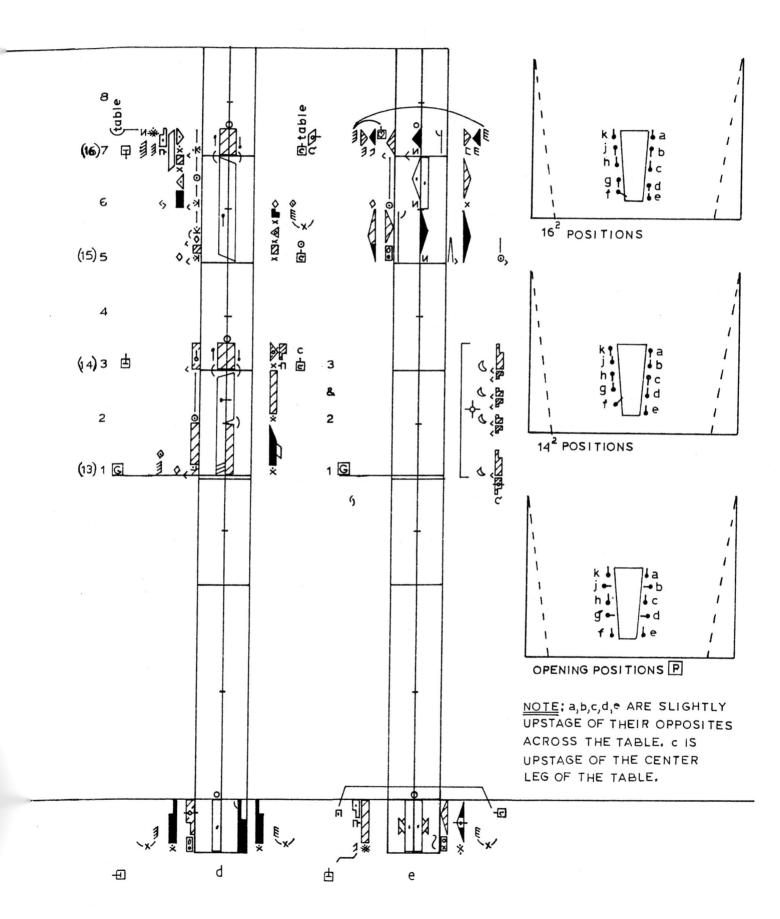

16² POSITIONS

14² POSITIONS

OPENING POSITIONS P

NOTE: a,b,c,d,e ARE SLIGHTLY
UPSTAGE OF THEIR OPPOSITES
ACROSS THE TABLE. c IS
UPSTAGE OF THE CENTER
LEG OF THE TABLE.

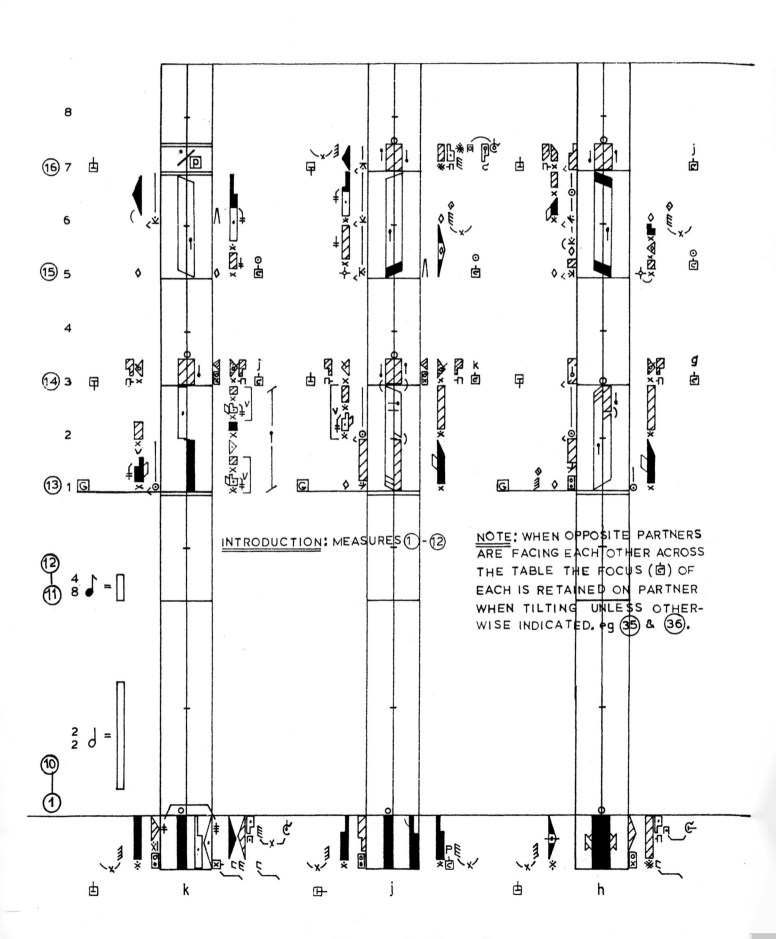

INTRODUCTION: MEASURES ① - ⑫

NOTE: WHEN OPPOSITE PARTNERS ARE FACING EACH OTHER ACROSS THE TABLE THE FOCUS (⌸) OF EACH IS RETAINED ON PARTNER WHEN TILTING UNLESS OTHERWISE INDICATED. eg ㉟ & ㊱.

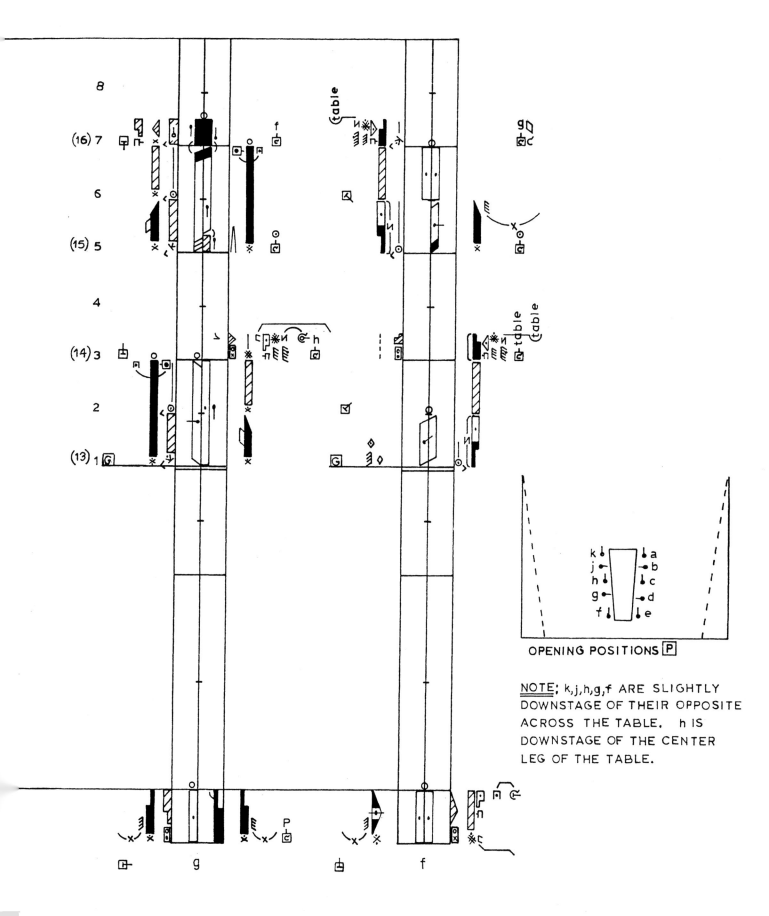

OPENING POSITIONS [P]

NOTE: k,j,h,g,f ARE SLIGHTLY
DOWNSTAGE OF THEIR OPPOSITE
ACROSS THE TABLE. h IS
DOWNSTAGE OF THE CENTER
LEG OF THE TABLE.

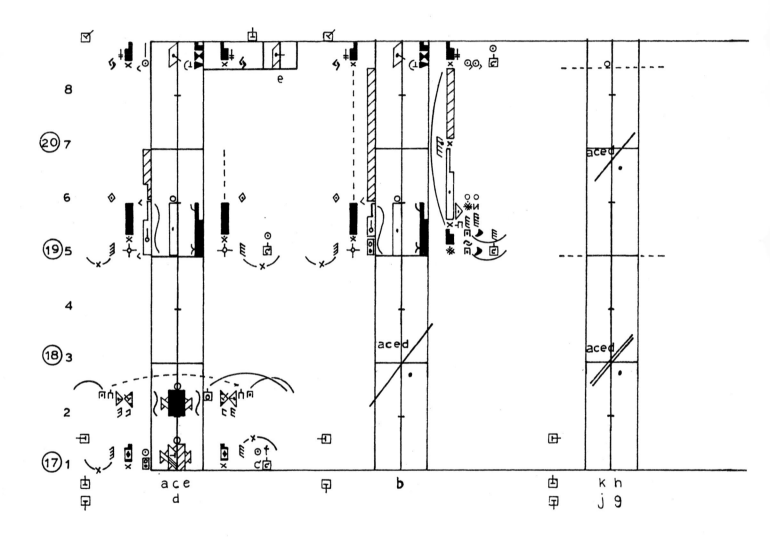

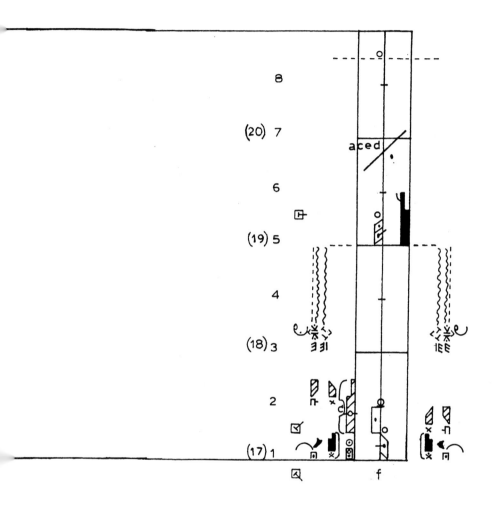

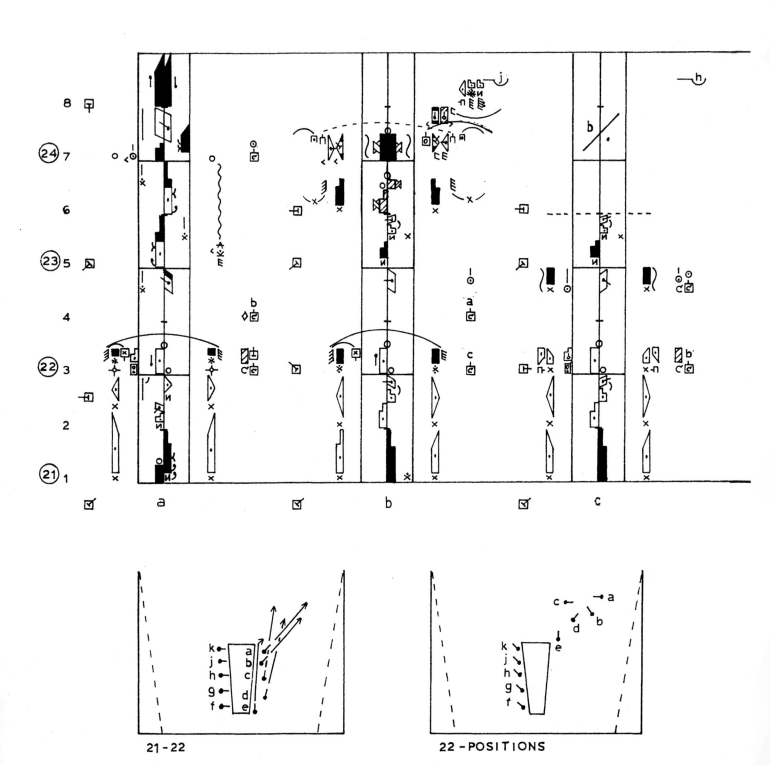

21-22

22-POSITIONS

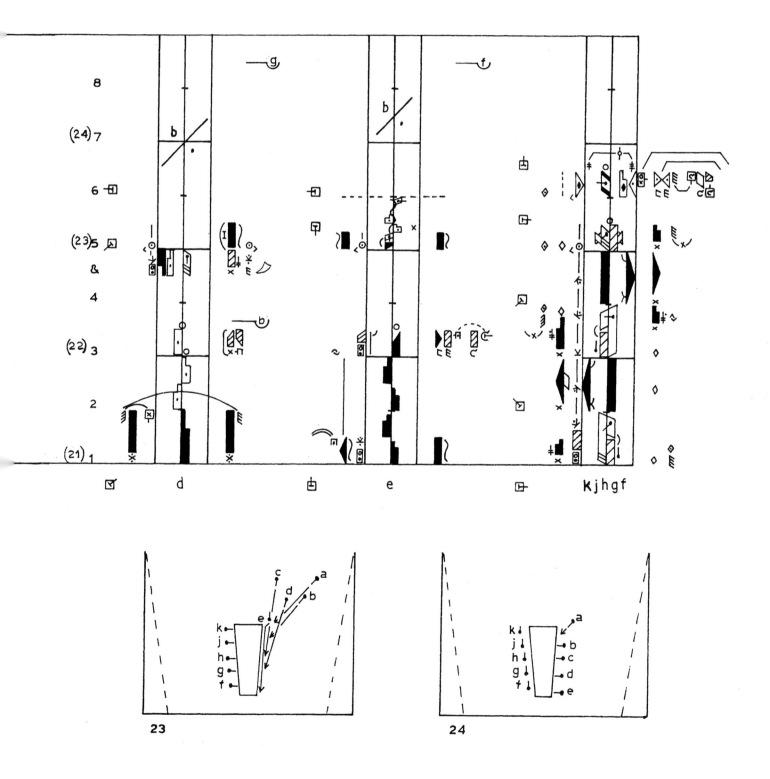

23

24

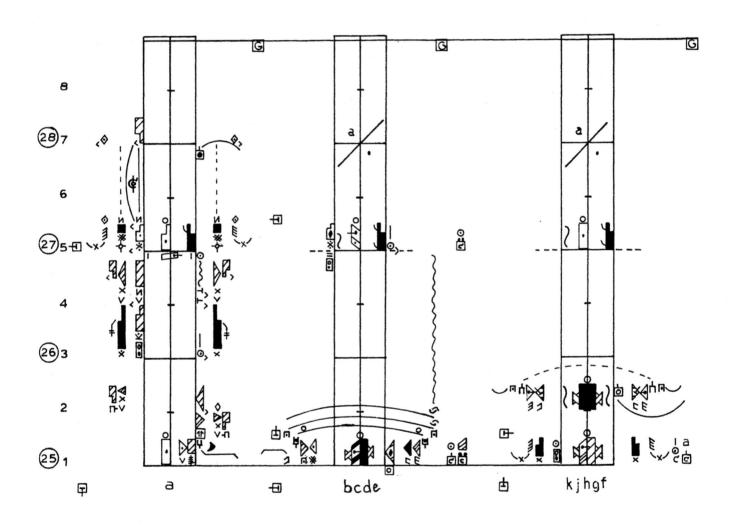

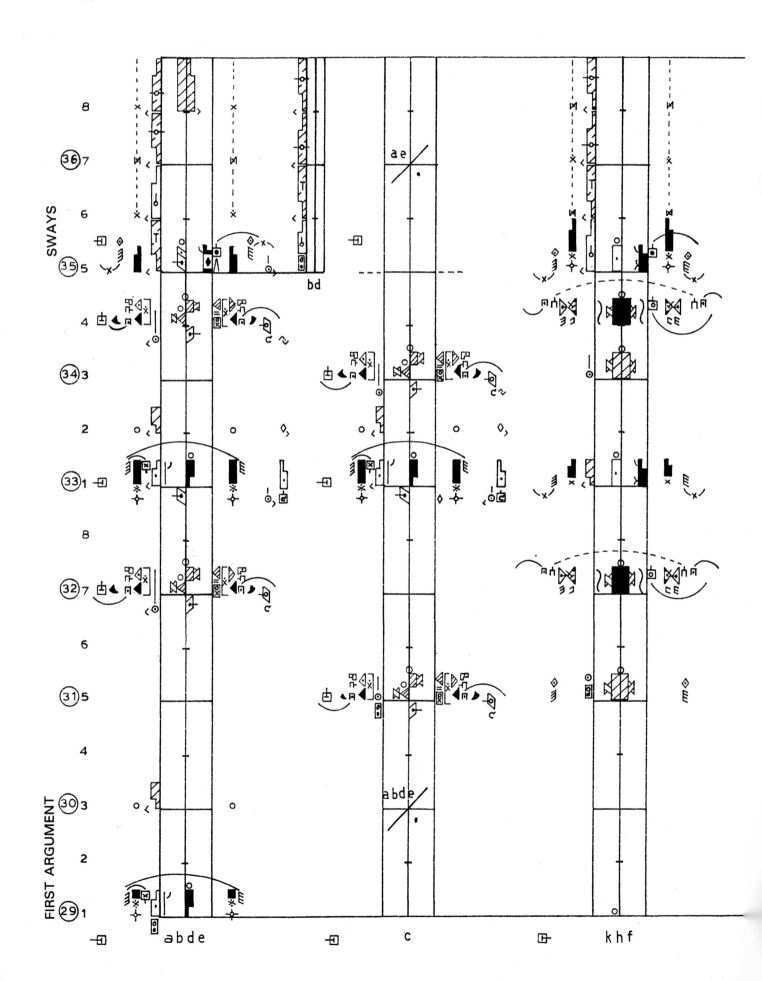

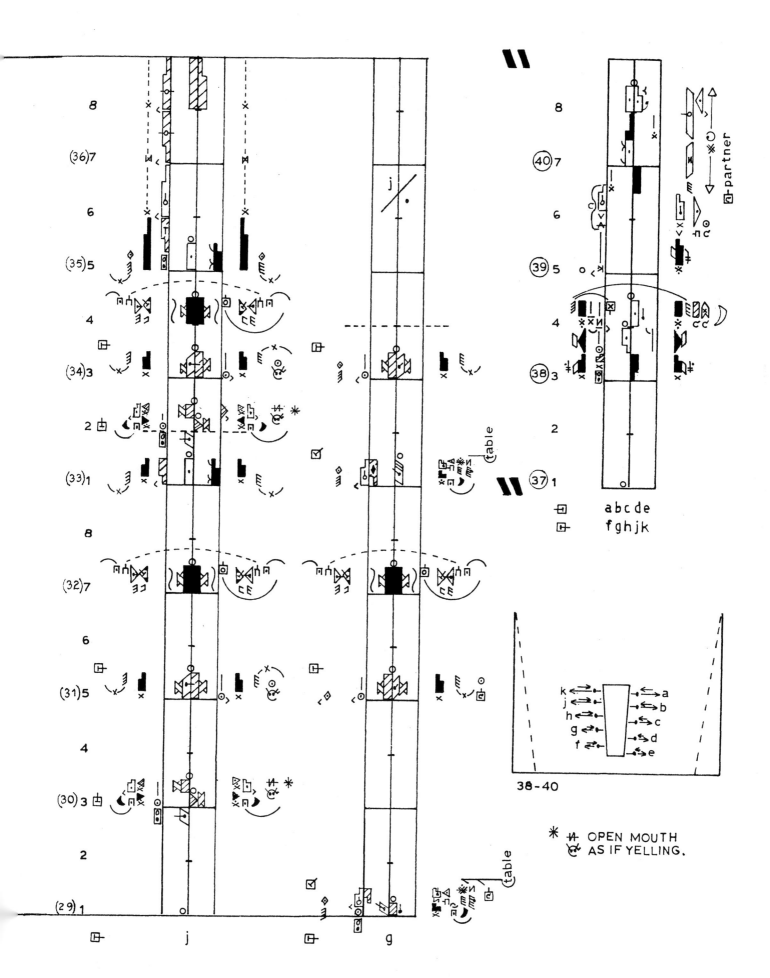

38-40

* ᴎ OPEN MOUTH
  AS IF YELLING.

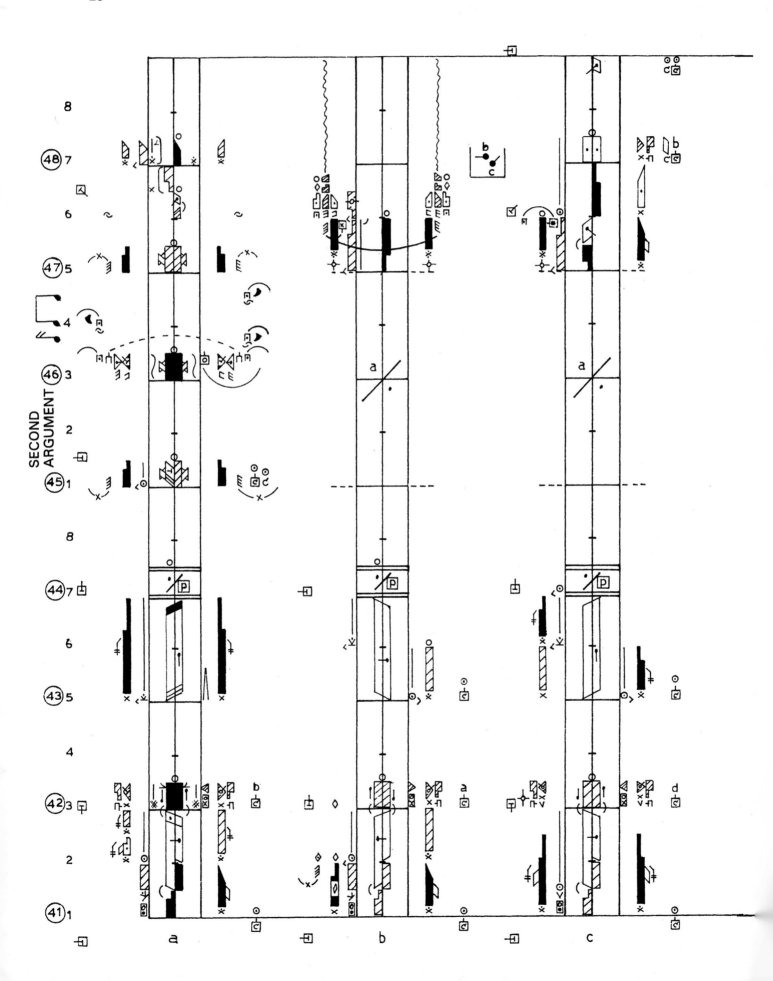

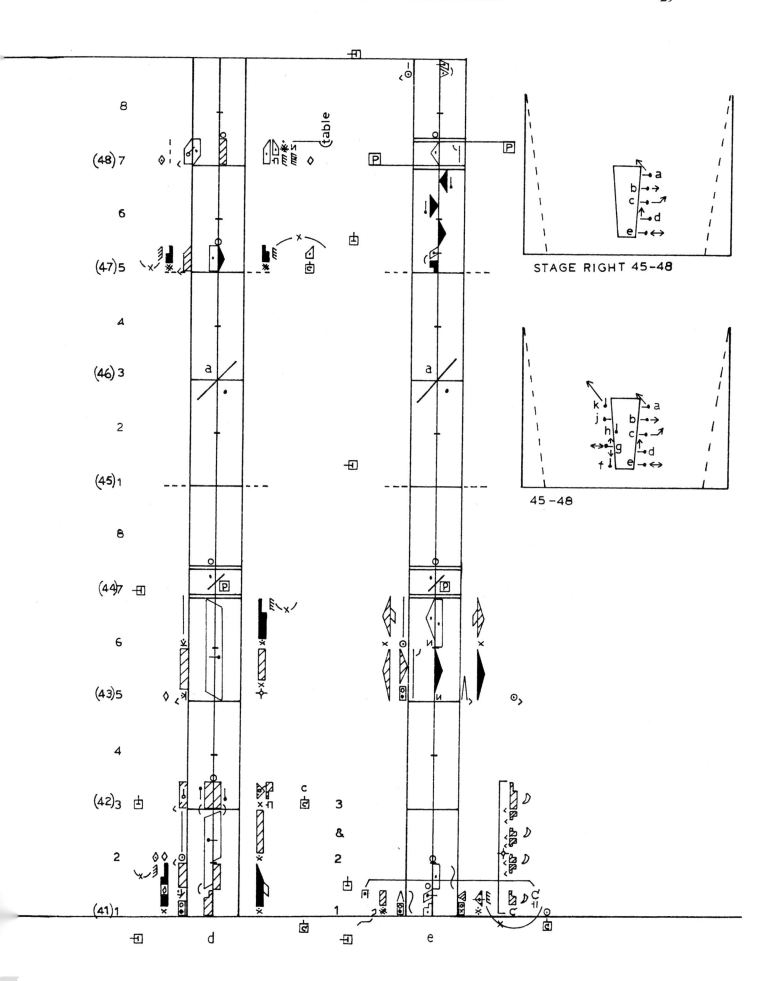

STAGE RIGHT 45-48

45-48

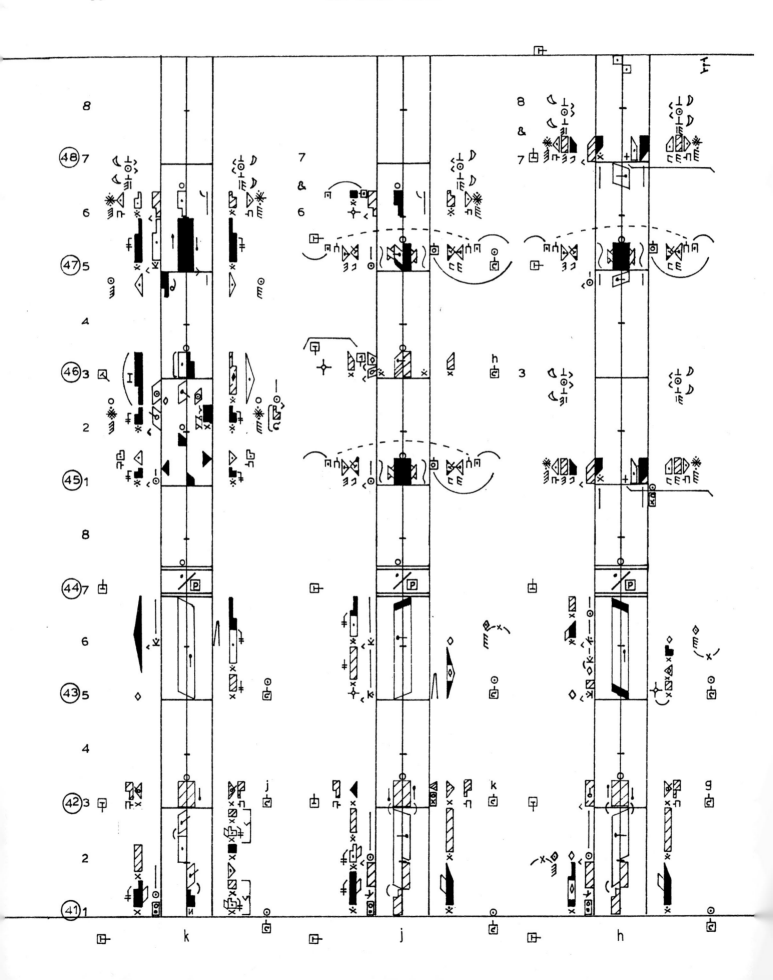

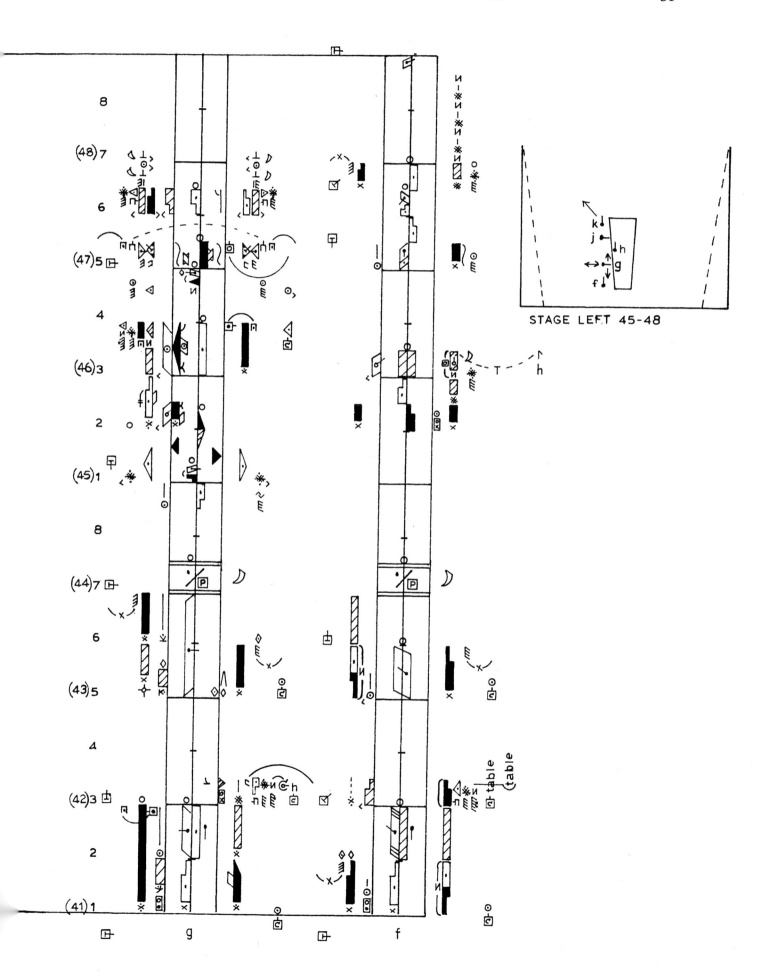

STAGE LEFT 45-48

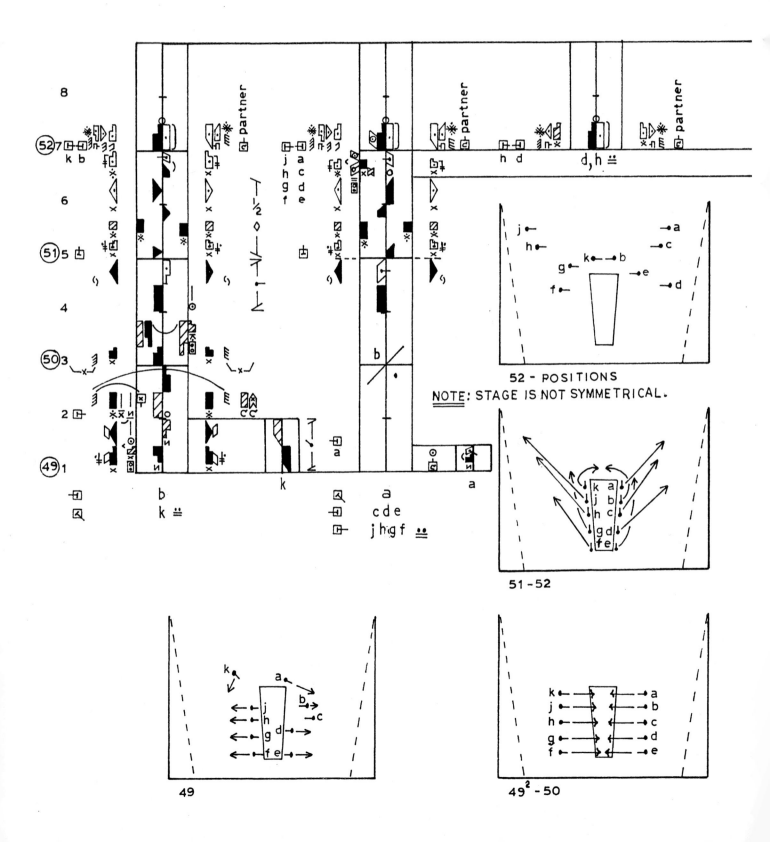

52 - POSITIONS

NOTE: STAGE IS NOT SYMMETRICAL.

51 - 52

49

49² - 50

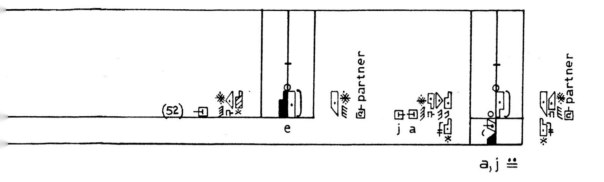

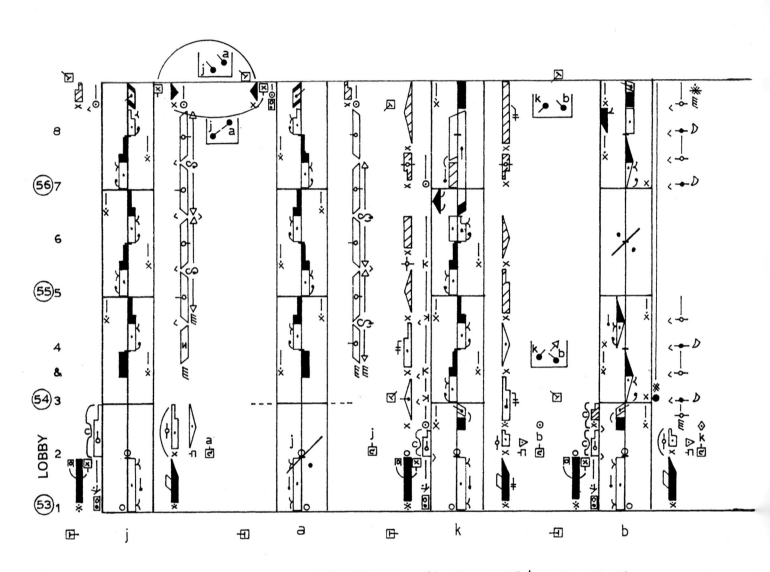

PARTNERS:
- a & j
- b & k
- c & g
- d & h
- e & f

WALKING-FIRST STEP ON: (⫴ LEFT FOOT; ⫲ RIGHT FOOT)

COUNT 3 – b⫲, k⫲

4 – a⫴, j⫴, g⫴, h⫴

5 – c⫴, d⫴, e⫴, f⫴

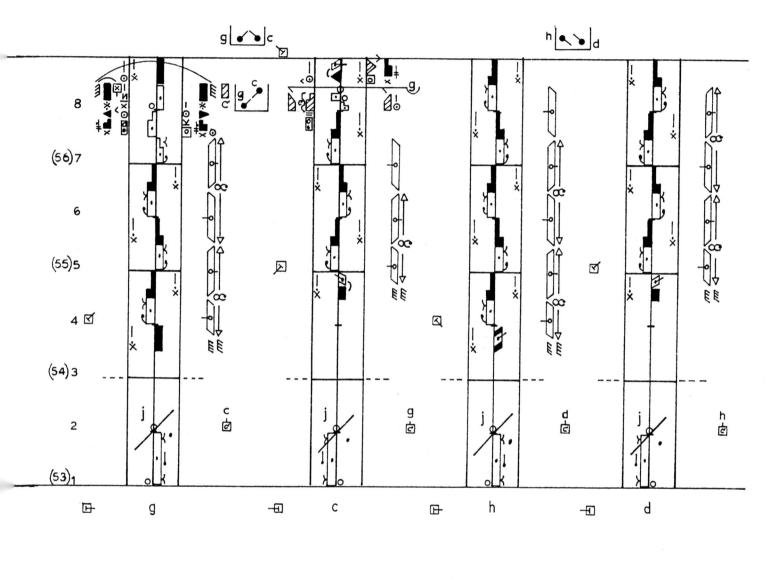

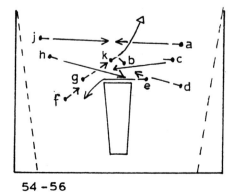

54 - 56

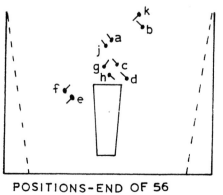

POSITIONS-END OF 56

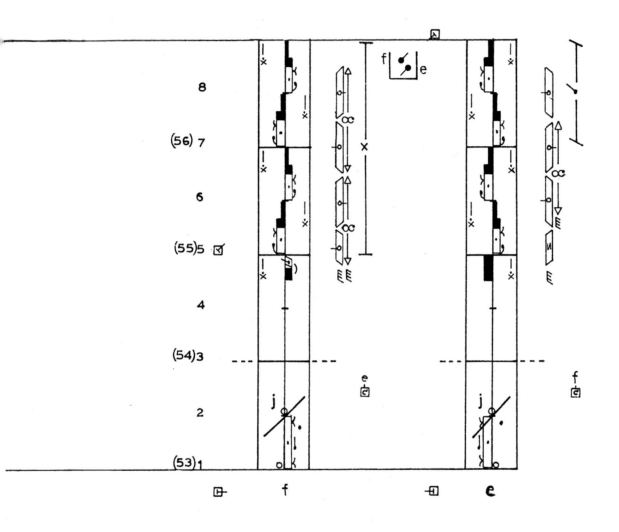

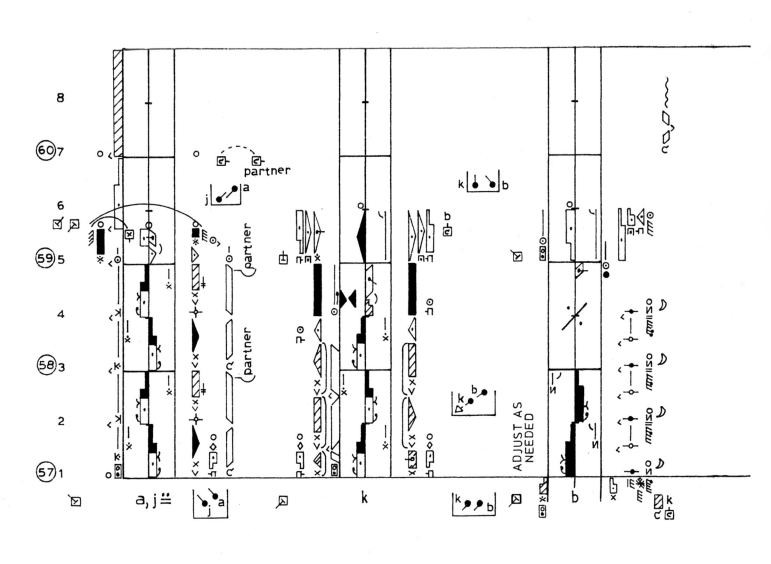

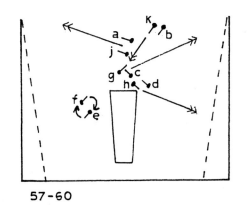

57-60

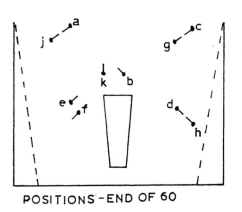

POSITIONS - END OF 60

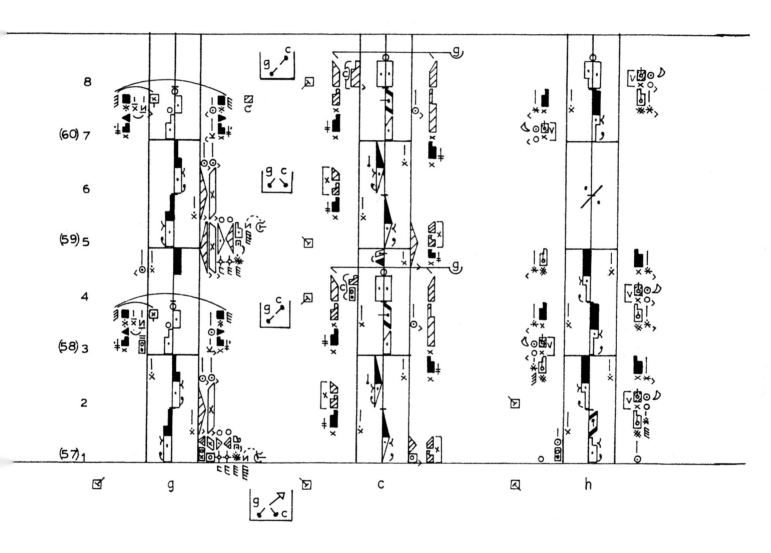

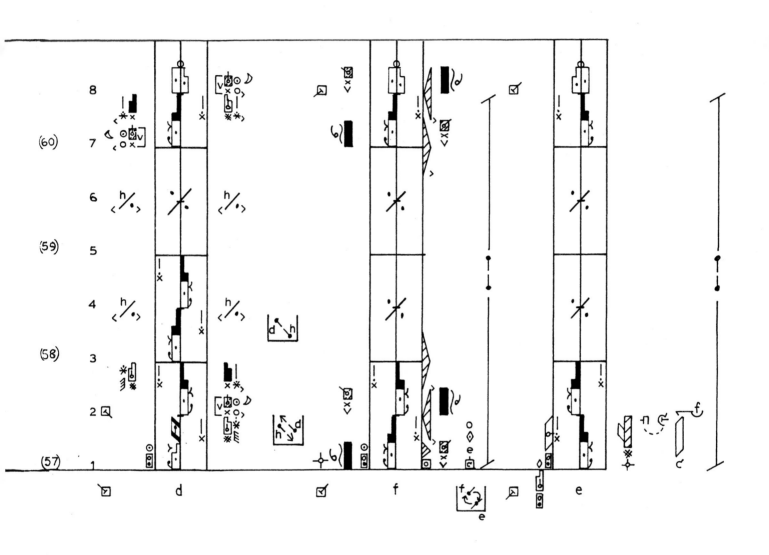

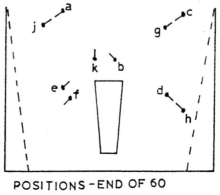

POSITIONS – END OF 60

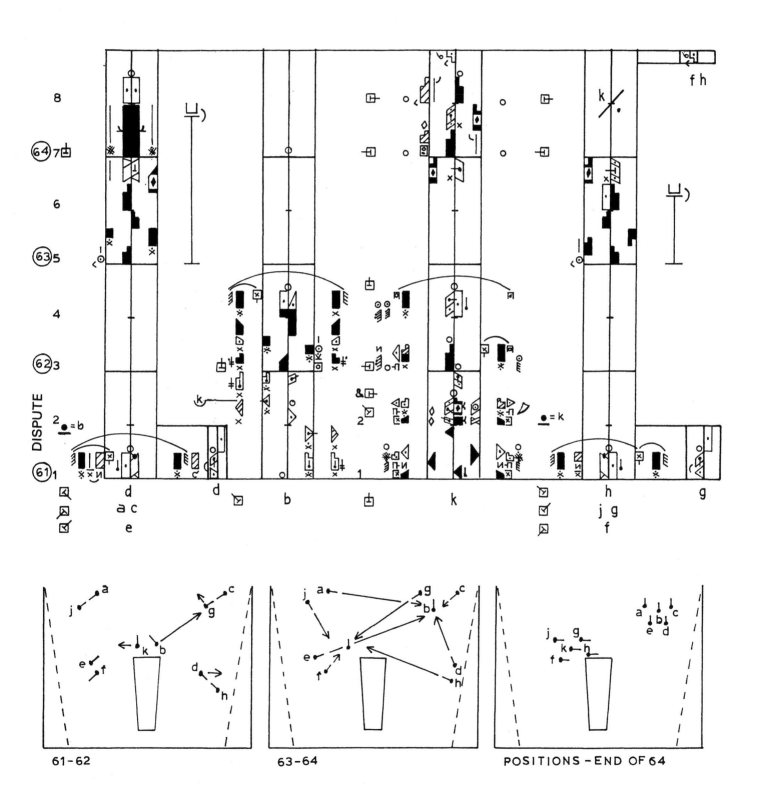

61-62   63-64   POSITIONS - END OF 64

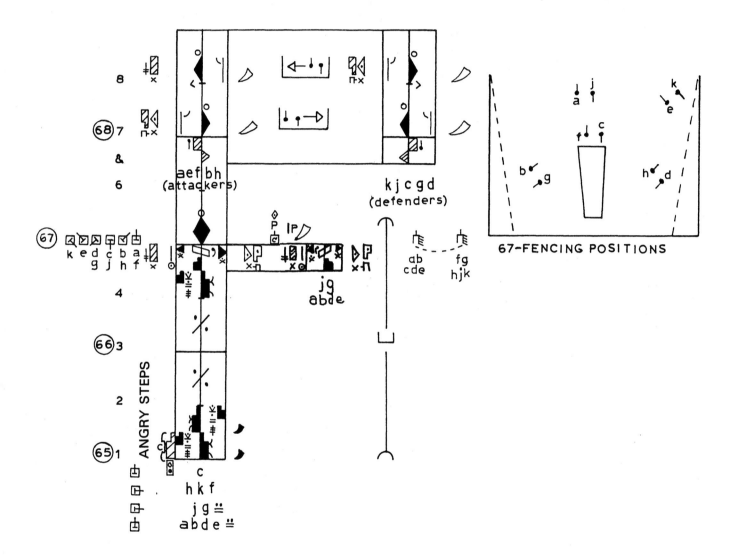

67–FENCING POSITIONS

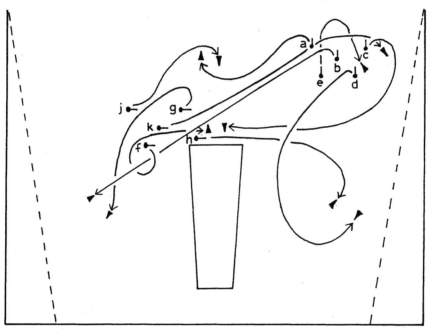

65-66 (ANGRY STEPS)
ENLARGEMENT

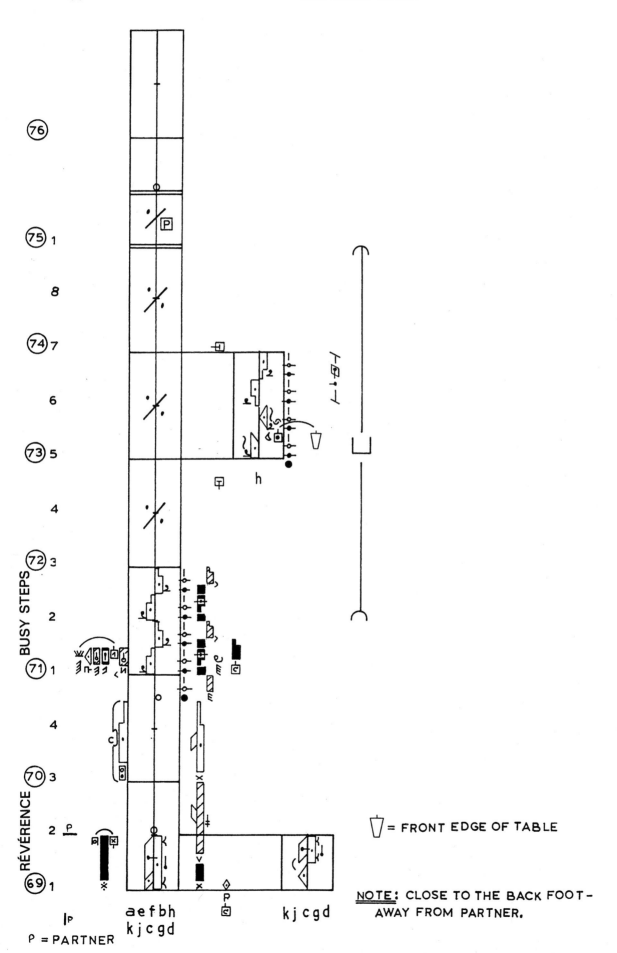

h

⬇ = FRONT EDGE OF TABLE

<u>NOTE:</u> CLOSE TO THE BACK FOOT -
AWAY FROM PARTNER.

BUSY STEPS

RÉVÉRENCE

P = PARTNER

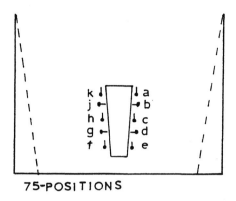

75-POSITIONS

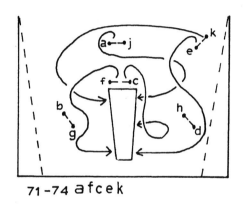

71-74 afcek

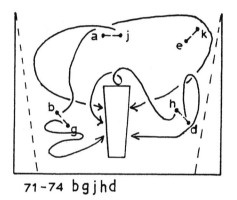

71-74 bgjhd

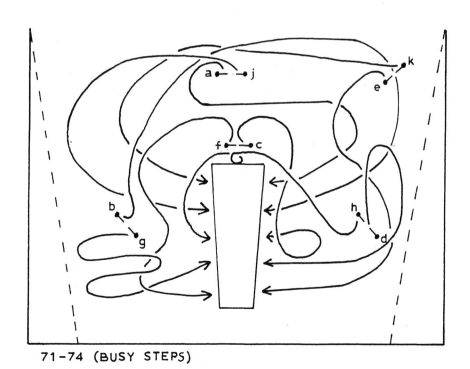

71-74 (BUSY STEPS)

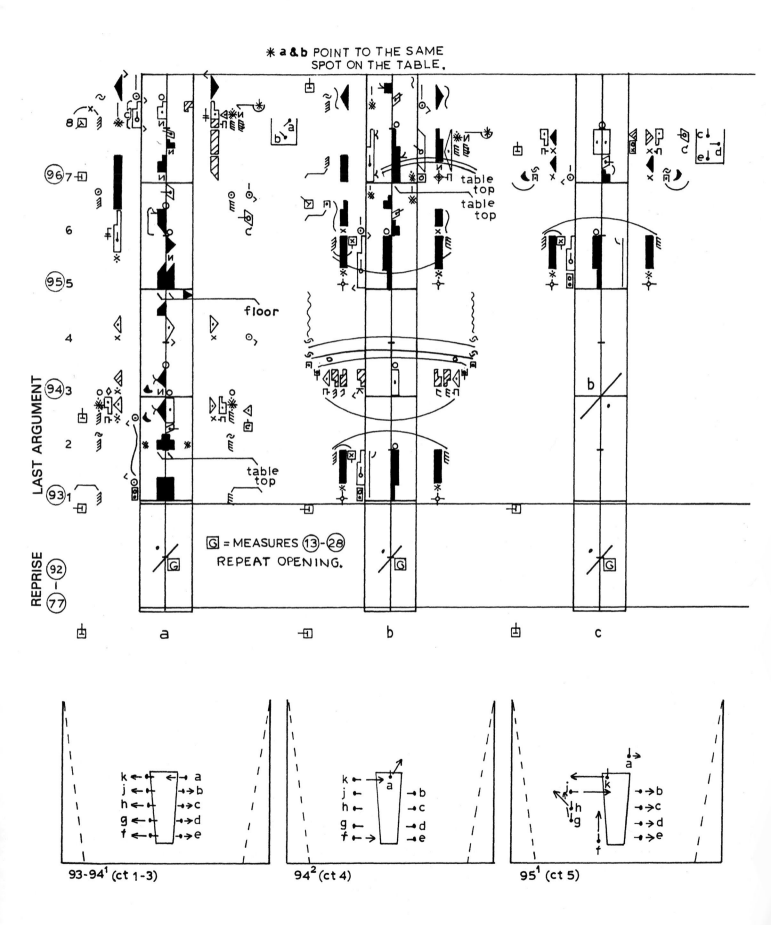

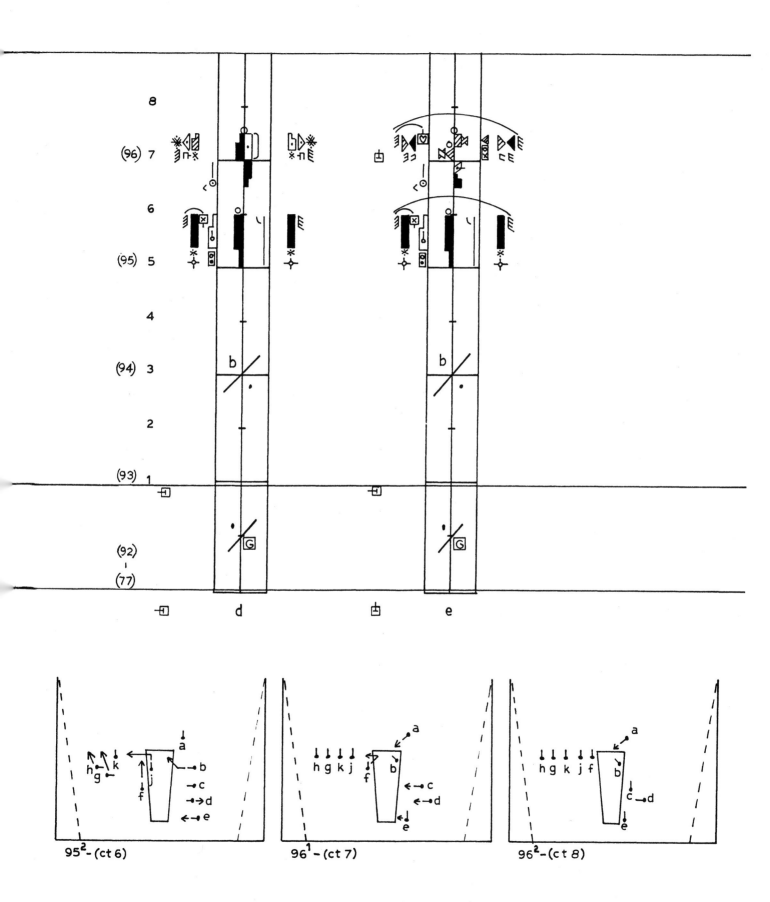

95²-(ct 6)   96¹-(ct 7)   96²-(ct 8)

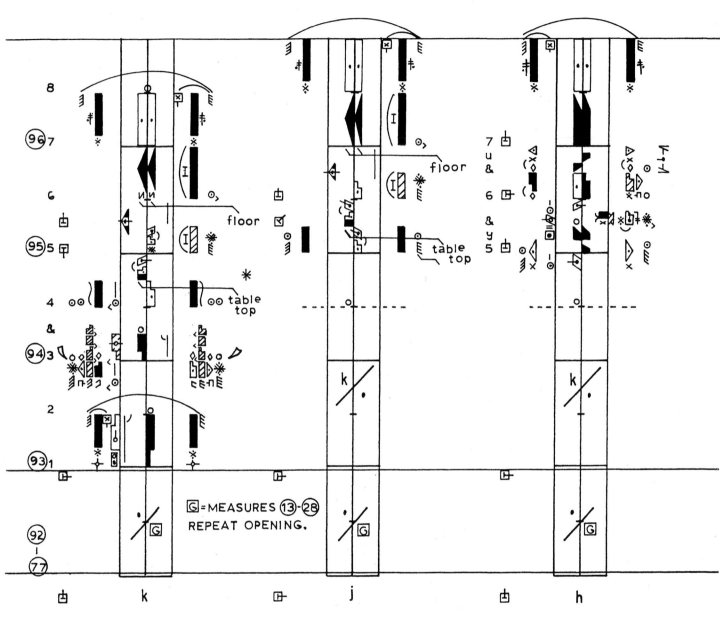

k   G = MEASURES 13-28   j   h
                     REPEAT OPENING.

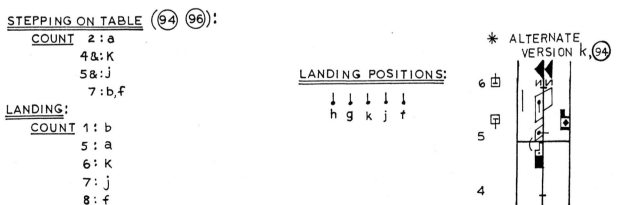

STEPPING ON TABLE (94)(96):

COUNT 2 : a
       4 & : K
       5 & : j
       7 : b, f

LANDING:

COUNT 1 : b
       5 : a
       6 : K
       7 : j
       8 : f

LANDING POSITIONS:

h g k j t

* ALTERNATE VERSION k, 94

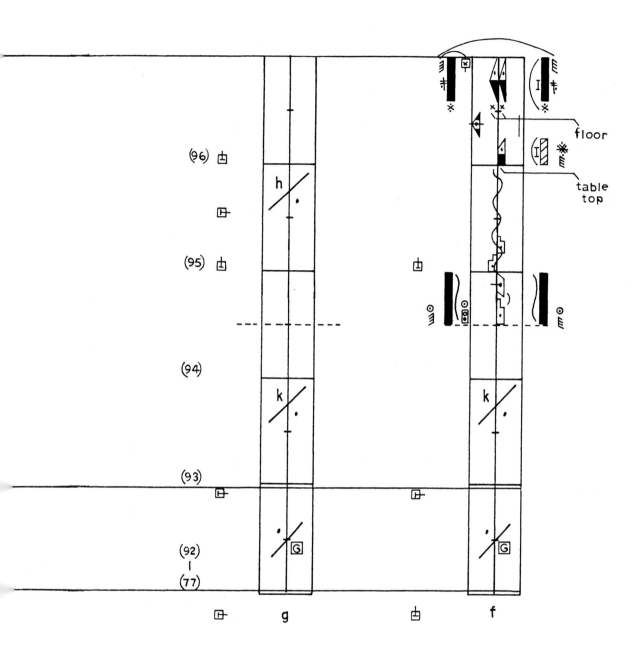

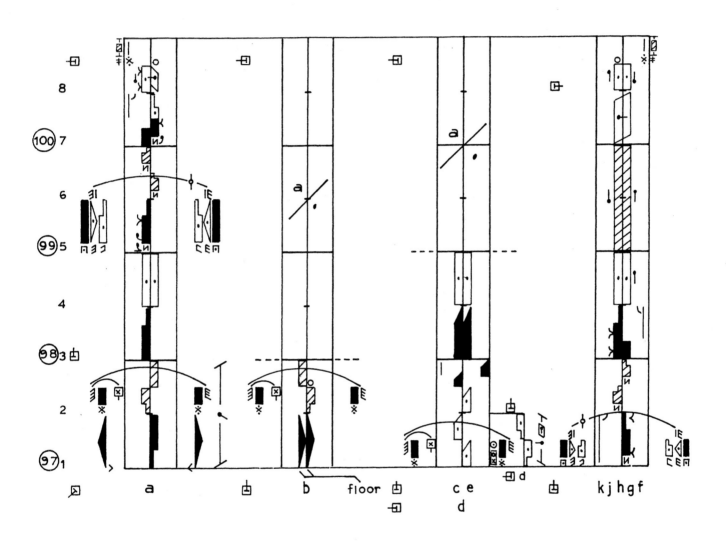

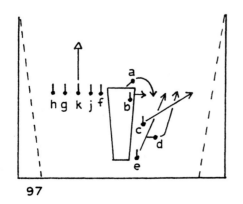

97

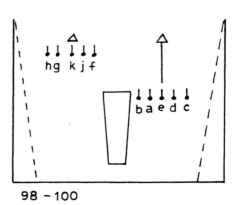

98 – 100

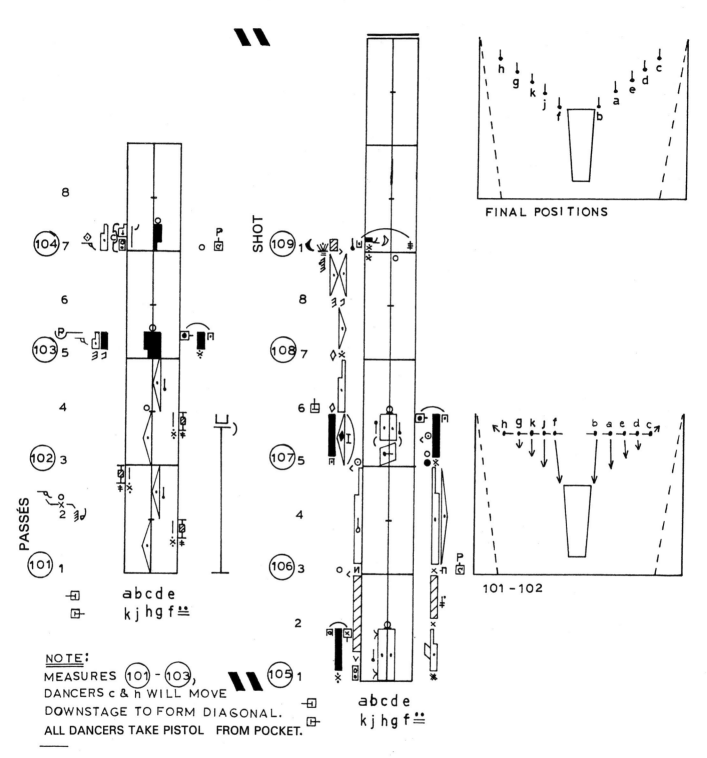

FINAL POSITIONS

PASSÉS

SHOT

101 - 102

NOTE:
MEASURES (101) - (103),
DANCERS c & h WILL MOVE
DOWNSTAGE TO FORM DIAGONAL.
ALL DANCERS TAKE PISTOL FROM POCKET.

abcde - PISTOL IS IN RIGHT POCKET.
kjhgf - PISTOL IS IN LEFT POCKET.

P = DANCER OPPOSITE

= PISTOL

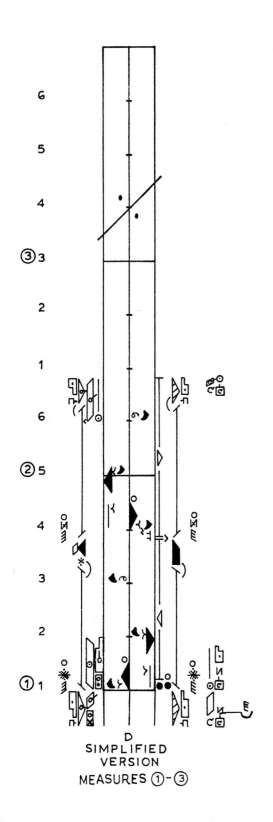

D
SIMPLIFIED
VERSION
MEASURES ①-③

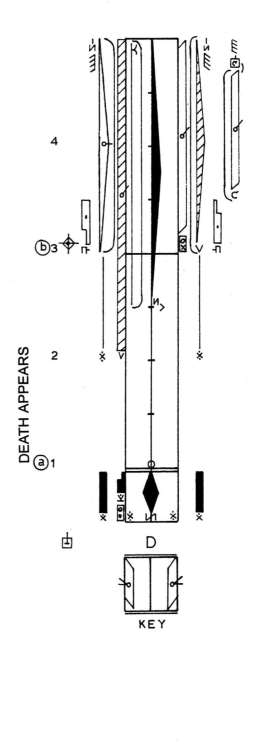

D

KEY

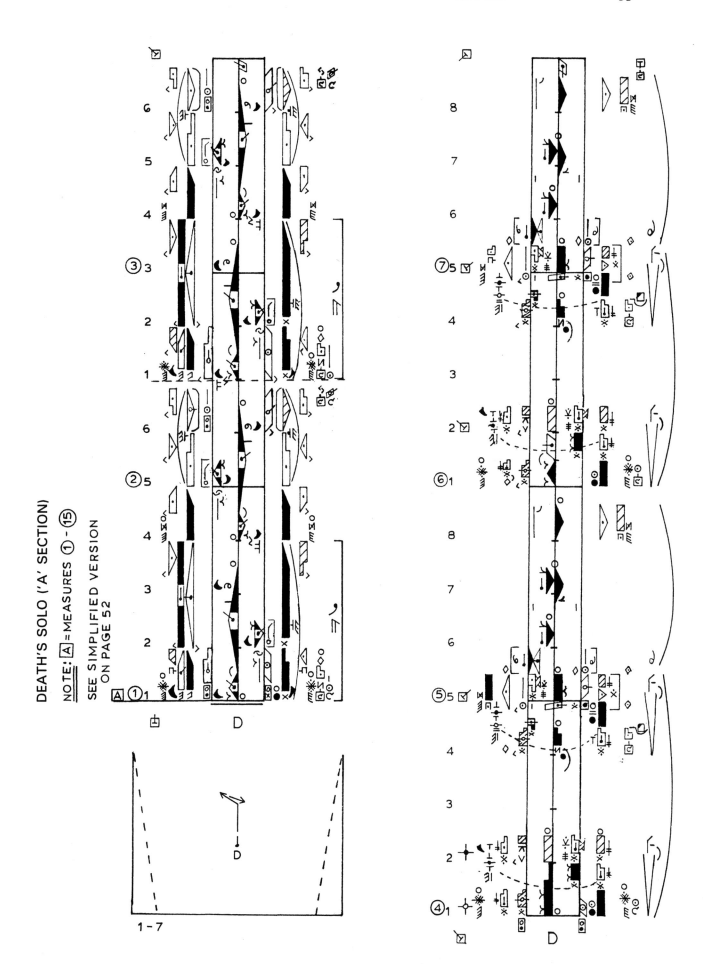

DEATH'S SOLO ('A' SECTION)

NOTE: Ⓐ = MEASURES ① - ⑮

SEE SIMPLIFIED VERSION
ON PAGE 52

1 - 7

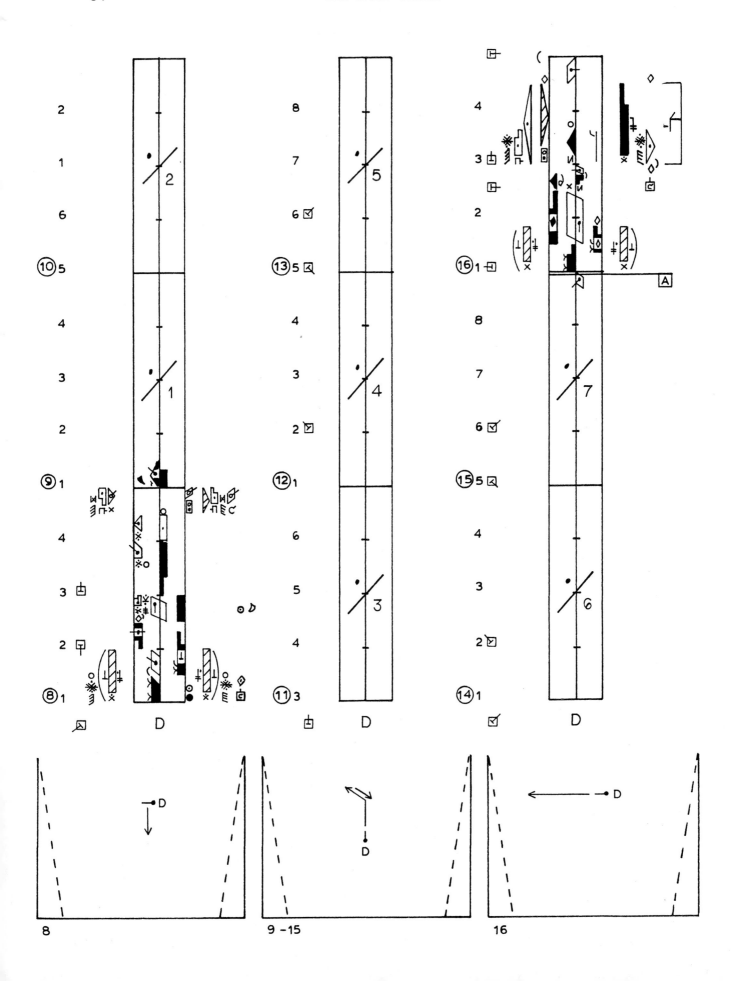

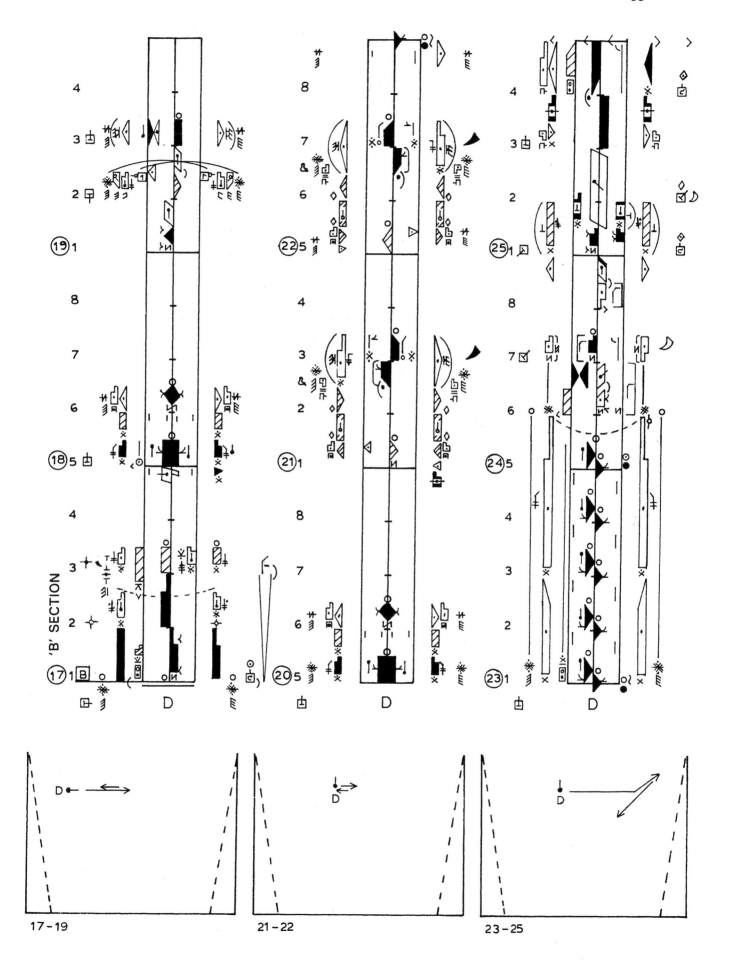

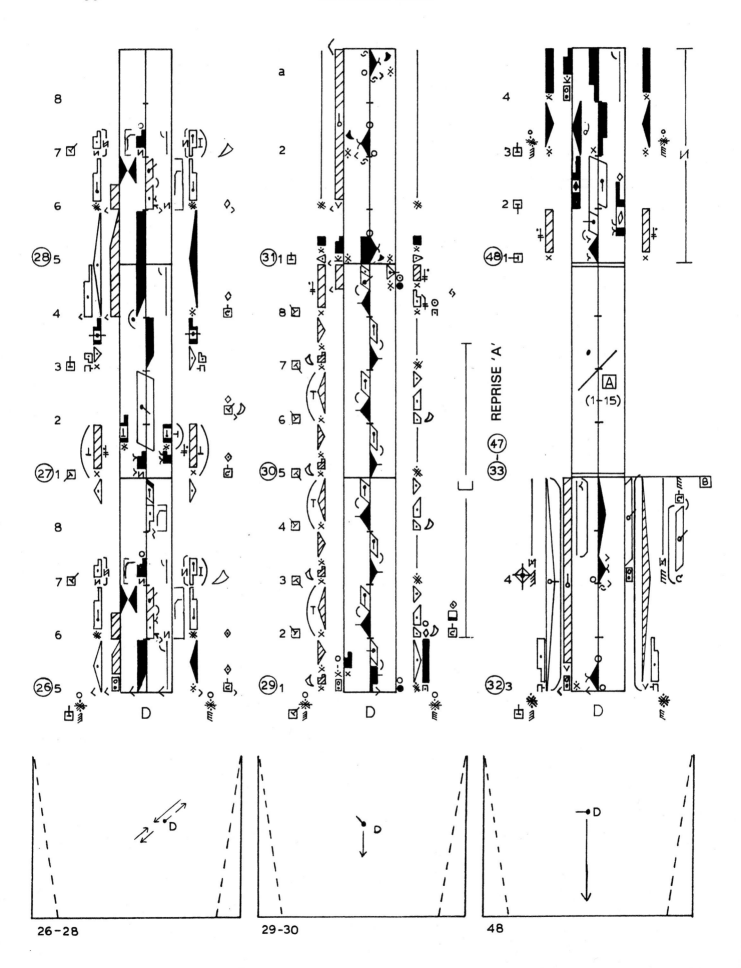

REPRISE 'A'

A
(1-15)

26-28

29-30

48

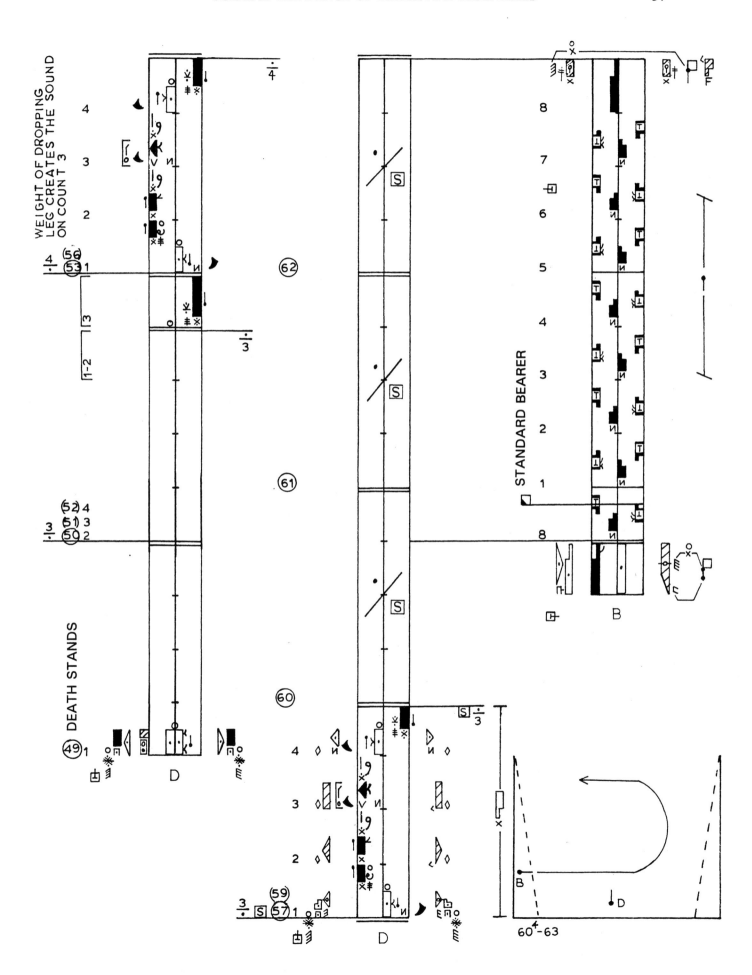

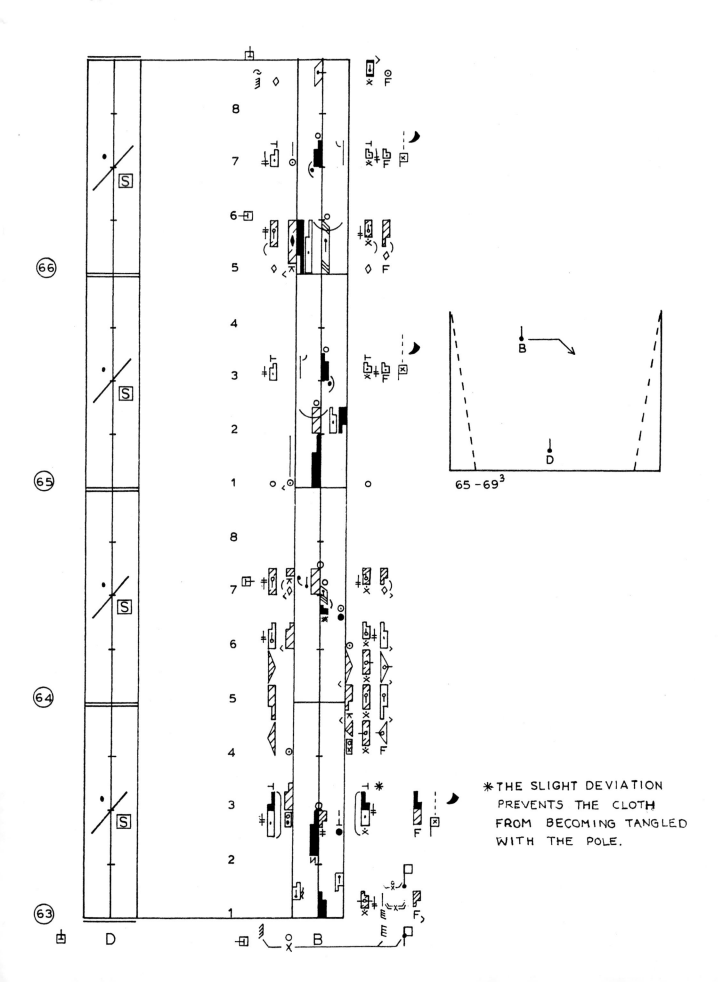

65 – 69³

*THE SLIGHT DEVIATION
PREVENTS THE CLOTH
FROM BECOMING TANGLED
WITH THE POLE.

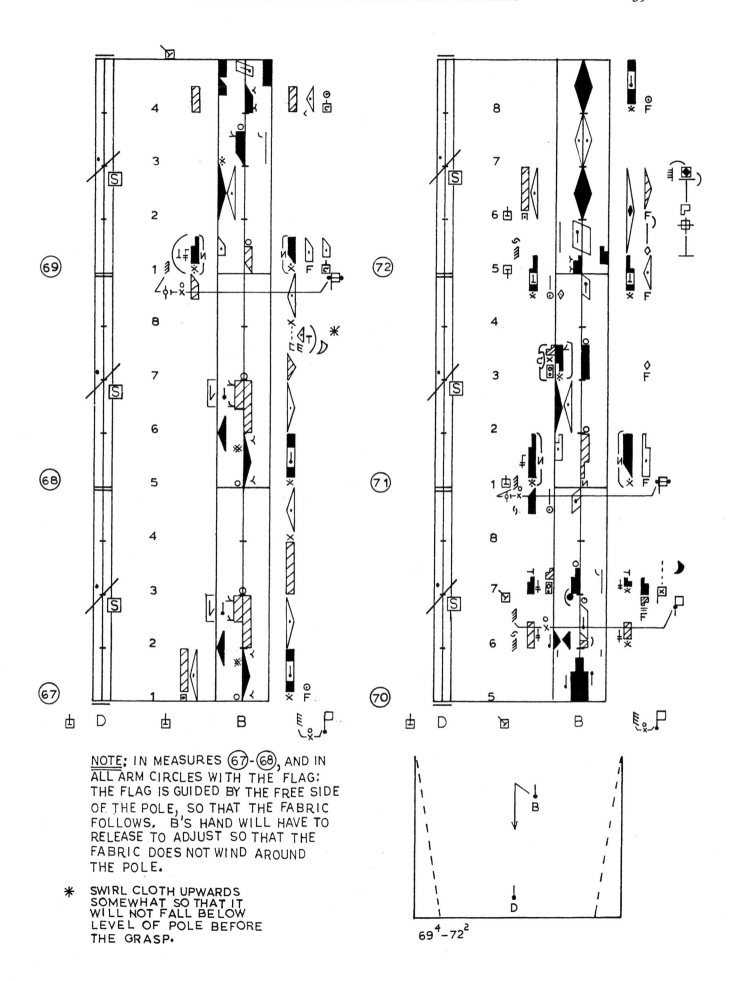

<u>NOTE:</u> IN MEASURES ⑥⑦-⑥⑧, AND IN ALL ARM CIRCLES WITH THE FLAG: THE FLAG IS GUIDED BY THE FREE SIDE OF THE POLE, SO THAT THE FABRIC FOLLOWS. B'S HAND WILL HAVE TO RELEASE TO ADJUST SO THAT THE FABRIC DOES NOT WIND AROUND THE POLE.

✳ SWIRL CLOTH UPWARDS SOMEWHAT SO THAT IT WILL NOT FALL BELOW LEVEL OF POLE BEFORE THE GRASP.

$69^4 - 72^2$

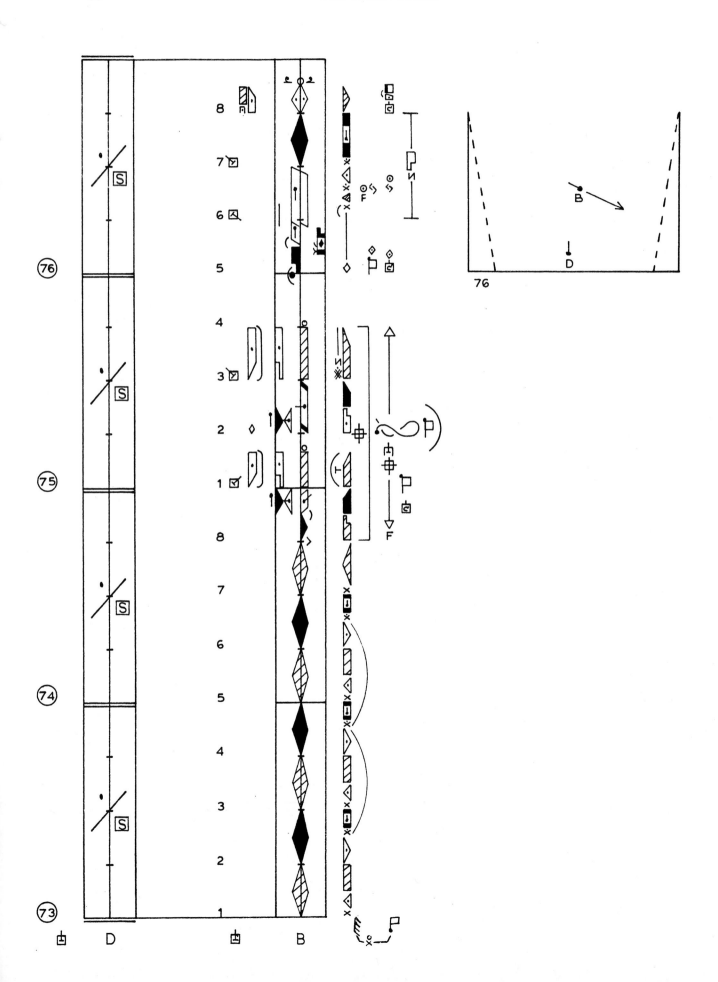

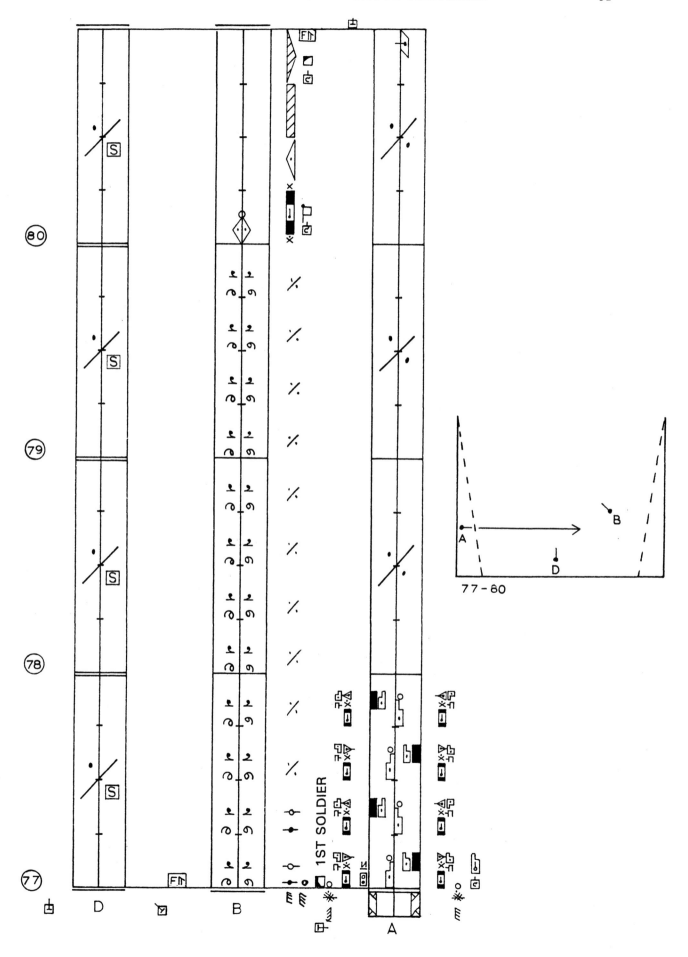

77-80

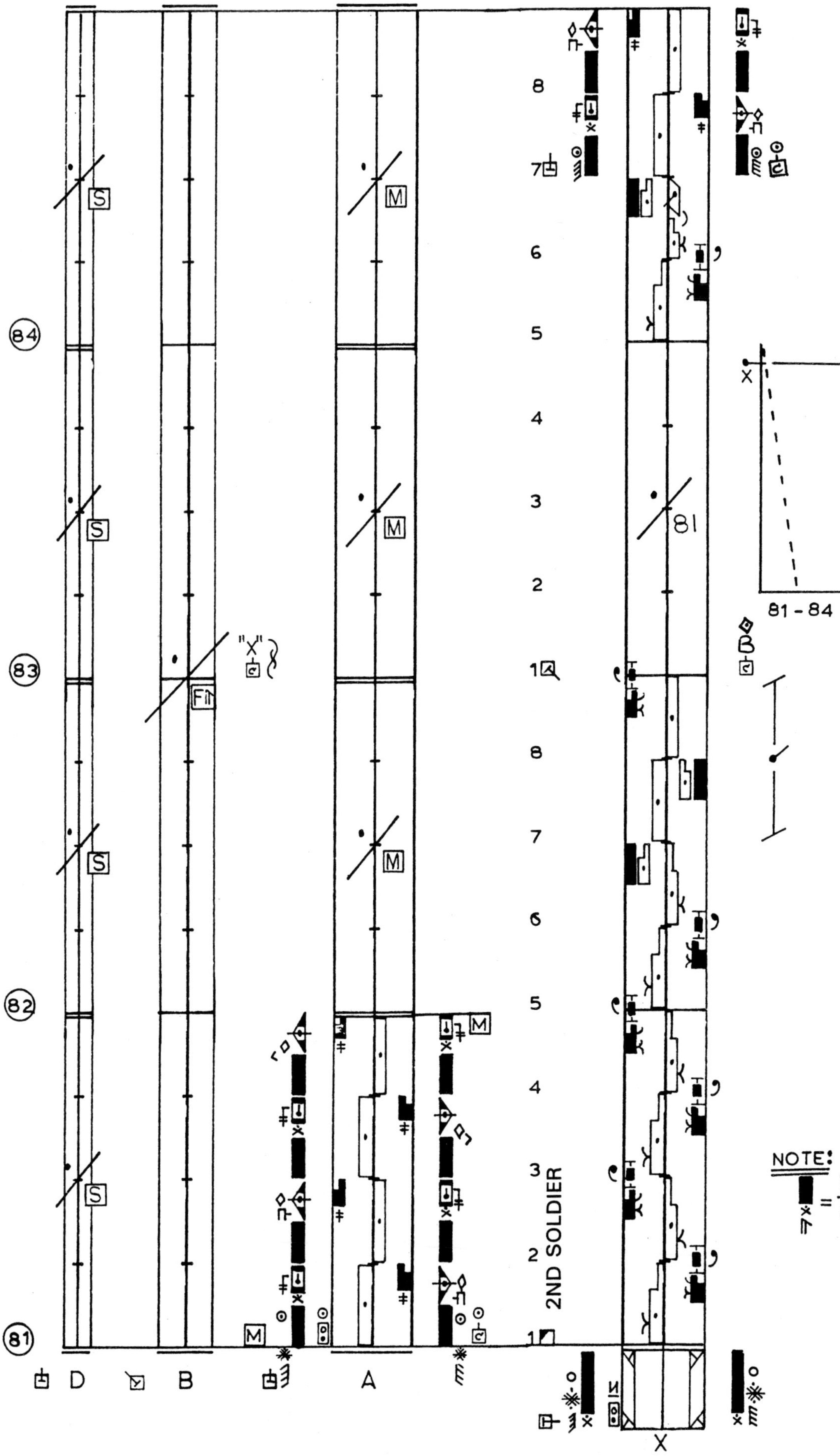

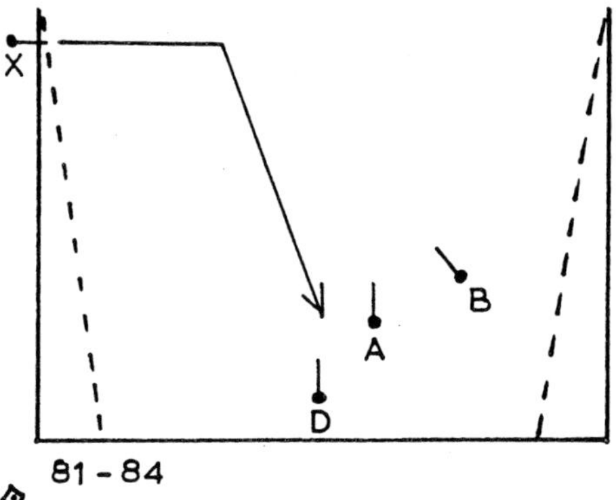

84

83

82

81

8
7
6
5
4
3
2
1
8
7
6
5
4
3
2
1

81

81 – 84

2ND SOLDIER

D   B   A   X

X

NOTE:

FOR SOLDIERS
ELBOWS ARE HELD
AWAY FROM THE BODY.

"X"

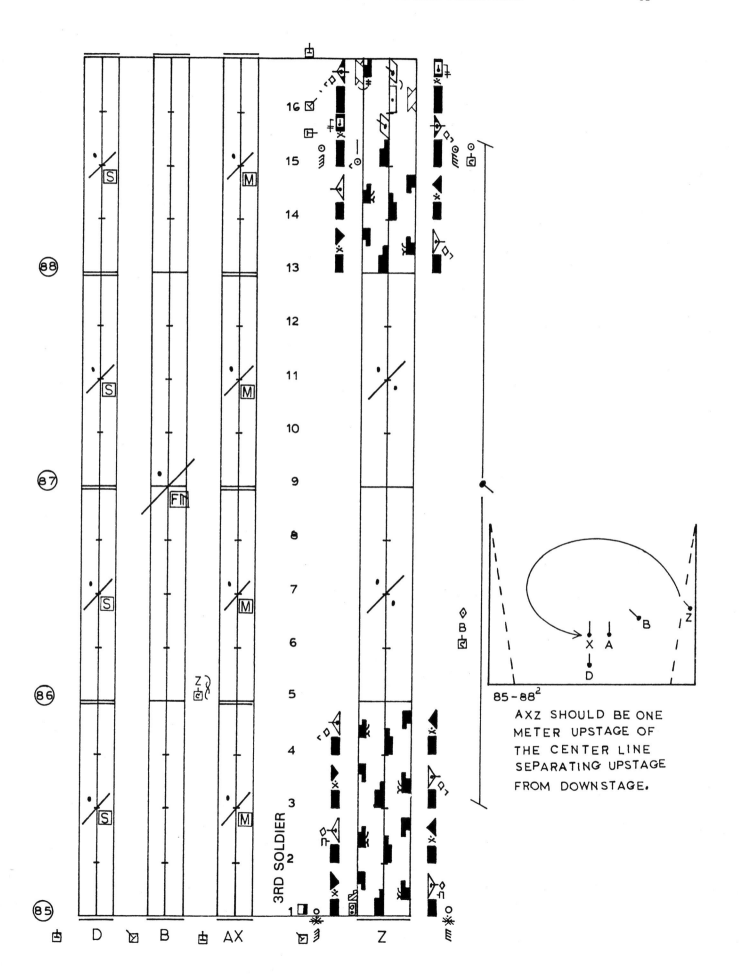

AXZ SHOULD BE ONE
METER UPSTAGE OF
THE CENTER LINE
SEPARATING UPSTAGE
FROM DOWNSTAGE.

85-88^2

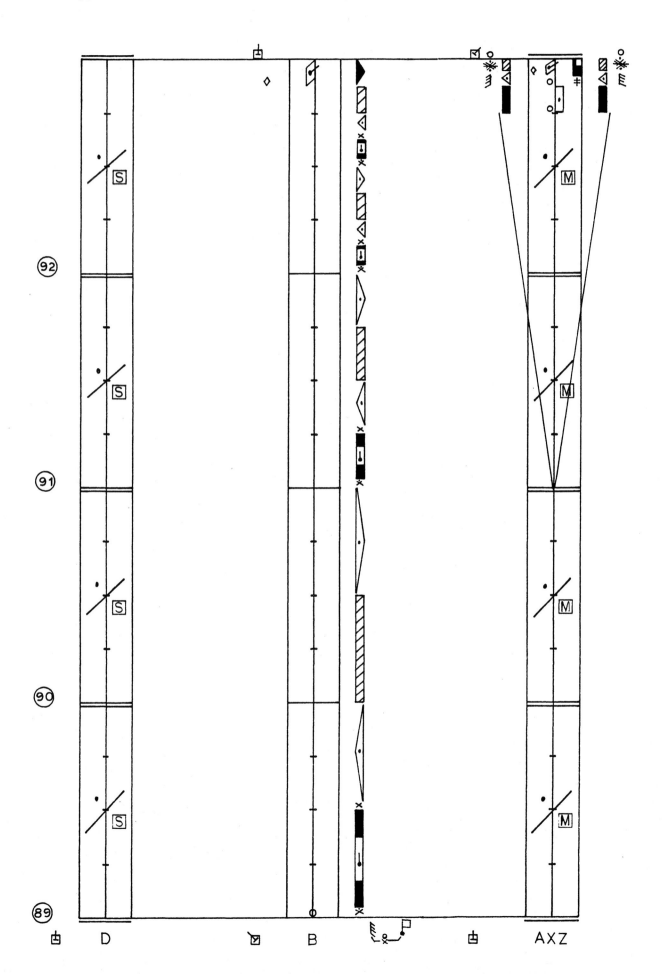

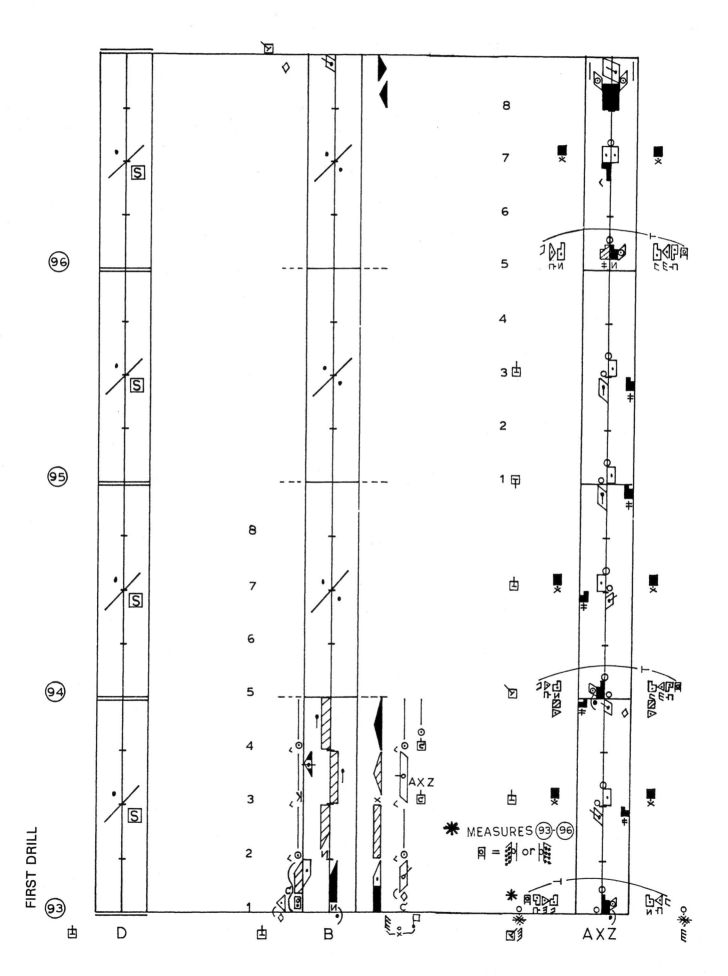

FIRST DRILL

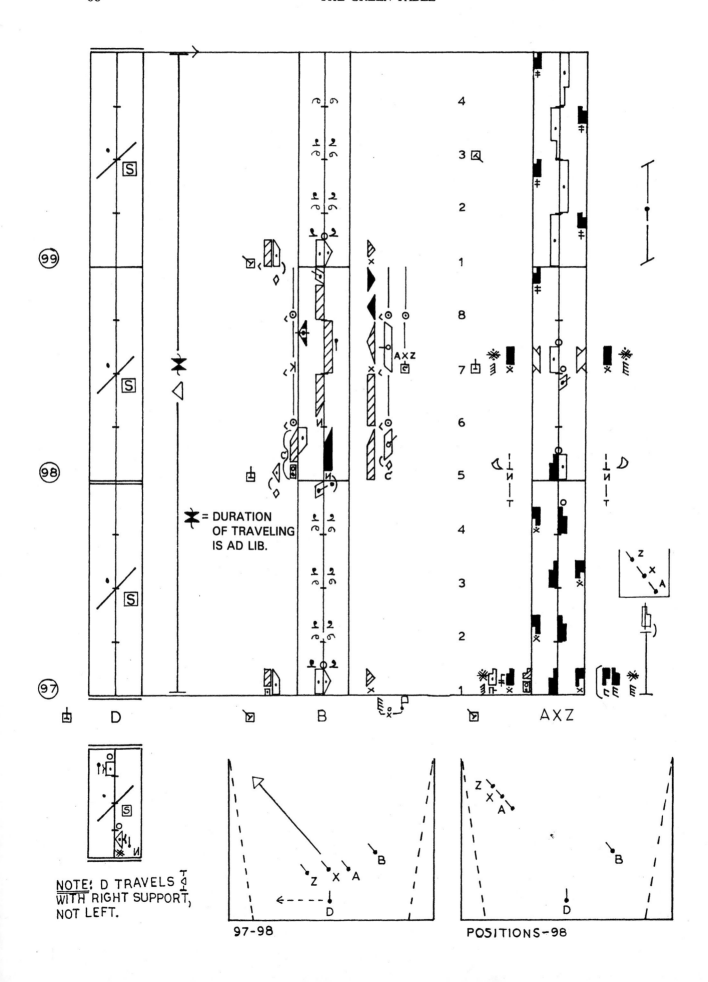

= DURATION
OF TRAVELING
IS AD LIB.

NOTE: D TRAVELS
WITH RIGHT SUPPORT,
NOT LEFT.

97-98

POSITIONS-98

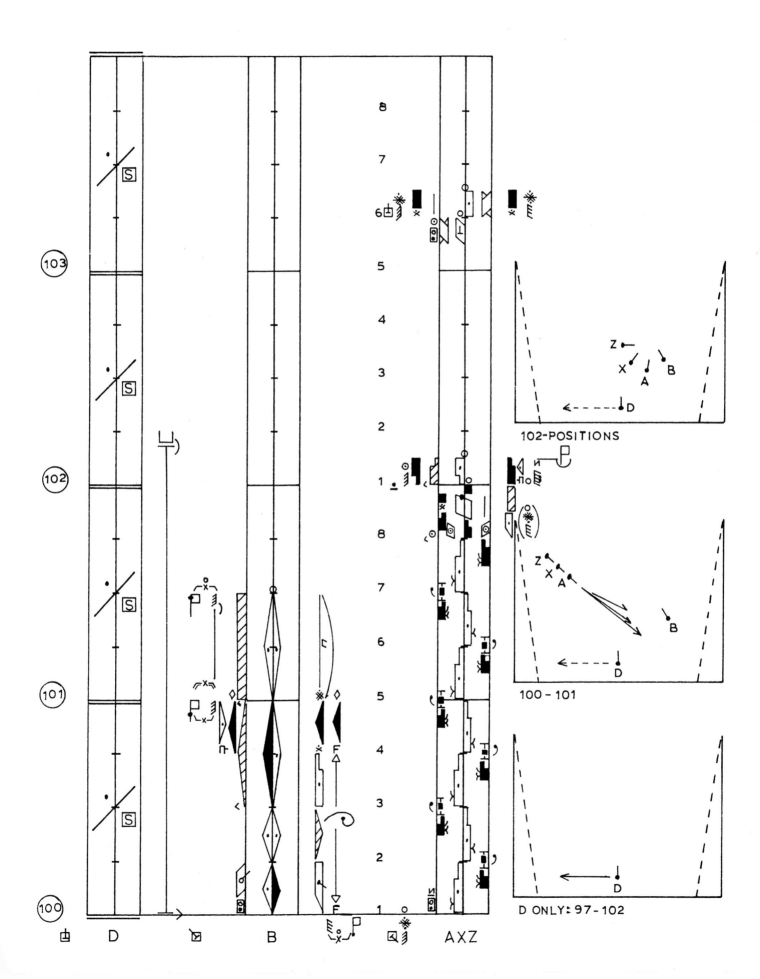

102-POSITIONS

100 - 101

D ONLY: 97-102

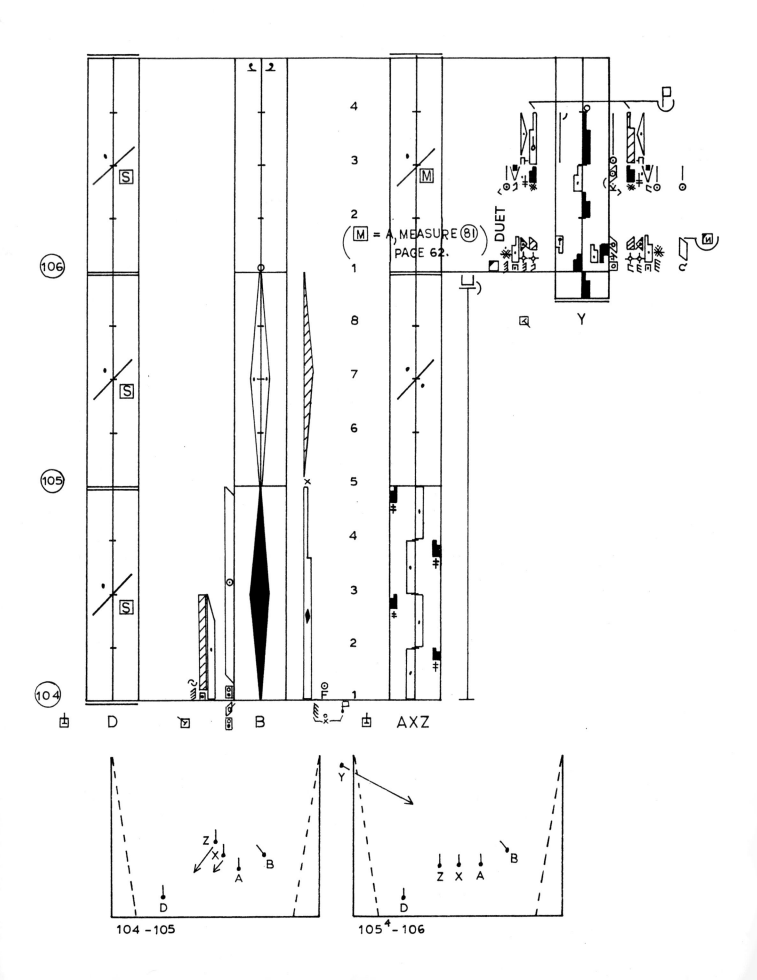

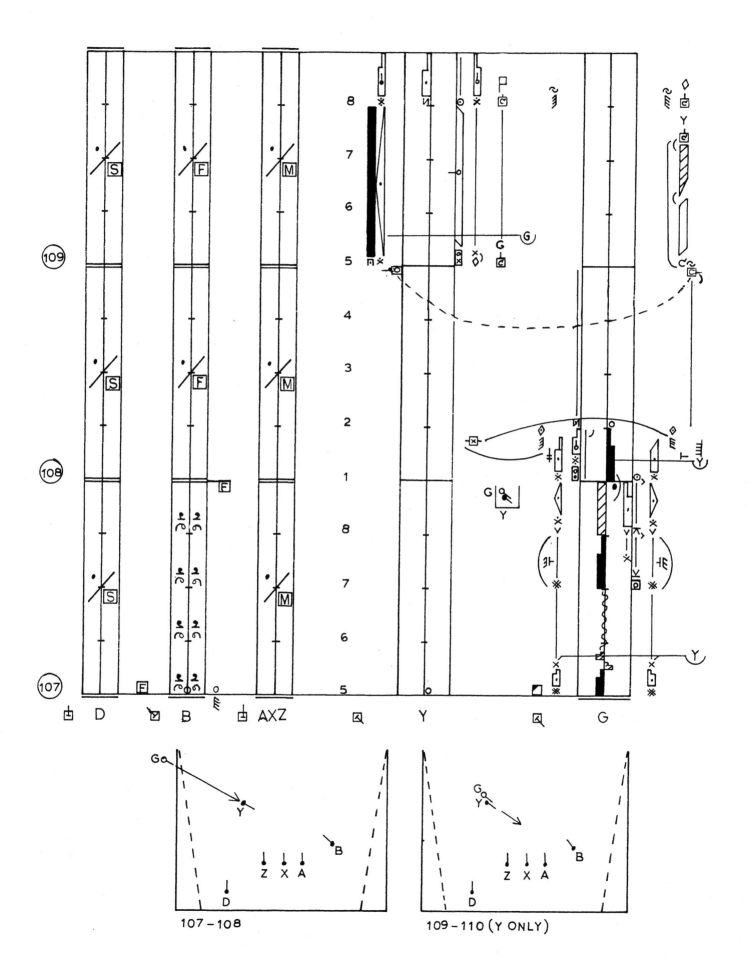

107 – 108

109 – 110 (Y ONLY)

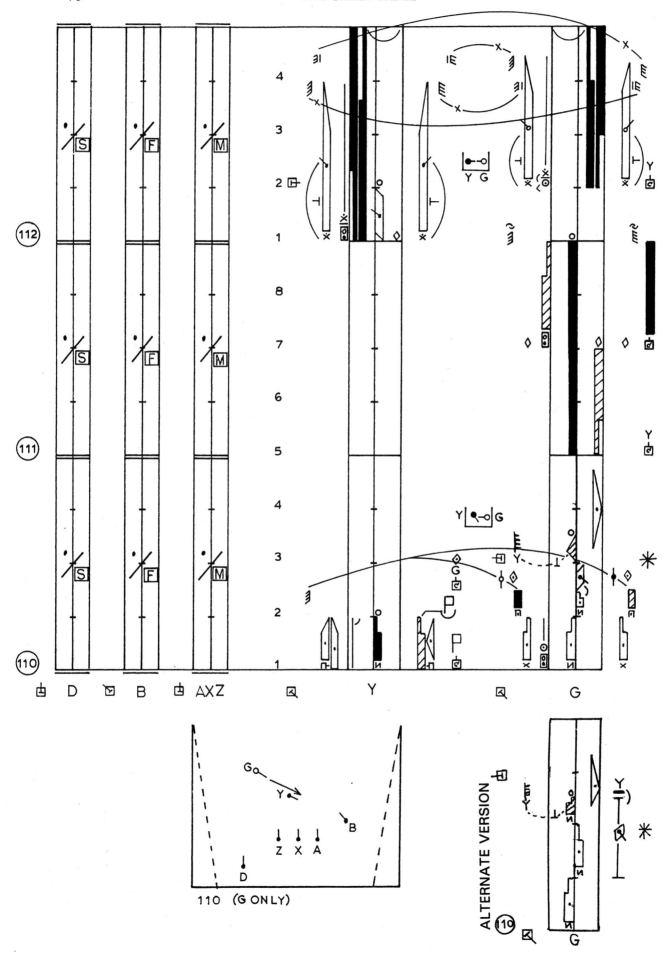

110 (G ONLY)

ALTERNATE VERSION

113

114^2–115

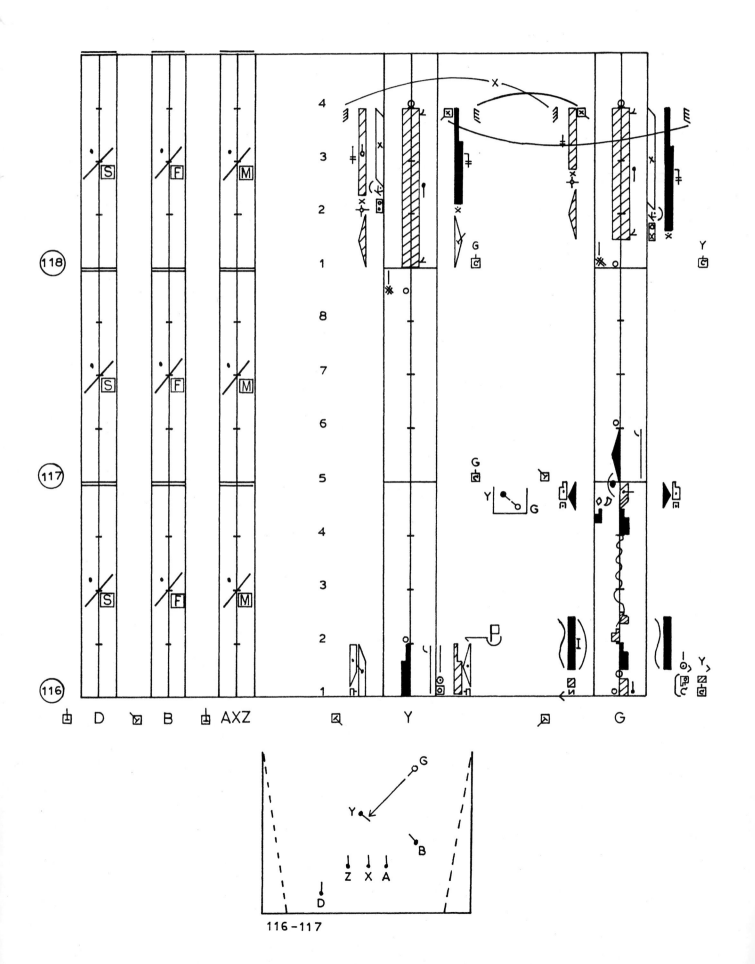

116–117

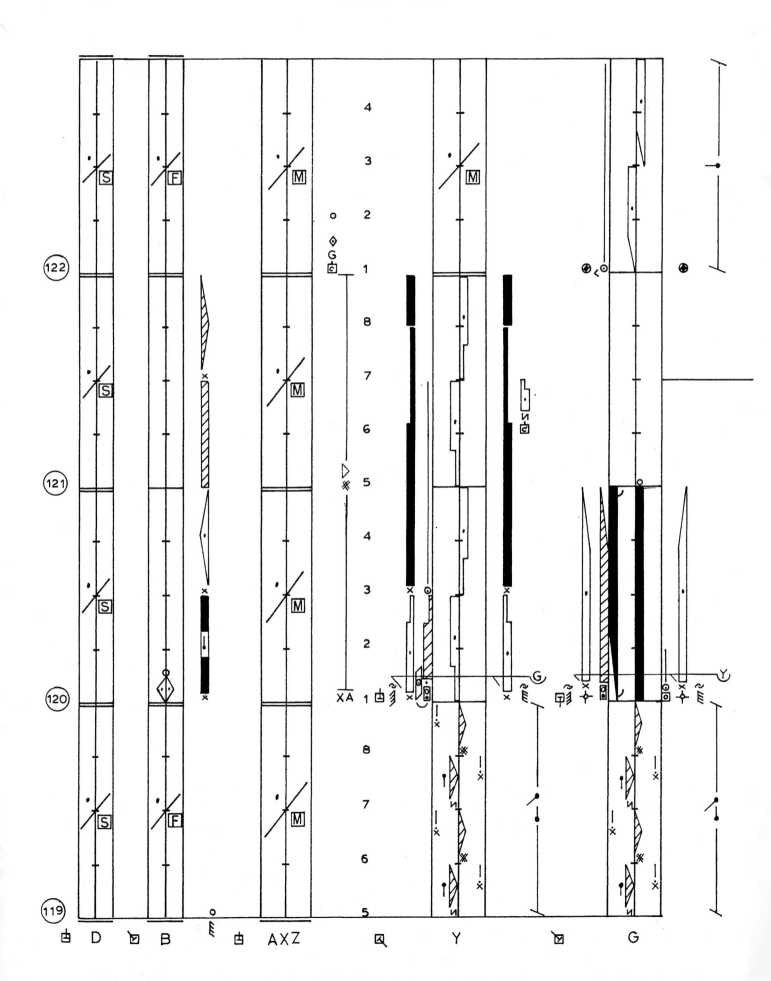

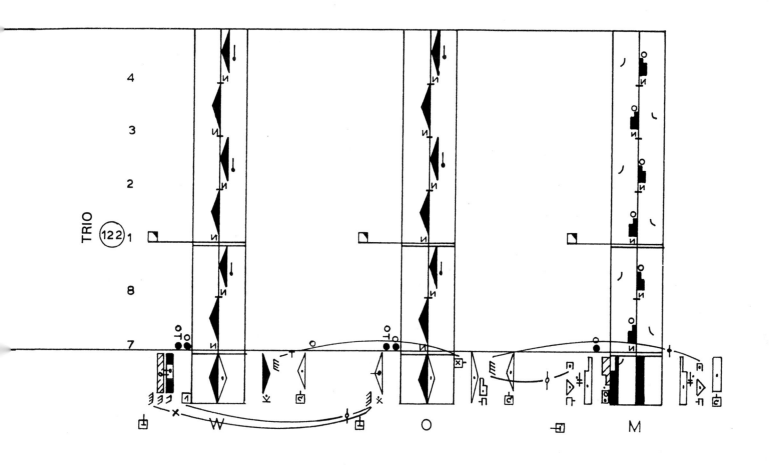

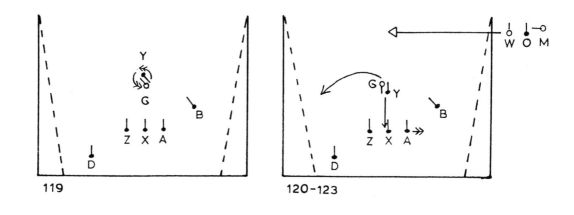

119

120-123

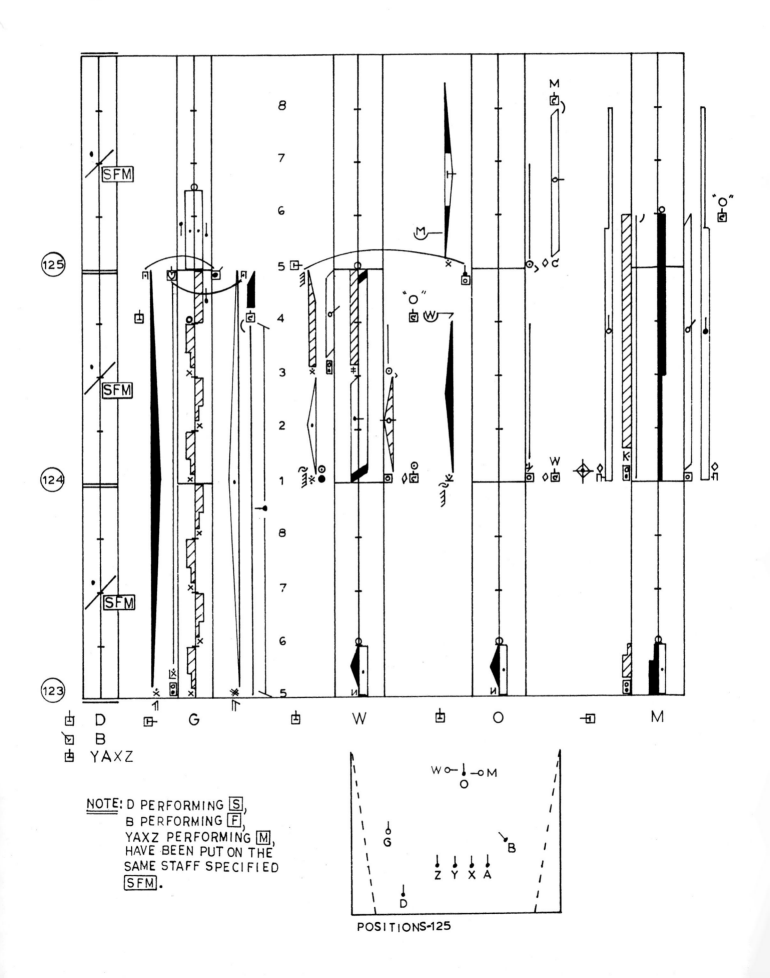

POSITIONS-125

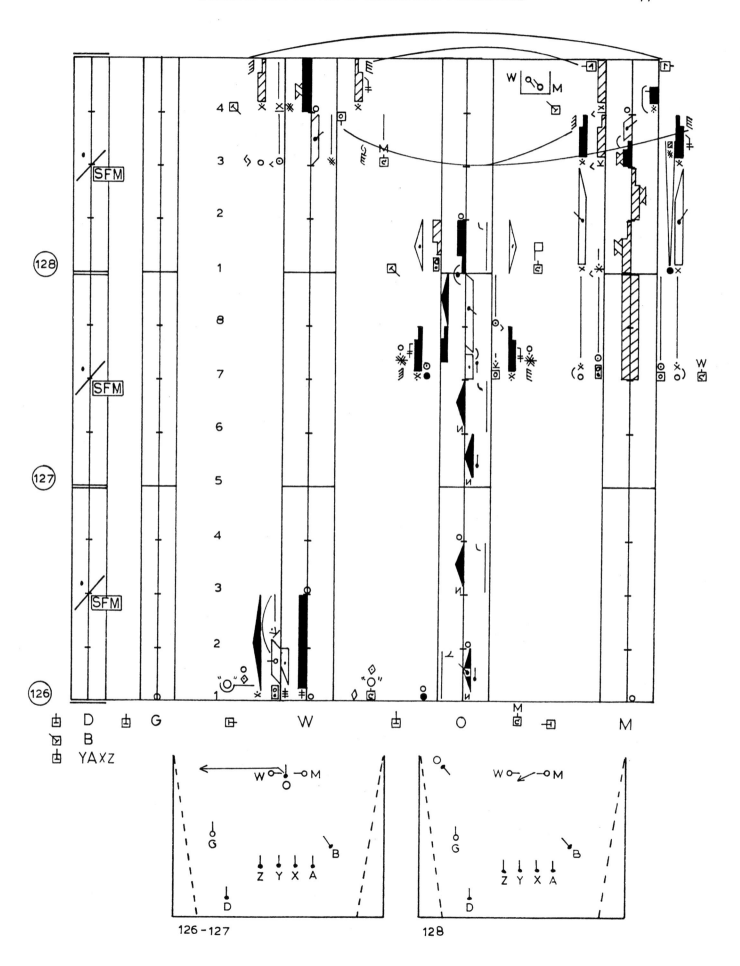

126-127

128

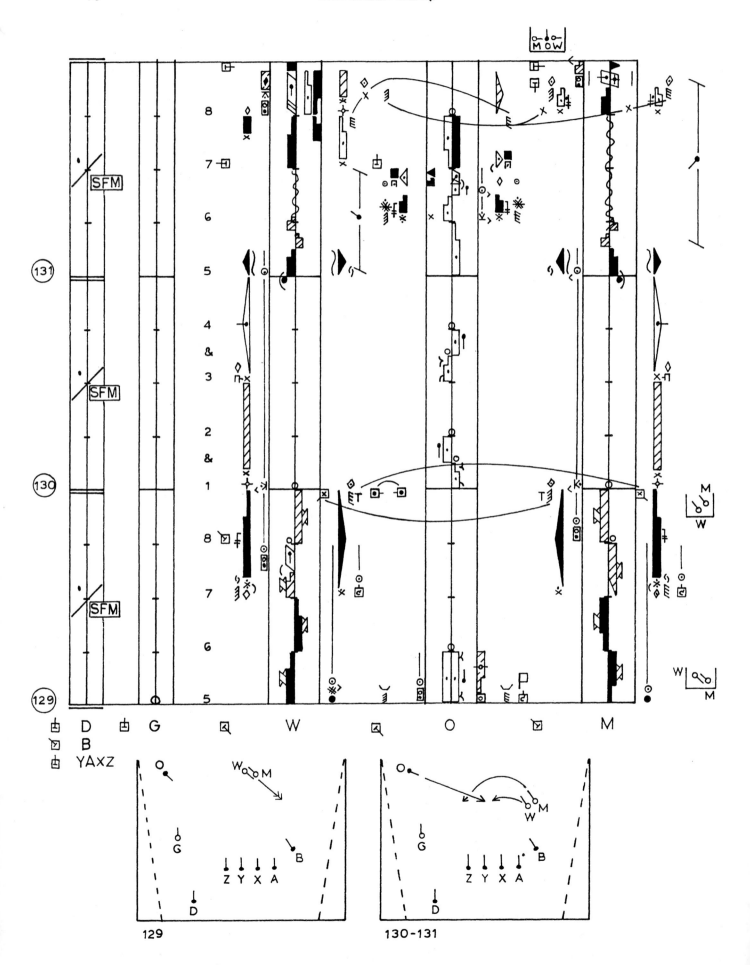

129

130-131

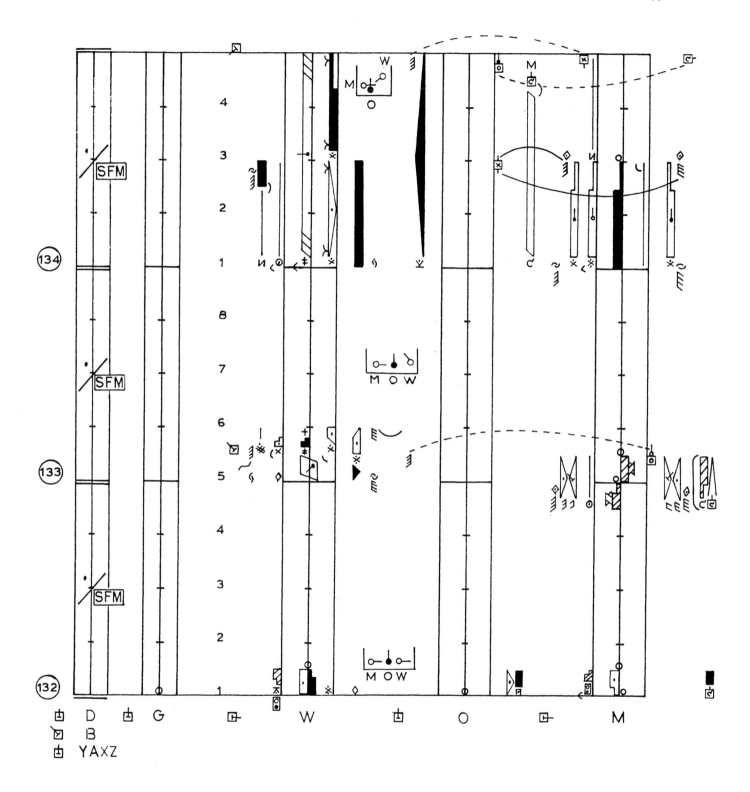

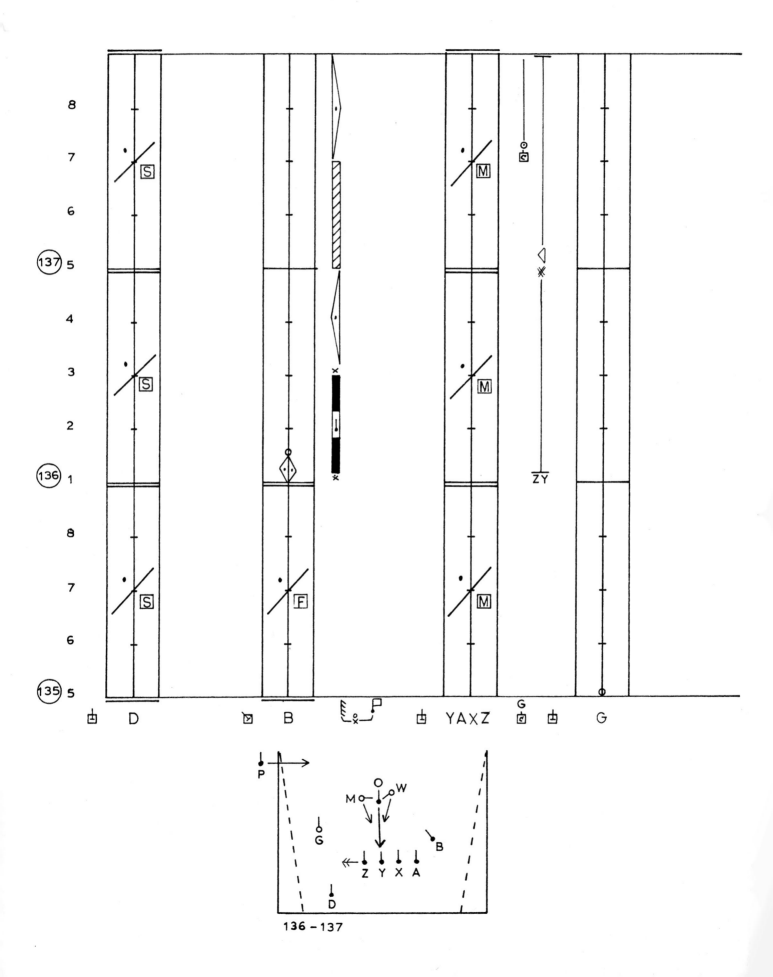

136 – 137

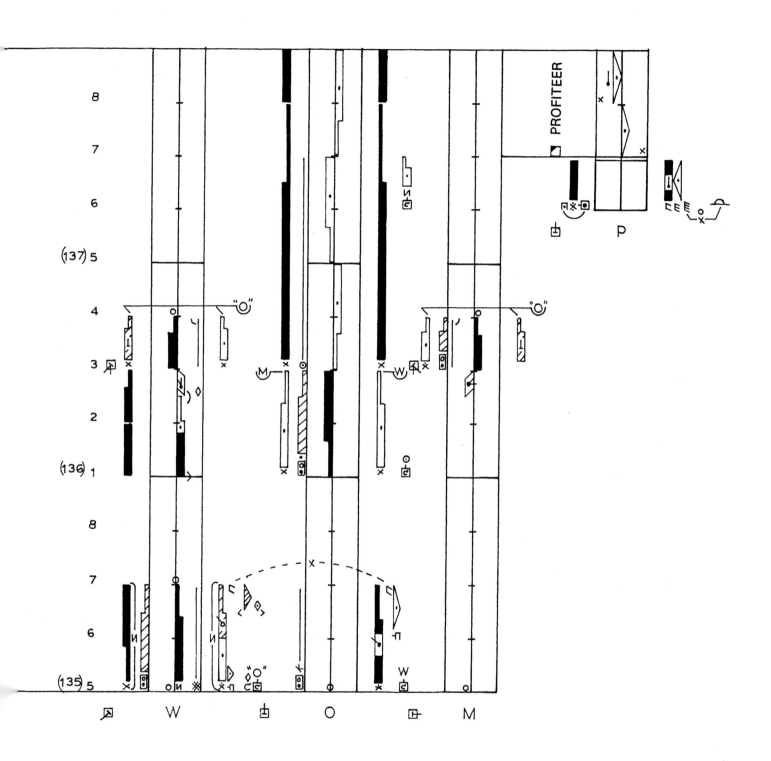

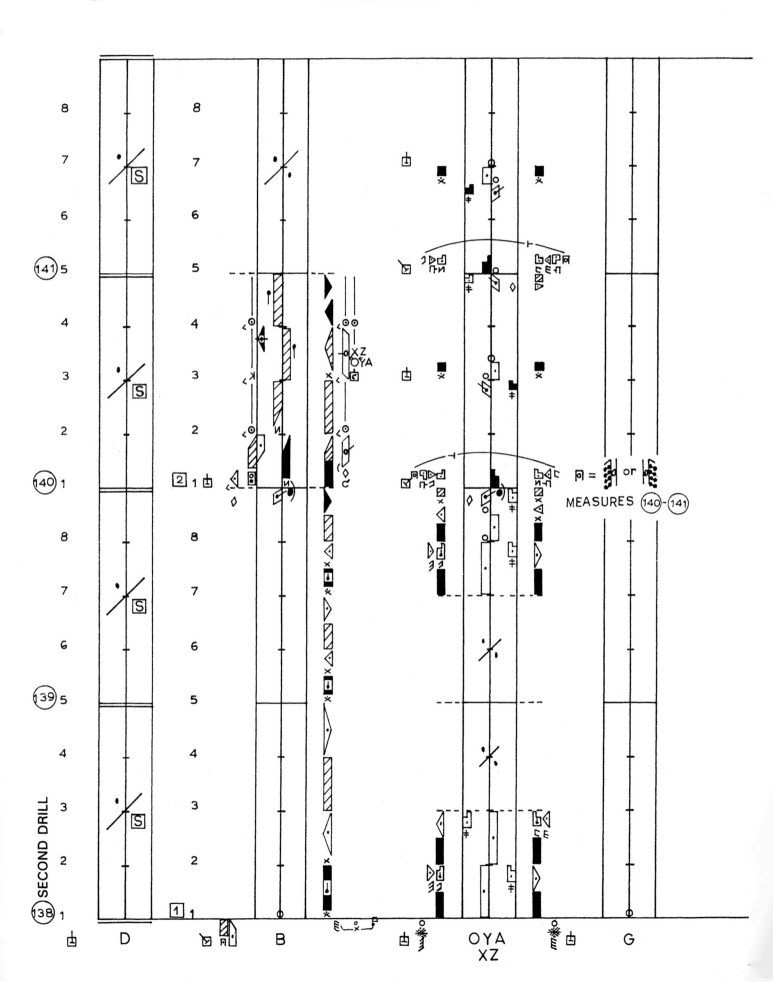

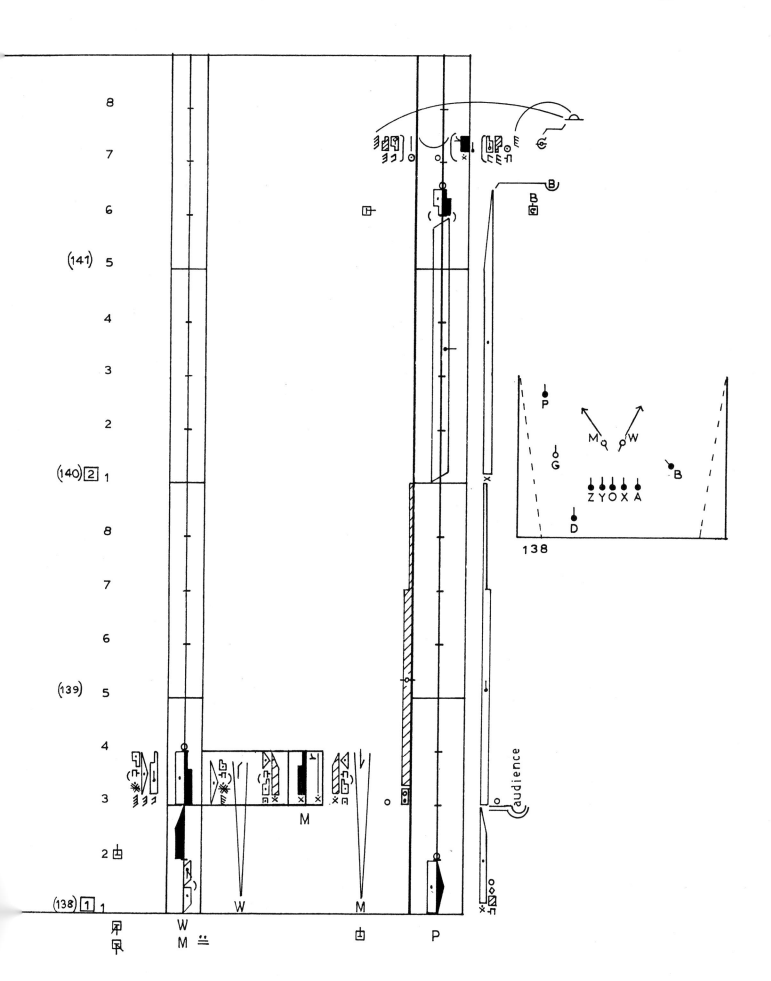

138

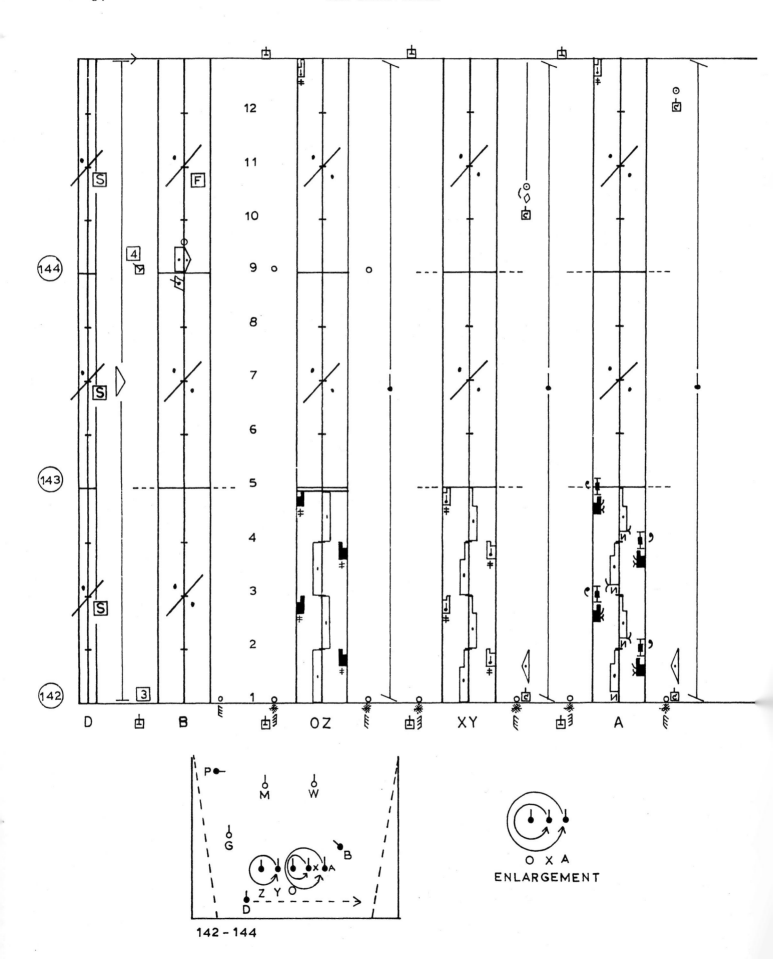

142 – 144

ENLARGEMENT

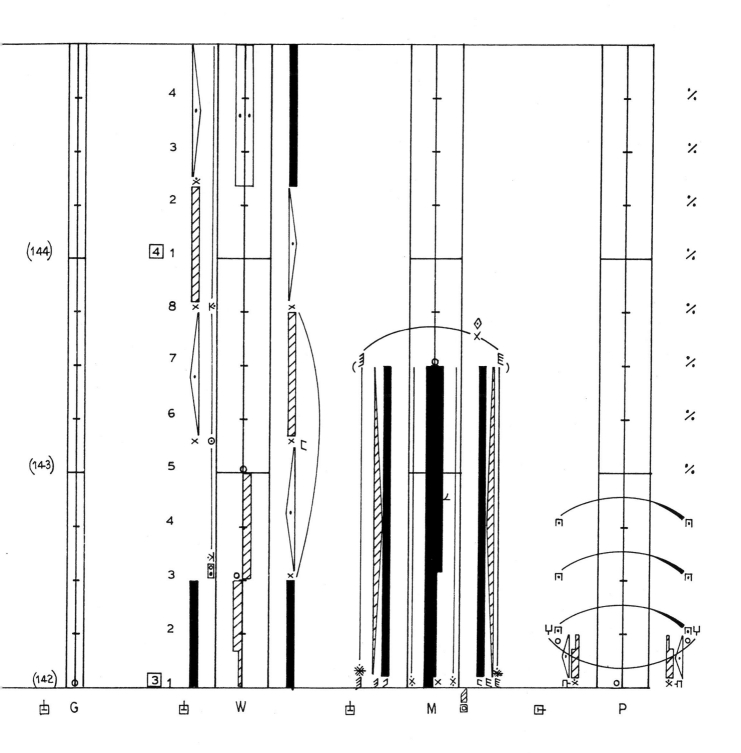

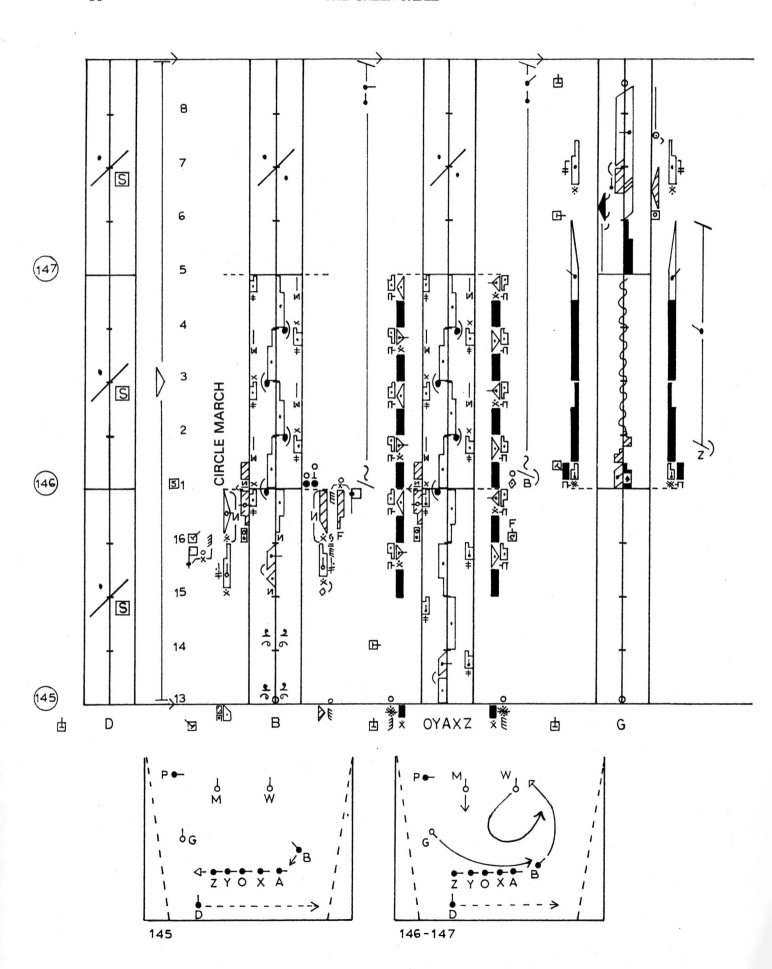

CIRCLE MARCH

145

146-147

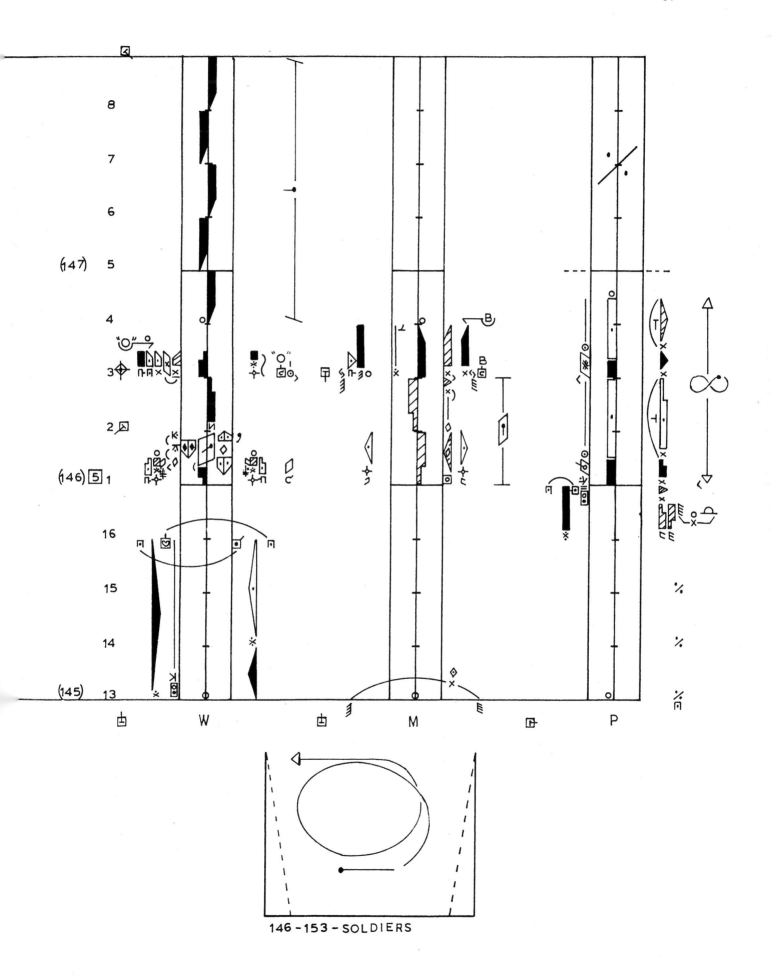

146 - 153 - SOLDIERS

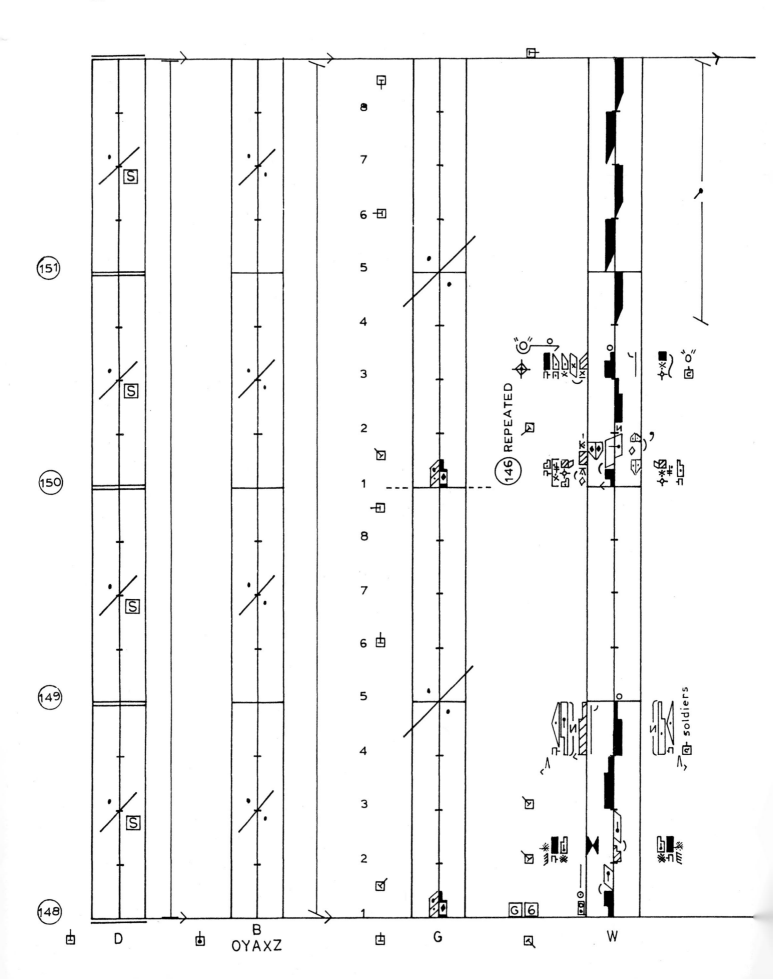

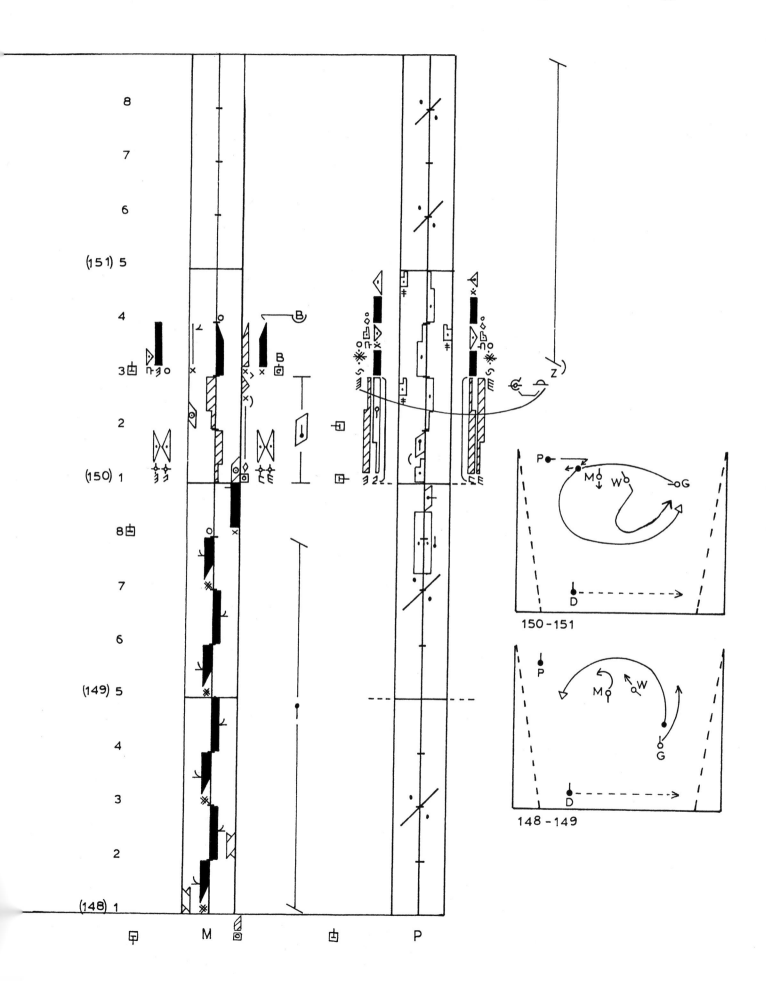

150-151

148-149

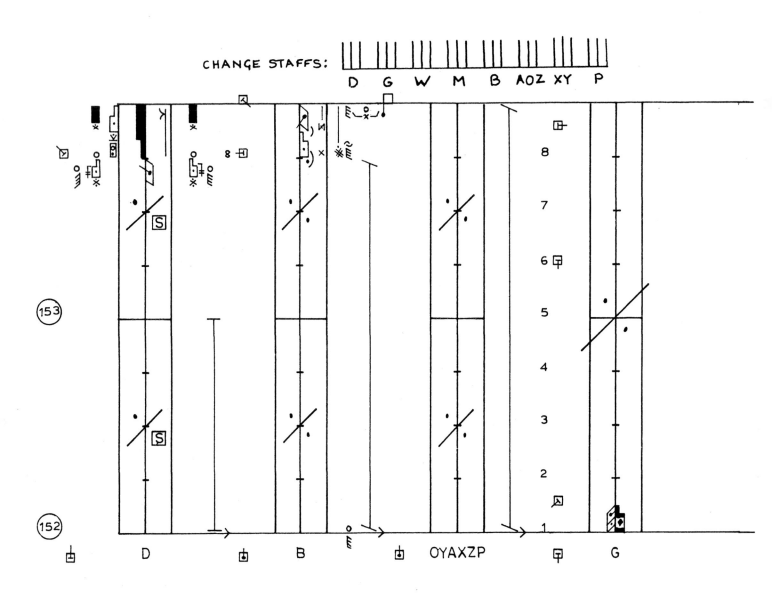

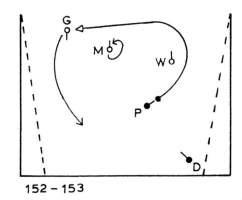

152 – 153

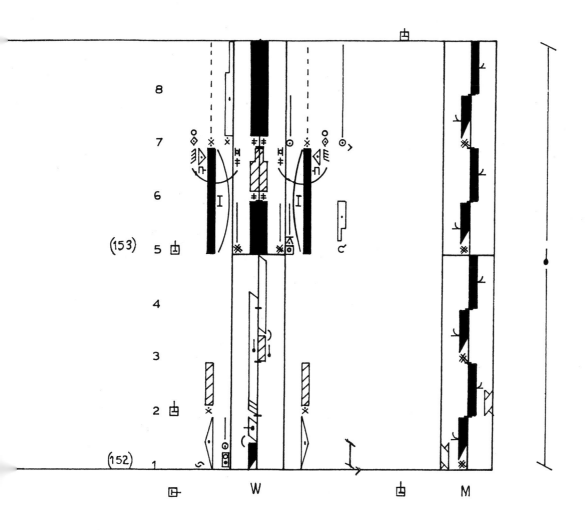

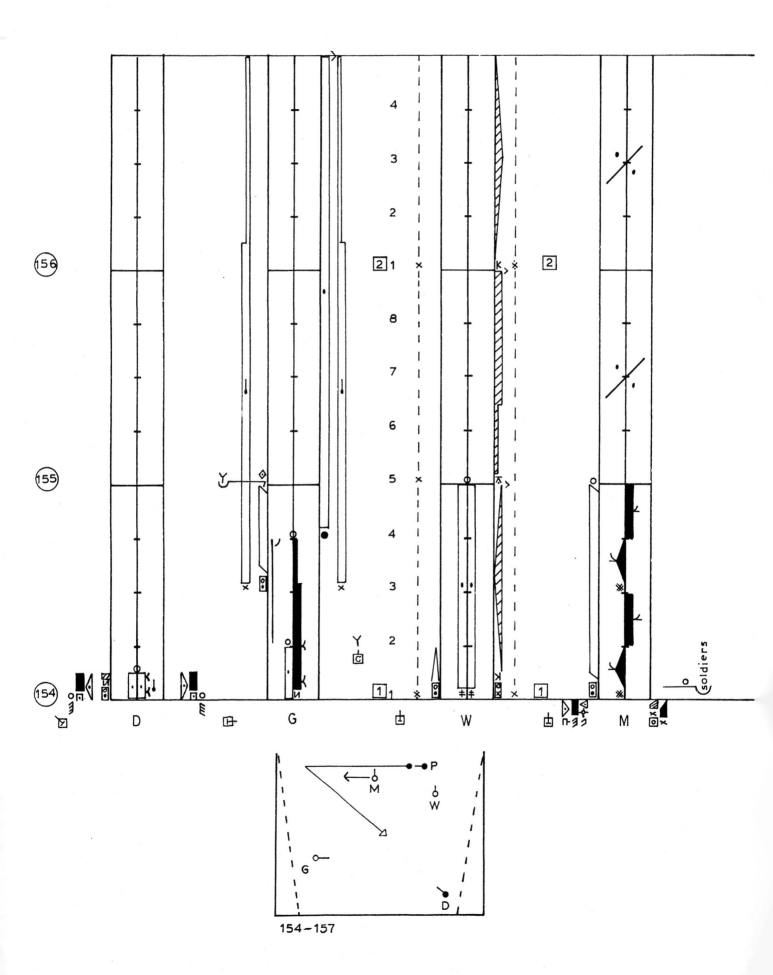

154–157

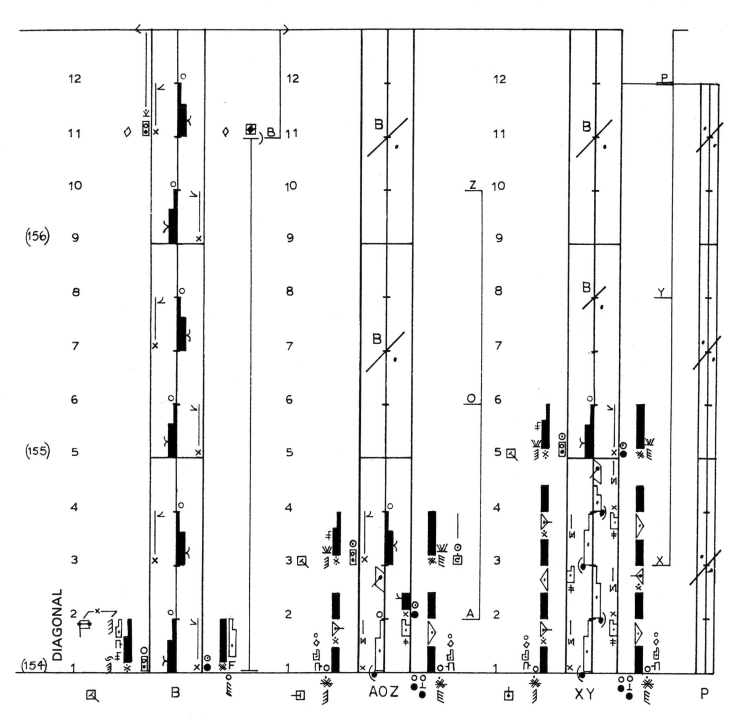

NOTE: DANCER'S COUNT FOR DIAGONAL

	TURN ON	FIRST STEP
B	8	COUNT 1
A	2 (TAP)	COUNT 3
X	4	COUNT 5
O	6 (TAP)	COUNT 7
Y	8 -	COUNT 9
Z	10 (TAP)	COUNT 11
P	12	COUNT 13

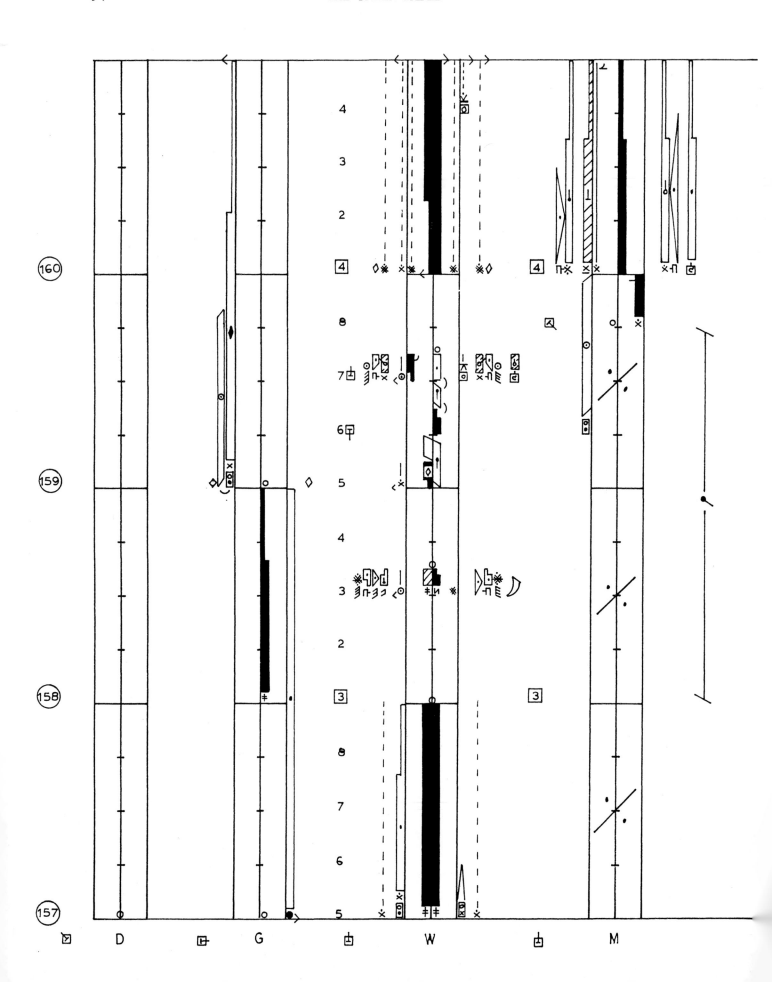

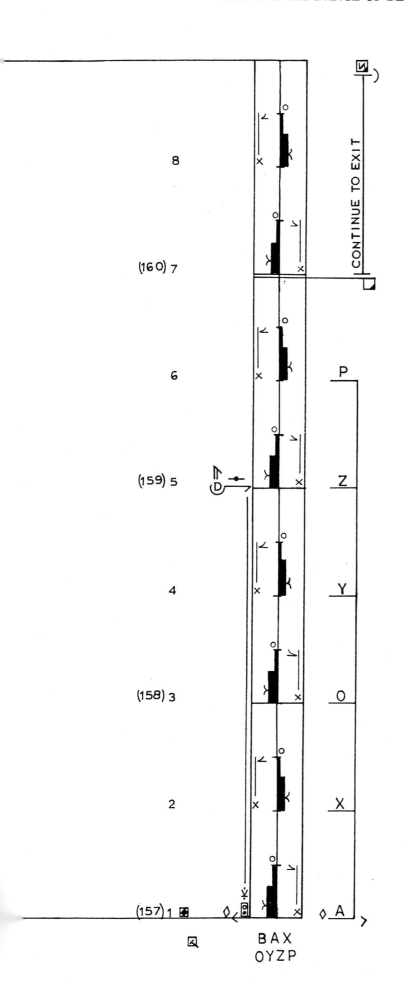

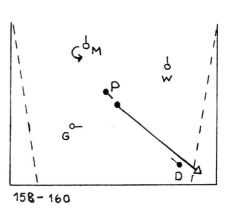

158 - 160

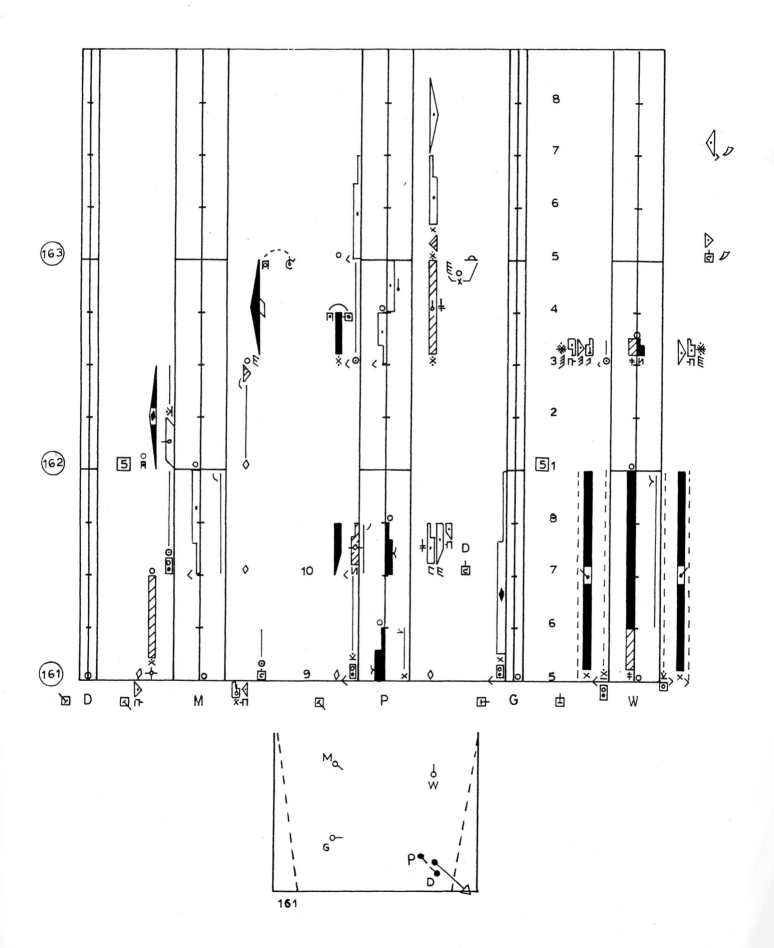

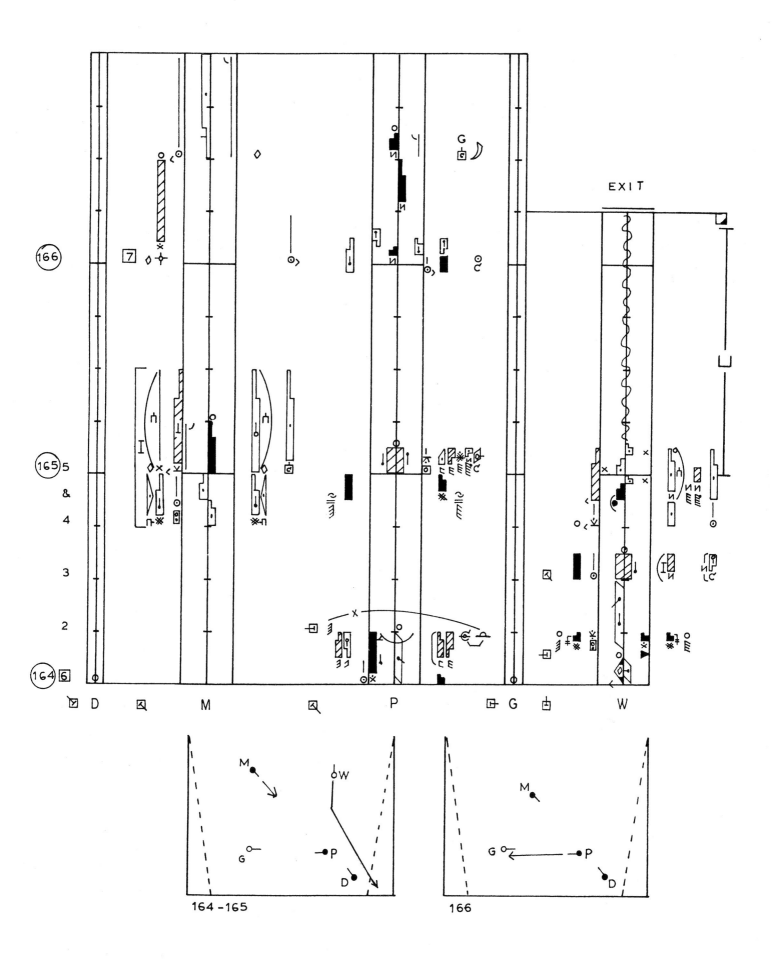

164 – 165

166

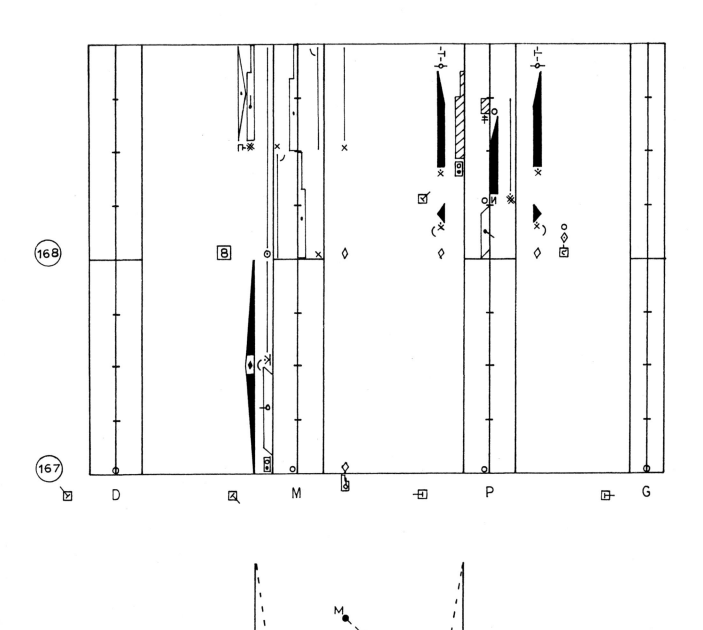

168

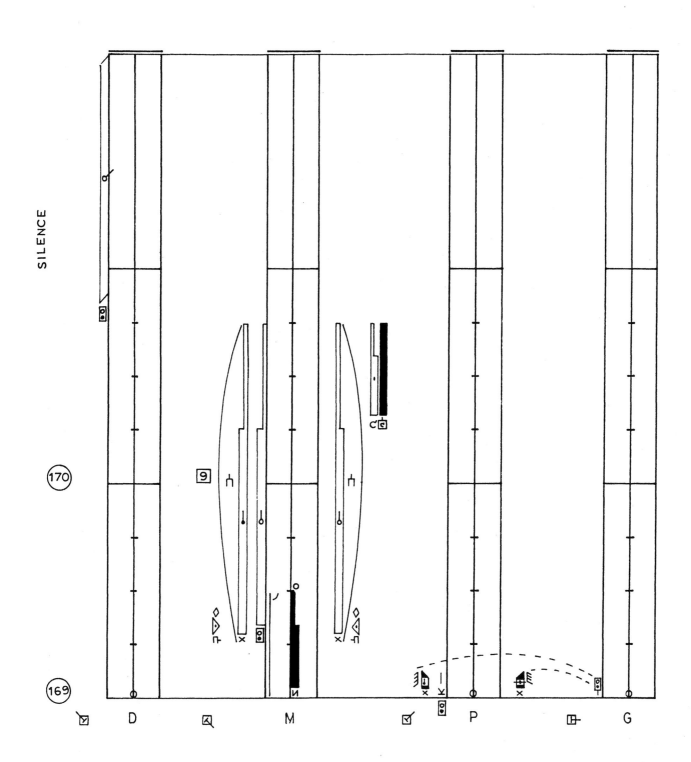

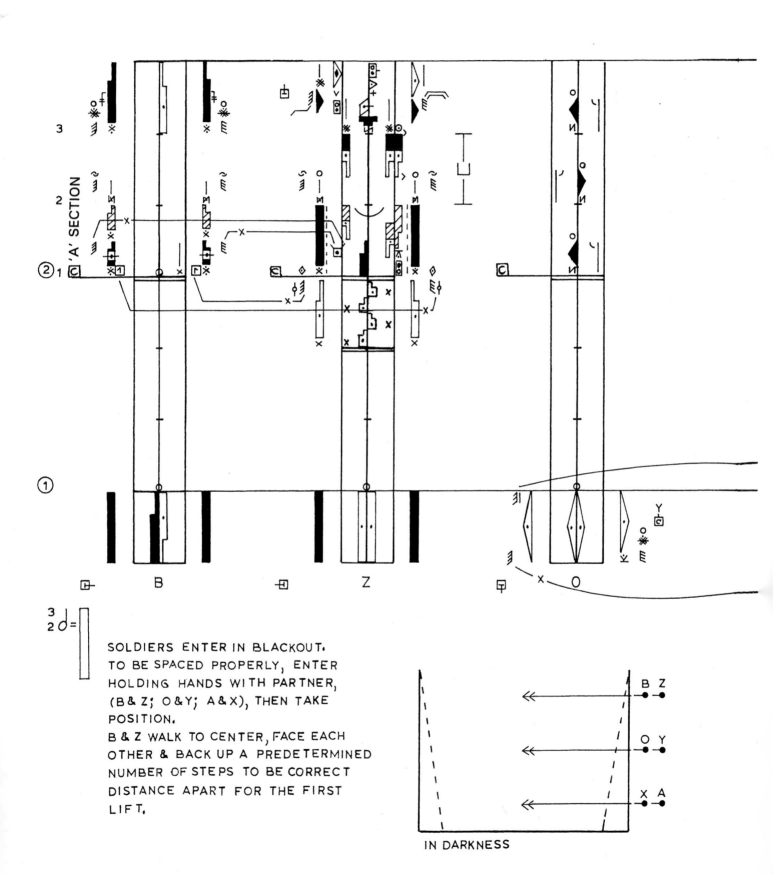

SOLDIERS ENTER IN BLACKOUT.
TO BE SPACED PROPERLY, ENTER
HOLDING HANDS WITH PARTNER,
(B & Z; O & Y; A & X), THEN TAKE
POSITION.
B & Z WALK TO CENTER, FACE EACH
OTHER & BACK UP A PREDETERMINED
NUMBER OF STEPS TO BE CORRECT
DISTANCE APART FOR THE FIRST
LIFT.

IN DARKNESS

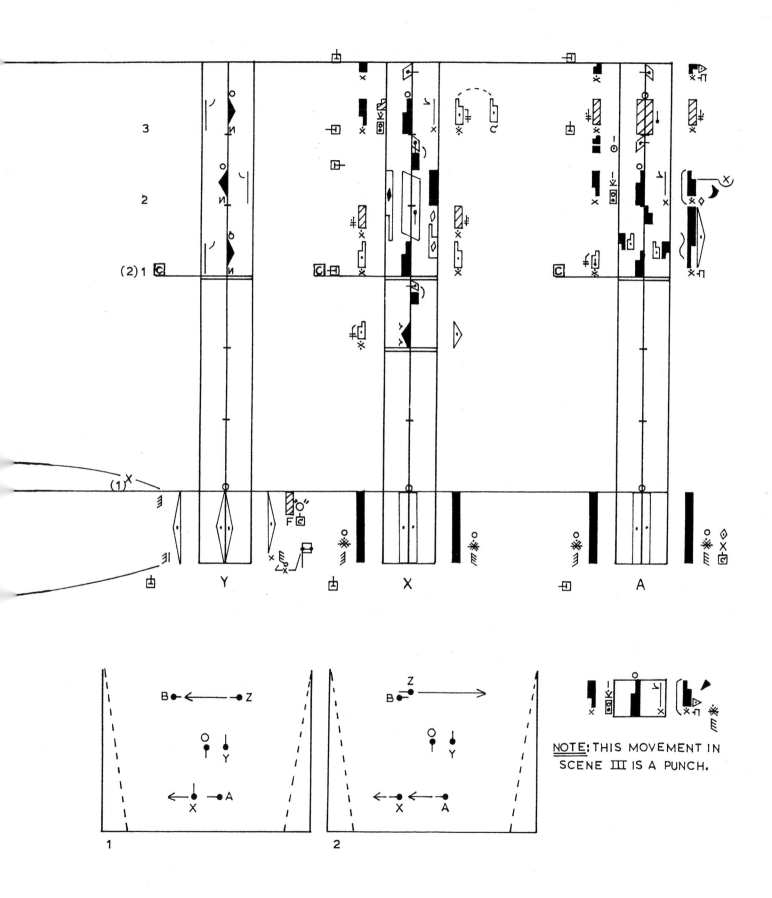

NOTE: THIS MOVEMENT IN SCENE III IS A PUNCH.

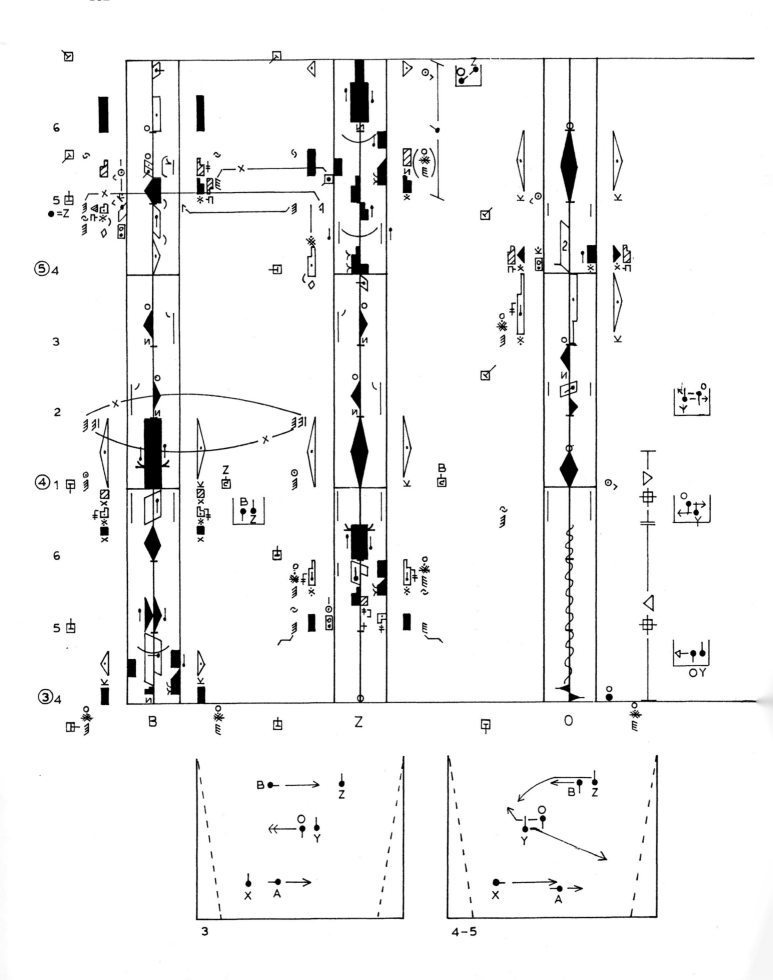

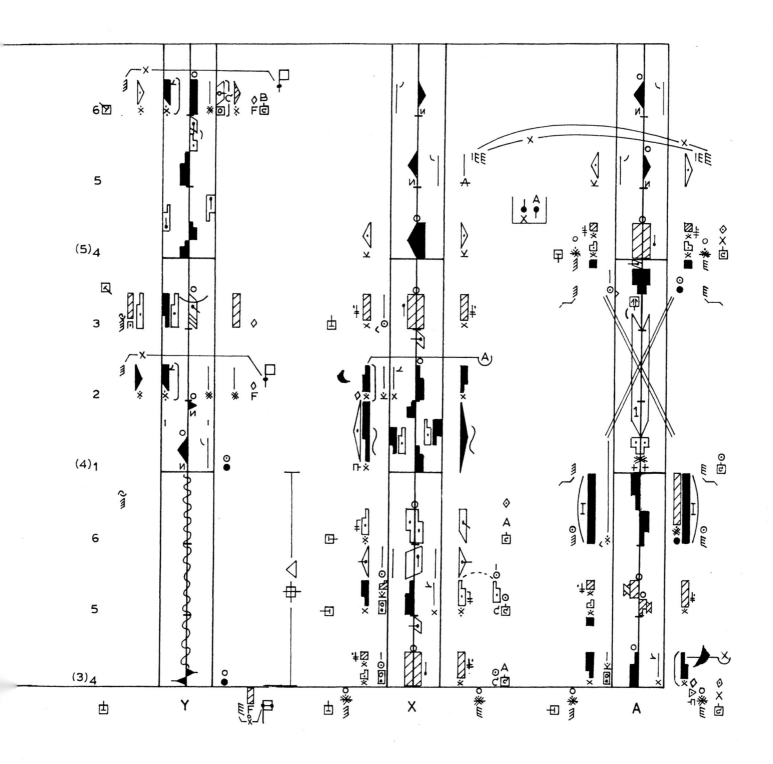

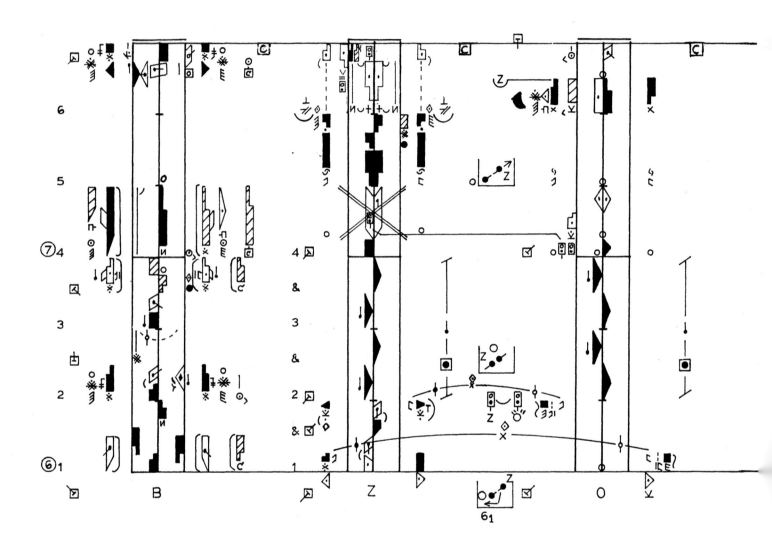

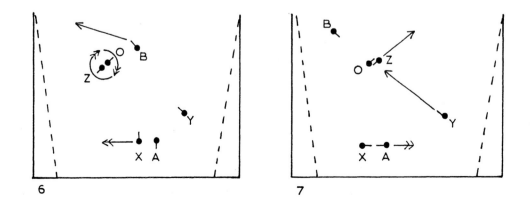

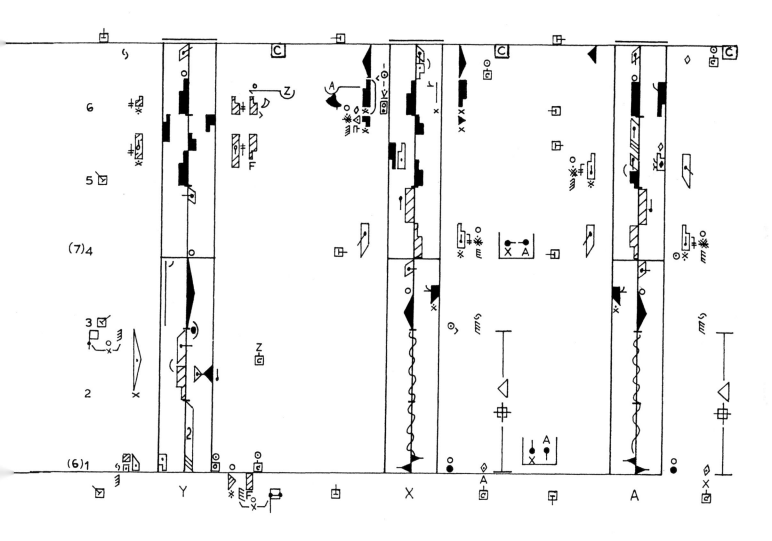

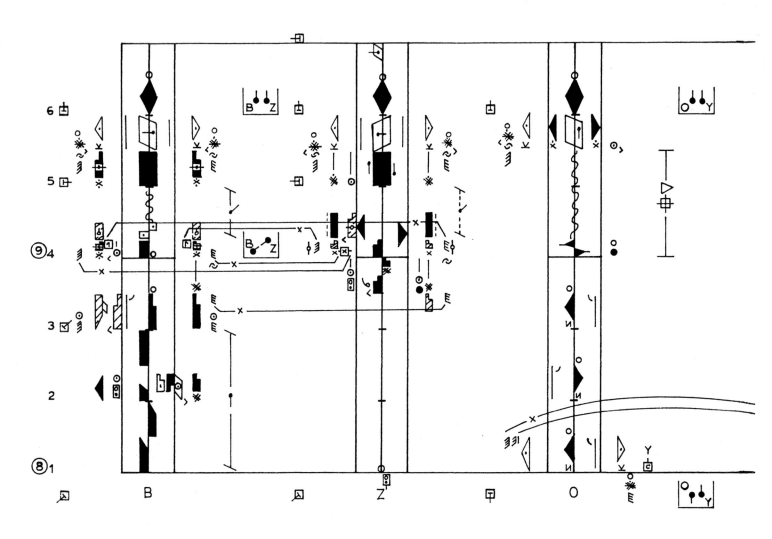

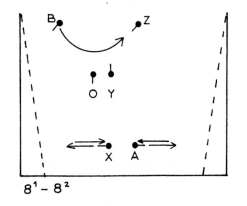

$8^1 - 8^2$

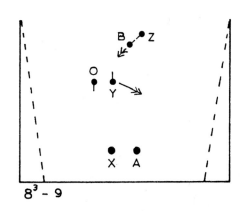

$8^3 - 9$

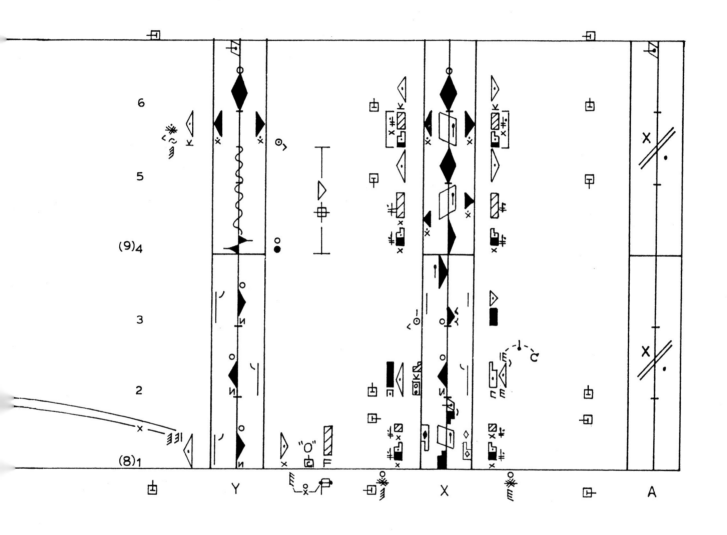

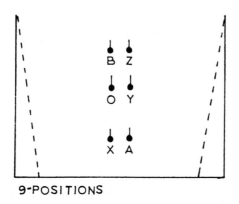

9-POSITIONS

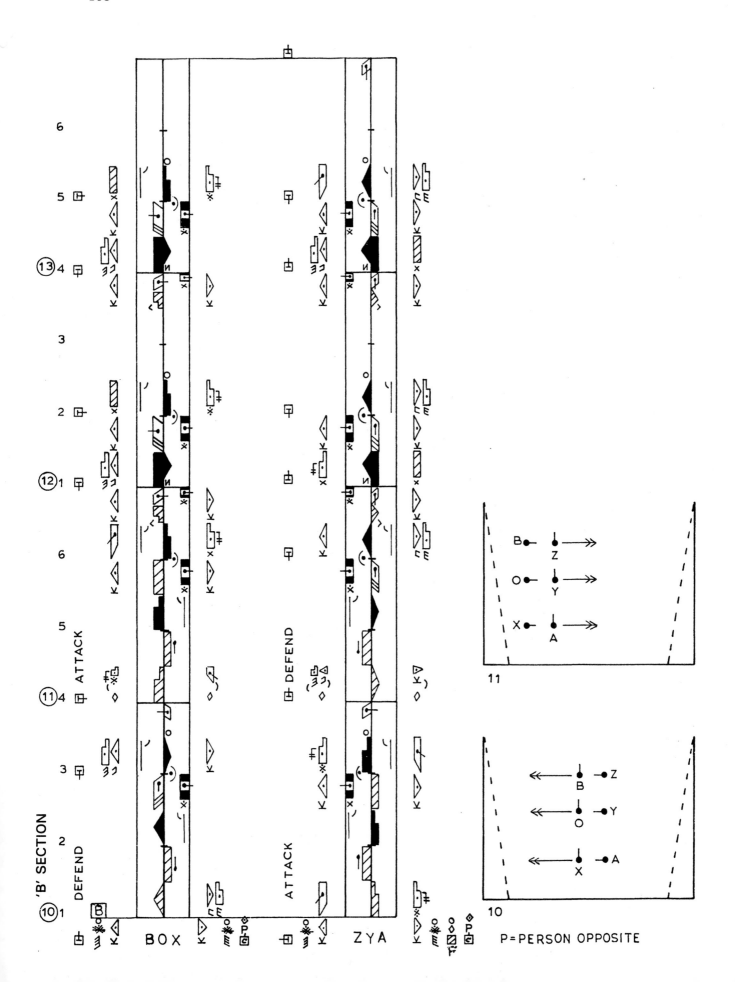

11

10

P=PERSON OPPOSITE

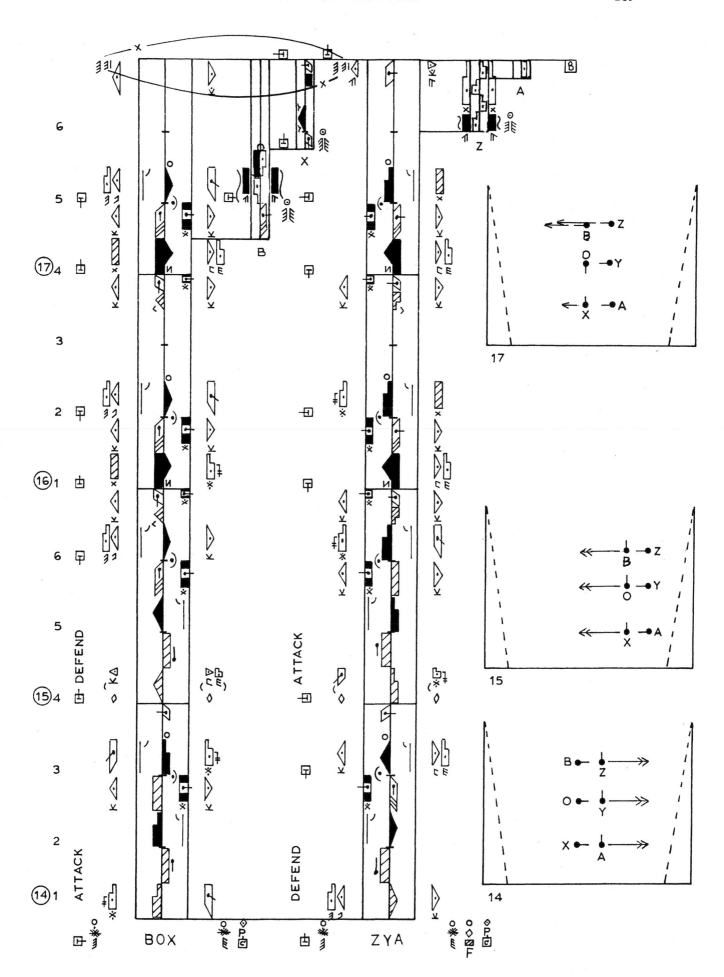

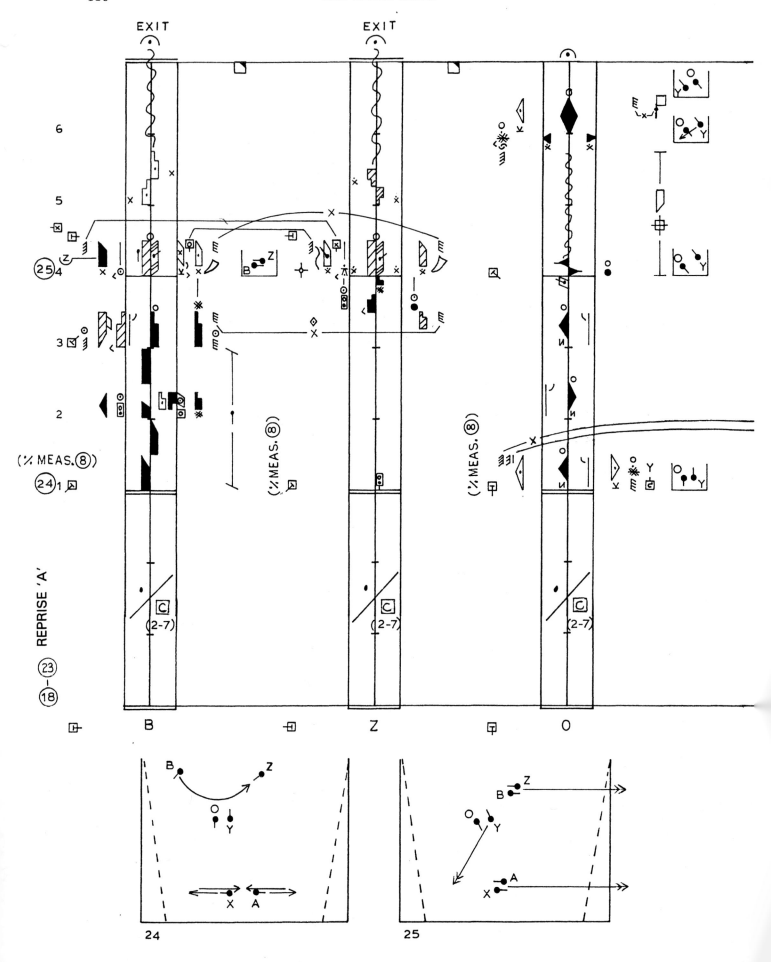

24

25

B   Z   O

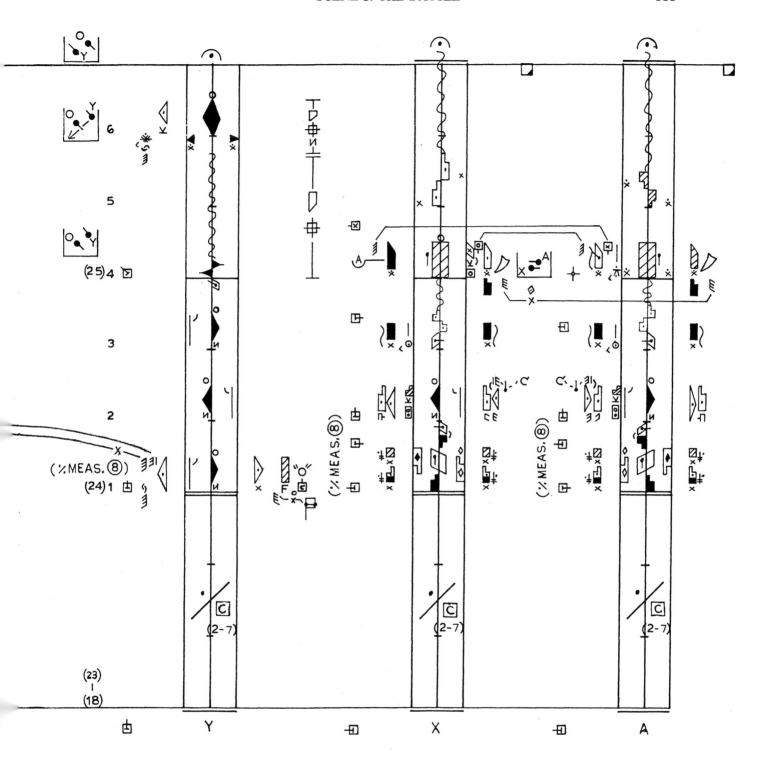

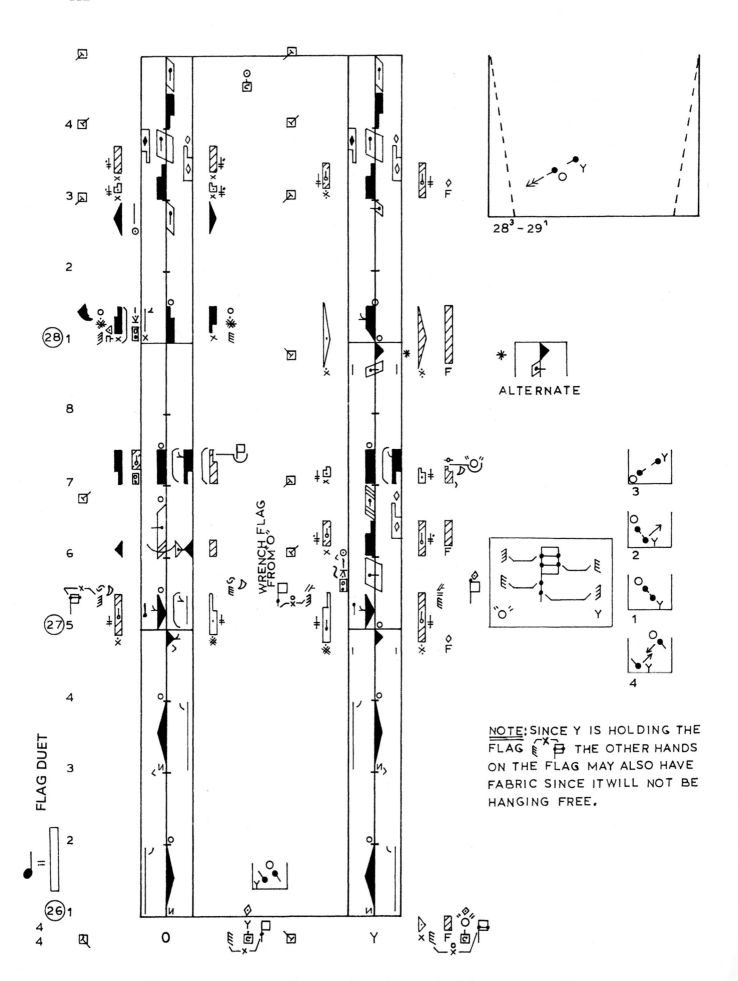

FLAG DUET

ALTERNATE

WRENCH FLAG FROM "O"

NOTE: SINCE Y IS HOLDING THE FLAG THE OTHER HANDS ON THE FLAG MAY ALSO HAVE FABRIC SINCE IT WILL NOT BE HANGING FREE.

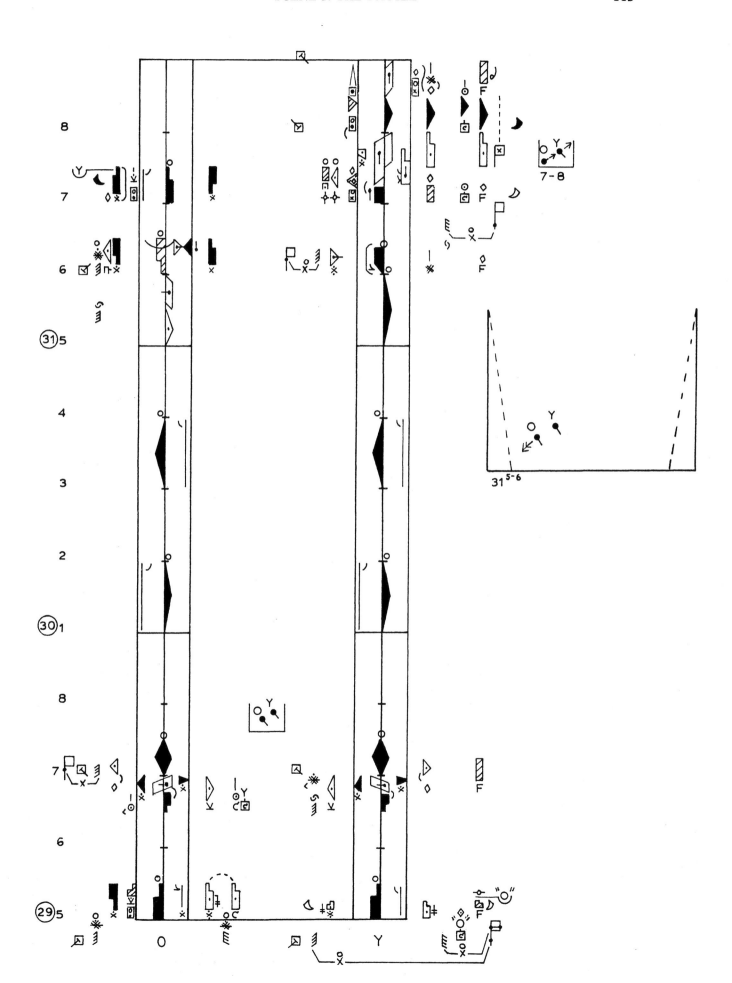

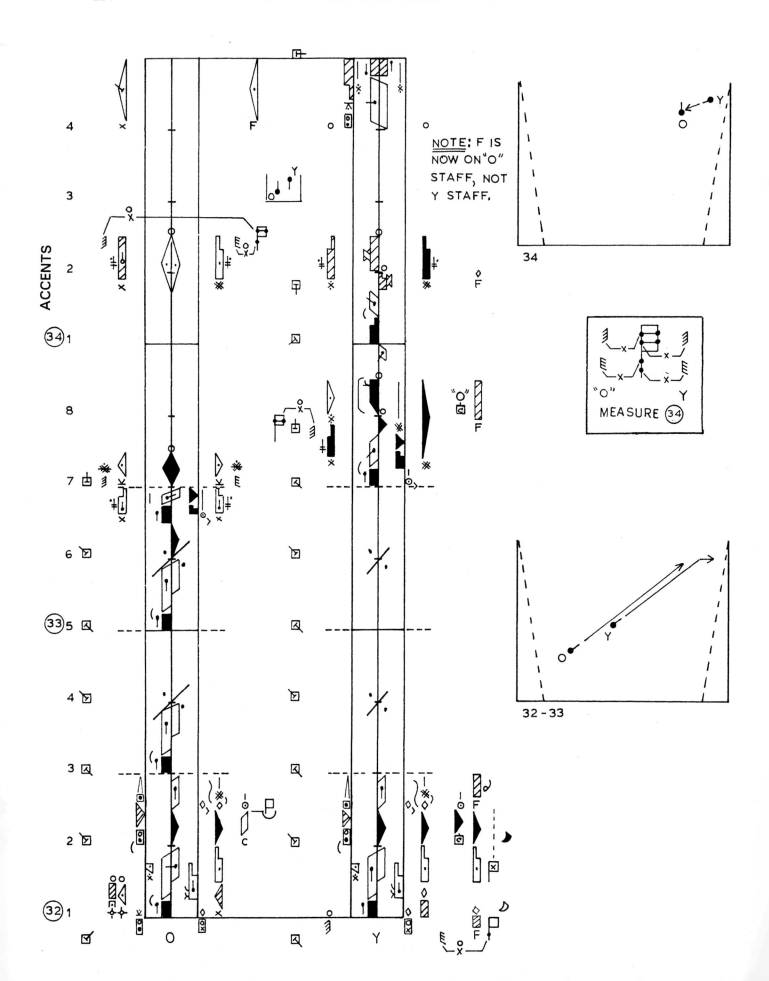

NOTE: F IS NOW ON "O" STAFF, NOT Y STAFF.

34

MEASURE 34

32 – 33

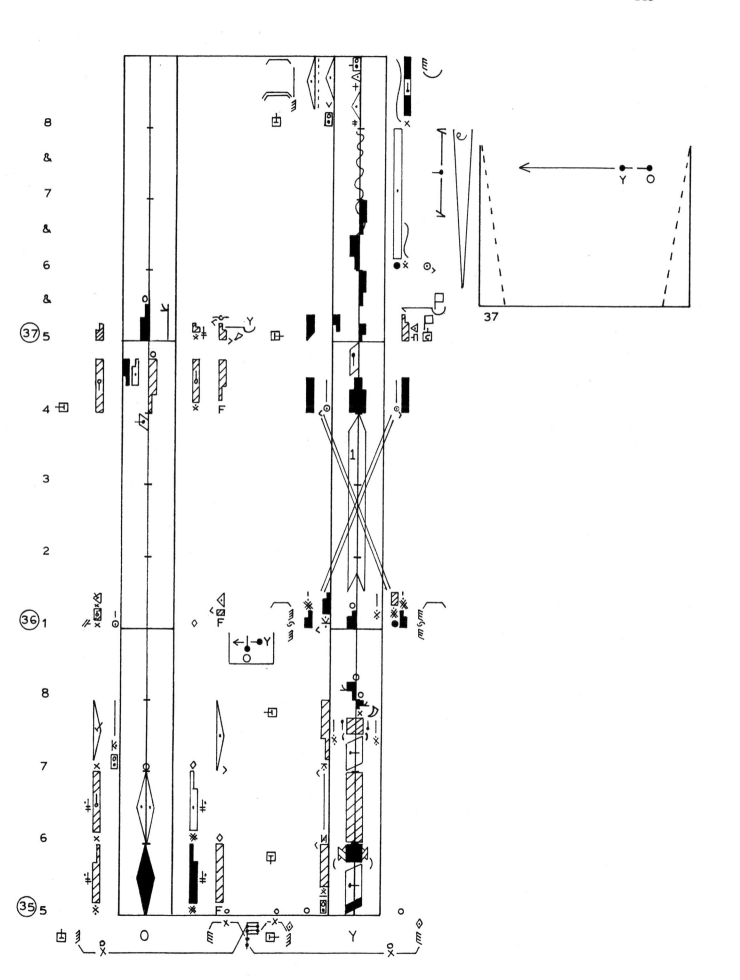

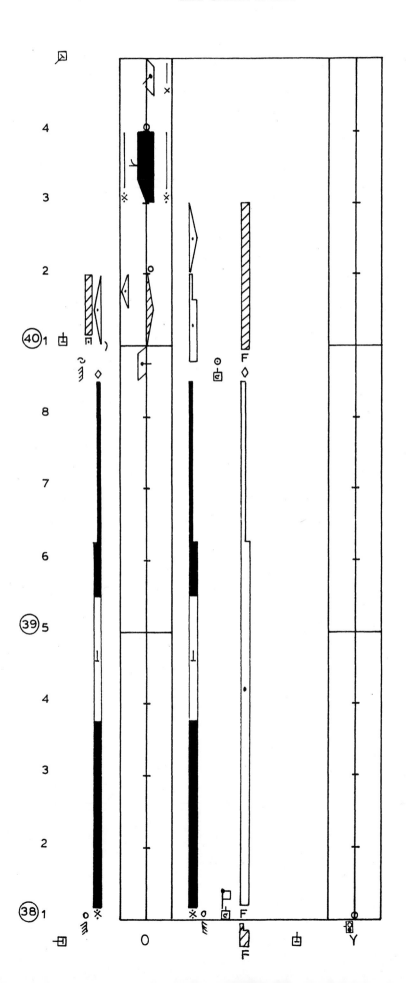

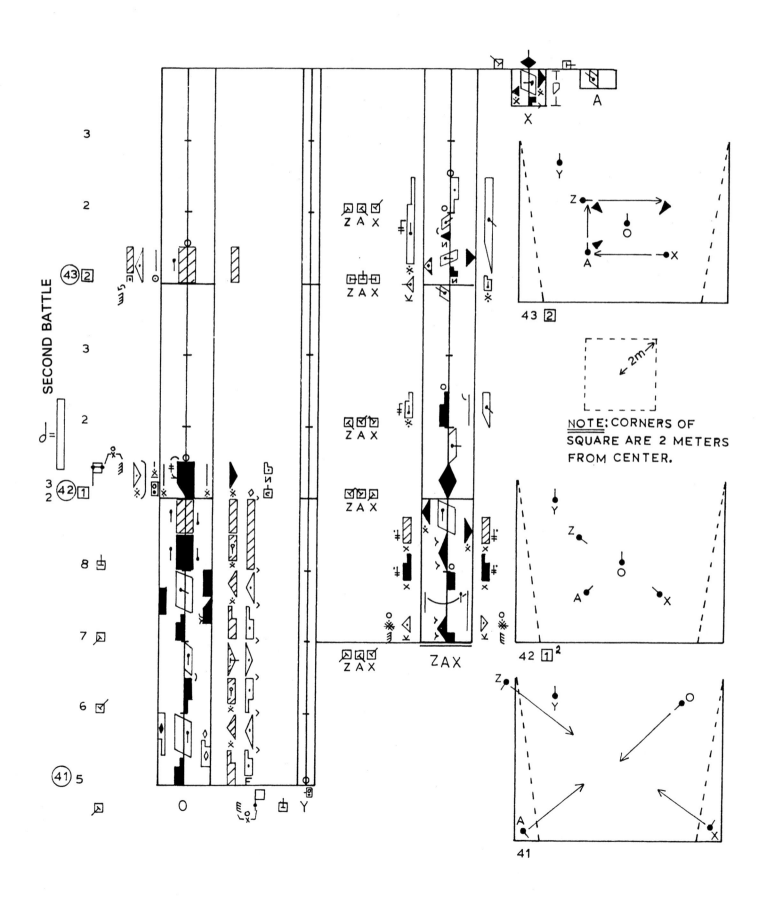

SECOND BATTLE

CHANGE STAFFS:

O B ZXA Y

44 3

45 4

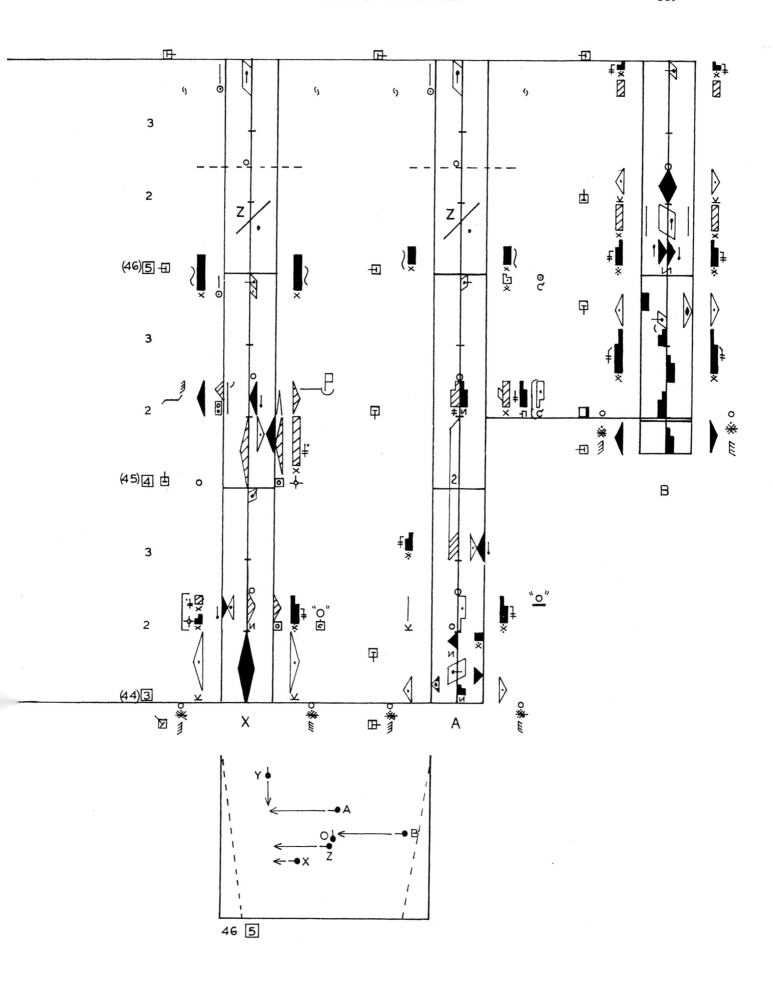

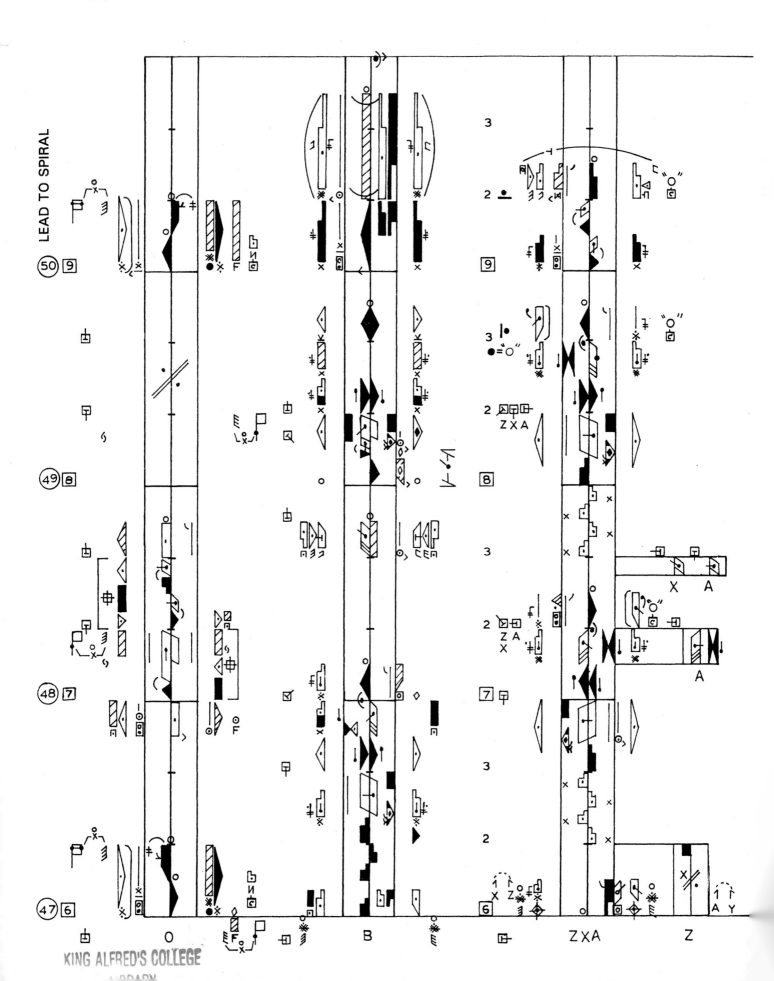

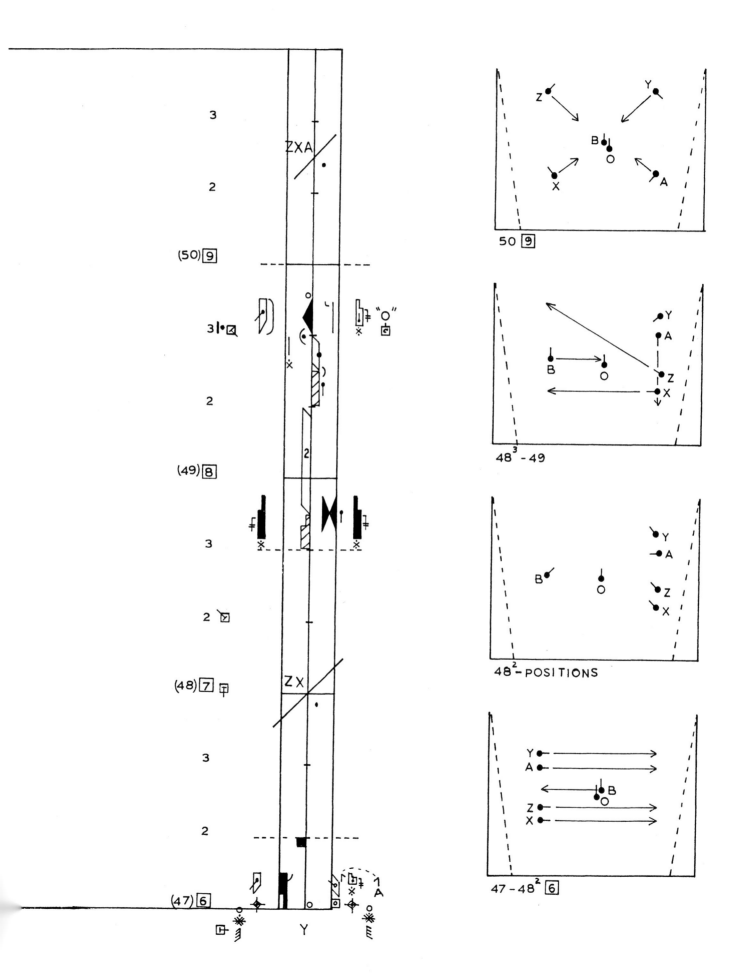

50 9

48³ – 49

48² – POSITIONS

47 – 48² 6

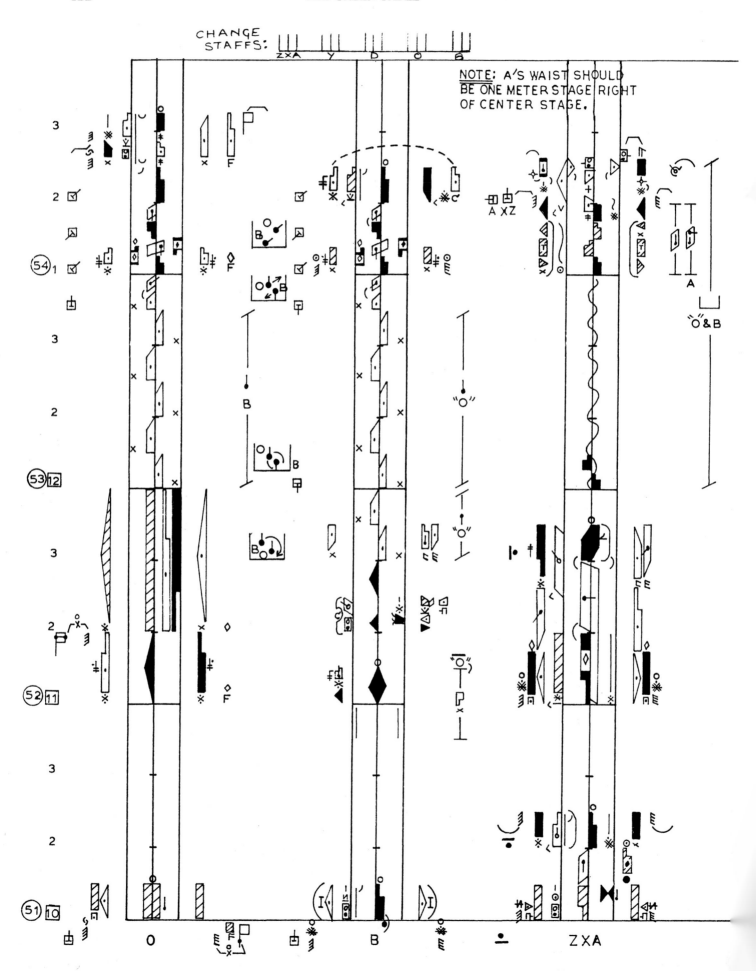

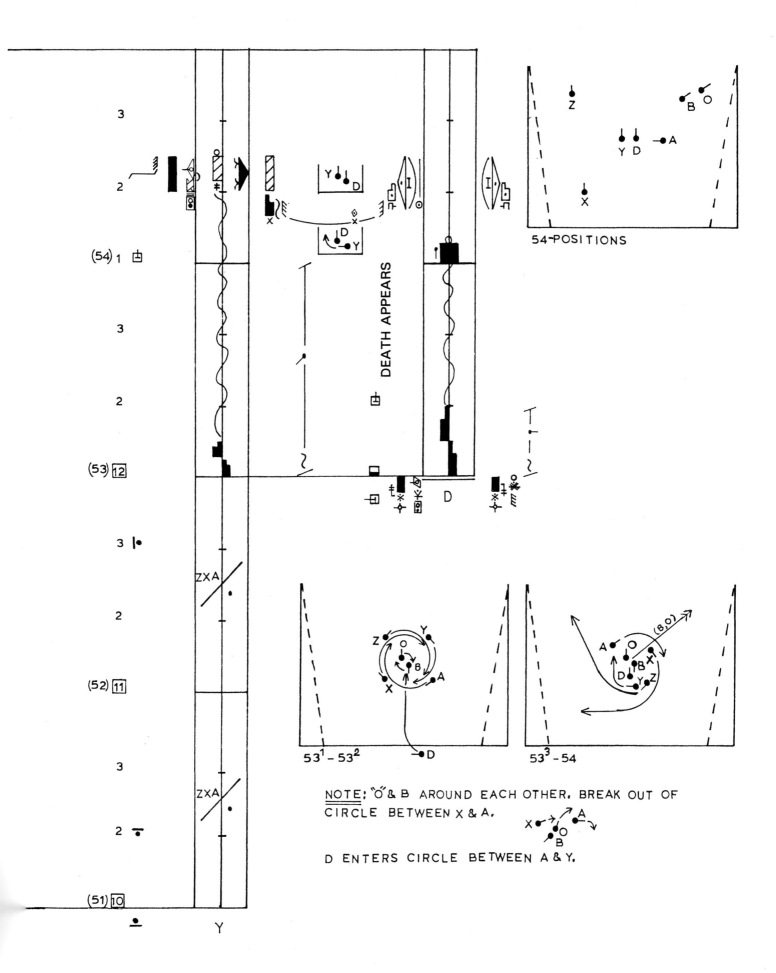

54-POSITIONS

DEATH APPEARS

ZXA

ZXA

$53^1 - 53^2$

$53^3 - 54$

(8,0)

NOTE: "O" & B AROUND EACH OTHER. BREAK OUT OF CIRCLE BETWEEN X & A.

D ENTERS CIRCLE BETWEEN A & Y.

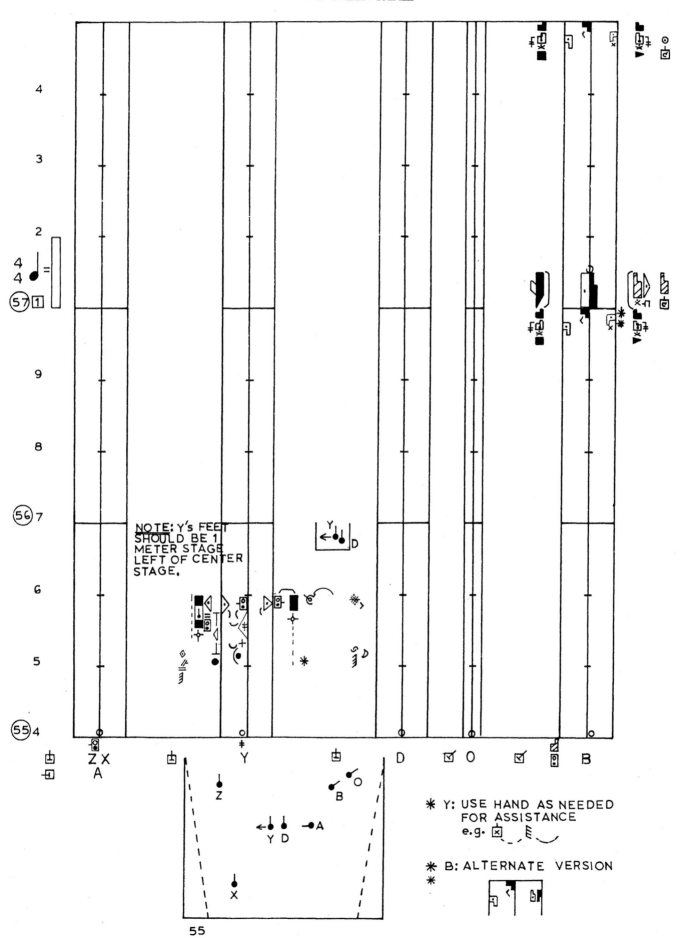

NOTE: Y's FEET
SHOULD BE 1
METER STAGE
LEFT OF CENTER
STAGE.

✳ Y: USE HAND AS NEEDED
FOR ASSISTANCE
e.g.

✳ B: ALTERNATE VERSION
✳

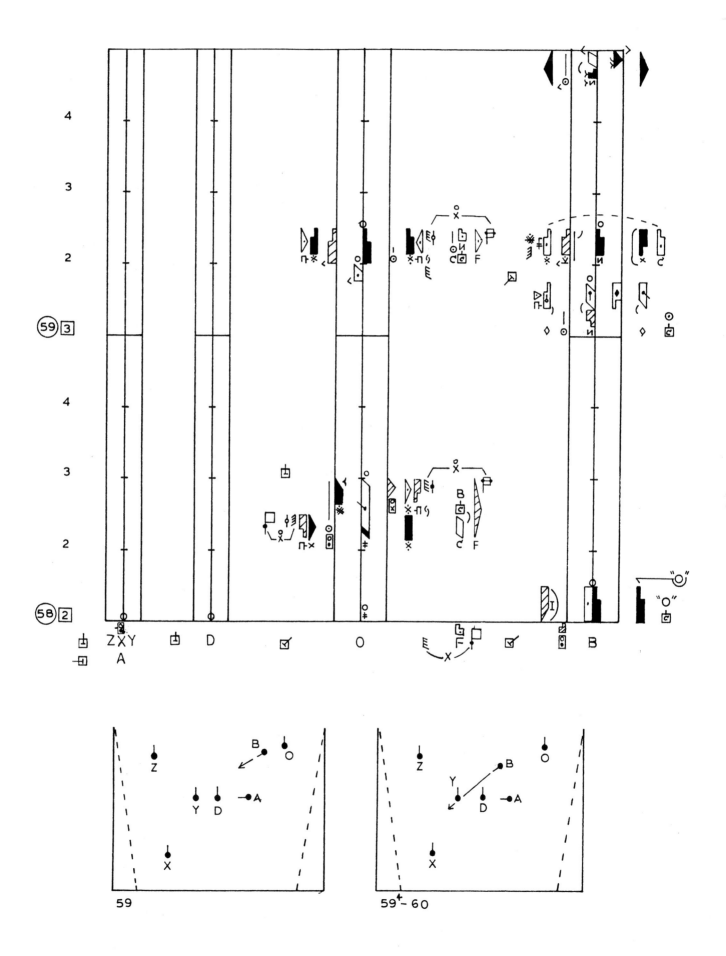

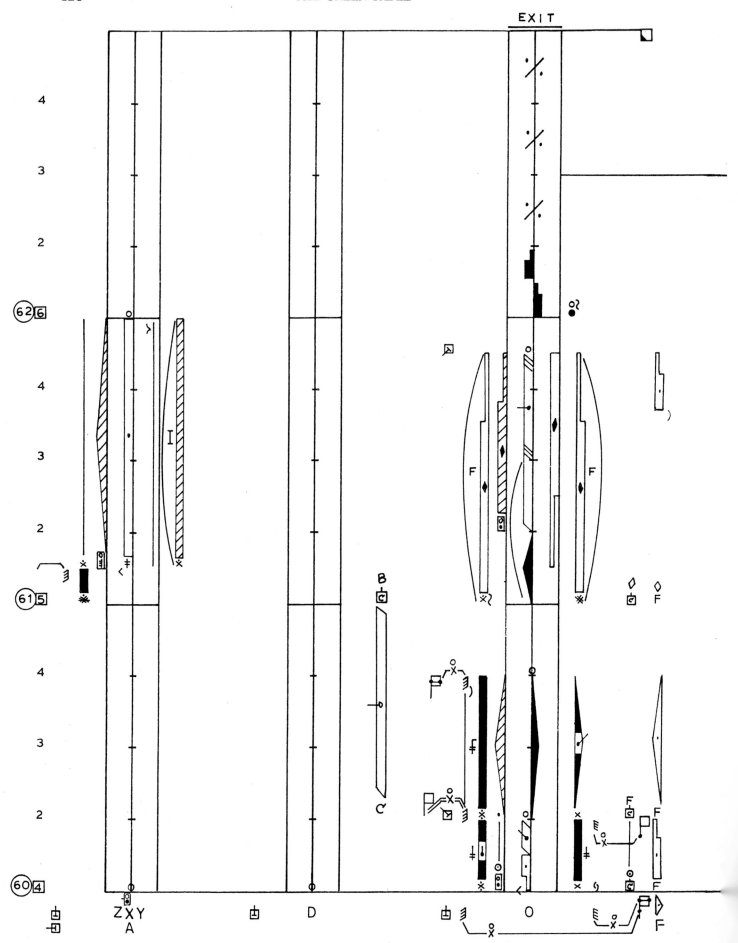

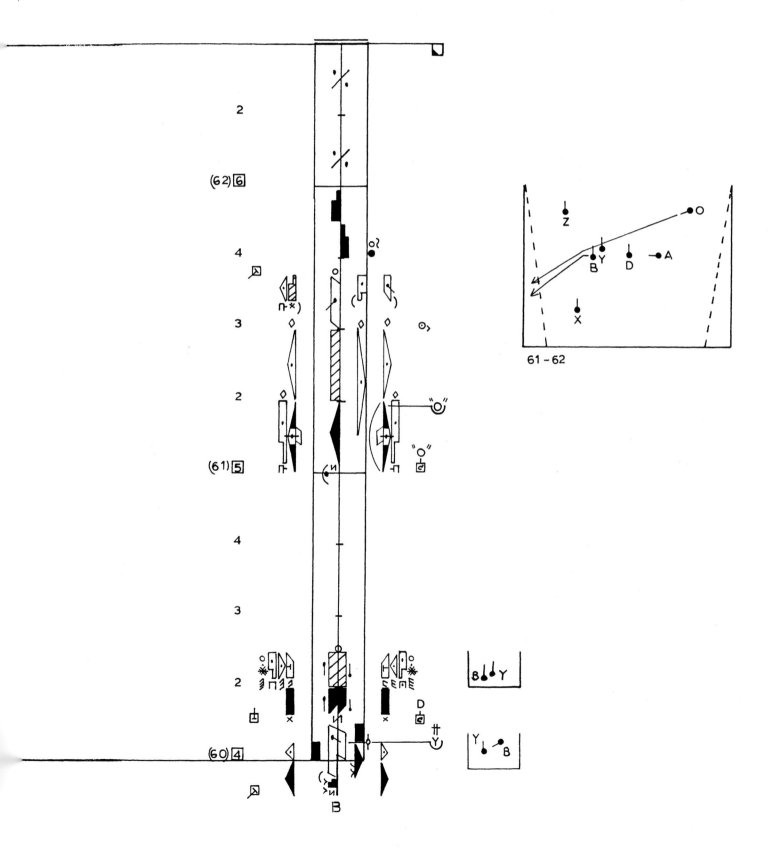

61 – 62

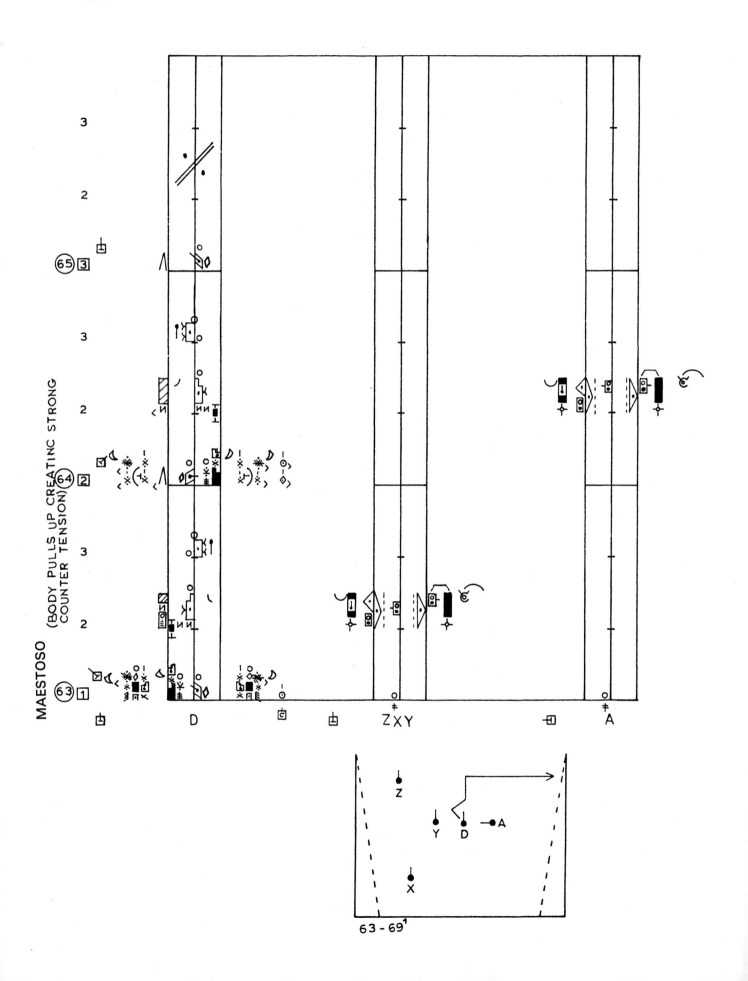

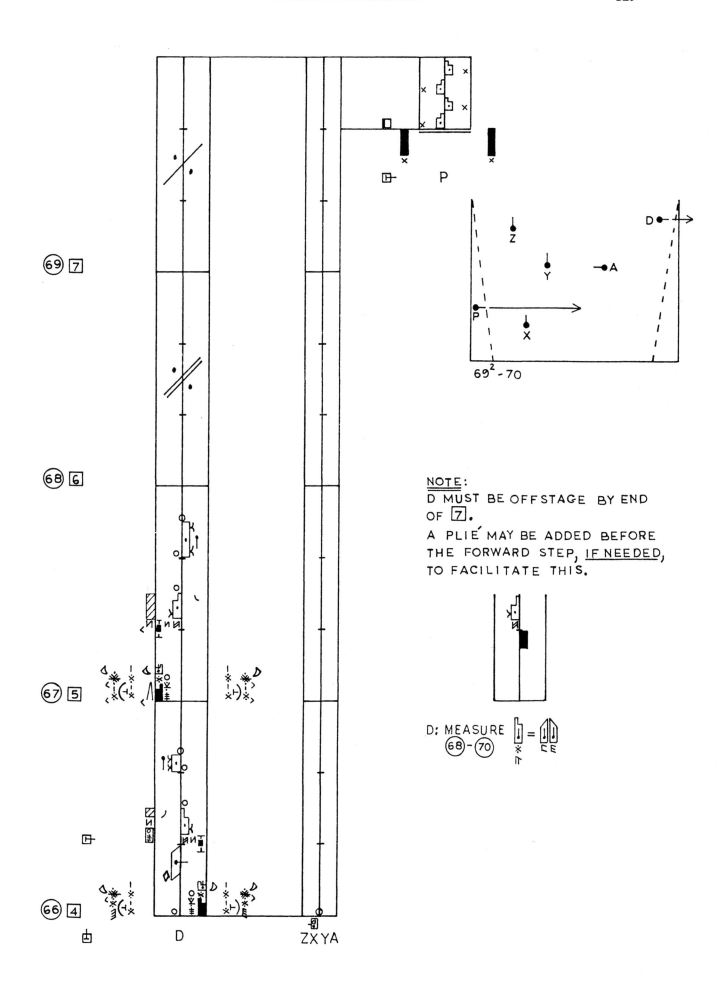

69² - 70

NOTE:
D MUST BE OFFSTAGE BY END
OF [7].
A PLIÉ MAY BE ADDED BEFORE
THE FORWARD STEP, <u>IF NEEDED</u>,
TO FACILITATE THIS.

D: MEASURE
(68) - (70)

69 [7]

68 [6]

67 [5]

66 [4]

D   ZXYA

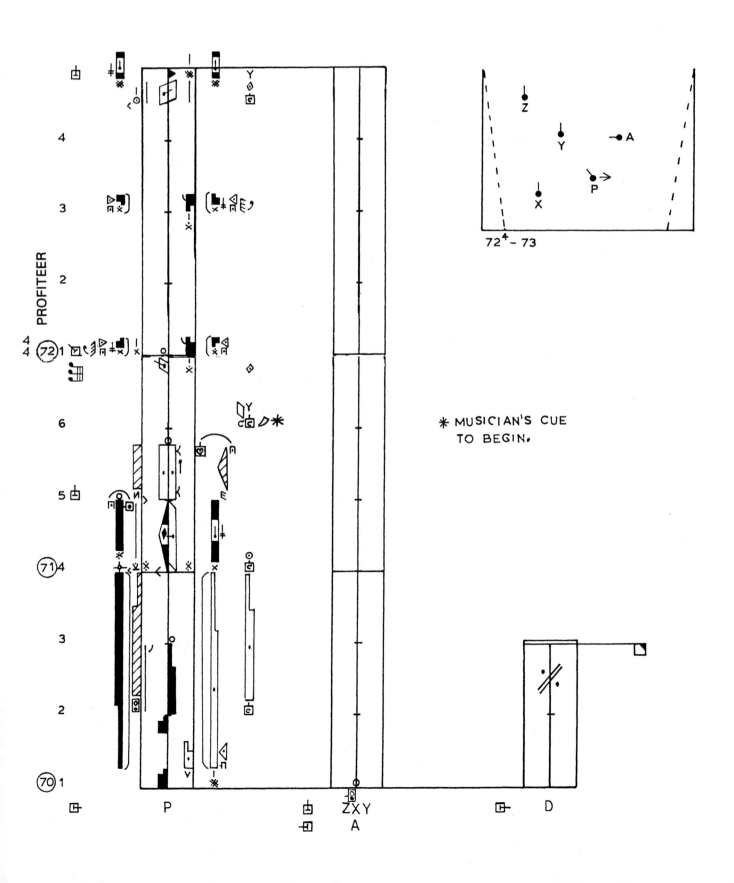

$72^4 - 73$

✳ MUSICIAN'S CUE
TO BEGIN.

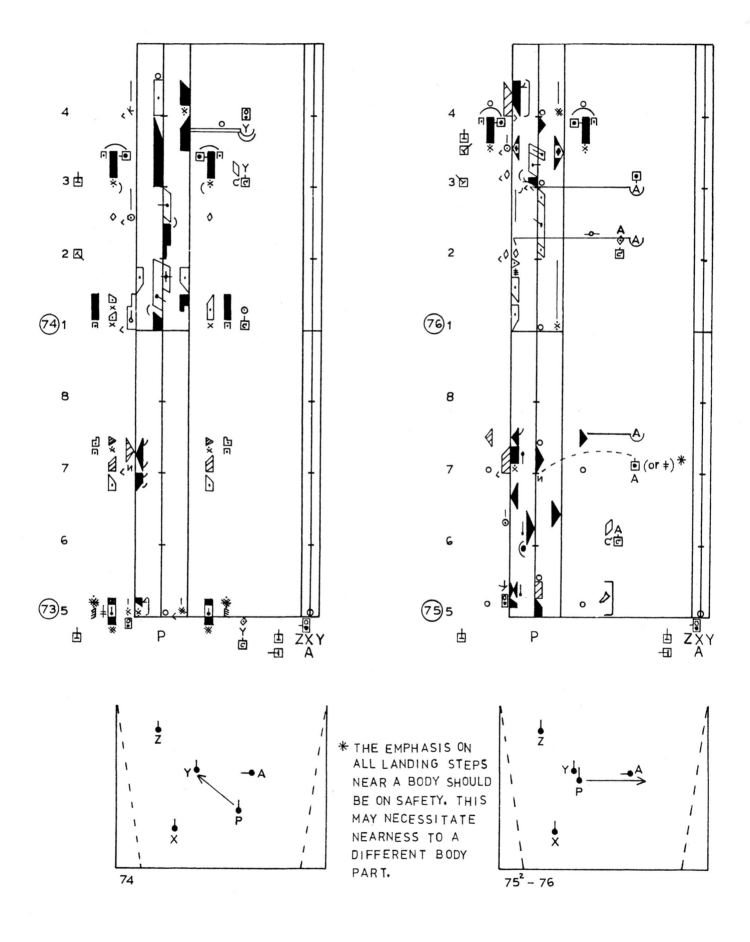

* THE EMPHASIS ON
ALL LANDING STEPS
NEAR A BODY SHOULD
BE ON SAFETY. THIS
MAY NECESSITATE
NEARNESS TO A
DIFFERENT BODY
PART.

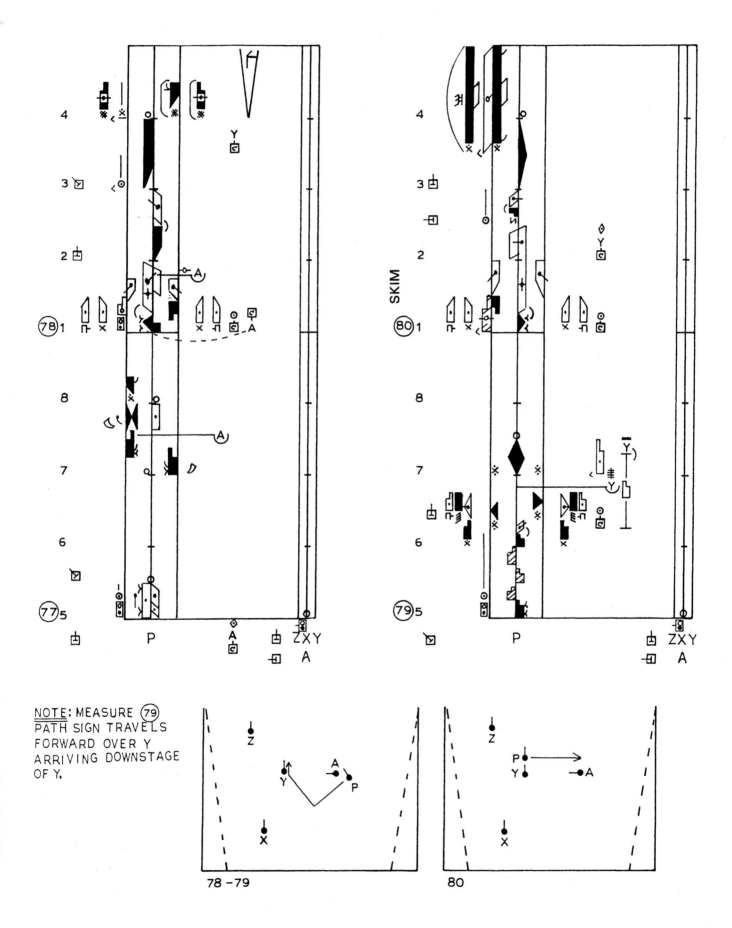

NOTE: MEASURE (79)
PATH SIGN TRAVELS
FORWARD OVER Y
ARRIVING DOWNSTAGE
OF Y.

78–79

80

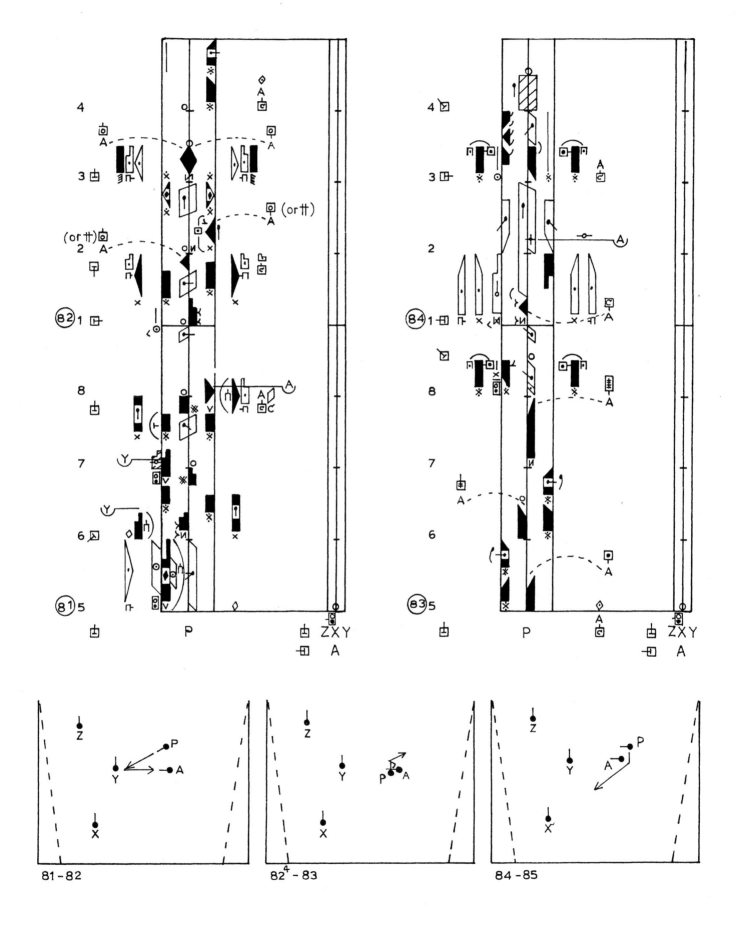

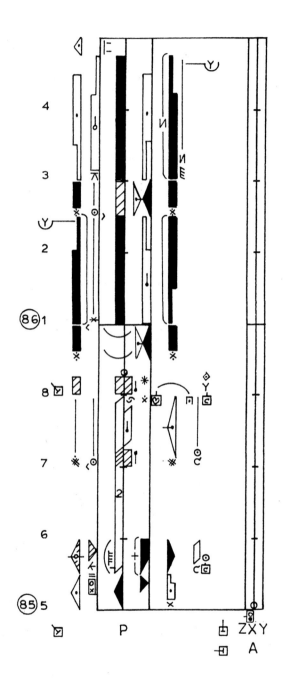

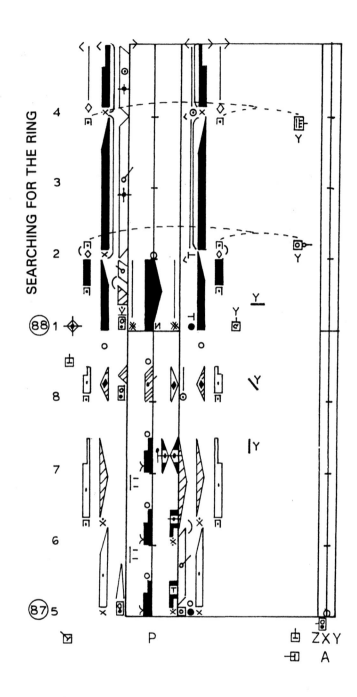

SEARCHING FOR THE RING

*THIS MAY BE DONE AS A
SOUTENU TURN, WITHOUT
THE STEP INTO 5th AT
THE END OF THE TURN.

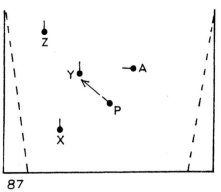

87

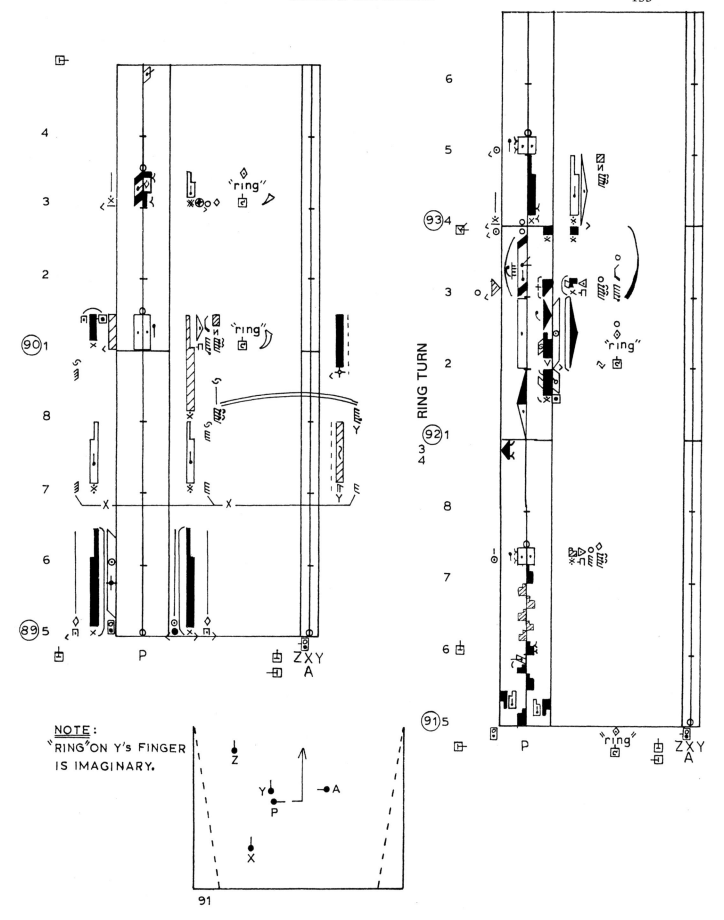

NOTE:
"RING" ON Y's FINGER
IS IMAGINARY.

RING TURN

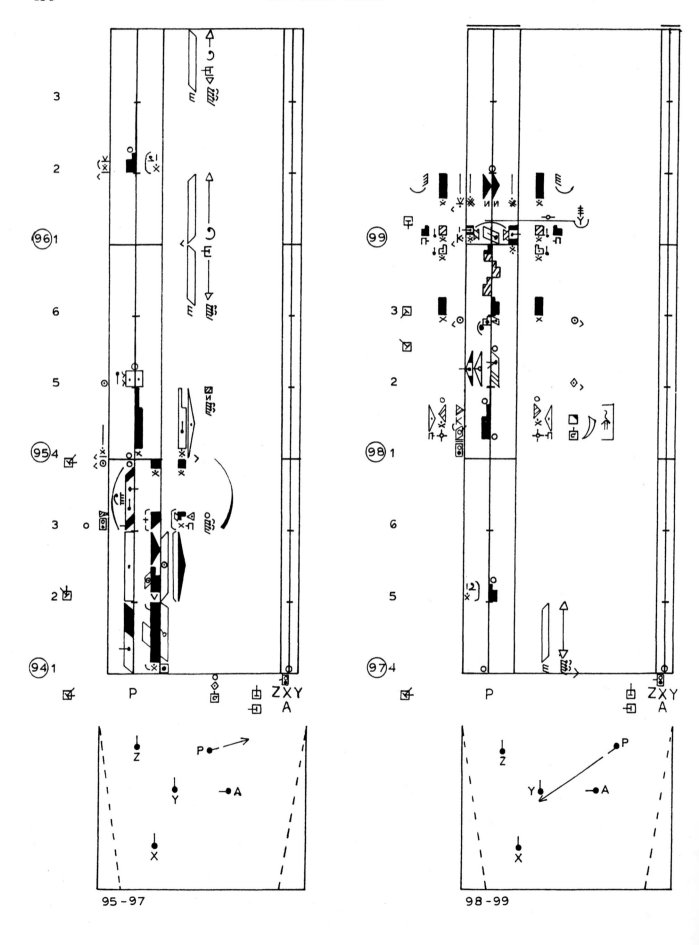

95 – 97

98 – 99

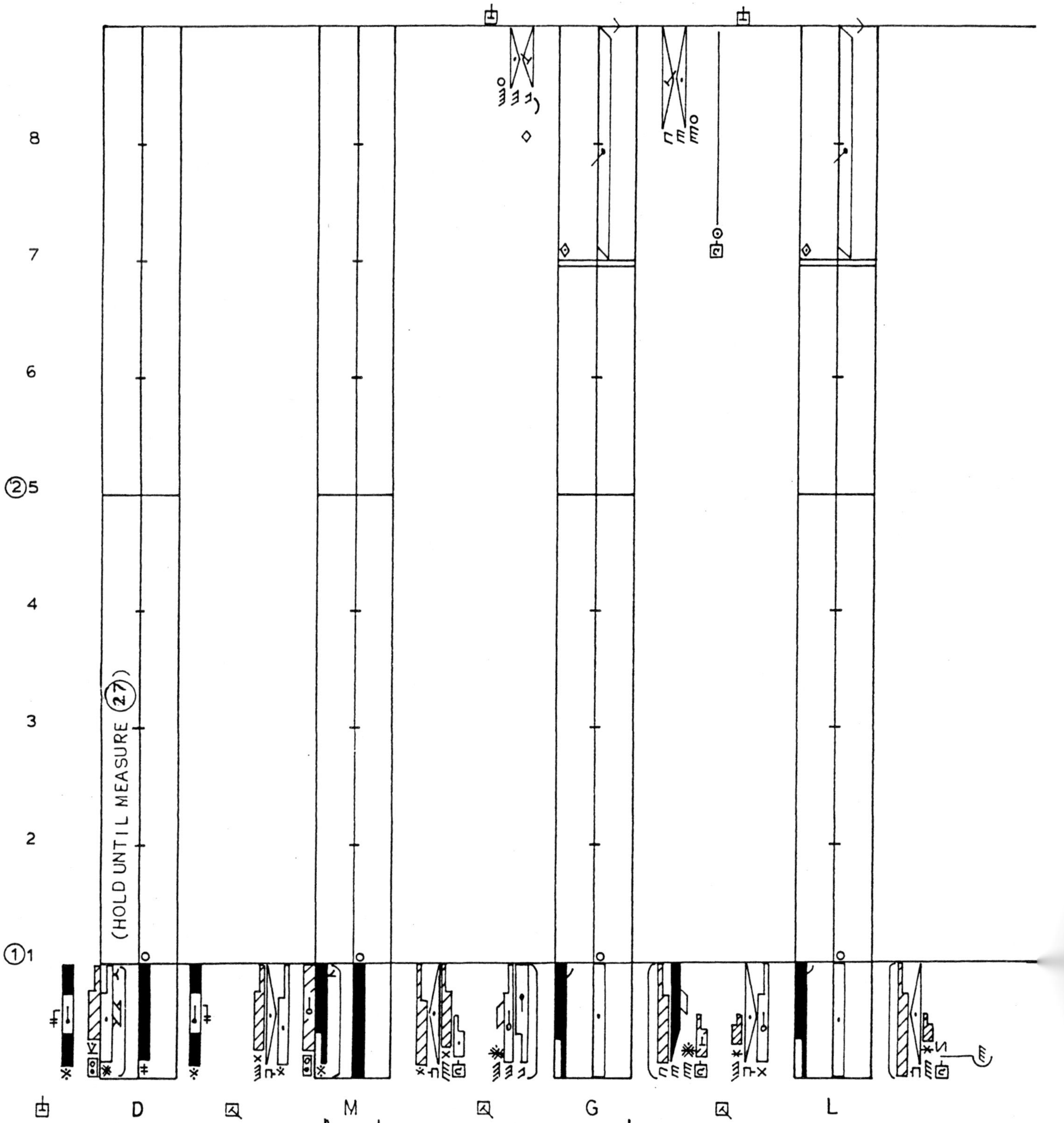

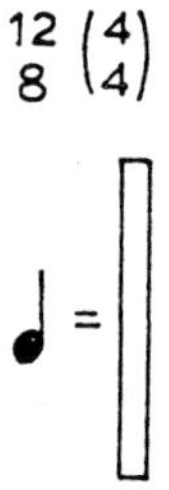

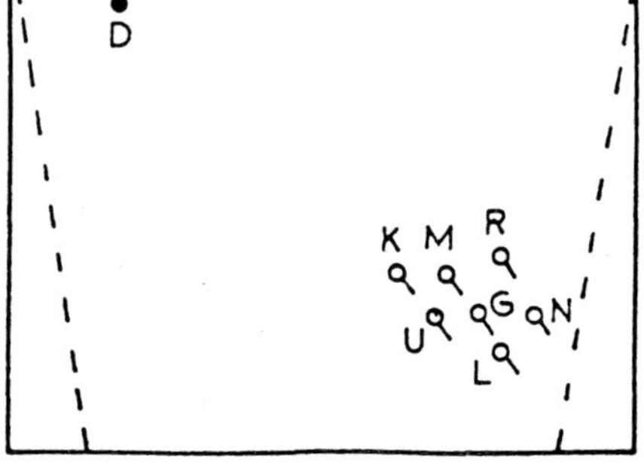

D   M   G   L

(HOLD UNTIL MEASURE 27)

12 (4)
8 (4)

WOMEN GET INTO FORMATION
OFF STAGE. TAKE HANDS,
ENTER IN A CLUMP, TURN
AND TAKE POSITIONS.

OPENING POSITIONS

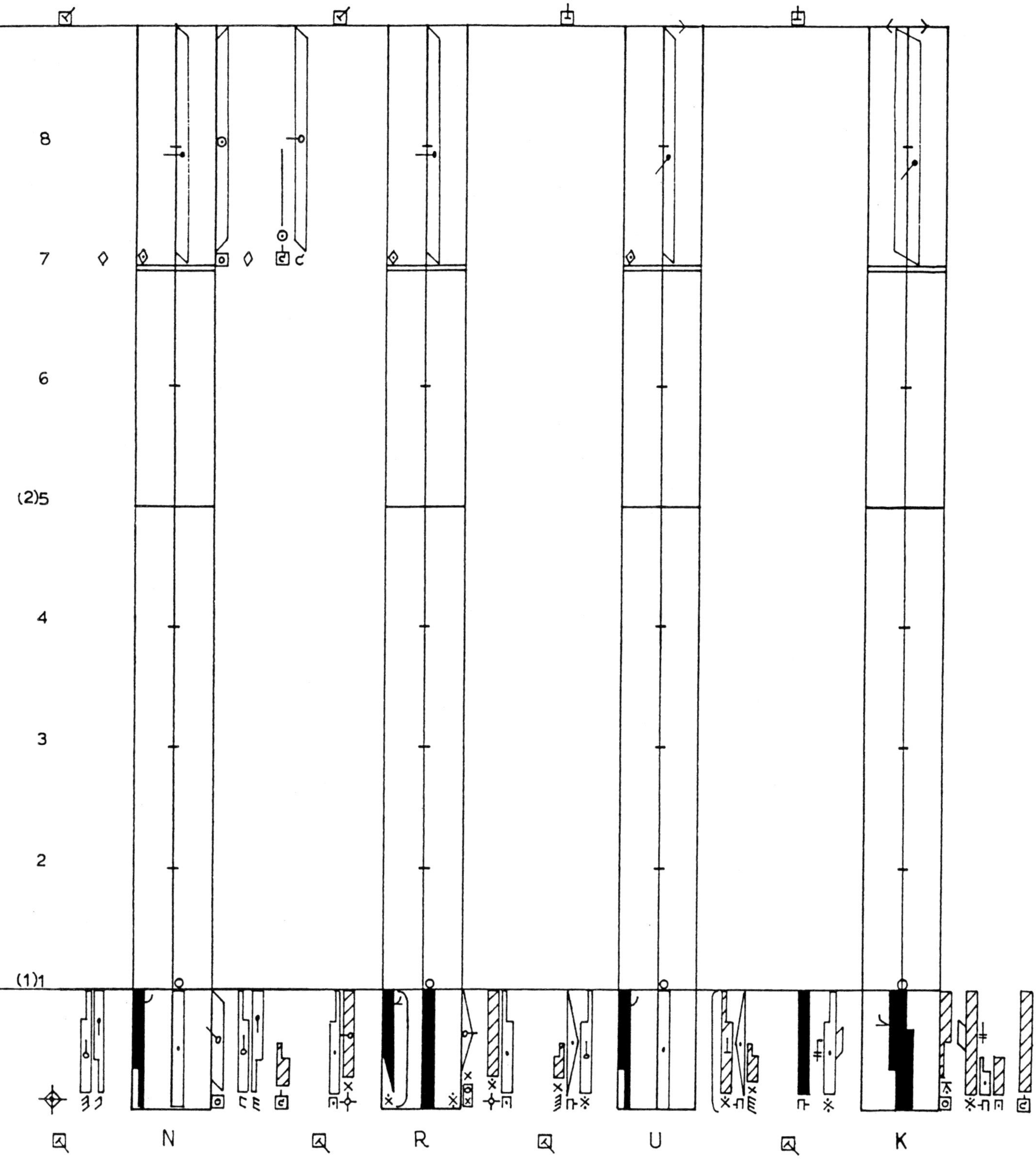
8
7
6
(2)5
4
3
2
(1)1
N
R
U
K

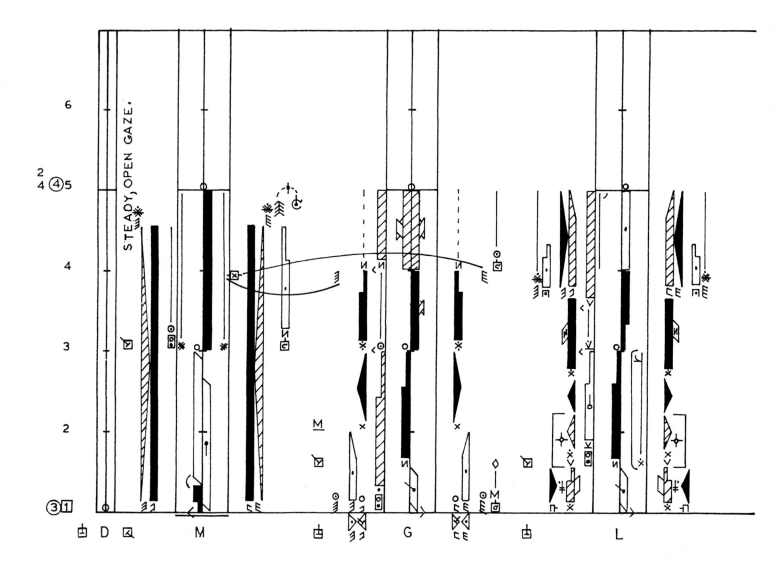

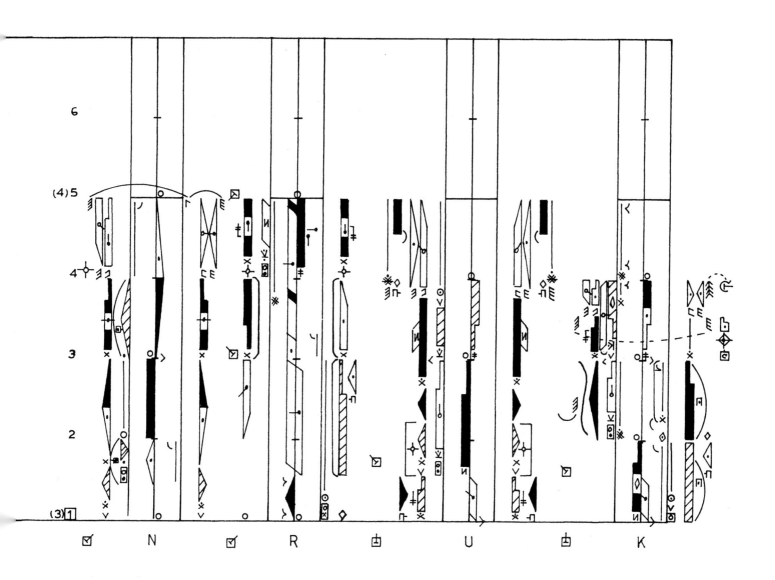

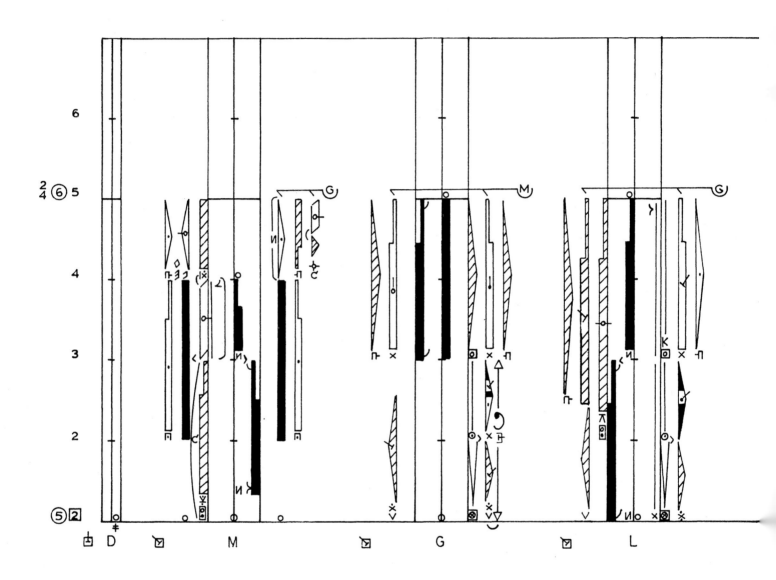

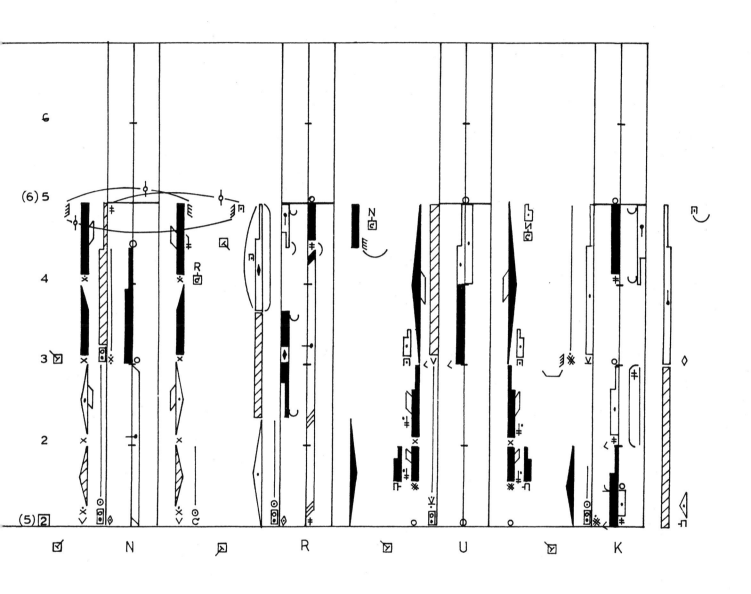

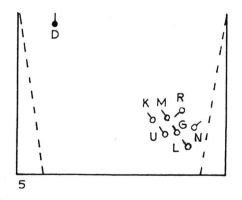

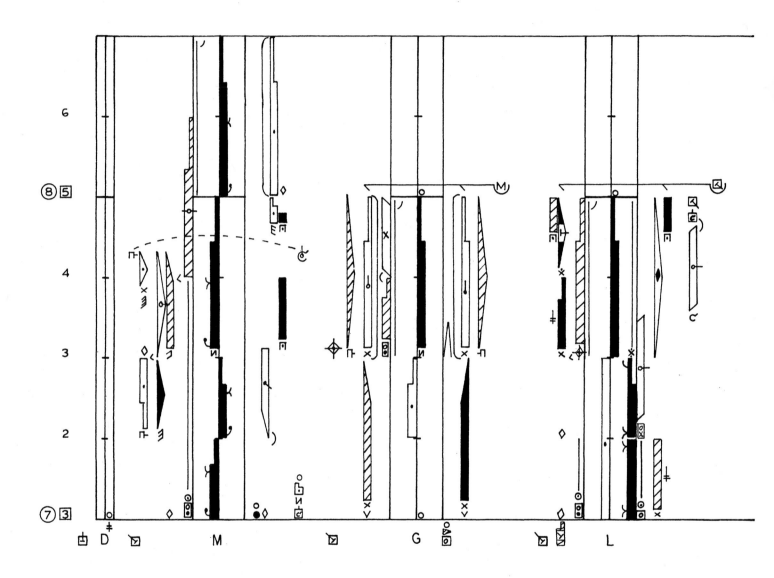

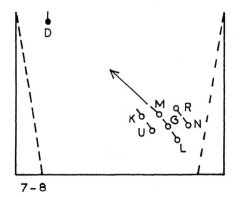

7-8

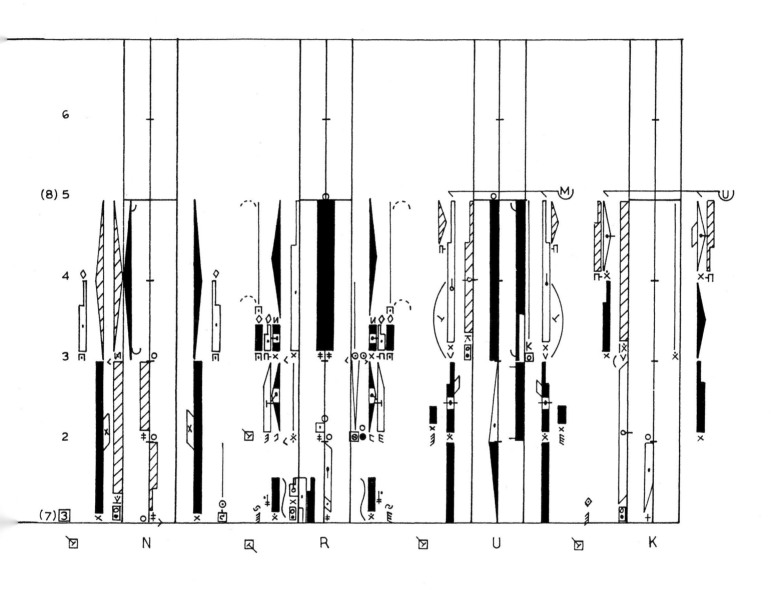

THE GREEN TABLE

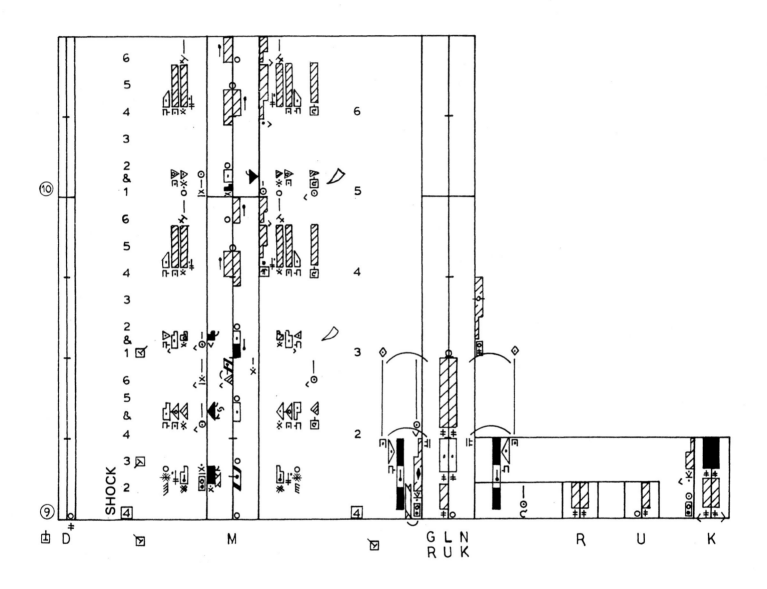

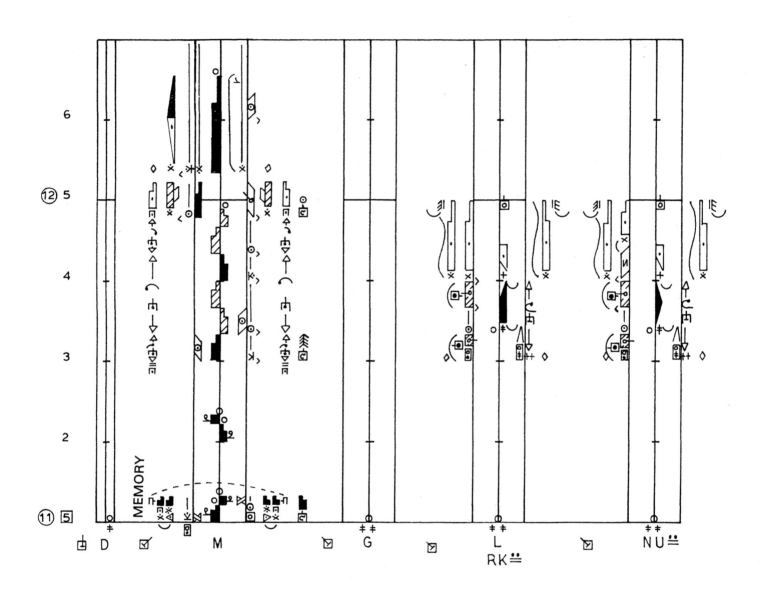

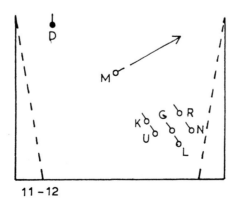

11 – 12

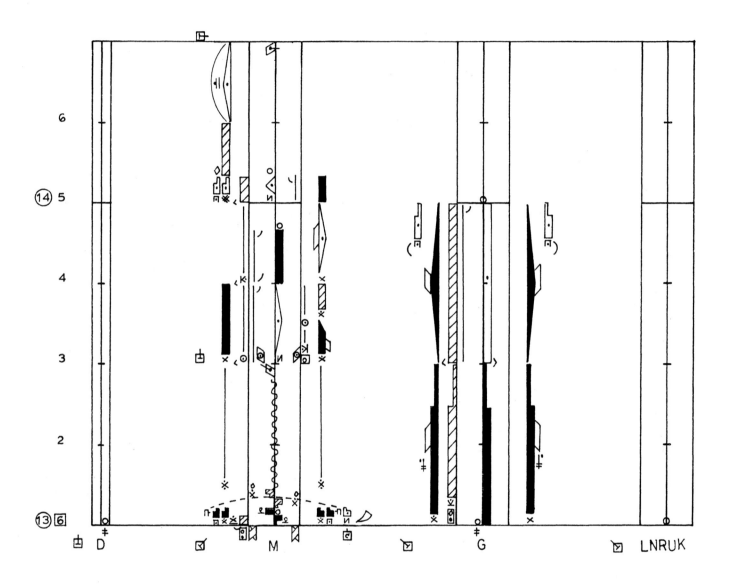

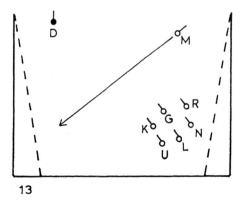

13

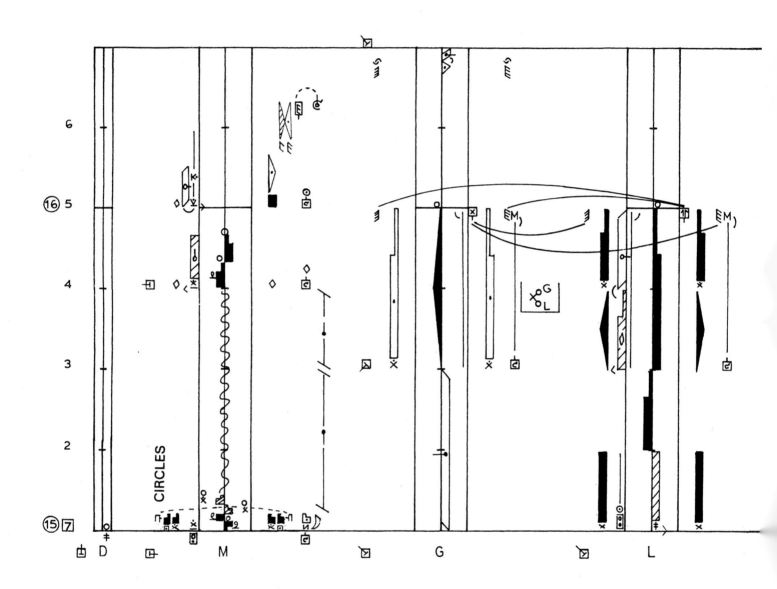

CIRCLES

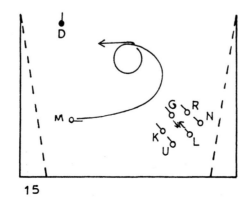

15

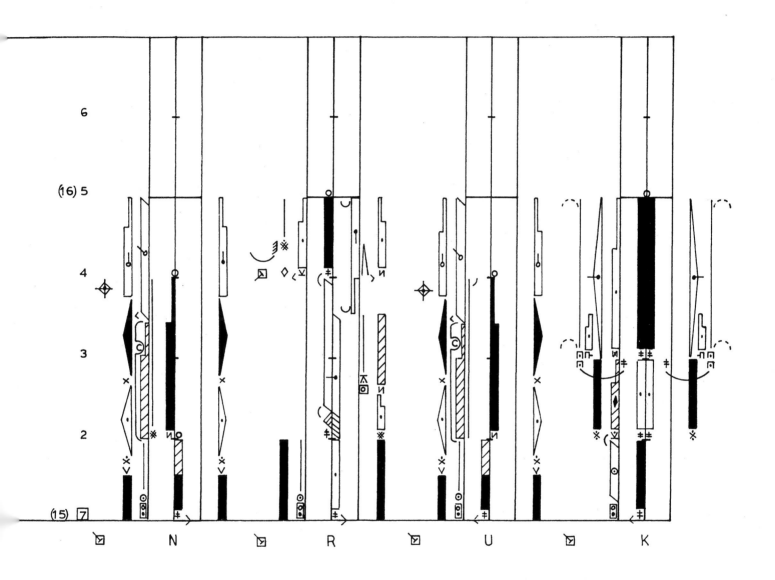

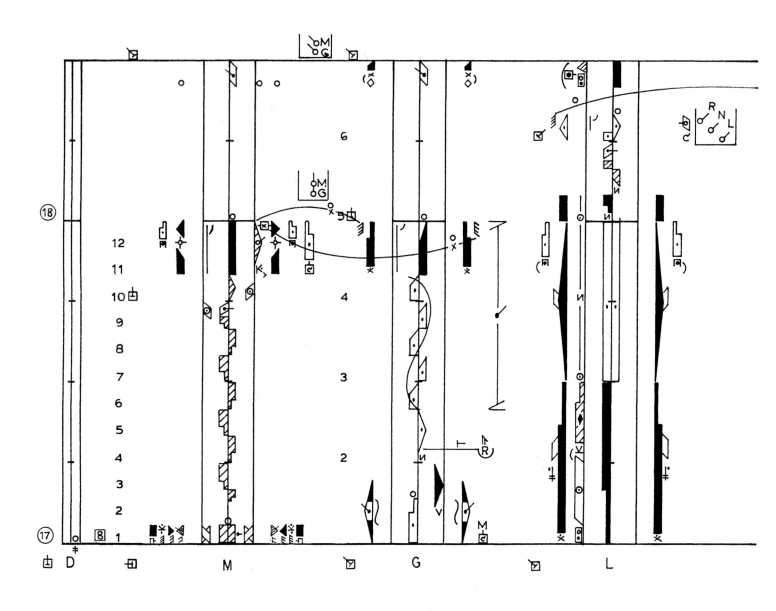

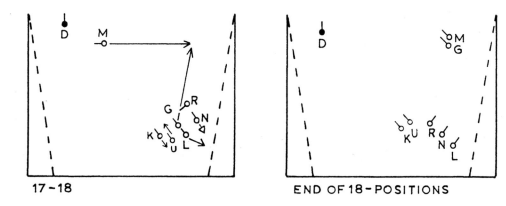

17~18   END OF 18-POSITIONS

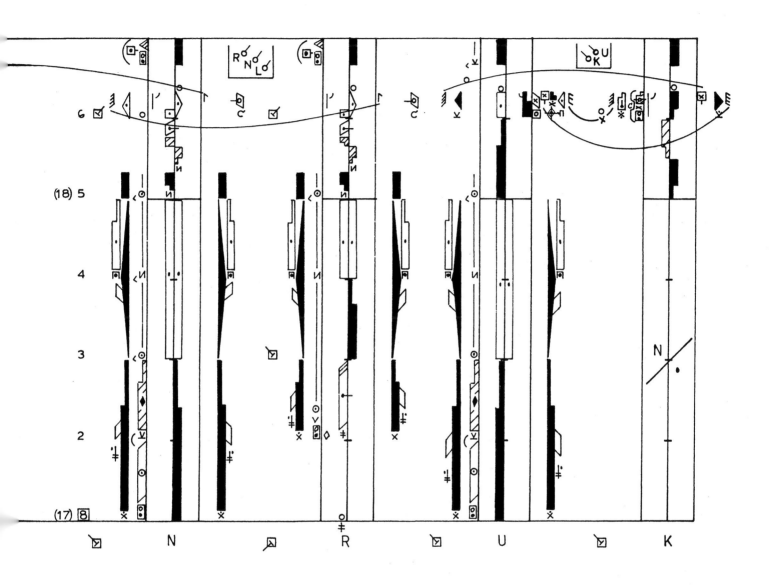

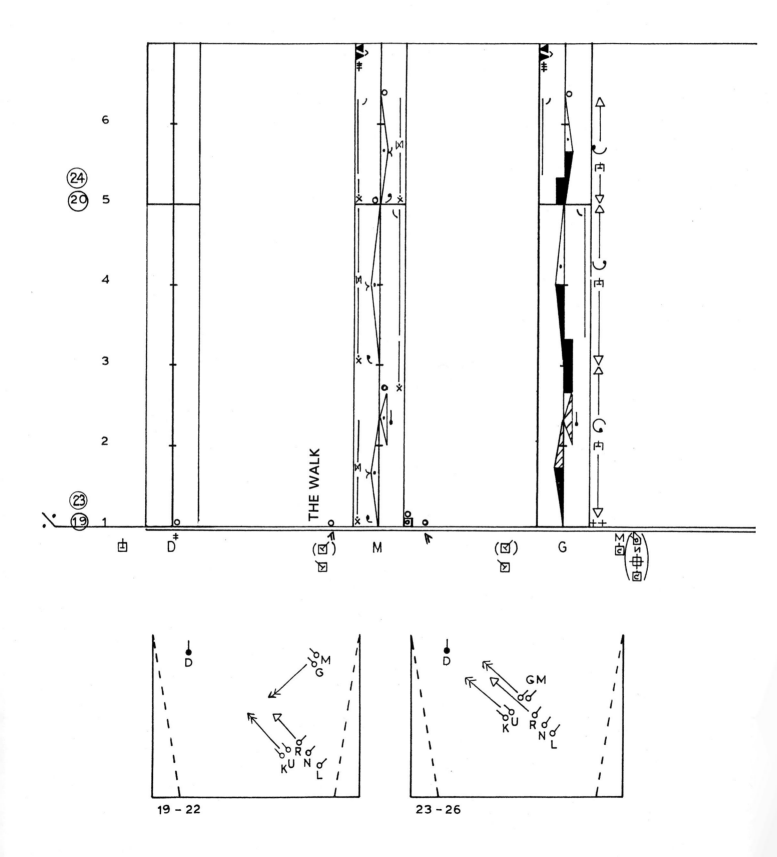

THE WALK

19 – 22

23 – 26

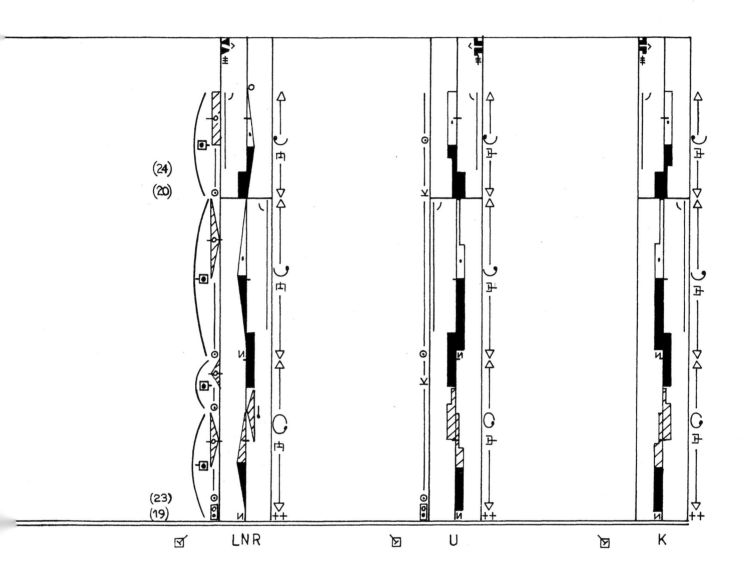

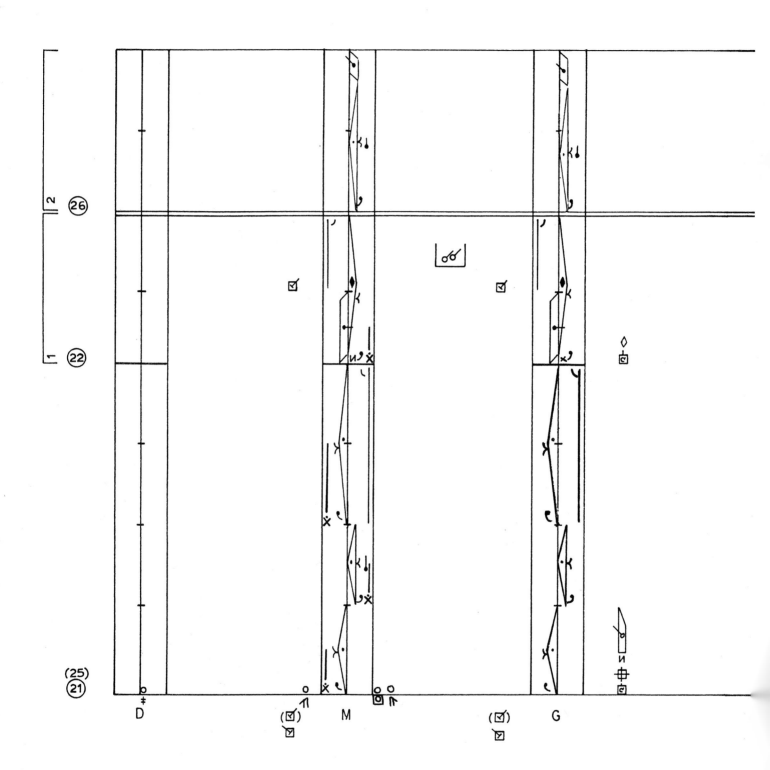

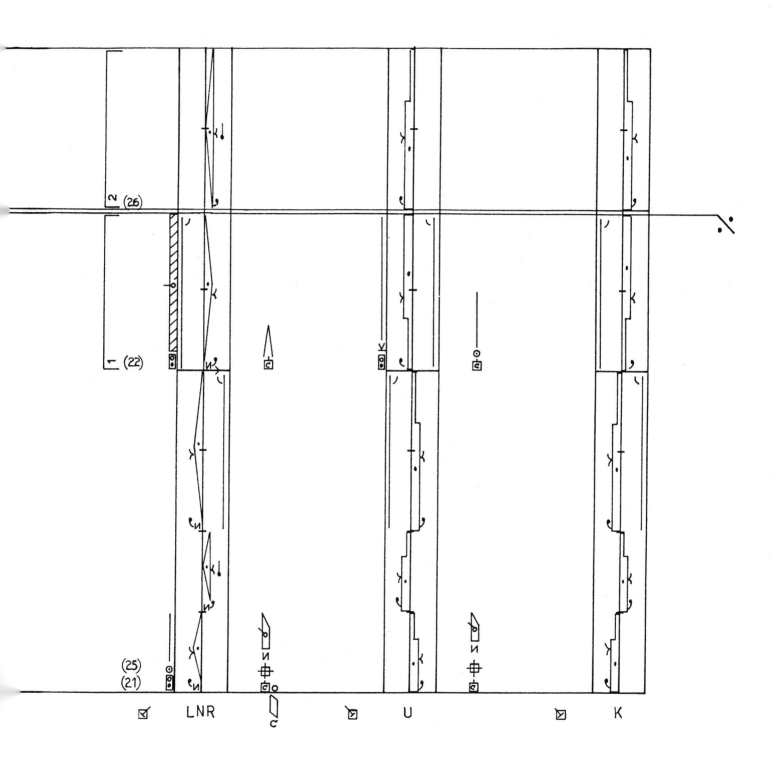

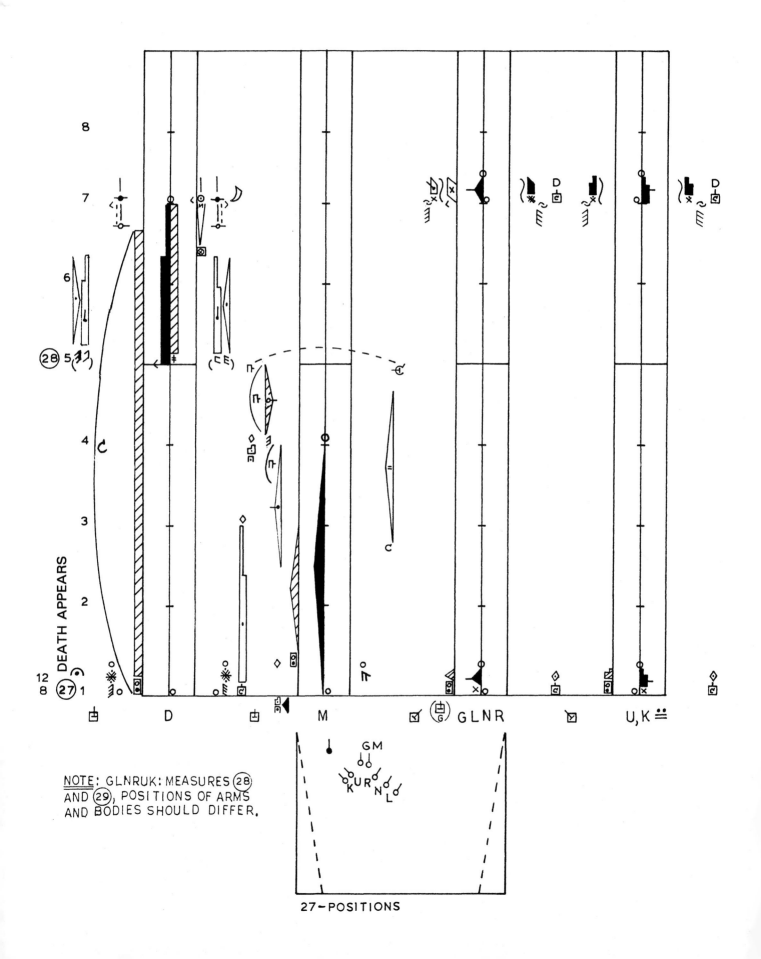

NOTE: GLNRUK: MEASURES ㉘
AND ㉙, POSITIONS OF ARMS
AND BODIES SHOULD DIFFER.

27–POSITIONS

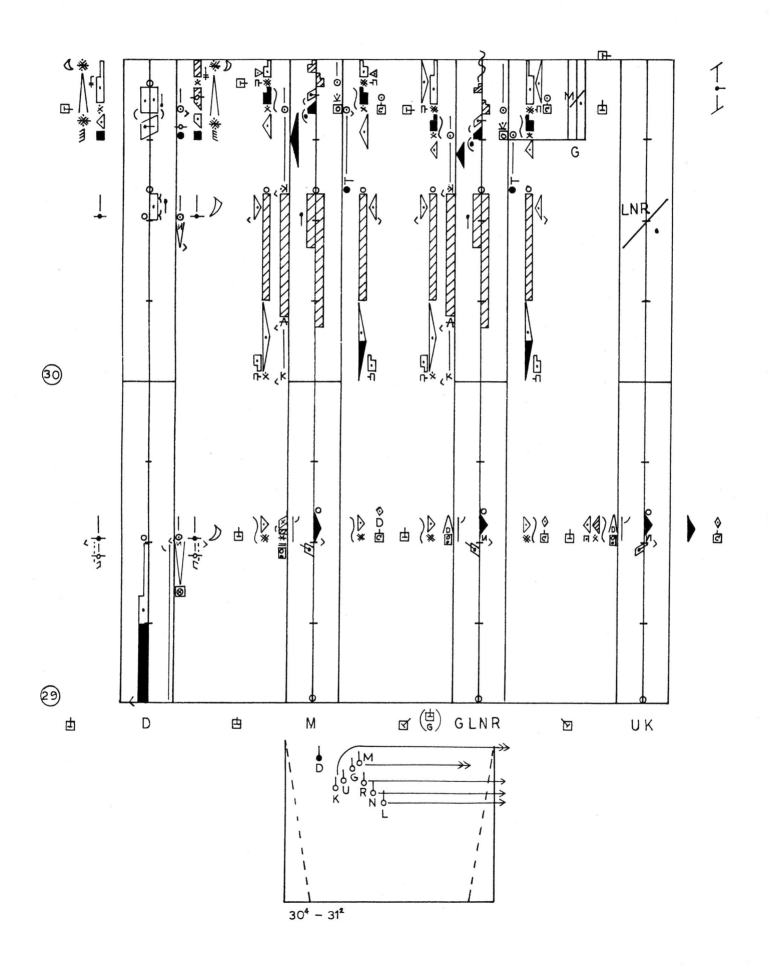

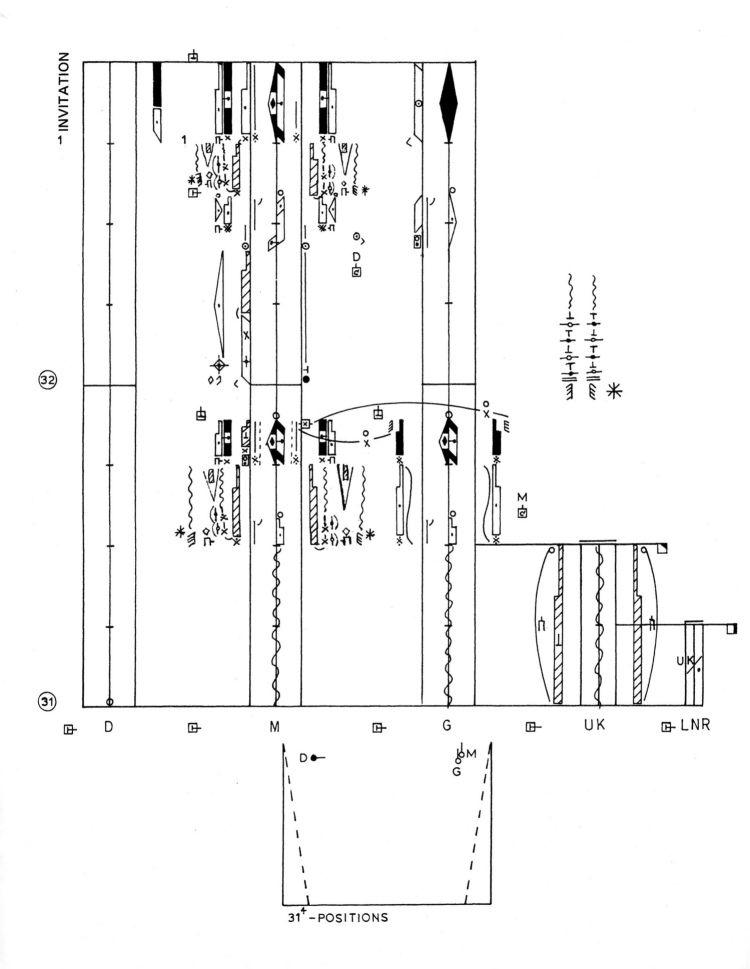

31⁴-POSITIONS

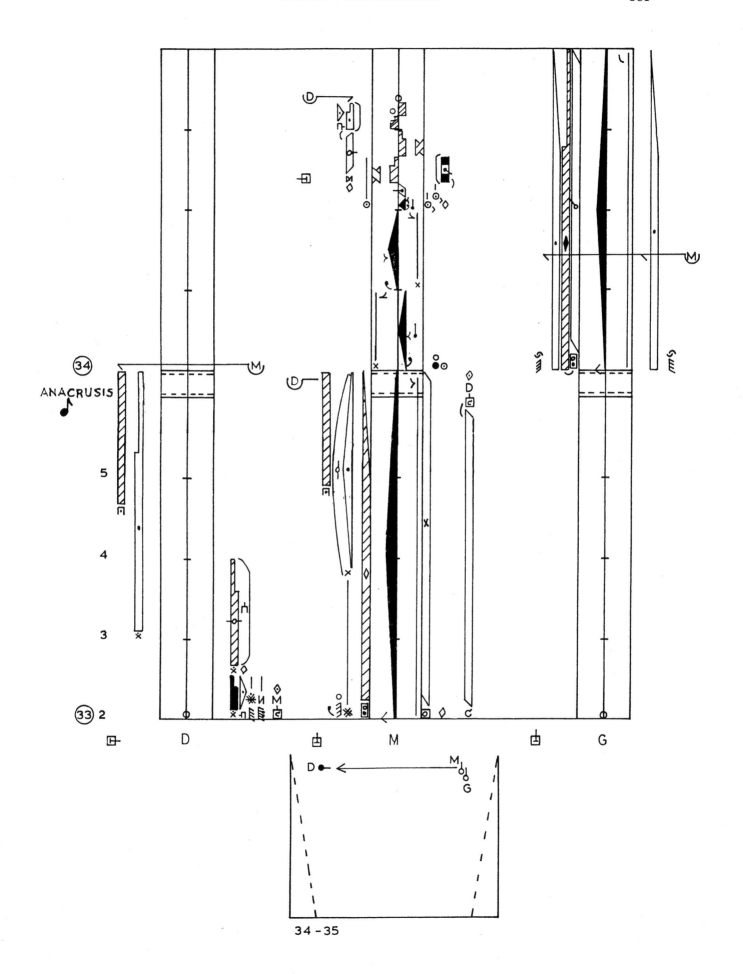

ANACRUSIS

34 - 35

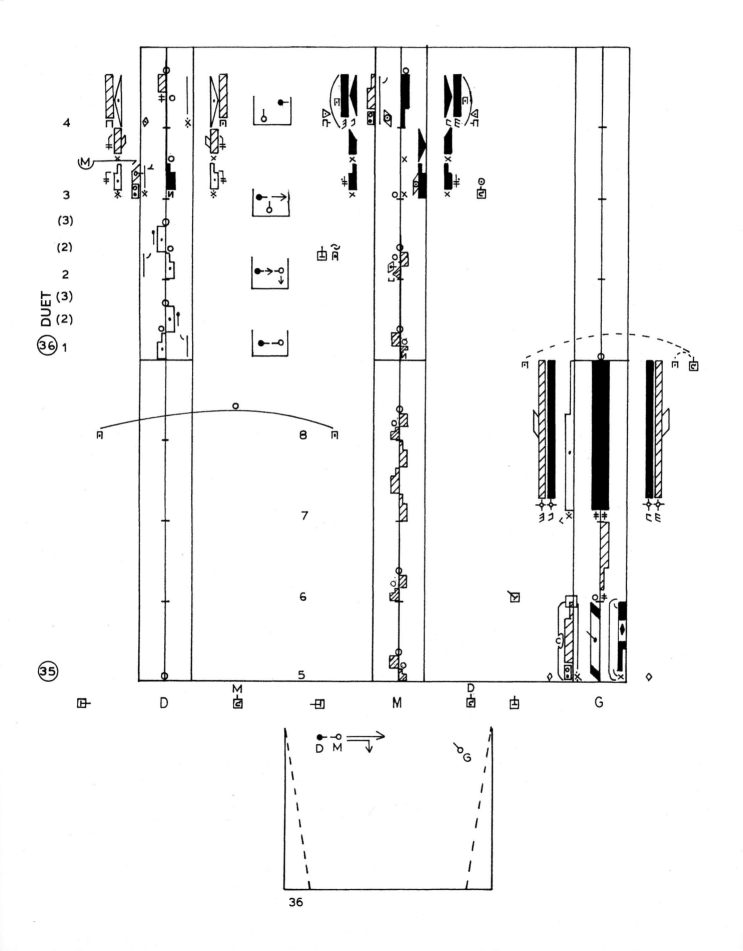

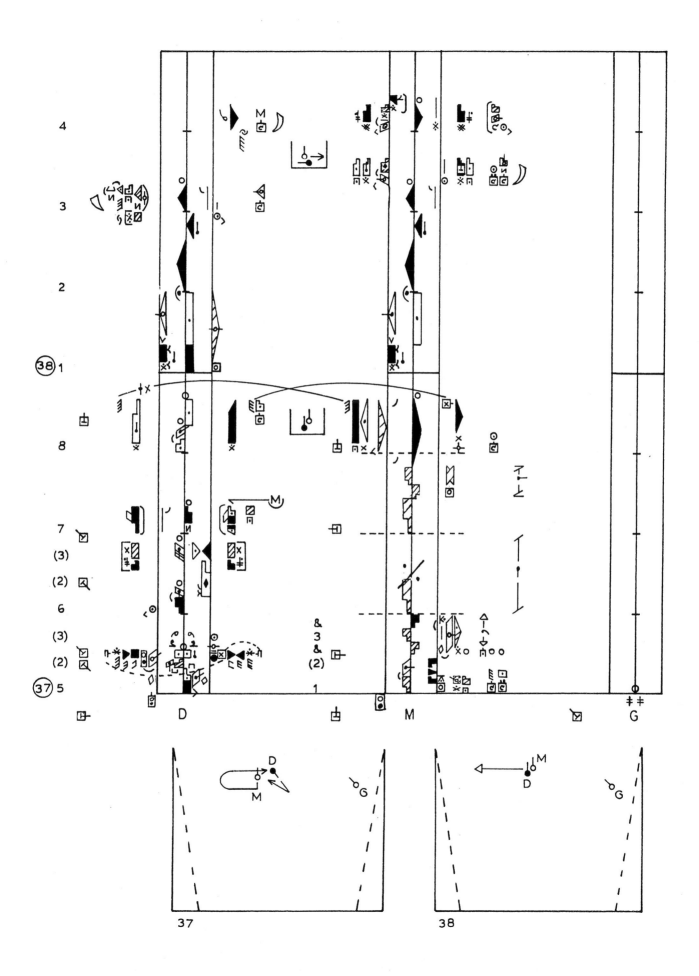

37   38

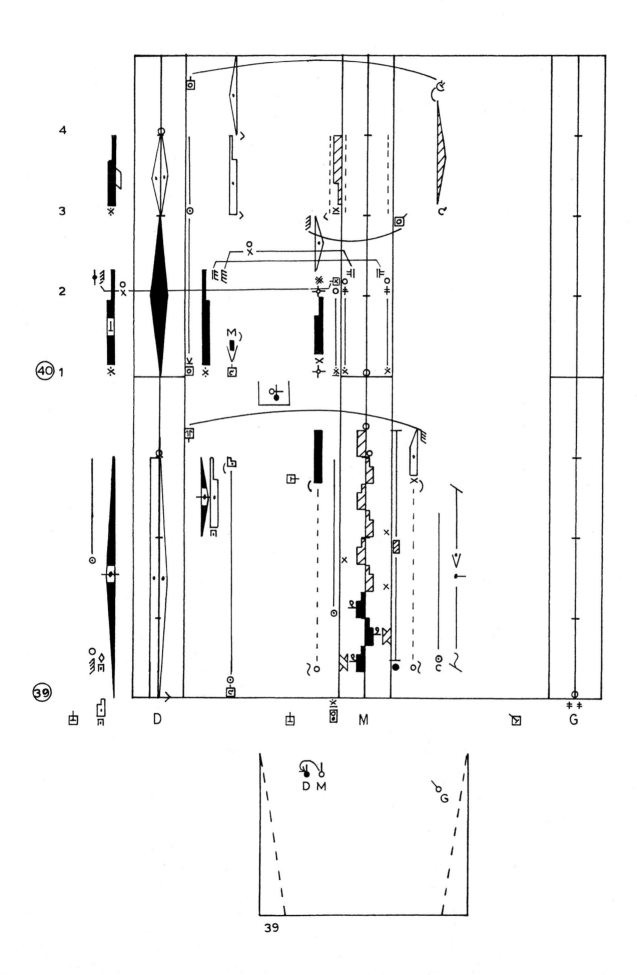

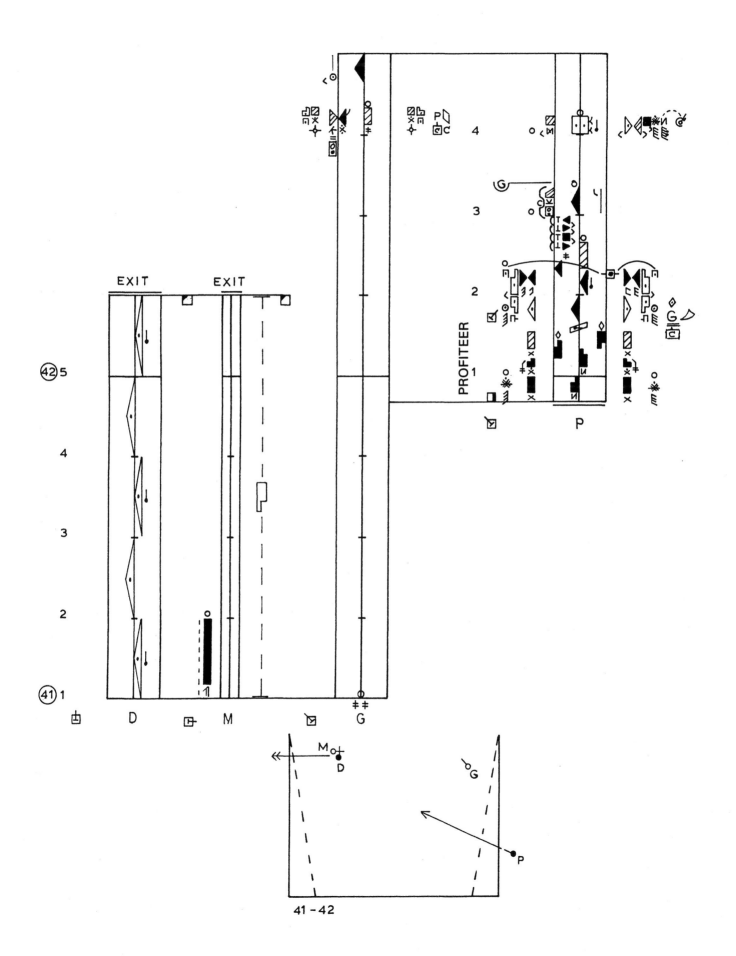

41 - 42

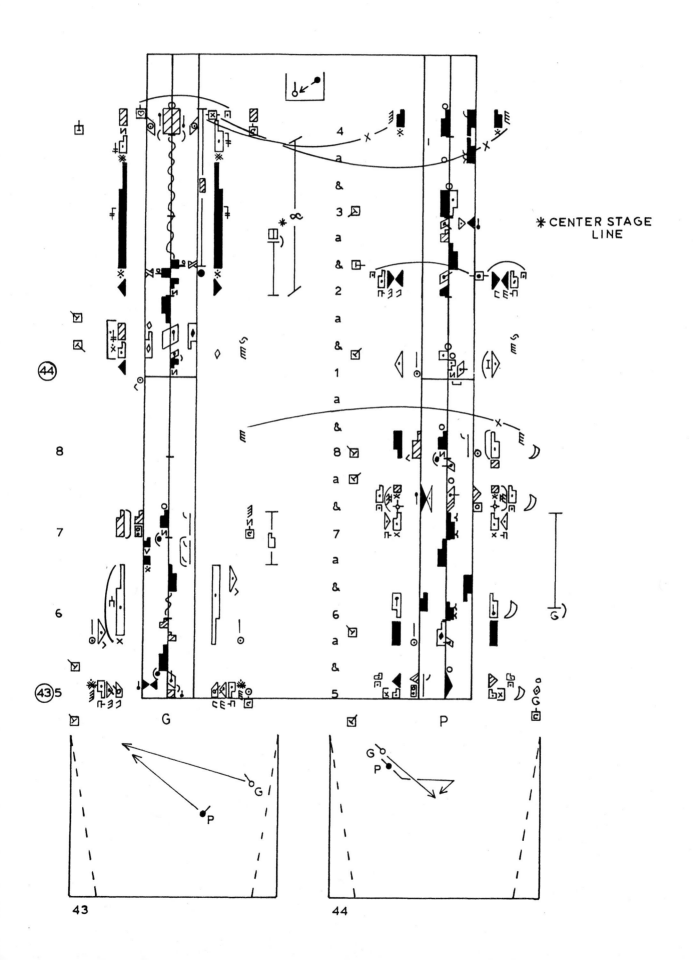

*CENTER STAGE
LINE

43   44

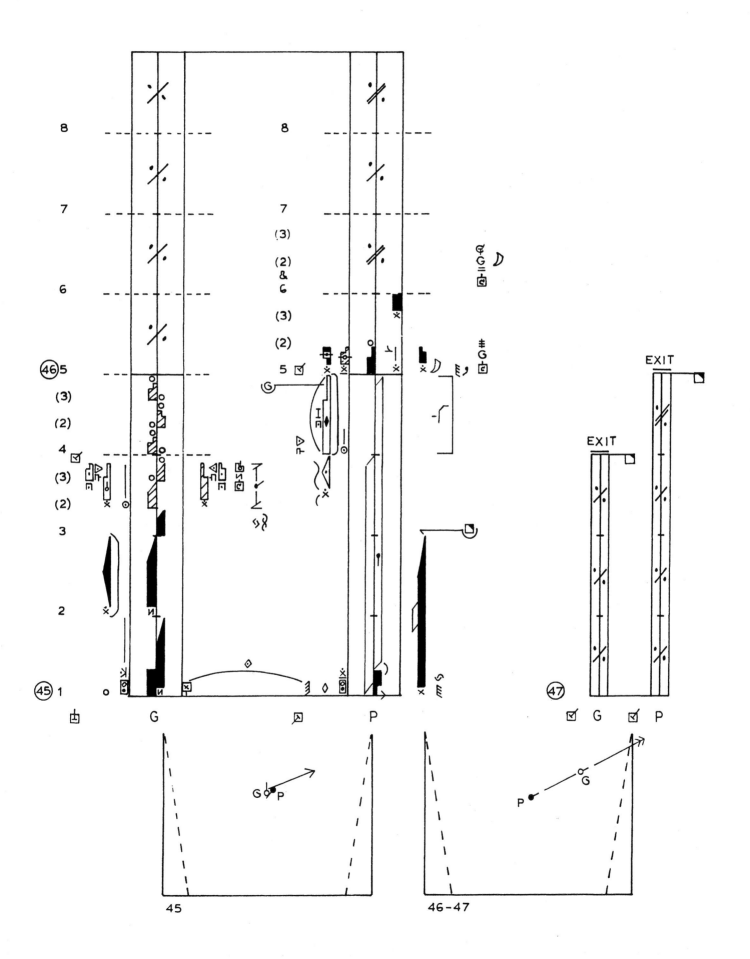

45

46-47

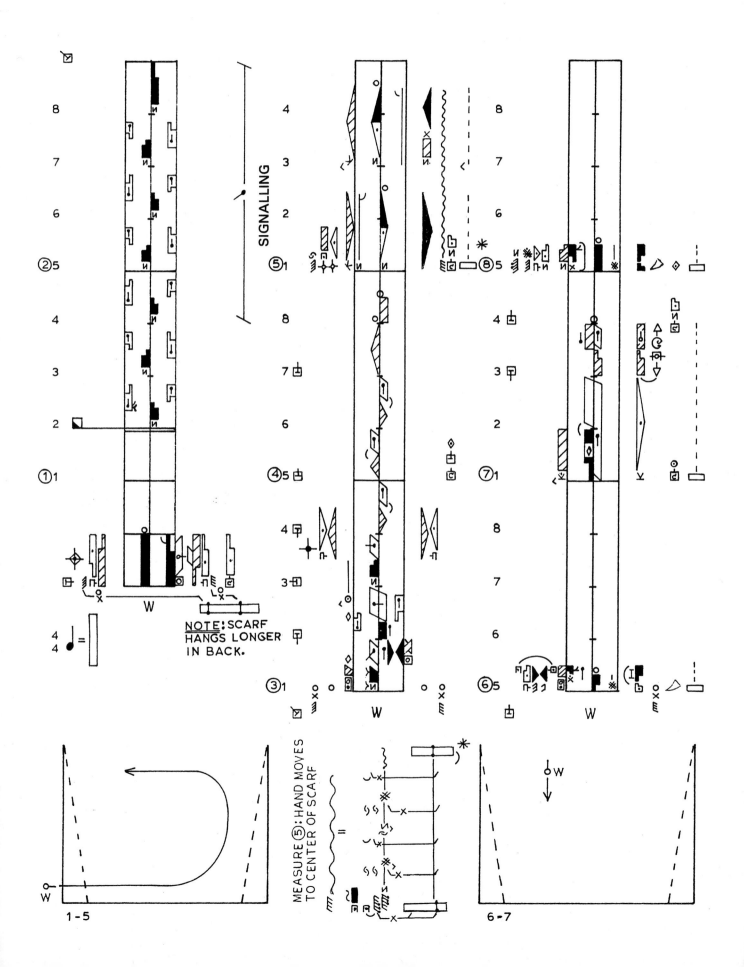

SIGNALLING

NOTE: SCARF
HANGS LONGER
IN BACK.

MEASURE ⑤: HAND MOVES
TO CENTER OF SCARF

1 - 5

6 - 7

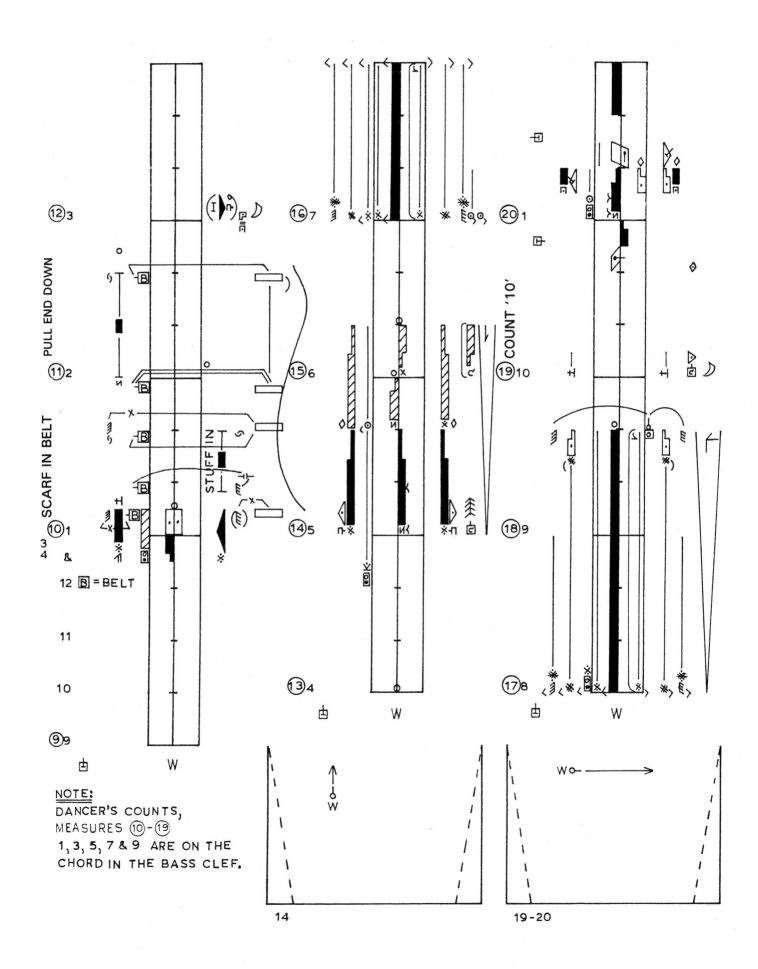

NOTE:
DANCER'S COUNTS,
MEASURES ⑩-⑲
1, 3, 5, 7 & 9 ARE ON THE
CHORD IN THE BASS CLEF.

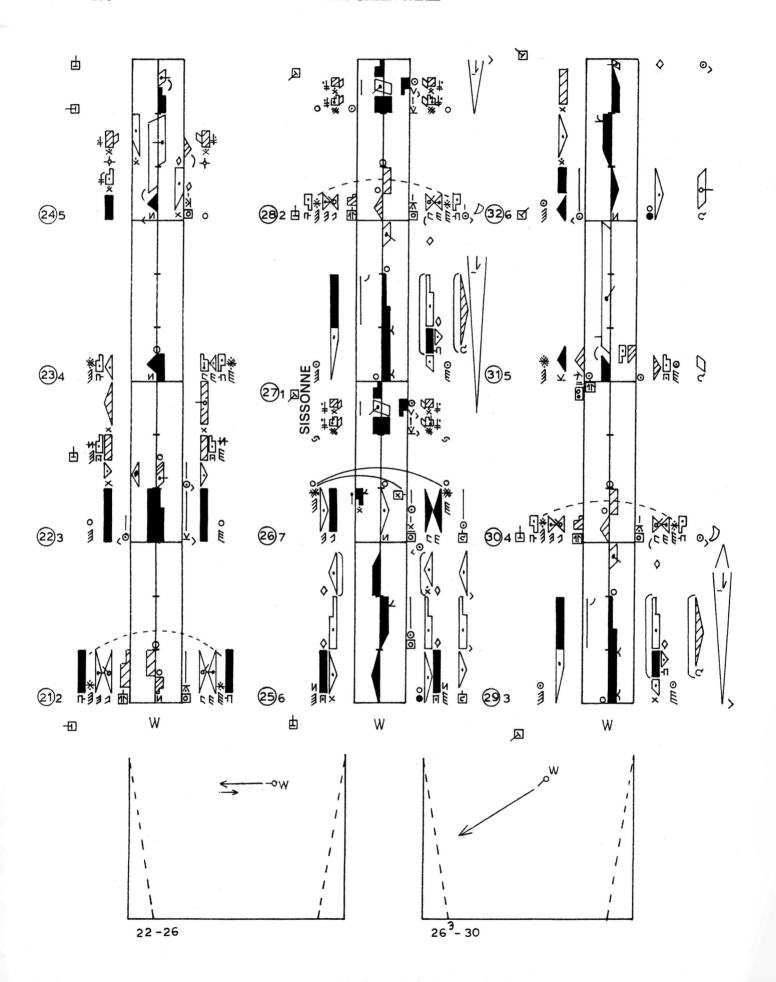

SISSONNE

24 5
23 4
22 3
21 2

28 2
27 1
26 7
25 6

32 6
31 5
30 4
29 3

W   W   W

22 – 26 26^3 – 30

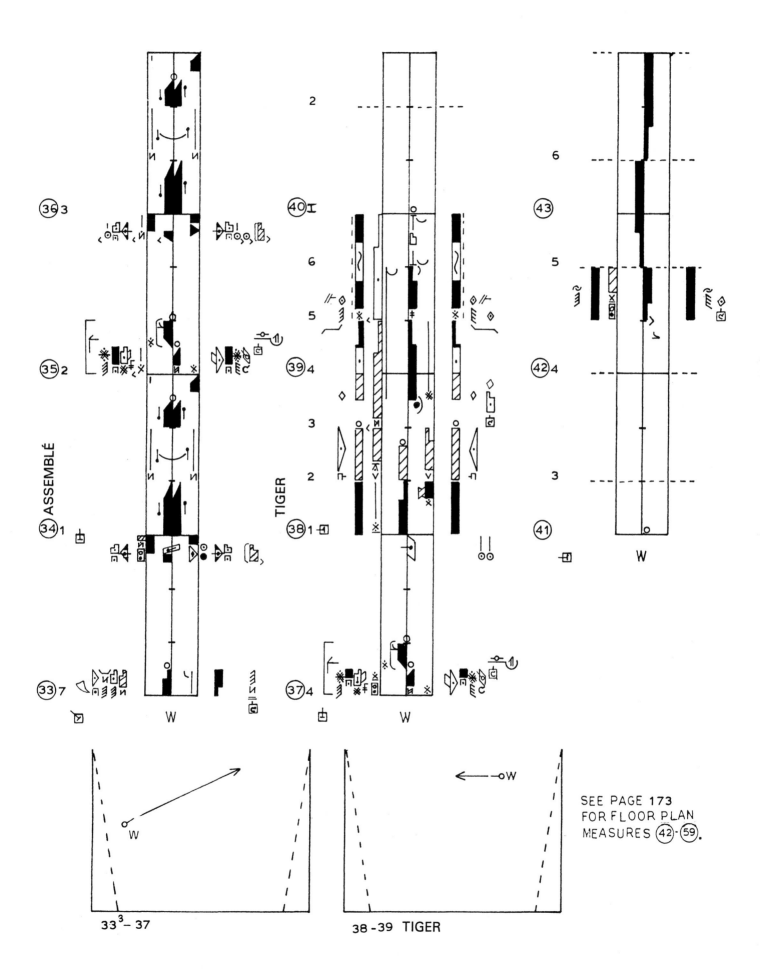

SEE PAGE **173**
FOR FLOOR PLAN
MEASURES ㊷-㊾.

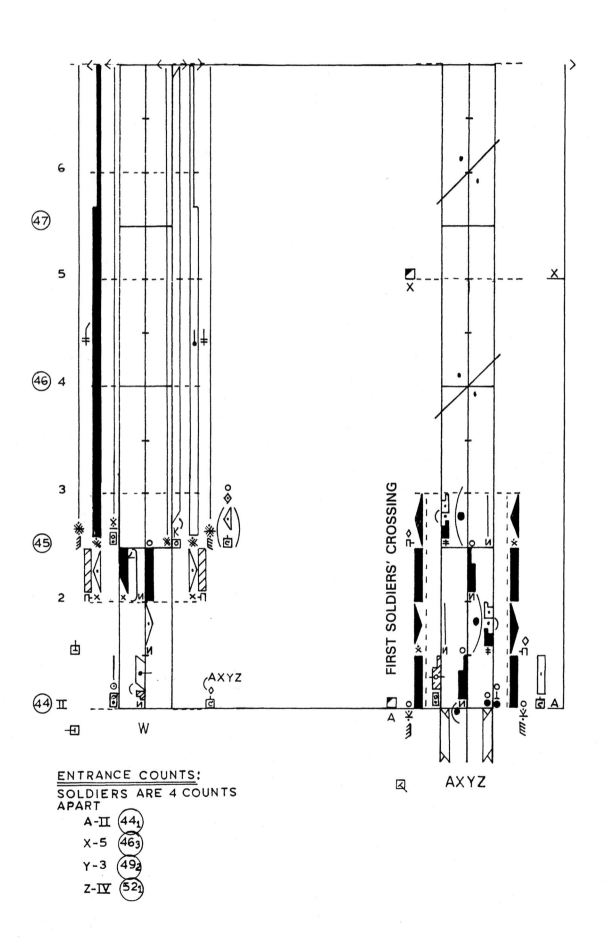

FIRST SOLDIERS' CROSSING

AXYZ

ENTRANCE COUNTS:

SOLDIERS ARE 4 COUNTS
APART

A-II (44₁)

X-5 (46₃)

Y-3 (49₂)

Z-IV (52₁)

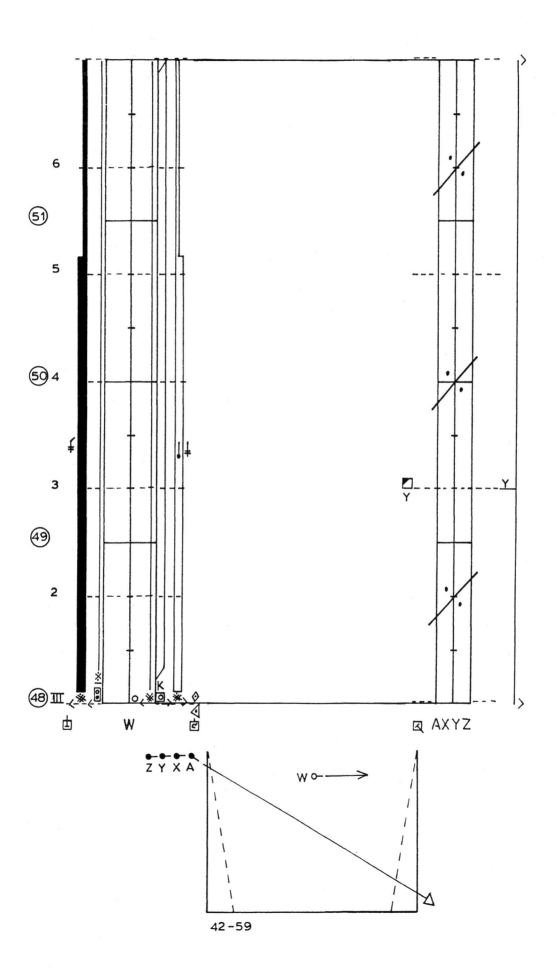

42-59

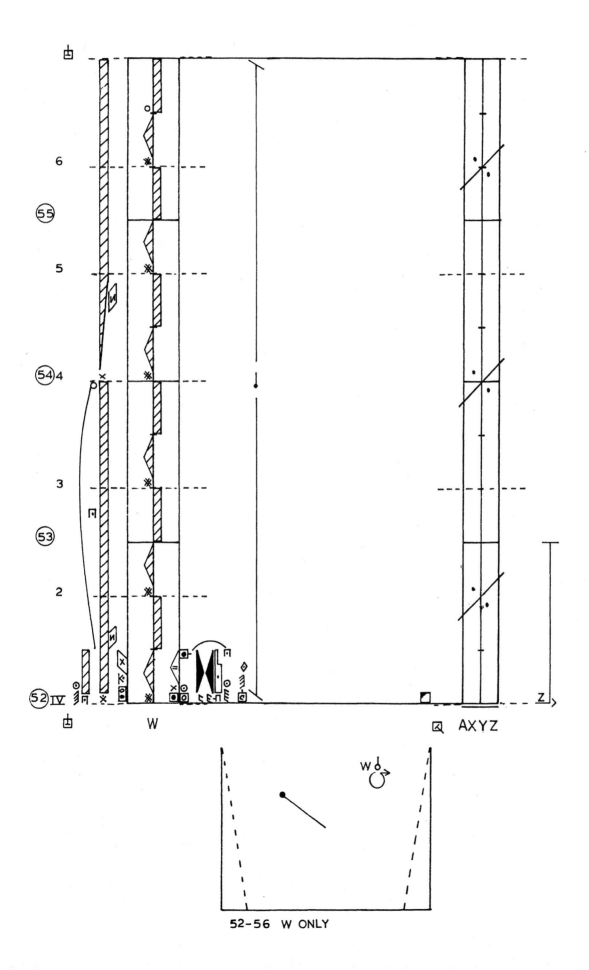

52-56 W ONLY

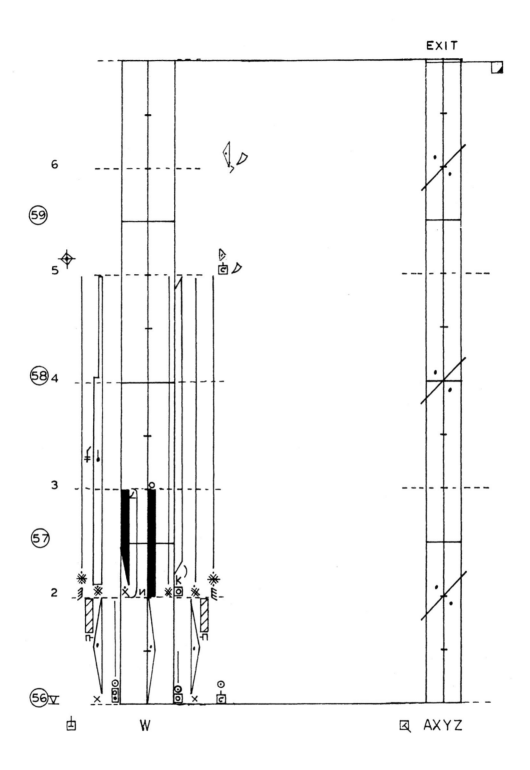

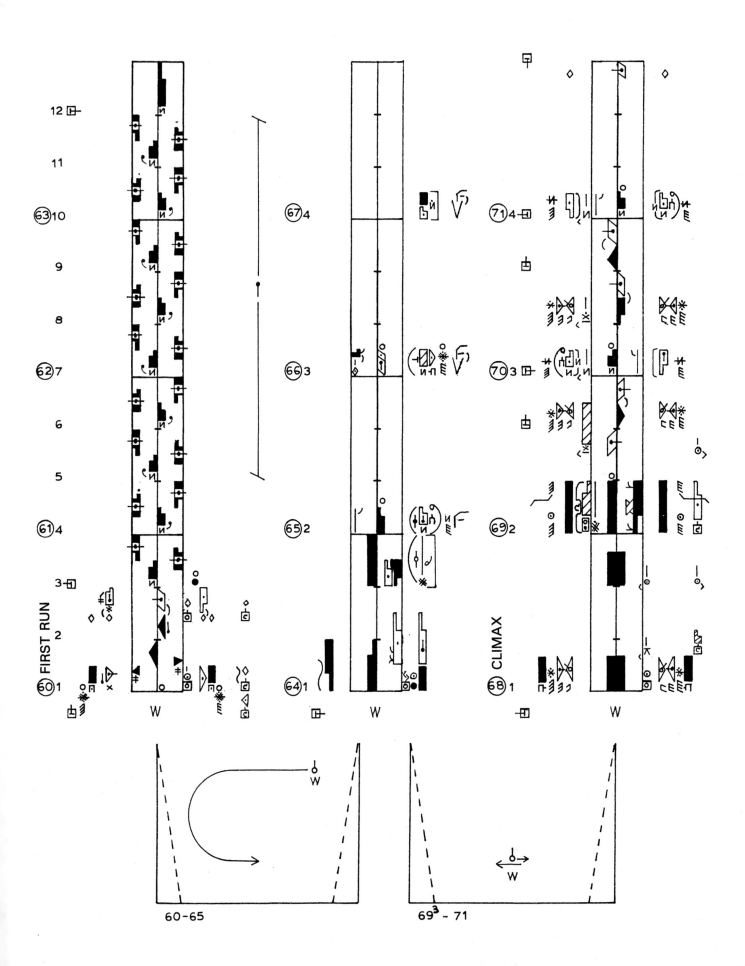

W   W   W

60-65   69³ - 71

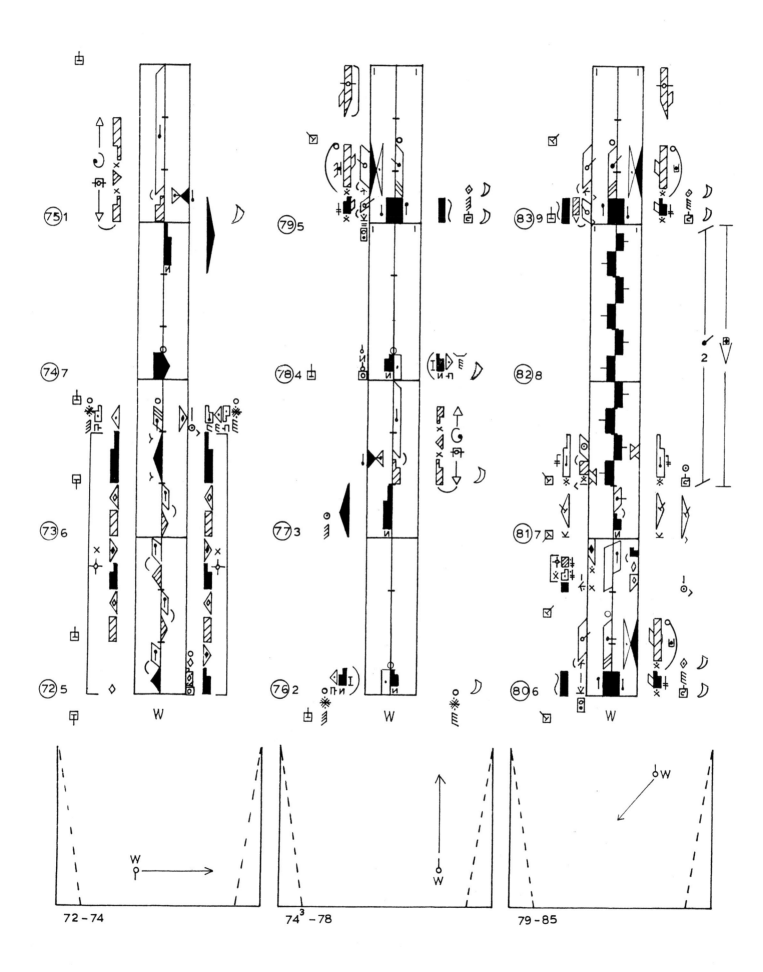

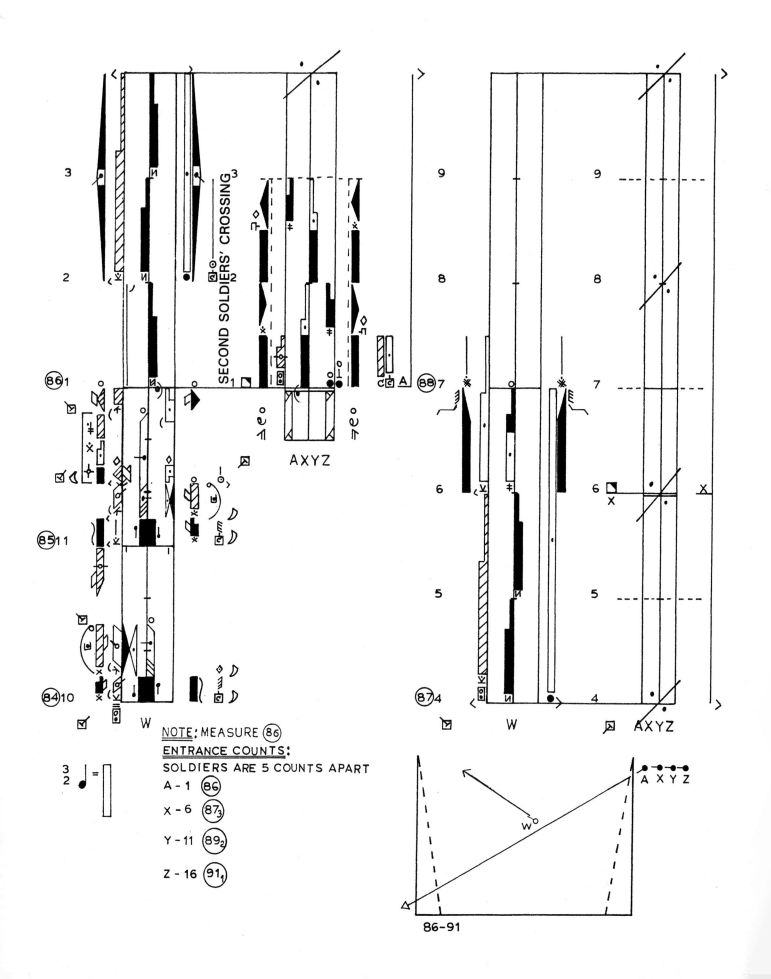

SECOND SOLDIERS' CROSSING

AXYZ

NOTE: MEASURE ⑧⑥

ENTRANCE COUNTS:

SOLDIERS ARE 5 COUNTS APART

A – 1 ⑧⑥

X – 6 ⑧⑦₃

Y – 11 ⑧⑨₂

Z – 16 ⑨¹₁

86–91

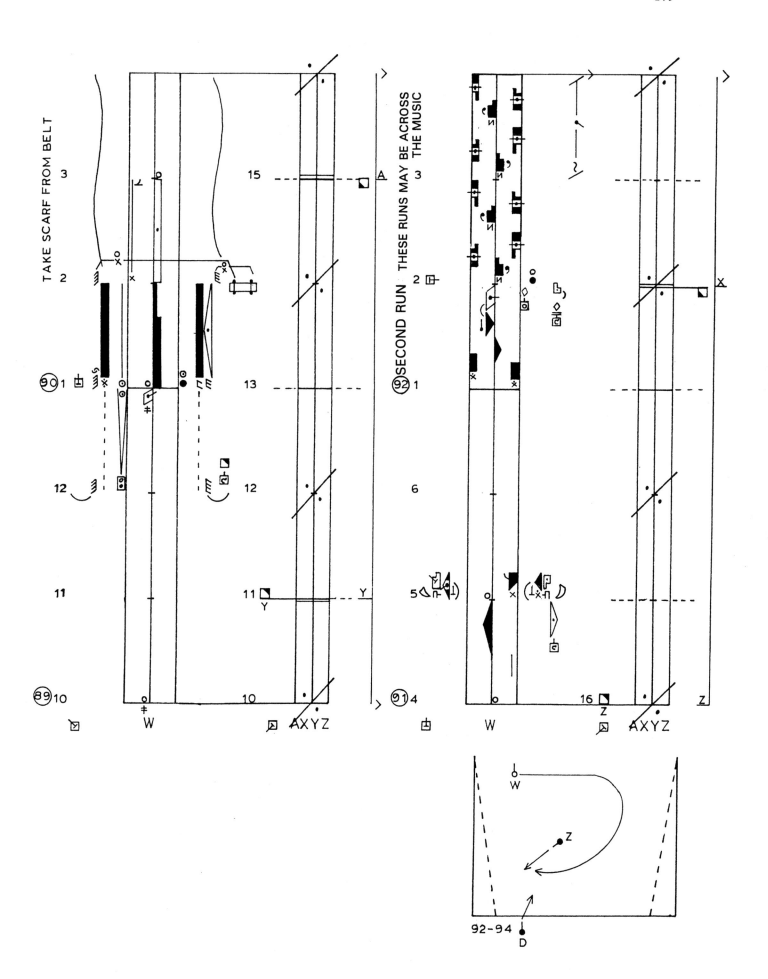

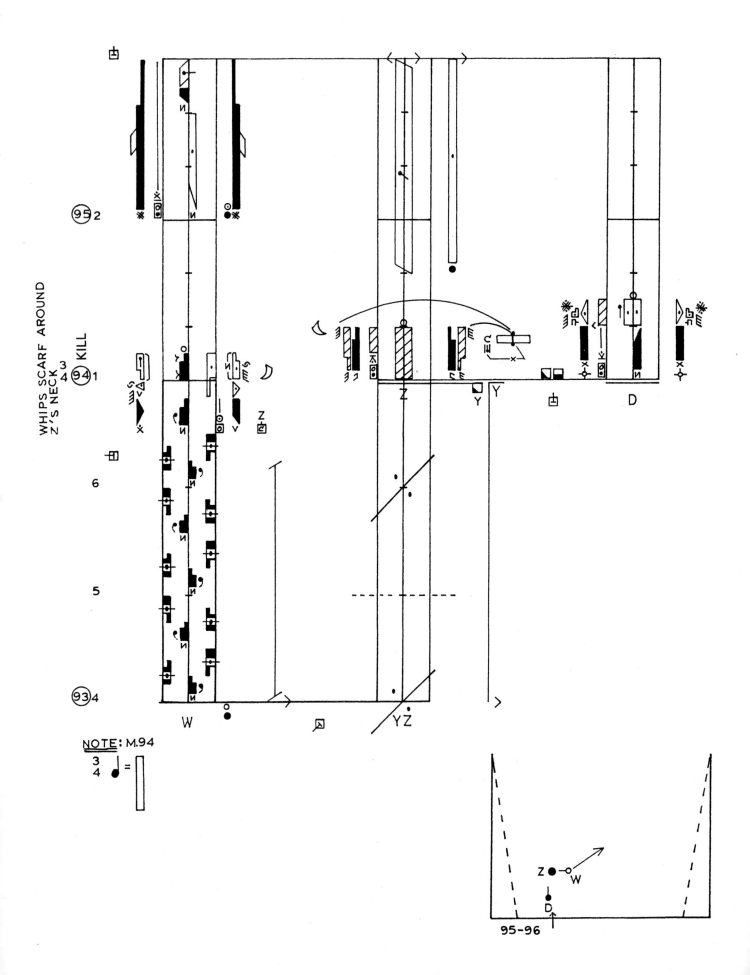

WHIPS SCARF AROUND
Z'S NECK

KILL

NOTE: M.94

$\frac{3}{4}$ ♩ =

W

YZ

Y

Z

D

95-96

CHANGE STAFFS:

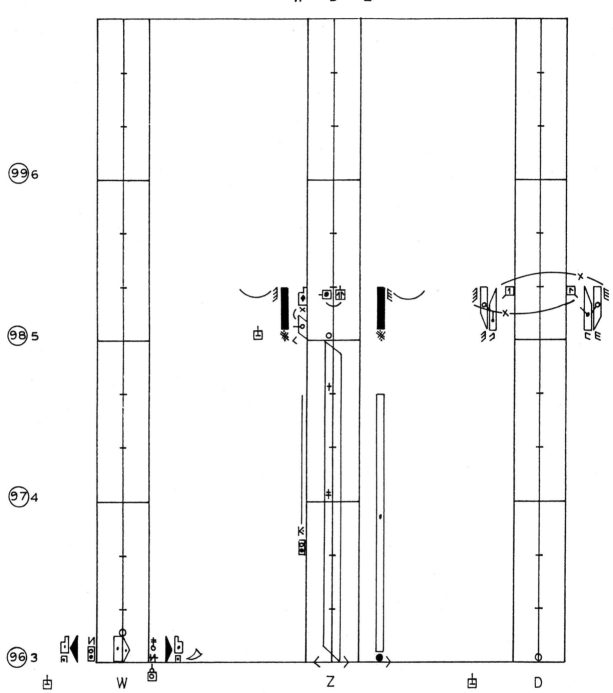

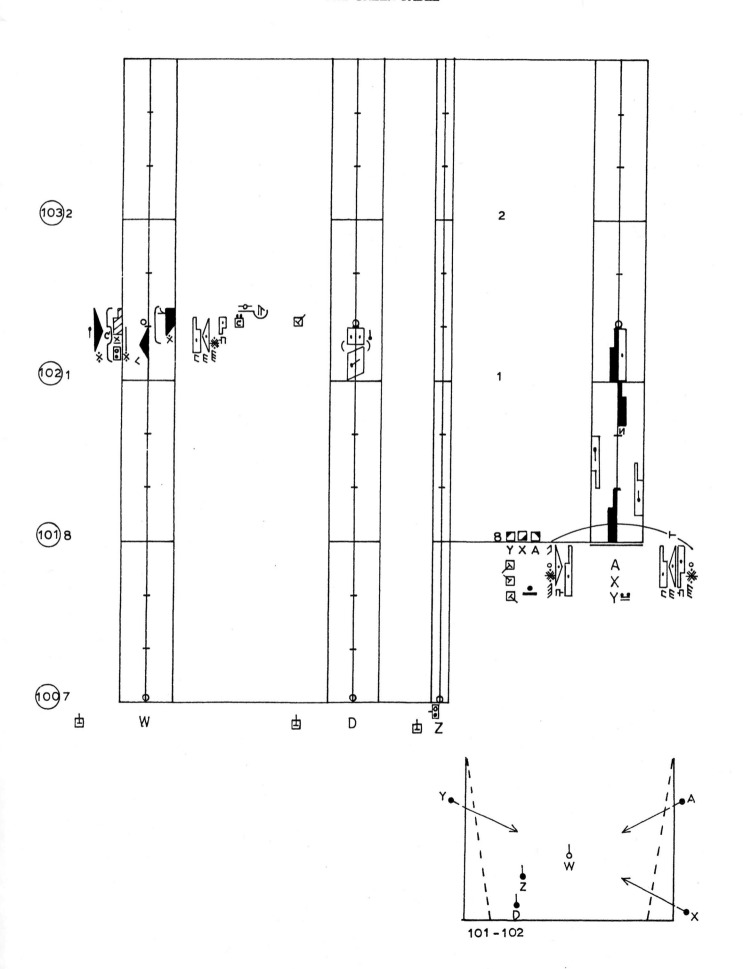

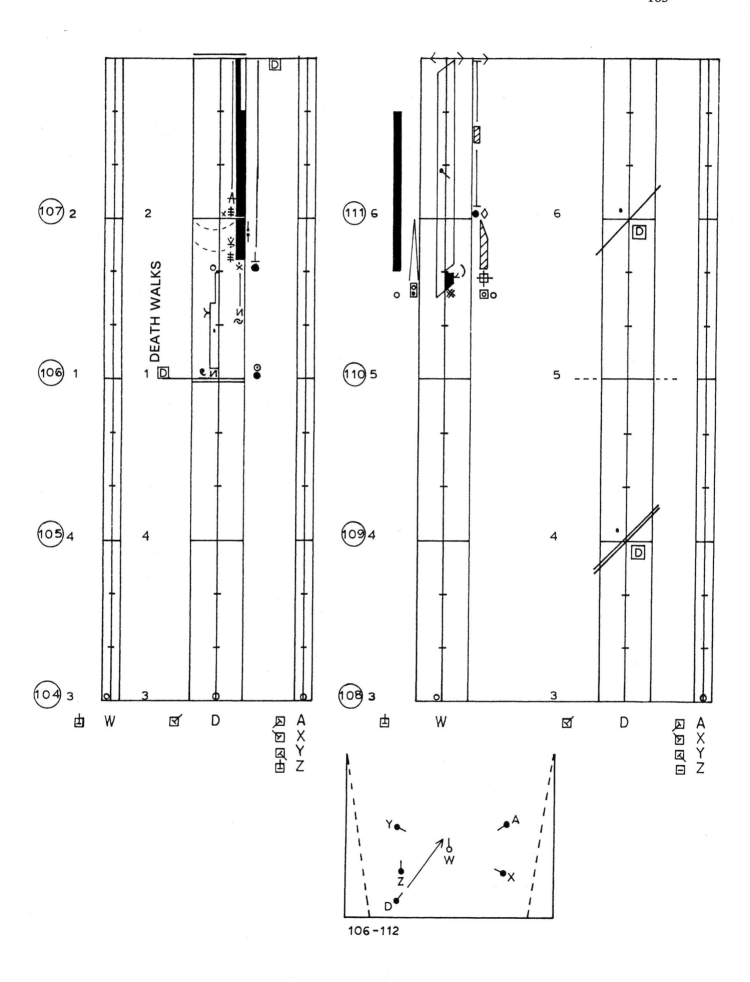

DEATH WALKS

106-112

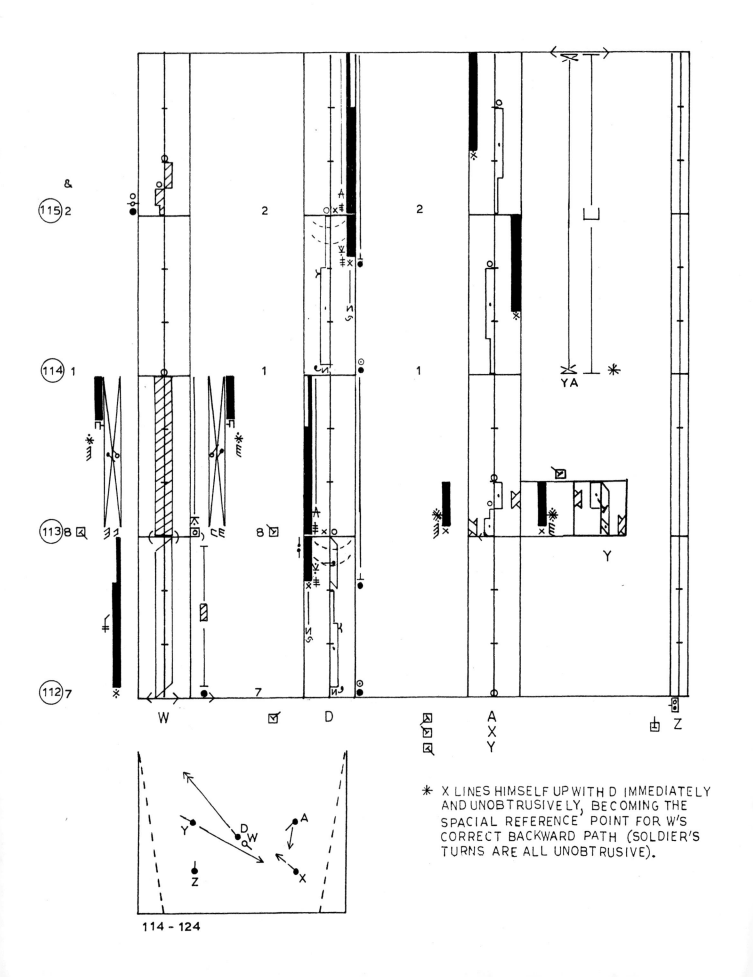

114 - 124

* X LINES HIMSELF UP WITH D IMMEDIATELY
AND UNOBTRUSIVELY, BECOMING THE
SPACIAL REFERENCE POINT FOR W'S
CORRECT BACKWARD PATH (SOLDIER'S
TURNS ARE ALL UNOBTRUSIVE).

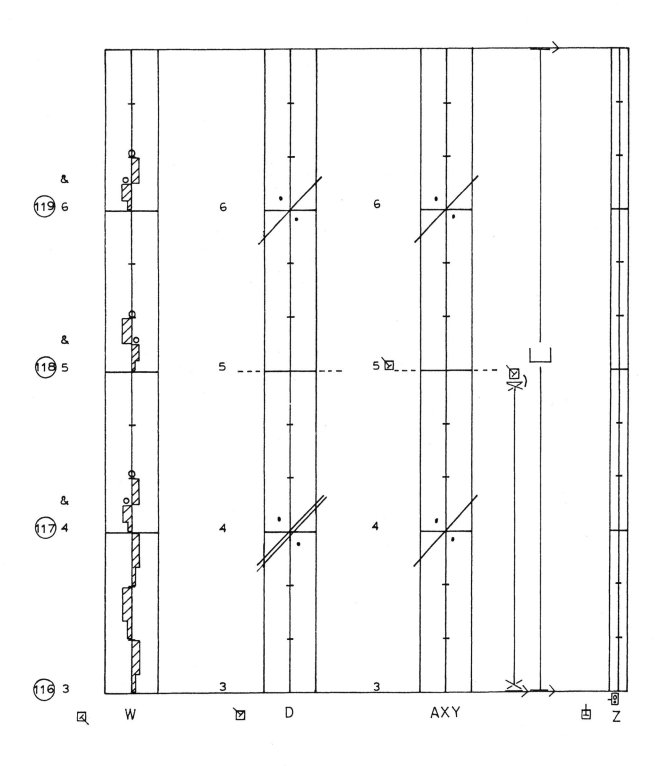

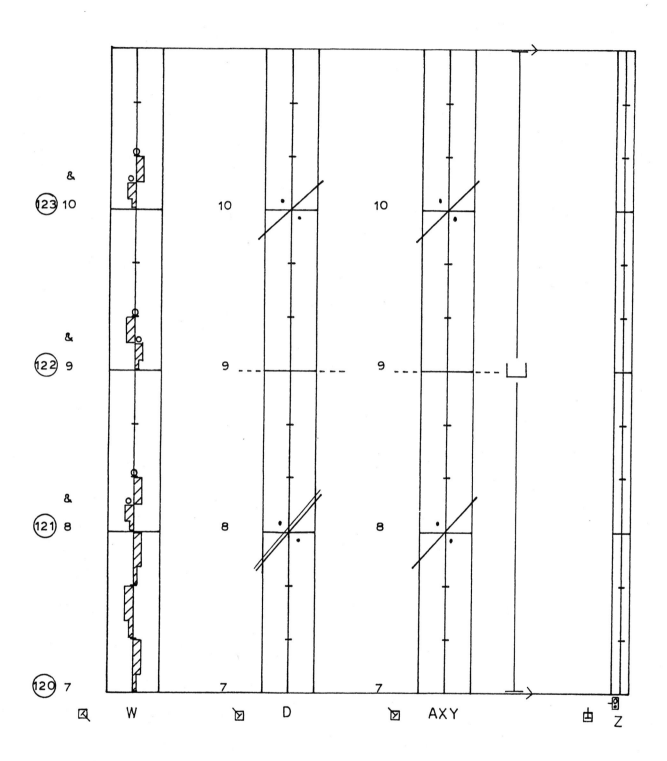

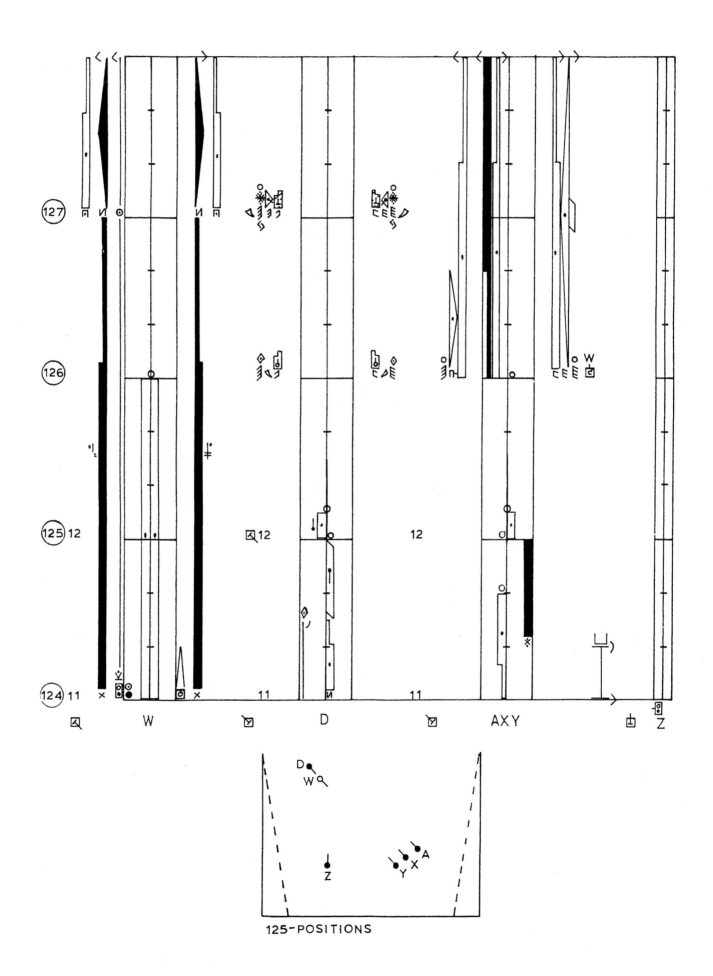

125-POSITIONS

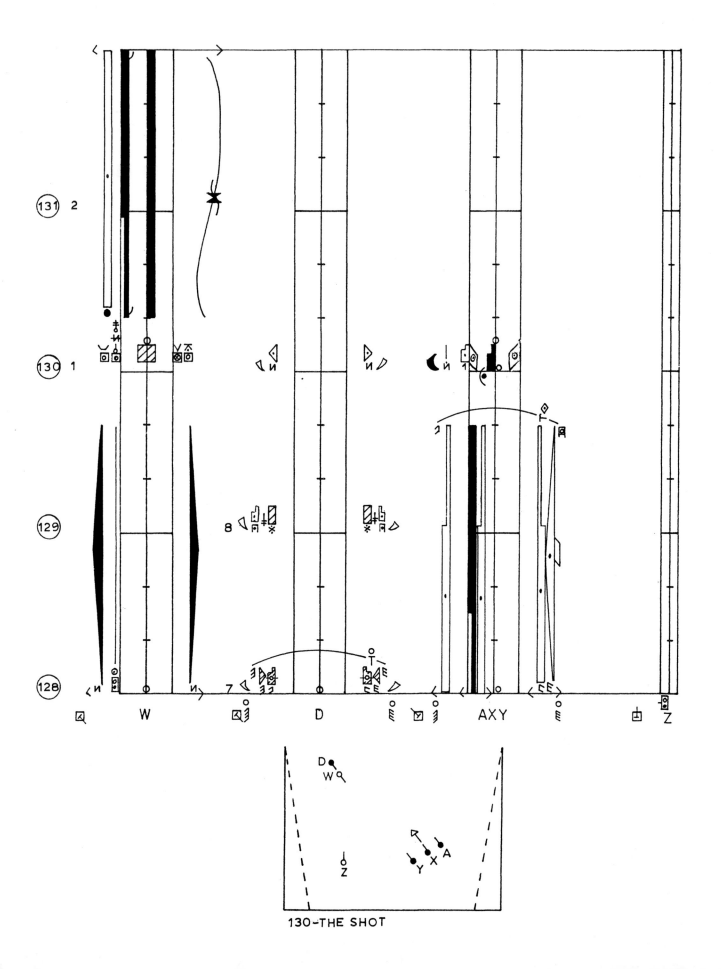

130–THE SHOT

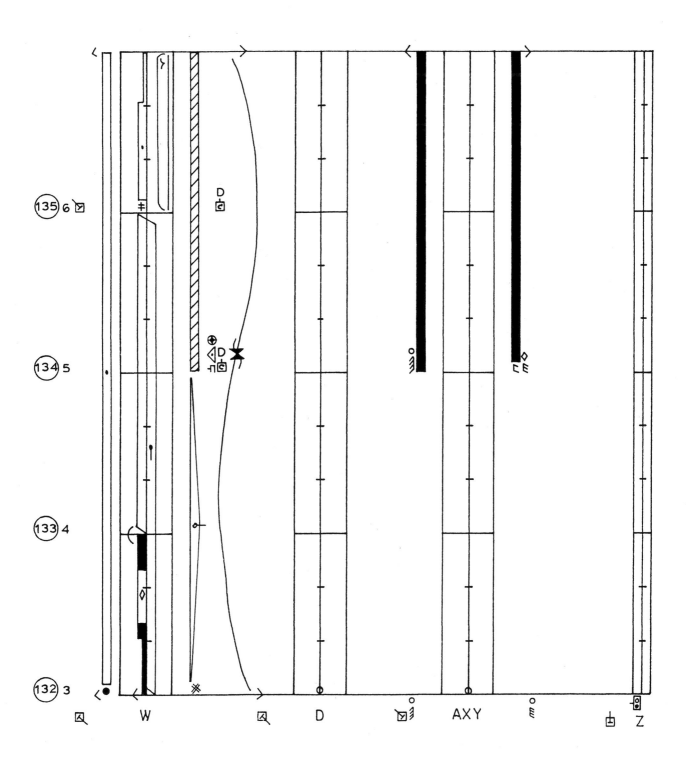

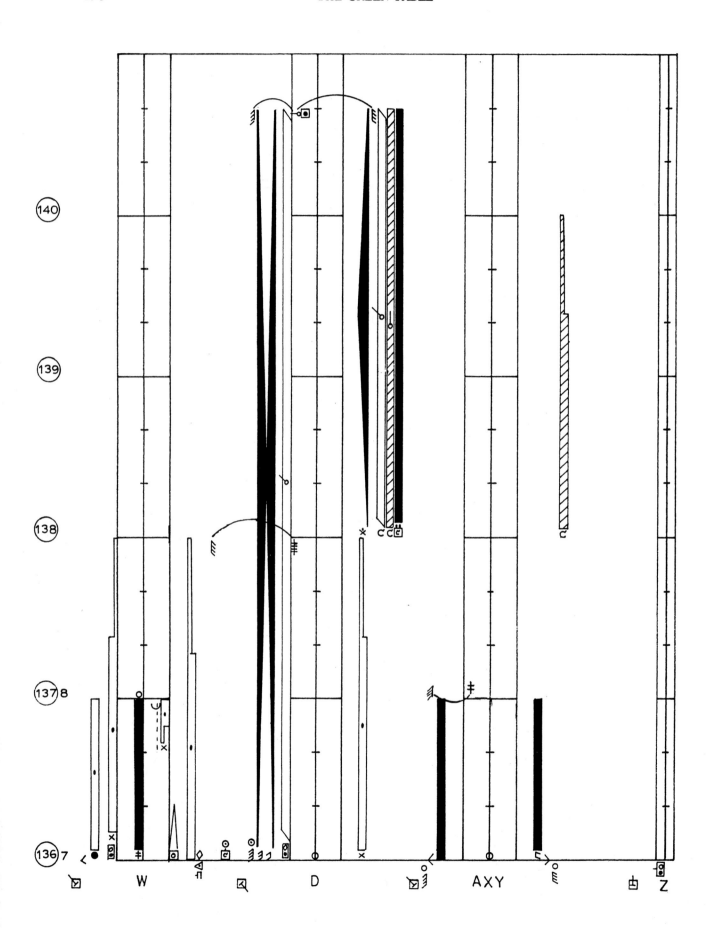

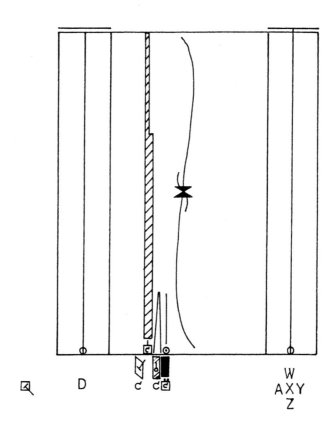

CHANGE STAFFS:

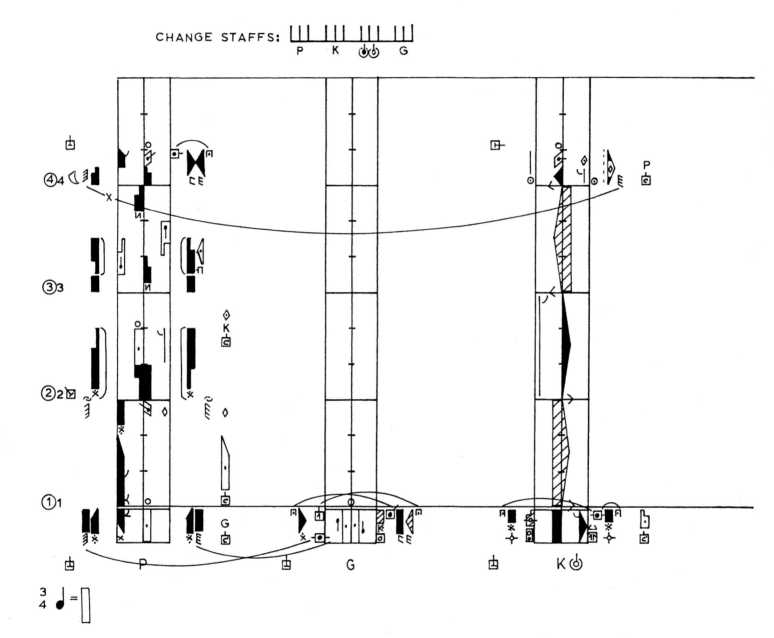

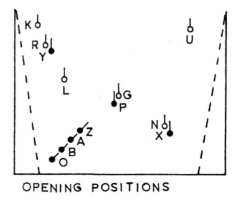

OPENING POSITIONS

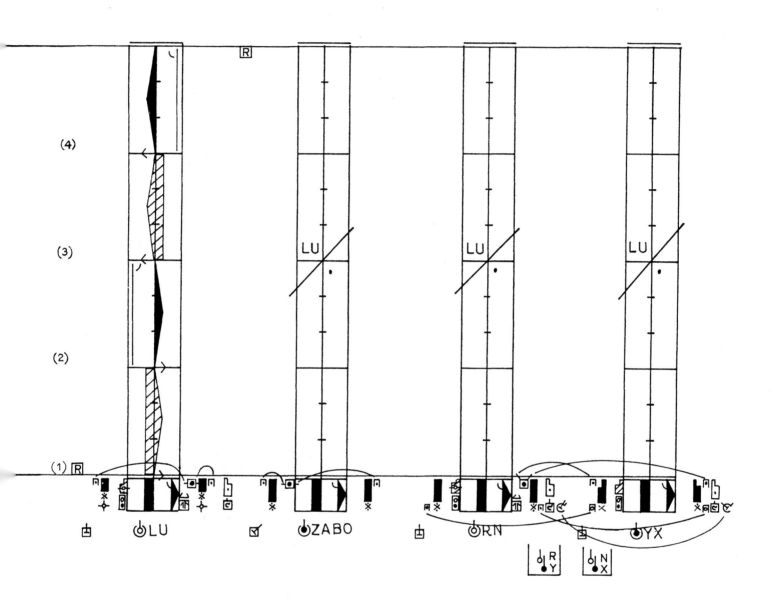

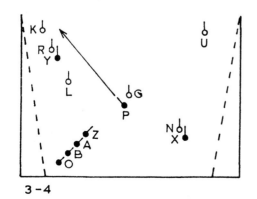

3 - 4

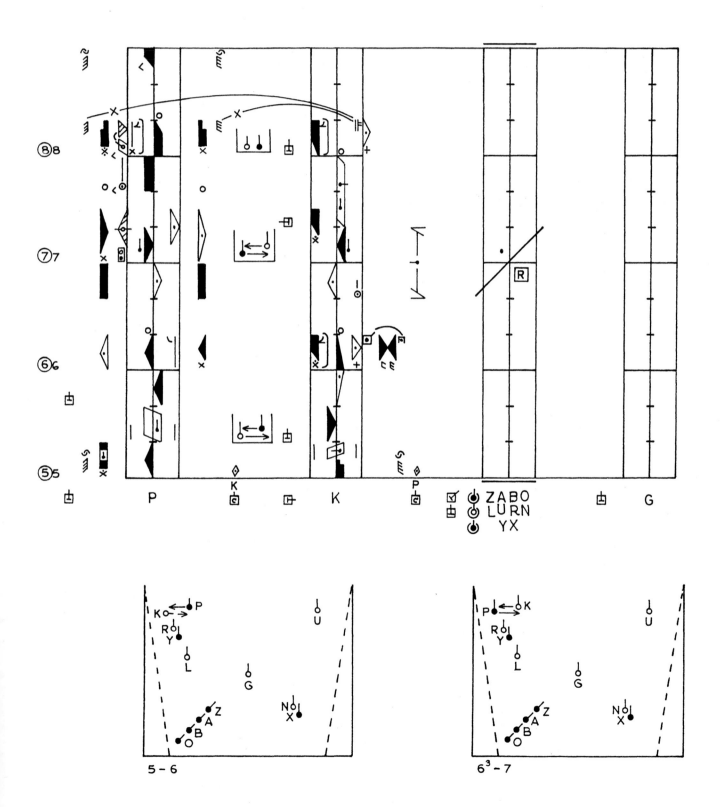

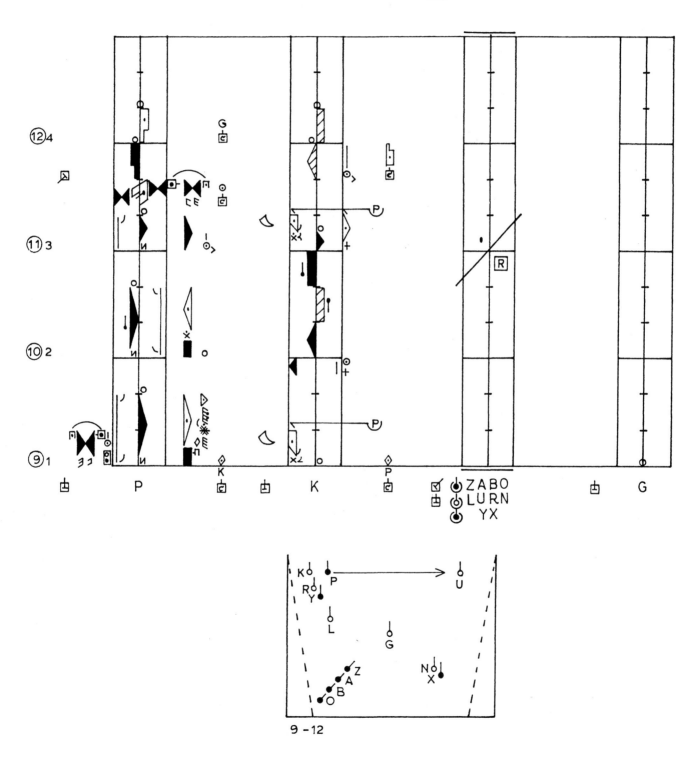

9 - 12

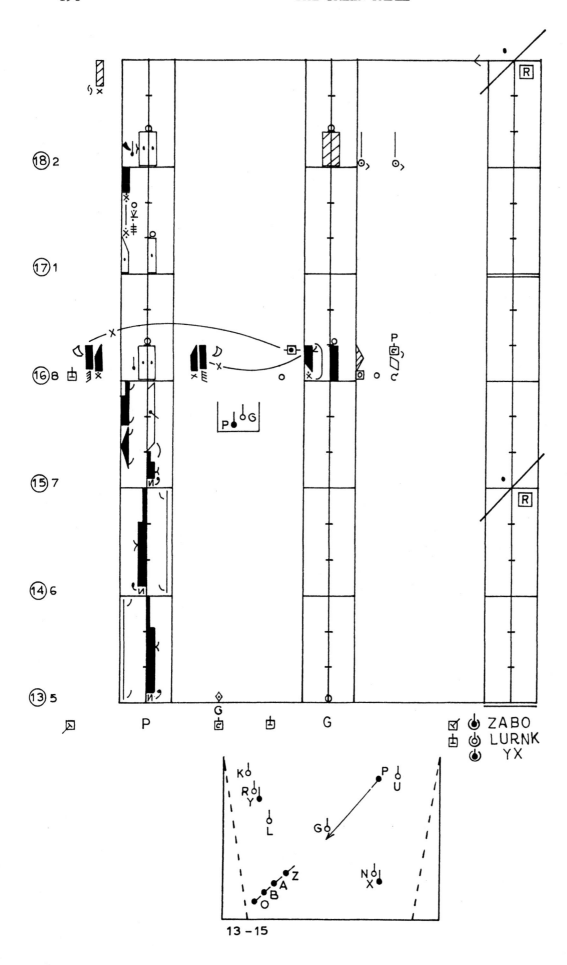

13 – 15

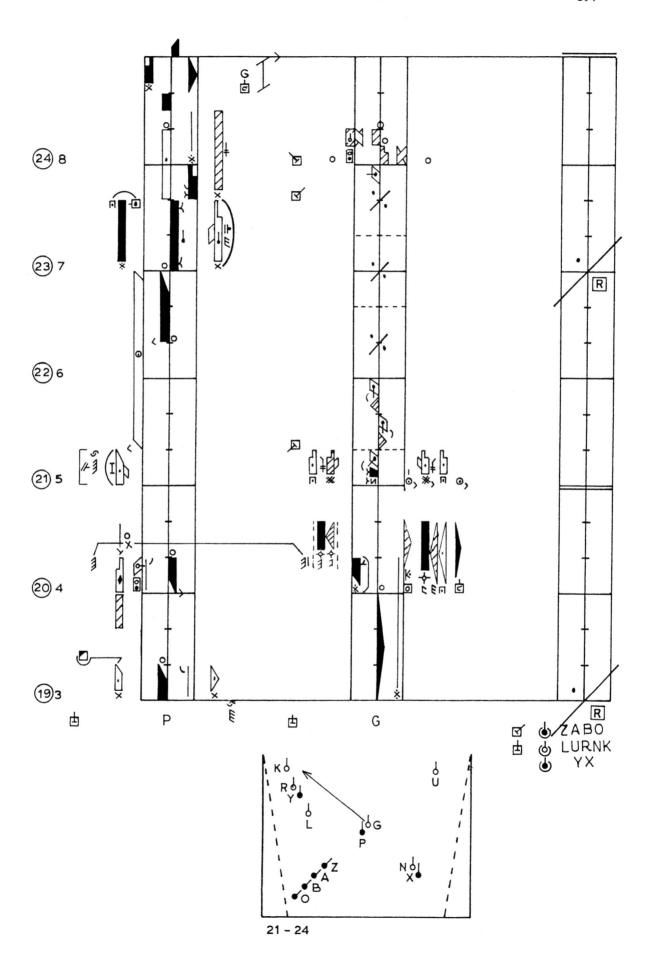

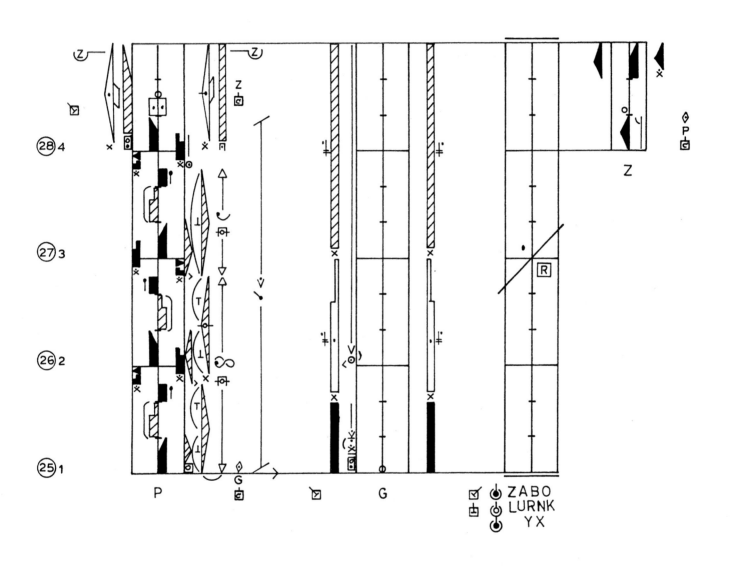

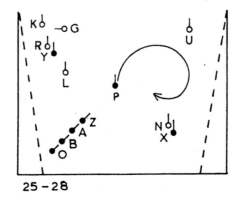

25 – 28

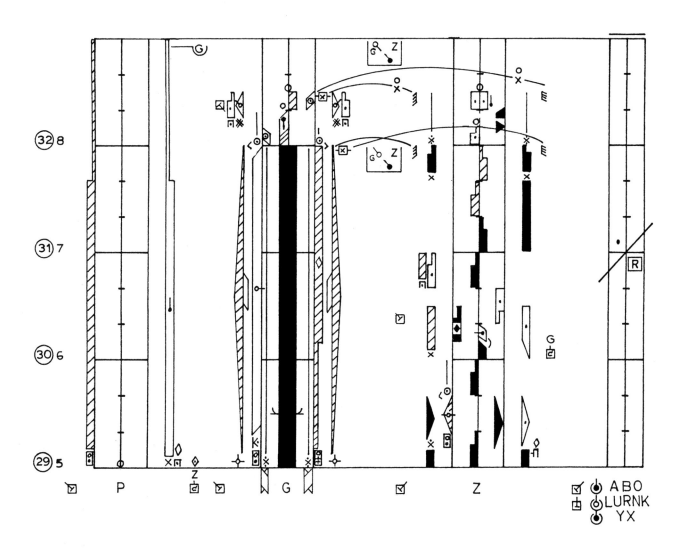

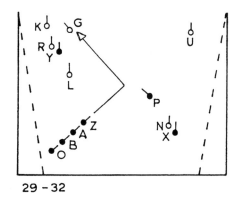

29 - 32

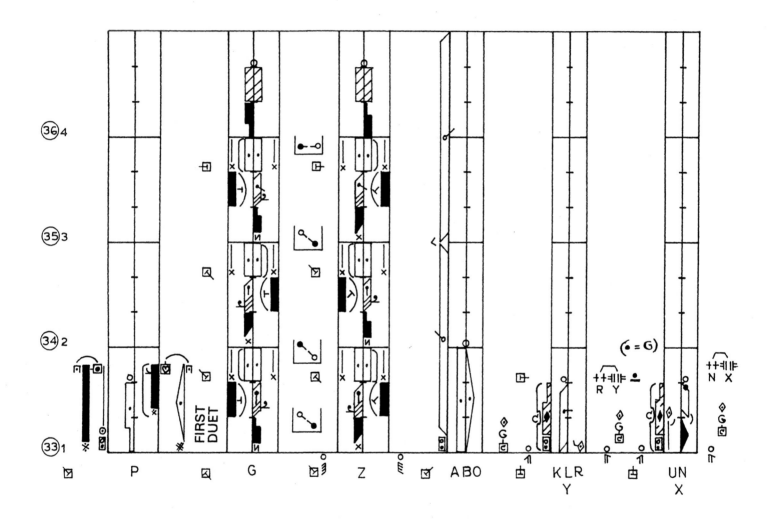

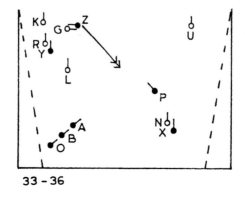

33 — 36

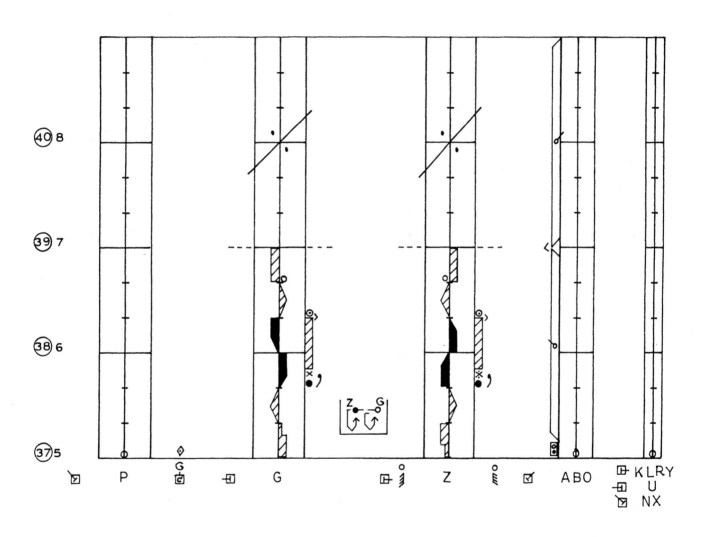

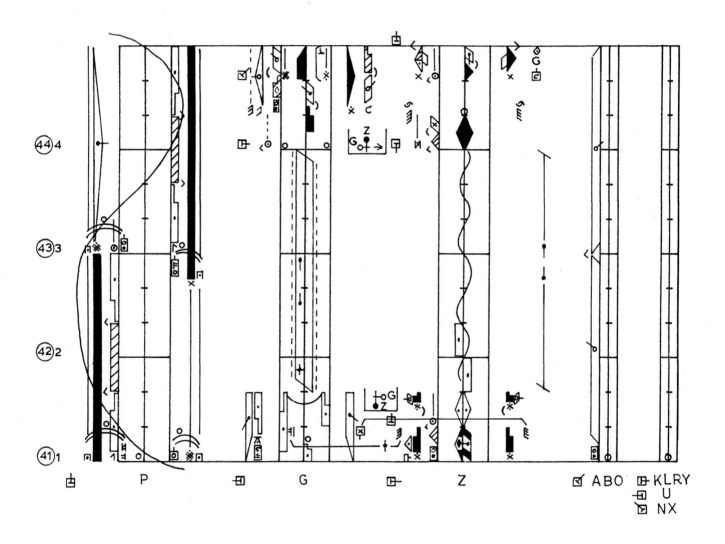

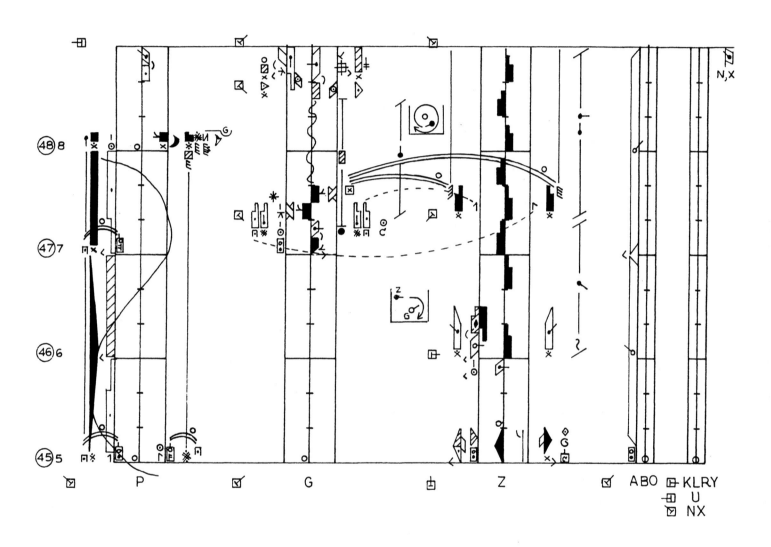

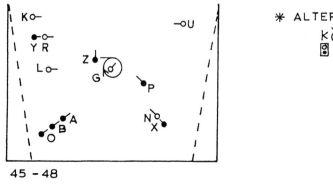

45 - 48

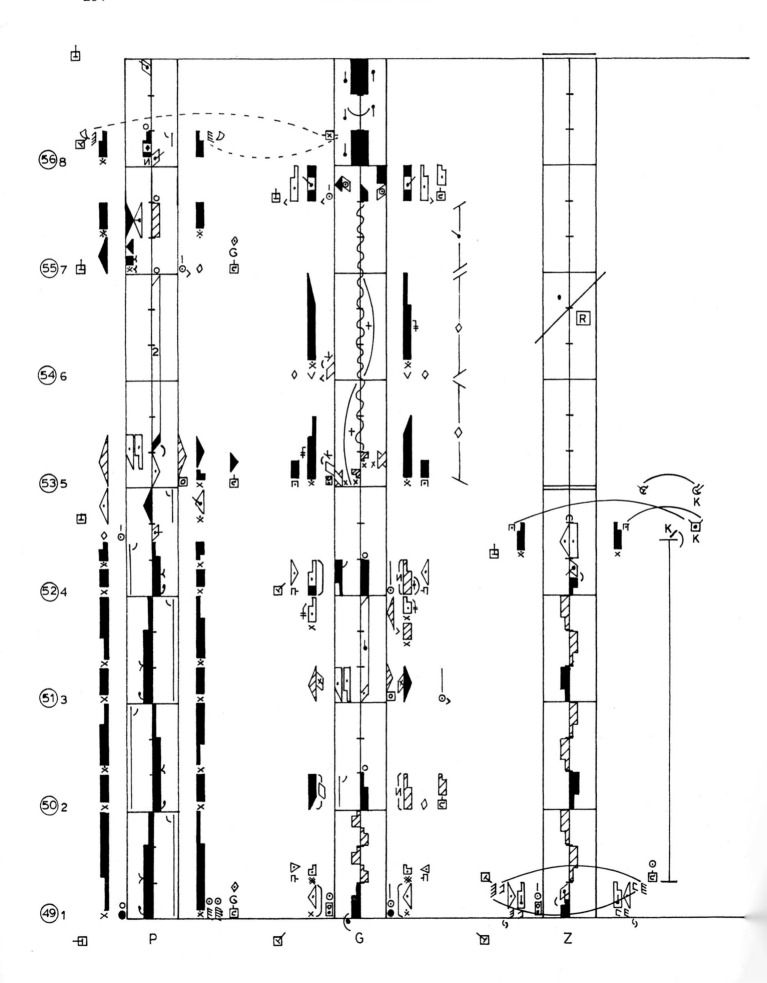

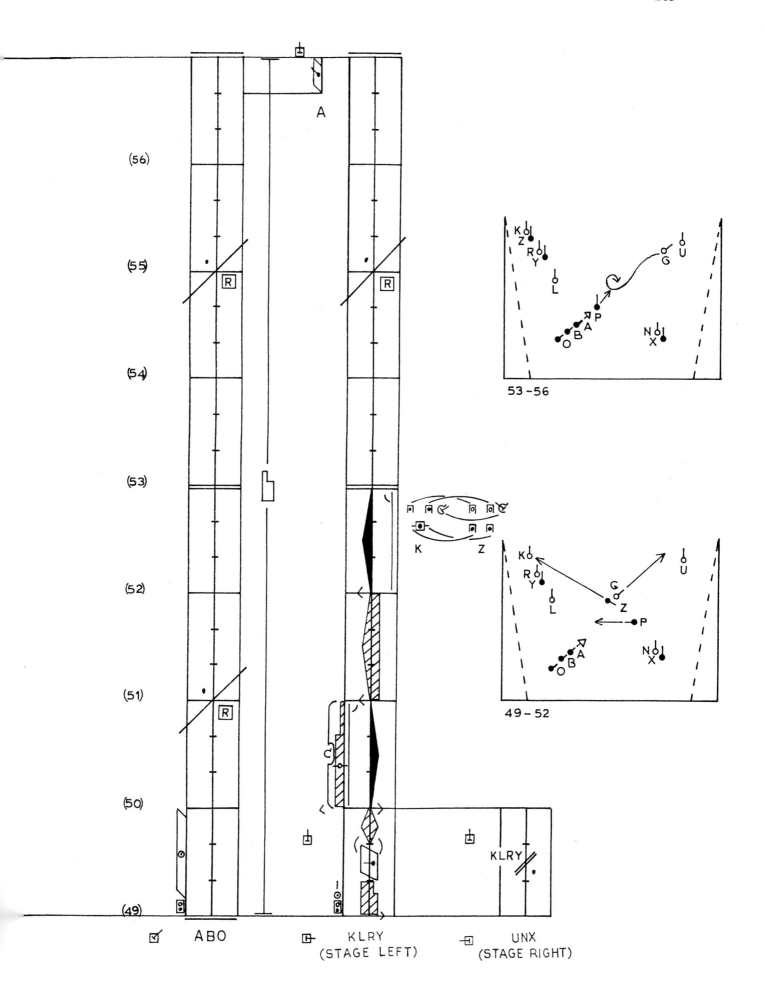

53-56

49-52

| ☑ | A B O | ⊞ | K L R Y | ⊞ | U N X |
| | | | (STAGE LEFT) | | (STAGE RIGHT) |

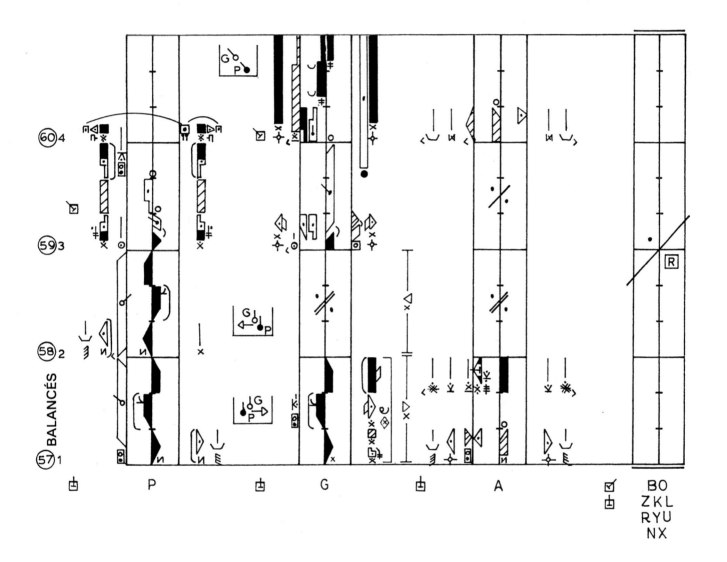

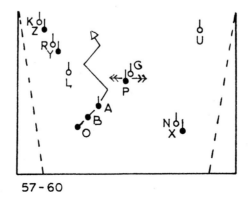

57 - 60

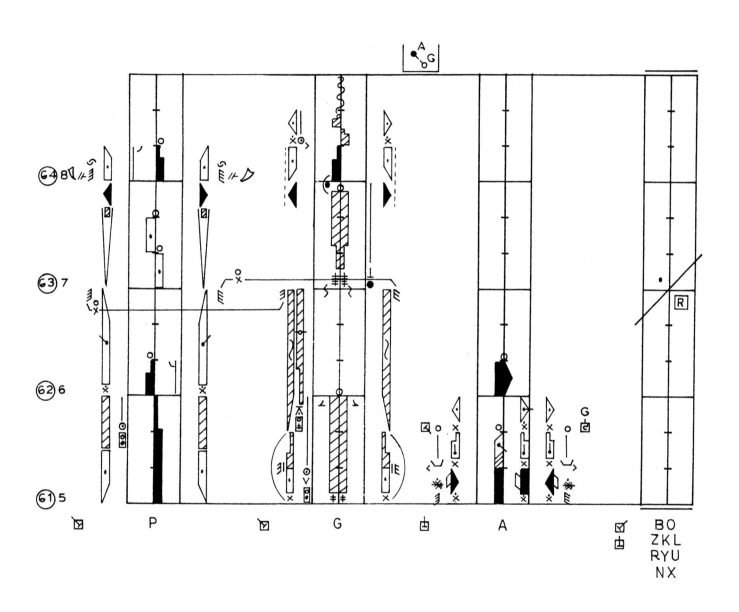

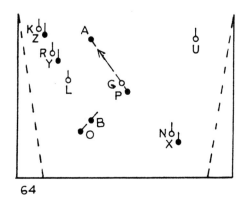

64

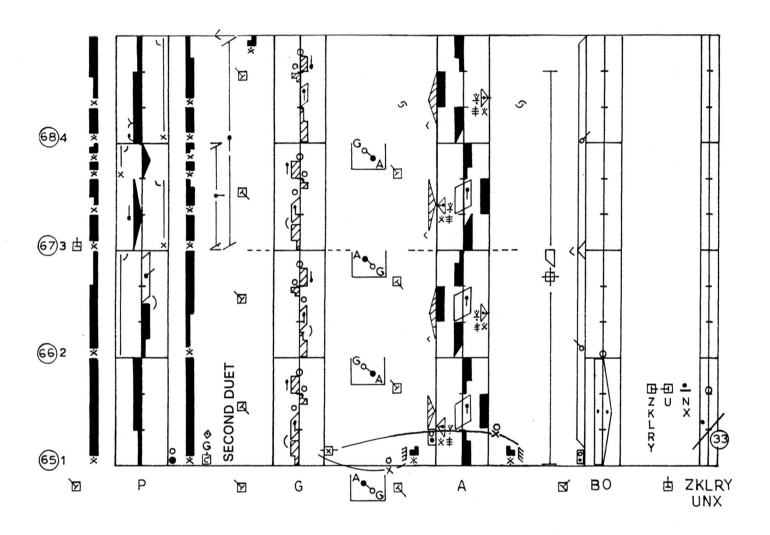

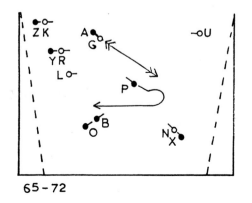

65-72

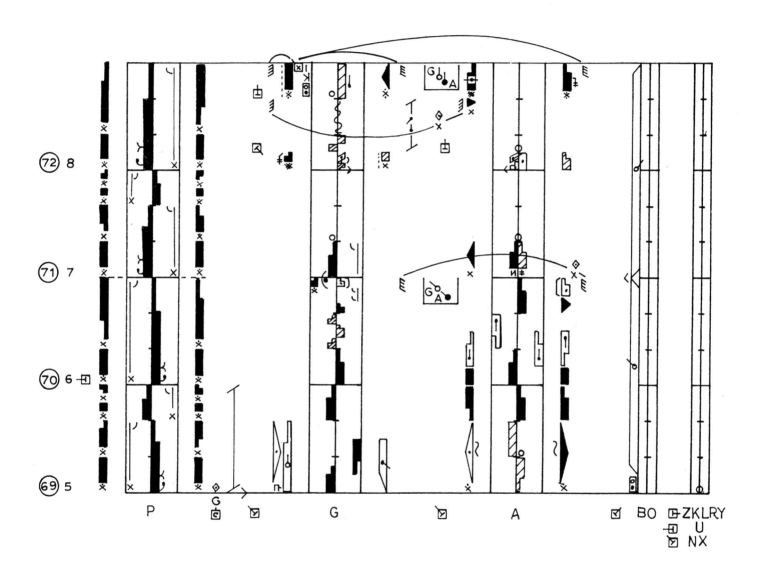

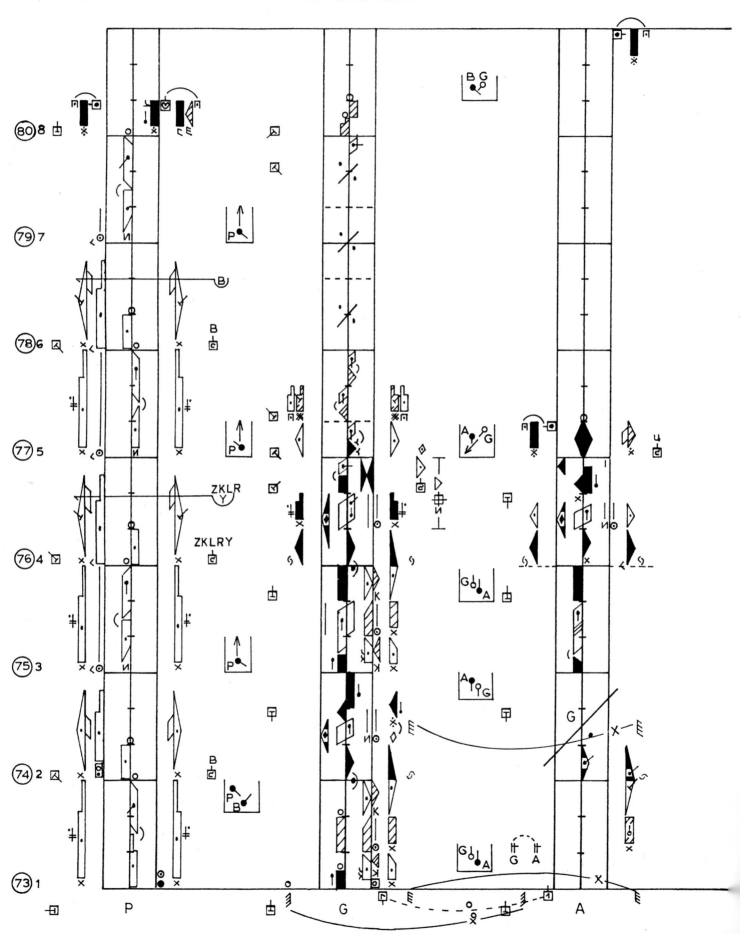

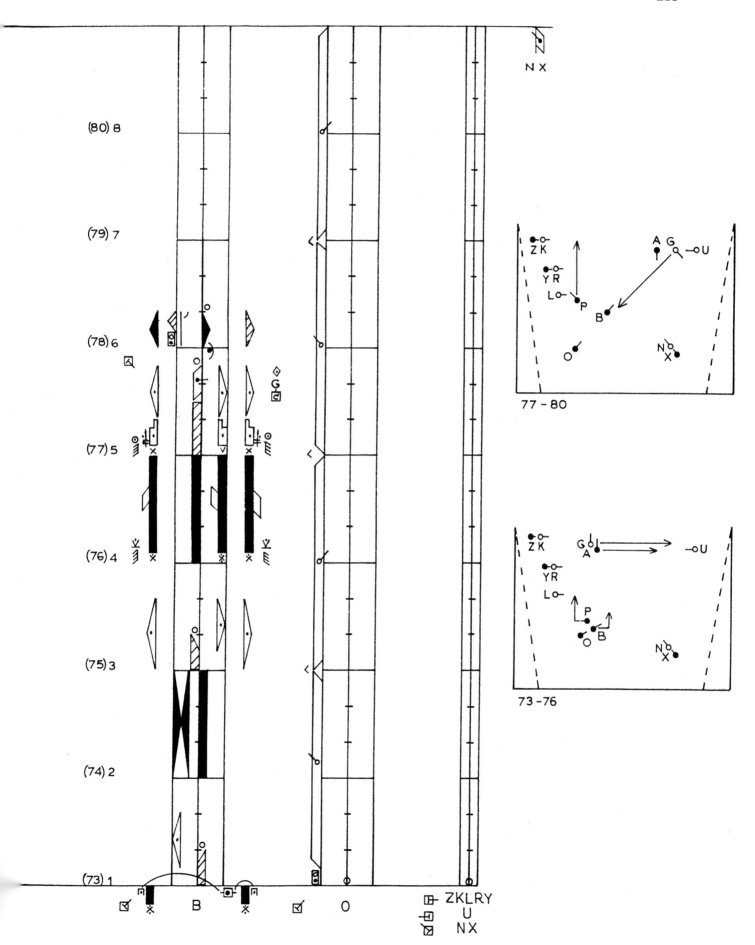

77 – 80

73 – 76

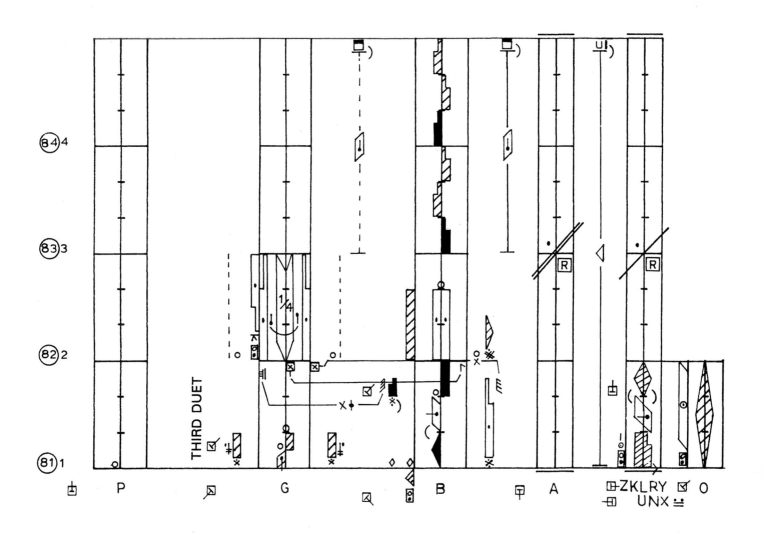

THIRD DUET

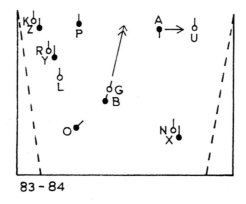

83 – 84

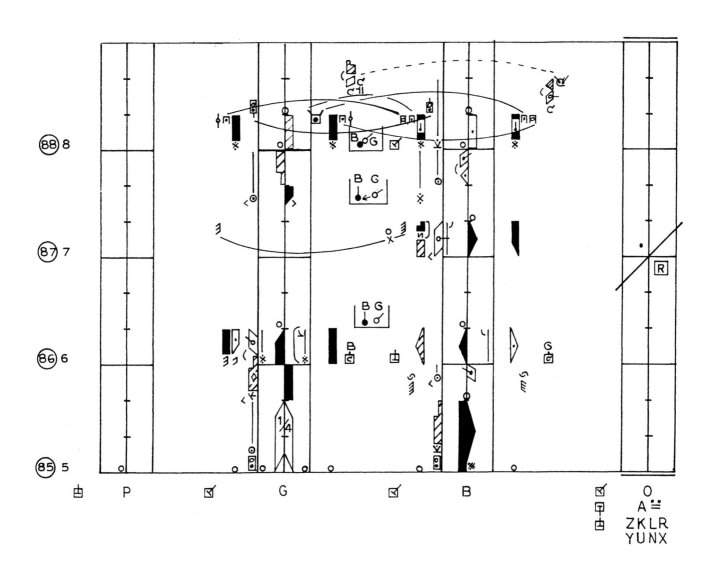

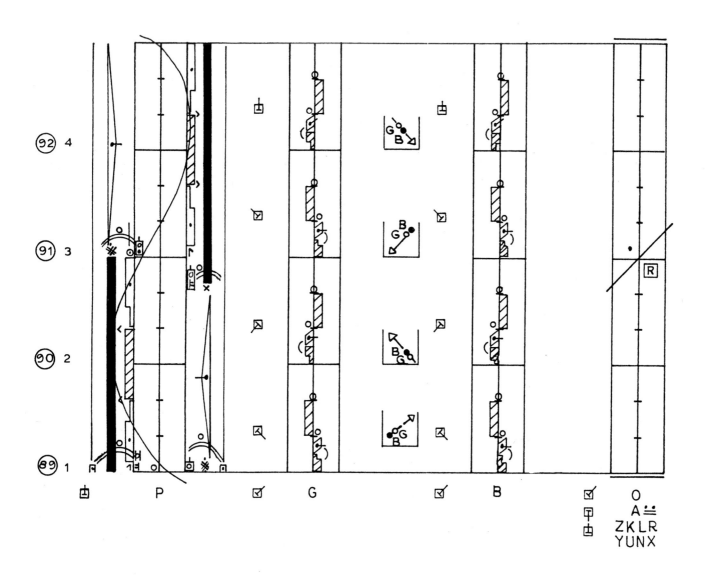

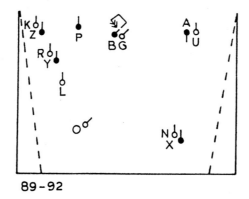

89-92

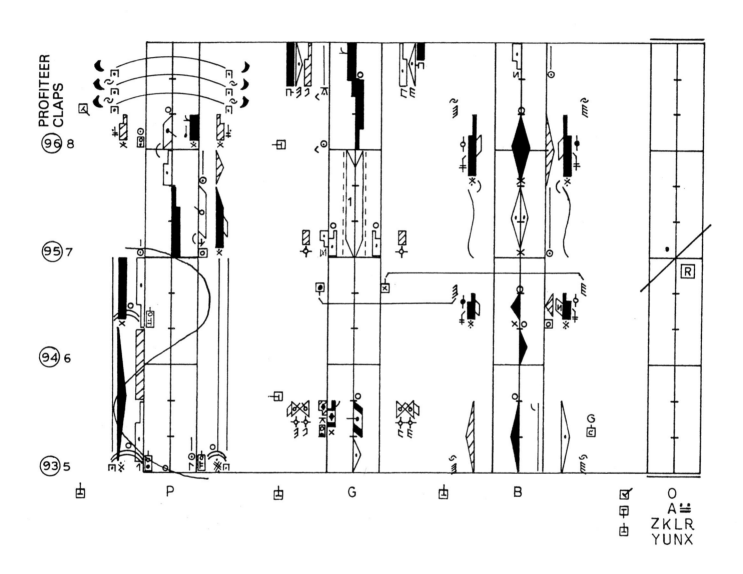

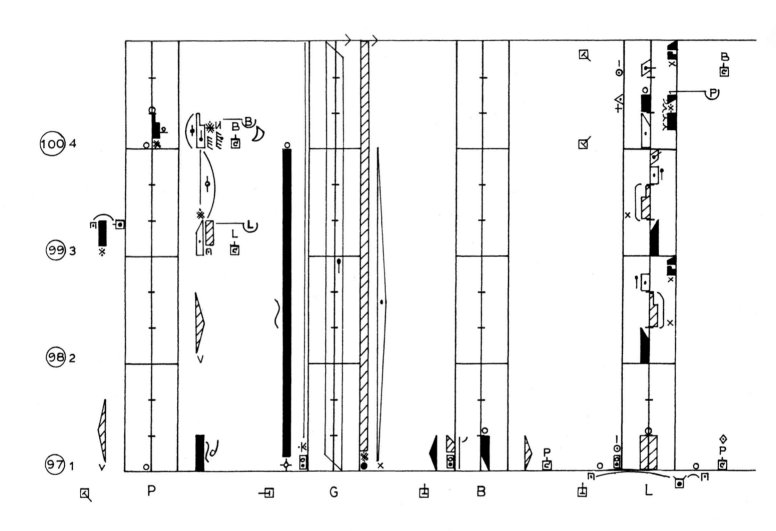

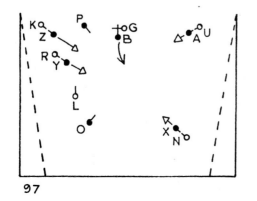

97

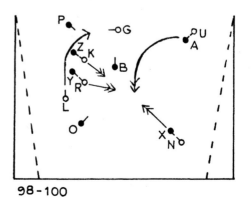

98-100

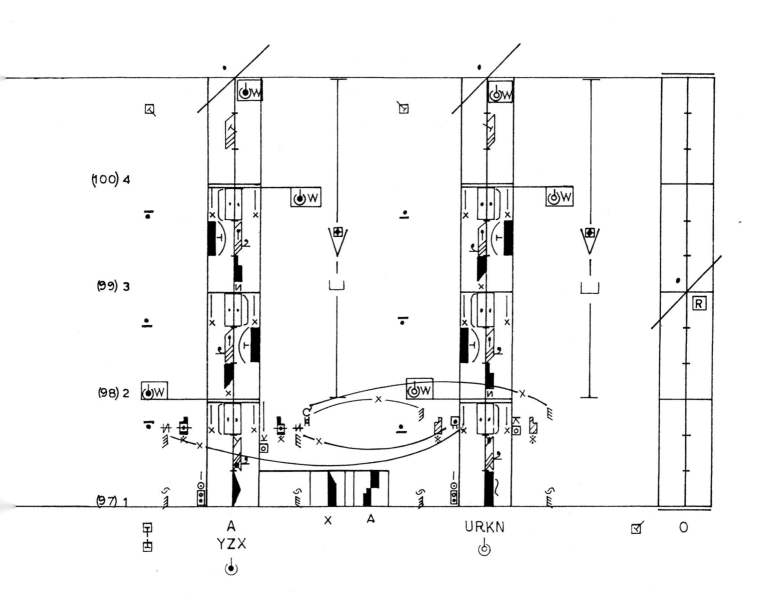

PARTNERS: THIS IS THE SAME WALTZ DONE BY G & Z (MEASURE ③③).

A & U
X & N
Z & K
Y & R

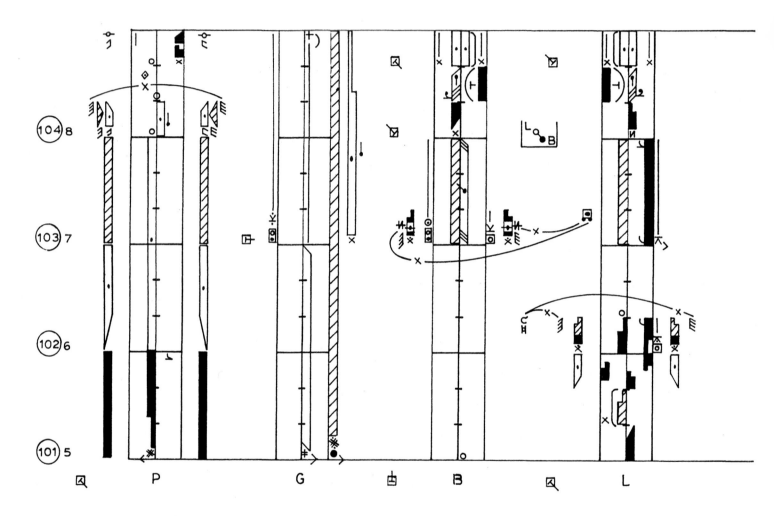

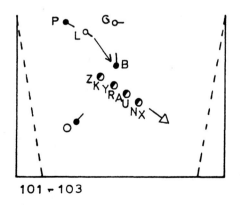

101 - 103

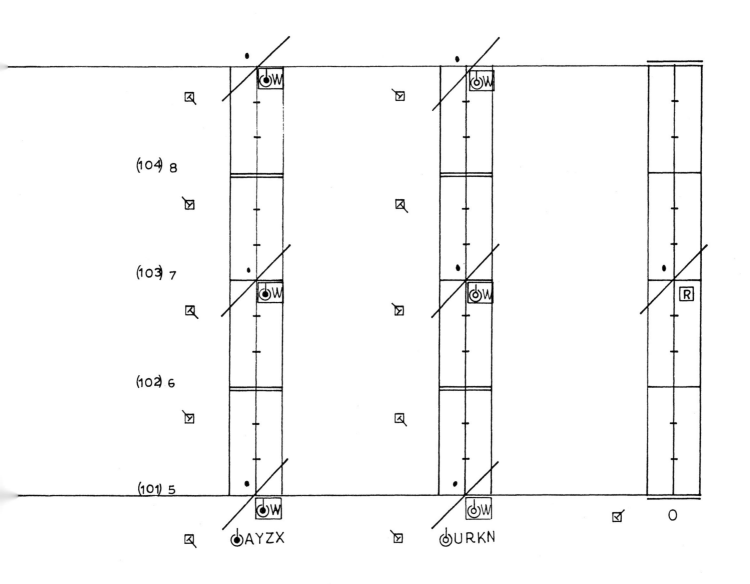

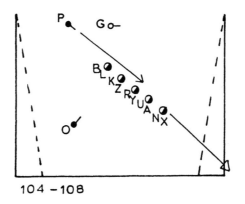

104 – 108

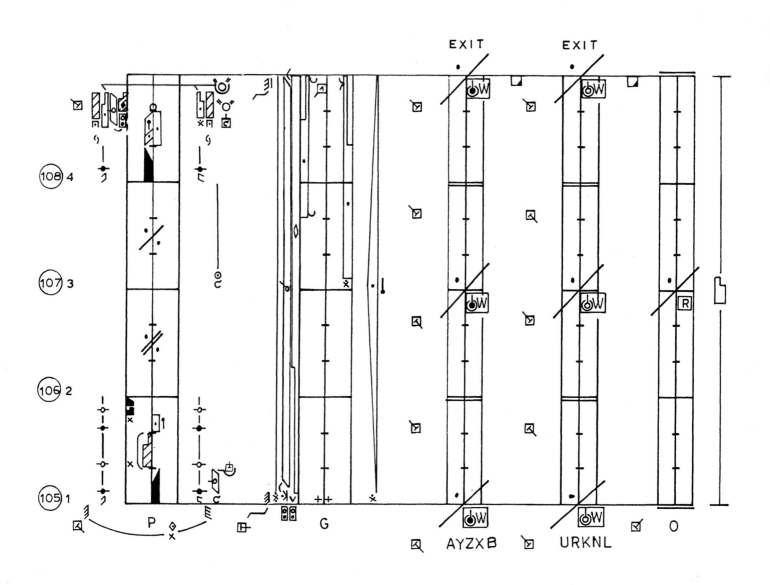

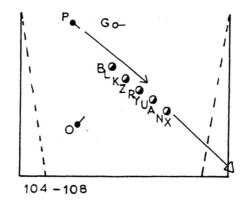

104 – 108

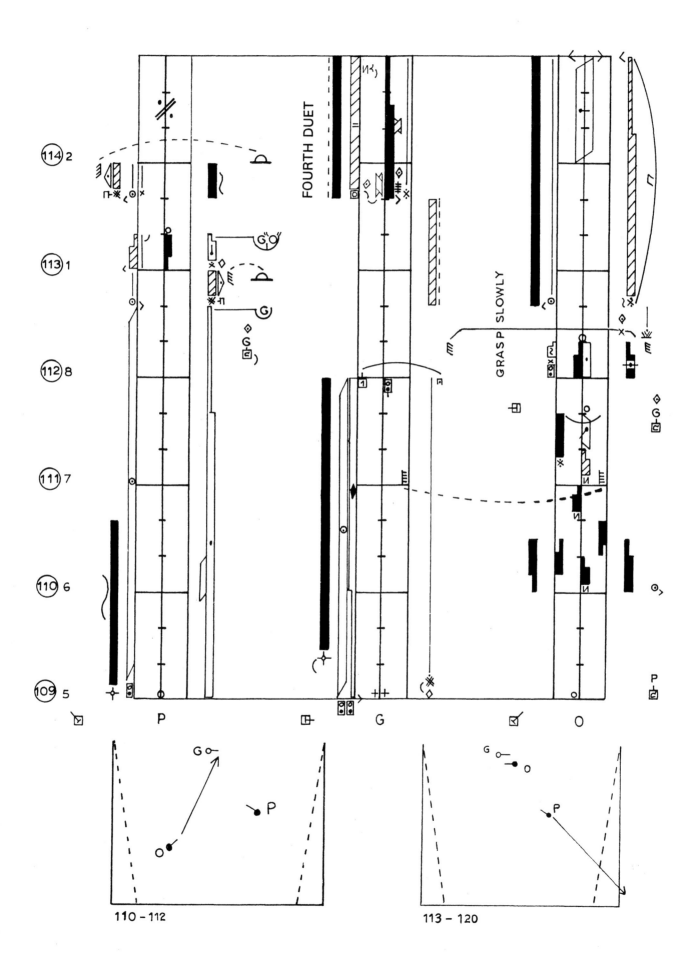

FOURTH DUET

GRASP SLOWLY

110 – 112

113 – 120

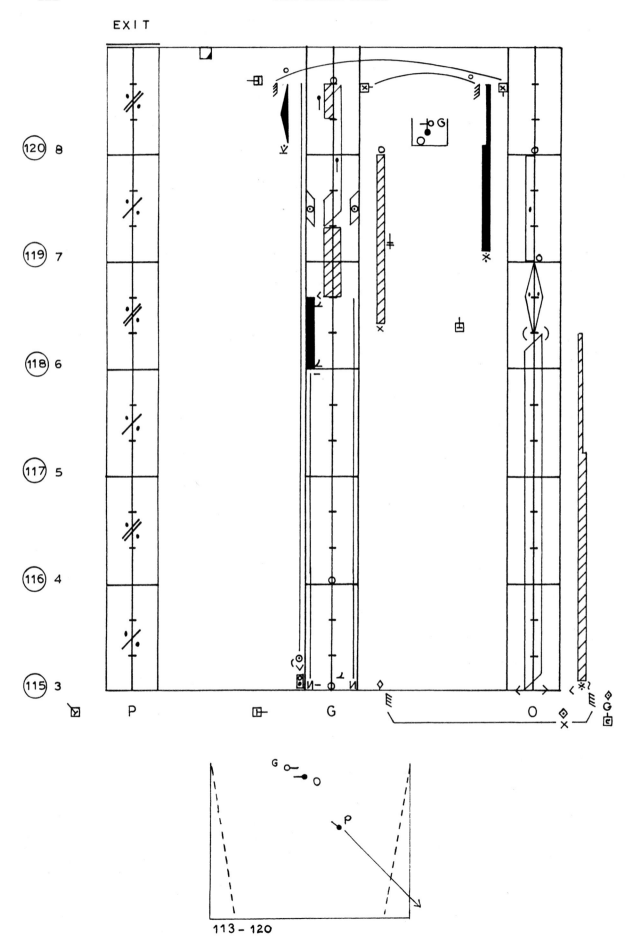

EXIT

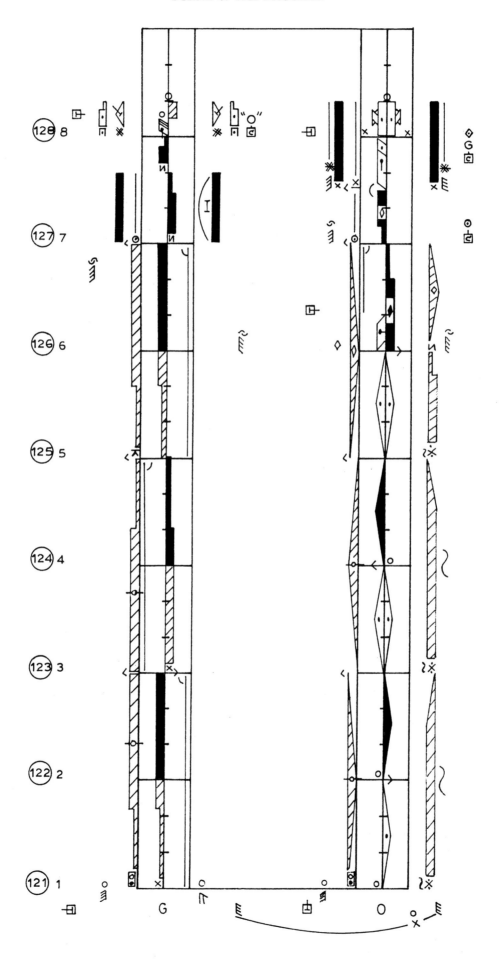

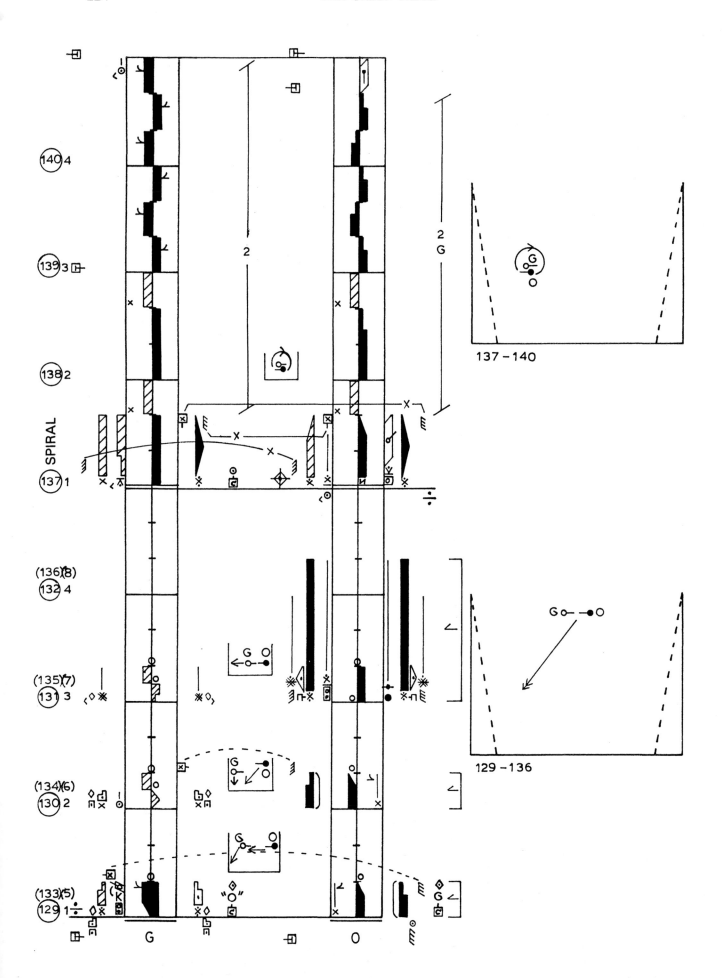

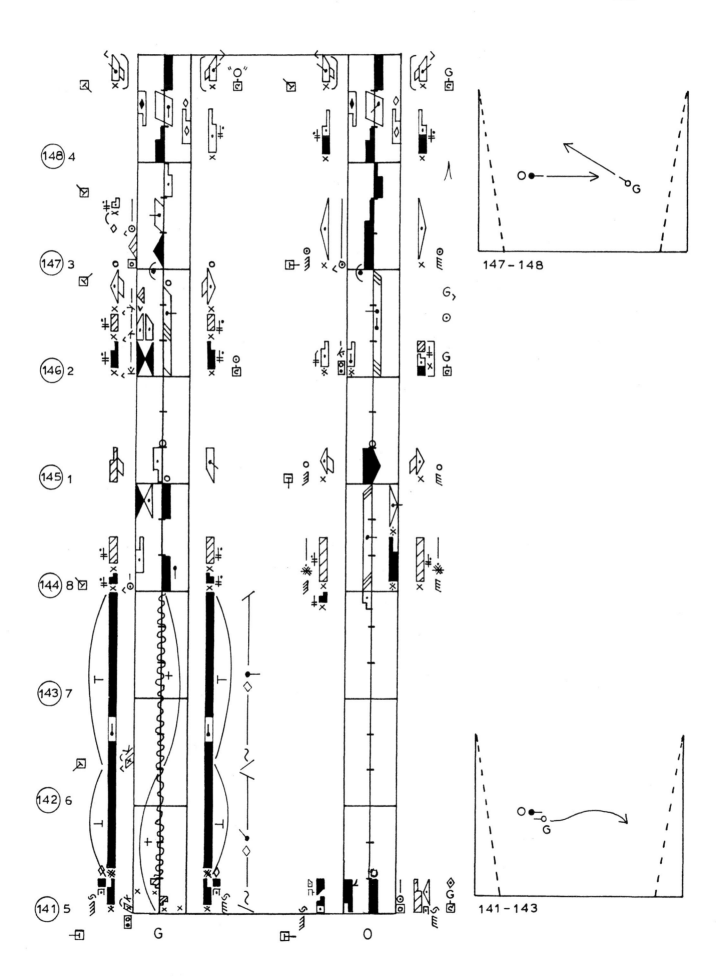

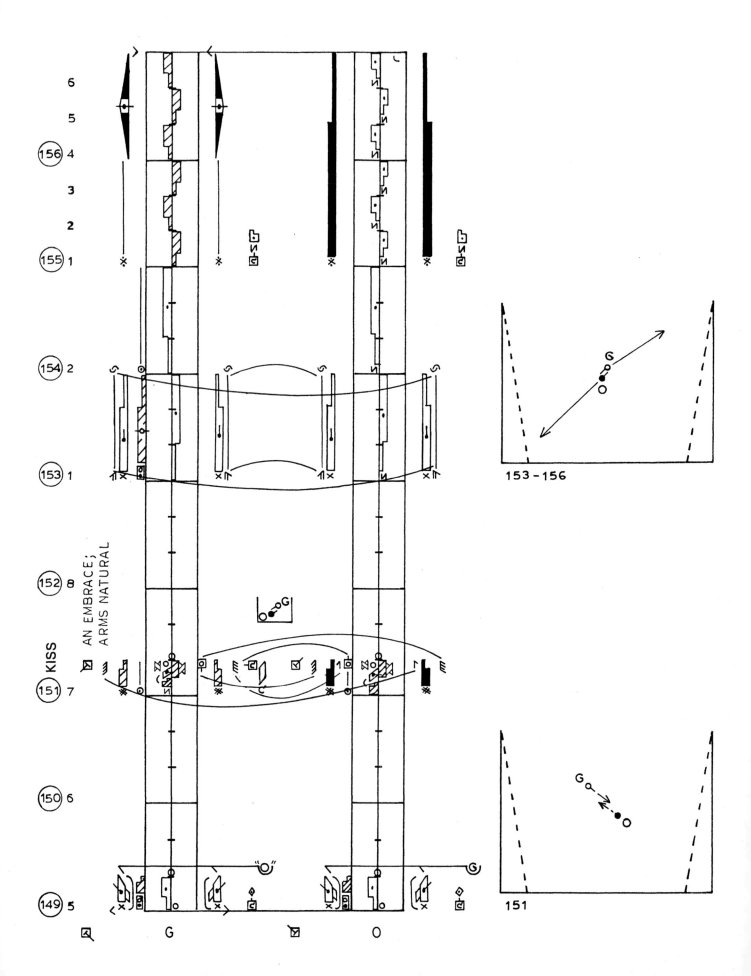

153 – 156

151

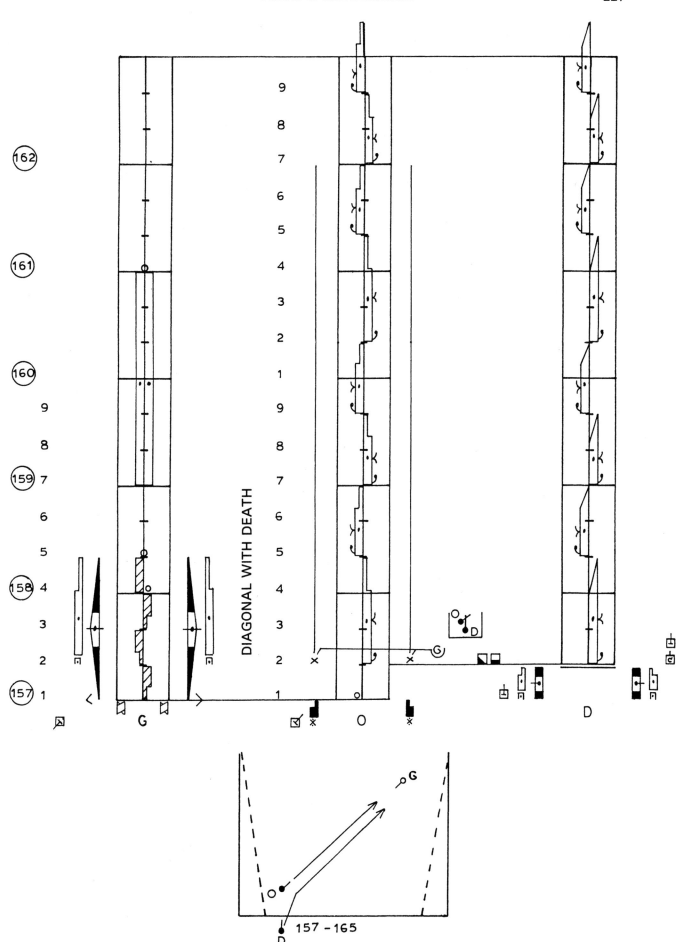

DIAGONAL WITH DEATH

157 – 165

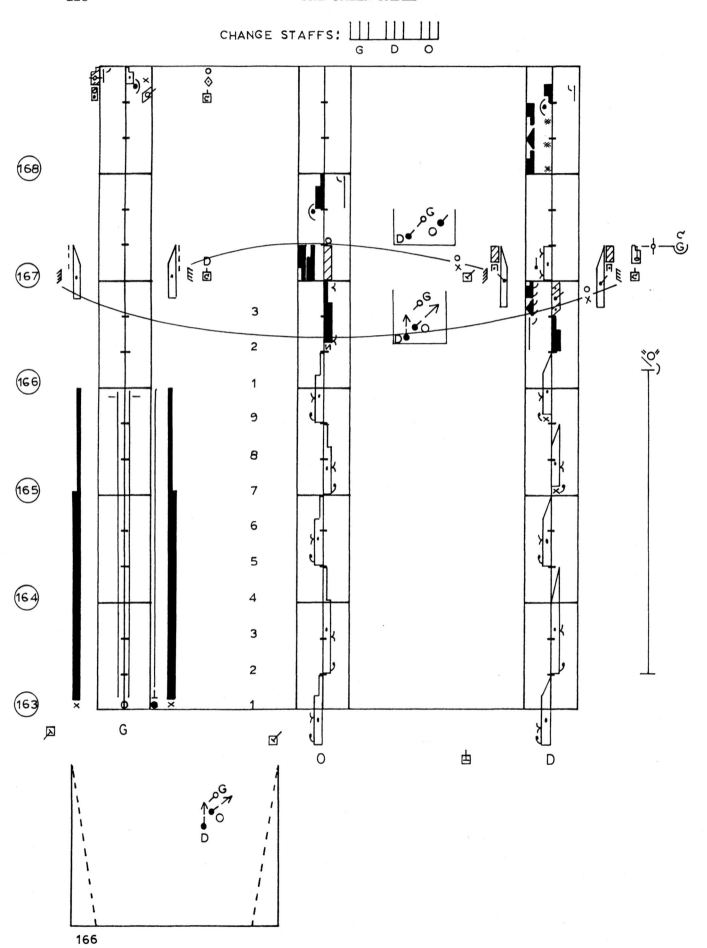

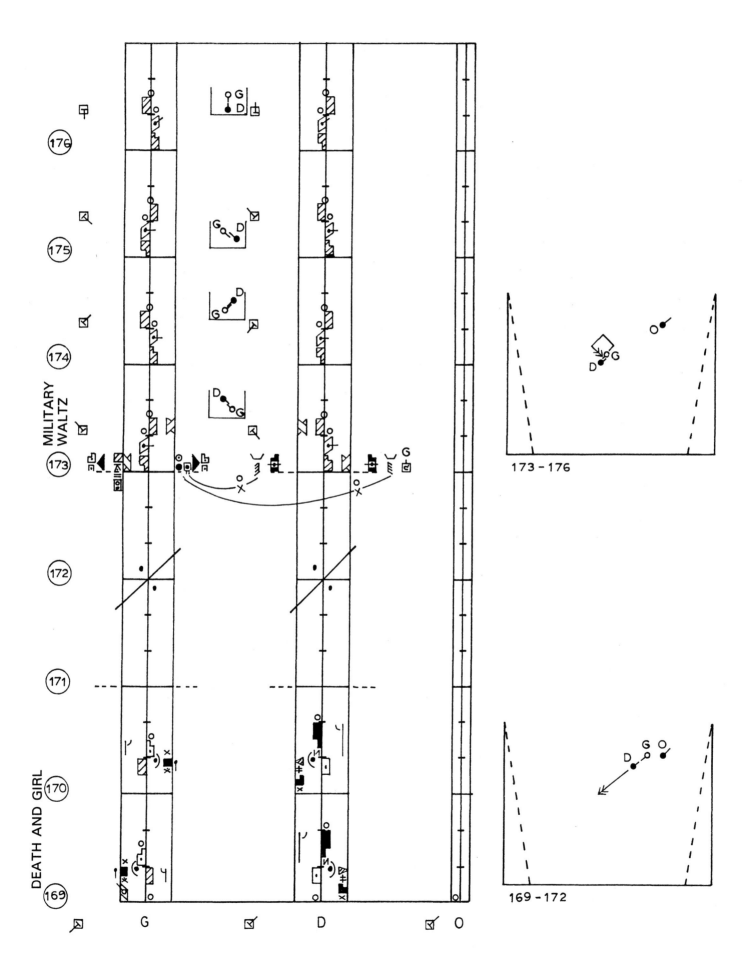

173 – 176

169 – 172

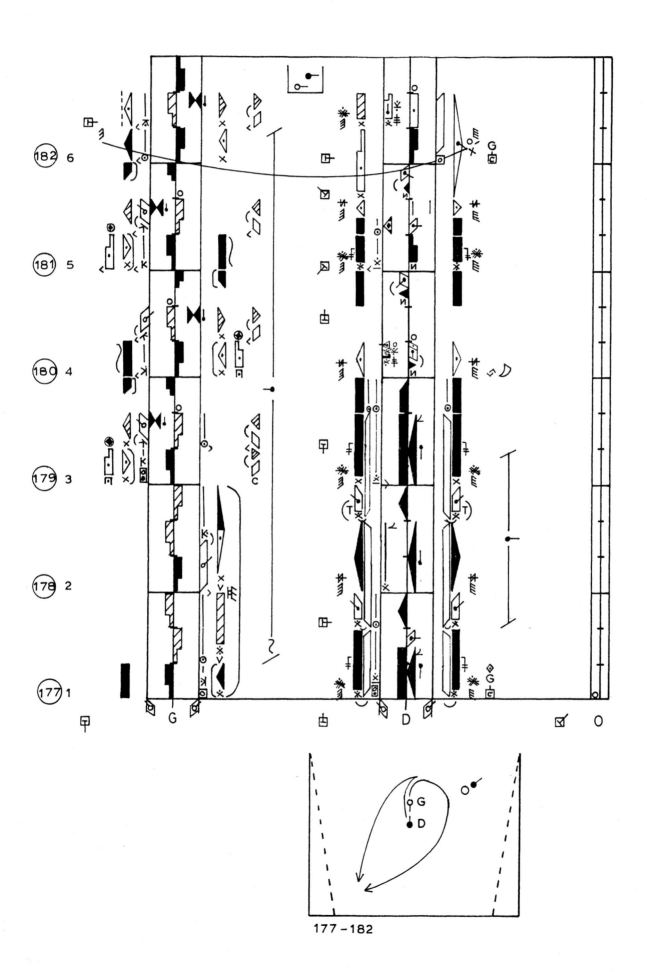

177 – 182

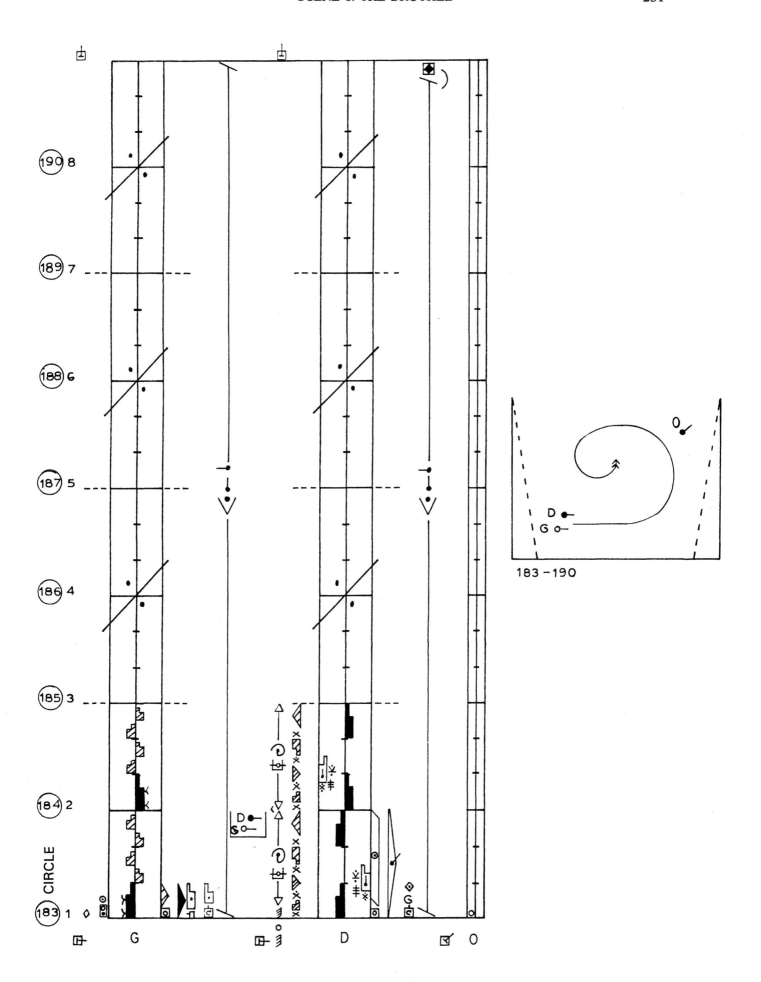

183 – 190

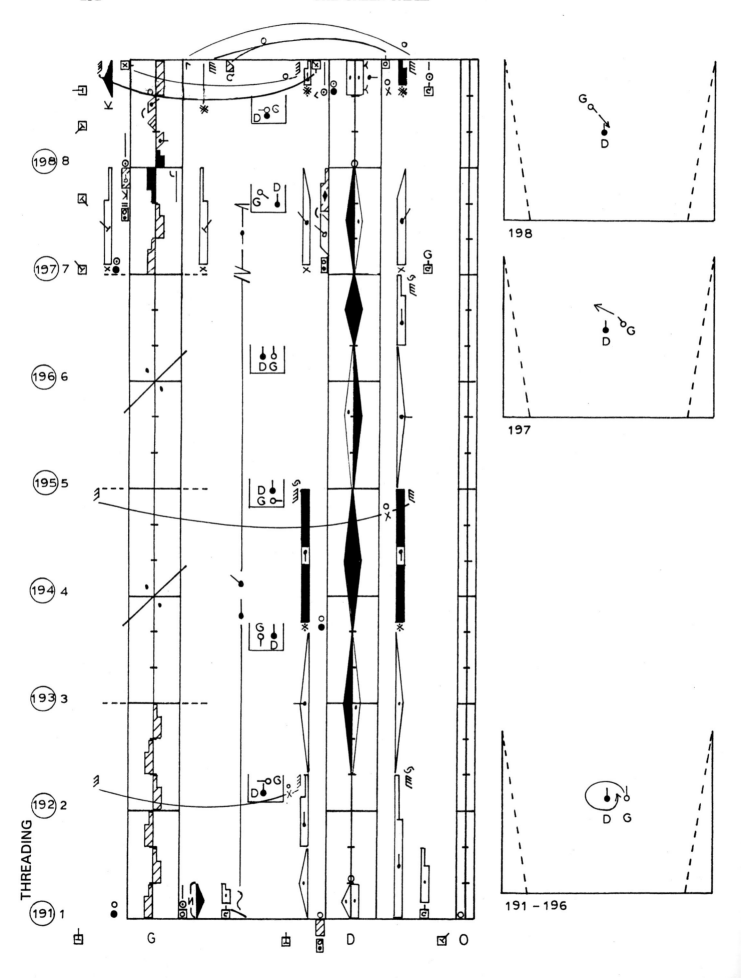

191 – 196

197

198

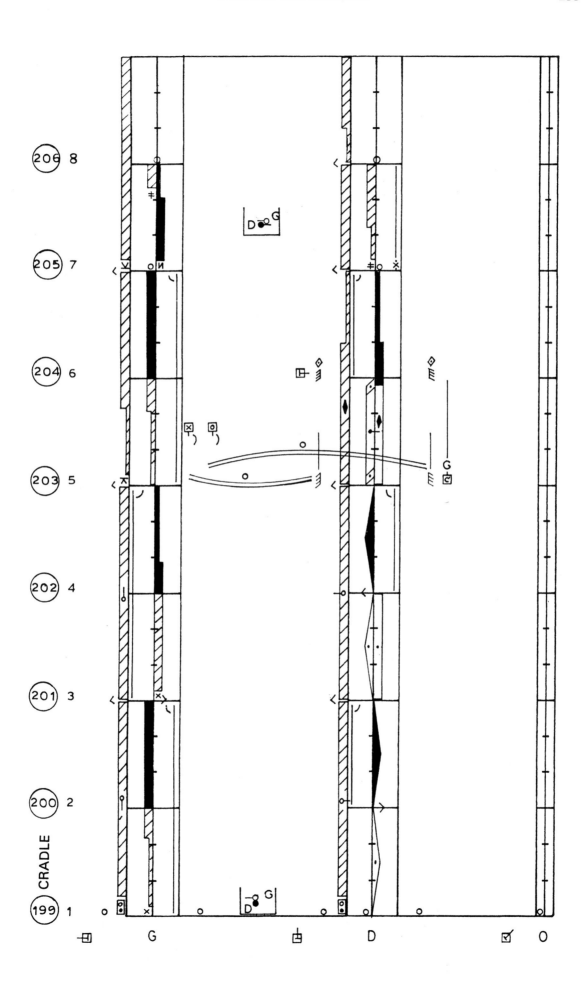

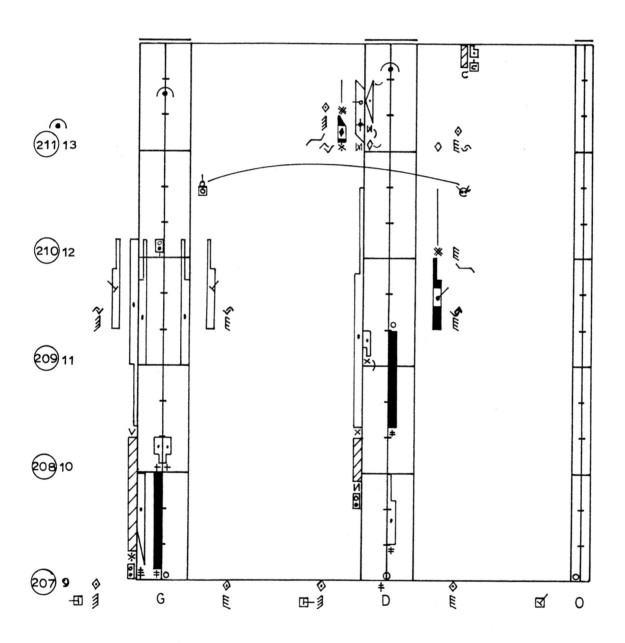

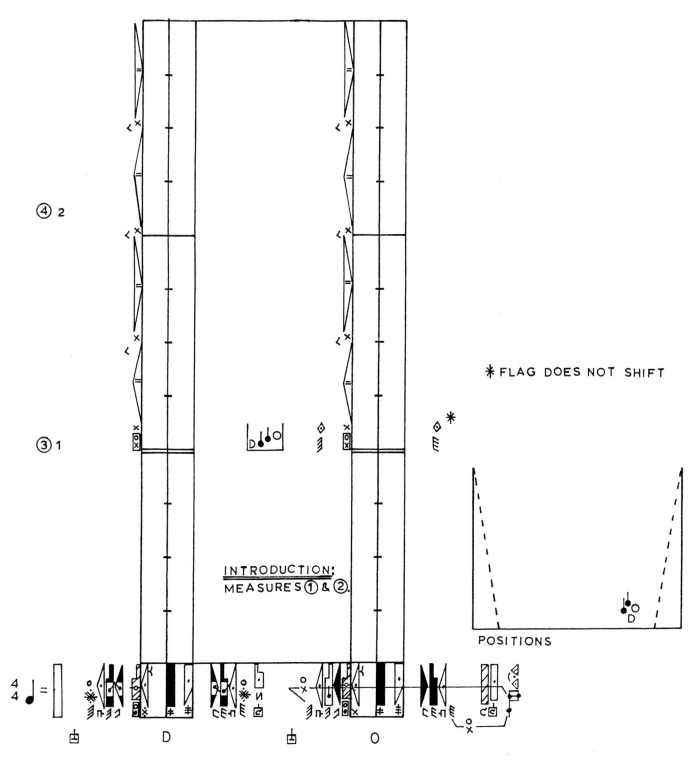

FLAG DOES NOT SHIFT

POSITIONS

INTRODUCTION:
MEASURES ① & ②.

D'S HEAD IS BEHIND "O"S LEFT SHOULDER.

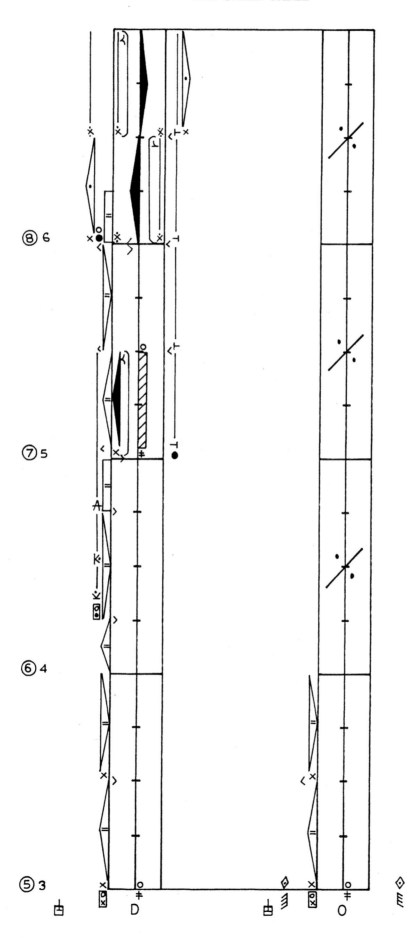

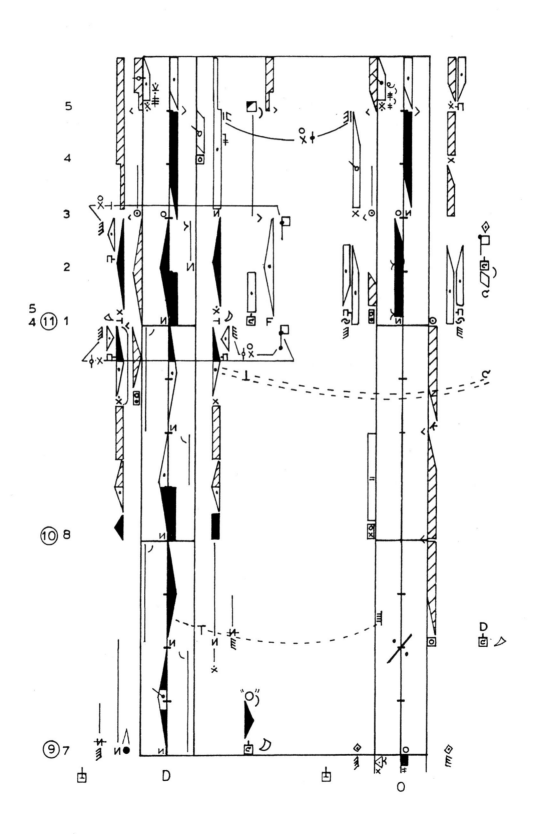

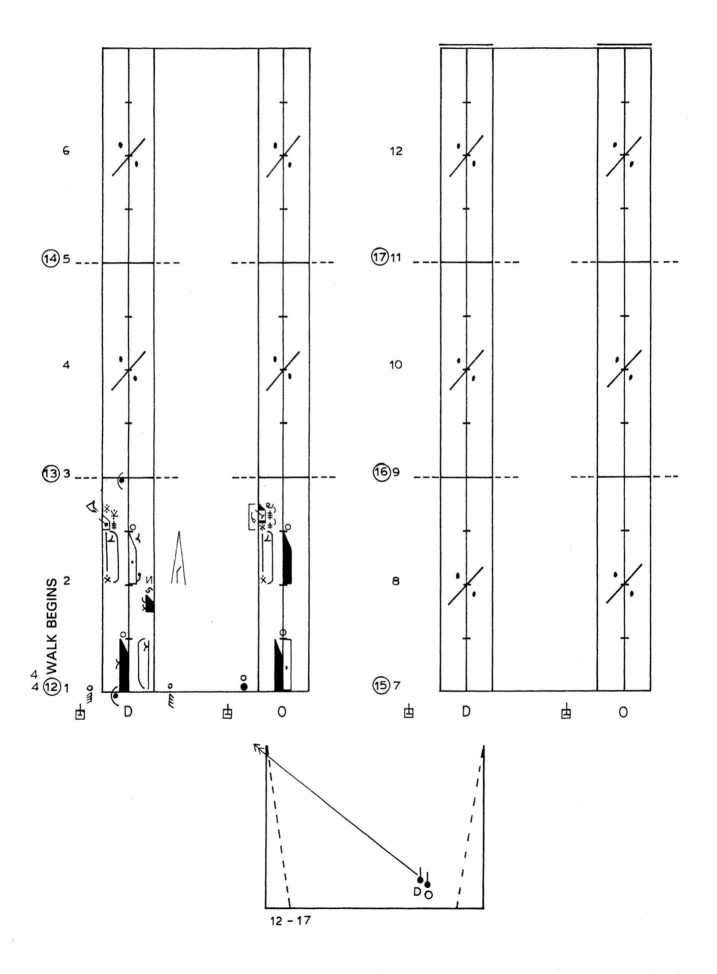

WALK BEGINS

12 - 17

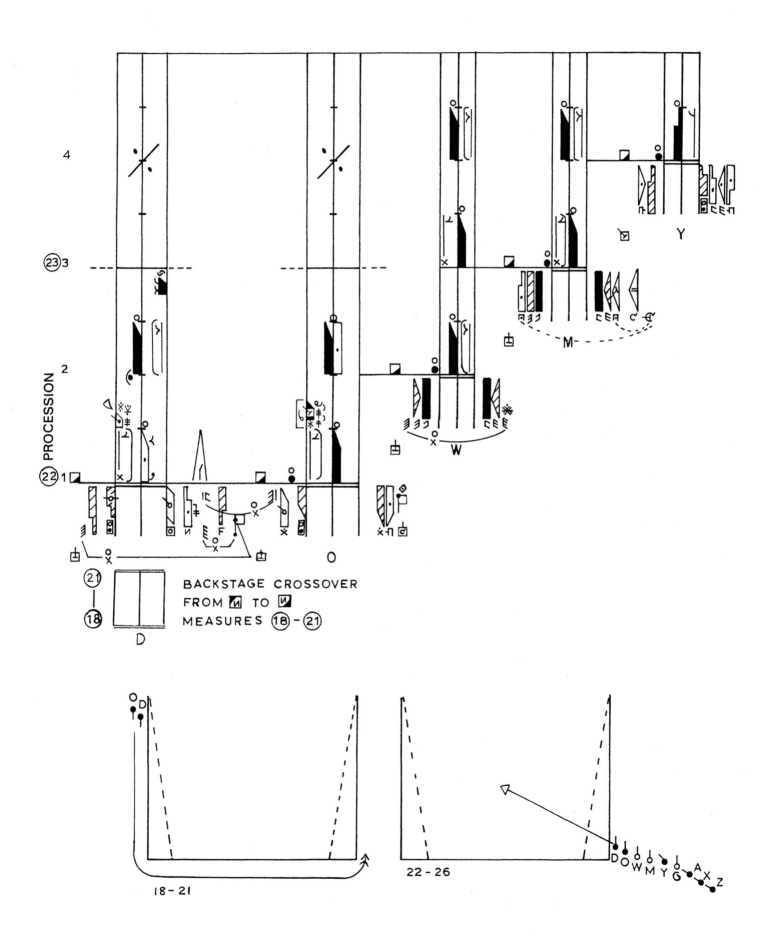

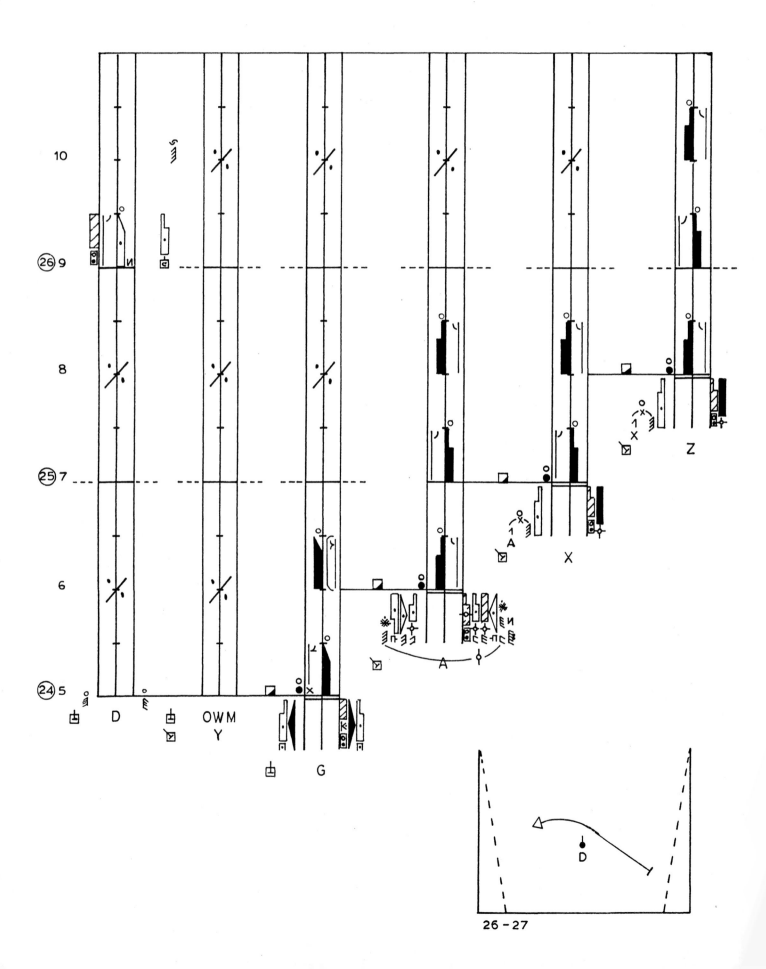

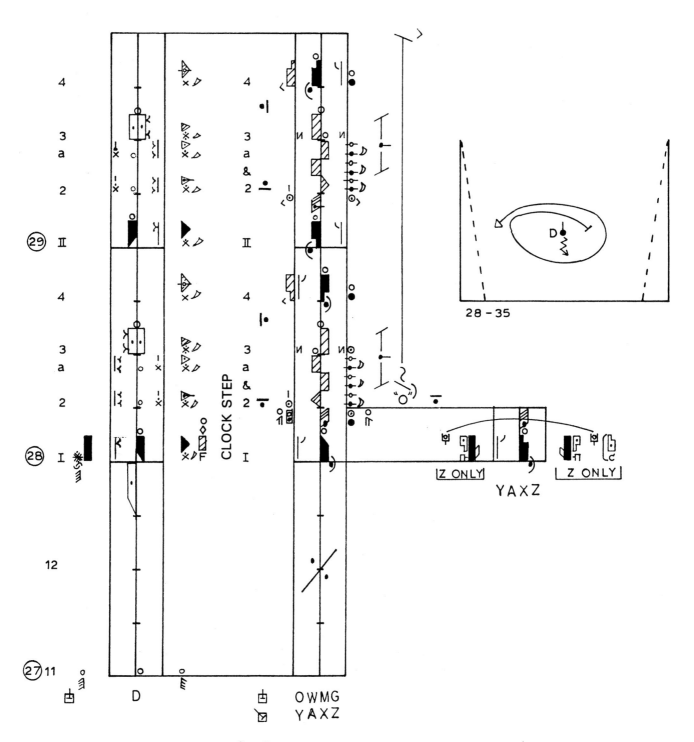

28 – 35

CLOCK STEP

Z ONLY   Z ONLY

YAXZ

D

OWMG
YAXZ

<u>NOTE:</u> MEASURES ㉘-㉟,
DANCERS KEEP THE ARM POSITIONS OF THEIR
ENTRANCE STEP, DURING THE CLOCK STEP

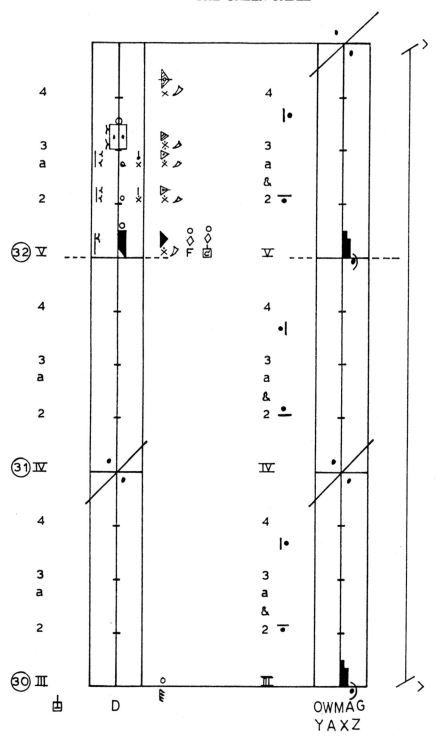

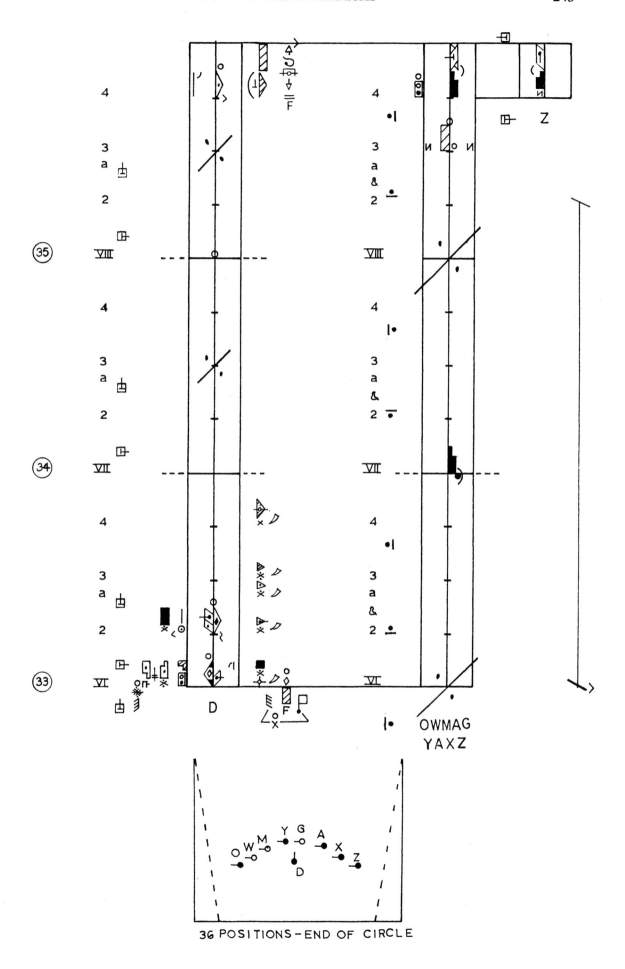

36 POSITIONS—END OF CIRCLE

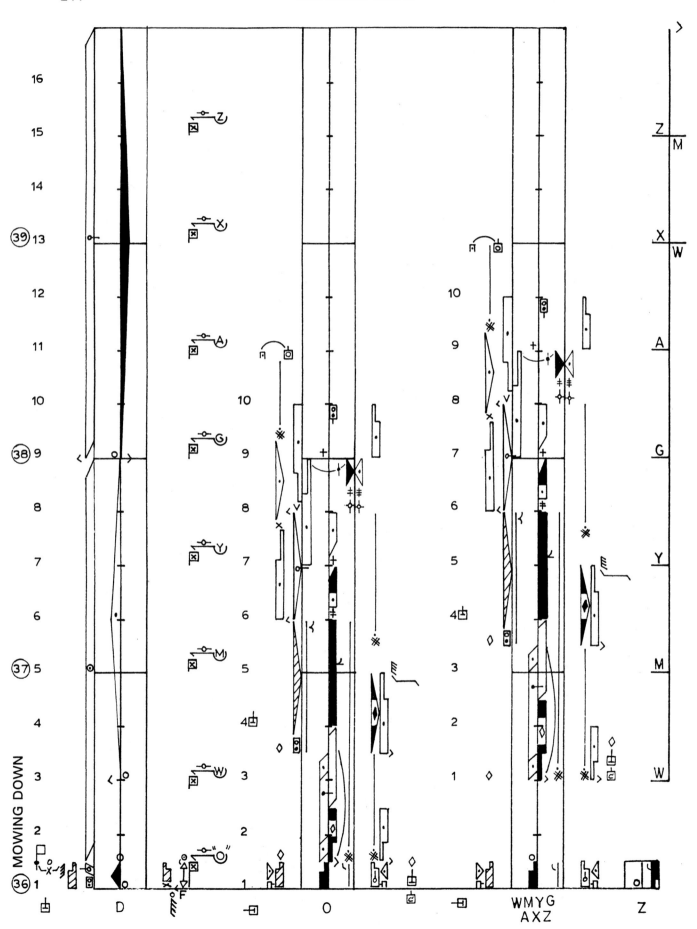

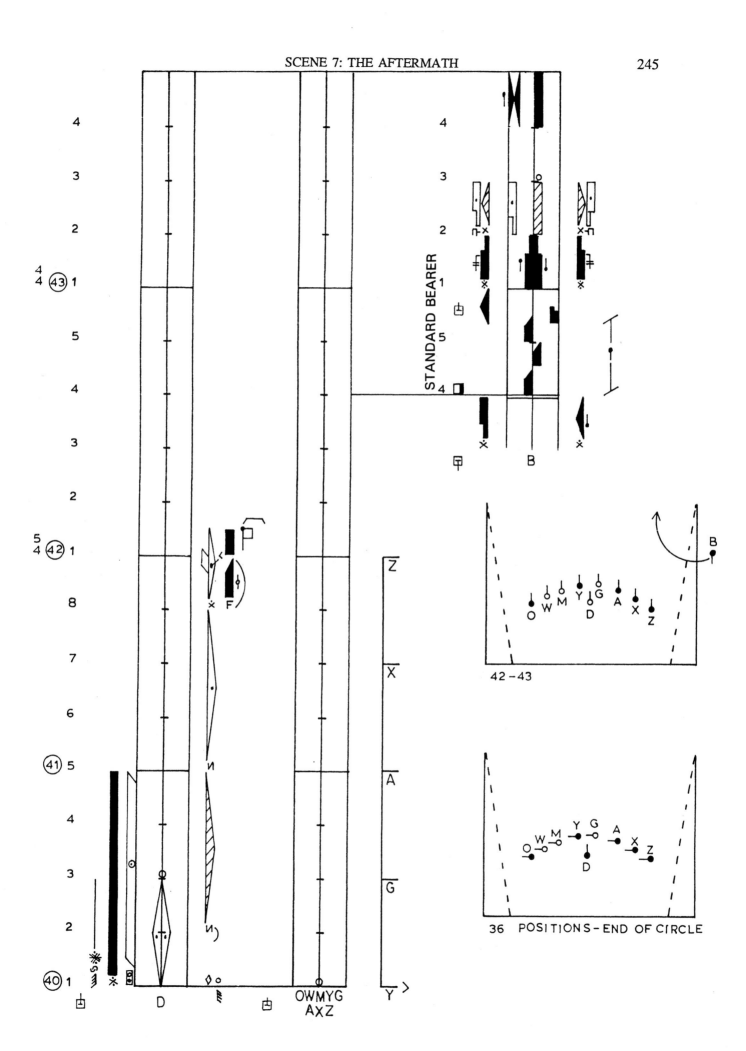

STANDARD BEARER

Z

X

A

G

Y

OWMYG
AXZ

D

42 – 43

36   POSITIONS – END OF CIRCLE

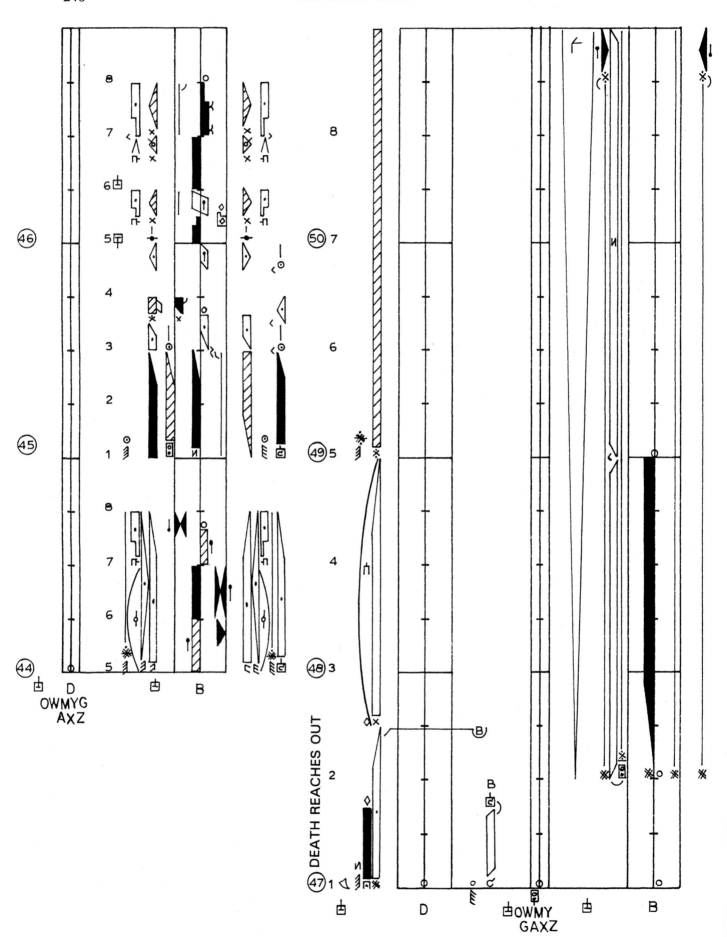

DEATH REACHES OUT

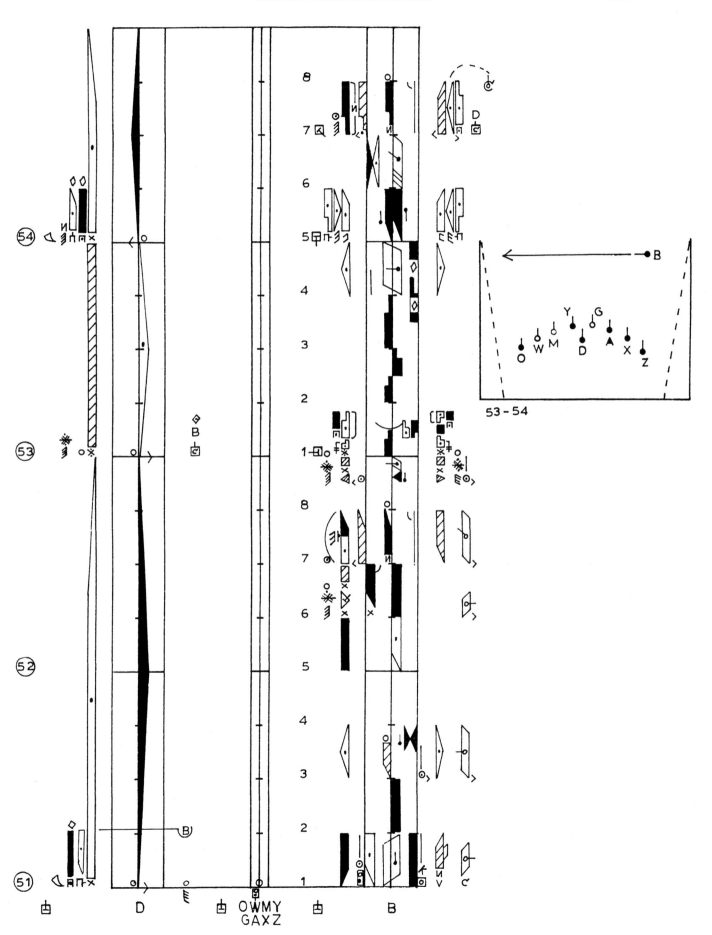

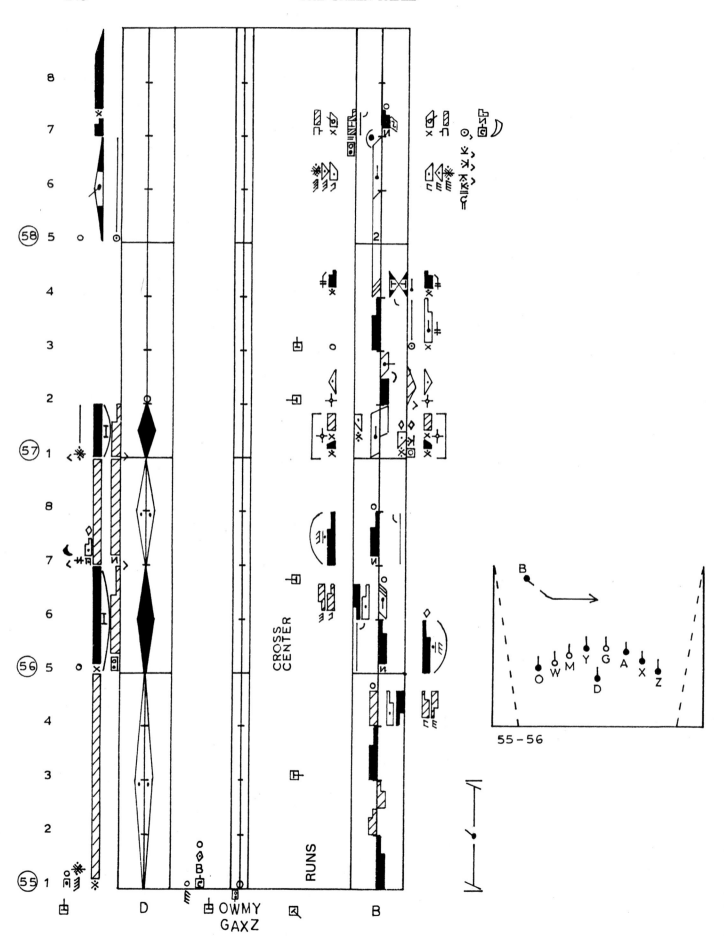

CROSS
CENTER

RUNS

55 – 56

D   OWMY
         GAXZ

B

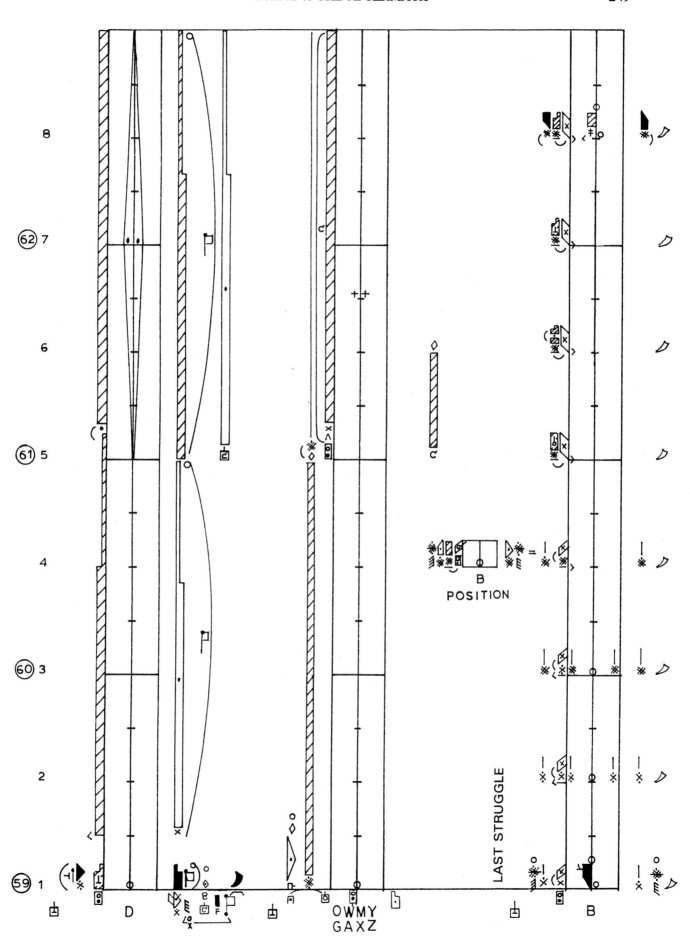

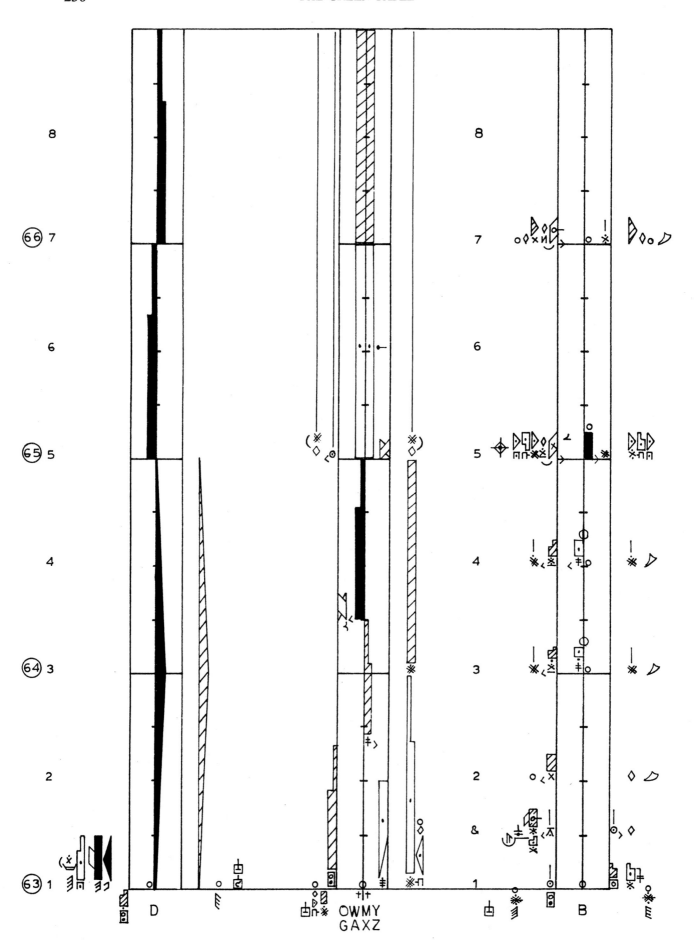

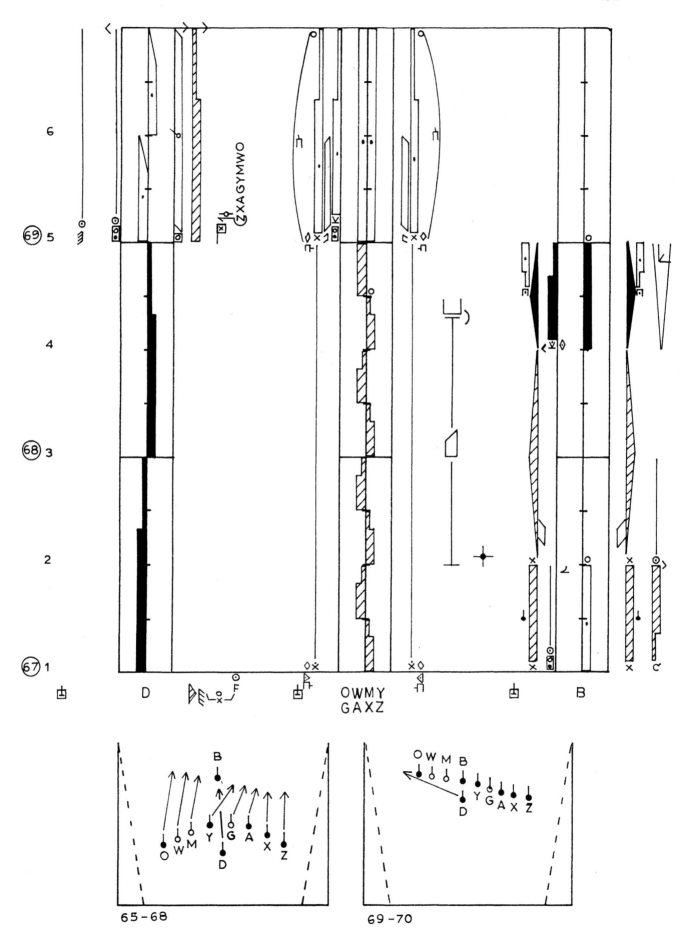

65-68

69-70

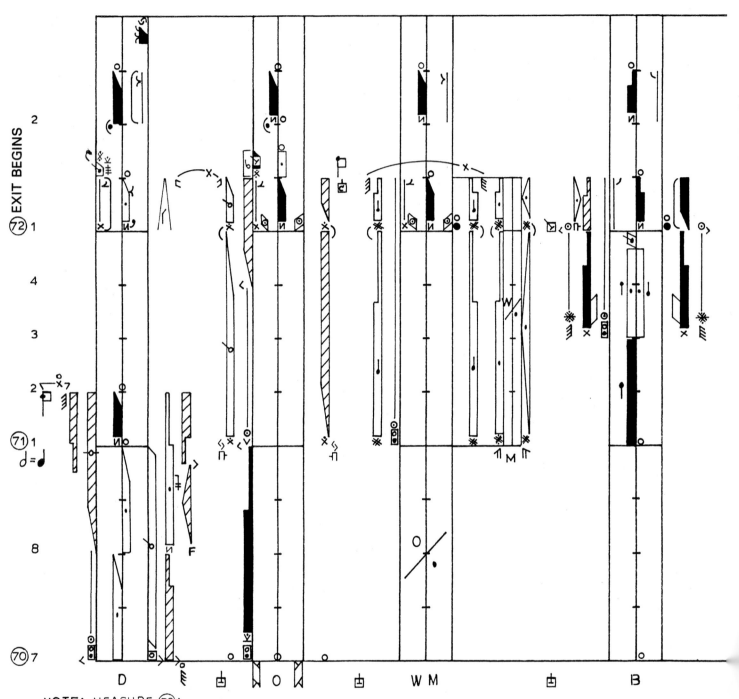

EXIT BEGINS

D   O   W M   B

NOTE: MEASURE ⑦:

DANCERS' POSITIONS ARE THE SAME AS
THEIR ENTRANCE IN THIS SCENE. SOME POSITIONS
HAVE BEEN WRITTEN DIFFERENTLY AND
SOME POSITIONS DO NOT HAVE HEAD,
TORSO, HANDS WRITTEN; THIS IS TO CONSERVE
SPACE ON THE PAGE. THE POSITIONS ARE EXACTLY
THE SAME AS THE ENTRANCE (PP. 239–240), DESPITE
THE DIFFERENCE IN NOTATION.

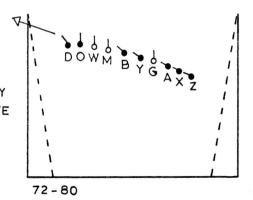

72 – 80

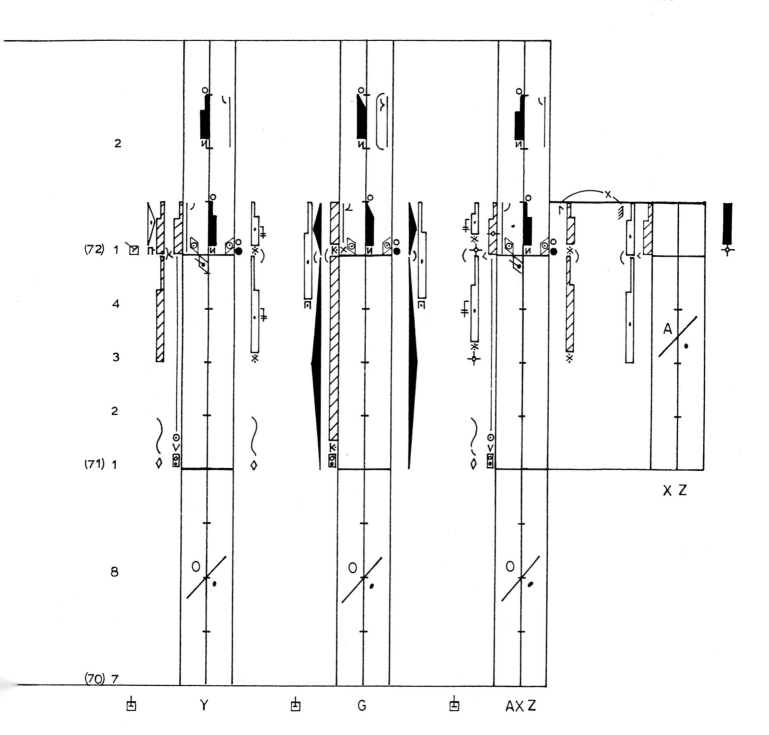

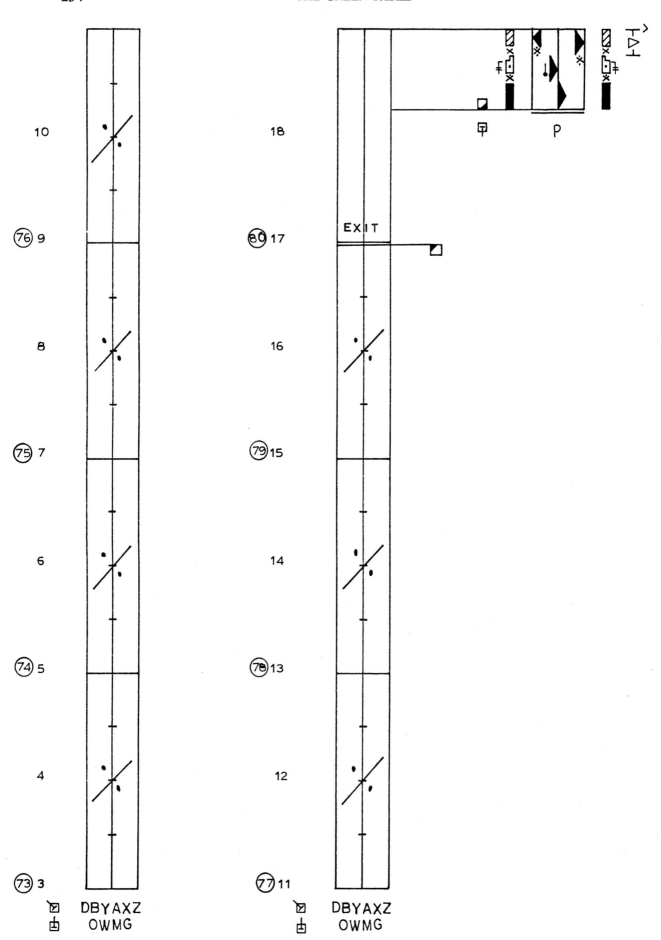

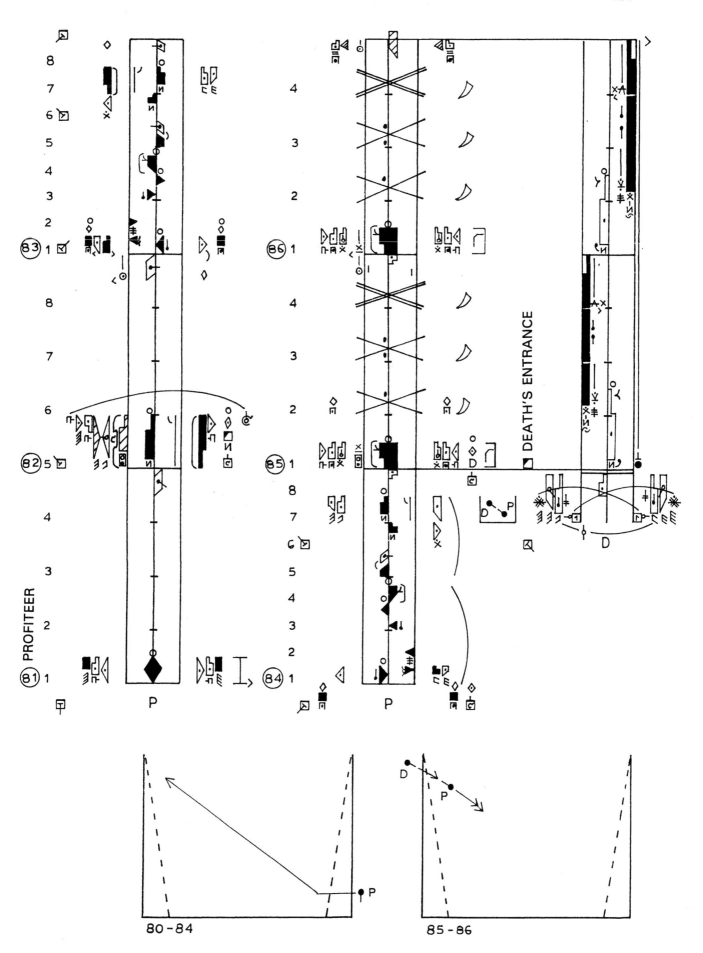

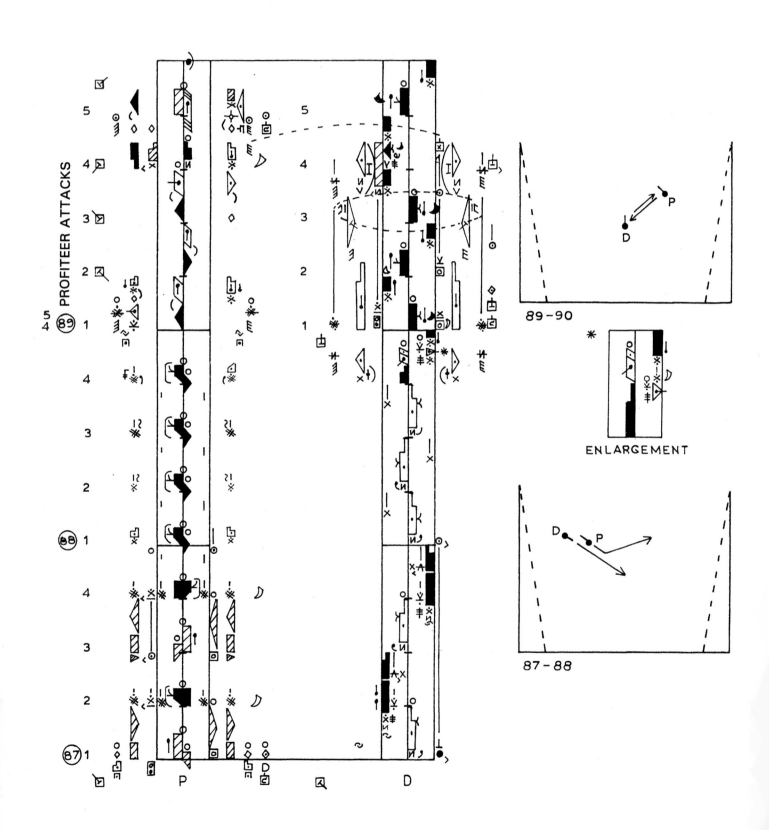

PROFITEER ATTACKS

ENLARGEMENT

89-90

87-88

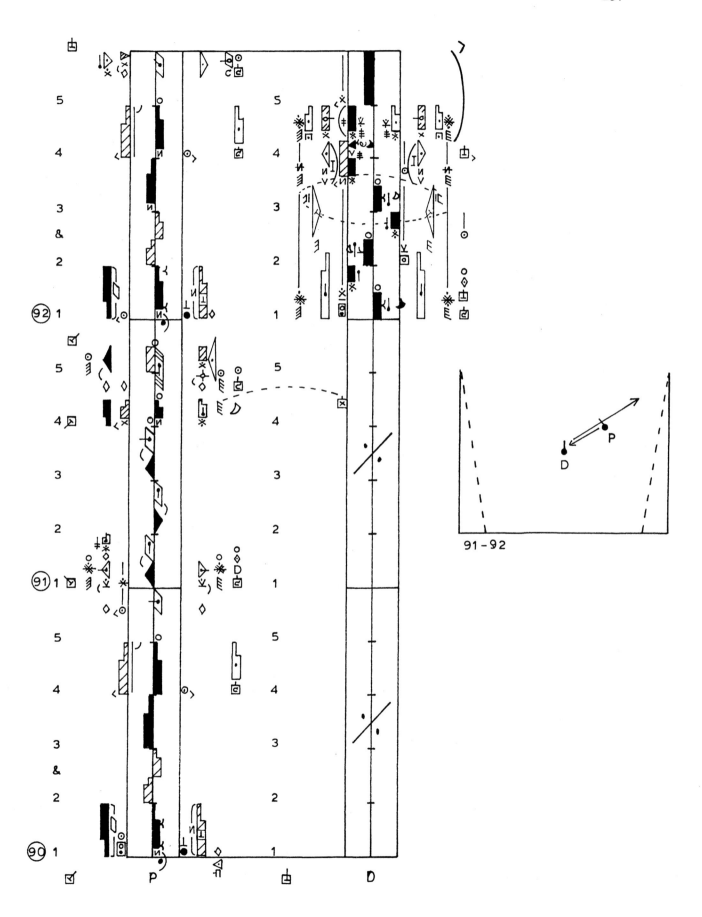

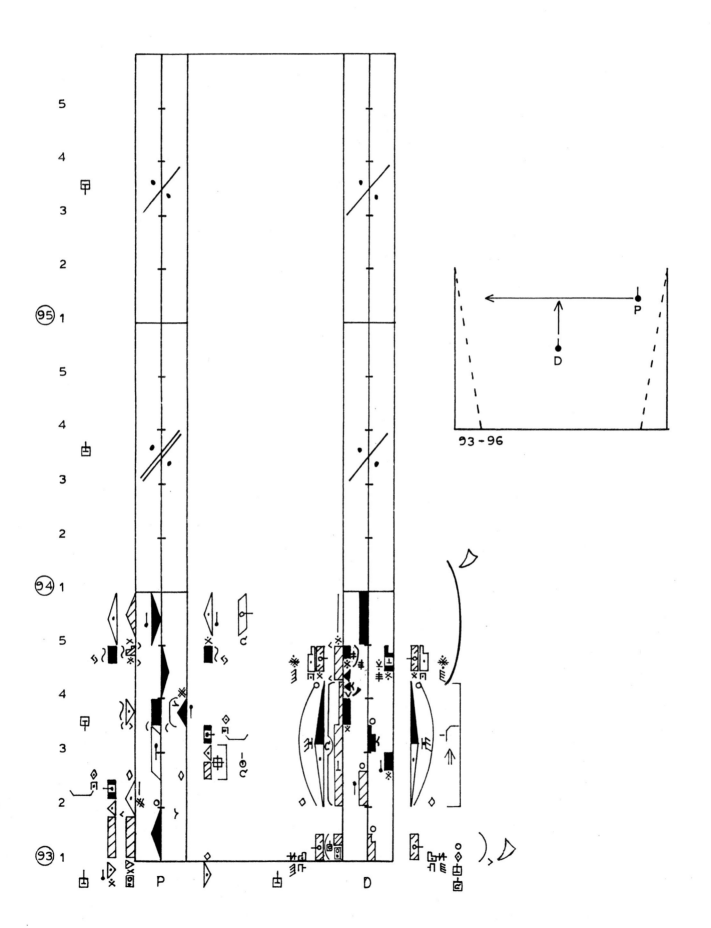

93 - 96

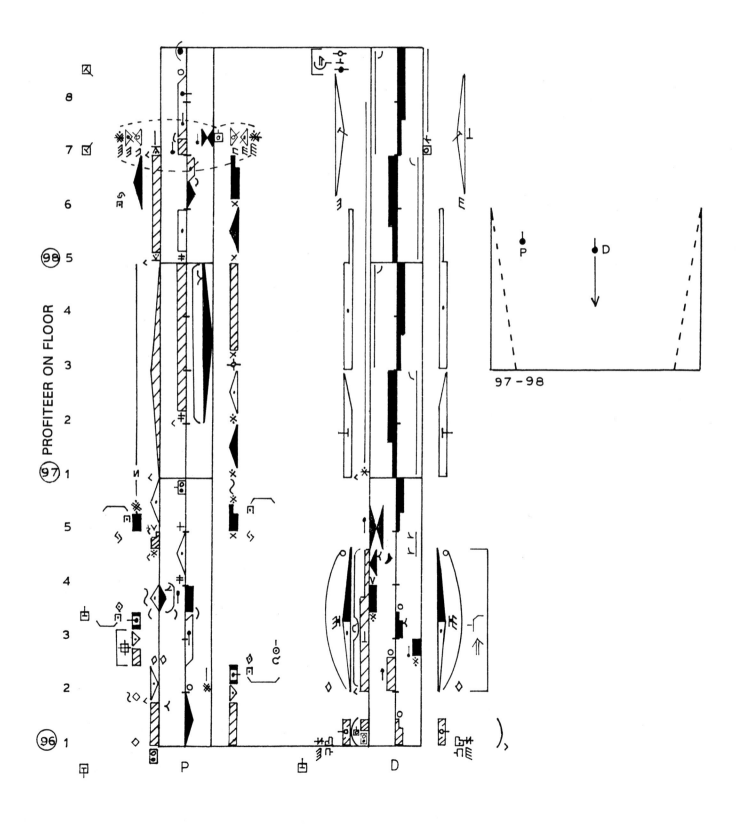

PROFITEER ON FLOOR

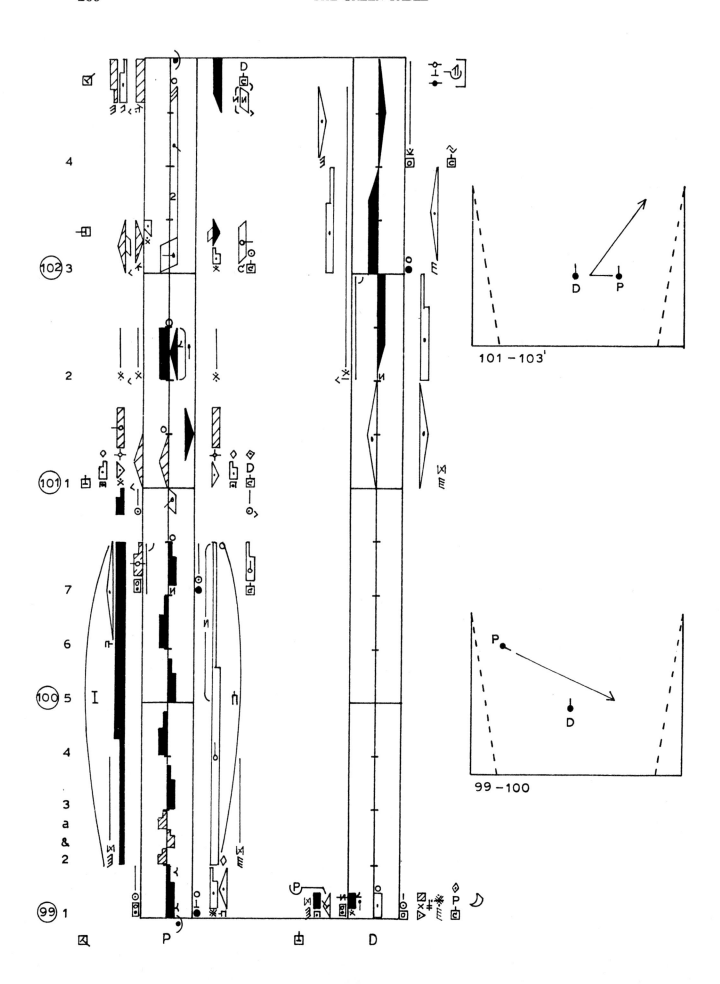

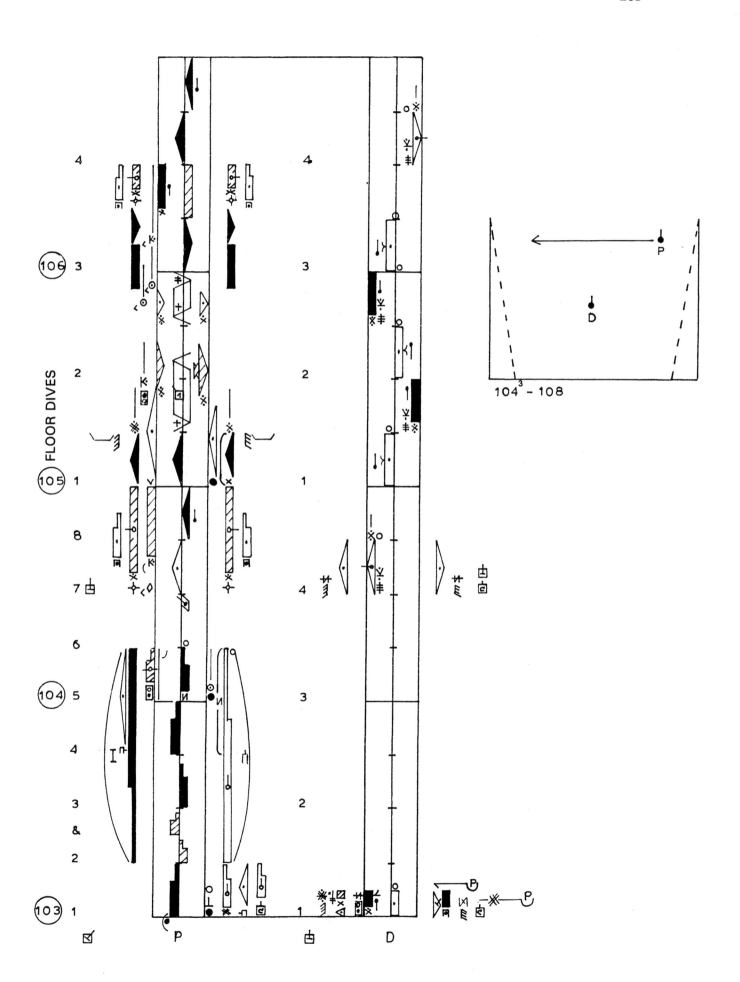

FLOOR DIVES

104 - 108

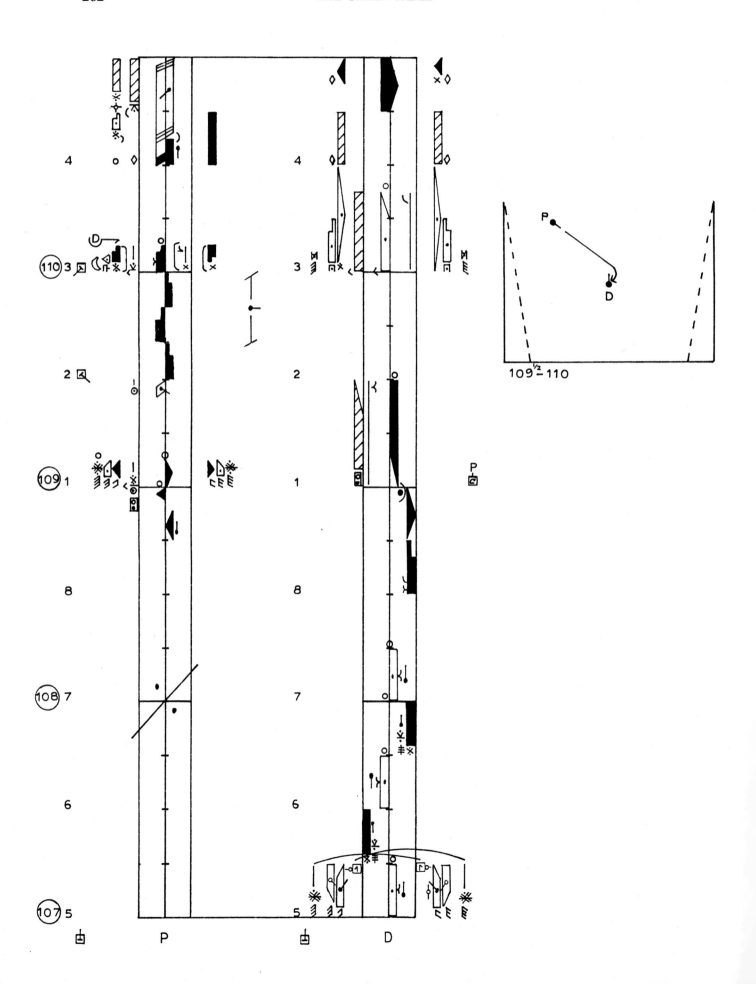

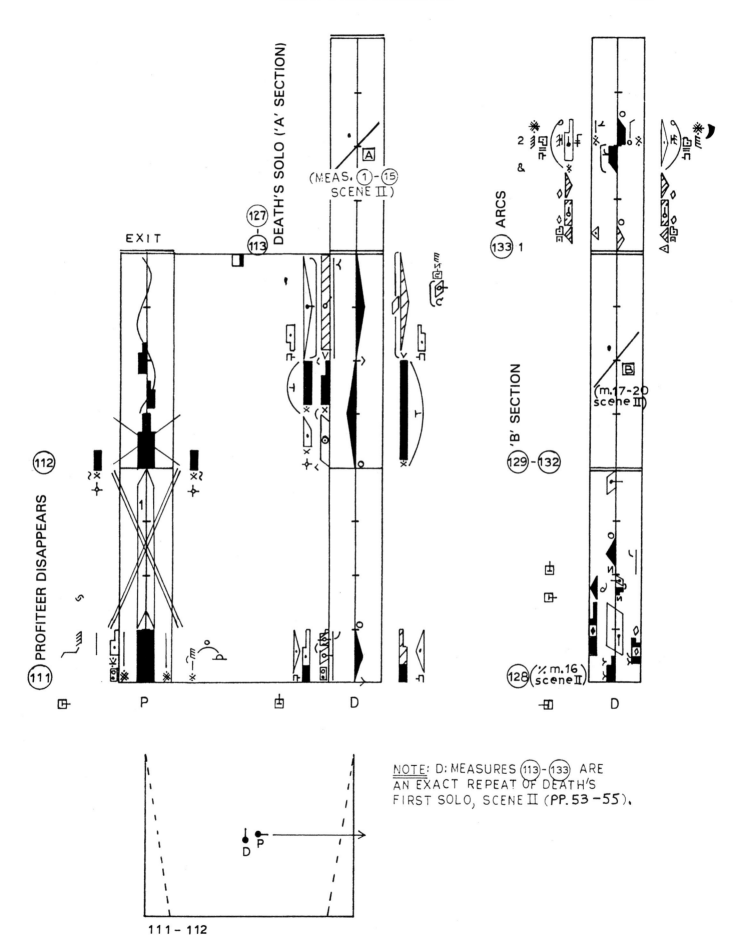

DEATH'S SOLO ('A' SECTION)

(MEAS. ①－⑮ SCENE Ⅱ)

Ⓐ

⑬

EXIT

⑪⑬

⑫ PROFITEER DISAPPEARS

⑪

P

D

ⒶRCS

⑬ 1

'B' SECTION

(m.17-20 scene Ⅱ)

Ⓑ

⑫⑨－⑬②

⑫⑧ (½ m.16 scene Ⅱ)

D

111－112

NOTE: D: MEASURES ⑬－⑬ ARE AN EXACT REPEAT OF DEATH'S FIRST SOLO, SCENE Ⅱ (PP. 53－55).

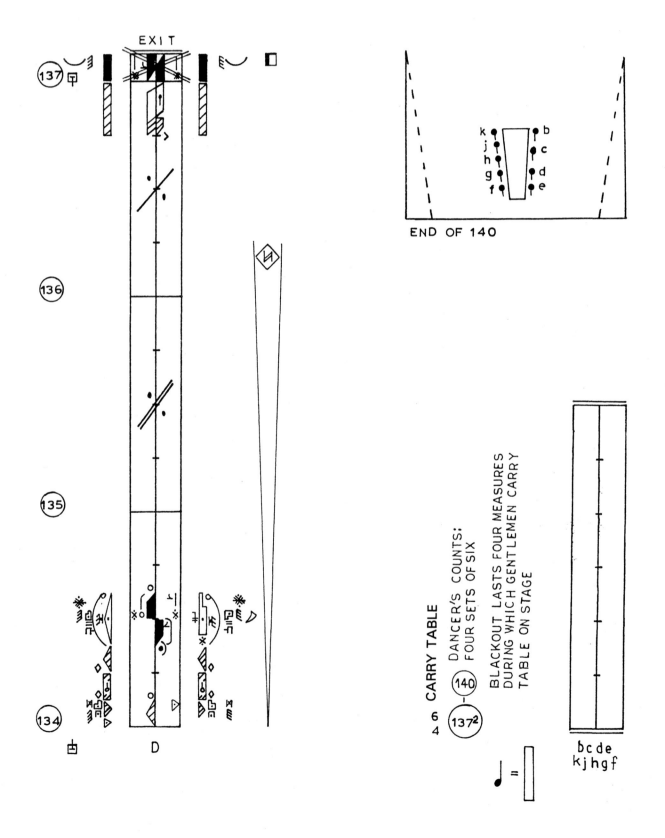

END OF 140

CARRY TABLE

DANCER'S COUNTS:
FOUR SETS OF SIX

BLACKOUT LASTS FOUR MEASURES
DURING WHICH GENTLEMEN CARRY
TABLE ON STAGE

bcde
kjhgf

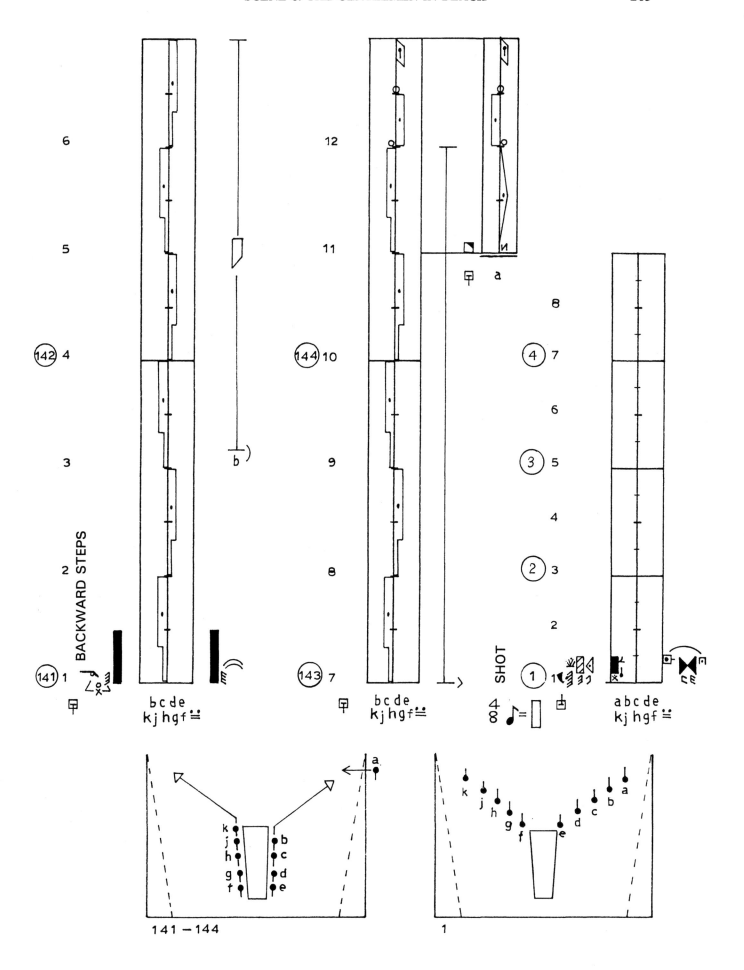

BACKWARD STEPS

SHOT

141 — 144

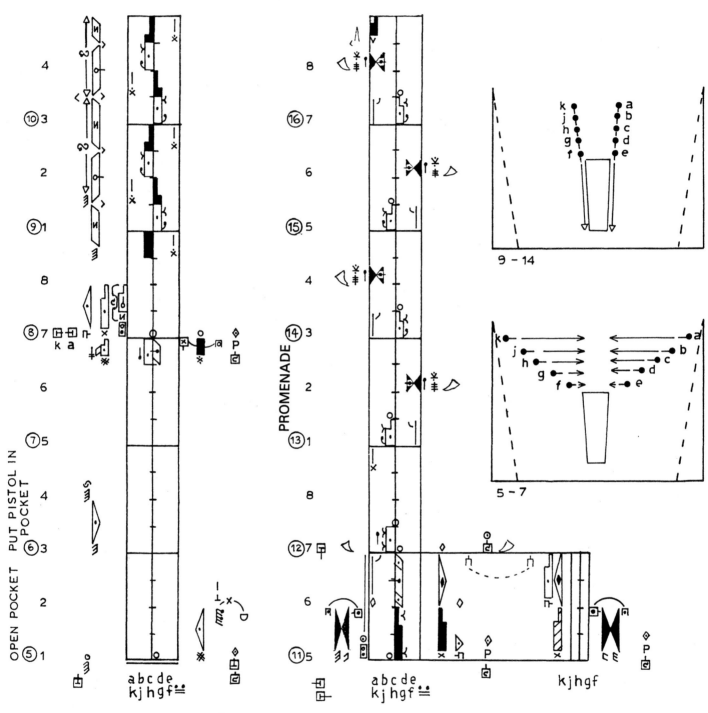

OPEN POCKET PUT PISTOL IN POCKET

PROMENADE

9 – 14

5 – 7

abcde
kjhgf

abcde
kjhgf

kjhgf

NOTE: MEASURE ④: $\frac{P}{\boxed{G}}$ = THE DANCER OPPOSITE.

OPPOSITES

k ——— a
j ——— b
h ——— c
g ——— d
f ——— e

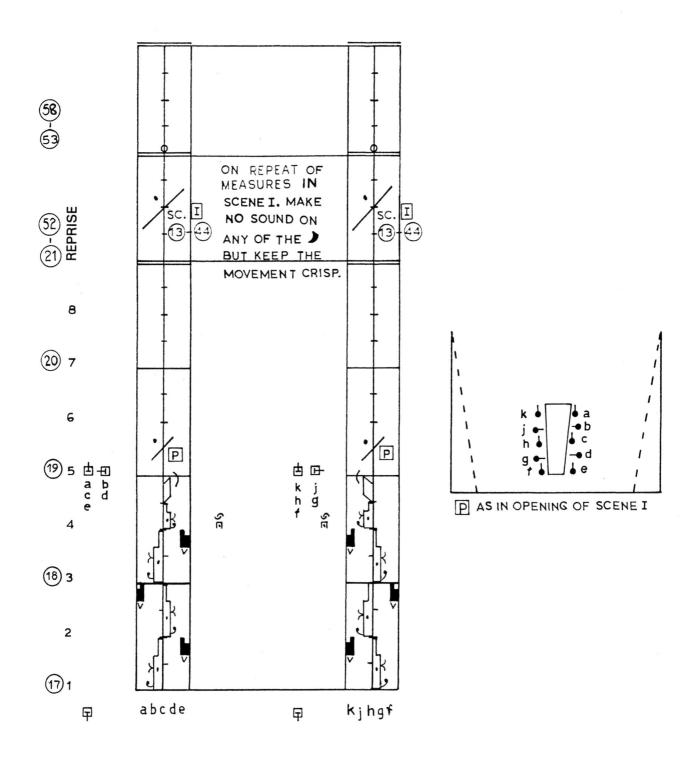

P AS IN OPENING OF SCENE I

Kurt Jooss
The Green Table

Part 2: Text, Photographs, and Music
Text written and compiled by Anna Markard
Edited by Ann Hutchinson Guest

CONTENTS

PART 2

INTRODUCTION

When I was about six, I was taken to the Barn Theatre in Dartington Hall, to see the Ballets Jooss. In that tiny theatre, on a stage with a proscenium opening of barely seven metres, they danced their full programme.

Already then *The Green Table* began to affect my life - choreographic discussions at home, rehearsals and performances accompanied my childhood and adolescent years. Then much later, when I had long entered the profession, *The Green Table* caught up with me again, and I began to learn, then teach, coach and finally to stage the full production.

For thirty-two years only my father's company performed *The Green Table*, in those days the dancers had mainly been trained in his school and were fully familiar with his choreographic language and style. The 'meaning' of a movement was clear to all and in rehearsals there was no need to analyse motivation, communicative rhythm or dynamics.

Later, however, this completely changed and for me it became an interesting challenge to teach the essence of this choreography to dancers with quite different professional backgrounds. The sparse, economic simplicity of the choreography is more demanding than it looks, and for today's high speed virtuoso dancers it is quite difficult to tune in to the style. Covering the space to reach the audience without losing the authenticity of the choreography is very hard in our vast new theatres. A clear understanding of the style becomes supremely important here, the borderline between honest, meaningful dancing and virtuoso showmanship is so very fine. When legs fly high, jumps become splits in the air or rhythms and dynamics are neglected, the content of the choreography becomes blurred or altogether lost.

My father would sometimes make small changes during rehearsal, but he always kept the original form and content; in his senior years he had become increasingly interested in detail and subtle characterisation and he was fascinated by the process of analysing and distilling his choreography.

Today, therefore, *The Green Table* appears as a highly complex composition requiring sensitive attention to detail. It is a taxing, but also rewarding challenge and I am happy now to be able to share and make available this wealth of information and accumulated experience, and - most importantly the fully notated choreography.

Everything that I could think of to help preserve this work is now in these two volumes, and I very much hope that they will be a valuable source of reference and inspiration to all those wishing to know more about *The Green Table*.

Anna Markard, February 1999

(Jooss Archive)

Hein Heckroth, Kurt Jooss and F.A.Cohen, Essen 1927

HISTORICAL BACKGROUND

During the Summer of 1931 Kurt Jooss was invited to participate in the first international competition of choreography, organised by *Les Archives Internationales de la Danse* in Paris. Only new works were accepted. At the time Jooss' company, the *Folkwang Tanzbühne*, belonged to the opera house in Essen. He had been planning a *Dance of Death* for many years inspired partly by the Medieval *Lübecker Totentanz* but also by the current political writings of Tucholsky and Ossietzky for *Die Weltbühne* which warned of new war preparations. In conceiving his libretto Jooss combined the idea of a *Dance of Death* with a strong pacifist message. Together with composer F. A. Cohen, his musical associate, Jooss created the work in six weeks. The choreography and music were developed simultaneously, piece by piece, in the studio. As well as designing the masks and costumes, Hein Heckroth textured the burlap curtains with black paint. These, however, were used for the first performances only.

The Green Table was a sensational success at the competition and was unanimously awarded first prize by the jury. At the first performance Jooss danced the leading rôle of Death. The other members of the cast (in order of appearance) were:

The Standard Bearer	Ernst Uthoff
The Young Soldier	Walter Wurg
The Young Girl	Lisa Czobel
The Woman	Elsa Kahl
The Old Soldier	Rudolf Pescht
The Old Mother	Frida Holst
The Profiteer	Karl Bergeest
Soldiers	Heinz Rosen, Peter Wolf, Hans Züllig
Women	Lola Botka, Lucie Lenzer, Mascha Lidolt, Hertha Lorenz, Trude Pohl.

F.A Cohen and Will Götze were the piano duo.

Jooss and his company became famous literally overnight and were immediately offered numerous touring opportunities and performance engagements. The *Folkwang Tanzbühne* was thus able to separate itself from the Essen Opera House and to develop into an independent Dance Theatre - the Ballets Jooss.

Performance History

World Première 3rd July 1932, Théâtre des Champs-Elysées, Paris.

From 1932-1968 *The Green Table* was almost continually in the repertory of Jooss' company. In 1933 after the initial series of performances in Germany, two European tours and a London season, Jooss and his company left Germany for political reasons. During the following years the Ballets Jooss presented *The Green Table* as a core work of its repertory on numerous world tours. With the exception of a production in 1948 for the Chilean National Ballet - a company founded and directed by former soloists of the Ballets Jooss - no other production rights for *The Green Table* were granted. It was not until 1964 that Jooss agreed to allow his works to enter the repertoire of international ballet companies. Since then about fifty productions have been mounted. *The Green Table* has retained its significant place in the international dance world for over sixty-five years.

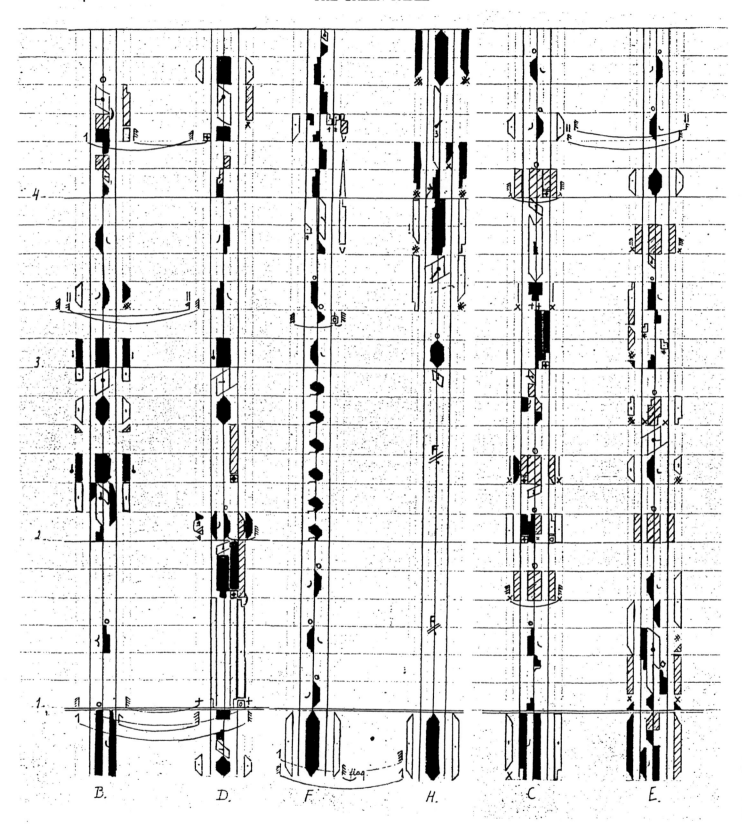

Excerpt from the original 1938 score notated by Ann Hutchinson,
showing the opening measures of the Battle scene.

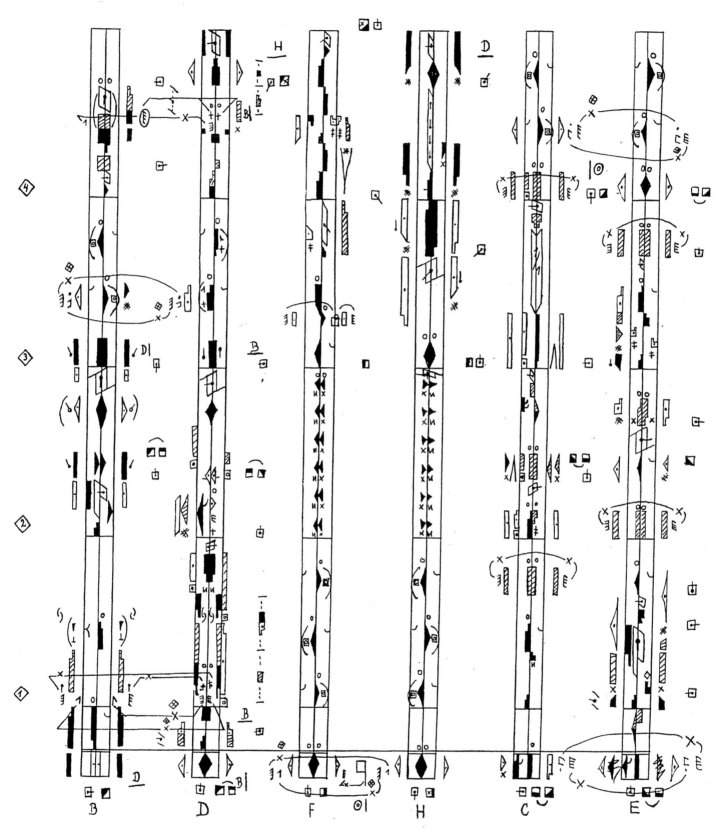

Excerpt from the 1958 notation by Albrecht Knust,
also showing the opening measures of the Battle scene.

(Renoldi)

(Shirali)

Albrecht Knust, Folkwangschule 1961   Kurt Jooss, Rudolf von Laban, Dartington 1939

THE STORY OF THE SCORE

The Green Table was the first complex choreographic work to be fully documented in a comprehensive system of dance notation. This system, originated by Rudolf von Laban, was first published in Germany in 1928. Entitled *Schrifttanz* it was also called *Kinetography Laban*, and in the 1940s the name *Labanotation* was registered in New York City by the Dance Notation Bureau.

In 1938 after her final year of training at the Jooss-Leeder School of Dance in England, Ann Hutchinson was asked to notate the famous signature program of the Ballets Jooss.[1]

Hutchinson's pencil scores were never checked or corrected, nor were they put to the test in the early days. Through constant performing, the dancers of the Ballets Jooss were familiar with every detail of the choreography and needed no memory prompt. But, as time went by, and the company was disbanded more than once, the scores and especially the floor plans became invaluable. Later, when Jooss began to stage *The Green Table* for other companies, he would often refer to the score, the 'bible' as he sometimes fondly called it, to check or ponder a choreographic detail. Thus, first in Santiago, then in Amsterdam, in New York, and in Stockholm, the 'bible' was consulted, but also amended and corrected, which greatly helped to keep the choreography authentic.

An interesting episode arose in Germany in 1951, just after the opening performances of the newly-formed Folkwang Tanztheater, which included *The Green Table*. News suddenly spread that a just-released film called "Sensation in San Remo" contained a wild scene with masked elderly gentlemen in black suits, white gloves and spats, gesticulating on two sides of a long green table! Immediate action had to be taken. Jooss filed a claim for plagiarism and a temporary injunction was granted. In the Lichtburg Cinema in Essen, on September 17th, 1951, the court was assembled to witness a live performance of "The Gentlemen in Black" from *The Green Table* given by the Folkwang Tanztheater (no film or video of the choreography being extant at that time), and then the excerpt from "Sensation in San Remo" was shown. The case appeared to be clear, the court had witnessed the obvious similarity of the two scenes, but they were unable to pass judgement merely on the strength of the live performance: clearer proof was necessary. Hutchinson's dance notation score was remitted to the court and the case was won. Legally, choreographic works are protected ".... if the action on stage is documented in writing or notated in some other way....".[2] Dance notation and *The Green Table* thus made choreographic copyright history!

Towards the mid 50s Albrecht Knust, leading authority on Kinetography Laban and teacher at the Folkwangschule in Essen, began to work on a new score. Unfortunately, his copious notes, based on interviews with the dancers were never assembled or completed. A few sections, however, were ready so that in 1958 Kinetography Laban could be presented in the West German Pavilion at the World Fair in Brussels with a sample of the Battle scene from *The Green Table*.

It was not until 1971, more than 30 years after Hutchinson notated the first score, that my father and I both felt we must begin preparing for a new updated score to be written. We planned to work together on the next production and asked dance notator Diana Baddeley to join us to take notes. Thus, during our rehearsals with Tanz Forum Köln, while I worked with the dancers, Jooss carefully reviewed, sifted and revised his choreography, making adjustments, corrections and definitive decisions where differences had crept in over the years.

We were now ready to take the next step. An agreement was signed with the Dance Notation Bureau, so that in 1977, when I started rehearsals for a new *Green Table* production with the José Limón Dance Company, work on the new score could also begin. First Muriel Topaz, followed by Charlotte Wile and then Gretchen Schumacher, worked on the project. After checking, amending and again correcting the notation through several productions - the Hartford Ballet, the Joffrey Ballet and again the Limón Company - it became Schumacher's task finally to rewrite and complete the score.

The first reading test for this new score was in 1985-86 when Odette Blum reconstructed *The Green Table* exclusively from the Labanotation with the repertory class at Ohio State University. I was amazed and overjoyed to witness the results and to see the entire choreography danced in the studio. Jane Marriett was responsible for notating final corrections and refinements of detail, and together with Odette Blum we carefully combed through the entire score. There was one more test in 1988 when *The Green Table* was mounted only from the score with the more experienced dancers of the University Dance Company and performed at Mersham Auditorium.

This testing has been a long and laborious process, and I sincerely hope that our publication will now meet the high standard we aimed for, and that it will enable all those genuinely concerned, interested, or merely curious to get closer to the essence of *The Green Table*.

Anna Markard

1.	Signature program:	Music	Costumes
	Big City	Alexandre Tansman	Hein Heckroth
	Pavane on the Death of an Infanta	Maurice Ravel	Sigurd Leeder
	A Ball in Old Vienna	Josef Lanner	Aino Siimola
	The Green Table	F.A. Cohen	Hein Heckroth

2.   Translation from the verdict of 20th September, 1951.

BIOGRAPHY OF KURT JOOSS

by Suzanne K. Walther

Kurt Jooss was born on January 12, 1901 in Wasseralfingen in the Baden-Wurttemberg region of Germany near the historic city of Stuttgart. His family owned farm land and his father expected Jooss to inherit and manage the estate. However, Jooss himself was drawn to the arts. Instead of thinking of a career in farm management, his attention was taken up with music, drama and the visual arts. He played the piano and studied singing and drama. Because he felt that he lacked the talent to paint or draw, he took up photography.

His father allowed him to pursue his artistic goals freely. Both of Jooss's parents had artistic talents themselves: his father was an amateur theatre producer and his mother a trained singer. As a teenager Jooss also tried his hand at amateur theatricals. Instinctively Jooss searched for a medium of expression that would consolidate his talents and give him personal satisfaction.

At the age of eighteen, after graduating from the *Realgymnasium* of Aalen, Jooss entered the Stuttgart Academy of Music. In spite of being a success at his studies, especially in acting and voice, he was dissatisfied. In an autobiographical essay he wrote: *I studied drama devotedly and with great success but I remained empty. Something was missing everywhere, and I no longer believed in my dream of the arts* (Markard & Markard, 1985, p.29). He was on the verge of giving up his quest for a suitable artistic expression and nearly resigned himself to a life of agricultural management when by chance he met Rudolf von Laban.[1] He had been taking lessons in movement from Grete Heid, a former Laban pupil. It was through her that the two men met: a meeting that changed the course of Jooss's life and to some extent the course of dance history.

During the years 1920 to 1922, Laban lived and taught in Stuttgart and served as Ballet Master at the Mannheim Opera. Shortly after Jooss became his student, Laban included him in a group of twenty-five dancers whom he trained for professional performances. They appeared at the Mannheim Opera together with the Opera Ballet in Laban's own works. Jooss instantly became one of the leading dancers of this group. As Jooss modestly remembers: *A few weeks later I danced the male lead in our first work,* **Die Geblendeten [The Deluded],** *with great success. At that time in Germany one did not need great proficiency for the 'Expressionist Dance': strong intensity was all-convincing. In the meantime though I have added to my abilities* (M. & M., 1985, p.31)[2].

Laban straight away recognised Jooss's exceptional ability and made him assistant and later regisseur of his company, the *Tanzbühne Laban.* While Jooss was a member of Laban's group, two important people entered his life. One was his future wife, the other a lifelong friend: both became his artistic collaborators.

In 1921, a year after Jooss's arrival, a new pupil entered the group. She had the exotic foreign name of Aino Siimola. She had been born in 1901 in the town of Narva, in Russian Estonia. This town was located inland from the Gulf of Finland, not far from the historic city of St. Petersburg. Siimola was educated in a private school that was directed by Maria Fedorovna, mother of the Russian Tzarina. Dance was one of the requirements of the curriculum.

Having chosen to become a professional dancer, Siimola decided to travel to Germany with the purpose of studying with Laban. After a short apprenticeship in Stuttgart, she became a member of the *Tanzbühne Laban*. She was a woman of great beauty and intelligence, and after she became Jooss's wife she also became his lifelong artistic collaborator.

While working with Laban in Hamburg in 1924, Jooss met a young native of that northern city named Sigurd Leeder. Leeder studied art at the Hamburg School of Arts and Crafts. He also studied acting and took movement classes from a former student of Laban. His skills and education complemented Jooss's, and so did his looks and temperament. Jooss had a strong personality: he was brimming with curiosity and overflowing with abundant creative energy. Leeder was frail and finely chiselled, with a sense for form, detail and craftsmanship.

Jooss began choreographing early in his career, while he was still working with Laban. He created a program of short dances or *Kammertänze*, 'chamber dances'. Shortly after they met, Jooss and Leeder put together a program called *Two Male Dancers*. The concept of a male duo of concert dancers appearing without props or a supporting cast was new and original. The choreography was experimental, influenced greatly by Laban's theories and movement studies. Only a few photographs remain of these dances, but Jooss stands out in them for his comic talent and character sketches.

In 1924 Niedecken-Gebhardt invited Jooss to join him at the Municipal Theatre of Münster as 'movement regisseur' and ballet master. Niedecken-Gebhardt's novel approach to opera staging included the conviction that movement should be an integral part of the production. He needed a movement specialist to accomplish this goal. Jooss, who was ready to strike out on his own, accepted the position. Jooss had achieved recognition as a choreographer and performer in his own right, with a distinctive style and original point of view. He wrote: *I needed independence for my further development, so, with regret, I left the Tanzbühne Laban* (M. & M., 1985, p.35).

Jooss then took the opportunity to establish his own company, *Die Neue Tanzbühne*. His group was small, initially consisting of three male and four female dancers. *Die Neue Tanzbühne* was technically a part of the Municipal Theatre of Münster, but it was artistically independent. It was entirely under the artistic direction of Jooss. In his productions he made use of the many talented people working in the Münster Theatre. Hein Heckroth created the designs for seven of the eight ballets Jooss choreographed during this period. His work contributed greatly to the unity of concept in these productions.

It was also during this time that the composer F.A. Cohen became Jooss's musical collaborator. Cohen had definite ideas about creating music for dance. He believed that the musical accompaniment should underlie the dramatic meaning of the dance, accentuate the choreographic form and rhythmically aid the dancer. Jooss and Cohen shared the belief that choreography and musical composition should proceed together to give expression of the dramatic idea in unified style and form. The greatest surviving example of this collaboration is *The Green Table*.

Performances were mainly held in the Münster Theatre, but the *Neue Tanzbühne* also toured throughout the country, stopping at such major cities as Berlin, Bonn, Hamburg, and Mannheim. The eight pieces Jooss choreographed during this two year period included shorter works such as *Larven* (1925), *Der Dämon* (1925), *Groteske* (1925) and *Kaschemme* (1926). Of *Groteske* he wrote: *A tiny piece which, however, showed clearly in which direction my work was to develop: away from the literal, aspiring toward a physically and spiritually motivated dance movement and art form* (M. & M., 1985, p.35).

Der Dämon was choreographed to music by Hindemith and it is described as *an expressionistic ballet with symbolic figures* (Häger, *International Encyclopedia of Dance*). The two longer pieces were entitled *Die Brautfahrt* (1925) and *Tragödie* (1926). *Tragödie* was a full length ballet in four acts for four soloists and a chorus, to music improvised by F.A. Cohen for each performance.

Meanwhile Jooss had been deeply concerned with the state of dance education in Germany. He believed that German modern dance lacked the kind of systematic dance training which gave classical dancers a highly developed technique. In the spring of 1925, he and Leeder worked out a plan for a professional dance school. He wrote: *We saw the greatest need for the New Dance to be a firmly consolidated system of teaching, and we decided to abandon all other wishes and work solely to this purpose. Laban's movement teachings and choreographic space principles, combined with the discipline of traditional ballet, were to make up our materials* (M., 1982, p.19).

In the fall of 1925, a group of artists including Jooss and Leeder established a new school which was named the *Westfälischen Akademie Für Bewegung, Sprache und Musik* (Westphalian Academy of Movement, Speech and Music). The school was under the overall direction of Rudolf Schulz-Dornburg, who was also the music director of the Münster Theatre. Jooss was the Director of the dance division, Vilma Mönckeberg headed the division of speech, and Hermann Erpf was in charge of the music division. The school developed rapidly, and two years later it moved to Essen to be incorporated into the newly-founded *Folkwangschule*.

Leeder had decided to dedicate himself to dance education. He had a genuine interest in teaching, and concerns about his health also contributed to his decision to change the direction of his career. From then on he concentrated on dance pedagogy and became one of the most significant European modern dance teachers. He was the greatest exponent of the Jooss-Leeder technique of dance. His positions included that of chief instructor at the Folkwangschule (1927-1934), co-director of the Jooss-Leeder School in England (1934-1940) and ballet master of the Ballets Jooss (1942-1947).

In order to enlarge the scope of their knowledge of dance, Jooss and Leeder decided to study abroad. So far Jooss had only mastered modern dance and he felt it necessary to acquire a first-hand knowledge of classical ballet. In December 1926 the two of them went to Paris to take class with the émigrée Russian ballerina Lubov Egorova. She was a graduate of the Imperial Ballet School and a principal dancer with the Maryinsky Theatre, now the Kirov Ballet. She exemplified the unsurpassed tradition of a school and the purity and artistry of a technique, the representatives of which like royalty form a lineage to the present day.

In a short period of time Jooss acquired an understanding of classical ballet that convinced him of its value, importance and historical significance. He never stopped defending his view, unique at the time, that ballet and modern dance are not opposing techniques but belong on a historical continuum in the realm of dance. He believed that all available means should be used for the expression of significant human emotion. He made this clear in a statement at the International Congress of the Dance in Paris in June 1932: *We aim therefore at discovering a choreography deriving equally from the contributions of modern art and from the classic Ballet. We find the basis of our work in the whole range of human feeling and all phases of its infinite expression; and by concentration on the 'Essential' we arrive at our form in the Dance.* The combined use of ballet and modern dance techniques in choreography was a completely novel position at the time. Modern dance was proclaiming its revolt against the academic restraints of ballet, and the various exponents of *Ausdruckstanz* feuded amongst themselves, each proclaiming to hold a superior point of view.

In 1926, as an addition to the program of *Two Male Dancers*, a masked dance was planned by Jooss and Leeder, tentatively called *Dance of Death*. Jooss described the plan as follows: *We intended to work with masks, which would enable us to quickly slip into different characters (beggar, peasant woman, bishop, king, courtesan), since we were only two people* (M., 1982, p.18). This was the small seed of a much greater concept that six years later came to fruition in Jooss's masterpiece, *The Green Table*.

Because of an unfortunate accident, the *Dance of Death* was never added to the program of concert dances. In January 1927 Jooss and Leeder were rehearsing in Vienna for Händel's *Herakles*. During one of the rehearsals Jooss leaped off a tall pedestal and wrenched his knee in landing. The performance of *Herakles*, as well as a *Two Male Dancers* performance in Vienna had to be cancelled. Within a month he was completely disabled, and spent ten weeks off his feet recuperating. The arthritis in his knee caused by this incident kept him in discomfort for the rest of his life.[3] Jooss remembered, with a note of dismay: *That was the end of our touring plans and as I thought also the end of my performing career. Buried was the tour of* **Two Male Dancers**, *buried the* **Dance of Death** *for which there were no performers* (M. & M., 1985, p.33).

Meanwhile the Municipal Theatre of Münster decided under public pressure that its artistic direction was too avant-garde. To ease the minds of the conservative municipal authorities, changes in programs and personnel were instituted. Among the people leaving were Niedecken-Gebhardt, Schulz-Dornburg, Cohen (for personal reasons)[4] and the entire *Neue Tanzbühne*, which at this time was under the direction of one of its members, Jens Keith. In early 1927 Jooss was concentrating all his efforts on a new pedagogical endeavor.

Fortunately for the *Neue Tanzbühne*, Schulz-Dornburg obtained the position of music director at the Essen Opera House and invited the entire company to join him there for the 1927-1928 season, with Keith as ballet master. In June 1927 the dance group performed two Jooss ballets, *Kaschemme* and *Groteske*, at the First German Dancer's Congress at Magdeburg.

In the spring of 1927, while Jooss was in Münster recuperating from his knee injury, he began negotiations with the mayor of Essen, who wanted Jooss to direct the dance division at a new school for the visual and the performing arts. Jooss accepted the position. Together with Rudolf Schulz-Dornburg and Max Fielder they moved the *Westfälishe Schule* to Essen, which became the core for the founding of the Folkwangschule.

In the early 1920's the city of Essen had acquired a sizable art collection named *Folkwang.*[5] In 1927 it was decided to sponsor a school of the performing arts. It was conceived as a sister school to the existing school of design, arts and crafts. The city wanted the museum and the two schools, to carry the mythological name *Folkwang.* Thus, when the school was brought to Essen it became the *Folkwangschule für Tanz, Musik und Sprechen.*

Meanwhile Jooss's knee did not get better. Hoping for a cure, he travelled to a small Hungarian town named Pistyan (consequently Piest'any in Slovakian as a part of Czechoslovakia) known for its medical hot springs. He stayed for six weeks at the spa, and while his knee was being treated with mud baths he spent the time working on dance notation. He started with the idea that movement sequences should be recorded on a vertical staff, where the right side represented the right side of the human body and the left the corresponding left side. Next he added the idea that the weight-bearing support of the body (the legs) should be represented on the middle shaft, while the arms and the head should be located on shafts further out. Jooss called this the *Linien System* (Linear System) of notation.

In the summer of 1927 Jooss and Leeder continued to work on the notation system and completed the notation of two solos, the *Courting Dance of the Princes (Werbetanz des Prinzen)* from Jooss's ballet *Die Brautfahrt,* and Leeder's *Maskentanz.* They attended a summer course of Laban's where they studied *Eukinetics* with Dussia Bereska, and took the occasion to present their developments for the notation system to Laban. Laban took up their scheme with enthusiasm and elaborated it extensively with the assistance of his disciples. This became the notation system known as Labanotation in English and Kinetographie Laban in German. Laban acknowledged Jooss's contribution to his notation system in a preface to one of his books: *I will mention here Kurt Jooss, who, after finishing his studies as a pupil of Bereska and myself, surprised us one day with a proposal to duplicate Feuillet's right-left division of the movement sequences. We proceeded then to record the movements of trunk and arms in separate columns instead of inserting them in the upper part of the cross.*[6]

In 1928, at the Second German Dancers Congress in Essen, Laban officially presented his notation system to the public. The Congress, which was organized by Jooss, ran from June 21st to 26th. In his opening statement Jooss addressed the issue of the relationship of classical ballet to modern dance. He maintained that it was important not to lose sight of the achievements of the classical tradition, and to consider how this tradition and technique might contribute to the evolution of German modern dance. He was a lone crusader in this advocacy of combining classical and modern dance techniques. *"I was nearly stoned for that,"* he said later, referring to the reactions of the participants to his speech (Häger, *International Encyclopedia of Dance*). Ultimately Jooss proved his point through his own choreography. It is fair to say that no choreographer in the history of dance has combined the classical and modern techniques in the service of theatrical dance drama as successfully as Jooss.

For Jooss, technique was a means for expression, choreography the form of content. By 1927, when he co-founded the Folkwangschule in Essen, he was a mature artist with a repertory of eight group works, at least four major solos, several duets and numerous dances staged and performed for operas and operettas. He had founded a school and developed a method of dance training. He was deeply committed to the theatre, to professional training for dancers, and to collaborative work with other art professionals.

In 1928 Jooss formed a small performing group of professional dancers and called it the Folkwang Tanztheater Studio. F.A. Cohen joined him as a composer, pianist and music teacher. When Jooss assumed the post of Ballet Director at the Essen Opera in 1929, he consolidated his studio group with the Opera dancers and gave it the name *Folkwang Tanzbühne Essen*. Of the sixteen major ballets Jooss choreographed for these groups, only four survive. They constitute his entire choreographic legacy.[7]

But Jooss's legacy includes more than his choreography. It includes an aesthetic and pedagogical method that is alive (though metamorphosed) in today's German *Tanztheater* and in the continued functioning of the Folkwangschule. Jooss outlined his theories on dance education in a memorandum he wrote in 1927 for the establishment of a German Dance Academy. Later he expanded this into a detailed proposal for a complete professional program for the choreographing, performing, directing, notating, and teaching of dance. He wrote: *The teaching method of the school combines 'classical ballet' and 'modern dance' as complementary factors in a new synthesis. Both technique and artistic usage are revealed to the student by use of **contrasting** characteristics of both these disciplines and the possibility of their harmonious synthesis* (M. & M., 1985, p.151). To the critics who accused him of not teaching a specific 'Jooss technique', Jooss had the following to say: *I am often reproached that the style we teach is not clearly identifiable. But we are not teaching a specific style; what we teach is the dancer's craft. Style is a result of choreographic intention and choice* (M. & M., 1985, p.33).

The *Folkwang Tanzbühne* was the resident company of the Essen Opera house. It gained world recognition at the *Grand Concours International de Chorégraphie* in Paris on July 3, 1932, when it performed *The Green Table*, the sensational winner of the first prize. During the fall of 1932 the company became a separate organization under the new name of *Ballets Jooss* and began an extensive touring program.

Jooss belonged to the generation of artists who matured between the two World Wars. He was a creative participant in the Weimar culture, and like many of his contemporaries he developed a strong social conscience. He had seen the ravages of war and felt emotionally close to the works of Otto Dix, George Grosz and Bertold Brecht, each of whom was concerned with the resulting social and political ills. He read the works of Kurt Tucholksky who was openly critical of the widespread right-wing militarism. His own work reflected the artistic trend known as *Die Neue Sachlichkeit* or New Objectivity. As its name suggests, the focus of the movement was to observe and depict everyday life, objectively presented. Humor, irony, caricature and real drama were characteristic of the movement, and Jooss used them all. Most of all, he was conscious of creating artistic forms that not only expressed but were a direct consequence of their content: *We are living in an age which is rediscovering **artistic form**. In dance this means that out of the chaos of arbitrary and haphazard movements only the essentially important will be developed, with an economy and restriction appropriate to art, and in the purest possible form* (M. & M., 1985, p.15).

In 1933 Jooss was forced to flee Nazi Germany. That year a German newspaper published an article with this lengthy title: *The Truthful Jacob, KURT JOOSS AS MOSES' TEMPLE DANCER: Without Cohen the Jew he Cannot Fulfil his Artistic Mission.* Jooss personally went to the headquarters of the Nazi Party to protest their demand that he dismiss the Jewish members of his company. His uncompromising attitude led the Nazis to escalate their rhetoric, and the Ballets Jooss was accused of harboring not only Jews, but also Kultur-Bolsheviks and homosexuals. Jooss had exposed himself to great danger, and was warned by the Freemasons that his arrest was imminent. An escape was arranged and Jooss fled to Holland with the entire company. These events brought to a sudden end the first and probably the most creative phase of Jooss's career.

After the flight from Nazi Germany, while the Ballets Jooss was on tour through Europe and America, Jooss received an invitation from a wealthy British couple, Leonard and Dorothy Elmhirst, to bring his school to England. Thus began a new chapter in Jooss's life and career. In April of 1934 his school re-opened at Dartington Hall in Devon, England, under the name of the 'Jooss-Leeder School of Dance'. Leeder left the Folkwangschule for Dartington Hall with the teaching staff and twenty-three students that formed the initial core of the school.

For more than a year the Ballets Jooss was without a permanent home. Nevertheless Jooss kept on creating important new works for them. His second version of *The Prodigal Son* dates from this period, as does a light humorous piece to Purcell's music entitled *The Seven Heroes*. The story of the ballet was based on a Grimm fairy tale set in an idyllic rural community.

Jooss left the company for a while to accept the invitation by the exotic ballerina Ida Rubenstein to choreograph and direct the world premiere of Stravinsky's *Persephone* for the Paris Opera. For a brief time his company had to disband for lack of financial support. Finally, in September 1935, exactly two years after Jooss's departure from Germany, the Ballets Jooss was re-established at Dartington Hall. A core group of dancers from the original company were joined by pupils of the school. Jooss added three new ballets to the repertory: *Ballade, Johann Strauss Tonight,* and *The Mirror*. The entire new program was produced that year in the newly built Barn Theatre at Dartington Hall.

The Mirror was a sequel to *The Green Table*. This ballet was also a collaboration between Jooss, F.A. Cohen and Hein Heckroth. Both works dealt with the impact of war. In *The Green Table* the focus is on the figure of Death and his victims, while in *The Mirror* Jooss shows us the survivors. The work *reflects the confusion and worries, the despair and the hopes of post-war mankind struggling to escape from the moral, social and political consequences of his own folly* (Coton, 1946, p.59). The scenario focused on the grim realities of postwar civilian existence.

Much later, after his return to Germany, Jooss choreographed a third ballet on the war theme entitled *Journey in the Fog*. This work was influenced by his own experiences during the Second World War. It consisted of four scenes, each one reflecting on a different aspect of hardship and suffering: *the loneliness of exile; the claustrophobia of internment camp; the shadow of bereavement; and the restlessness of attempted rehabilitation* (Häger, *International Encyclopedia of Dance*). These three works, *Table, Mirror* and *Fog,* form a trilogy focused on the gravest events of our twentieth century, the century shaped by global warfare.

In 1939 Jooss choreographed *Chronica*, a full length ballet dealing with another timely topic: the horrors of dictatorship. His portrayal of a medieval despot and the suffering he inflicts on his subjects made allegorical reference to Hitler and Germany. With the entire new repertory, the Ballets Jooss travelled to the United States in 1940 for an extensive tour, including a long engagement in New York City. Jooss stayed in England, expecting to devote his time to the Jooss-Leeder School of Dance. However, England adopted the wartime policy of evacuating aliens from the costal areas, and the school had to close down. Teachers and students alike were obliged to leave.

Jooss, as a German national, was interned as an 'enemy alien'. This was a devastating experience for him. He was freed after six months, following the intervention of some prominent intellectuals. His devoted wife Aino Siimola worked relentlessly for his release.

In 1942 the Ballets Jooss was disbanded once again. Jooss himself was unable to leave England and could not look after his company. The final performances were in New York City, following an extended tour of the United States and Latin America. Ernst Uthoff, his wife Lola Botka, and Rudolph Pescht went to Santiago, Chile to form their own ballet company. Some company members got jobs in theatres in New York, and others were offered one-way passage on convoys travelling from the United States to England. This was arranged as a favour to Jooss by the British government, following Jooss's successful staging of Mozart's *Magic Flute* and *Marriage of Figaro* for the Sadler's Wells Opera Company.

The Ballets Jooss was re-established for the third time in Cambridge in 1942. Again Jooss added new works to the company's repertory: *Company at the Manor,* to Beethoven's "Spring Sonata", and *Pandora.* Häger describes the latter work as *deeply disturbing.* He writes: *Refraining from his customary clarity of message, he created visions of future dangers for humanity, warning against unrestrained curiosity and ingenuity. It was as if he had a presentiment of the atom bomb a year before it happened, and of the evils to follow in its wake* (Häger, *International Encyclopedia of Dance*).

The new repertory of the Ballets Jooss was premiered at The Haymarket in London two days before D-Day in June 1944. From 1942 on there was a shortage of male dancers so Jooss began performing again.

In 1947 Jooss was finally granted British citizenship. Also in that year, despite government support and popular success, the Ballets Jooss disbanded for the final time. Post-war conditions made it too difficult to continue performing. Jooss embarked on a journey to Chile at the invitation of the Uthoffs. He choreographed *Juventud* for their company, the Chilean National Ballet. He also gave his farewell performance in his greatest role, the part of Death in *The Green Table.* With this another chapter of Jooss's career came to an end.

The final phase of his career began with an invitation from the Folkwangschule in Essen to return as Director of the dance division once again. He was also offered a subsidy from the municipality of Essen for a new dance company. He accepted, and in 1949, with great hopes for the future, he returned to Germany for good. For the next two years he worked at re-establishing the dance program at the Folkwangschule. A leading soloist and teacher at the school, Hans Züllig became his assistant and shared many of the responsibilities. Once again Jooss founded a company, naming it the *Folkwang-Tanztheater der Stadt Essen.* By 1951 the new company went on a West German and European tour. Included in the repertory were restagings of the original Ballets Jooss program. This was the first time that postwar Germany experienced *The Green Table*. Also included on the program were two ballets by Züllig (*Le Bosquet* and *Fantasie*) and four new ballets by Jooss: *Colombinade, Dithyrambus, Journey in the Fog,* and *Night Train*. Keeping life in proper perspective in *Night Train* Jooss created a humorous piece about people's dreams during an overnight train journey.

Unfortunately the Folkwang-Tanztheater was short-lived. The municipality of Essen reneged on its promise and refused to extend its financial support. The final curtain came down on the company in 1953. The following comment appeared in a Dutch newspaper, the *Algemeen Handelsblad*: *It would be tragic and absolutely irresponsible if the most famous German dance group should now be obliged to end its successful activity* (M. & M., 1985, p.69). Jooss's disappointment was especially keen because he believed that the company was on the verge of becoming self-supporting.

Meanwhile Jooss continued his mission as an educator, working at the Folkwangschule and teaching in summer schools in Switzerland. From 1954 to 1956 he directed the Düsseldorf Opera Ballet with the hope of establishing a *Tanztheater* there. The administration promised him to help found an independent dance company. When they broke their promise he left. In the next few years he travelled in Europe teaching and choreographing. He established a post graduate Master's Program for Dance under the name of *Folkwang Dance Studio*. The members of these classes were given opportunities to choreograph and to perform. From these Master Classes evolved Jooss's last company, the *Folkwangballet*. In addition to Jooss's choreography, the repertory included works by other distinguished artists such as Antony Tudor's *Jardin Aux Lilas*, Jean Cébron's *Struktur,* and Lucas Hoving's *Songs of Encounter* and *Icarus*. Pina Bausch tried her wings as a choreographer and her first effort *Fragment* was included in the program.

Jooss retired from his post at the Folkwangschule in 1968. He continued to work as a guest choreographer, and re-staged his ballets for several companies and arts festivals. In 1972 he delegated the responsibility for restaging the original Ballets Jooss program to his daughter, Anna Markard. To this day Miss Markard continues to set these ballets, most importantly *The Green Table*, for dance companies all over the world.

Jooss lost his wife Aino in 1971, she had been his lifetime companion and his most trusted artistic adviser. He moved from Essen to Kreuth in Bavaria, where he spent the rest of his life. During the 1970's Jooss was often asked to serve as guest choreographer, but he usually refused. He did accept an invitation to the Salzburg Festival to choreograph Cavalieri's *Rappresentatione di anima e di corpo,* which he considered his last significant work. Jooss died in 1979 in Heilbronn, from injuries sustained in an automobile accident.

In 1976, in celebration of Jooss's seventy-fifth birthday, Robert Joffrey revived the original Ballets Jooss program at the City Center 55th Street Theater. These four ballets - *Big City, Pavane on the Death of an Infanta, A Ball in Old Vienna,* and *The Green Table* - are all that remain of the forty to fifty ballets Jooss choreographed in his lifetime. Appropriately, their survival owes much to Labanotation, which in turn owes so much to Jooss. But Jooss's artistic legacy goes far beyond those four ballets. He pioneered an approach to dance expression in which content determines form and technique is the direct outcome of dramatic necessity. He was thus a founder of the newest movement in theatrical dance, the German *Tanztheater*.

1.   Laban dropped the 'von' from his name in the 1940's and referred to himself from then on plainly as Rudolf Laban.

2.   Laban himself alternately refers to this work as a 'play' and as 'pure dance', suggesting that Jooss's dramatic abilities made up for his lack of technical proficiency.

3.   Personal notes of Elsa Kahl Cohen, in the author's possession.

4.   As the oldest son, F.A. Cohen had taken over the running of the family publishing house after his father died.

5.   In North German mythology *Folkwang* was the banquet hall of the goddess of love and fertitlity Freya. It was located in a great meadow in the sky where deceased heroes were invited to be her guests. The owner of the paintings who donated them for the establishment of the Essen museum chose the name because he intended the museum to be a place where people met to be inspired by creativity.

6.   This system of notation was published first in 1928, during Laban's lifetime. (Laban, 1976, p. x).

7.   The four works are *Pavane on the Death of an Infanta* (1929), *The Green Table* (1932), *Big City* (1932), and *A Ball in Old Vienna* (1932).

JOOSS'S WISE COVENANT WITH DEATH

by Claudia Jeschke

Anyone perusing today's dance theater programs will search in vain for any other evidence of the period of German *Ausdruckstanz* but Kurt Jooss's *The Green Table*. After more than six decades since its premiere in 1932, this work still forms a part of both German and international ballet repertoires, thus belonging to the modern classics. What are the reasons behind the success of this particular work? Looking for explanations in the many publications on Jooss's piece, one comes across a number of interpretations that have at least two ideas in common: the political affiliation of the work, represented by the "Gentleman in Black", and the structural openness and transparency of the work, represented by Jooss's decision to link the Dance of Death and war. The correlation between these two topics is of a dynamic nature and encourages different, even if very specific, views on this work.

Before I comment on a few significant interpretations of *The Green Table*, I shall present Jooss's own memories of its genesis. *I went to Lübeck [...] and saw the Totentanz in the Marienkirche (Church of St. Mary). You know, the Totentanz, the Dance of Death. This is one of those medieval dances of death. [...] One is not quite sure of the meaning, whether it meant that the skeletons come out of the graves and dance in the graveyard, or whether these skeletons always meant Death. It was Death dancing with the bishop, with an old man, with a mother with her still-born child and so on. I took it that way.*

[...] in Münster. There was a group of actors whose leading man was Holtoff, actually a painter. He had a small company and did the Totentanz taken from motifs of the Totentanz in Lübeck. That struck me deeply and got stuck in me too.

Then Sigurd [Leeder] and I had our program - Two Dancers. We were supposed to go on this tour, but the program which we had was not enough. [...] So I remembered the Totentanz and we decided to do this in a special way. Since we were only two people, it was obvious that it had to keep moving. [...] We had the idea of doing it as different types dancing with Death as an invisible partner [...]. Sigurd devised masks for it and we agreed that I would dance first the figure of Death with the scythe.

[...], Aino [Jooss's wife] had given me a subscription to the Weltbühne. The Weltbühne was a slightly, or rather not so very slightly, rather leftist, periodical in which the main writer - Tucholsky who published in every issue - wrote about secret things which were going on about preparations for the new war, and that nobody noticed it. [...] In the meantime, I had been reading Tucholsky and got that political aspect of people arranging wars and so on.[1]

Jooss explains the topic of the Dance of Death in his memories very pragmatically in visual terms when he speaks about how he was influenced by the image of the Dance of Death in Lübeck. He also alludes to the broader metaphorical potential of that topic when speaking about the omnipresence of Death and about the cycle of life and death that is equally valid for all human beings. In so doing, he refers in particular to the organisational and structural implications that interested him as creative principles of composition. His last statement notes how these principles can be applied to the political situation of the Weimar Republic.

Political Affiliations

Jooss's memories show the various influences that ultimately materialize in *The Green Table*. Any interpretation of this work automatically re-constructs these influences in a particular way. Jooss himself had a rather philosophical point of view on this issue. When asked about his political intentions, he said: *I didn't mean anything specific. I meant that which one doesn't know, but which somehow exists, these powers are just to be felt and not seen.*[2]

In her quest to identify the political implications of German *Ausdruckstanz*, American scholar Susan Manning emphasizes the affiliation of *The Green Table* with the political left, which *[...] was more apparent in 1932 than decades later, when the generalizing power of the work and its survival in the repertory have supported multiple interpretations. Created during the last year of the Weimar Republic, the production affirmed leftist politics through a simple structural device, the juxtaposition of framed and framing sections. While the framed sections associate the Dance of Death with war, the framing sections assign responsibility for war's Dance of Death to the Gentleman in Black and to the Profiteer.*

The choreography supports the thesis of an alliance between capitalism and militarism by drawing a connection between the Gentlemen in Black and the figure of the Profiteer. [...] Significantly, the Profiteer is the only figure within the framed sections to escape Death, dropping to the floor and rolling offstage just before the blackout that precedes the reappearance of the Gentlemen in Black. [...] Within the framed sections the Profiteer represents the workings of entrepreneurial capitalism, thus functioning as the Gentlemen's surrogate. His actions realize the large designs of capitalism on a day-to-day level.[3]

The German journalist Norbert Servos, one of the leading theoreticians of West German *Tanztheater* of the seventies and eighties, sees Kurt Jooss as a transitional as well as integrative figure in the German dance scene of the 20th century. Like Susan Manning, Servos speaks about the political dimension of *The Green Table*, but in contrast to her findings, his synopsis is to evaluate it as different from the aesthetics of *Tanztheater* that consider the body to reflect societal norms. *Jooss shows himself thoroughly conscious of tradition, examining the obsolete formal canon of the Danse d'école for what is still useable for the new dance. At the same time, he is more explicitly political than the majority of Ausdruck dancers in his selection and treatment of themes.*

Where people were generally attuned to Eurhythmie's cosmic harmony, to the unity of body and Nature, Jooss attempted in the Green Table to intervene in current events. He thus escapes that fuzzy mysticism in which a good part of the revolutionary spirit of Ausdruckstanz got trapped, relegating itself to political insignificance. Where Ausdruckstanz often behaved naively in the face of mass unemployment, inflation, worldwide economic recession, thinking to bring the world order back into line by dint of choreographed harmonization, Jooss acted with decisive sociopolitical commitment.

[Jooss] embraced the general penchant [of Ausdruckstanz] for everyday motions, but used them to typify society. [...] Jooss logically makes the connection between the general conditions and the behavior specific to social strata and class.

Jooss [...] furnishes proof that a modern narrative ballet is perfectly capable of making choreographically precise statements on current affairs[4].

In her interpretation, the American dance historian Suzanne K. Walther starts with Jooss's own notion, that "art never should be political", and proceeds to defend the humanist aspects of the work. *Despite Jooss's disclaimer, the ballet is considered a monument to pacifism. But The Green Table is not political propaganda. It does not exhort, instruct or coerce; it does not label or pass value judgements; it does not take sides.*

Jooss's impartiality is more damning than any apportionment of blame would be. The evil cannot be assigned to an army or a cause. It lies deeper in man: in irrational ways of thinking, fanaticism, greed and aggression.

Death is also a normal part of human existence, [...]. The ballet's personification of death gives shape and character to pure amorphous notions. This terrifying half-knight and half-skeleton, the elegant and mythical monster figure of Death, is a composite of our fearful imaginings.

Nevertheless, Jooss shows us how an individual's own personal character affects his death. [...] Personal decisions shape our lives, our deaths and the fate of those around us. Jooss's focus on the individual always brings with it a commentary on society as well.[5]

Multilayered Structure

All interpretations of *The Green Table* stress the fact that the value and timeless quality of the work cannot exclusively be explained by its ever valid call for pacisfism. The continuing effect of this work that has to be evoked afresh every time relies equally on the organisation (or the outer and inner structure) of the composition that carries the message: the Dance of Death. The knowledge of the ubiquitious nature of death effectively exists beyond all chronological, geographical and social boundaries. The Dance of Death itself, however, consists of two motifs: the dance of the personified death and the dance of a person with Death (which means a dying person) - i.e., the dance of (the) Death and the dance towards death.

Dance, Art, and (Dance) History

Jooss was not the only one at the beginning of the 20th century, who dealt with the motif of the Dance of Death. The dance of the Death and dance towards death also came up in literature, fine art, and dance in general - proceeding from the notion that movement and transcience, the two essential elements of the Dance of Death, are often considered to be synonymous. Gabriele Brandstetter comments on the relationship of those elements in the following way: *It is the moment of the ultimate and last breaking up of the boundaries of the self: the dance in the face of death. It is the moment of the cross-over to another universe that is called up in dance itself as the motion along the borderline of the ever irretrievable moment of the movement which is as such transient and always already in the past.*[6]

According to another voice, the motif of the Dance of Death works beyond its usage in art as "one of the supreme symbols of our centrifugal and paradoxical century"[7], as it supposedly combines the orgiastical in an ironic way with the nihilistic. Modris Eksteins comes to this general statement in his analysis of Stravinsky's *Le Sacre du Printemps* which has also been seen as a Dance of Death. It is probably not appropriate to ascribe Jooss to this rather existentialist interpretation of the Dance of Death[8]: even though he too makes use of the symbol of the Dance of Death and thus reactivates the symbolic function of Death, he does not do so in an orgiastic or nihilistic manner at all. The unique quality of his choreographical composition rather lies in his integration of the figure of Death into the development of a story. The complexity of the outer structure of *The Green Table* stems from this process: Death as a symbol is of a continuous and unchangeable nature, it, nevertheless, provokes emotions and causes human tragedies. Jooss tells us stories about people who are in the face of death and he develops individual movement vocabularies to express their emotional situation and their actions. Anna and Hermann Markard comment on the importance in the history of dance that has to be seen in this dramatic and thus also dynamic re-evaluation of the traditional motif of the Dance of Death: it is an innovative and highly specific combination of narrative and structural elements for the construction of a ballet that replaces an understanding of dramatic action of the 19th century classical dance based on isolated units. *The Green Table is dramatic dance theatre and as such it had no precedents. The dance works of its time were either still rooted in the expressionistic cult forms of the late 1920s or were variations on the developments within the classical tradition. For Jooss's concept of Dance Drama new ways of expression had to be found. He developed an articulate 'Language of movement' that could convey what he wanted to say. In the classical tradition, mime was used as narrative interspersed between the dance sections. Jooss's choreography communicates directly; but he does not merely use realistic movement, he reshapes and condenses the movement, transforming the realism by distilling it to the essence; he gives the movement clearly defined rhythmic and spatial components, without loosing the recognisable origin or meaning. In fact because of this stylisation the movements become increasingly meaningful. Jooss developed his movement vocabulary according to his theme, guided by the belief that 'there is no external movement without internal movement' or, the source of all movements is sensed motivation.*[9]

The Movement Idea

The foundation of *The Green Table* in the then contemporary aesthetic debates on art and its historical liability as a renewal of the story ballet are the two aspects that constitute the significance of this work. Both aspects are determined by its inner structure, for which Jooss applied the ideas that had been identified and categorized by Rudolf von Laban. Laban had been working on a new concept of movement analysis, notation, and composition for many years.[10] His research led him to Plato and to the Icosahedron which he found to be an appropriate structure for the organisation of the Kinesphere, the space around the human body whose peripherey is reachable by extended limbs. In the Icosahedron, Laban identified laws of space which enabled the analysis of all forms of human physical action, whether behaviour, work, traditional dance forms or the new, free way of dancing. Laban organized his findings as "Choreographische Harmonielehre", that was concerned with a theory of space, its laws and dramatic content, and a theory of expression, the laws of dynamics and their expressive potential. When Jooss and Sigurd Leeder began their artistic and pedagogical partnership, they filtered and gradually systematized these theories and developed them - as Choreutics and Eukinetics[11].

Anna Markard points out that *Choreutics is a tool for choreographic composition, for meaningful, communicative movement* and that: *the practice of Choreutics achieves discipline, co-ordination and sensitivity through awareness of gestural paths and directional focus through space. An understanding of the contrasting dimensional and diagonal directions stimulates the spatial imagination. Observation shows that there is also an inseparable relationship between human emotion and the direction of spontaneous physical action. A specific emotion will always favour a certain direction or directional path in space. [...] Choreutics therefore also reveals the psychological content of movement and is thus one of the keys to dramatic dance.*[12]

As a theory of dynamics, Eukinetics concerns the expressive qualities of the movement, which are the relative properties of speed, quick or slow, designated as the element of time and the muscular strength, strong or weak, defined as the element of intensity. A spatial element has to be included to make the other two visible. Jooss called this element modus. It defines the starting point and guidance of movement which can be central or peripheral: *Central movement originates and remains in the center of the body or the base joint of the limb concerned; peripheral movement originates and remains at the extremities.*[13] Furthermore, Eukinetics also defines sequential flow, the radiating or converging of movement and a multitude of dynamic shadings and degrees of change.

While the focus of Choreutics lies in the spatial laws of structuring movement, Eukinetics deals with the temporal and dynamic occurences within the rendering of expression. In *The Green Table*, Jooss is particularly successful not only in identifying formal and expressive aspects of a language of movement and of composition, but also in giving them a recurrent pulse and combining them with each other, so that the various individual scenes seem like repeatedly recalled memories. On the level of the macrostructure, this is achieved through the dramaturgical order of the scenes within the action, which is determined by the tension between identity and contrast. The first and last scenes, "The Gentlemen in Black", are identical; and the rhythm of the other scenes is of a repetitious nature, as Death connects the individual scenes through his appearances, while also influencing the action in all scenes actively or passively. Another character that appears in all the inner scenes is the Profiteer functioning as a contrasting figure to Death: the movement vocabularies of these two characters demonstrate on the level of microstructure, how the choreutic and eukinetic material influences the choreographical solutions and their effects. The figure of Death often shows repetitious, unrelenting movement motifs; his stance is upright, mainly using the dimensional direction high-deep; he employs direct and strong trace forms for his gestures, for example the cutting down and gathering of the opening scene. The Profiteer's avarice, alternating with hesitant cowardice, is characterized by fast, small advancing steps, punctuated with staccato holds and sharp retreats; his gestures are often organized on the horizontal plane, following 'rond' and 'tortillé' traces. From the performer's point of view, every movement suggests a particular dramatic action, which renders motoric intensity and kinesthetic meaning; it requires, as Marcia Siegel puts it, *an investment of feeling, of risk, of total presence, in addition to the choreographed positions and timings. Through this commitment, the dancer infuses the choreography with feeling.*[14]

On both the macrostructure and the microstructure level of the choreography, these few examples already show a dense and evocative network of never-ending movement sructures that are diverse, but that always relate to each other and that give relevance to each of the various interpretations of the work that I presented in the beginning. While it certainly is possible to see *The Green Table* as a treatise on and against the political situation of the Weimar Republic, or on and against war, or in favour of humanism, the work also represents choreography that is primarily based on means of movement and thus becomes a fictional work of movement-art that always is more than the sum of its supposed tendencies. In *The Green Table*, Kurt Jooss manages to achieve the paradoxical combination of traditional motifs with innovative structures. By putting a story (and thus dynamics and variability) around the Dance of Death that has a static nature due to its symbolic character, he rejects - idealistically, hypothetically, and at least temporarily - the inevitability of dying: he evokes the possibility of human intervention against the figure of Death that can and should prevent a pointless and early death with the force of humanistic intelligence. While this surely is an illusionary mission that is doomed to failure (as is shown by the repetition of the first scene at the end or by the victory of Death over all characters except the Profiteer),[15] it still must never be abandoned (and the various images and their construction and composition can be interpreted in this way). The composition and the interrelations of macro- and microstructures represent an artistic as well as humanistic balance and they portray a state of uncertainty that is very typical of our cultures: in modern age, there is the motif of a dance of the dead or of Death, but there is no dance of the living. Instead, dance as such exists here as a metaphor for life. Thus, the Dance of Death is based on the inevitability of an end to life, while dance as such represents being alive and enables changes in the current situation and the construction of individual stories within the lifetime. It probably is the immanence of dance, the being alive in the face of death, that makes *The Green Table* so much a modern and contemporary work of art: *The Green Table* dramatizes and structures the immanences at the heart of human beings like no other choreography of the modern age.

1.   "The Green Table - A Dance of Death." Kurt Jooss in an interview with Michael Huxley in 1978. In: *Ballett International*. 8/9, 1982: 4-10, here: 9.

2.   Ibid.

3.   Manning, Susan A.. *Ecstasy and the Demon. Feminism and Nationalism in the Dances of Mary Wigman*. Berkeley/Los Angeles/London: University of California Press, 1993: 160-165.

4.   Servos, Norbert. "The Green Table. A piece holds its own for 50 years in dance theater repertoire". In: *Ballett International*. 8/9, 1982: 10-12, here: 12.

5.   Walther, Suzanne K.. *The Dance of Death. Kurt Jooss and the Weimar Years*. Chur: Harwood Academic Publishers, 1994: 71-73.

6.   Brandstetter, Gabriele. "'Tanzt die Orange'. Literatur und Tanz in der Moderne." In: Adelsbach, Karin and Andrea Firmenich (eds.). *Tanz in der Moderne. Von Matisse bis Schlemmer*. Emden: Wienand, 1996: 277-286, here: 282. The issue of dance as a methaphor for death ("Der Tanz - Metapher des Todes") is also dealt with by the following text but from a point of view of cultural and socio-historical studies: Koch, Marion. *Salomes Schleier. Eine andere Kulturgeschichte des Tanzes*. Hamburg: Europäische Verlagsanstalt, 1995: 111-157. - A view of Jooss's work in the context of general aesthetic innovations of its time is presented in: Schlicher, Susanne. "The West German dance theatre. Paths from the twenties to the present." In: *Choreography and Dance*. 3/2, 1993: 29-33.

7.   Eksteins, Modris. *Rites of Spring. The Great War and the Birth of the Modern Age*. Boston: Houghton Mifflin, 1989: xiv.

8.   Marcia Siegel mentions two further examples for the use of the motif of the Dance of Death in German expressionist dance: One is Mary Wigman's satirical Charleston for skeletons which formed the entr'acte for the 1927 revue *Hoppla, wir leben!* by Ernst Toller and Erwin Piscator, while the other is Harald Kreutzberg's *Ewiger Kreis*. See Siegel, Marcia. "The Green Table - Sources of a classic." In: *Dance Research Journal*. 21/1 (Spring 1989): 15-21, here: 17.

9.   Markard, Anna and Hermann. "Der grüne Tisch." In: Dahlhaus, Carl et alii (eds.). *Pipers Enzyklopädie des Musiktheaters*. Bd. 3. München: Piper, 1989: 218-220. I have quoted here Anna Markard's English version of the article.

10.   The exposition of the choreographic principles of harmony by Laban and Jooss follows Anna Markard's article "Jooss the teacher. His pedagogical aims and the development of the choreographic principles of harmony". In: *Choreography and Dance*. 3/2, 1993: 45-51, here: 49-51.

11. For the genesis and application of Choreutics and Eukinetics see also Maletic, Vera. *Body - Space - Expression. The Development of Rudolf Laban's Movement and Dance Concepts.* Berlin et alii: Mouton de Gruyter, 1987.

12. Markard, Anna. "Jooss the teacher": 50. Choreutics includes four fundamental trace forms in any direction, these are droit, ouvert, rond, tortillé; it also features six dimensional directions: high, deep, side narrow, side wide, backward and forward; it gives three dimensional planes, combining two dimensional directions: the "flat", lateral or door plane (high-deep, side-side), the "steep", sagittal or wheel plane (high-deep, backward-forward), and the "floating", horizontal or table plane (backward-forward, side-side). Furthermore, Choreutics combines the six dimensional directions into the so-called dimensional scale. It also refers to the space diagonals which are the four diagonals of a cube; it uses the four diagonals of a dimensional plane called diameters, and it combines the twelve directions relating to the Icosahedron in the "A-Scale" and "B-Scale", alternating "flat", "steep", "floating".

13. Ann Hutchinson, ibid.: 51.

14. Siegel, "The Green Table": 16.

15. Anna Markard remembers her father's comments on the role of the profiteer as follows: The exceptional situation of this character in the ballet does not necessarily mean, that he actually escapes death (as Susan Manning states), it might also show that Death condemns the Profiteer as not even worthy of his mere attention. This last reading refers to Jooss's conviction that good choreography should offer multiple choice of interpretation.

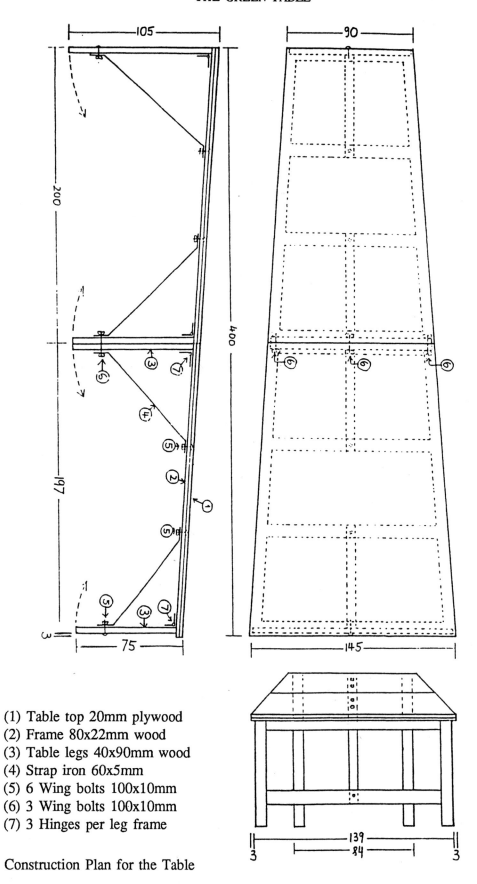

(1) Table top 20mm plywood
(2) Frame 80x22mm wood
(3) Table legs 40x90mm wood
(4) Strap iron 60x5mm
(5) 6 Wing bolts 100x10mm
(6) 3 Wing bolts 100x10mm
(7) 3 Hinges per leg frame

Construction Plan for the Table

REHEARSAL REQUIREMENTS

The following will cover the requirements for every form of class or studio study.

Space:

The choreography requires an average of 10 x 10 meter dance space.

Music:

Rehearsals should be with live music. The accompanying tape in intended as a guideline only.

Table:

Scenes 1 and 8 must be rehearsed with a table made according to the construction plan (see opposite page). The low wide edge of the table is downstage. 'C' must be placed just upstage of the middle table leg, 'H' almost opposite him, just downstage of the middle table leg.

Shoes:

Death should work in boots with a widebased 1cm. heel, and a full, soft flexible sole. All other dancers must wear soft ballet shoes in every rehearsal.

Flags:

The two flags are made with lightweight wooden poles, 1.40m long, 22cm diameter, a taffeta silk rectangle is firmly attached so that 1m is along the pole and 1.20m flows freely.

Bowler Hat:

For Scene 2 the Profiteer must practice with a classic bowler hat. It is also advisable to wear the bowler hat for all Profiteer rehearsals.

Scarf:

The Woman's scarf for Scene 4 is 2m x 35cm. It should be wool crêpe or fabric of a similar weight, a loose-fitting, non-elastic belt is also worn for this scene.

Pistols:

These are never used in studio rehearsals. Please work on the choreography imagining both the pistol and the pocket!

Rehearsal, Dartington 1935

CASTING

The Green Table requires sixteen dancers: eight men, eight women, some dancing two rôles.

Rôles:

Ten Gentlemen in Black, Death, The Standard Bearer, The Young Soldier, The Young Girl, The Woman, The Old Soldier, The Old Mother, The Profiteer, Three Soldiers, Five Women.

The Gentlemen in Black - a,b,c,d,e,f,g,h,j,k
The ten Gentlemen in Black (in Scenes 1 and 8) are cast with seven men and three women, i.e. all the men except Death. The three women are the Mother, the Woman and one woman from the group of five.

a:	Small, extrovert, oily. (Frequently the Profiteer).
b:	Tall, pompous 'elder statesman'. Team leader (usually the Old Soldier or sometimes the Profiteer, if tall).
c,d:	Average height. Minor rôles (usually soldiers).
e:	Deaf, zealous. One of the five women (U or L).
f:	Puffed up, fanatic (Mother or Woman).
g:	Dutiful, business-like (Mother or Woman).
h:	Average height or tall, strong, aggressive.
j:	Average height, bright, quick-tempered.
k:	Tallest (usually the Standard Bearer), 'elder statesman', team leader, aloof, vain.

The Standard Bearer must always be on stage left of the table and the Profiteer must always be on stage right of the table.

D = Death
Tall. An extremely complex, multi-faceted rôle requiring intelligence, sensitivity and the ability of rapid change of attitude. Dynamically he must be capable of the full range of qualities from brutal strength to extreme gentleness and be able to project a sense of awesome power. Requires strong, clean, powerful technique, a sense of weight, good jumps, coordination, rhythm and stamina.

B = The Standard Bearer
Tall, handsome, heroic, military enthusiast with ability to project victorious confidence. Requires strong technique, good jumps and clean line.

Y = The Young Soldier
Patriotic idealist. Torn between the glamour of the military and a budding romance. A small rôle requiring good technique.

G = The Young Girl
Innocent, vulnerable with both lyrical and dramatic qualities. An important rôle requiring fast light footwork and a mobile, expressive torso.

W = The Woman
Mature woman emotionally torn between hesitancy and fanaticism. An important, dramatic rôle. Requires a strong, dynamic dancer, very good elevation, weight and a mobile, expressive torso. Should also be cast as f or g in Scenes 1 and 8.

O = The Old Soldier
Average or tall. The mature family man, sadly brave. Resigned to his duty to join the army and fight. An important rôle. Requires good solid technique and an understanding of meaningful weighted movement.

M = The Old Mother
Wise with age, perceptive, fragile yet strong. An important rôle requiring fine, slow control, light, lifted footwork, sensitive hands. Should be cast as f or g in Scenes 1 and 8.

P = The Profiteer
Small, average or tall. Strong stage personality. Sardonic, gleeful, two-faced. A voyeur and coward who lives on the sufferings of others. Requires articulate, fast, sharp technique, expressive hands. Must be capable of projecting every detail and nuance.

A,X,Z = Three Soldiers
These should fit together as a unit.
A: the tallest.
Z: the shortest.
A and X are minor rôles.
Z is technically demanding. He must be able to do acrobatic lifts. Z also dances the first duet in Scene 6 (The Brothel).
Either A or X, depending on suitability, dance the second duet in Scene 6. All three soldiers require strong, virile, high energy technique and a good sense of weight.

K,U,L,N,R = Five Women
Different types. K should be small, U and L should be tall. Either U or L will be cast as e in Scenes 1 and 8.

STUDY AND REHEARSAL NOTES

Scene 1: The Gentlemen in Black

Synopsis:
Ten Gentlemen (**a, b, c, d, e, f, g, h, j, k**), powerful manipulators of world affairs (as in politics, high finance or industry), are in discussion. At the height of an argument they draw pistols and shoot. War breaks out.

Rehearsal Notes:
Despite their frequently abrupt movements, the Gentlemen must be clearly understood as human beings, not puppets. Special attention should be paid to the multiple changes of mood and movement qualities - e.g. formal politeness, emotional antagonism. The conversational gestures and *révérences* begin with central (inner) initiation on the downbeat, there are no peripheral (exterior) upbeats. All gestures must 'stay alive' until the very end of the pause. Work on articulate, sensitive hands and clear focus.

Breakdown of Scene:

[11-12] Opening pose.

[13-16] The Gentlemen converse with elaborate, persuasive, exaggerated gestures.

[17-28] All are startled by **f,** and **b**'s significant statement [19-20] causes general astonishment. The conference continues.

[29-37] 'First argument'. Strong statements from one side provoke the other side, and the argument increases.

[38-44] The high tension is relieved, each side condescendingly bows to the other, and the original conversations are resumed.

[45-52] 'Second argument'. New, more insistent provocations from both sides lead to an angry, aggressive confrontation.

[53-60] However, in the 'Lobby' both sides again bow condescendingly, then individually, the Gentlemen seek one another out, and the corrupt business of scheming and bribery begins.

[61-64] A dispute breaks out between the team leaders **b** and **k** - all negotiations stop abruptly and both sides dutifully team up.

[65-76] Chaos breaks out - angry steps lead to a brief fencing confrontation. As though startled, the opponents fake an elaborate pompous bow and busily hasten back to the table.

[77-92] The conference routine repeats.

[93-100] **a** threateningly stamps on the table, a dramatic clash is unleashed.

[101-104] Both sides line up, and, confronting each other, produce their pistols.

[105-109] An exaggerated reconciliation precedes the impartial ceremony which culminates in a mutual pistol shot.

[105-1] "Let there be war!"

Scene 2: The Dance of Death and Farewells

Synopsis: Dance of Death
From the smoke of pistols, the raging power of destruction, God of war appears. Death, the merciless reaper establishes his omnipotent presence.

Rehearsal Notes:
Work on a well-grounded earthbound quality, powerful *relevés* and jumps with assertive, strong landings. Rehearse in boots or at least heeled practice shoes. Pay careful attention to 45° turnout, the locking of the knee and flexed foot [4 ct.2].

Breakdown of Scene:

[a-b] **D** rises with space-encompassing power.

[1-3] Solid, earthbound, crushing motif - powerful wielding of the scythe while relentlessly reaching out to cut again. All-embracing focus.

[4-7] Fierce, triumphant, warrior-like, left arm (ct.2) as though brandishing a shield, right arm (ct.4) like a heavy sledge hammer, malicious, fast, lightning-like changes (cts.7,8).

[8] Suspended in air with bull-like horns and landing with explosive power.

[9-15] Repeat of [1-7].

[16] Light, wind-blown jump, slowly taking aim to attack (cts.3,4).

[17-24] An increase in dynamic contrasts: raging, unleashed fury, fast savage accents.

[25-28] High suspension, slow threatening aim, aggressive attack.

[29-30] Ferocious ball of fire.

[31-32] Repeat of [a-b] with additional powerful accents.

[33-52] Full repeat of [1-15], last jump to central commanding position.

[53-153] Relentless dominating of the entire scene and every mortal being.

Synopsis: Farewells
A scene of patriotic enthusiasm. The Standard Bearer summons the recruits. Men and women are forced to part and the Profiteer enters the scene. The army goes to war passing under the 'gate' of Death. The Woman rushes off after the soldiers but the Profiteer, recognising Death, turns the other way.

Rehearsal Notes:
The roles are introduced as archetypes, each with his/her individual characterisation. The Standard Bearer (**B**) - a dashing, victory-confident commanding officer; the three Soldiers (**A,X,Z**) - dutiful to the flag and the cause; The Young Soldier (**Y**) - torn between his duty to the flag and tender ties to the Young Girl; The Young Girl (**G**) - desperate in her attempt to keep her young lover from joining the force; The Woman (**W**) - passionate, torn between family concern and the irresistible desire to become involved in the cause; The Old Soldier (**O**) - the mature man, not blinded by militarism but resigned to his duty to obey the flag; The Old Mother (**M**) - worried, alarmed, perceiving the tragedy which will inevitably follow the military parade; The Profiteer (**P**) - just in time to mock-praise the army and to take advantage of the grieving Young Girl.

The entire scene is built on the dynamics of an energetic, strong march. The tempo must be kept steady and crisp.

Breakdown of Scene:

[61-76] **B:** Takes the stage with confident sweeping assurance, enjoying the flurry and crackle of the flag. He positions himself proudly and summons the army.

[77-92] **A,X,Z:** Obeying **B,** they join up.

[93-105] **B,A,X,Z:** Army drill. **A,X,Z** swear allegiance to the flag [102].

[106-122]   **Y,G:** Y enters leaping towards the flag. G follows, desperately attempting to hold him back. **Y,** torn between patriotism and tender love, is finally drawn into the ranks while **G** is left alone.

[122-137]   **W,O,M:** W determined, pulls **O** to the scene dragging **M** along. O reluctnantly leaves the women, and advances towards the flag. **W** and **M** comfort each other, then hurl themselves passionately at **O** before the final parting.

[138-145]   **P:** Slyly appears on the side to applaud the army.
             B: Commands the drill of the assembled forces.
             G: Stands aside, forlorn.
             W: Prepares to fight.
             M: Apprehensive of the catastrophe.

[146-153]   **All men except D:** The victory-confident march, even **P** appears to join the army.

[154-170]   The atmosphere changes as each man realises the imminent danger of war.
             D: Awaits his victims to pass under his 'gate'.
             G: Gives up in sorrow and sinks to the ground.
             P: Recognising **D** turns to go the other way, and just happens to notice **G**.
             W: Unable to resign herself to staying, she rushes to follow the army.
             M: Remains behind in hopeless sorrow.

Scene 3: The Battle

Synopsis:
Soldiers fighting man-to-man on the battlefield. The Old Soldier covets the flag and overpowers the Young Soldier. Death appears, the soldiers are scattered and stamped out. The Standard Bearer, still on his feet, commands the Old Soldier to follow him and defying Death, they leave the battlefield together. Stealthily the Profiteer searches the corpses.

Rehearsal Notes:
Soldiers: high energy, well-grounded, weighted quality. Avoid preparatory movements or 'upbeats'. Profiteer: work without bodies on the floor, later risk placing nimble feet close to bodies for take-offs so that all jumps clear easily.

Breakdown of Scene:

[1-9]   All men in single combat.

[10-17]   Ranks are formed and the opposing armies close in to attack or defend.

[18-25]   Single combat is resumed, **A** and **Z** succumb to **X** and **B,** but **O** and **Y** still fight on.

[26-30]   **O** and **Y** struggle for the flag, **Y** holds it successfully.

[31-33]   **Y** triumphantly takes off with the flag, **O** follows closely.

[34-37]   **Y** attacks **O**, but is overpowered and loses the flag.

[38-41]   **O** is fascinated with the flag.

[42-52]   The fighting continues, **Z, A,** and **X** enter. **O** is surrounded and threatened. **B** returns [45-46] reaffirming his central command.

[53]   All are caught up in a violent spiralling swirl.

[54]   The explosive appearance of **D** in their midst, catching **Y** in mid-action, throws all to earth, only **B** keeps his stance.

[55]   **D** lets **Y** drop.

[57]   **B:** Regaining his strength, calls to action.

[58-62]   **O** responds to **B**'s call and both leave the scene.

[63-70]   **D** strides across the battlefield, obliterating every breath of life.

[70-71]   **P:** Eagerly following on **D**'s heels, finds himself alone with the dead.

[72-75]   **P:** Stealthily, driven by avarice, he scurries nervously amongst his prey.

[76-79]   **P:** Almost lustfully he straddles **A**, then shrinks back, changes his attention and leaps across **Y**.

[80-85]   **P:** His excitement quickens, bewitched by temptation, he springs to and fro, unable to make a decision. He sees a ring on **Y** [85, ct.8], his goal is set.

[86-91]   **P:** Gleefully he pursues his intent and steals the ring.

[92-97]   **P:** He twists and turns, obsessed by his sparkling prize.

[98-99]   **P:** In sudden panic he takes to his heels.

Scene 4: The Refugees

Synopsis:
A group of homeless women are on their way. Death interrupts their journey: he assumes the rôle of courtly suitor to the Old Mother, dances with her and takes her gently into his arms. The bereaved Young Girl is trapped by the Profiteer.

Rehearsal Notes:
Very slow, steady tempo. Be sure to start each movement clearly on the downbeat. Work carefully on slow, sequential movements, include focus and the whole body in each gesture. Silent steps, no swish. Old Mother: very light; 'frozen' accents in contrast to slowness; work on delicate qualities. Young Girl: very fast, high runs.

Breakdown of Scene:

[3-18]   **G,L,N,R,U,K:** Calm, supportive, with concern for **M** and one another.

[7-18]   **M:** Seeking a path, she separates from the group: slightly nervous, apprehensive [9-10]: and haunted by memories, perhaps of a lost child, [11] she momentarily gives up, but shunning her thoughts [13] gathers strength again. Running, scanning her whereabouts, she halts suddenly, on the fringe of the unknown, then controlling her weakness, she accepts the support of **G.**

[19-26] **All:** The endless journey.

[27-30] **D:** Appearing like a rock in the pathway, he gradually draws up to his full awesome stature.

[27-31] **M,G,L,N,R,U,K:** Sensing an obstacle, they stop, riveted in their tracks. They see and recognise the threat of **D** and flee.

[32-35] **M:** Her strength failing, she hesitantly submits and obeys **D**'s call.

[32-36] **G:** Unable to comprehend or accompany **M,** she sinks to the ground.

[36-42] **D,M:** Seeming to begin a courtly dance, **M** drifts off into fantasies, and finally sinks into her partner's arm. **D** briefly permits the illusion, then breaks the spell [38, ct.3] and awaits **M**'s obedience. **M,** her momentary fear changing to grateful surrender, obeys, and is gently lifted and carried away.

[42-47] **P:** Bursting in on **G,** he chases her, traps her and obliges her to proceed his way.
        G: Panic-stricken, she tries to escape in vain then gives in weakly.

Scene 5: The Partisan

Synopsis:
A fanatical woman, desperately involved in the cause, kills a soldier. Surrounded and challenged she bravely faces execution. Death ignores her desperate plea for mercy.

Rehearsal Notes:
Be aware of the friction between the lilt of the music and the strong, independent choreographic accents. Work on clear focus and the quality of risk, combined with strong jumps and a use of weight in relation to the floor.

Breakdown of Scene:

[1-4]   **W:** Destined to fight, she charges onto the scene brandishing a long scarf.

[5-13]   **W:** She signals with her scarf, seeking far distant allies [5-8], then resolutely prepares to fight.

[14-19]   **W:** A moment of doubt or hesitation, before she reinforces her decision.

[20-39]   **W:** She is torn between despair, strength of purpose and heroism. Eventually she takes aim, and, pouncing like a tigress [38-39], awaits the approaching soldiers.

[40-44]   **W:** Lies in ambush, then retreats to prepare.

[44-59]   **A,X,Y,Z:** Resigned, dutiful soldiers appear, their endless march crossing **W**'s path.[

[52-67]   **W:** After a moment of weakness her resolve prevails, she charges after the soldiers.

[68-85]   **W:** Desperate, almost deranged, her inner conflict continues.

[86-93]   **A,X,Y,Z:** Appear again.

[86-89]   **W:** Utterly spent, she drags herself out of the soldiers' path.

[90-94]   **W:** Handling the scarf like a weapon, and with desperate determination she rushes at the last soldier, **Z,** and strangles him.

[94-125]   **D:** Appears. He marshals the death of **Z,** and approaches **W** who is forced to follow in his stride.
W: Courageously she accepts her destiny.
A,Y,X: As though summoned they surround **W,** then line up to form a firing squad.

[124-129] **W:** Prepares to die.

[126-130] **D:** Commands the execution.

[130-138] **W:** She sinks to the ground beseeching **D** to be received with mercy.

[131-141] **D:** Coldly ignores **W**'s plea, while symbolically sheathing his sword and asserting his omnipotent power.

Scene 6: The Brothel

Synopsis:
A tavern run by the Profiteer. The scene is in full swing to a bawdy waltz, soldiers and women are having a good time. The Profiteer sells the Young Girl to one man after another. Recognising the Young Girl's pitiful state, the Old Soldier treats her with consideration - she responds trustingly, but is suddenly confronted by Death.

Rehearsal Notes:
The waltz is heavy and vulgar. All should be careful not to bounce off the last beat of the measure. Young Girl with partners: the man leads, she only reacts and must never anticipate the beginning of a new phrase.

Breakdown of Scene:

[1-32] **All except P,G:** The 'rocking' motif is a high energy routine with an outgoing focus to attract attention. **Z,A,B,O** are 'in line' behind an imaginary door.
P is in control, after a brief scrimmage with one of the women, **K**, [4-8], he stalks **G**. He frightens her, grabs her and sends her to dance with a customer, **Z**. Gleefully, he then dances a circular path and places himself as 'watch dog'.
G: Trapped, she stands unhappily until she is forced to dance.

[33-48] **K,L,R,Y,U,N,X:** Twist round to watch **G**'s helplessness.
Z: Dances with **G** politely, he sweeps her off her feet, but his attempted embrace fails and he leaves her for another woman, **K**.
G: Weakly complies while trying to keep her distance.
P: Impatiently he stops the duet [48].

[49-64] **K,L,R,Y,U,N,X:** Back to the routine.
G: Runs away from **Z** but unable to escape, she again finds herself in **P**'s power.
P: Watching **G** trying to flee, he traps her, flings her to another 'suitor', **A**, and forces her to dance with him.

[65-80] **Z,K,L,R,Y,U,N,X:** Twist round to watch again.
A: Clumsily takes his turn, forcing **G** into his tight step [73-77]. He loses her and jumps to another woman, **U.**
G: Petrified and rigid with fear, she obeys; but when she succeeds in freeing herself from **A's** grip she finds her escape blocked by another man, **B.**
P: Takes a stroll, checking his customers and bowing to all sides.

[81-96] **Z,K,L,R,Y,U,N,X,A:** The rocking motif is resumed with increased energy.
B: Barring **G's** way, he catches her and throws her across his shoulder. As she collapses to the floor, he brutally pulls her into a tight clutch and forcefully tries to kiss her. Finally, he whirls her through the air and abandons her.
G: Cruelly victimised by **B,** she no longer has the strength to resist or escape.
P: Stands aloof, biding his time [81-88]. He begins to get impatient, suddenly stops the turbulent scene [96] and sends all the couples 'upstairs'.

[97-113] **All except P,G,O:** Take partners and leave with a bawdy two-step waltz.
P: Watches the couples leave, then follows, relishing the certitude of 'good business'. On his way out he catches sight of a remaining 'customer', **O,** and bows to him sarcastically as he leaves.
G: Alone in her misery, she sinks to the floor.
O: Waits patiently, then eagerly approaches his helpless victim, **G.**

[113-148] While **P** backs out, chuckling and bowing, the whole atmosphere changes to bleak emptiness.
O: Carefully pulls **G** up from the floor. Wondering who she might be, he begins to cradle her, but she slips from his arms. Controlling his desire to possess her, he treats her gently.
G: Weak and bewildered she allows herself to be taken into **O's** arms, but her fear returns and she backs away until, realising his considerate attitude she trustingly returns to him.

[149-156] **O,G:** Passionately embrace and their brief separation seems to contain the promise of return.

[157-165] **O,G:** Entirely oblivious of **D** entering [157], they trustingly expect to be reunited.

[166-211] **O:** Drifts past **G,** and **D** takes his place, inviting **G** to dance.
G: Powerless she hesitatingly obeys and becomes **D's** victim.
D: He leads her majestically then suddenly changes [173], becoming a violent seducer, vexatious ring master, tyrant. But finally, as the fatherly comforter he takes her gently in his arms, cradles her and lays her to eternal rest.

Scene 7: **The Aftermath**

Synopsis:
The Old Soldier is still on duty, keeping watch, Death overpowers him and seizes the flag. The processional march of Death begins. The Standard Bearer, unaware, bursts in on the scene with his battle cry, but he too must join the victims and follow Death. The Profiteer, alone, is confronted by Death. After a futile struggle he is tossed aside and disappears. Death, reigns omnipotent.

Rehearsal Notes:
All shades (**O,W,M,Y,G,A,X,Z**) work for a weightless, void quality throughout and a distinct, light staccato for [28-35].

Breakdown of Scene:

[3-6] **O:** Dutifully keeping watch, is quite unconscious of the shadow of **D.**

[7-10] The presence of **D** increases and looms gigantically over **O.** Hypnotised by **D**'s commanding gaze [9 ct.3] **O** helplessly surrenders.

[11] **D:** Seizes the flag.

[12-17] **D:** The triumphant march begins.

[22-27] **D:** Now leads the full procession.

[28-42] At **D**'s will the victims rotate like clockwork then all are mown down to the ground [36] and **D** establishes himself as sole vanquisher [42].

[43-46] **B** bursts in on the scene, repeating his confident call to arms.

[47] **D** directs his attention towards **B.**

[48-58] **B** bewildered, questioning, he tries to resist and fight the unknown power. Suddenly recognising **D** [54 ct.3], he rushes to attack but is caught in mid-action [58 ct.2'and''a'].

[59-71] **O,W,M,Y,G,A,X,Z:** At **D**'s command the shades slowly rise, advance and like a huge wave, they smother **B** and absorb him into their file.

[72] **D:** Again at the head of the procession, leads onwards.

[81-85] **P:** Alone, overcurious and apprehensive is trailing the procession. Suddenly he is confronted by **D** [85].

[85] **D:** Approaches menacingly.

[85-88] **P:** Trapped, recoiling helplessly like a hypnotised rat.

[89-108] **P:** Panic-stricken, desperate, he attempts futilely to combat **D**. The menace of **D** increases.

[109-111] **P:** Incapable of escape, musters his last strength to attack but succumbs feebly.

[113-133] The Dance of Death resumes its course.

Scene 8: **The Gentlemen in Black**

Synopsis:
The Gentlemen reappear with a pistol shot. After elaborate gestures of reconciliation they return to the Table and resume their discussions. These are exactly as before.

Rehearsal Notes:
[48-54] are performed with full energy as in Scene 1, and with sharp, but silent accents, despite the change in the mood of the Tango.

Breakdown of Scene:

[141-144] Silent 'invisible' steps.

[1-4] The Gentlemen appear with the shot.

[5-20] Deftly they return their pistols to their pockets, then politely bow, advance towards one another and take partners for a stately promenade back to the table.

[21-50] An eerie quality pervades the never-ending conference routine.

(van Leeuwen)

Jean Cébron; Kurt Jooss, Pina Bausch, Erika Fabry, Folkwangschule 1963

SELECTED PHOTOGRAPHS FROM
THE GREEN TABLE
(COVERING 63 YEARS OF PRODUCTION)

For the full list of Companies, Dancers, Dates and Photographers, please see pages 67-69.
For all photographs marked with *, please see Comments, page 70.

1. Meas. 11, The Gentlemen in Black

2. Meas. 19-20, The Gentlemen in Black

3. Meas. 32, The Gentlemen in Black

4. Meas. 50, The Gentlemen in Black

5. Meas. 94, The Gentlemen in Black

6. Meas. 1, ct. 3, Death

7. Meas. 4, ct. 2, Death

8. Meas. 65, ct. 3, Standard Bearer

9. Meas. 102, ct. 1, Standard Bearer, Soldiers*

10. Meas. 109, Young Soldier, Young Girl*

11. Meas. 125, Mother, Old Soldier, Woman

12. Meas. 1, ct. 1, Standard Bearer, Soldiers*

13. Meas. 12, ct. 2, Standard Bearer, Soldiers

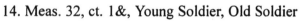

14. Meas. 32, ct. 1&, Young Soldier, Old Soldier

15. Meas. 34, ct. 4, Young Soldier, Old Soldier

16. Meas. 37, ct. 6&, Old Soldier, Young Soldier

17. Meas. 54, ct. 2, Death, Soldiers*

18. Meas. 86, ct. 4, Profiteer, Young Soldier

19. Meas. 96, ct. 2, Profiteer

20. Meas. 3, ct. 4, Mother, Young Girl, Women

21. Meas. 38, ct. 4, Mother, Death*

22. Meas. 41, ct. 2, Death, Mother

23. Meas. 44, ct. 4, Profiteer, Young Girl*

24. Meas. 46, ct. 7, Young Girl, Profiteer

25. Meas. 20, Woman   26. Meas. 38, ct. 2&, Woman

27. Meas. 59, ct. 6, Woman

28. Meas. 94, ct. 1, Woman, Soldier*

29. Meas. 98, Woman, Death

30. Meas. 2, ct. 3, Women, Soldiers

31. Meas. 16, Young Girl, Profiteer   32. Meas. 115, Old Soldier, Young Girl

33. Meas. 126, Old Soldier, Young Girl

34. Meas. 198, Death, Young Girl

35. Meas. 211, ct. 3, Death, Young Girl

36. Meas. 8, ct. 3, Death, Old Soldier*

37. Meas. 12, Old Soldier, Death*

38. Meas. 26, Mother, Woman, Death

39. Meas. 42, ct. 1, Death, Shadows*

40. Meas. 47, ct. 2, Standard Bearer

41. Meas. 59, ct. 1, Standard Bearer, Death

42. Meas. 65, ct. 5, Death, Standard Bearer, Shadows

43. Meas. 106, Profiteer, Death

44. Meas. 107, Death, Profiteer

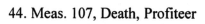

Photo	Company	Dancers	Photographer	Year

Scene 1: The Gentlemen in Black

1.	Folkwangballett Essen		W.D.R. Düsseldorf	1963
2.	Folkwang Tanzbühne Essen		Renger-Patzsch Essen	1932
3.	Birmingham Royal Ballet		Spatt London	1992
4.	Het Nationale Ballet Amsterdam		Fatauros Amsterdam	1984
5.	Birmingham Royal Ballet		Spatt London	1992

Scene 2: The Dance of Death and Farewells

6.	Essener Ballett	Holder (Guest)	Wenzel Essen	1985
7.	Staatsoper Dresden	Hartmann	Döring Dresden	1979
8.	Birmingham Royal Ballet	Bailey	Spatt London	1992
9.	Folkwangballett Essen	Diekamp, Thorpe, Pop, Patsalas	Crickmay London	1966
10.	Folkwangballett Essen	Röhm, Schwerdtfeger	W.D.R. Düsseldorf	1963
11.	Staatsoper Dresden		Döring Dresden	1979

Scene 3: The Battle

12.	Folkwangballett Essen	Patsalas, Diekamp	Crickmay London	1966
13.	Staatsoper Dresden		Döring Dresden	1979
14.	Ballet du Rhin Strasbourg	Boruel, Imbert	Philippe Paris	1991

Photo	Company	Dancers	Photographer	Year
15.	Folkwang Tanzbühne Essen	Rosen, Pecht	Renger-Patzsch Essen	1932
16.	Het Nationale Ballet Amsterdam	Schumann, Knill	van Leeuwen Amsterdam	1965
17.	Folkwang Tanztheater Essen	Alexander	Particam Pictures Amsterdam	1951
18.	Het Nationale Ballet Amsterdam	Fisher	Regeling Amsterdam	1971
19.	Deutsche Oper Berlin	Gelvan	Kranich Berlin	1977

Scene 4: The Refugees

20.	Staatsoper Dresden		Döring Dresden	1979
21.	Folkwang Tanztheater Essen	Tona, Alexander	Enkelmann Deutsches Tanzarchiv Köln	1951
22.	Het Nationale Ballet Amsterdam	Bell, Davis	Jansen Hilversum	1995
23.	Folkwang Tanztheater Essen	Unanue, de Mosa	Boje Hamburg	1951
24.	Staatsoper Dresden	Schwab, Hermann	Döring Dresden	1979

Scene 5: The Partisan

25.	Ballet van Vlaanderen Antwerpen	Wilderijck	Schellens Antwerpen	1973
26.	Het Nationale Ballet Amsterdam	Vondersaar	Fatauros Amsterdam	1978
27.	Birmingham Royal Ballet	Waldie	Spatt London	1992
28.	Folkwang Tanzbühne Essen	Kahl, Rosen	Renger-Patzsch Essen	1932
29.	Het Nationale Ballet Amsterdam	Valentine. Bell	van Duin Amsterdam	1995

Photo	Company	Dancers	Photographer	Year

Scene 6: The Brothel

Photo	Company	Dancers	Photographer	Year
30.	Cleveland Ballet		Edwards Cleveland	1979
31.	Deutsche Oper Berlin	Holz, Gelvan	Buhs Berlin	1983
32.	Het Nationale Ballet Amsterdam	Jürriens, Paire	Regeling Amsterdam	1971
33.	Ballet du Rhin Strasbourg	Amm, Imbert	Philippe Paris	1991
34.	Het Nationale Ballet Amsterdam	Jürriens, Schnabel	Fatauros Amsterdam	1984
35.	Het Nationale Ballet Amsterdam	Bell, Lord	Spatt London	1995

Scene 7: The Aftermath

Photo	Company	Dancers	Photographer	Year
36.	Tanz Forum Köln	Jaquin, Hall	Weigelt Köln	1982
37.	Folkwang Tanzbühne Essen	Pescht, Jooss	Lipnitzki Paris	1932
38.	Het Nationale Ballet Amsterdam	Langenstraat, Vondersaar, Sinceretti	Fatauros Amsterdam	1978
39.	Folkwang Tanztheater Essen	Alexander	Giessner München	1951
40.	Staatsoper Dresden	Binke	Döring Dresden	1979
41.	Het Nationale Ballet Amsterdam	Johansen, Bell	Jansen Hilversum	1995
42.	Het Nationale Ballet Amsterdam	Lord, Bell, Johansen, Pronk, Davis	van Duin Amsterdam	1995
43.	Het Nationale Ballet Amsterdam	Ebelaar, Sinceretti	Fatauros Amsterdam	1978
44.	Het National Ballet Amsterdam	Bell, Barat	Jansen Hilversum	1995

Comments

The following comments are for all photographs marked *

9.   Soldiers, lengthen left arm.

10.   Young Soldier, wear chin strap

12.   Standard Bearer, left leg forward.
            Soldier A, parallel *pas de chat,* curl torso and arms.

17.   Standard Bearer, reverse arms.
            Soldier A, face opposite direction.

21.   Young Girl, tight, curled kneel, wear head scarf.

23.   Young Girl, wear head scarf.

28.   Woman, right leg *en l'air.*

36.   Death, Old Soldier, full *en face.*

37.   Old Soldier, should not hold flag.

39.   Shadows, lie in accurate semicircle, see floor plan.

APPENDIX A

Choreographic Works by Kurt Jooss

This list does not include the many regular Opera or Operetta productions. Also not listed are Solo Recital Dances and various works choreographed for school performances.

Title	Music	Design	Date	Company	Place
Persisches Ballett	Wellesz	Heckroth	July 1924	Neue Tanzbühne	Donaueschinger Musiktage
Tanz-Suite*	Toch	Heckroth	1924	Neue Tanzbühne	Theater der Stadt Münster
Der Dämon	Hindemith	Heckroth	March 1925	Neue Tanzbühne	Theater der Stadt Münster
Die Brautfahrt*	Rameau, Couperin	Heckroth	May 1925	Neue Tanzbühne	Theater der Stadt Münster
Groteske*	-	Heckroth	1925	Neue Tanzbühne	Theater der Stadt Münster
Larven*	Jooss (percussion)	Leeder	October 1925	Neue Tanzbühne	Theater der Stadt Münster
Tragödie*	Cohen	Heckroth	May 1926	Neue Tanzbühne	Theater der Stadt Münster
Kaschemme*	Cohen	Heckroth	October 1926	Neue Tanzbühne	Theater der Stadt Münster
Seltsames Septett*	-	Leeder	1928	Folkwang-Tanztheater-Studio	
Drosselbart*	Mozart	Heckroth	March 1929	Folkwang-Tanztheater-Studio	
Zimmer Nr. 13*	Cohen	Heckroth	October 1929	Folkwang-Tanztheater-Studio	

Title	Music	Design	Date	Company	Place
Suite 1929*	Cohen	Heckroth	October 1929	Folkwang-Tanztheater-Studio	Opernhaus Essen
Pavane auf den Tod einer Infantin/Pavane on the Death of an Infanta*	Ravel	Leeder	October 1929	Folkwang-Tanztheater-Studio	Folkwang Museum
Petrouchka	Strawinsky	Heckroth	February 1930	Folkwang-Tanztheater-Studio	Opernhaus Essen
Gaukelei	Cohen	Haerdtlein	2.5.1930	Folkwang-Tanztheater-Studio	Opernhaus Essen
Le Bal	Rieti	Heckroth	November 1930	Folkwang Tanzbühne Essen	Opernhaus Essen
Polowetzer Tänze	Borodin	Heckroth	November 1930	Folkwang Tanzbühne Essen	Opernhaus Essen
Coppélia	Delibes	Heckroth	25.2.1931	Folkwang Tanzbühne Essen	Opernhaus Essen
Die Geschichte vom Soldaten	Strawinsky	Heckroth	1931	Folkwang Tanzbühne Essen	Opernhaus Essen
Der verlorene Sohn/The Prodigal Son	Prokofjew	Heckroth	28.5.1931	Folkwang Tanzbühne Essen	Opernhaus Essen
Pulcinella	Strawinsky	Heckroth	April 1932	Folkwang Tanzbühne Essen	Opernhaus Essen
Der Grüne Tisch/The Green Table*	Cohen	Heckroth	3.7.1932	Folkwang Tanzbühne Essen	Théâtre des Champs-Elysées, Paris
Grosstadt von Heute/Big City*	Tansman	Heckroth	21.11.1932	Folkwang Tanzbühne Essen	Opernhaus Köln
Ein Ball in Alt-Wien/A Ball in Old Vienna*	Lanner (arr. Cohen)	Siimola	21.11.1932	Folkwang Tanzbühne Essen	Opernhaus Köln
Seven Heroes/Die sieben Schwaben*	Purcell (arr. Cohen)	Heckroth	1.10.1933	Ballets Jooss	Schouwburg Maastricht, Niederlande
The Prodigal Son/Der verlorene Sohn*	Cohen	Heckroth	6.10.1933	Ballets Jooss	Stadschouwburg, Amsterdam
Persephone	Strawinsky	Barsacq	30.4.1934	Ida Rubinstein	Opéra. Paris
Big City/Grosstadt*	Tansman	Heckroth	1935	Ballets Jooss	Dartington Hall

Title	Music	Design	Date	Company	Place
Ballade*	Colman	Heckroth	23.9.1935	Ballets Jooss	Opera House, Manchester
The Mirror/Der Spiegel*	Cohen	Heckroth	28.9.1935	Ballets Jooss	Opera House, Manchester
Johann Strauss, To-night!*	Strauss (arr. Cohen)	Kirsta	21.10.1935	Ballets Jooss	Gaiety Theatre, London
Seven Heroes/Die sieben Schwaben*	Purcell (arr. Cohen)	Heckroth	9.10.1937	Ballets Jooss	Lyric Theatre, Baltimore, USA
A Spring Tale/Die Brautfahrt*	Cohen	Heckroth	8.2.1939	Ballets Jooss	New Theatre, Oxford
Chronica*	Goldschmidt	Bouchêne	14.2.1939	Ballets Jooss	Arts Theatre, Cambridge
The Prodigal Son/Der verlorene Sohn*	Cohen	Bouchêne	October 1939	Ballets Jooss	Prince's Theatre, Bristol
Company at the Manor*	Beethoven (arr. Cook)	Zinkeisen	15.2.1943	Ballets Jooss	Arts Theatre, Cambridge
Pandora*	Gerhard	Heckroth	26.1.1944	Ballets Jooss	Arts Theatre, Cambridge
Juventud*	Händel	Bouchêne	1948	Ballet del Instituto Musical	Santiago de Chile
Dithyrambus*	Händel	Bouchêne	1951	Folkwang Tanztheater/Ballets Jooss	Opernhaus Essen
Colombinade*	Strauss/Montijn	Gliese	1951	Folkwang Tanztheater/Ballets Jooss	Opernhaus Essen
Weg im Nebel/Journey in the Fog*	Montijn	Pudlich	1952	Folkwang Tanztheater/Ballets Jooss	Opernhaus Essen
Nachtzug/Night Train*	Tansman	Pudlich	1952	Folkwang Tanztheater/Ballets Jooss	Opernhaus Essen
Persephone	Strawinsky	Hartmann	16.4.1955		Opernhaus Düsseldorf

Title	Music	Design	Date	Company	Place
Der verlorene Sohn/ The Prodigal Son	Cohen	Hartmann	23.5.1956		Opernhaus Düsseldorf
Catulli Carmina	Orff	Hartmann	22.10.1956		Opernhaus Düsseldorf
Die Feenkönigin/ The Fairy Queen	Purcell	Ponnelle	1959	Direction: Schumacher	Schwetzinger Festspiele (Opernhaus Essen)
Castor und Pollux	Rameau	Ponnelle	1962	Direction: Schumacher	Schwetzinger Festspiele (Opernhaus Essen)
Persephone	Strawinsky	Heckroth	7.2.1965	Folkwangballett	Opernhaus Essen
Der Nachmittag eines Fauns/Afternoon of a Faun	Debussy	Markard	8.3.1965		Leverkusen
Phasen/Phases*	Sehlbach	Markard	1966	Folkwangballett	Stadthalle Mülheim
Dido und Äneas Epilog*	Purcell	Grübler	1966	Direction: Schumacher	Schwetzinger Festspiele (Opernhaus Essen)
Rappresentazione di anima e di corpo	Cavalieri	Colosanti/ Moore	1968	Direction: Graf	Salzburger Festspiele
Belsazar	Händel	Corrodi	March 1972	Direction: Graf	Grand Théâtre Genève
Acis und Galathea	Händel	Colosanti/ Moore	1972	Direction: Graf	Salzburger Festspiele

*   Libretto Jooss
/   This list gives precedence to the original title.

APPENDIX B

Short Biographies

Frederic Alexander Cohen 1904-1967

Born in Bonn, Germany. Attended the music conservatories of Leipzig and Cologne and the University of Bonn.

1924-1933 Opera director, composer and conductor at the Municipal Theatres of Münster, Würzburg and Essen.

1926 Composes his first ballet, *Tragödie*, for Kurt Jooss in Münster.

1927 Marries Elsa Kahl, dancer and later leading member of Ballets Jooss.

1932-1942 Musical director and pianist with Ballets Jooss.

1933 Leaves Germany with Ballets Jooss.

1942 Following the dissolution of Ballets Jooss in the USA, Cohen takes up opera direction again. Partly free lance, then for the Juilliard Opera Theatre, he directs over 33 productions including many American premieres.

1946 Founding director of the Juilliard Opera Studio.

Between 1926 and 1939 Cohen composes 10 ballets including *The Green Table* in close collaboration with Kurt Jooss, and arranges further ballet scores for Jooss with music by Mozart, Purcell, Lanner, Strauss and others.

Hein Heckroth 1901-1970

Born in Giessen, Germany, and studied painting at the Städel Schule - the Art Academy in Frankfurt/Main.

1924-1927 Stage designer at the Municipal Theatre Münster, also the beginning of his long collaboration with Kurt Jooss.

1927 Stage designer at the Municipal Theatre Essen, also teaches stage design at the Folkwangschule.

1932 Awarded the Kuntpreis Rheinische Sezession.

1933 Leaves Germany together with Ballets Jooss. On tour and later in Southern England, their new home, Heckroth designs almost all the new productions for Ballets Jooss. He continues to paint and also designs many productions for opera and drama. During the war Heckroth is interned for over a year; after his release he moves to London.

1944 Begins to work extensively for films.

For *The Red Shoes* (1948) and *The Tales of Hoffmann* (1951) he is awarded three Oscars.

1956 Moves to Frankfurt on Main, Germany, and works as leading stage designer at the Opera. He continues painting and designs internationally for all fields of the theatre, films and television.

Aino Siimola 1901-1971

Born in Narva in Russian Estonia. Educated at the school of Maria Fedorovna (Mother of the Tzarina) where she received regular instruction in dancing.

1921 Travels to Germany to work with Rudolf von Laban. After studying with him in Stuttgart she joins the Tanzbühne Laban.

1924-1932 Soloist member of the dance companies at the Municipal Theatres of Münster and Essen directed by Kurt Jooss, and subsequently member of the Folkwang Tanztheater.

1929 Marriage to Kurt Jooss. Aino Jooss-Siimola is Kurt Jooss' artistic partner and close collaborator. Together they direct the Folkwang Tanztheater and later Ballets Jooss.

1932 Ill health obliges her to leave the stage. She becomes Kurt Jooss' choreographic assistant, from now on contributing greatly to the artistic success of his work.

1933 Kurt and Aino Jooss leave Germany as political refugees. They live in England for 17 years and return to Germany in 1949.

Despite her ill health Aino Jooss continues to work professionally until the mid-sixties.

(Gray)   (Anthony)   (Pesci)

Hein Heckroth 1964   Aino Siimola 1933   F.A.Cohen 1935

APPENDIX C

International Productions of *The Green Table*

Company	Date
Bayerische Staatsoper, Munich	May 1964
Het Nationale Ballet, Amsterdam	July 1965
City Center Joffrey Ballet, New York	March 1967
Cullberg Baletten, Stockholm	October 1968
Het Nationale Ballet, Amsterdam (2nd prod.)	April 1971
Tanz-Forum, Köln	December 1971
Teatr Wielki, Lodz	March 1972
Northern Dance Theatre, Manchester	May 1973
Ballet van Vlaanderen, Antwerpen	November 1973
Städtische Bühnen, Wuppertal	January 1974
Deutsche Oper am Rhein, Düsseldorf	July 1974
Royal Winnipeg Ballet	November 1974
CAPAB, Cape Town	September 1975
Batsheva Dance Company, Tel Aviv	November 1975
City Center Joffrey Ballet, New York (2nd prod.)	March 1976
José Limón Dance Company, New York	April 1977
Star Dancers Ballet, Tokyo	September 1977
Deutsche Oper, Berlin	December 1977
Malmö Stadstheatern	March 1978
Opernhaus, Zürich	May 1978
Het Nationale Ballet, Amsterdam (3rd prod.)	December 1978
Cleveland Ballet	April 1979
Staatstheater, Dresden	November 1979
The Joffrey Ballet, New York (3rd prod.)	May 1981
Hartford Ballet	August 1981
Teatro Regio, Torino	March 1982
Tanz-Forum, Köln (2nd prod.)	July 1982
Suomen Kansallisbaletti, Helsinki	November 1982
Deutsche Oper, Berlin (2nd prod.)	February 1983
Ballet de l'Opéra de Lyon	November 1983
Het Nationale Ballet, Amsterdam (4th prod.)	February 1984
Companhia Nacional de Bailado, Lisboa	May 1984
Oakland Ballet	September 1984
Bühnen der Stadt, Essen	March 1985
Louisville Ballet	January 1986
Companhia Nacional de Bailado, Lisboa (2nd prod.)	February 1987
Ballet dell L'Arena, Verona	October 1987
Komische Oper, Berlin	January 1988
Staatstheater am Gärtnerplatz, Munich	February 1989
Deutsche Oper, Berlin (3rd prod.)	September 1989

Company	Date
Ballet Nacional Chileno, Santiago	October 1989
Richmond Ballet	February 1990
The Joffrey Ballet, New York (4th prod.)	May 1990
Ballet du Rhin, Strasbourg	January 1991
Les Grands Ballets Canadiens, Montreal	May 1991
Het Nationale Ballet, Amsterdam (5th prod.)	November 1991
Birmingham Royal Ballet	October 1992
Star Dancers Ballet, Tokyo (2nd prod.)	January 1993
Richmond Ballet (2nd prod.)	February 1993
Star Dancers Ballet, Tokyo (3rd prod.)	January 1994
Landestheater, Dessau	February 1994
Ballett im Aalto, Essen (2nd prod.)	November 1994
Deutsche Oper, Berlin (4th prod.)	June 1995
Het Nationale Ballet, Amsterdam (6th prod.)	September 1995
Oakland Ballet (2nd prod.)	November 1995
Les Grands Ballets Canadiens, Montreal (2nd prod.)	March 1996
Stadttheater, Bern	October 1996
The Joffrey Ballet of Chicago (5th prod.)	March 1998
Ballet Arizona, Phoenix	September 1998
Tulsa Ballet	February 1999
Les Grands Ballets Canadiens, Montreal (3rd prod.)	March 2000
SNG Opera in Balet Ljubljana	April 2000
Theater Krefeld Mönchengladbach	March 2001
Ballet du Rhin, Strasbourg (2nd prod.)	September 2001
Aalto Ballett Theater, Essen (3rd prod.)	November 2001

APPENDIX D

Reference Materials

Bibliography

Coton, A.V. *The New Ballet, Kurt Jooss and his work.* London: Denis Dobson, 1946.

Häger, B. "Kurt Jooss". In *International Encyclopedia of Dance* (S.J. Cohen, Ed.). Vol. 3, (p.624-631). Oxford: Oxford University Press, 1998.

Markard, A. "Kurt Jooss and his work". *Ballet Review,* Vol. X, No. 1, Spring, pp.15-67: 1982.

Markard, A. & Markard, H. *Jooss: Dokumentation von Anna und Hermann Markard.* Köln: Ballett-Bühnen-Verlag, 1985.

Partsch-Bergsohn, I. *Modern Dance in Germany and the United States.* Choreography and Dance Studies, Vol. 5. London: Harwood Academic Publishers, 1994.

Pipers Enzyklopädie des Musiktheaters, Vol. 3, Munich/Zurich: 1989.

Oral History, Dance Collection, Library of the Performing Arts, Lincoln Center, New York.

Venezia Danza Europa '81. *Jooss Catalogue.* Venice: Masillio Editori, 1981.

Walther, S.K., (Ed.). *The Dance Theatre of Kurt Jooss.* Choreography and Dance Journal, Vol. 3, Part 2. London: Harwood Academic Publishers, 1993.

Walther, S.K. *The Dance of Death - Kurt Jooss and the Weimar Years.* Choreography and Dance Studies, Vol. 7. London: Harwood Academic Publishers, 1994.

Dissertations:

Lidbury, C., Ph.D., University of Birmingham, 1992: *Kurt Jooss and The Green Table - the man and his masterpiece.*

Walther, S.K., Ph.D., New York University, 1990: *The Form of Content: The Dance Drama of Kurt Jooss.*

Annotated Videography

1963   WDR Köln
Danced by The Folkwangballett
Directed by Truck Branss
Black/White
Adaptation for a studio production using a cyclorama.
Special effects: Frequent large shadows.
Remarks: The music is partially not synchronised with the choreography.

1966   BBC London
Danced by The Folkwangballett
Directed by Peter Wright
Black/White
Filmed in the studio using a cyclorama.
Special effects: The use of smoke in some scenes.
Remarks: Some choreographic adjustments for the TV screen and unusual camera positions. Difficult conditions due to a slippery concrete floor.

1970   Sveriges Radio Stockholm
Danced by The Cullberg Ballet
Directed by Birgit Cullberg
Colour
Filmed in the studio.
Special effects: Blue Box technique with specially designed projected décor.
Remarks: Some choreographic adjustments for the TV screen.

1979   NHK Tokyo
Danced by Star Dancers Ballet
Directed by Motoko Sakaguchi
Colour
Filmed on stage.
Special effects: Some double images.
Remarks: A straight documentary of the original theatre production. Cameras 'front of house' only.

1982   EBC New York
Danced by The Joffrey Ballet
Directed by Emile Ardolino
Colour
Studio production using a specially constructed stage with black wings to emulate the original production.
Special effects: None.
Remarks: Meticulously 'framed' pictures also preserving almost 100% of the choreography.

1996 NPS Hilversum
Danced by The National Ballet, Amsterdam
Directed by Jellie Dekker
Colour - High Definition 16x9
Studio production using a specially constructed stage with black wings to emulate the original production.
Special effects: None.
Remarks: Straight documentary, cameras 'front of house' only.

There is no definitive film or video of *The Green Table*. The films made for television are not generally available. In some cases however they can be found in research libraries.

Exhibitions

Kurt Jooss and his work

1981   Venezia Danza Europa '81, Teatro Fenice, Venice

1982   Public Library of the Performing Arts, Lincoln Center, New York

1985   Festival Folkwang '85, Museum Folkwang, Essen

1985   Akademie der Künste, Berlin

1986   Biennale Internationale de la Danse, Lyon

Materials

The two original Labanotation scores, all photographs (except page x - Part 1) and press materials are lodged at the Jooss Archive, Amsterdam.

APPENDIX E

Excerpts from the Press

It occurs to me that *The Green Table* is probably the most famous ballet made since Diaghilev's death. Although I am carried on the tide of reaction against the intellectual ballet of the twenties and thirties I can still admit that Jooss's work is one of the very best - a masterpiece of dance drama. Music, movement, production, lighting, all blend to produce a series of unforgettable pictures, the theatrical equivalent of Goya's "Diasters of War".

Richard Buckle in the Sunday Observer, April 26th 1953

The great ones of the repertory are *The Green Table* and *The Big City*. About *The Green Table* (dance-drama by Jooss; music by F.A. Cohen; costumes by Hein Heckroth), it only remains to say that it is still Jooss's masterpiece choreographically, still (unfortunately) topical, and is one of the most significant works in ballet history.

Clive Barnes in Dance and Dancers, 1953

What is it about Kurt Jooss' 35-year-old ballet *The Green Table* that makes it so peculiarly effective today? Topicality, of course. Yet this is only part of the issue. Perhaps more important still is the manner in which its very flexible dramatic style seems to make sense in today's theater.

In *The Green Table*, Mr. Jooss arrived at a form of theater of enormous suggestibility. It is a work where great stress is placed upon image and metaphor, and as a result it springs alive in the mind's eye. The happenings on stage are instantly reinforced by the tiny explosions of the imagination that Jooss' vivid imagery sets off, so that each dramatic note is vibrated into a poetic chord.

Clive Barnes in the New York Times, March 22nd 1967

The Green Table must be one of the most **shocking** ballets ever created, in the proper sense of the word, but its impact remains the same after repeated performances.

John Percival (ca. 1977)

If you are planning to see just one ballet this year, make sure it is the Joffrey Ballet's revival of Kurt Jooss's *The Green Table*.

Anna Kisselgoff in the New York Times, November 7th 1981

That war is not inescapable destiny but a conflict of interests, into which those who 'have' drag those who 'have not', was never more clearly shown on the dance stage than in the opening and closing scenes of *The Green Table*. The piece really is as good as its legendary reputation: it is **the** ballet of the twentieth century, not just because of its subject matter, a violent indictment of war. Its form also is unsurpassedly impressive: like a woodcut in which the artist's knife has been guided by a fondness and compassion for the figures it portrays.

Jochen Schmidt in Kultur heute in Deutschlandfunk, July 1982

Jooss' *The Green Table*, which closes the program, packs a universal message that transcends the passing of time and remains as potent as the day it was rendered in 1932: when the heads of state decide their egos are bigger than their brains, war breaks out and innocent people die.

Kathryn Greenaway in The Gazette, Montreal, May 5th 1991

The Green Table should be in the dance repertory of every country; it should be required study for diplomats, war profiteers, oil magnates, you name it. Actions speak louder than words and *The Green Table* speaks for us all, since no man is an island; the bell tolls for Us [sic] as loudly as it does for Them [sic], and maybe even louder.

Janet Sinclair in Dance and Dancers, July 1992

What keeps the ballet alive and freshly effective in the theatre, apart from its terrifying relevance to current European events, is the power of its dance imagery. Jooss was a true creator, and his metaphors still catch the imagination.

Nicholas Dromgoole in The Sunday Telegraph, October 25th 1992

The continued popularity of this ballet on stages all over the world proves the artistic validity of this indisputable classic and of its *cri de coeur* against the dangers that gave birth to the work and from whose grip mankind is not yet delivered.

Walter Sorrell in Choreography and Dance Journal, Volume 3, Part 2, 1993

The *tour de force* Dance Drama should be required viewing for every politician and diplomat from Washington to Belgrade and Kosovo.

Hedy Weiss in Chicago Sun Times, March 14th 1998

APPENDIX F

Production History and Performance Information

Production History

The Green Table is always produced and performed in the original version. The overall concept adheres to the original of 1932 in every detail. Over the years a number of minor adjustments and additions were made for practical reasons. Jooss, in the rôle of Death, danced the first performances wearing elaborate body make-up with the black harness. Later the make-up was replaced by painted body tights. Originally the stage was draped with black textured burlap, this was changed to black velour in 1933.

The masks were not originally designed on paper. By 1935 the first set had deteriorated and Willi Soucop, resident sculptor at Dartington Hall was commissioned to recreate the masks. Then in 1961 Hermann Markard, in consultation with Jooss redesigned a slightly modified version - precise copies of these masks are now made for all productions. Markard also revised the lighting, together with Jooss; this lighting design is an integral part of all productions.

Performance Information

For any form of performance, a performance licence must be negotiated with the Jooss Estate. The Jooss Estate has the sole right to designate the production team and to furnish the designs, musical score and all production details.

The Green Table requires a technically well-equipped company capable of handling a demanding, complex production.

The costumes, the black velour set and the lighting design are integral to the production.

The eight scenes are separated by blackouts of approximately 15 seconds. There are over 40 accurately timed light cues. The original two piano score should be played live, the grand pianos are placed in the pit with a view of the stage floor.

The Green Table is 35 minutes long and must always be presented as the last work on any program.

For permission to produce the ballet contact:
Anna Markard/The Jooss Estate
Keizersgracht 73
1015 CE Amsterdam
The Netherlands

APPENDIX G

The Rehearsal Music

Reduction for one piano arranged by W. Hilsley from the original score.
Edited for publication by Jonathan Still.

INTRODUCTION

F. A. Cohen 1904 - 1967

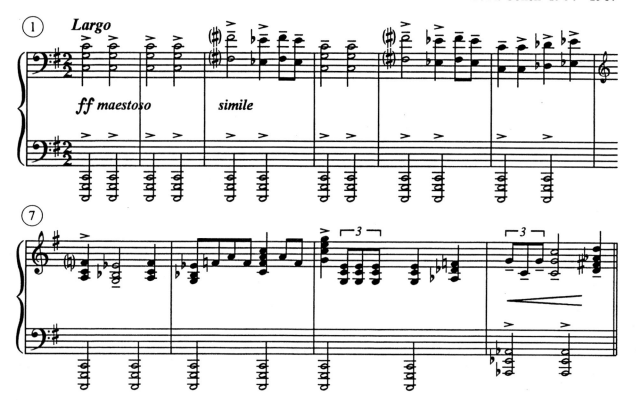

SCENE 1:

THE GENTLEMEN IN BLACK

SCENE 2:
THE DANCE OF DEATH AND FAREWELLS

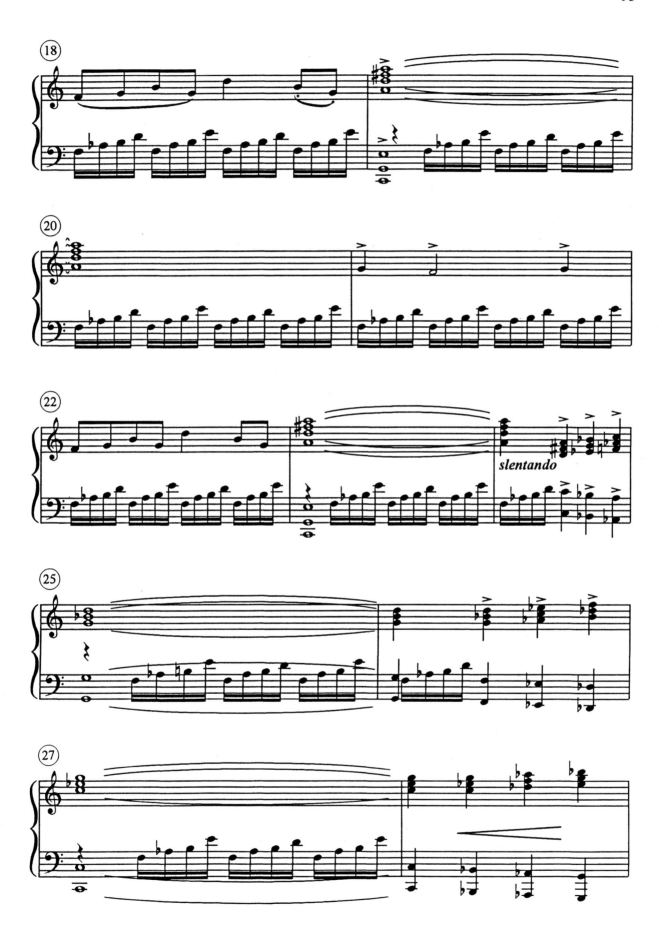

slentando

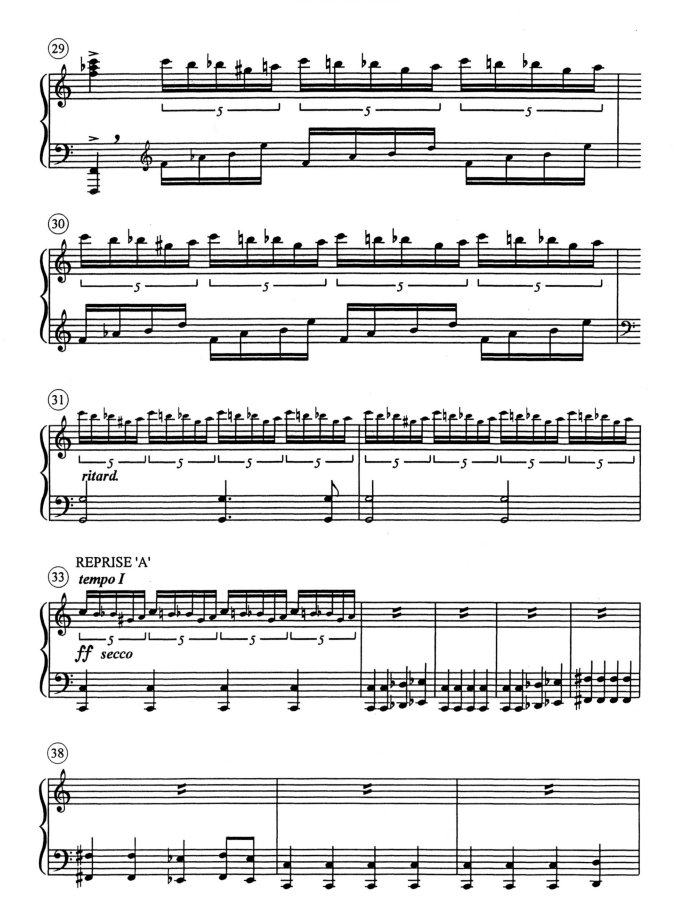

SCENE 3:
THE BATTLE

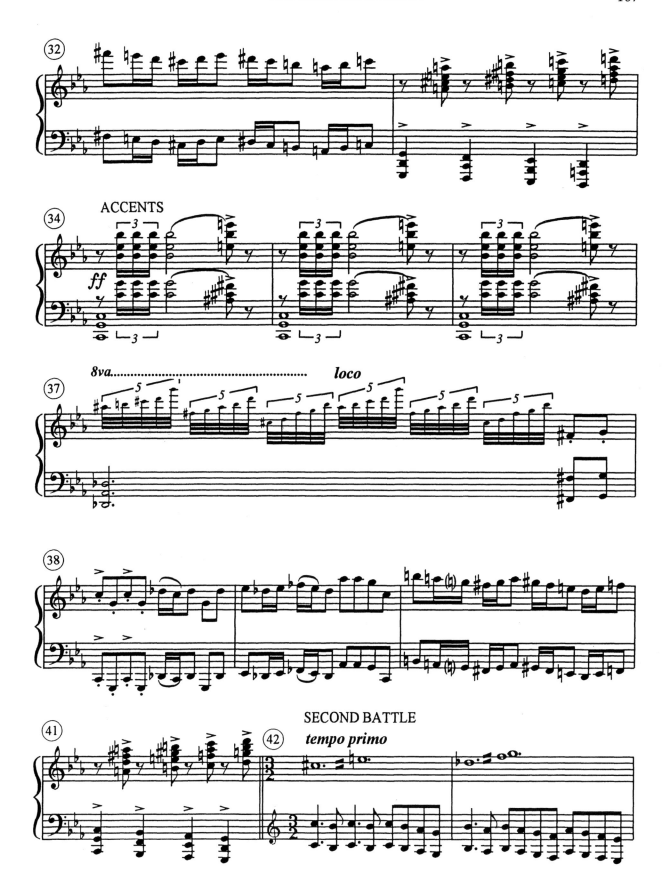

SCENE 4:
THE REFUGEES

SCENE 5:
THE PARTISAN

DEATH WALKS

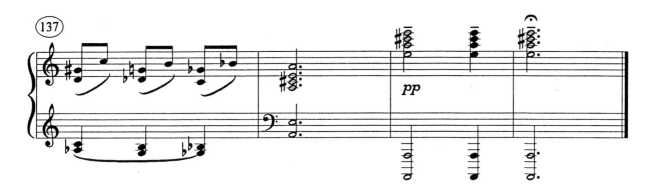

SCENE 6:
THE BROTHEL

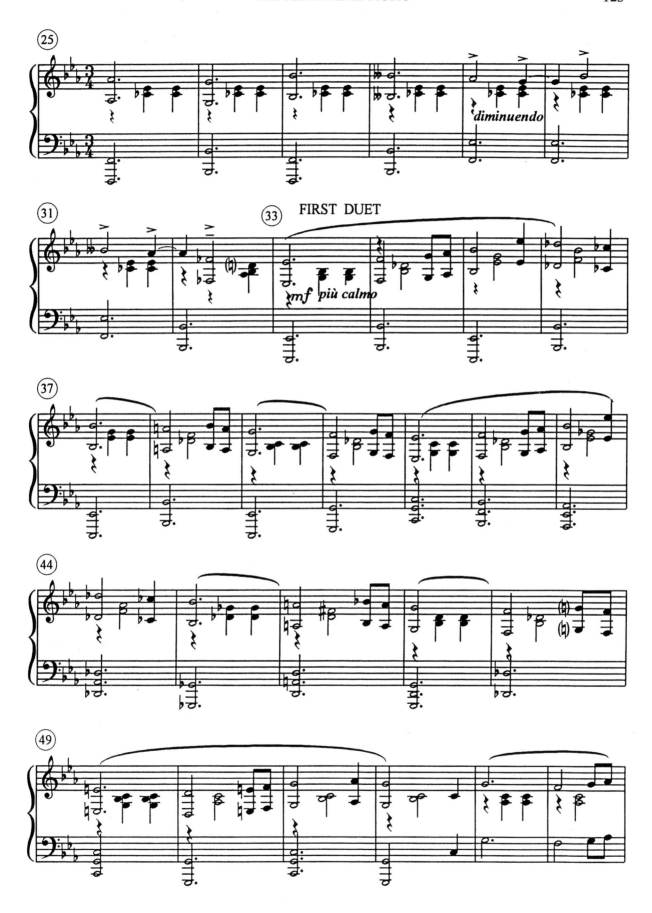

SCENE 7:

THE AFTERMATH

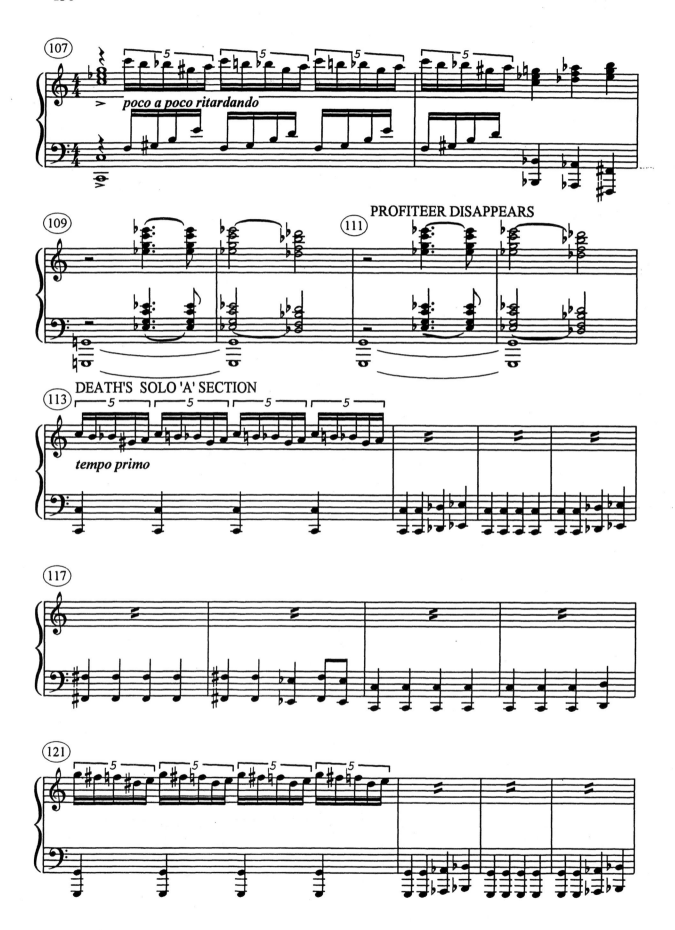

SCENE 8:

THE GENTLEMEN IN BLACK

INDEX

This index only lists the works mentioned within the text, for the complete list of Choreographies by Kurt Jooss please see Appendix A, page 71. All Part 1 entries are indicated in parentheses. The underlined page numbers refer to photographs.

The Green Table
by Anna Markard
LANGUAGE OF DANCE SERIES, No. 8

No other twentieth century ballet has achieved such world-wide renown, has been more unanimously acknowledged as a choreographic masterpiece, or proved more timeless, than The Green Table, the ballet by Kurt Jooss which won the 1932 International Choreographic Prize in Paris. This is now the first publication of the entire choreography in Labanotation, together with the annotated rehearsal music. The two volumes also include the historical background, performance and production history, extensive study and rehearsal notes, a wide selection of photographs spanning 65 years of performances as well as technical information, biographies and a complete list of works by Kurt Jooss.

About the Author

Born in 1931 in Essen, Germany as the eldest daughter of Kurt and Aino Jooss, Anna came to England when her family emigrated in 1933. She studied dance, first in London at the Sigurd Leeder School, then at the Folkwangschule in Essen and subsequently spent several years in Paris studying with Madame Nora Kiss. After dancing, and then teaching both in the USA and Germany, Anna Markard entered into close collaboration with her father; by teaching and staging his choreographic works, she became the authority on the Jooss repertoire. *The Green Table*, Jooss' masterpiece, has been in continual demand by companies all over the world. Anna Markard has staged well over 50 productions of *The Green Table* as well as several of Jooss' other works. In addition to the continuing production work, she now also devotes much time to the building of the Jooss Archive, writing, giving workshops and lecture demonstrations. Anna Markard is married to the painter Hermann Markard and lives in Amsterdam.

OPERATIVE LAPAROSCOPY & HYSTEROSCOPY

OPERATIVE LAPAROSCOPY & HYSTEROSCOPY

Edited by

STEPHEN M. COHEN, M.D.
Associate Professor
Department of Obstetrics and Gynecology
University of Massachusetts Medical School
Director
Reproductive Surgery
Department Of Obstetrics and Gynecology
University of Massachusetts Hospital
Worcester, Massachusetts

CHURCHILL LIVINGSTONE

New York, Edinburgh, London, Madrid, Melbourne, San Francisco, Tokyo

Library of Congress Cataloging-in-Publication Data

Operative laparoscopy and hysteroscopy / edited by Stephen M. Cohen.
      p.   cm.
     Includes bibliographical references and index.
     ISBN 0–443–08950–7
     1. Generative organs, Female—Endoscopic surgery. I. Cohen,
Stephen M.
     [DNLM: 1. Surgery, Laparoscopic—methods. 2. Hysteroscopy—
methods. WO 500 O616 1996]
RG104.7.O646 1996
618.1´059—dc20
DNLM/DLC
for Library of Congress   95–47254
                                                        CIP

Distributed in the United Kingdom by Churchill Livingstone, Robert Stevenson House, 1–3 Baxter's Place, Leith Walk, Edinburgh EH1 3AF, and by associated companies, branches, and representatives throughout the world.

Accurate indications, adverse reactions, and dosage schedules for drugs are provided in this book, but it is possible that they may change. The reader is urged to review the pack-age information data of the manufacturers of the medications mentioned.

The Publishers have made every effort to trace the copyright holders for borrowed mate-rial. If they have inadvertently overlooked any, they will be pleased to make the neces-sary arrangements at the first opportunity.

Assistant Editor: *Jennifer Hardy*
Production Editor: *Paul Bernstein*
Production Supervisor: *Sharon Tuder*
Cover Design: *Jeannette Jacobs*

Printed in Singapore

First published in 1996   7 6 5 4 3 2 1

*To my son Bryan, who taught his Dad the true meaning of
enthusiasm and who makes every moment of my life worthwhile,
and to my mother, father, and Aunt Bernice, for their undying
love and encouragement.*

Contributors

Johnny T. Awwad, M.D.

Instructor, Department of Obstetrics, Gynecology, and Reproductive Biology, Harvard Medical School; Fellow, Division of Reproductive Endocrinology and Infertility, Vincent Memorial Obstetrics and Gynecology Service, Department of Gynecology, Massachusetts General Hospital, Boston, Massachusetts

Jose P. Balmaceda, M.D.

Professor and Director, Division of Reproductive Endocrinology and Infertility, Department of Obstetrics and Gynecology, University of California, Irvine, College of Medicine, Irvine, California

Ronald K. Burke, M.D.

Associate Professor, Division of Reproductive Endocrinology, Department of Obstetrics and Gynecology, University of Massachusetts Medical School, Worcester, Massachusetts; Chief, Department of Gynecology, Mercy Hospital, Springfield, Massachusetts

Stephen M. Cohen, M.D.

Associate Professor, Department of Obstetrics and Gynecology, University of Massachusetts Medical School; Director, Reproductive Surgery, Department of Obstetrics and Gynecology, University of Massachusetts Hospital, Worcester, Massachusetts

Alan DeCherney, M.D.

Luis E. Phaneuf Professor and Chairman, Department of Obstetrics and Gynecology, Tufts University School of Medicine, Boston, Massachusetts

James H. Dorsey, M.D.

Assistant Professor, Department of Obstetrics and Gynecology, The Johns Hopkins University School of Medicine; Chairman, Department of Gynecology, Greater Baltimore Medical Center; Director, The Institute of Conservative and Minimally Invasive Surgery, Baltimore, Maryland

Harrith M. Hasson, M.D.

Director, University of Chicago Hospitals Gynecologic Endoscopy Center, Weiss Memorial Hospital, Chicago, Illinois

Robert B. Hunt, M.D.

Instructor, Department of Obstetrics, Gynecology, and Reproductive Biology, Harvard Medical School, Boston, Massachusetts

Paul D. Indman, M.D.

Associate Professor, Department of Gynecology and Obstetrics, Stanford University School of Medicine, Stanford, California; Senior Consultant, Gynecologic and Endoscopic Surgery, Santa Clara Valley Medical Center, San Jose, California

Keith Isaacson, M.D.

Assistant Professor, Department of Obstetrics, Gynecology, and Reproductive Biology, Harvard Medical School; Chief, Division of Reproductive Endocrinology and Infertility, Vincent Memorial Obstetrics and Gynecology Service, Department of Gynecology, Massachusetts General Hospital, Boston, Massachusetts

J. M. Lomano, M.D.

Director, The South Florida Women's Center, Fort Myers, Florida

Raymond Lui, M.D.

Assistant Professor, Department of Obstetrics and Gynecology, Tufts University School of Medicine, Boston, Massachusetts

Thomas L. Lyons, M.D.

Assistant Professor, Department of Gynecology–Obstetrics, Emory University School of Medicine; Director, Center of Women's Care and Reproductive Surgery, Atlanta, Georgia

Saul Maloul, M.D.

Clinical Research Fellow, Division of Reproductive Endocrinology and Infertility, Department of Obstetrics and Gynecology, University of California, Irvine, College of Medicine, Irvine, California

Dan C. Martin, M.D.

Associate Professor, Department of Obstetrics and Gynecology, University of Tennessee, Memphis, College of Medicine; Reproductive Surgeon, Department of Obstetrics and Gynecology, Baptist Memorial Hospital, Memphis, Tennessee

Kenneth L. Noller, M.D.

Professor and Chair, Department of Obstetrics and Gynecology, University of Massachusetts Medical School; Chair, Department of Obstetrics and Gynecology, University of Massachusetts Hospital, Worcester, Massachusetts

Ganson Purcell, Jr., M.D.

Professor, Department of Obstetrics and Gynecology, University of Connecticut School of Medicine, Farmington, Connecticut; Chairman/Director, Department of Obstetrics and Gynecology, St. Francis Hospital and Medical Center, Hartford, Connecticut

Harry Reich, M.D.

Associate Professor, Department of Obstetrics and Gynecology, Columbia University College of Physicians and Surgeons; Director, Advanced Laparoscopic Surgery, Columbia Presbyterian Medical Center, New York, New York

Eli Reshef, M.D.

Assistant Professor, Section of Reproductive Endocrinology and Infertility, Department of Obstetrics and Gynecology, University of Oklahoma College of Medicine, Oklahoma City, Oklahoma

Jacques E. Rioux, M.D., M.P.H.

Professor, Department of Obstetrics–Gynecology, Laval University Faculty of Medicine, Quebec City, Québec, Canada; Chief, Reproductive Medicine, Department of Gynecology–Reproduction, Le Centre Hospitalier de l'Université Laval, Ste–Foy, Québec, Canada

Joseph S. Sanfilippo, M.D.

Professor and Chief, Division of Endocrinology, Department of Obstetrics and Gynecology, University of Louisville School of Medicine, Louisville, Kentucky

Thomas Sedlacek, M.D.

Adjunct Professor, Department of Obstetrics and Gynecology, Hahnemann University School of Medicine; Chairman, Department of Gynecology, The Graduate Hospital, Philadelphia, Pennsylvania

Howard T. Sharp, M.D.

Assistant Professor, Department of Obstetrics–Gynecology, University of Utah School of Medicine, Salt Lake City, Utah

James Shwayder, M.D.

Associate Clinical Professor, Department of Obstetrics and Gynecology, Eastern Virginia Medical School of the Medical College of Hampton Roads, Norfolk, Virginia; Clinical Consultant, Department of Gynecologic Endoscopy and Ultrasound, James River Gynecology and Infertility, P.C., Newport News, Virginia

Alvin M. Siegler, M.D., D.Sc.

Professor, Department of Obstetrics and Gynecology, State University of New York Health Science Center at Brooklyn College of Medicine, Brooklyn, New York

Duane Townsend, M.D.

Clinical Professor, Department of Obstetrics and Gynecology, University of Utah School of Medicine; Director, Gynecologic Oncology and Gynecologic Endoscopy, LDS Hospital, Salt Lake City, Utah

Preface

It is an exciting time to be involved in the field of endoscopic surgery. Although hysteroscopy was described 150 years ago, and laparoscopy was performed at the turn of the century, it is only within the last few years that we have witnessed the dramatic growth in minimally invasive surgery. The rapid advances in technology, coupled with a new understanding of many disease processes, have allowed us to apply laparoscopy and hysteroscopy to treatments, whereas in the past they remained mainly diagnostic tools. We are now able to perform procedures via endoscopy that one could not even imagine five years ago.

Endoscopic surgery provides the gynecologist with many advantages compared to traditional surgery. These include a magnified and improved view of the operating field, observation of the pelvic organs in a more natural state, less tissue handling, smaller incisions that reduce pain and the length of hospital stay, improved cosmetics, and decreased costs as procedures are moved into less expensive venues such as ambulatory or office surgery.

Moreover, operative endoscopic surgery is still in its infancy. There is much to be learned: which procedures should be done via the laparoscopic versus the hysteroscopic approach; which procedures involve complication rates too high to justify their performance; whether a reduced hospital stay for certain procedures justifies increased operating time; whether procedures can be made less costly by changing the method or the instruments; and what new instruments can be manufactured that could enable procedures to be performed more safely, quickly, and easily by more surgeons.

Operative Laparoscopy & Hysteroscopy is intended for both those physicians who are more experienced in the field of operative endoscopy and those less experienced who are just beginning the journey. The experts who have contributed to this book offer advanced tips to knowledgeable gynecologists on methods to improve their techniques and avoid complications; they also describe the basics in detail, so that gynecologists just beginning to expand their abilities will have a strong foundation to build on.

I wish to greatly acknowledge the help I received from Jennifer Hardy and Paul Bernstein at Churchill Livingstone, and extend my personal thanks to my secretary, Jean Foran, whose extraordinary efforts have made this book a reality.

Stephen M. Cohen, M.D.

Contents

Laparoscopy

1 History of Laparoscopy

ALVIN M. SIEGLER

ORIGINS

During the early decades of the twentieth century, physicians developed an interest in exploring body cavities with various forms of specula and optics. Almost a century before, Bozzini[1] in 1807 described a light conductor in which a candle served as the illumination for a special "vaselike" instrument whose purpose was to enable the physicians to explore the cavities of various organs. At the time, the medical profession was opposed to this type of "curiosity." Not until 1880 when Nitze[2] developed the cystoscope were such investigations begun again. This new instrument could be passed into the bladder so that the physician could locate bladder stones and remove them without the need for an abdominal incision. In 1901, Kelling[3] reported his findings of a celioscopic examination of a living dog after pneumoperitoneum had been created with filtered air. Jacobeaus[4] coined the term *laparoscopy* after having explored the peritoneal cavity in humans by "direct" insertion of a Nitze cystoscope without pneumoperitoneum. He described the use of the laparoscope in 17 patients who had ascites. Kelling and Jacobaeus should be regarded as the pioneers of modern laparoscopy. The technique of the abdominal entry was varied and controversial. The early laparoscopes were primitive, the lens systems were of inferior quality, and adequate light and image transmission could be achieved only with wide lenses requiring large-bore telescopes. Distally placed incandescent light bulbs generated heat within the abdominal cavity, and they had the disconcerting habit of failing just at the critical point of a procedure. In 1938, Veress[5] described a new needle for inducing pneumothorax for the treatment of tuberculosis, and this instrument currently is used most frequently for the creation of pneumoperitoneum.

DEVELOPMENT OF OPERATIVE PROCEDURES

Ruddock[6] described a good optic system including a built-in biopsy forcep with the capability of electrocoagulation. He was able to report on its use in more than 2,000 patients. Apparently the first gynecologic report was published by Hope[7] on the use of the laparoscope for the diagnosis of tubal pregnancy. In the same year, Anderson[8] suggested tubal fulguration as a method for tubal sterilization but did not report the description of any cases. Decker and Cherry[9] were able to achieve good observation of the pelvic organs with the patients in the knee-chest position using a culdoscope. Indeed, this endoscopic method was practiced almost exclusively in the United States for the next 25 years. In 1941 Power and Barnes[10] reported the performance of tubal sterilization by coagulation of the isthmic portions of the fallopian tubes under laparoscopic control. In France, Palmer[11] adopted the deep Trendelenburg position and designed forceps for ovarian biopsy. In 1947 he published the results of his first 250 laparoscopic operations. Laparoscopy and other endoscopic procedures in general attained a wide acceptance after the introduction in 1952 of "cold light" concept by Fourestier, Gladu, and Vulmiere.[12] In the same year, Hopkins and Kapany[13] in England introduced fiberoptics to the field of endoscopy. Frangenheim[14] and Albano and Cittidini[15] incorporated the new techniques of laparoscopy and published their findings in textbooks on the subject. The first book published in the English language was written by Steptoe[16]; and in it he described the instruments available at the time. Details of many endoscopic procedures including tubal sterilization, ovarian biopsy, uterine suspension, appendectomy, and lysis of adhesions were included. Books by Cohen[17] and Semm[18] also included discussions on laparoscopy, culdoscopy, hysteroscopy, and gynecography.

TECHNICAL ADVANCES

In response to the worldwide interest in sterilization and population control with the use of the laparoscopic and concern about potential complications, The American Association of Gynecologic Laparoscopists was formed in 1972. The initial enthusiasm for laparoscopy was based in no small part on the fact that for the first time female sterilization was available at a reasonable cost and the procedure could be accomplished in many women on an outpatient basis. Advanced operative endoscopic surgery represents a continuation of these early developments. Enormous technical advances have taken place since the idea of using reflected light in the deeper body cavities for diagnostic purpose was first conceived, and these have led to significant advances in modern endoscopic techniques. Initially, development was slow and only since 1980 have many of the technical problems been solved. Large disposable trocars, high-flow insufflating apparatuses, ancillary instruments for additional trocars, and safer electrosurgical and laser equipment have been devised. These advances in gynecologic endoscopy have had a significant impact on our specialty.

VIDEO LAPAROSCOPY

Laparoscopy is the most frequently performed gynecologic procedure in North America. The rapid improvement in technology has led to important advances in the quality and reliability of available endoscopic equipment. Parallel to the advances in the design of the telescopes, light sources and a wide range of ancillary instruments have been developed, and thus patient care has been improved, costs have been reduced for hospitalization, and many difficult diagnostic problems have been resolved without the need for a laparotomy. Until 1980 the cost of specific surgical procedures was of relatively small concern to health care providers. The implementation of diagnostic related groups and other cost-containing government policies have made physicians increasingly aware of the economic impact of their therapeutic decision. In gynecology, the selection of the optimal and cost-effective surgical procedure for a given disease process is becoming an area for concern, especially when there is more than one method of treatment available. The ability to retrieve oocytes by laparoscopy led to the development of in vitro fertilization techniques and opened new vistas for research. No reproductive surgeon would consider performing a laparotomy without initially doing an endoscopic survey of the pelvis to assess the need for a laparotomy. Laparoscopic fertility-promoting procedures give the opportunity to decline further treatment to some couples and to avoid a laparotomy in others. The ability to make an early diagnosis of tubal pregnancy and, in appropriate circumstances, to treat the condition by laparoscopic techniques represents the present standard of care. Laparoscopy provides access to the peritoneal cavity for diagnosis and for many surgical interventions previously only possible by laparotomy. Laparoscopy is valuable to the patient and her physician when performed accurately and safely with proper indications. Familiarity with the instruments, meticulous attention to details of technique, sound clinical judgment, and continued practice and application are prerequisites for successful operative laparoscopy. To quote DeCherney,[19] "The obituary for laparotomy for pelvic reconstructive surgery has been written; it is only its publication that remains." It is estimated that 70 percent of gynecologic laparotomies can be avoided by operative laparoscopy with the use of available instruments. The interest in advanced operative laparoscopy has been ignited by video monitoring and laser technology. Photographic and television imaging represent the leading edge of progress in this type of minimally invasive surgery. Safe automatic high-flow insufflators, and effective methods of hemostasis including intra-abdominal suturing, electrosurgery, lasers, and stapling have extended the safety and efficiency of operative laparoscopy.

Good training is necessary before some of these complex operations are undertaken. The specific form of training in terms of duration, location, and intensity will depend on the level of difficulty of procedures to be learned and the experience of the gynecologist seeking the training. Aside from the physician's responsibility, the hospitals have the obligation to maintain the equipment purchased for laparoscopic operations in good condition and thereby not dangerous or harmful to the patient. Perhaps the time is not too distant when a laparotomy will be required to manage only selected patients who have pelvic malignancies or require organ transplantation.

REFERENCES

1. Bozzini P: Der Lichtleiter oder Beschreibung einer einfachen Vorrichtung und ihrer Anwendung zur Erleuchtung innerer Hohlen und Zwischenraume des lebenden animalischen Korpers. Landes Industrie, Comptoir, Weimar, 1807

2. Nitze M: Uber eine neue Beleuchtungsmethode der Hohlen des menschlichen Korpers. Wein Med Presse 20:251, 1879

3. Kelling G: Uber Oesophagoskopie, Gastroskopie und Koelioscopie. Munch Med Wochenschr 49:21, 1902

4. Jacobaeus H: Uber die Moglichkeit, die Zystoskopie die Untersuchungen seroser Hohlungen anzuwenden. Munch Med Wochenschr 57:2090, 1910

5. Veress J: Neues Instrument zur Ausfuhrung von Brust-oder Bauchpunktionen und Pneumothorax behandlung. Dtsch Med Wochenschr 64:1480, 1938

6. Ruddock JC: Peritoneoscopy. West J Surg 42:392, 1934

7. Hope R: The differential diagnosis of ectopic gestation by peritoneoscopy. Surg Gynecol Obstet 64:229, 1937

8. Anderson ET: Peritoneoscopy. Am J Surg 35:36, 1937

9. Decker A, Cherry T: A new method in the diagnosis of pelvic disease. Am J Surg 64:40, 1944

10. Power FH, Barnes AC: Sterilization by means of peritoneoscopic tubal fulguration: a preliminary report. Am J Obstet Gynecol 41:1038, 1941

11. Palmer R: La coeloscopie gynecolgique, ses possibilites et ses indications actualles. Sem Hop Paris 30:441, 1954

12. Fourestier M, Gladu A, Voulmiere J: Perfectionments de l'endoscope medicale. Presse Med 60:1292, 1952

13. Hopkins HH, Kapany NS: Flexible fiberscope using static scanning. Nature 173:39, 1954

14. Frangenheim H: Die Laparoskopie und die Culdoscopie in der Gynakologie. G Thieme, Stuttgart, 1959

15. Albano V, Cittidini E: La Celioscopia in Ginologia. Denaro, Palermo, 1962

16. Steptoe PC: Laparoscopy in Gynaecology. Livingstone, Edinburgh, 1967

17. Cohen M: Laparoscopy, Culdoscopy, and Gynecography. WB Saunders, Philadelphia, 1970

18. Semm K: Atlas of Gynecologic Laparoscopy and Hysteroscopy. WB Saunders, Philadelphia, 1975

19. DeCherney AH: "The leader of the band is tired . . ." Fertil Steril 44:299, 1985

2 Indications and Contraindications of Laparoscopy

JOHNNY T. AWWAD
KEITH ISAACSON

Although described several decades ago, laparoscopy has developed into one of the more important diagnostic and therapeutic tools in gynecology during the past few years. The growth of this technique and its applications have developed exponentially, and it currently accounts for a large proportion of all gynecologic surgical procedures.

The main attributes of laparoscopic surgery are the reduction of trauma due to small skin incisions and reduction in adhesion formation. New concepts in methodology and considerable technologic advances, such as electrical and laser technology, have rendered laparoscopy a particularly useful tool for the surgical treatment of a variety of gynecologic conditions. The growing interest in laparoscopy is mostly attributable, however, to cumulative evidence suggesting a reduction in patient morbidity, shortening in hospitalization stay, and decreased cost.

Nevertheless, laparoscopy has been criticized as it moved toward newer dimensions. Newly introduced surgical applications in the field have triggered controversial opinions about their appropriateness. Amid these controversies, a universal agreement on indications and contraindications for laparoscopy is far from being realistic as more advances are constantly shaping the horizons of the field. Growing experience, cumulative data, and improved patient selection will shape our acceptance to different aspects of laparoscopy and ultimately determine its usefulness. The indications and contraindications of laparoscopy displayed in this chapter subsequently represent general guidelines that will keep evolving as we accumulate more experience.

INDICATIONS

Laparoscopy is a minimal access approach that allows direct visualization and remote handling of pelvic organs. It is invaluable in the identification of lesions that would not be otherwise detected by other diagnostic techniques. Also, laparoscopy allows the surgeon to assess and at the same time treat various diseases. It is a safe and effective technique in the presence of sound clinical judgment and adequate surgical skills.

General Guidelines

Several prerequisites need to be addressed before considering a patient for laparoscopy. These are derived from common sense and are related to factors that can influence the safety and efficacy of the procedure. Should they be underestimated, serious consequences and shortcomings in patient care may result.

1. *Surgical skills:* Experience and knowledge in a particular approach should be at a level to permit the performance of a safe and effective procedure. Common sense should be such that one can recognize one's own limitations as well as those of the laparoscopic approach. Because laparoscopy often entails the use of electrical and laser technology, an adequate knowledge of the basic physical properties of these modalities is required to avoid major injuries. Also, the use of video imaging requires the development of spatial perception with delicate hand-mind coordination.

   At present, there are no well-defined criteria and prerequisites on a national basis for licensing physicians in laparoscopic surgery. Some general guidelines have been issued by the American College of Obstetricians and Gynecologists[1] and the American Fertility Society.[2] Many of these credentialing procedures, however, remain largely institutional.

2. *Surgical equipment:* Critical to any procedure is the availability of well-maintained surgical equipment and an operating room staff familiar with the workings of this equipment. Appropriate instrumentation determines the safety and feasibility of a procedure, especially with the use of electrical or laser energy.

3. *Consideration of alternative therapy:* The feasibility of a surgical procedure through the laparoscope is not necessarily an indication for such a surgical approach. When a procedure can be performed more safely and with a better outcome by conventional surgery, laparoscopy should be abandoned. Laparoscopic surgery of unproved benefits should be performed only under proper experimental protocol.

4. *Estimation of operating time:* The length of time anticipated to conclude a procedure laparoscopically is an important consideration before surgery. It may be poor judgment to subject the patient to prolonged operating time and risks of general anesthesia if the surgery can be performed by the conventional approach in a much shorter duration. It should be acknowledged, however, that the duration of a procedure is frequently prolonged with initial exposure to new techniques. Speed is acquired with experience and personal confidence.

5. *Assessment of indications:* Even though laparoscopy is perceived as a minimally invasive surgery, this does not condone its overuse in patients in whom observation is a reasonable approach. The overuse of laparoscopy may result in the unnecessary rise in health care expenditure that would defeat a key benefit of cost-effectiveness.

The basic prerequisites for laparoscopic surgery therefore include adequate surgical skills, appropriate equipment, and the proper indications based on an assessment of the risks and the benefits involved.

Diagnostic Laparoscopy

Evaluation of the Acute Abdomen

Laparoscopy is a valuable tool for the diagnosis of acute pelvic pain or an acute abdomen in which the differential diagnosis includes pelvic inflammatory disease (PID), appendicitis, adnexal torsion, or ectopic pregnancy (Table 2-1). Advantages of diagnostic laparoscopy in patients presenting with acute pelvic pain are the following: (1) the avoidance of an exploratory laparotomy, and (2) the prevention of delayed surgical intervention associated with expectant management.

Diagnostic laparoscopy is also useful to confirm the diagnosis of acute salpingitis. It is estimated that the diagnosis of PID is incorrectly made in 30 to 50 percent of women.[2–4] The advantages of laparoscopy in the management of suspected PID include the immediate establishment of an accurate diagnosis, the ability to obtain culture specimens, and pelvic lavage and drainage of purulent material. Nonetheless, cost-effectiveness remains a major concern, and laparoscopy has failed to become an essential component of PID management because of economic considerations.

The risk of a missed appendicitis as a cause of pelvic pain can be particularly detrimental. The old rule of thumb, "if you can't rule it out, take it out," reflects the presence of diagnostic insecurity. The availability of diagnostic laparoscopy has created significant changes in the management of suspected appendicitis by providing a more accurate and confident diagnosis.

Whereas laboratory and radiologic tests can only improve the suspicion of ectopic pregnancy, correct diagnosis is made with certainty with the use of laparoscopy. The introduction of this tool in the management of extrauterine pregnancies has led to early detection and treatment, and this in turn has resulted in a reduction in maternal mortality and an improvement in subsequent fertility.

Laparoscopy is also useful in assessing uterine and intraperitoneal trauma occurring in the event of uterine perforation. Uterine perforation occurs in 0.02 to 1.5 percent of elective abortions and in 0.3 percent of premenopausal women and 2.6 percent of postmenopausal women undergoing dilation and curettage. It has also been reported in up to 10 percent of patients undergoing adhesiolysis for Asherman syndrome. Once suspected, the diagnosis of uterine perforation is made by direct visual evaluation of the uterine rent and adjacent organ damage.

Elective Diagnostic Laparoscopy

The most frequent indications for laparoscopy are pelvic pain and infertility. The membership survey of the American Association of Gynecologic Laparoscopists (AAGL) revealed that pelvic pain and infertility accounted for 58 percent and 42 percent, respectively, of laparoscopic procedures performed in 1991.[5]

Chronic Pelvic Pain

Chronic pelvic pain is one of the most frustrating gynecologic problems both to the patient and physician, often resulting in multiple surgical interventions with disappointing results. Chronic pelvic pain that persists beyond 6 months despite conservative therapy becomes an indication for laparoscopic evaluation.

Table 2-1. Indications for Laparoscopy

Diagnostic Laparoscopy
    Emergency laparoscopy
        Acute pelvic pain
        Uterine perforation
    Elective laparoscopy
        Chronic pelvic pain
        Infertility
Therapeutic Laparoscopy
    Indications
        Ectopic pregnancy
        Pelvic adhesions
        Endometriosis
        Ovarian endometriomas
        Benign ovarian teratomas
        Tubal sterilization
    Controversial indications
        Management of ovarian cysts
        Laparoscopic tubal reconstructive surgery
        Ovarian torsion
        Laparoscopic ovarian drilling
        Laparoscopic myomectomy
        Laparoscopically assisted vaginal surgery
        Laparoscopic uterosacral ablation
        Second-look laparoscopy

Diagnostic laparoscopies in women presenting with chronic pelvic pain have revealed organic pelvic pathology in 8 to 70 percent of cases.[6–11] This incidence rises to 83 percent when the criteria for patient selection include only those presenting with persistent pelvic pain in the same location for at least 6 months.[12] Preoperative physical evaluation is not predictive of pelvic findings in patients with chronic pelvic pain. Among women with initially normal examination, 50 to 63 percent showed disease at laparoscopy.[6,11] By contrast, no organic disease was identified in 17.5 to 33 percent of those who had abnormal examinations.

Interestingly, 22 percent of patients with no identifiable pathology at laparoscopy were pain-free on their 6-week follow-up appointment and 58 percent were pain-free after 6 months in the absence of any psychiatric assistance.[13] Consistent with this finding is the observation that an abnormal psychosocial history can be elicited in 50 percent of women with chronic pelvic pain who have no evidence of organic pathology at laparoscopy.[7] In addition to its diagnostic and therapeutic role, laparoscopy may also provide the benefit of patient reassurance.

Infertility

Laparoscopy is an essential and valuable step of the infertility evaluation. Its role is to allow the surgeon to visualize tubal patency and integrity, endometriosis, and pelvic adhesions.

Although hysterosalpingography (HSG) is a well-established diagnostic modality for tubal disease, additional information will be gained through laparoscopy.[14,15] Misleading information can result from technical limitations of the HSG, however. Most false information is due to the occurrence of tubal spasm. Investigations have revealed a negative predictive value of HSG ranging from 57 to 92 percent[16,17] and a positive predictive value ranging from 30 to 84 percent.[14,17] While the reporting of proximal tubal obstruction and peritubal loculation by HSG is often unconfirmed surgically, unilateral and bilateral distal tubal obstruction, by contrast, are associated with significant pelvic disease in 92 and 95 percent of cases, respectively.[18]

Laparoscopy is an important complementary tool to HSG in determining the extent and subsequent therapy for tubal disease. Currently, the preservation of distal tubal rugae with a mild hydrosalpinx demonstrated by laparoscopy may favor the use of microsurgery. However, damaged fimbrial mucosa, due to its relatively poor prognosis, favors laparoscopic tuboplasty with reduced patient morbidity. The complete absence of an identifiable fimbria is an indication for assisted reproductive technology. These recommendations will undoubtedly change as we accumulate data on the success of laparoscopic repair.

Therapeutic Laparoscopy

In recent years, the spectrum of gynecologic indications appropriate for operative laparoscopy has expanded dramatically. Due to major advances in instrumentation including safe high-flow peritoneal insufflators, cold-light illumination, sophisticated lens systems, high-resolution cameras, and instruments to ensure hemostasis, complex laparoscopic gynecologic procedures can now be performed safely. The laparoscope has provided easier access to areas deep in the pelvis normally poorly accessible through laparotomy. Because of the unique video-camera magnification system, diagnosis of minimal disease on the basis of visual features can be made more accurately and vital structures identified more easily. The possibility of taperecording pathologic findings can be very valuable for the assessment of disease progression and further consultations.

Operative laparoscopy is associated with a 69 to 96 percent reduction in postoperative hospital stay when compared with laparotomy.[19,20] With the use of this minimally invasive approach, the convalescence period is also decreased from a few weeks to a few days, with significant reduction in postoperative pain and disability. Levine[19] reported 79 percent economic savings on drugs and medical supplies with the use of laparoscopy compared with conventional surgery. Nonetheless, the decision for laparoscopy must be primarily based on the evidence of proven clinical benefits. Financial considerations should not be allowed to sway the balance of clinical practice unless these clinical benefits clearly outweigh alternative conventional techniques.

Ectopic Pregnancy

The first laparoscopic diagnosis of an extrauterine gestation was made by Hope in 1937,[21] while the first laparoscopic removal of a tubal pregnancy was performed by Shapiro in 1973.[21a] Today, laparoscopy is the preferred surgical approach to the treatment of ectopic pregnancies. Subsequent pregnancy rates after laparoscopic management of ectopic pregnancy are comparable with those obtained with laparotomy.[22–25] Nager and Murphy[26] found that 65 percent of women who desired pregnancy after laparoscopic management of an ectopic pregnancy achieved an intrauterine pregnancy, whereas 17 percent had a repeat ectopic pregnancy. Moreover, laparoscopic treatment of extrauterine pregnancy has been shown to reduce postoperative adhesions, days of hospitalization, postoperative analgesia requirement, and convalescence time when compared with laparotomy.[27–30]

Tubal rupture is no longer considered an absolute contraindication to laparoscopy provided the patient is hemodynamically stable. With the availability of efficient suction-irrigation systems and reliable hemostatic tools, several investigators have reported safe and effective laparoscopic management of the ruptured ectopic pregnancy.[31–33] The only limitations to the laparoscopic management of ectopic pregnancy are the experience of the operator and the hemodynamic status of the patient.

It has recently been demonstrated that a variety of medical regimens are also effective in treating ectopic pregnancy. At present, no well-defined guidelines are available to define the standard treatment of ectopic pregnancy. The advantages of the laparoscopic approach over medical therapy are the ability of making an accurate diagnosis of a presumptive condition, the prognostic evaluation of tubal damage, the avoidance of potential side effects of chemotherapy, and the alleviation of the anxiety associated with the uncertainty of the diagnosis.

Pelvic Adhesions

The first reported operative procedure performed under laparoscopic guidance was lysis of adhesions by Fervers in 1933.[34] Adhesiolysis is the second most frequent gynecologic condition treated exclusively by laparoscopy.[35] The general incidence of pelvic adhesions is unknown; however, they are encountered in 26 to 48 percent of patients with chronic pelvic pain.[36,37]

Indications for lysis of adhesions are mostly pelvic pain and infertility. Although it is well established that the presence of pelvic adhesions is likely to interfere with fertility, very little evidence is available to support the contention that pelvic adhesions are a primary cause of pelvic pain. The duration and severity of pain often do not correlate with the extent and location of adhesions. Even though several studies suggest that pelvic pain is independent of the presence of pelvic adhesion,[36,38–41] there are good data that demonstrate that laparoscopic adhesiolysis in patients with chronic pelvic pain will result in a reduction in pain.[42–44]

Pelvic adhesions have been implicated as a cause of infertility in 15 to 20 percent of infertile couples. Suggested mechanisms include kinking and obstruction of the fallopian tubes, interference with ovum pick-up, and coating of the ovary interfering with egg release. The intrauterine pregnancy rate after laparoscopic salpingoovariolysis is 50 to 85 percent and the ectopic gestation rate 4 to 8 percent.[45–48] This compares favorably with pregnancy rates of 32 to 83 percent and ectopic rates of 1 to 8 percent obtained with adhesiolysis via laparotomy.[46,47,49–53]

In a carefully designed animal study, Luciano et al.[54] found that adhesions tend to reform less frequently after laparoscopic adhesiolysis when compared with laparotomy. A prospective multicenter human clinical trial using second-look laparoscopy (SLL) confirmed that 67 percent of laparoscopically lysed adhesions tend to reform while the incidence of de novo adhesion formation was minimal.[55]

Endometriosis

Endometriosis is mostly a pelvic disease diagnosed by direct vision and tissue biopsy. In its membership survey of 1988, the AAGL recognized endometriosis as the most common gynecologic condition managed predominantly by laparoscopy.[56] Surgical treatment consists of desiccation, fulguration, vaporization, or resection of well-defined lesions. The accessibility of the laparoscope to areas previously barred to the naked eye as well as the magnified visualization of peritoneal lesions have dramatically improved the diagnostic yield.

Because endometriosis is a benign condition, the only indication to diagnose and treat the disease is the symptoms of pain or infertility. No data demonstrate that surgically treating early-stage endometriosis will reduce the likelihood of advanced endometriosis being present at a later date. Therefore, endometriosis should only be diagnosed and treated because of current symptoms.

Although it is well recognized that the degree of pelvic pain does not correlate to the stage of the disease, Sutton et al.[57] demonstrated in a prospective randomized clinical trial that laparoscopic treatment of endometriosis is successful in alleviating pelvic pain. It remains unclear, however, whether laparoscopic treatment of stage I or II endometriosis is useful in improving fertility outcome.[58,59] Hughes et al.,[60] in a review of controlled trials, reported a benefit in these patients with laparoscopic treatment. Pregnancy rates achieved after the surgical treatment of endometriosis using either laparoscopy or laparotomy have been comparable for mild[61–64] and for moderate and severe forms of the disease.[58,61,64–68] Only recently have the pregnancy rates associated with laparoscopy for the treatment of endometriosis been reported to be superior to those for laparotomy when endometriosis was the sole cause of infertility.[69]

Ovarian Endometriomas

Initially, the size of an endometrioma was an important criterion in defining the feasibility of the laparoscopic approach for endometrioma resection. Concerns were based on the fear of a potential risk for malignancy with cysts of larger size[70] and the fear of incomplete resection. Almost all endometriomas can now be removed laparoscopically in appropriately selected patients thought to be at low risk for ovarian carcinoma.

The pregnancy rates reported after resection of ovarian endometriomas by laparoscopy compare favorably with laparotomy. Equivalent pregnancy rates were found by Adamson et al.,[71] who compared both laparoscopic and laparotomy approaches.

Benign Ovarian Teratomas

Teratomas with their characteristic radiologic features are most often benign ovarian tumors in young women. After the report of Kistner[72] in 1952, in which he described severe morbidity associated with intraperitoneal rupture of teratomas, laparotomy emerged as the exclusive approach for surgical resection of these tumors. As a result, the presence of a ter-

atoma was considered a contraindication for the laparoscopic approach, mainly for fear of inadvertent spillage of the sebaceous cyst contents into the peritoneal cavity. This dictum was re-evaluated in 1986 when Semm described the laparoscopic treatment of 70 dermoid cysts with no complications. A similar experience was later reported by others.[73–76] With sufficient irrigation of the peritoneal cavity, the risk of chemical granulomatous peritonitis appears to be minimal. Also, with the use of endoscopic bags, the chances of intra-abdominal spillage can be significantly reduced.

Tubal Sterilization

The first tubal sterilization in the United States was by Power and Barnes in 1941.[77] This procedure represents the earliest widely accepted operative use of laparoscopy. Even though the failure rates among different ligation techniques are all similar,[78] failures associated with coagulation techniques have been shown more likely to be extrauterine.[79,80] The 1988 membership survey of the AAGL observed a 73 percent ectopic pregnancy rate with unipolar coagulation failures as opposed to 16 percent with clip failures.[81]

Controversial Indications

Although definite indications represent conditions in which laparoscopic surgery has been found to have a definite positive beneficial role with respect to patient care outcome, several other indications remain of controversial value. These are conditions in which a clinical benefit has not been confirmed by sufficient clinical data, methodology has not been refined, and patient selection criteria have not been defined. Cumulative clinical experience and developing surgical skills will ultimately determine our acceptance to these procedures.

Management of Ovarian Cysts

Management of ovarian cysts is one of the most common and controversial applications of operative laparoscopy. The 1990 survey conducted by the AAGL reported the incidence of unsuspected ovarian cancer as 0.04 percent of patients with ovarian cysts treated laparoscopically.[56] The value of cytologic examination of the cyst fluid for malignancy has not been established as the false-negative rate of malignant cysts aspirates range from 10 to 66 percent.[82]

The main reservation for the use of this technique in the management of ovarian cysts derives from the fear of delaying the diagnosis of ovarian cancer and disseminating the disease.[83] In a group of 42 patients with unsuspected ovarian tumors in whom cautious preoperative screening was not performed, 71 percent had a delay of 4.8 weeks in the management of their cancer.[84] Laparotomy was performed immediately only in 17 percent of patients and was never performed in 12 percent. More than 50 percent of these patients had advanced-stage ovarian disease, and only 40 percent had frozen sections performed at the time of surgery. This emphasizes the utmost importance of preselection criteria for patients with ovarian cysts under consideration for laparoscopy, as well as the surgeon's anticipation and readiness for the possibility of cancer. It is estimated that about 0.4 percent of nonsuspicious ovarian cysts managed laparoscopically have stage I ovarian cancer.[85]

Careful preoperative evaluation is therefore necessary to select the proper patients to undergo laparoscopic evaluation and treatment of an adnexal mass. The patient's menopausal status, clinical examination, ultrasound findings, and CA-125 titers can provide useful information that helps in defining the risk for malignancy. The positive predictive value of ultrasound alone in the detection of an adnexal malignancy was found to be 73 percent and the negative predictive value 91 to 95 percent.[86–88] The size of the adnexal mass is an important selection criterion because larger cysts are associated with a greater risk of malignancy.[88,89] Sonographic findings of irregular borders, papillations, solid components, thick septa, and ascites are all associated with ovarian malignancy. Recently, the use of transvaginal color Doppler sonography was studied for the preoperative evaluation of pelvic masses. Although still investigational, one study reported a sensitivity of 94 percent and a specificity of 97 percent.[90]

The value of CA-125, a tumor-associated antigen, in the preoperative screening for malignant disease has also been evaluated. In a group of women with a pelvic mass and elevated CA-125 levels (greater than 35 units/ml), 80 percent of those older than 50 years of age had a malignancy compared with 15 percent of those younger than 50 years.[91] Hence, preoperative CA-125 screening is useful in postmenopausal women. Only 50 percent of patients with stage I ovarian cancer have elevated CA-125 values greater than 35 units/ml.[92] When CA-125 levels were added to the ultrasound impression for the preoperative evaluation of ovarian masses, marked improvement in the negative prediction was noted only in postmenopausal women.[93]

Even though every surgeon is concerned about cancer dissemination from inadvertent rupture of a malignant cyst, the rate of spillage from unsuspected ovarian cancer is quite low (3.2 per 1,000 procedures).[94] Studies have suggested that rupture of an ovarian tumor does not have an adverse effect on prognosis.[95,96] The concern that cancer spill into the peritoneal cavity could reduce survival derives from early studies with inadequate staging that did not account for tumor grade, extent of adhesions, and volume of ascites. These three factors were found later to influence the rate of relapse in women with stage I epithelial ovarian cancer.[96] Although unusual, the development of peritoneal seeding at the site of trocar insertion after laparoscopic treatment of an ovarian cancer has also been described.[97]

Comparing adnexal surgery using either laparoscopy or laparotomy, the overall operating time was found to be similar for both procedures, but the hospital stay and recuperation period were significantly in favor of laparoscopy.[98] Ovarian cysts can be approached laparoscopically only if the clinical, biochemical, and radiologic evaluation of the tumor is compatible with a benign profile.

Laparoscopic Tubal Reconstructive Surgery

Although the laparoscope has proved to be a valuable diagnostic tool for the evaluation of infertility, its usefulness in tubal reconstructive surgery has remained controversial. Technically, laparoscopic tuboplasties can be performed, but their virtues remain to be determined.

Laparoscopic salpingostomy for hydrosalpinx and terminal tubal occlusion has been described. Even though Gomel's earliest experience with laparoscopic salpingostomy was favorable,[99] the literature later revealed conflicting reports. Although pregnancy rates after laparoscopic salpingostomy ranged between 23 and 50 percent,[47,99–101] pregnancy rate of 10 percent was observed by Fayez[45] with no viable pregnancies. With the absence of well-controlled randomized clinical trials, the comparison of pregnancy outcomes of various uncontrolled studies, often with different patient characteristics, falls short of a meaningful and conclusive interpretation.

Ovarian Torsion

The presence of ovarian torsion can easily be diagnosed by laparoscopy. Torsion occurs more commonly in the presence of ovarian cysts but can also occur in their absence.[102] Traditionally, the practice of untwisting the torsed ovary was discouraged for fear of releasing blood emboli from the occluded ovarian venous plexus into the main circulation.[103] As more clinical observations accumulated, however, the conservative management of torsed ovaries has proved to be safer than initially anticipated, with no observed thromboembolic events reported.[104–106] Unwinding of ischemic ovaries in patients presenting with ovarian torsion has resulted in the salvage of the organ with return of ovarian function as demonstrated by ultrasound evidence of follicular development.[107,108] Oocytes recovered from these patients during assisted reproduction are microscopically normal and retain their fertilization capacity.[107]

Laparoscopic Ovarian Drilling

Ovarian drilling is a laparoscopic alternative to ovarian wedge resection in patients with polycystic ovary (PCO) disease. It consists of drilling multiple symmetrically placed holes into the ovarian stroma using either electrical or laser energy.

When used in PCO patients, an improvement in the hormonal profile was observed with a reduction in androstenedione, testosterone, estradiol, and luteinizing hormone serum levels.[109,110] Spontaneous ovulations have been reported in 45 to 92 percent of women refractory to clomiphene citrate therapy within 3 months of the ovarian drilling.[110–114] A favorable reproductive outcome has been found to be associated with this therapy.[112,114] Armar and Lachelin[115] reported that 86 percent of women with PCO and an otherwise normal pelvis in one series conceived after laparoscopic ovarian drilling. A lower incidence of pelvic adhesions after laparoscopic ovarian drilling was noted when compared with wedge resection.[112,116] As long-term effects are yet unknown, concerns remain regarding the theoretic risk of premature menopause from uncontrollable damage to ovarian tissue.

Laparoscopic Myomectomy

The usefulness of laparoscopy for uterine myomectomy has not yet been proved. Nezhat et al.[117] reported a series of 154 laparoscopic myomectomies with no intraoperative complications related to the procedure. A similar experience was also reported by others.[118,119] Although the laparoscopic procedure is associated with a shorter hospital stay,[117–119] the removal of the fibroids from the abdominal cavity is frequently a time-consuming process.[117,118]

The three main surgical concerns with laparoscopic myomectomy are intraoperative blood loss, the strength of the uterine incision, and postoperative pelvic adhesions. Hemostasis may be difficult to obtain, as traditional means of reducing blood loss during conventional surgery are not applicable laparoscopically, namely, the use of hemostatic tourniquets and suture ligatures. Nonetheless, the average estimated blood loss associated with the procedure was reported to be 75 to 78 ml[118,119] and appears to be lower compared with open myomectomy.[120,121] These results, however, are likely to be affected by patients selection bias of those selected to undergo the laparoscopic procedure.

The strength of the uterine incision after laparoscopic myomectomy has been challenged. Because meticulous repair of uterine defects during laparoscopic myomectomy is technically difficult, concerns regarding the weakening of the uterine wall after the procedure are present. The observation of indentations along the healed uterine incision after the laparoscopic removal of intramural fibroids may represent uterine structural defects[117] and raises doubts about the ability of the uterus to safely accommodate a term pregnancy and withstand labor.

There are yet no sufficient data to compare postoperative adhesions after laparoscopic myomectomy with laparotomy. A higher incidence of adhesion formation was noted when sutures were used to approximate the uterine walls during laparoscopic myomectomy.[117] By contrast, a reduced risk of postoperative adhesions in association with the laparoscopic approach was claimed by others and was associated with a favorable fertility outcome.[118] The long-term risks and benefits of laparoscopic myomectomy for infertility, however, remain largely unknown.[122]

Laparoscopically Assisted Vaginal Surgery

The first laparoscopic hysterectomy in the United States was performed in 1988 by Reich et al.[123] Laparoscopically assisted vaginal hysterectomy (LAVH) represents the most common form of hysterectomies performed through the laparoscope.[124–126]

Although the indications for LAVH remain poorly defined, the procedure may potentially be useful in certain conditions. LAVH appears to be particularly useful with the suspicion of pelvic adhesions in patients with a history of previous surgeries or peritonitis. It becomes also helpful when inspection of the pelvis and adnexa is needed to evaluate pelvic symptoms and rule out pelvic disease. LAVH is also a means of converting an abdominal hysterectomy into a vaginal one in women with no significant pelvic relaxation and uterine descent. Despite the reported high incidence of successful oophorectomies via the vaginal approach in experienced hands,[127–129] LAVH remains a viable option for patients in whom the ovaries are inaccessible vaginally.

LAVH can help expand the limits of vaginal hysterectomy and not replace it. When the use of LAVH was compared with vaginal hysterectomy in a prospective well-controlled randomized approach, a comparable surgical outcome was found, but higher costs and increased postoperative pain were observed with LAVH.[126] Theoretically, LAVH offers several advantages over an abdominal hysterectomy with respect to reduced patient morbidity and hospital stay. Also, the incidence of postoperative ileus is less common after LAVH due to minimal bowel manipulation. However, elevated intraoperative costs constitute a major criticism in clinical studies evaluating the cost-effectiveness of LAVH.[129,130] These enormous expenditures were determined to be mainly the result of prolonged operating time and the use of disposable instruments.[130] Longebrekke et al.[131] reported the incidence of serious complications from LAVHs at 20 percent. Although this is higher than most reports, ureteral injuries are a far too common complication of the procedure, particularly when linear cutters are used.[132]

Laparoscopic Uterosacral Ablation

The concept of laparoscopic uterosacral nerve ablation (LUNA) consists of transecting the afferent pain fibers within the uterosacral ligaments with the intention of alleviating pelvic pain in women with no identifiable pelvic pathology.

The use of LUNA for refractory dysmenorrhea appears to have a maintained beneficial effect in 50 to 60 percent of patients for 12 months.[133,134] The high failure rate of the procedure may be partially explained on the basis of individual anatomic variations. Alternate pathways for the T10–L1 sympathetic fibers passing through the uterosacral ligaments are present in 30 percent of patients. In one series, no significant improvement in pain was observed in women undergoing LUNA compared with diagnostic laparoscopy.[134] The two most commonly described complications of the procedure are ureteral injury and hemorrhage.

Second-Look Laparoscopy

SLL for the lysis of postoperative adhesions remains the subject of many criticisms. Although shown to be effective in reducing the incidence of postoperative adhesions, it did not improve reproductive outcome.[135,136]

The appropriate timing of postoperative adhesiolysis has varied from 3 days to 6 weeks postoperatively among studies.[137,138] Early SLL performed 4 to 6 weeks postoperatively showed that 15 percent of reformed adhesions were moderate to severe, compared with 63 percent when the procedure was performed at 16 to 19 months.[139]

CONTRAINDICATIONS

As in conventional surgery, the standard general surgical principles apply to laparoscopy. Nevertheless, some principles exist that are peculiar to the laparoscopic approach. these are related to the physiology of the pneumoperitoneum, patient positioning, and the method of surgical access. This risk is largely dependent on the disease process involved, procedure performed, acuity of the patient, and operator experience. As we are becoming more sophisticated, the map of contraindications is constantly changing, and many previous contraindicated procedures are now common practice (Table 2-2).

Contraindications have been divided into absolute and relative. Absolute contraindications were thought to increase patient morbidity irrespective of the surgeon's skill. With dramatic advances in the field recently, the line separating these two categories of contraindications appears to get thinner. For this reason, the conventional separation between the two categories of contraindications does not appear in the following section. The choice is left to the readers to draw their own conclusions and formulate their own contraindications.

Severe Medical Disease

The presence of severe cardiopulmonary disease has traditionally been considered an absolute contraindication to laparoscopy. Unfortunately, no well-defined set of criteria exists to select for medically compromised patients at higher risk for the procedure. As a result, many ill patients who may benefit from reduced postoperative discomfort and shortened convalescence time with laparoscopy could be denied access to this treatment modality. Therefore, there is a strong need for a more meaningful definition of medical risk for laparoscopy at all category levels.

An understanding of the basic physiologic changes associated with laparoscopy is essential for a better appreciation of the risk involved. Two main events during the induction of the pneumoperitoneum can have significant physiologic changes in the patient: (1) CO_2 gas insufflation and (2) increased intra-abdominal pressure (IP).

Table 2-2. Contraindications of Laparoscopy

Severe medical disease
    Severe cardiac disease
    Cardiac arrhythmias
    Severe pulmonary disease
    Hemodynamic instability
    Critically ill patients
    Generalized sepsis
Neurologic disease
Coagulopathies
Previous abdominal surgery
Abdominal ileus
Large abdominal mass
Hiatal hernia
External hernia

Although previously recognized, the physiologic consequences of laparoscopy have been poorly appreciated in clinical practice, as most laparoscopies were diagnostic and were performed in young healthy women. As more medically compromised patients are now undergoing the procedure and with the shift toward operative laparoscopy, the significance of these hemodynamic changes is assuming a new dimension.

Severe Cardiac Disease

The induction of general anesthesia is accompanied by a reduction in MAP, CVP, and SV, resulting in a decreased coronary and myocardial perfusion pressure flow. With the establishment of the pneumoperitoneum, the abrupt increase of IP leads to a dramatic increase in MAP, SV, and venous resistance. With reduced cardiac preload, heart rate (HR) increases to maintain an adequate CO, which results in increased myocardial oxygen consumption. Concomitantly, the increase in the cardiac afterload raises ventricular wall tension, further compromising transmural coronary artery flow. Patients with coronary artery disease may be at high risk for transient myocardial ischemia during laparoscopy. Careful intravascular volume expansion aimed at improving cardiac preload seems to offset the effects of increased IP and can be an important mode of myocardial protection in these patients.

Patients with aortic outflow obstruction are also at increased risk of myocardial ischemic changes with laparoscopy. As blood flow decreases across the aortic valve during the induction of general anesthesia, a reduction in coronary perfusion occurs. The compensatory increase in HR, resulting from reduced preload, leads to shortened diastolic filling time and increased left ventricular work. Increased IP then raises MAP, SV, and left ventricular wall tension, increasing myocardial oxygen demand and the potential for ischemia. Careful afterload reduction becomes essential for unloading the left ventricle and controlling left ventricular stroke work.

Cardiac Arrhythmias

Cardiac arrhythmias are common during laparoscopy. Their incidence was noted to be 47 percent in one study, with bradyarrhythmias accounting for 30 percent of cases.[153] Nearly all episodes occurred during carbon dioxide insufflation or traction on pelvic structures. Because cardiac arrhythmias can result from respiratory acidosis and reflex sympathetic nervous system stimulation, as well as from hypoxia and vagal stimulation,[154,155] Scott and Julian[156] suggested that the

1. *CO_2 gas insufflation:* Because of its high diffusibility through the peritoneal membranes, CO_2 gas can potentially attain elevated serum levels that could cause cardiovascular impairment. Significant elevations in serum CO_2 (pCO_2) and end-tidal CO_2 ($ETCO_2$) with concomitant fall in serum pH have been observed with laparoscopy.[140,141] Elevations in systolic and mean arterial pressures (SAP, MAP), central venous pressure (CVP), cardiac output (CO), and left ventricular stroke volume (SV) are well-known effects of hypercarbia.[142,143] In current practice, however, this condition is largely avoided by the use of controlled mechanical ventilation during general anesthesia. Nonetheless, persistent elevations in arterial carbon dioxide tension ($PaCO_2$) with resultant hypercapnia and acidosis can still occur in patients. Those with cardiopulmonary disease appear to be particularly susceptible.[141,144]

2. *Increased IP:* Acute increases in IP during the pneumoperitoneum may have several hemodynamic consequences. The increase in IP impedes diaphragmatic mobility and excursion, resulting in a restricted pulmonary compliance. As a consequence, peak airway pressure rises and vital lung capacity falls.[145–148] Compression of the basilar lung fields leads to decreased functional residual capacity and increased alveolar dead space and results in V/Q mismatch.[148] This may further be worsened when the patient is placed in the Trendelenberg position.[149]

An increase in IP during the establishment of the pneumoperitoneum in healthy patients results in an approximate 15 percent increase in MAP, a 23 percent fall in SV, a 79 percent increase in total peripheral resistance index, and a 0 to 17 percent decrease in CO.[138,147,149–152] This is accompanied by a 30 percent reduction in cardiac index.[152]

Although these changes are well tolerated by healthy individuals, they may increase physiologic stress in patients with pre-existing conditions, placing them at increased risk for perioperative complications.

culprit was CO_2 gas used for abdominal distention and demonstrated a lower rate of cardiac arrhythmias with the use of nitrous oxide gas. Some inhaled anesthetics and muscle relaxants may also sensitize the myocardium and predispose them to arrhythmias.

Severe Pulmonary Disease

Chronic obstructive pulmonary disease patients have a large ventilatory dead space and therefore are unable to cope efficiently with the increased CO_2 load because their main CO_2 disposal mechanism is impaired. Consequently, the patient's body acts as a CO_2 sink, resulting in significant hemodynamic alterations due to profound hypercarbia and acidemia. In these patients, intraoperative hemodynamic complications may be preventable by meticulous intraoperative monitoring. Controlled ventilation with continuous adjustment of ventilatory rate and volume settings based on changing serum $PaCO_2$ levels during the procedure is necessary.

Hemodynamic Instability

Intraperitoneal insufflation with CO_2 for laparoscopy may be hazardous in acute hypovolemic patients. A direct association was found between the volume status and CO at elevated IPs.[157,158] At low right-sided filling pressures as in hypovolemia, elevated IP compresses the inferior vena cava (IVC), impeding venous return and reducing CO. This is not seen at high right-sided pressures presumably because of facilitated emptying of the splanchnic circulation. Also, a significant drop in baseline SV and cardiac index was noted in moderately hemorrhaged animals when compared with euvolemic animals after induction of the pneumoperitoneum.[159] These effects were thought to be mediated through the accumulation of CO_2 in the system. In view of limited diaphragmatic mobility during spontaneous breathing, hypercarbia tends to occur, thereby increasing intraoperative risks. Associated physiologic changes may not be readily detectable until after patient decompensation. The use of controlled mechanical ventilation with adequate monitoring reduces the risks of hypercarbia.

Laparoscopy, therefore, may not be advised for patients with hemorrhagic volume depletion presenting with evidence of hemodynamic decompensation.

Critically Ill Patients

Laparoscopy in the critically ill patient with acute respiratory failure should be approached very cautiously especially when positive end-expiratory pressure (PEEP) is required for respiratory assistance. By increasing the functional residual capacity and decreasing intrapulmonary vascular shunting, PEEP can be very helpful in improving oxygenation in patients with acute respiratory failure. However, when used with intraperitoneal insufflation, it can result in deleterious circulatory effects.[160] The pneumoperitoneum was found to exacerbate the known side effects of PEEP in animals, raising concerns about the potential risks of laparoscopy in critically ill patients on PEEP.[161] The resulting decrease in stroke index, left ventricular stroke index, cardiac index, and pulmonary vascular resistance index observed in animals may exacerbate ischemic changes in bowel and other organs. Clinical human studies are required to determine whether these reported deleterious effects are relevant.

An intensive care patient with metabolic acidosis and reduced reserve may decompensate in the presence of the metabolic changes associated with the pneumoperitoneum. Aggressive preoperative stabilization and intraoperative monitoring are required to prevent potentially fatal complications.

Generalized Sepsis

Patients with significant medical disease appear to be more susceptible to hemodynamic changes during CO_2 insufflation despite controlled mechanical ventilation.[144] Profound hypercarbia and acidemia in these patients may reflect a limited homeostatic reserve easily overwhelmed by the increase in CO_2 load. Particularly susceptible are patients with high metabolic and cellular respiratory rates, as occurs in generalized sepsis.

Until recently, no systematic investigations had been performed to define the intraoperative response of patients with pre-existing cardiac disease to laparoscopy. In a unique report, Safran et al.[162] evaluated the effects of laparoscopic cholecystectomy in 15 patients with cardiac disease ASA III and IV (American Society of Anesthesiologists). Pulmonary artery and radial artery catheters were placed for intraoperative monitoring, and mixed venous oximetry, an indicator of total body oxygen demand and delivery, was used to signal cardiovascular decompensation. Under well-monitored conditions, all patients tolerated the procedure safely without cardiovascular morbidity. The authors therefore recommended aggressive preoperative optimization of hemodynamic function and vigilant intraoperative monitoring in patients with severe cardiopulmonary disease undergoing laparoscopy.

The CO_2 pneumoperitoneum can cause substantial alterations in acid-base and blood gas metabolism, pulmonary mechanics, and cardiorespiratory physiology. Although it is becoming more evident that laparoscopy can result in serious hemodynamic stress in patients with significant co-morbidity, the procedure may be performed in high-risk patients with the use of aggressive intraoperative monitoring. Optimal perioperative management involves anticipation of hemodynamic stress and early intervention.

Neurologic Disease

One potential hazard of laparoscopy in the patient with neurologic disease is the increase in intraperitoneal pressure that can potentially alter intracranial pressure (ICP) and cerebral perfusion pressure (CPP).

Until recently, no studies had been performed to investigate the effects of the pneumoperitoneum on ICP. The effects of hypercarbia and acidemia on raising ICP, however, are well known. Using an animal model, Josephs et al.[163] demonstrated an elevation in ICP during the induction of the pneumoperitoneum that was independent of $PaCO_2$ and pH. Despite the fact that hypercarbia can now be monitored and controlled by mechanical ventilation during general anesthesia, elevations in ICP can still potentially occur through different mechanisms. This may be very concerning in patients with certain neurologic diseases that are susceptible to variations in ICP. CPP may be secondarily affected in the presence of neurologic disease because of impaired autoregulation, increasing the risk for cerebral ischemia. These effects may be even more pronounced in the Trendelenberg position during gynecologic surgery. Because of the potential for significant increase in ICP and alteration in CPP, laparoscopy should be considered with extreme caution in patients with neurologic disease.

Coagulopathies

Bleeding disorders should be corrected and managed before laparoscopic surgery in the same way as with conventional surgery. In a retrospective evaluation of only four patients on warfarin anticoagulation therapy, laparoscopic cholecystectomy was performed safely and with no hemostatic complications after heparinization.[164] Although minimally invasive, laparoscopy has yet to be proved safe in patients whose condition requires anticoagulation therapy.

Previous Abdominal Surgery

The presence of previous abdominal scars increases the risk of bowel damage during the blind introduction of instruments. The consideration of the laparoscopic approach should take into account the type, indications, and circumstances of previous surgeries. A history of peritonitis, carcinomatosis, or previous colostomies may significantly increase the risks of inadvertent bowel injury during laparoscopy.

Alternate access sites of abdominal entry should be sought when adhesions are suspected. Reich[165] described the insertion of the Veress needle in the left ninth intercostal space along the anterior axillary line for the purpose of establishing the pneumoperitoneum. Placement of the Veress needle through the cul-de-sac of Douglas has also been described. The technique of open laparoscopy, involving the direct insertion of the trocar under direct vision, has initially been proposed by Hasson[166] as a means of reducing inadvertent bowel injury. Although reported to have failed in reducing the risk of bowel and vascular injuries, it remains a viable option for many gynecologists. As a result of recent technologic advances, a new generation of trocars has been developed, permitting the entry of the abdominal wall layers under continuous laparoscopic monitoring. The efficacy of this technology in reducing the risk of bowel injury remains unknown.

Abdominal Ileus

Mechanical and paralytical ileus secondary to intestinal obstruction or peritonitis may significantly increase the likelihood of bowel trauma and perforation during laparoscopy. Distented bowel loops against the anterior abdominal wall are susceptible to the blind insertion of the Veress needle and trocar.

Large Abdominal Mass

The presence of a large abdominal mass may increase the risk of inadvertent injury to the mass by the blind-access technique. It may be useful in these circumstances to use alternate entry ports for the induction of the pneumoperitoneum or the open trocar insertion technique. Conventionally, a mass size larger than a 14-week pregnant uterus has been considered a contraindication to laparoscopy.

Hiatal Hernia

Hiatal hernias are frequently asymptomatic and are found in 33 percent of the population.[167] Large symptomatic hernias theoretically carry the potential of abdominal contents being pushed into the thoracic cavity with increasing IP. This may be further enhanced with the use of the steep Trendelenberg position. The direct placement of the trocar without prior abdominal distention has been proposed to avoid the above complication.[168]

External Hernia

A strangulated irreducible external hernia may exacerbate ischemic changes by the pulling effect of the pneumoperitoneum. Alternatively, the direct trocar insertion technique without prior peritoneal insufflation may be useful in this context. Also, umbilical hernias when associated with obesity may cause entrapment of abdominal contents in at least one-third of patients.[169] This can increase the risk of injury during needle or trocar insertion.

CONCLUSION

Strict indications and contraindications to laparoscopy are yet to be defined. These appear to be intimately related to recent technologic developments and improved surgical techniques. Unfortunately, they also appear to be driven at times by fashionable trends in surgical practice long before critical scientific evaluations are available. Strong public enthusiasm and aggressive media promotion commonly help feed these trends. However, as Pitkin[170] reminded us in 1992, the capability of the laparoscope does not define its indications, and therapeutic appropriateness should remain separate and independent from technical feasibility.

The principal attraction of laparoscopic surgery is its minimal access attribute that translates into shorter hospitalization, reduced convalescence, and decreased costs. The clinical benefits of many laparoscopic procedures over conventional laparotomy remain unclear. Scientific confirmation of the clinical virtues of many of these procedures still awaits accumulating clinical data. In the interim, situations exist in which laparoscopy appears to have important clinical use such that it would be inappropriate to withhold it from many patients. In these circumstances, decisions should be driven by common sense and sound clinical judgment.

REFERENCES

1. ACOG Committee Opinion: Credentialing guidelines for operative laparoscopy. Proceedings of the meeting of the American College of Obstetricians and Gynecologists, 1992
2. Society for Reproductive Surgeons, The American Fertility Society: Guidelines for attaining privileges in gynecologic operative endoscopy. Fertil Steril 62:1118, 1994
3. Jacobson L: Differential diagnosis of acute pelvic inflammatory disease. Am J Obstet Gynecol 7:1006, 1980
4. Sellors J, Mahony J, Goldsmith C et al: The accuracy of clinical findings and laparoscopy in pelvic inflammatory disease. Am J Obstet Gynecol 164:113, 1991
5. Hulka JF, Peterson HB, Phillips JM, Surrey MW: Operative laparoscopy. American Association of Gynecologic Laparoscopists 1991 membership survey. J Reprod Med 38:569, 1993
6. Lundberg WI, Wall JE, Mathers JE: Laparoscopy in evaluation of pelvic pain. Obstet Gynecol 42:872, 1973
7. Beard RW, Belsey EM, Lieberman BA et al: Pelvic pain in women. Am J Obstet Gynecol 128:566, 1977
8. Levitan Z, Eibschitz I, DeVries K et al: The value of laparoscopy in women with chronic pelvic pain and a normal pelvis. Int J Gynaecol Obstet 23:71, 1985
9. Vercellini P, Fedele L, Arcaini L et al: Laparoscopy in the diagnosis of chronic pelvic pain in adolescent women. J Reprod Med 34:827, 1989
10. Vercellini P, Fedele L, Molteni P et al: Laparoscopy in the diagnosis of gynecologic chronic pelvic pain. Int J Gynaecol Obstet 32:261, 1990
11. Cunanan RG, Courey NG, Lippes J: Laparoscopic findings in patients with pelvic pain. Am J Obstet Gynecol 136:589, 1983
12. Kresch AJ, Seifer DB, Sachs LB, Barrese I: Laparoscopy in 100 women with chronic pelvic pain. Obstet Gynecol 64:672, 1984
13. Baker PN, Symonds EM: The resolution of chronic pelvic pain after normal laparoscopy findings. Am J Obstet Gynecol 166:836, 1992
14. Swolin K, Rosencrantz M: Laparoscopy versus hysterosalpingography in sterility investigations: a comparative study. Fertil Steril 23:270, 1972
15. Keirse MJNC, Vandervellen R: A comparison of hysterosalpingography and laparoscopy in the investigation of infertility. Obstet Gynecol 41:685, 1973
16. El-Minawi MF, Abdel-Hadi M, Ibrahim AA, Wahby O: Comparative evaluation of laparoscopy and hysterosalpingography in infertile patients. Obstet Gynecol 51:29, 1978
17. Opsahl MS, Klein TA: Tubal and peritoneal factors in the infertile woman: use of patient history in selection of diagnosis and therapeutic surgical procedures. Fertil Steril 53:632, 1990
18. Opsahl MS, Miller B, Klein TA: The predictive value of hysterosalpingography for tubal and peritoneal infertility factors. Fertil Steril 60:444, 1993
19. Levine RL: Economic impact of pelviscopic surgery. J Reprod Med 30:655, 1985
20. Azziz R, Steinkampf MP, Murphy A: Postoperative recuperation: relation to the extent of endoscopic surgery. Fertil Steril 51:1061, 1989
21. Hope R: The differential diagnosis of ectopic pregnancy by peritoneoscopy. Surg Gynecol Obstet 64:229, 1937
21a. Shapiro HI, Adler DH: Excision of an ectopic pregnancy through the laparoscope. Am J Obstet Gynecol 117:290, 1973
22. Koninckx PR, Witters K, Brosens J et al: Conservative laparoscopic treatment of ectopic pregnancies using the CO_2-laser. Br J Obstet Gynaecol 98:1254, 1991
23. Lundorff P, Thornburn J, Lindblom B: Fertility outcome after conservative surgical treatment of ectopic pregnancy evaluated in a randomized trial. Fertil Steril 57:998, 1992
24. Murphy AA, Kettel LM, Nager CW et al: Operative laparoscopy versus laparotomy for the management of ectopic pregnancy: a prospective trial. Fertil Steril 57:1180, 1992
25. Sultana CJ, Easley K, Collins RL: Outcome of laparoscopic versus traditional surgery for ectopic pregnancies. Fertil Steril 57:285, 1992
26. Nager CW, Murphy AA: Ectopic pregnancy. Clin Obstet Gynecol 34:403, 1991
27. Brumsted J, Kessler C, Gibson C et al: A comparison of laparoscopy and laparotomy for the treatment of ectopic pregnancy. Obstet Gynecol 71:889, 1988
28. Vermesh M, Silva P, Rosen G et al: Management of unruptured ectopic gestation by linear salpingostomy: a prospective randomized clinical trial of laparoscopy versus laparotomy. Obstet Gynecol 73:400, 1989

29. Lundorff P, Hahlin M, Källfelt B et al: Adhesion formation after laparoscopic surgery in tubal pregnancy: a randomized trial versus laparotomy. Fertil Steril 55:911, 1991

30. Zouves C, Urman B, Gomel V: Laparoscopic surgical treatment of tubal pregnancy: a safe, effective alternative to laparotomy. J Reprod Med 37:205, 1992

31. Pouly JL, Mahnes H, Mage G et al: Conservative laparoscopic treatment of 321 ectopic pregnancies. Fertil Steril 46:1093, 1986

32. Dubuisson JB, Aubriot FX, Cardone V: Laparoscopic salpingectomy for tubal pregnancy. Fertil Steril 47:225, 1987

33. Reich H, Johns DA, DeCaprio J et al: Laparoscopic treatment of 109 consecutive ectopic pregnancies. J Reprod Med 33:885, 1988

34. Fervers C: Die Laparoskopie mit dem Cystoskope. Ein Beitrag zur Vereinfachung der Technik und zur endoskopischen Strangdurchtrennung in der Bauchole. Med Klin 29:1042, 1933

35. Peterson HB, Hulka JF, Phillips JM: American Association of Gynecologic Laparoscopist's 1988 membership survey on operative laparoscopy. J Reprod Med 35:587, 1990

36. Rapkin AJ: Adhesions and pelvic pain: a retrospective study. Obstet Gynecol 68:13, 1986

37. Rock JA, Katayama P, Martin EJ et al: Factors influencing the success of salpingostomy techniques for distal fimbrial obstruction. Obstet Gynecol 52:591, 1978

38. Walker E, Katon W, Harrop-Griffiths J et al: Relationship of chronic pelvic to psychiatric diagnoses and childhood sexual abuse. Am J Psychiatry 145:75, 1988

39. Lehmann-Willenbrock E, Mecke H, Riedel HH: Sequelae of appendectomy, with special reference to intra-abdominal adhesions, chronic abdominal pain, and infertility. Gynecol Obstet Invest 29:241, 1990

40. Peters AAW, Van Dorst E, Jellis B et al: A randomized clinical trial to compare two different approaches in women with chronic pelvic pain. Obstet Gynecol 77:740, 1991

41. Stout AL, Steege JF, Dodson WC, Hughes CL: Relationship of laparoscopic findings to self-report of pelvic pain. Am J Obstet Gynecol 164:73, 1991

42. Goldstein DP, DeCholnoky C, Emans SJ et al: Laparoscopy in the diagnosis and management of pelvic pain in adolescents. J Reprod Med 14:251, 1980

43. Daniell JF: Laparoscopic enterolysis for chronic abdominal pain. J Gynecol Surg 5:61, 1989

44. Sutton C, MacDonald R: Laser laparoscopic adhesiolysis. J Gynecol Surg 6:155, 1990

45. Fayez JA: An assessment of the role of operative laparoscopy in tuboplasty. Fertil Steril 39:476, 1983

46. Gomel V: Salpingo-ovariolysis by laparoscopy in infertility. Fertil Steril 40:607, 1983

47. Reich H: Laparoscopic treatment of extensive pelvic adhesions, including hydrosalpinx. J Reprod Med 32:736, 1987

48. Gomel V: Operative laparoscopy: time for acceptance. Fertil Steril 52:1, 1989

49. Young PE, Egan JE, Barlow JJ, Mulligan WJ: Reconstructive surgery for infertility at the Boston Hospital for Women. Am J Obstet Gynecol 108:1092, 1970

50. Bronson RA, Wallach EE: Lysis of periadnexal adhesions for correction of infertility. Fertil Steril 28:613, 1977

51. Diamond E: Lysis of postoperative pelvic adhesions in infertility. Fertil Steril 31:287, 1979

52. Hulka JF: Adnexal adhesions: a prognostic staging and classification system based on a five-year survey of fertility surgery results at Chapel-Hill, North Carolina. Am J Obstet Gynecol 144:141, 1982

53. Tulandi T: Salpingoovariolysis: a comparison between laser surgery and electrosurgery. Fertil Steril 45:489, 1986

54. Luciano AA, Maier DB, Koch EI et al: A comparative study of postoperative adhesions following laser surgery by laparoscopy versus laparotomy in the rabbit model. Obstet Gynecol 74:220, 1989

55. Operative Laparoscopy Study Group: Postoperative adhesion development after operative laparoscopy: evaluation at early second-look procedures. Fertil Steril 55:700, 1991

56. Peterson HB, Hulka JF, Phillips JM: American Association of Gynecologic Laparoscopist 1988 membership survey on operative laparoscopy. J Reprod Med 35:587, 1990

57. Sutton CJG, Ewen SP, Whitelaw N, Haines P: Prospective, randomized, double-blind, controlled trial of laser laparoscopy in the treatment of pelvic pain associated with minimal, mild, and moderate endometriosis. Fertil Steril 62:696, 1994

58. Garcia C-R, David SS: Pelvic endometriosis: infertility and pelvic pain. Am J Obstet Gynecol 129:740, 1977

59. Schenken RS, Malinak LR: Conservative surgery versus expectant management for the infertile patient with mild endometriosis. Fertil Steril 37:183, 1982

60. Hughes EG, Fedorkow DM, Collins JA: A quantitative overview of controlled trials in endometriosis-associated infertility. Fertil Steril 59:963, 1993

61. Rock JA, Guzick DS, Sengos C et al: The conservative surgical treatment of endometriosis: evaluation of pregnancy success with respect to the extent of disease as categorized using contemporary classification systems. Fertil Steril 35:131, 1981

62. Fayez JA, Collazo LM, Vernon C: Comparison of different modalities of treatment of minimal and mild endometriosis. Am J Obstet Gynecol 159:927, 1988

63. Damewood MD, Rock JA: Treatment independent pregnancy with operative laparoscopy for endometriosis in an in vitro fertilization program. Fertil Steril 50:463, 1988

64. Nezhat C, Cravgey S, Nezhat F: Video laseroscopy for the treatment of endometriosis associated with infertility. Fertil Steril 51:237, 1989

65. Buttram VC Jr: Conservative surgery for endometriosis in the infertile female: a study of 206 patients with implications for both medical and surgical therapy. Fertil Steril 31:117, 1979

66. Nezhat C, Crowgey SR, Garrison CP: Surgical treatment of endometriosis via laser laparoscopy. Fertil Steril 45:778, 1986

67. Canis M, Mage G, Manhes H et al: Laparoscopic treatment of endometriosis. Acta Obstet Gynecol Scand, suppl. 150:15, 1989

68. Davis GD: Management of endometriosis and its associated adhesions with the CO_2 laser laparoscope. Obstet Gynecol 68:422, 1986

69. Adamson GD, Hurd SJ, Pasta DJ, Rodrigez BD: Laparoscopic endometriosis treatment: is it better? Fertil Steril 59:35, 1993

70. Ranney B: Endometriosis. III. Complete operations. Am J Obstet Gynecol 109:1137, 1971

71. Adamson GD, Subak LL, Pasta DJ et al: Comparison of CO_2 laser laparoscopy with laparotomy for treatment of endometriomata. Fertil Steril 57:965, 1992

72. Kistner RW: Intraperitoneal rupture of benign cystic teratomas: review of the literature with a report of two cases. Obstet Gynecol Surv 7:603, 1952

73. Nezhat C, Winer WK, Nezhat F: Laparoscopic removal of dermoid cysts. Obstet Gynecol 73:278, 1989

74. Reich H: New techniques in advanced laparoscopic surgery. Baillieres Clin Obstet Gynecol 3:655, 1989

75. Mage G, Canis M, Manhes H et al: Laparoscopic management of adnexal cystic masses. J Gynecol Surg 6:71, 1990

76. Reich H, McGlynn F, Sekel L, Taylor P: Laparoscopic management of ovarian dermoid cysts. J Reprod Med 37:640, 1992

77. Power FH, Barnes AC: Sterilization by means of peritoneoscopic fulguration: a preliminary report. Am J Obstet Gynecol 41:1038, 1941

78. Bhiwandiwala PP, Mumford S, Feldblum PJ: A comparison of different laparoscopic sterilization occlusion techniques in 24,439 procedures. Am J Obstet Gynecol 144:319, 1982

79. Makar AP, Vanderheyden JS, Schatteman EA et al: Female sterilization failure after bipolar electrocoagulation: a 6 year retrospective study. Eur J Obstet Gynecol Reprod Biol 37:237, 1990

80. Holt VL, Chu J, Daling JR et al: Tubal sterilization and subsequent ectopic pregnancy. JAMA 266:242, 1991

81. Hulka JF, Peterson HB, Phillips JM: American Association of Gynecologic Laparoscopists 1988 membership survey on laparoscopic sterilization. J Reprod Med 35:584, 1990

82. Trope C: The preoperative diagnosis of malignancy of ovarian cysts. Neoplasia 28:117, 1981

83. Larsen JF, Pederson OD, Gregersen E: Ovarian cyst fenestration via the laparoscope. Acta Obstet Gynecol Scand 65:539, 1986

84. Maiman M, Seltzer V, Boyce J: Laparoscopic excision of ovarian neoplasms subsequently found to be malignant. Obstet Gynecol 77:563, 1991

85. Hulka JF, Parker WH, Surrey MW, Phillips JM: Management of ovarian masses. AAGL 1990 Survey. J Reprod Med 37:599, 1992

86. Herrman V, Locher G, Goldhirsch A. Sonographic patterns of ovarian tumors: prediction of malignancy. Obstet Gynecol 69:777, 1987

87. Benacerraf BR, Finkler NJ, Wojciechowski C, Knapp RC: Sonographic accuracy in the diagnosis of ovarian masses. J Reprod Med 35:491, 1990

88. Granberg S, Norstrom A, Wikland M: Tumors in the lower pelvis as imaged by vaginal sonography. Gynecol Oncol 37:224, 1990

89. Rulin M, Preston A: Adnexal masses in postmenopausal women. Obstet Gynecol 72:578, 1987

90. Weiner Z, Thaler I, Beck D et al: Differentiating malignant from benign ovarian tumors with transvaginal color flow imaging. Obstet Gynecol 79:159, 1992

91. Vasilev S, Schlaerth J, Campeau J, Morrow P: Serum CA-125 levels in preoperative evaluation of pelvic masses. Obstet Gynecol 71:751, 1988

92. Jacobs I, Bast R: The CA-125 tumor associated antigen: a review of the literature. Hum Reprod 4:1, 1989

93. Finkler N, Benacerraf B, Lavin F et al: Comparison of serum CA-125, clinical impression, and ultrasound in the preoperative evaluation of ovarian masses. Obstet Gynecol 72:659, 1988

94. Hulka J, Parker W, Surrey M, Phillips J: Management of ovarian masses: AAGL 1990 Survey. J Reprod Med 7:599, 1992

95. Grogan R: Accidental rupture of malignant ovarian cysts during surgical removal. Obstet Gynecol 30:718, 1987

96. Dembo AJ, Davy M, Stenwig AE et al: Prognostic factors in patients with stage I epithelial ovarian cancer. Obstet Gynecol 75:263, 1990

97. Gleeson NC, Nicosia SV, Mark JE et al: Abdominal wall metastases from ovarian cancer after laparoscopy. Am J Obstet Gynecol 169:522, 1993

98. Goodman MP, Johns DA, Levine RL et al: Report of the study group: advanced operative laparoscopy (pelviscopy). J Gynecol Surg 5:353, 1989

99. Gomel V: Salpingostomy by laparoscopy. J Reprod Med 18:265, 1977

100. Mettler L, Giesel H, Semm K: Treatment of female infertility due to tubal obstruction by operative laparoscopy. Fertil Steril 32:384, 1979

101. Daniell JF, Herbert CM: Laparoscopic salpingostomy utilizing the carbon dioxide laser. Fertil Steril 41:558, 1984

102. Hibbard LT: Adnexal torsion. Am J Obstet Gynecol 152:456, 1985

103. Jeffcoate TNA: Torsion of the pelvic organs. p. 280. In Tindall VR (ed): Principles of Gynaecology. 4th Ed. Butterworths, London, 1975

104. Vancaillie T, Schmidt E: Recovery of ovarian function after laparoscopic treatment of acute adnexal torsion. J Reprod Med 32:561, 1987

105. Mage G, Canis M, Mahnes H et al: Laparoscopic management of adnexal torsion: a review of 35 cases. J Reprod Med 34:520, 1989

106. Bider D, Mashiach S, Dulitzki M et al: Clinical, surgical, and pathologic findings of adnexal torsion in pregnant and nonpregnant women. Surg Gynecol Obstet 173:363, 1991

107. Oelsner G, Bider D, Goldenberg M et al: Long-term follow-up of the twisted ischemic adnexa managed by detorsion. Fertil Steril 60:976, 1993

108. Zweizig S, Perron J, Grubb D, Mishell DR: Conservative management of adnexal torsion. Am J Obstet Gynecol 168:1791, 1993

109. Greenblatt E, Casper RF: Endocrine changes after laparoscopic ovarian cautery in polycystic ovarian syndrome. Am J Obstet Gynecol 156:279, 1987

110. Armar NA, Holownia N, McGarrigle HHG et al: Laparoscopic ovarian diathermy in the management of anovulatory infertility in women with polycystic ovaries: endocrine changes and clinical outcome. Fertil Steril 53:45, 1990

111. Campo S, Garcea N, Caruso A, Siccardi P: Effect of celioscopic ovarian resection in patients with polycystic ovaries. Gynecol Obstet Invest 15:213, 1983

112. Gjönnaess H: Polycystic ovarian syndrome treated by ovarian electrocautery through the laparoscope. Fertil Steril 41:20, 1984

113. Aakvaag A, Gjonnaess H: Hormonal response to electrocautery of the ovary in patients with polycystic ovarian disease. Br J Obstet Gynaecol 92:1258, 1985

114. Daniell JF, Miller W: Polycystic ovaries treated by laparoscopic laser vaporization. Fertil Steril 51:232, 1989

115. Armar NA, Lachelin GCL: Laparoscopic ovarian diathermy: an effective treatment for anti-oestrogen resistant anovulatory infertility in women with the polycystic ovary syndrome. Br J Obstet Gynaecol 100:161, 1993

116. Dabirashrafi H, Mohamad K, Behjatnia Y, Moghadami-Tabrizi N: Adhesion formation after ovarian electrocauterization on patients with polycystic ovarian syndrome. Fertil Steril 55:1200, 1991

117. Nezhat C, Nezhat F, Silfen SL et al: Laparoscopic myomectomy. Int J Fertil 36:275, 1991

118. Hasson HM, Rotman C, Rana N et al: Laparoscopic myomectomy. Obstet Gynecol 80:884, 1992

119. Daniell JF, Gurley LD: Laparoscopic treatment of clinically significant symptomatic uterine fibroids. J Gynecol Surg 7:37, 1991

120. Jansen RP: Early laparoscopy after pelvic operations to prevent adhesions, safety, and efficacy. Fertil Steril 49:26, 1988

121. Smith DC, Uhlir JK: Myomectomy as a reproductive procedure. Am J Obstet Gynecol 162:1476, 1990

122. American Fertility Society: The American Fertility Society Guideline for Practice: Myomas and Reproductive Function. American Fertility Society, Birmingham, AL, 1992

123. Reich H, DeCaprio J, McGlynn F: Laparoscopic hysterectomy. J Gynecol Surg 5:213, 1989

124. Maher PJ, Wood EC, Hill DJ, Lolatgis NA: Laparoscopically-assisted hysterectomy. Med J Aust 156:316, 1992

125. Minelli L, Angiolillo M, Caione C, Palmara V: Laparoscopically-assisted vaginal hysterectomy. Endoscopy 23:64, 1991

126. Summitt RL Jr, Stovall TG, Lipscomb GH, Ling FW: Randomized comparison of laparoscopy-assisted vaginal hysterectomy with standard vaginal hysterectomy in an outpatient setting. Obstet Gynecol 80:895, 1992

127. Smale LE, Smale ML, Wilkening RL et al: Salpingo-oophorectomy at the time of vaginal hysterectomy. Am J Obstet Gynecol 131:122, 1978

128. Hoffman MS: Transvaginal removal of ovaries with endoloop sutures at the time of vaginal hysterectomy. Am J Obstet Gynecol 165:407, 1991

129. Sheth SS: The place of oophorectomy at vaginal hysterectomy. Br J Obstet Gynaecol 98:662, 1991

130. Boike GM, Elfstrand EP, DelPriore G et al: Laparoscopically assisted vaginal hysterectomy in a university hospital: report of 82 cases and comparison with abdominal and vaginal hysterectomy. Am J Obstet Gynecol 168:1690, 1993

131. Longebrekke A, Skar SO, Urnes A: Laparoscopic hysterectomy. Acta Obstet Gynecol Scand 71:226, 1992

132. Woodland MB: Ureter injury during laparoscopy-assisted vaginal hysterectomy with the endoscopic linear stapler. Am J Obstet Gynecol 167:756, 1992

133. Doyle JB: Paracervical uterine denervation by transection of the cervical plexus for the relief of dysmenorrhea. Am J Obstet Gynecol 70:1, 1955

134. Lichten EM, Bombard J: Surgical treatment of primary dysmenorrhea with laparoscopic uterine nerve ablation. J Reprod Med 32:37, 1987

135. Trimbos-Kemper TCM, Trimbos JB, Van Hall EV: Adhesions formation after tubal surgery: results of the eighth-day laparoscopy in 188 patients. Fertil Steril 43:395, 1985

136. Tulandi T, Falcone T, Kafka I: Second-look operative laparoscopy 1 year following reproductive surgery. Fertil Steril 52:421, 1989

137. Raj SG, Hulka JF: Second-look laparoscopy in infertility surgery: therapeutic and prognostic value. Fertil Steril 38:325, 1982

138. Semm K: Technique of second look pelviscopic surgery: prevention of recurrence of adhesions, abstracted (82). Third World Congress on the Fallopian Tube, Kiel, Germany, 1990

139. DeCherney AH, Mezer HC: The nature of posttuboplasty pelvic adhesions as determined by early and late laparoscopy. Fertil Steril 41:643, 1984

140. Baratz RA, Karis JH: Blood gas studies during laparoscopy under general anesthesia. Anesthesiology 1:241, 1969

141. Liu SY, Leighton T, Davis I et al: Prospective analysis of cardiopulmonary responses to laparoscopic cholecystectomy. J Laparoendosc Surg 1:241, 1991

142. Rasmussen JP, Dauchot PJ, DePalma RG et al: Cardiac function and hypercarbia. Arch Surg 113:1196, 1978

143. Versichelen L, Serreyn R, Rolly G et al: Physiopathologic changes during anesthesia administration for gynecologic laparoscopic. J Reprod Med 29:697, 1984

144. Wittgen CM, Andrus CH, Fitzgerald SD et al: Analysis of the hemodynamic and ventilatory effects of laparoscopic cholecystectomy. Arch Surg 126:997, 1991

145. Alexander GD, Noe FE, Brown EM: Anesthesia for laparoscopy. Anesth Analg 48:14, 1969

146. Brown DR, Fishburne JI, Roberson VO, Hulka JF: Ventilatory and blood gas changes during laparoscopy with local anesthesia. Am J Obstet Gynecol 124:741, 1976

147. Johannsen G, Anderson M, Juhl B: The effect of general anesthesia on the haemodynamic events during laparoscopy with CO_2 insufflation. Acta Anaesthesiol Scand 33:132, 1989

148. Puri GD, Singh H: Ventilatory effects of laparoscopy under general anesthesia. Br J Anaesth 68:211, 1992

149. Kelman GR, Swapp GH, Smith I et al: Cardiac output and arterial blood-gas tension during laparoscopy. Br J Anaesth 44:1155, 1972

150. Motew M, Ivankovich AD, Bienarz J et al: Cardiovascular effects and acid-base and blood gas changes during laparoscopy. Am J Obstet Gynecol 115:1002, 1973

151. Lenz RJ, Thomas TA, Wilkins DG: Cardiovascular changes during laparoscopy. Anaesthesia 31:4, 1976

152. Westerband A, Van De Water JM, Amzallag M et al: Cardiovascular changes during laparoscopic cholecystectomy. Surg Gynecol Obstet 175:535, 1992

153. Myles PS: Bradyarrhythmias and laparoscopy: a prospective study of heart rate changes during laparoscopy. Aust NZ J Obstet Gynecol 31:171, 1991

154. Carmichael DE: Laparoscopy: cardiac considerations. Fertil Steril 22:69, 1970

155. Harris MNE, Plantevin OM, Crowther A: Cardiac arrhythmias during anaesthesia for laparoscopy. Br J Anaesth 56:1213, 1984

156. Scott DB, Julian DG: Observations on cardiac arrhythmias during laparoscopy. BJH 1:411, 1972

157. Diamant M, Benumof JL, Saidman LJ: Hemodynamics of increased intraabdominal pressure: interaction with hypovolemia and halothane anesthesia. Anesthesiology 48:23, 1978

158. Kashtan J, Green JF, Parsons EQ, Holcroft JW: Hemodynamic effects of increased abdominal pressure. J Surg Res 30:249, 1981

159. Ho HS, Saunders CJ, Corso FA, Wolfe BM: The effects of CO_2 pneumoperitoneum on hemodynamics in hemorrhaged animals. Surgery 114:381, 1993

160. Burchard KW, Ciombor DM, McLeod MK: Positive end-expiratory pressure with increased intraabdominal pressure. Surg Gynecol Obstet 161:313, 1985

161. Moffa SM, Quinn JV, Slotman GJ: Hemodynamic effects of carbon dioxide pneumoperitoneum during mechanical ventilation and positive end-expiratory pressure. J Trauma 35:613, 1993

162. Safran D, Sgambati S, Orlando R: Laparoscopy in high-risk cardiac patients. Surg Gynecol Obstet 176:548, 1993

163. Josephs LG, Este-McDonald JR, Birkett DH, Hirsch EF: Diagnostic laparoscopy increases intracranial pressure. J Trauma 36:815, 1994

164. Fitzgerald SD, Bailey PV, Liebscher GJ, Andrus CH: Laparoscopic cholecystectomy in anticoagulated patients. Surg Endosc 5:166, 1991

165. Reich H: Laparoscopic bowel injury. Surg Laparosc Endosc 2:74, 1992

166. Hasson HM: Open laparoscopy: a report of 150 cases. J Reprod Med 12:234, 1974

167. Dyer NH, Pridie RB: Incidence of hiatus hernia in asymptomatic subject. Gut 9:696, 1968

168. Dingfelder JR: Direct laparoscopic trocar insertion without prior pneumoperitoneum. J Reprod Med 21:45, 1978

169. Baccari EM, Breiling B, Organ CH: A study of the maturity onset of adult umbilical hernia. Am Surg 37:385, 1971

170. Pitkin RM: Operative laparoscopy: surgical advance or technical gimmick? Obstet Gynecol 79:441, 1992

3 Lasers in Gynecology: CO$_2$ and Fiber Lasers

JAMES SHWAYDER

The introduction of lasers to gynecologic surgery opened up a world of imagination and innovation. This technology served as the impetus for development of operative laparoscopes and the accompanying instrumentation, which has flourished in recent years. Although improvements in electrosurgical instrumentation have replaced many laser applications, lasers remain an integral part the armamentarium of the gynecologic surgeon. Thorough knowledge of the various types of lasers and their applications is mandatory for the well-versed endoscopic surgeon.

PHYSICAL PRINCIPLES

LASER is an acronym for light amplification through the stimulated emission of radiation. The basic concept of laser energy was introduced by Einstein in 1917. He proposed the concept of stimulated emission, thus laying the foundation for lasers as we know them today.[1]

An atom or molecule in its normal energy state or ground state is capable of becoming excited to a higher energy level by absorption of thermal, electric, or optic energy (Fig. 3-1). After energy is absorbed, an atom, or more specifically an electron, spontaneously returns to its ground state (*spontaneous emission of radiation*) and releases the absorbed energy (photon) (Fig. 3-2). With stimulated emission, an atom in its excited state is bombarded by a photon, releasing two waves of energy simultaneously (Fig. 3-3).[2]

To produce the potent energy of lasers, a larger population of atoms must exist in the excited state than at the ground state. Such a situation is referred to as *population inversion*. These excited atoms/molecules are thus prepared to simultaneously release their energy photons under appropriate stimulation.

BASIC LASER COMPONENTS

Certain basic components are found in all medical laser systems.[3] An active medium is the collection of atoms capable of undergoing stimulated emission. The most common active mediums used in gynecology include CO$_2$, neodymium, and argon. The active medium is typically contained within a closed space, the resonator or optic cavity, which has two parallel mirrors (Fig. 3-4). The rear mirror reflects 100 percent of the energy that strikes it, whereas the front mirror reflects only a portion of the impingent energy. The front mirror is designed with an exit port to allow the controlled release of the energy that has accumulated in the resonator tube. A shutter is present that, when activated by a foot pedal, opens, allowing the release of laser energy.

CHARACTERISTICS OF LASER LIGHT

Laser light possesses three characteristics that render it highly effective.

Coherence (Fig. 3-5): all waves are exactly in step or in phase with each other, both in space and in time.

Collimated (Fig. 3-6): All rays are virtually parallel to each other. Thus, even over long distances the laser beam diverges only slightly.

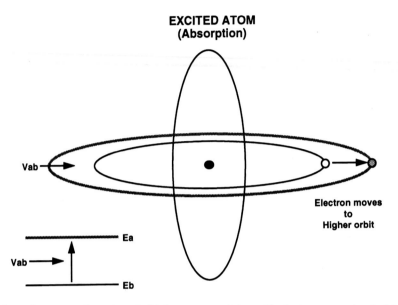

Fig. 3-1. Absorption of energy raises atom to higher energy state, with electrons moving to higher orbit.

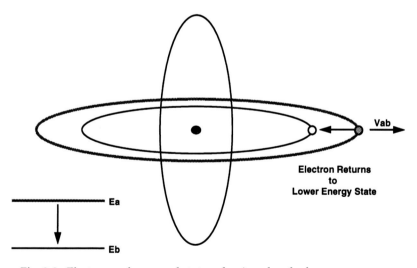

Fig. 3-2. Electron seeks ground state, releasing absorbed energy.

STIMULATED EMISSION

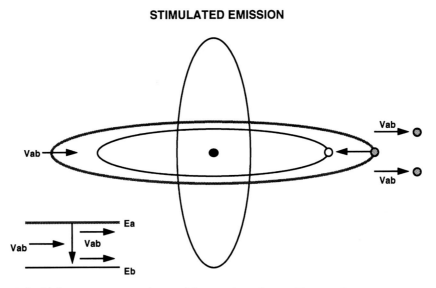

Fig. 3-3. Photon at the highest energy state is struck by another photon. This produces two photons in phase and of the same wavelength.

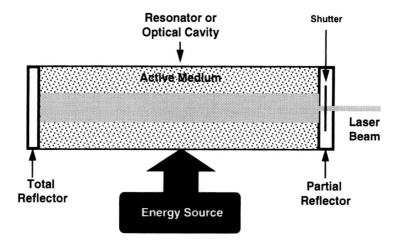

Fig. 3-4. Components of laser resonator or optic cavity.

**Laser Light
(Coherent)** **Ordinary Light
(Non-Coherent)**

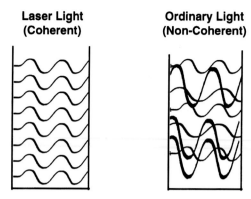

Fig. 3-5. Coherent light waves are in phase.

Monochromatic: All waves have essentially the same wavelength and the same energy. Thus, all energy from a particular laser beam will have identical and reproducible effects on tissue.

TISSUE ACTION OF LASER ENERGY

The mechanism by which lasers create their tissue effect is determined by a rise in the temperature of the tissue resulting from absorption of the laser beam. If tissue is heated above 60°C for more than a few seconds, protein denaturation and coagulation will take place. As the temperature approaches 100°C intracellular water begins to evaporate, causing tissue shrinkage and loss (*vaporization*). Temperatures beyond this lead to carbonization and burning (Table 3-1).

The effect of laser light on tissue depends on the following interactions: reflection, transmission, scattering, and absorption (Fig. 3-7). Ultimate tissue effects of lasers depend on the absorption of the laser beam. If a laser is transmitted through or reflected from tissue it has no effect. If light is scattered, it will be absorbed over a broader area so that its effects are more diffuse (Fig. 3-8). Although the final mechanism of the tissue effects of lasers is typically heat, each laser possesses a unique profile of tissue absorption, depending on the frequency of the laser light produced and the delivery system used (Table 3-2 and Fig. 3-9).

Certain modifications of a laser's action are independent of the type used. *Power density* refers to the concentration of energy at the point of impact of a laser beam. At a constant beam power, the surface area at the point of impact affects the concentration of energy.[4] Specifically, the power density is inversely proportional to the square of area of impact. Thus, doubling the size of impact (spot size) effectively reduces the power delivered by one-fourth. Conversely, reducing the spot size by one-half increases the power delivered by a factor of 4[5] (Fig. 3-10).

Focal length refers to the distance from the focusing lens at which the concentration of power (i.e., power density) is greatest (Fig. 3-11). This is a factor of the focal length of the lens, the delivery system, and the type of laser. When using lasers in laparoscopy, the surgeon must be aware of the potential for working with a laser in a "prefocused" fashion. Although the tissue effect seen is fairly constant, the greatest tissue damage is at the focal length of the laser, actually deeper in the tissue. Thus, unintended injury to deeper structures can

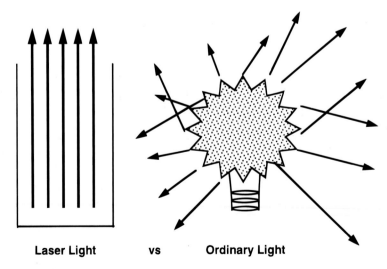

Laser Light vs **Ordinary Light**

Fig. 3-6. Collimated light waves are parallel with each other.

Table 3-1. Effects of Tissue Heating

Temperature (°C)	Visual Change	Tissue Effect
<43	None	Thermal conductivity and repair
43–60	Retraction	Denaturation and death of normal cells
60–65	Blanching	Coagulation
65–90	White puckering	Necrosis
100	Plume	Vaporization of water
>150	Char formation	Carbonization

(Data from Martin,[7] Keckstein,[42] and Absten.[43])

occur. It is thus recommended to work at the true focal length of the laser delivery system or withdraw the laser and work with a "defocused" beam, which is actually "postfocused." As a result, the area of greatest power density is actually in "free space," before laser impact, thus preventing inadvertent destruction of deeper tissues.

SURGICAL LASERS

A variety of laser media are currently being used in gynecology. The most commonly used in gynecology include CO_2, neodymium:yttrium-aluminum-garnet (Nd:YAG), potassium-titanyl-phosphate (KTP), and argon (Fig. 3-12). Many new types are in development and will perhaps be available in the near future.[6]

Carbon Dioxide Laser

The CO_2 laser is one of the most commonly used and versatile surgical lasers. It is used externally, in the treatment of lower tract disease, intra-abdominally at laparotomy, and laparoscopically, either through a sec- ondary probe or via the operating channel of the laser laparoscope. The active medium in the laser cavity is the CO_2 molecule. However, energy transfer requires nitrogen and helium. Thus, a mixture of all three gases is present in the laser cavity. The laser emits energy in the nonvisible portion of the light spectrum at 10,600 nm (10.6 μm). Thus, a second laser, a visible helium-neon (HeNe) laser is used as an aiming beam. Proper alignment of the HeNe and CO_2 lasers are required, such that the appropriate point of impact can be determined. To provide for safe application, proper alignment of the laser beams must be confirmed at the beginning of each surgical case. If the two lasers are not aligned, the CO_2 laser cannot be safely used at surgery. Typically, lack of alignment is due to misalignment of the mirrors in the laser arm.

Tissue Effects

The CO_2 laser is highly absorbed by water. Tissue is composed of 70 to 90 percent water, which acts as the primary absorbing medium. The absorption coefficient is so high that 98 percent of the incident energy is absorbed in the first 0.01 mm of tissue (Fig. 3-12).[7–10] As such, the CO_2 laser has very predictable tissue action, penetration, and thermal effect.[11] Because there is minimal tissue effect beyond the initial 0.01 mm, the typical action of the CO_2 laser is "what you see is what you get." As the laser energy is absorbed, the temperature of the water in the tissue is immediately brought to "boiling" and the cells are vaporized, resulting in the production of a "smoke" vapor (Fig. 3-13). At la-

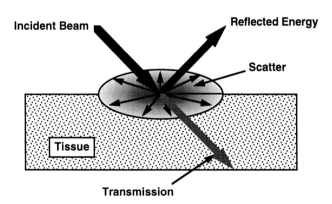

Fig. 3-7. Tissue interaction of laser energy.

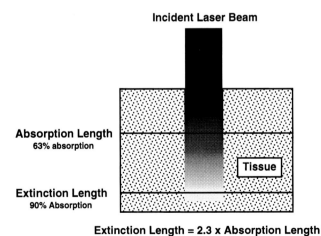

Fig. 3-8. Transfer of energy into tissue is dependent on the absorption of the laser.

Table 3-2. Tissue Action of Lasers

Name	Wavelength (nm)	Preferential Absorption		Depth of Penetration of Tissue (mm)	Hemostatic Ability
CO_2	10,600	Water		0.1–0.2	Poor
Nd:YAG	1,064	Dark color	Contact	0.3–2.0	Good
			Noncontact	3.0–7.0	Excellent
KTP	532	Hemoglobin		0.3–2.0	Excellent
Argon	488–514.5	Hemoglobin		0.3–2.0	Excellent

(Data from Martin[7] and Luciano et al.[44])

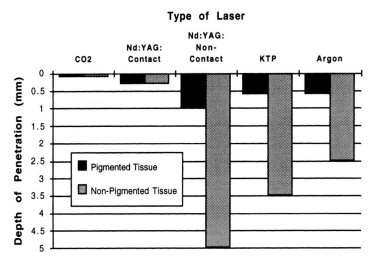

Fig. 3-9. Each laser possesses unique tissue-dependent absorptive characteristics.

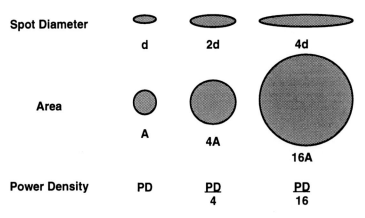

Fig. 3-10. Power density is inversely proportional to the square of the area of impact.

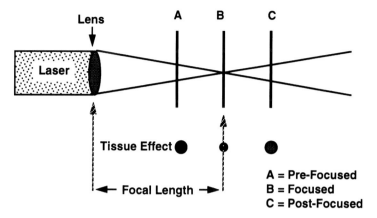

Fig. 3-11. The maximum power density, thus tissue effect, is at the focal length of the lens that the laser energy passes through.

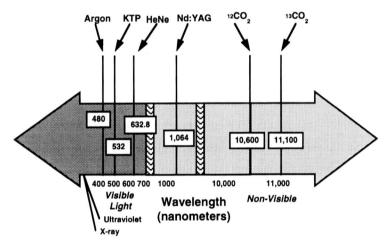

Fig. 3-12. Lasers encompass a wide spectrum of energy. Argon, KTP, and HeNe lasers are in the visible light spectrum. CO$_2$ and Nd:YAG lasers are not visible, thus requiring "aiming" lasers, such as the HeNe, for safe use.

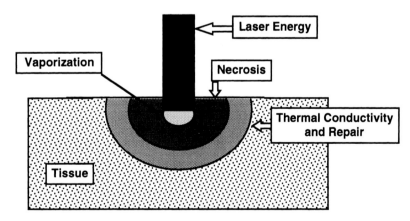

Fig. 3-13. The maximum tissue effect of laser energy is that of vaporization. Surrounding this are zones of nonreversible thermal necrosis, with resultant tissue death, and zones of thermal conductivity, which undergo repair and regeneration.

paroscopy, this smoke must be evacuated to provide adequate visualization and avoid interaction with the laser energy.[12]

Delivery Systems

The CO_2 laser is delivered to the patient via several methods: (1) coupled to an operating microscope or colposcope[9]; (2) via a hand piece for "free-hand" use; (3) via a second puncture probe through a suprapubic port at laparoscopy; (4) via a "wave guide" or fiber[6]; or (5) via the operating channel of a specially designed laser laparoscope.[13] Each delivery system imparts unique absorptive characteristics (Fig. 3-14). At laparoscopy, the use of a wave guide or "fiber" allows the surgeon to defocus the laser beam, thus exponentially decreasing the power density. By contrast, if the CO_2 laser is directed through the operating channel of the laser laparoscope, the focal length is essentially at infinity; thus the laser is always "in focus." Tissue destruction and vaporization will occur wherever the laser impacts. Thus, use of a backstop, such as fluid with "hydrodissection" or in the cul-de-sac, or specially "brushed" instruments, which diffuse the laser beam on impact, should always be entertained when using the CO_2 laser laparoscopically.[13]

Pulsing of the CO_2 Laser

Energy of the CO_2 laser can be applied to tissue in various ways. The laser is activated via a foot pedal that opens the shutter of the optical cavity, releasing the CO_2 laser beam. This continuous mode releases laser energy until the foot pedal is released. Various modifications are available that alter the release of laser energy or its effects at the tissue level. The interval between laser pulses and the time the laser is activated can be controlled at the control panel of the laser. This allows either single or repeated firing of the laser with one application of the foot pedal. The actual time the laser is activated with each firing can also be similarly controlled.

Pulsing of the laser results in altered tissue effects by allowing a cooling period between firings and thus limiting the thermal effect on tissue. By pulsing the laser via computer control, the firing of the laser can be limited to microsecond intervals, obviously much faster than humanly feasible. Thus, the development of superpulse, Chopped Pulse (Sharplan Lasers, Israel), Ultrapulse (Coherent, Inc., Palo Alto, CA), and Powerpulse (Surgilase, Inc., Warwick, RI) by laser manufacturers are modifications designed to limit the tissue effect beyond the immediate area of impact (Fig. 3-15). Some companies have even altered the frequency of the laser emitted (Coherent 5000L, Coherent). The use of an isotope of CO_2 ($^{13}CO_2$ as opposed to $^{12}CO_2$) avoids absorption of the laser beam by the CO_2 gas used for insufflation, thus minimizing *blooming,* which is the spread of lateral thermal damage beyond the original zone of vaporization, due to dispersion of the beam[14] (Fig. 3-16). Surgeons must acquaint themselves with the characteristics and features of the particular laser they use.

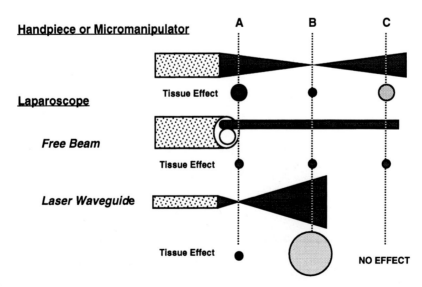

Fig. 3-14. The delivery system used affects the focal characteristics and resultant tissue effect of the CO_2 laser.

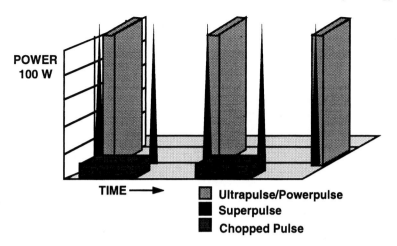

Fig. 3-15. Pulsing characteristics of CO$_2$ lasers.

Nd:YAG laser

The active medium of this laser is a crystal of YAG combined with 1 to 3 percent of Nd ions. The energy released is in the near-infrared spectrum at 1,060 nm (1.06 μm).

Tissue Effects

The Nd:YAG laser is poorly absorbed by water or blood. Thus, its penetration of tissue at point of impact is relatively deep. Also, transfer of thermal energy oc-

curs beyond the point of impact, resulting in subsequent tissue necrosis. With a "bare fiber," the Nd:YAG laser penetrates up to 3 to 4 mm into tissue. This deep penetration was used when performing endometrial ablation via the hysteroscope. However, the scattering of laser energy that occurs with a bare fiber makes it inappropriate for use via the laparoscope (Fig. 3-17). The advent of fiber delivery systems, however, allowed conversion of the somewhat "uncontrolled" Nd:YAG laser energy to predictable "heat energy" at the tip of various fibers, thus making it feasible to use this laser

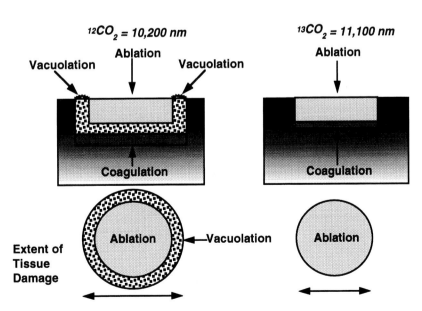

Fig. 3-16. Using an isotope of CO$_2$ (^{13}CO$_2$) reduces the tissue damage (vacuolation) surrounding the area of vaporization, so-called blooming.

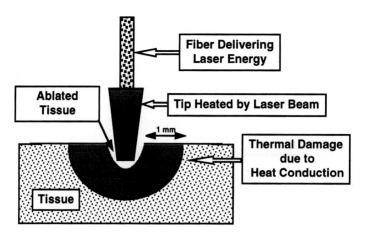

Fig. 3-17. Use of a sapphire tip or extruded fiber converts laser energy into thermal energy. Tissue action is dependent on the transfer of thermal energy.

at the time of operative laparoscopy.[15,16] These fibers limit the depth of penetration to about 0.1 to 0.3 mm, slightly deeper than the CO_2 laser.

Delivery Systems

The Nd:YAG laser is delivered via fibers. As noted above, its initial application was via a bare fiber at the time of hysteroscopy.[17] Because this laser is poorly absorbed by water, its energy passed easily through the fluid mediums used at operative hysteroscopy. The advent of sapphire-tipped fibers allowed safe application to operative laparoscopy. Subsequent development of extruded or sculptured fibers has added alternative delivery systems for laparoscopy. However, the use of the various fiber tips, in fact, alters the true tissue effect

of the Nd:YAG laser. Rather than emitting pure Nd:YAG laser energy, these fibers actually use Nd:YAG energy to heat the tips of the fibers, thus converting laser energy to thermal energy (Fig. 3-18). The shape of the various tips determines the zone of impact and the thermal effect of the laser. Recognition of this effect is quite important as thermal damage and subsequent tissue necrosis occurs beyond the visualized area of impact. Thus, extreme caution must be exercised when using these fibers near the bowel, the ureters, the bladder, and major blood vessels.

Pulsing of the Nd:YAG

Pulse technology has been developed (Xintec Corporation, Oakland, CA) for various YAG lasers (Nd:YAG and Ho:YAG) that significantly alters the tissue effects

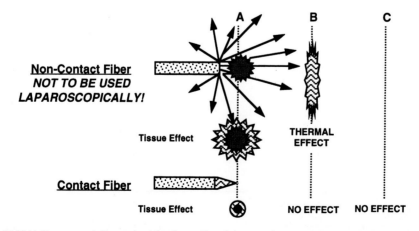

Fig. 3-18. Nd:YAG energy delivered with a bare fiber has significant and uncontrolled scatter of laser energy, thus requiring a contact tip or fiber to safely harness and deliver the Nd:YAG energy. Use of these fibers converts the Nd:YAG energy into thermal energy.

of this laser energy. Pulsing allows the laparoscopic use of noncontact, as well as contact fibers, to accomplish cutting as well as coagulation. Cutting occurs in the contact and near-contact modes. By withdrawing the fiber slightly, coagulation can be accomplished. Coupled to a sensor system that automatically reduces the power when off of tissue, this laser possesses an excellent safety profile and ease of use when applied laparoscopically.

Argon/KTP-532 Lasers

Although having slightly differing wavelengths, the argon and KTP lasers will be addressed together, as their tissue effects are virtually identical. Argon lasers use argon gas as their active medium. They emit laser light at 480 to 515 nm.[18,19] The KTP laser is a frequency-doubled YAG laser that uses a KTP crystal in the path of an Nd:YAG beam to convert to frequency of the emitted light from 1,064 to 532 nm.[20,21] Current KTP lasers, in fact, allow switching between these two frequencies, resulting in a more cost-effective and versatile laser.

Tissue Effects

The tissue effects of laser light emitted in the range of 480 to 532 nm are indistinguishable. This light is readily absorbed by chromogens, melanin, and hemoglobin. Tissue penetration is limited to 0.5 to 2 mm, thus slightly deeper than CO_2 lasers. In gynecology, selective absorption by blood and pigment makes these lasers applicable to the treatment of pigmented endometriosis and control of bleeding during endoscopic surgery. As the KTP and argon lasers are not well absorbed by nonpigmented lesions, endometrotic lesions that are white or fibrotic are better suited to excision than vaporization with these lasers.

Delivery Systems

Both the argon and KTP lasers are delivered to tissue by flexible fibers. They can be coupled to hand pieces, an operating microscope, or delivered via the laparoscope. They can be used with sculptured and plain fibers. With plain fibers, a contact mode is used to produce cutting, whereas a noncontact mode results in coagulation or vaporization (Fig. 3-19). Use of a sculptured fiber, as with the Nd:YAG fiber, converts the emitted energy from pure laser energy to heat or thermal energy.

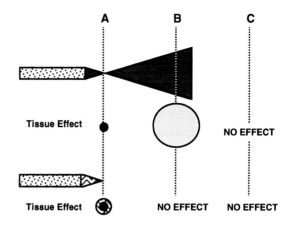

Fig. 3-19. Argon and KTP lasers can be used with a bare fiber, thus retaining their inherent laser characteristics. The use of contact tips or fibers converts the laser energy into thermal energy.

LASER SELECTION

Understanding the basic physics of each laser wavelength allows proper selection of the appropriate laser, depending of the tissue to be treated and the tissue effect desired[22] (Fig. 3-20).

Hysteroscopic Surgery

The CO_2 laser has no practical application to hysteroscopic surgery. The requirement of fluid for distention of the uterine cavity, which would thus absorb the energy of the CO_2 laser, precludes the use of the CO_2 laser for hysteroscopic surgery. The fiber lasers (i.e., Nd:YAG, KTP, and argon) are ideally suited to hysteroscopic surgery, as their energy readily passes

LASER	ABSORPTION		TISSUE EFFECT
	Water	Hemoglobin	
CO_2	Strong	Strong	Consistent
Nd:YAG	Weak	Weak	Variable
Argon	Weak	Strong	Variable
KTP	Weak	Strong	Variable

Fig. 3-20. Each laser possesses unique absorptive characteristics that alter its tissue effect.

through a fluid medium. The first application of lasers to hysteroscopic surgery was using a bare fiber Nd:YAG for endometrial ablation.[17] By using a bare fiber, the Nd:YAG penetrates 3 to 4 mm into tissue, effectively destroying the endometrium. It is typically used in either a noncontact mode or contact, or dragging, motion.[23–25] Although initial reports highlighted the success of the Nd:YAG laser for endometrial ablation, the use of the resectoscope, which uses less costly and more readily available technology, has essentially supplanted the use of lasers for this procedure. Other fiber lasers have no particular advantage over Nd:YAG lasers or electricity, thus they also have no practical application for endometrial ablation.

In a similar fashion, the resectoscope has replaced lasers in the treatment of submucous fibroids and endometrial polyps.[26,27] However, the ability to fire a laser directly forward allows the use of any fiber laser for the treatment of a uterine septum. Two words of caution: (1) never use a coaxial Nd:YAG fiber in the uterine cavity, as deaths have been reported when CO_2 gas was used for cooling a coaxial fiber at hysteroscopy[28]; and (2) always use a laparoscope when applying energy away from the hysteroscope to prevent, or identify, uterine penetration and avoid subsequent bowel injury. Again, with the introduction of resectoscopic "knives," the treatment of uterine septi has largely come under the domain of the resectoscope.

Laparoscopic Surgery

All lasers discussed have application to laparoscopic surgery.[29] Availability and cost largely determine the selection of a particular laser. It must be remembered that lasers do not impart any magical qualities to the basic surgical skills of a laparoscopic surgeon. Thus, they should be viewed as another tool in the surgeons armamentarium to treat pelvic disorders. It is recommended that each surgeon master the techniques of pelviscopic and laser surgery and select the energy source that is most suitable for the pathology encountered.

The basic tissue effects of each laser must be considered when selecting the particular wavelength. Vaporization and desiccation are used for primary destruction and for excision of lesions. Several basic concepts must be kept in mind when using the various lasers at laparoscopic surgery.

CO_2 Laser

The CO_2 laser was the first laser used at laparoscopic surgery.[30] In its early use, it was plagued with an ineffective beam alignment system and the accumulation of laser plume, requiring evacuation and lengthy re-establishment of the pneumoperitoneum. However, newer laser arms are far more reliable, and the introduction of direct couplers and CO_2 "fibers" has greatly enhanced the ease with which the CO_2 laser is used at laparoscopic surgery.[31–33] High-flow insufflation systems have reduced the time required to redistend the abdomen after evacuation of the laser plume. However, management of the plume created remains a major challenge in effective application of the CO_2 laser at laparoscopy.[12]

The CO_2 laser has been rated as a class 3 laser. Technically, this means that eye protection is not required when it is fired inside the abdomen via the laparoscope.[11] However, when confirming appropriate alignment of the HeNe beam, the laser is fired outside of the patient. Thus, all operating room personnel should still wear suitable protective eye wear during use of the CO_2 laser.

Nd:YAG Laser

The Nd:YAG laser was not applicable to laparoscopic surgery until the advent of sapphire tips.[34] As previously discussed, these tips convert the laser energy present in a bare fiber to heat, which can be applied via various tip designs, thus accomplishing coagulation or vaporization.[15] These tips require cooling to avoid fracturing at high temperatures. This is accomplished via a gas or liquid flowing through a coaxial fiber. The introduction of sculptured or extruded fibers avoids the necessity of cooling the fiber with coaxial gases or fluids, making the use of the Nd:YAG even easier. It must be remembered, however, that use of sapphire tips or sculptured fibers changes the actual characteristic tissue interactions from those of the Nd:YAG energy to one of heat. Thus the tissue interaction is now more a characteristic of the shape of the tip used (i.e., pointed [excision] or rounded [coagulation]) than the energy wavelength used.[35]

One distinct advantage of the Nd:YAG laser over the CO_2 laser is the lack of smoke generated at laparoscopic surgery. Thus, maintenance of the pneumoperitoneum is less difficult with this laser. Probes are available that allow suctioning, irrigation, and insertion of the laser fiber via the same probe through a secondary port. If desired, the fiber can also be directed via the operating port of the laparoscope, thus freeing other probes for surgical assistance.

If viewed directly, a special filter must be applied over the laparoscope lens to prevent eye injury due to back scatter of the Nd:YAG energy. However, using a camera directly applied to the lens eliminates this requirement. However, operating room personnel should wear protective goggles, specifically designed for the Nd:YAG, in the event a break occurs in the fiber, thus placing one at risk for eye injury.

KTP and Argon Lasers

The KTP and argon lasers have similar characteristics at tissue; thus they will be discussed together. Both lasers are delivered laparoscopically via either bare fibers or sculptured fibers. The advantage of the bare fiber is the retention of the tissue interaction characteristics that are inherent to these wavelengths.[21] Specifically, these lasers are selectively absorbed by pigmented lesions, thus treatment of endometriosis by direct vaporization is easily accomplished with these lasers.[18–20] Coagulation and transection of moderate-sized vessels can also be performed with application of energy via a bare fiber at varying distances from the tissue, as one can "defocus" the laser by withdrawing it from tissue.

Application of these wavelengths via sculptured fibers alters the tissue effects, converting the pure laser energy into heat at the tip. Thus, tissue interaction becomes similar to that seen with the Nd:YAG laser delivered via sapphire tips or sculptured fibers. Thus, to some degree these tips and fibers negate many of the advantages found when using the KTP or argon laser via bare fibers.

Use of special filters when viewing surgery directly or with a beam splitter is required, as these lasers seek out and selectively coagulate the vessels on the retina (a characteristic used by ophthalmologists in the treatment of proliferative retinopathy). These lens filters impart significant changes to the view obtained at laparoscopic surgery, as they open and close as the laser is activated. However, use of a direct lens coupler with the video camera eliminates the requirement for filters and the distortion they create. However, as with all fiber lasers, operating personnel are cautioned to wear specially designed goggles to prevent eye injury in the event a fiber breaks during laparoscopic surgery.

Summary

Laparoscopic application of the various lasers should be approached only with a thorough knowledge of the tissue interaction of the various wavelengths. One can thus select a laser based on the tissue to be treated and the action desired (Fig. 3-20). Using the various lasers to treat adhesions, endometriosis, ovarian cysts, ectopic pregnancy, and other disorders becomes a function of the type of tissue being treated and the attributes of each laser, while avoiding its disadvantages.

As an example, adhesiolysis can be performed with all the lasers discussed, particularly when treating filmy adhesions. However, well-vascularized adhesions require special precautions. The CO$_2$ laser is a poor coagulator. Thus, with the exception of small vessels, less than 0.1 mm in diameter, coagulation should be performed before transection of larger vessels with the CO$_2$ laser. The Nd:YAG laser, using a sapphire tip, can first be used to coagulate a vessel, by using the side of the tip, and then transecting it with the point of the fiber. The KTP, using a bare fiber, can be defocused to accomplish coagulation and then focused to transect the treated vessel.

LASER SAFETY

Lasers were initially thought to be hazardous, with somewhat "space-age" powers. However, time and familiarity have removed the mystery surrounding lasers. We now recognize that lasers merely represent an alternative to conventional surgical tools. They are very safe when used under strict policies and procedures. Laser safety is the responsibility of the laser team and laser manufacturers. The safety classifications of lasers and the basic precautions for medical lasers are reviewed.

Laser Classification

Class 1: self-contained units that do not inflict harm under normal circumstances and are subject to general controls.

Class 2: devices that could cause damage if viewed for extended periods of time. The helium-neon laser (such as used in laser pointers) is in this category.

Class 3: lasers that require special training to operate and have high potential for injury. These lasers require procedural controls and protective equipment. The CO$_2$ laser is a class 3 laser, having been downgraded from a class 4 laser. When used laparoscopically, no special eye protection is required. In all other uses, protective eye wear is mandatory.

Class 4: lasers that are potentially hazardous and could cause fire, skin burns, and retinal damage either by direct or indirect reflective contact. Nd:YAG, argon, and KTP lasers are class 4 lasers.

The Laser Team

The laser team consists of surgeons, nurses, safety officers, biomedical technicians, and support personnel. Safe operation of lasers depends on a thorough knowledge of the physics, tissue effects, and delivery systems pertinent to each laser.

To ensure patient safety, surgeons must be properly trained in the safe application of each laser they use. The operating room nurses who operate the laser are integral to the safe use of lasers. They must understand the basics of each laser used, the various functions of the control panel, and basic trouble-shooting of the laser. The laser nurse is responsible for ensuring that the laser is in the standby mode when not being used by the physician. Open verbal communication between the surgeon and the nursing staff is mandatory.

Preoperative Preparation

Each laser should be tested before each surgical procedure. This involves ensuring appropriate power supply to the laser and proper alignment of the laser and the aiming beam, if applicable.

Safety signs should be placed on all doors that lead into the operating room. This is intended to limit access to the room and warn of potential danger for those who enter.

Ocular Safety

Eye protection is required for all lasers. Because each laser has a specific wavelength, different types of eye wear are necessary. The CO_2 laser requires the use of clear plastic or glass eye wear. Prescription glasses are acceptable, but side shields are highly recommended. When used via the laparoscope, no eye protection is required as long as the laparoscope is in the abdominal cavity. However, when removed from the abdomen, eye protection should be in place. Nd:YAG lasers require eye wear that will stop a wavelength of 1,060 nm (green tint). Protective eye wear for argon and KTP lasers must stop a wavelength of 488 to 532 nm (orange tint). As these goggles are designed for specific wavelengths and are not interchangeable, they should be carefully marked.

Eye protection does not stop with the operating room personnel. The patient's eyes should also be protected. If anesthetized, eye pads can be taped over the patient's eyes; if awake, appropriate eye wear should be worn by patients.

Windows in operating rooms should also have appropriate coverings when in lasers are in use. Typically, opaque covers that prevent transmission of laser light are used for Nd:YAG, argon, and KTP lasers. The glass present in windows serves as adequate protection for the CO_2 laser.

Some laser protocols require baseline eye examina-

tions and periodic retesting. This testing may also be required for a facility's legal protection.

Fire and Electrical Safety

The potential for fire exists with all lasers. The use of moistened cloth towels is preferable for protection of the patient. However, paper drapes are commonly used in most operating rooms today. Thus, extreme care must be exercised when these drapes are used. Appropriate fire extinguishers should be readily accessible in the operating room.

Special precautions are necessary when performing laser surgery in the vicinity of the rectum. The potential for methane gas explosion at the time of lower genital tract surgery is reduced by packing the rectum with a wet sponge.

Electrical hazards are always a potential at the time of laser surgery. Most lasers produced today are internally cooled. However, some older lasers required external cooling via water supplies. Ensuring electrical isolation of the laser is mandatory to avoid electrical shock hazards.

Hazards of Laser Plume

Special care must be taken when using lasers to treat human papillomavirus in external applications.[36-39] Many questions remain as to the exact composition of the laser plume produced. Thus, special masks and appropriate evacuation of the laser plume are required.[40]

Risks of the laser plume are minimized at the time of laparoscopic surgery due to the confined nature of the abdominal cavity.[41] However, special filters should be present in the suction line to avoid blockage of the vacuum system of the operating room. High-flow insufflators are mandatory to allow rapid recreation of the pneumoperitoneum.

SUMMARY

Lasers have assumed a permanent place in the world of gynecologic surgery. Acquiring knowledge of the basic physics of each laser, its surgical applications, and its safe use rewards the surgeon with a unique and valuable surgical instrument.

REFERENCES

1. Patel CKN, Wood OR: History of laser. p. 1. In Baggish MS (ed): Basic and Advanced Laser Surgery in Gynecology. Appleton-Century-Crofts, East Norwalk, CT, 1985
2. Gardner FM: Laser physics I. p. 23. In Baggish MS (ed): Basic and Advanced Laser Surgery in Gynecology. Appleton-Century-Crofts, East Norwalk, CT, 1985

3. Baggish MS, Chong AP: Intraabdominal surgery with the CO_2 laser. J Reprod Med 28:269, 1983
4. Fuller TA: Laser tissue interaction: the influence of power density. p. 51. In Baggish MS (ed): Basic and Advanced Laser Surgery in Gynecology. Appleton-Century-Crofts, East Norwalk, CT, 1985
5. Wright VC, Riopelle MA: Gynecologic Laser Surgery. Biomedical Communications, Houston, 1982
6. Baggish M, El Bakry M: A flexible CO_2 laser fiber for operative laparoscopy. Fertil Steril 46:16, 1986
7. Martin DC: Tissue effects of lasers. Semin Reprod Endosc 9:127, 1991
8. Martin DC: Infertility surgery using the carbon dioxide laser. Clin Gynecol Briefs 1–4, 1983
9. Daniell JF: The CO_2 laser in infertility surgery. J Reprod Med 28:265, 1983
10. Coherent: Laser Tissue Interaction: A Surgeon's Guide. Coherent, Inc., Palo Alto, CA, 1991
11. Reich H, MacGregor TS, Vancaillie TG: CO_2 laser used through the operating channel of laser laparoscopes: in vitro study of power and power density losses. Obstet Gynecol 77:40, 1991
12. Feste JR, Lloyd JM: A new valving system for removal of laser plume during pelvic CO_2 laser endoscopic procedures. Obstet Gynecol 69:669, 1987
13. Nezhat C, Crowgey SR, Nezhat F: Videolaseroscopy for the treatment of endometriosis associated with infertility. Fertil Steril 51:237, 1989
14. Nezhat C, Nezhat F: Laparoscopic surgery with a new tuned high-energy pulsed CO_2 laser. J Gynecol Surg 8:251, 1992
15. Kojima E, Yanagibori A, Yudo K et al: Nd:YAG laser endoscopy. J Reprod Med 33:907, 1988
16. Shirk GJ: Use of the Nd:YAG laser for the treatment of endometriosis. Am J Obstet Gynecol 160:1344, 1989
17. Goldrath MH, Fuller R, Segal S: Laser photovaporization of endometrium for the treatment of menorrhagia. Am J Obstet Gynecol 140:14, 1981
18. Keye WRJ, Dixon J: Photocoagulation of endometriosis by the argon laser through the laparoscope. Obstet Gynecol 62:383, 1983
19. Keye WRJ, Hansen LW, Astin M et al: Argon laser therapy of endometriosis: a review of 92 consecutive patients. Fertil Steril 47:208, 1987
20. Daniell JF: Laparoscopic evaluation of the KTP/532 laser for treating endometriosis—initial report. Fertil Steril 46:373, 1986
21. Daniell JF: p. 1. In KTP/532 Clin Update, No. 28, December,1988
22. Baggish M: Selecting a laser in 1990. Contemp Obstet Gynecol Dec:49, 1990
23. Loffer F: Hysteroscopic endometrial ablation with the Nd:YAG laser using a nontouch technique. Obstet Gynecol 69:679, 1987
24. Indman PD, Lovoi PA, Brown WW, Lucero RT: Uterine surface temperature changes caused by endometrial treatment with the Nd:YAG laser. J Reprod Med 36:505, 1991
25. Indman PS: High-power Nd:YAG laser ablation of the endometrium. J Reprod Med 36:501, 1991
26. Loffer FD: Removal of large symptomatic intrauterine growths by the hysteroscopic resectoscope. Obstet Gynecol 76:836, 1990
27. Neuwirth RS: Hysteroscopic management of symptomatic submucous fibroids. Obstet Gynecol 62:509, 1983
28. Challener RC, Kaufman B: Fatal venous air embolism following sequential unsheathed (bare) and sheathed quartz fiber Nd:YAG laser endometrial ablation. Anesthesiology 73:548, 1990
29. Feste J: Laser laparoscopy: a new modality. J Reprod Med 30:413, 1985
30. Tadir Y, Kaplan I, Zuckermann Z et al: New instrumentation and technique for laparoscopic carbon dioxide laser operations: a preliminary report. Obstet Gynecol 63:582, 1984
31. Davis GD: Management of endometriosis and its associated adhesions with the CO_2 laser laparoscope. Obstet Gynecol 68:422, 1986
32. Davis GD, Brooks RA: Excision of pelvic endometriosis with the carbon dioxide laser laparoscope. Obstet Gynecol 72:816, 1988
33. Martin DC: CO_2 laser laparoscopy for endometriosis associated with infertility. J Reprod Med 31:1089, 1986
34. Lomano JM: Photocoagulation of early pelvic endometriosis with the Nd:YAG laser through the laparoscope. J Reprod Med 30:77, 1985
35. Corson SL, Unger M, Kwa D et al: Laparoscopic laser treatment of endometriosis with the Nd:YAG sapphire probe. Am J Obstet Gynecol 160:718, 1989
36. Baggish M, Elbakry M: The effects of laser smoke on the lungs of rats. Am J Obstet Gynecol 156:1260, 1987
37. Baggish MS, Baltoyannis P, Sze E: Protection of the rat lung from the harmful effects of laser smoke. Lasers Surg Med 8:248, 1988
38. Garden JM, O'Baniou MK, Shelnitz LS et al: Papillomavirus in the vapor of carbon dioxide laser-treated verrucae. JAMA 259:1199, 1988
39. Walker NPJ, Matthews J, Newsom SWB: Possible hazards from irradiation with the carbon dioxide laser. Lasers Surg Med 6:84, 1986
40. Wisniewski PM, Warhol MJ, Rando RF et al: Studies on the transmission of viral disease via the CO_2 laser plume and ejecta. Obstet Gynecol Surv 46:3, 1990
41. Nezhat C, Winer WK, Nezhat F et al: Smoke from laser surgery: is there a health hazard? Lasers Surg Med 7:376, 1987
42. Keckstein J: Tissue effects of different lasers and electrodiathermy. p. 60. In Sutton C, Diamond MP (eds): Endoscopic Surgery for Gynaecologists. WB Saunders, London, 1993
43. Absten GT: Fundamentals of laser surgery. In Dorsey JH (ed): Gynecologic Laser Surgery. Medcom, Baltimore, MD, 1991
44. Luciano AA, Whitman G, Maier DB et al: A comparison of thermal injury, healing patterns, and postoperative adhesion formation following CO_2 laser and electromicrosurgery. Fertil Steril 48:1025, 1987

4 Electrosurgery: Clinical and Comparative Concepts

RONALD K. BURKE

The role of radio-frequency electricity in electrosurgery is aptly described by the Hegelian dialectic (Georg Wilhelm Hegel, 1770–1831)—a process of arriving at the truth by stating a *thesis,* developing a contradictory *antithesis,* and combining and resolving them into a coherent *synthesis* (Fig. 4-1). Electrosurgery was universally used in the 1960s, highly (albeit somewhat unjustifiably) criticized in the 1970s, virtually supplanted by lasers in the 1980s, and is in the process of assuming its rightful place in the 1990s.

This chapter provides a basic introduction to the physics of electricity, an understanding of which should significantly improve the gynecologist's ability to perform electrosurgery in an appropriate and efficacious manner. A comparison is drawn between laser and electricity and the concept of power density (PD) is described. I believe that PD is an appropriate common ground on which to compare most methods of energy applied to tissue and is particularly appropriate when applied to laser and electricity. Simply stated, tissue effect, regardless of the source of power, is directly related to the PD applied to the tissue and the duration of application.

HISTORY

Electricity, in its varied delivery modes, has been of marked value to the field of medicine. Although Cushing and Bovie[1] are credited with the introduction of electricity as an operating room modality in the United States in 1928, there are others whose work should be credited. In 1910, Clark[2] reported the use of high-frequency current in a paper presented at the American Electrotherapeutic Association meeting and was the first to use and coin the term *dessication.* Edwin Beer, another early investigator in the realm of electrosurgery, advocated the use of "fulguration" for tumor destruction.[3] By the 1960s, most operating rooms contained a "Bovie machine" and radio-frequency electricity had become the "gold standard" energy modality for surgery.

Electrosurgical generators or electrosurgical units (ESU) remained unchanged from the design of Bowie (a spark gap generator for coagulation and a vacuum tube generator for fulguration) until the introduction of solid-state ESU in the early 1970s by Valleylab and EMS.

In the 1970s, driven by the widespread acceptance of laparoscopic sterilization, electrosurgery for "electrocoagulation" of the fallopian tubes achieved universal acceptance in the field of gynecology. Gynecologists used electric energy for ever-widening indications including dissection, hemostasis, and ablation of tissue.

The stage for calamity was set. In the early 1970s, few postgraduate courses and even fewer residency training programs included the physics of electricity as an integral part of the curriculum, and surgeons were relatively unaware of the potential dangers inherent in electrosurgical endoscopy. By the mid-1970s, many reports of patient injury as well as several deaths sec-

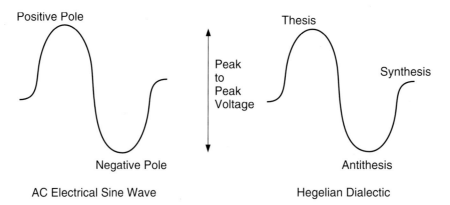

Fig. 4-1. Comparison of the Hegelian dialectic and the radio-frequency electrical sine wave.

ondary to complications resulting from electrical energy began to appear in the literature and at national conferences. The American Association of Gynecological Laparoscopists cautioned against the use of unipolar electrical delivery systems. Simultaneously, the laser appeared in the operating room, and unsubstantiated reports of the superiority of laser to electricity were quickly and widely accepted in the lay press.

By the onset of the mid-1980s, electricity as an operating energy had fallen on hard times. Lasers were hyped by the same media that publicized malpractice cases arising from electrosurgical complications. Patients appeared in gynecologists' offices demanding the healing powers of the laser. Medical centers throughout the United States established "laser centers." Although no such standard had ever been required for the use of electrical energy, an impressive knowledge of laser physics was required of any surgeon seeking credentialing in the use of lasers.

BASIC ELECTRICITY

Electrosurgery is a useful asset in laparoscopy for sterilization, treatment of endometriotic implants, removal of adnexa, excision of ectopic pregnancy, and the management of hemorrhage or the division of adhesions. It is therefore important for the practicing laparoscopist to be familiar with the biophysical principles involved. Only the most frequently used terms and concepts are defined and explained.

Terminology

Electric current is a stream of electrons flowing through a conducting body, much as a stream of water molecules flows through a hose, and with quite similar physical principles. There are three basic types of electric current:

1. *Direct current* (DC) (synonym—galvanic current): the electron exchange is unidirectional and continuous between poles of opposite signs. This type of current is used in medicine for purposes other than electrosurgery (e.g., acupuncture, endothermy).
2. *Pulsed current:* a relatively high amount of electrical energy is discharged in a short period. It is used for nerve and muscle stimulation (e.g., electromyography).
3. *Alternating current* (AC): The electron exchange is bidirectional. The polarity changes rhythmically in a sinusoidal fashion. There is no net gain of electrons at either pole of the electric circuit. This is the type of current used for electrosurgery.

Alternating current is characterized by power output and frequency. The power output is the rate of power delivered at any given time.

Average power (watts) = average voltage × average current (ampere)

An understanding of basic electrical concepts requires the knowledge of volts, ohms, watts, and amperes.

Volts	Power
Ohms	Resistance
Watts	Work
Amperes	Current (flow)

Volt (Count Alasandro Volta, Italian physicist, 1740–1827): the unit of electromotive force that, when steadily applied to a resistance of 1 Ω, will produce a current of 1 A. A volt is a measure of electric pressure. In short, voltage is the pressure force to push electrons.

Ampere (Andre Marie Ampere. French physicist, 1775–1836); the amount of current produced by 1 V applied across a resistance of 1 Ω. The ampere is a measure of the rate at which current flows.

Ohm (Georg Simon Ohm, German philosopher, 1787–1854): the electric resistance (or impedance) equal to the resistance of a circuit in which a potential difference of 1 V produces a current of 1 A.

Watt (James Watt, Scottish engineer, 1736–1819): the basic unit of power or rate of work represented by a current of 1 A under pressure loss of 1 V (watts = volts × amperes). Because the practical purpose of electricity is to generate energy, most electric appliances, including coagulation generators, are described in terms of watts, with voltage and amperage characteristics varying considerably.

Current: a flowing stream of electrons.

Electrons behave much the same as molecules of water. In Figure 4-2, the water in tank A will flow into tank B until the water level is equal in both tanks. Decreasing the diameter of the pipe connecting the two tanks increases the resistance and decreases the rate of flow while increasing the pressure. This "water tank" analogy is useful to the understanding of one of the basic electric concepts: *potential difference* or that force that causes free electrons to move as an electric current through a conductor—just as the difference in water pressure between the two tanks caused water to flow from tank A to tank B through the connecting pipe. This potential difference is also called *electromotive force* (emf) or, more commonly, *voltage.*

Whereas the volume of water may be measured in cubic centimeters, the volume of electrons is measured in coulombs. If we push a volume of water through a conduit at a given pressure over a specific period, we create current. In electricity, current (measured in amperes or coulombs per second) refers to the passage of a given quantity of electrons through an area over a given period. With either water or electricity, as resistance increases, the flow of current decreases (given constant pressure or voltage). Increasing the diameter of a pipe will decrease the resistance to water flow just as increasing the size (i.e., from 14-gauge to 16-gauge) of a wire will decrease the resistance to electron flow. Increasing the density of the material through which water flows will also affect the ability of water to flow through that material just as increasing the density of tissue will affect the freedom with which electrons can flow.

The difficulty of pushing electrons through tissue or other material can be defined as the *resistance* or *impedance,* which is measured in ohms.

As a last definition, electrical power or watts is the energy produced or consumed over a period of time. The electrical power may be defined as pressure × current, or volts × current, or volts × electron flow per second.

The relationship between voltage (E), current (I), and resistance (R) is expressed by Ohm's law, which states that

$$I = \frac{E}{R}$$

or "the intensity of a current (in amperes) is any electrical circuit is equal to the difference in the potential (in volts) across the circuit, divided by the resistance (in ohms) of the circuit." In other words, an electric current is directly and inversely related to the resistance.

The relationship between power, voltage, and current can be stated by the equation

$$P = E \times I$$

or power (P) is directly related to the voltage (E) across a circuit and the current (I) flowing in the circuit.

Combining the two relationships, where only voltage and current are known, we can solve for power as follows:

$$1) \ P = EI$$
$$2) \ P = E\left(\frac{E}{R}\right)$$
$$3) \ P = \frac{E^2}{R}$$

or power is inversely related to the resistance or directly related to the square of the voltage.

Clinical Significance

The resistance (or impedance) of tissues in the human body varies between 100 and 1,000 Ω. The human fallopian tube has a resistance of approximately 400 to

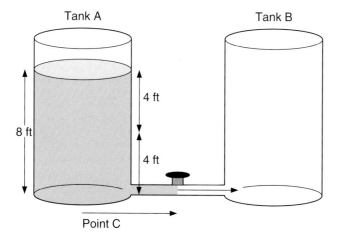

Fig. 4-2. Water pressure in tank A will drive water through point C until the level of water molecules in tank A is equal to the level in tank B. The principles are quite similar to electrons that flow under the force of voltage.

500 Ω. As tissue is coagulated, water in the cells evaporates and resistance increases, preventing further passage of current, a process similar to turning off the nozzle of a hose. As with water, electricity will flow in the path of least resistance. Because the human fallopian tube has a relatively low resistance, it is easily heated to coagulation with a 60- to 100-W generator. As the tissue is dessicated, the resistance increases. If possible, the electrons will then flow in the path of least resistance, which, in this case, would be proximally in the direction of the uterus or through any contiguous organ. Inadvertent damage is more likely to occur if current dispersed though a large amount of tissue was then forced to flow through a small area (as with a piece of bowel in contact with the uterus). Understanding the relationship of $P = E^2/R$ will discourage the surgeon from turning up the power when the expected result from electrosurgery is not observed.

Generators and Circuits

Electrons are not absorbed by tissue—only their energy is. All electrons doing work must return to the ground. These electrons seek the path of least resistance in their journey, as water does during its downhill flow. Instrumentation designed to affect electrocoagulation in the body must ensure that electrons flow at a controlled rate through the tissue intended, with no leaks through tissue offering less resistance. To this purpose, grounding, particularly in the case of unipolar current, is a concept that must be understood. Electrons energized through electric generators pass through the body and must then be allowed to exit from the patient to the ground. Today, flexible material is available for this purpose. The grounding plate must contact the body over a large area to ensure wide dispersal of electrons. The prior rigid metal plates have been replaced by flexible grounding material, making it less likely that only a small area of grounding material can come into contact with the body. The latter condition may establish an area of resistance leading to severe skin burns at the cite where electrons were to leave the body.

AC flows to and fro, increasing to a maximum voltage in one direction, dropping to zero, and increasing to the same voltage in the opposite direction. The United States has settled on electricity supplied as an AC of 60 cycles/sec (50 in Europe). The frequency of the waves measured in seconds is described as hertz (Heinrich Rudolf Hertz, German physicist, 1857–1894). One hertz is a frequency of 1 cycle/sec. Voltage is measured from zero to one maximum (peak voltage) or from the maximum in one direction to the maximum in the other (peak-to-peak voltage). The ordinary household (and hospital) power supply is 60 Hz, which means that the current flows 60 times to one pole of the electric circuit and 60 times to the other in 1 sec. Because nerves and muscles respond to frequencies less than 10,000 Hz, modern electrocoagulation generators convert the 60-Hz house current into high-frequency patterns using solid-state transformers. These generate frequencies between 300,000 and 4,000,000 Hz, with no particular biologic advantage as these frequencies are increased beyond 10,000 Hz.

Clinical Currents

Cutting and coagulating currents, in modern solid-state generators, can be produced by varying the voltage. Modern generators vary the wave patterns as well. High-frequency electric current generates intense heat in tissue when applied through a small electrode and will literally explode the cells by evaporating them. This is the pure sine wave supplied when a modern ESU is set to cutting (undamped, unmodulated) current. Bursts of electric waves separated by intervals in which no energy is passing through the body are believed to generate a different type of heat for coagulation for hemostasis. With modern high-frequency generators, this is the damped (modulated) wave, and it is what is supplied as a coagulating current. Varying "blends" of cutting and coagulating current can be set, as in "blend 1," "blend 2," and "blend 3," which, respectively, refer to a ratio of 80/20, 50/50, and 60/40 cutting to "coag." The greater the "pure" cutting, the less the peripheral zone of necrosis. The larger the coagulation portion, the greater the hemostatic effect. Therefore, understanding the frequencies and the respective sine waves allows for a more efficacious use of electrode and ESU.

Capacitance

The following section defines and explains a capacitor. An understanding of the following material leads to the conclusion that an all-metal trocar is safer than a plastic trocar and that a combined metal and plastic trocar is the least safe of the three.

Essentially, a capacitor is a device that stores electricity (Fig. 4-3). A capacitor can be charged and discharged. Capacitors are important components of electronic devices because of their ability to maintain

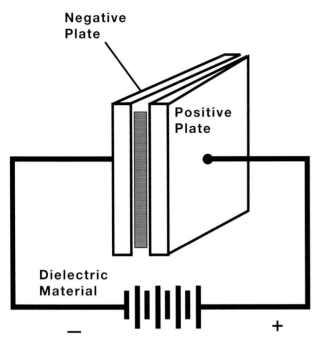

Negative Plate

Positive Plate

Dielectric Material

−   +

Fig. 4-3. Simple capacitor.

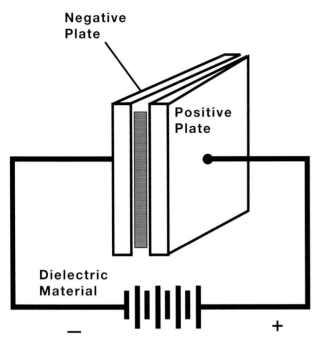

continuous flow of electricity. *"Unplanned"* or *"natural" capacitance* is the term used by electrical engineers to describe undesired, deleterious, and potentially dangerous electron buildup in electronic circuits. Anyone who has received a shock from a doorknob has experienced the result of unplanned "natural" capacitance. Although a shock may be unpleasant, unplanned capacitance discharge in the operating room can result in significant tissue embarrassment or even fatalities. An understanding of capacitance can prevent the operating endoscopist from creating a potentially dangerous natural capacitor.

The simplest arrangement for a capacitor consists of a positive and a negative plate separated by a dielectric (insulated material that will not conduct electricity—a nonconductor of electricity, especially a substance with electric conductivity less than a millionth $[10^{-6}]$ of a siemens) material through which an electric current flows. A body with an excess of electrons is negatively charged, and a body with a deficiency of electrons is positively charged. When a capacitor is connected across a voltage source, such as an ESU, the voltage forces electrons onto one plate, creating a positive charge while at the same time pulling electrons off the other plate, making it negative. Electrons cannot flow through the dielectric material. An important concept is that for any given dielectric material there is a spe-

cific "charge" that it will hold, a specific capacity for electrons. A capacitor that has been "filled up" will then overflow or discharge. A capacitor is actually much like a water closet (toilet), which first fills up with water and then discharges or flushes. As with the water closet, once the electric capacitor begins to discharge it does so completely.

There are several models in endoscopy in which the trocar and electrode may create a capacitor situation.

1. A combined metal and plastic trocar through which an electrode has been placed can function as a capacitor. This configuration is the most dangerous as it has the highest dielectric constant and can store the most electrons. The plastic material is a nonconducting dielectric. The positive charge builds up proximal to the plastic and the negative charge distally. Electron discharge usually occurs in the direction of the flow.
2. An all-plastic trocar through which an electrode has been placed through a metal carrier (as in a suction-irrigation probe) can produce a capacitance effect. The plastic is the insulated dielectric material, and the metal probe proximally is the negative plate and the metal probe distally the negative.
3. An all-metal trocar whose dielectric constant is significantly different from the shielded wire and metal carrying probe passing through may serve as a capacitor, although this third example has the least potential of storing a significant charge.

As electrons pass through an insulated unipolar forceps, they generate an electromagnetic field. This field has the capacity to activate a neon light held close enough to the length of the conducting insulated wire electrode. This electromagnetic field, in turn, will create an electric charge in any configuration whose dielectric constants differ. In an operating laparoscope, the forceps are completely insulated from the surrounding metal laparoscope and sleeve. The charge induced in the surrounding metal can adsorb 50 to 70 percent of the current in the forceps. In a bipolar forceps, the electric currents within the forceps running in both directions cancel out each other's electromagnetic fields, and no charge is created in the laparoscope.

The danger, of course, occurs when the capacitor discharges. The larger the area through which the discharged electrons can flow, the less the danger of electric burns. The safest situation is to avoid the inadvertent creation of a "natural" capacitor. This can be effected by using a large-diameter all-metal trocar. Nevertheless, the surgeon using electrosurgery must realize that all metals, except certain superconductors or metal at extremely cold temperatures, are imperfect conductors with natural capacitance.

UNIPOLAR INDUCTION OF CAPACITANCE

Under normal laparoscopic conditions, the electrical charge is rapidly dissipated by the metal sleeve over its relatively large surface in contact with the patient's abdominal wall, and no damage occurs. If, as we have seen above, the trocar sleeve in contact with the abdominal wall is nonconducting (such fiberglas sleeves were introduced in the 1970s), this electrical energy may be stored on the trochar and discharged through a relatively small area, such as the laparoscope touching the bowel.

For these reasons, the Food and Drug Administration (FDA) National Advisory Committee has recommended that metal sleeves be used for any laparoscope greater than 7 mm in diameter. In the case of a 5-mm second-puncture sleeve, however, the surgeon can visualize the entire sleeve and its electrode and can be certain there is no inadvertent bowel contact. One can therefore use a Fiberglas sleeve for the second puncture with the advantage of being able to elevate the tube away from adjacent structures, sometimes to the point of touching the live forceps to the sleeve, without fear of causing a skin burn by such contact.

Surgeons should realize that electrical discharges after dissipation of capacitance may travel upward, as well as downward, causing electric eye burns in the operating laparoscopist as well as soft tissue burns in the patient.

Effects of Current

Electric currents have several specific effects on tissue:

1. *Coagulation:* denaturization of protein in tissue from heat produced by a current. A general term that has been used to describe (erroneously) both dessication and fulguration.
2. *Desiccation:* in this technique, the electrode is in direct contact with the tissue. The tissue is heated until cellular water has evaporated completely and the tissue is dry. In an electric generator designed by Dr. Richard K. Kleppinger for a bipolar system, an ammeter (measuring amperes, or current flow) initially jumps when the forceps hold the tube and the current is turned on; the tissue turns white (electrocoagulation) with the maintenance of a steady flow of electric current. The electric current slowly drops back as desiccation of the tissue causes the resistance of the tube to increase. When the tube is completely desiccated (dry), there is no electrolytic solution left in the cells to conduct electricity, current flow stops, and the ammeter returns to zero. It is currently recommended, particularly with the extensive use of bipolar electricity in extensive pelvic dissection, that all operating room electric generators be fitted with an ammeter to demonstrate when complete desiccation has occurred.
3. *Fulguration:* in this technique, the electrode is not permitted to actually touch the tissue. A spark gap is created, causing sparks to fly from an electrode to tissue. This technique may be used to create a surface char and underlying coagulation with little tissue separation. This technique may also be used to cause a spark to leap from a fine electrode, rapidly destroying small cells and resulting in separation of tissue and little underlying coagulation. Fulguration can be contrasted with dessication in several ways. First, sparking to tissue with any generator (ESU) always produces necrosis wherever the sparks land (although, as we discover below, the zone of necrosis can be minimized by predetermining the PD and the length of time over which the electrode delivers the energy to the tissue). This is not surprising when one considers that each cycle of voltage produces a new spark, and each spark has an extremely high current density. In dessication, the current is no more concentrated than the area of contact between the electrode and the tissue. As a result, dessication may or may not produce necrosis, depending on current density. For a given level of current flow, fulguration is always more efficient at producing necrosis. In general, fulguration requires only one-fifth the average current flow of dessication.

   For example, if a ball electrode is pressed against moist tissue, the electrode will begin in the dessication mode, regardless of the waveform. The initial tissue resistance is quite low, and the resulting current will be high, typically 0.5 to 0.8 A RMS. As the tissue dries out, its resistance rises until the electric contact is broken. Because moist tissue is no longer touching the electrode, sparks may jump to the nearest moist tissue in the fulguration mode, as long as the voltage is high enough to make a spark.
4. *Electrosurgery:* electrosurgery is accomplished by passing a high-frequency AC in the radio-frequency range (400 kHz to 1 MHz) produced by an electrical generator (ESU) through a small electrode, through tissue to a large dispersive or return electrode. The effect of electrosurgery is dependent on the inherent tissue impedance, which, in turn, is related to tissue resistance and tissue capacitance. (Note that, when referring to live tissue, the term *impedance* is more appropriate than the term *resistance*, the latter term being more correct when applied to inanimate objects such as a metal wire.) Each tissue has its inherent capacitance, which, for the most part, is directly related to its bilayer lipid membranes and is an indication of the tissues ability to store electrons. Tissue resistance, however, is the characteristic of a particular tissue to dissipate energy as heat. Electrosurgery is the result of the thermal process in which current flowing through tissue creates heat and resultant tissue destruction. The amount of heat generated in tissue (E) is directly related to the square of the current flowing through the tissue (I) times the tissue resistance (R):

$$E = I^2 R$$

5. *Electrocautery:* it is important that electrocautery be differentiated from electrosurgery. The word *cautery* is derived from the Greek *kauterion*—"hot iron." Electrocautery refers to the application of heat to tissue by conduction from a heated electrode resulting in a direct burn. Original cautery instruments were powered with galvanic current, heating a metal ball or wire. In this application, no dispersive electrode is involved. This type of application is currently used, for example, in the Semm endothermy equipment. The term *cautery* is also used to describe coagulation, as in bipolar cautery. Electrocautery thus means transfer of heat from an electrically heated source to the tissue and should not be confused with electrosurgery. In electrosurgery, the electrons are energized and exert their effect by actual dispersal through the tissue.

Because all electrons must eventually seek ground to return to the wire in which they were generated, several different grounding systems are available:

1. *Traditional grounded system:* the current is delivered through an active electrode to the site required in the patient. The electrons then dissipate through the patient's tissues to a ground plate, usually connected to the thigh, which is in turn connected to a metallic connector in the operating room through which the electrons go into the ground (as water in a hose flows onto pavement).

2. *Isolated system:* the current going into the patient returns via a return plate, which is not connected to the ground but returns electrons to the isolated circuit of the generator. The patient forms part of a circuit isolated from the grounded current coming from the wall, as well as the metal in the room connected to the ground. The water cooling system of an automobile, in which water is recirculated but isolated from the great water cycle of the earth, is a good analogy for the isolated circuit.

   The great safety advantage of this isolated system is that no current will flow if the return electrode is not correctly connected to the circuit, whereas traditionally grounded systems with faulty ground connections will allow electrons to seek the path of least resistance through electrocardiogram electrodes or other small areas where the patient's body is in contact with metal during surgery, causing electrical burns, which may be quite extensive.

Unipolar and Bipolar

The terms *unipolar* and *bipolar* as commonly used by physicians are technically incorrect, confusing, and often misused in the medical literature and terminology. As all high-frequency electric current used for electrosurgery uses AC, there are no positive and negative poles. Of the three current types mentioned above, only galvanic current is polar. As advocated by Sebben,[4] the terms *monoterminal* and *biterminal* are more correct than *monopolar* and *bipolar*. Nevertheless, *mono* and *bipolar* have become deeply engrained in the medical literature and vocabulary. Most gynecologists have adopted the terminology of unipolar and bipolar—*unipolar* referring to current that flows from the ESU into the electrode through the body and is dispersed via a grounding plate; *bipolar* referring to current that flows into the electrode, through only the tissue being treated to a second electrode, and back to the ESU.

A unipolar electrode that is split at the ends, as in unipolar scissors, is, nevertheless, unipolar just as a bipolar electrocautery tip with a dispersive electrode remains bipolar. The newer bipolar scissors are examples of a monoterminal, bipolar electrode.

Monoterminal

The electrode delivering the electric energy through the body can be designed in two ways. The unipolar system considers the electrode as one electrode through which the electric current flows to the ground plate or return plate. In this arrangement, a large portion of the patient becomes part of the circuit as electrons must flow from the point at which they are delivered by the forceps to the ground or return plate. Risks of accidental burns are higher with this system because electrons seek the path of least resistance, which may be the adjacent bowel, as electrocoagulation desiccates the tube touching the bowel. Because of unexplained bowel injuries reported by surgeons using the unipolar technique, alternative mechanical and electric techniques have been sought. Conventional wisdom today, however, attributes many of the bowel injuries of the 1970s to the mechanical trocar or local inadvertent application of heat to the bowel rather than to arcing.

Biterminal

The bipolar system is essentially a miniaturized isolated circuit, in which one prong of the forceps is the source of the current and the second prong is the return plate. With high-frequency AC, both prongs are equal in design and function. The current does not travel through the body to an externally placed return plate but only through the tissue held between the electrodes. The patient does not become a part of circuit, only the tissue between the electrodes does. When the two prongs coagulate the tissue excessively, the prongs come into contact at some point and no current flows through the highly resistant tissue, preferring the low resistance of the metal prongs. For these biophysical reasons, bipolar systems have greatly reduced the hazards of intra-abdominal accidental burns.

Electrode Shape and Electron Concentration or Density

Current density is a central and markedly important concept that the surgeon using power, whatever its source, must understand.

The limitations of voltage and output power are determined in direct proportion to the impedance of the electric circuit, or in other words, the mass (or diameter) of the electrode. The amount of mass that makes contact with the tissue determines two electric effects:

1. whether the electrode will cut and destroy tissue cells within a narrow area
2. whether the electrode will coagulate and destroy tissue cells in a wide area

It is for this reason that the concepts of "cutting current" and "coagulating current" can be both confusing and interchangeable, depending on the size of the electrode. A 4-mm-diameter ball electrode, for example, cannot cut even if it is used with nonmodulated cutting current.

The area of electrode contact with the tissue, or the amount of mass in contact with the tissue, determines the impedance or electric resistance of the circuit. All electrosurgical equipment is designed to operate within certain impedance parameters. There is no general surgical system on the market that can deal with an impedance of 10,000 Ω and 500 Ω on an equal basis. Wire-thin microelectrodes produce an impedance of approximately 10,000 Ω. When a general surgical unit is connected to such an electrode, the result is that the excess voltage not only destroys the thin electrode material but it also discharges to the tissue, producing an arc to the tissue. The resultant high temperature is what produces the tissue burning, necrosis, and resultant adhesions later.

When different tissue effects are desired in conservative surgery, it is not reasonable or possible to produce them with the same size electrode without compromising safety. If the desired effect is to cut, the preference is for a thin cutting electrode. If the desired effect is to coagulate, the preference is for a larger surface electrode to produce contact coagulation. Many surgeons who use electrosurgery in conservative surgery tend to regard the electrode as generic, varying the waveform or increasing the voltage to produce cutting or coagulation. Such an approach will lead to the needless destruction of unnecessarily large amounts of

tissue and may increase the probability of inadvertent electric injury.

Tables 4-1 and 4-2 reflect the newest ElMed Co. electric generator. Notice the low levels of voltage required to cut with a microelectrode when the unit is in the micro mode.

The amount of heat an electric current generates is directly related to the electron density passing through the tissue, which is determined by the metal contact area of the electrode. In the least-damaging configuration, two large metal plates are placed with a sore shoulder or other body part between them, and a diathermy current is passed through the body to generate warmth with no burning. If just the wire to one of those plates touches the skin, the same number of electrons will be flowing into that small area. Electron concentration or density in the skin touching the wire will be great enough to heat the skin to the point of burning.

The second example illustrates the principle in the unipolar coagulating forceps, where the small electrode area is in a forceps configuration to distribute electrons densely through the tube to coagulate it. The electrons then dissipate into adjacent structures such as the uterus or vessels and thereby are no longer concentrated enough to heat these tissues. The bipolar forceps similarly has a relatively small surface, grasping the tube between two prongs, limiting the entire circuit to the tube, and allowing electric current to generate heat between the two prongs to the point of coagulation and desiccation.

In using coagulation to control hemorrhage (such as applying a unipolar lower-voltage current to a hemo-

Table 4-1. Output Measurement Chart (ESU 100 L M/M Unipolar Generator)[a]

Output Level	Macro		Micro	
	Watts	Volts	Watts	Volts
0.5	0.05	28	0.05	40
1	1.90	40	1.08	60
2	9	150	2	100
3	20	275	10	200
4	49	450	20	275
5	59	510	25	325
6	69	560	29	350
7	875	600	30	375
8	88	660	35	400
9	95	700	39	425
10	100	720	40	430

[a] All voltage measurements are peak to peak. The measurements were taken under the condition of a 500-Ω load, through a standard laparoscopic cable and electrode.

Table 4-2. Output Measurements (ESU 100 L M/M Bipolar Generator)[a]

Output Level	Watts	Volts
0.5	1.01	40
1	2.5	50
2	6	75
3	15	125
4	28	160
5	33	175
6	37	190
7	42	200
8	47	210
9	49	225
10	50	225

[a] All voltage measurements are peak to peak. The measurements were taken under the condition of a 100-Ω noninductive load, through an ELMED laparoscopic bipolar forceps and bipolar radio-frequency cable.

stat on a bleeder in an abdominal incision), the rapidity of the coagulation is directly dependent on the amount of tissue grasped in the forceps. A lower density of low-energy electrons is distributed by the forceps over a wider area, and the lower energy load coagulates rather than evaporates the tissue. If the area of contact is large, coagulation or hemostasis will not occur because the electrons are dissipated over too wide a surface to generate sufficient heat. Ringer's lactate or saline are also excellent dissipators of electrons. When irrigation is useful to facilitate visualization, as in laparoscopy or microsurgery, glycine or sorbitol, both poor conductors of electrons, are more useful in allowing microcurrents of electricity to coagulate bleeders.

If the electrode is reduced to a point (such as an electrocoagulation knife or fine needles in microsurgery) and a higher-voltage current is used, the concentration of electrons and energy at the cells making contact with the electrode will cause these cells to vaporize; the spent electrons will then rapidly dissipate into adjacent tissues without further damage.

Timing

Considerations of electrode shape and electron density enter into the timing of applying the electric current, depending on the surgeon's objective.

In cutting, the electric current should be turned on before touching the needle to the tissue to be cut, so that the minimum amount of contact between the electrode and tissue will take place (actually, a fine spark should do the exploding of the cells without the electrodes ever touching the body). The point of the needle, rather than its side, should be used for cutting, and of course, a cutting current should be used.

For coagulation, however, the coagulating forceps should be applied first, mechanical hemostasis achieved, and the coagulating current turned on after grasping to ensure coagulation of the vessels grasped within the forceps. Applying the current before firmly grasping the tissue will result in charring of the surface without hemostasis.

HEALING AFTER LAPAROSCOPY

In the abdominal cavity, the bacteria introduced are left on the peritoneal surface, where blood supply combined with the peritoneal cavity's extensive macrophage defense system makes the bacteria introduced rapidly disappear. In short, the more dead or injured tissue left behind after surgery, the greater the chance for postoperative infection. In the past, lasers were touted as being associated with less tissue necrosis than electrocautery. With more extensive laparoscopic dissection, this was viewed as even more important. One reason for the minimal peripheral necrosis after laser was the phenomenon of "reactive hyperemia," an observation that, after cutting or coagulation by laser, there was a compensatory growth of blood vessels, which resulted in improved healing. A second reason may well be that "laser surgeons" understood the physical principles of lasers better than "electrical surgeons" understood the physics of electricity. The appropriate laser power density was used for each type of tissue, thereby minimizing peripheral destruction. The concept of PD applies to electric as well as laser energy.

Most surgeons using lasers understood that for each type of tissue there was the highest recommended power setting for collimated energy brought to the tissue in the smallest spot size for the briefest duration. This resulted in minimal peripheral tissue damage and rapid healing. Were these principles applied to electric current, the same benefits would accrue.

CONCEPT OF POWER DENSITY

Laser instruments can operate at varying power levels selected by the operator by simply dialing the desired level on the instrument console. The power (or watts) produced by a particular instrument affects the intensity of the beam. Maximum powers for surgical lasers commonly range from 20 to 100 W at the exit point of the optical cavity. Concentrating the beam with laser focusing lenses can result in enormous beam intensity at the focal spot (Fig. 4-4). The magnitude of power concentration is described most commonly as the PD or power per unit area of the beam. It usually reflects the beam intensity at the focal length of the laser focusing lens. PD is a function of the beam power and the surface area of the focal spot. Power and spot diameter are considered together, and a combination is selected to produce the appropriate PD.

$$PD = \frac{\text{power in the focal spot}}{\text{area of the focal spot}}$$

PD varies directly with power and inversely with surface area. For constant beam power, the larger the surface area the less the concentration, hence the lower the PD. The smaller the surface area, the higher the PD (Fig. 4-1).

The relationship of surface area to beam diameter is an important one when considering PD. Assuming an ideal beam with a rectangular cross-sectional intensity profile, surface area (A) is

$$A = \pi r$$

where r is beam radius. Because the radius is half the beam diameter ($d/2$), area can be expressed as

$$A = \pi \frac{d^2}{2^2} \quad \text{or} \quad A = \pi \frac{d^2}{4}$$

The surface area, therefore, varies as the square of the beam diameter. This means that doubling the beam diameter will increase the surface area by four times. Inversely, halving the beam diameter (from, for example, 2 mm to 1 mm) will yield only one-quarter the area. This means that PD varies inversely with the square of the beam diameter.

Therefore, doubling the beam diameter (from d to $2d$) reduces the PD to one-fourth (PD/4), and halving the spot diameter increases power density by a factor of 4. Increasing spot size by a factor of 4 (from d to $4d$, or 0.5-mm diameter to 2.0 mm) reduces PD by 16 times because the area is increased by a factor of 16 (4^2).

PD determines the effect of a laser instrument's beam on any particular target. It is the most important operating parameter of a laser at a given wavelength. The concept of PD and how it is affected by focal spot surface area, focal spot beam diameter, and wattage must be mastered by anyone intending to use the laser. The actual calculation of PD will vary depending on the transverse electromagnetic mode (TEM) of the particular instrument (remember that, for CO_2, the TEM_{00} (donut mode) or gaussian distribution is operative); however, its direct relationship to wattage and inverse square relationship with focal spot diameter are fundamental.

PD, then, for laser, is a function of the spot size and the applied power in watts. The flow of an electric radio-frequency AC through tissue is dependent on its density. Electric density refers to the amount of current flowing through a given cross-sectional area of tissue. Whereas laser density is expressed in watts per square centimeter, current density is expressed in amperes per square centimeter. Heat generated in tissue is directly proportional to the square of the current density. As with lasers, the smaller the "spot size" of the electrode,

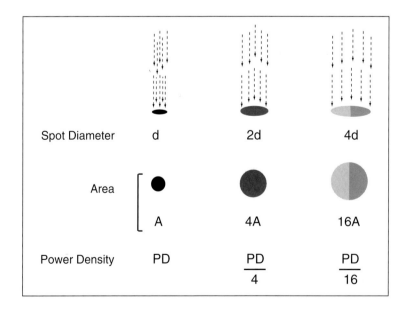

Fig. 4-4. Spot size, area, and power density.

the smaller the cross-sectional area of the tissue through which the electrons are forced to flow and, therefore, the greater the temperature rise.

PD, in comparison, for electricity, is a function of the "spot size" (diameter) of the electrode and the applied power in watts.

The spot size for laser, in turn, is determined by the focal length of the lens, the TEM of the beam, and the characteristic wavelength of the laser.

The spot size for electricity, in turn, is determined by the diameter and composition (resistance) of the electrode and the characteristic radio frequency ("wavelength") of the electric current (nonmodulated continuous sinusoidal waveform for cutting, modulated sinusoidal waveform for coagulating).

Electrosurgical Principles

Electrosurgery, as described above, is the use of flowing electrons to fulgurate or desiccate tissue. ESUs are machines that produce an alternating current of electricity at a radio frequency that will not stimulate muscle activity (approximately 500,000 to 1 million cycles/sec). Whereas DC flows in one direction only, AC flows to and fro, first increasing to a maximum in one direction and then increasing to a maximum in the other direction. This "sinusoidal waveform" can be interrupted or varied, resulting in different surgical effects (Fig. 4-5).

The waveform of AC has a negative and a positive excursion or peak. The measurement from zero polarity to positive or negative polarity is called the *peak voltage* of the waveform (the relationship is the same for peak current). The measurement from plus peak to negative peak, which is twice peak voltage, is called *peak-to-peak voltage*. An output waveform that is interrupted or varied (modulated or damped) is called a *coagulating waveform*. When using modulated coagulation current, the sinusoidal waveform is active less

than 10 percent of the time, and power is generated by a marked increase in the peak-to-peak voltage.

A pure *cutting waveform* is a simple sinusoidal, undamped or nonmodulated waveform and is generally produced by continuous energy. Because of this continuous flow, the amount of peak voltage of a pure cutting waveform required to produce a given amount of wattage is less than the amount of damped waveform required to create the same wattage. However, when a coagulation effect is desired, the damped waveform is preferable. In coagulation using modulated current, bursts of damped waveforms are pushed through the tissue, and for an instant, extremely high voltage may be present within the electric circuit. A combination of undamped and damped waveforms is called a *blended current*. With blended current, the sinusoidal waveform is on for 80 percent, 60 percent, or 50 percent of the time, resulting in cutting with varying degrees of coagulation.

As electrons, pushed with a given voltage, are concentrated in one specific location, heat within the tissue increases. This concentration phenomenon, as mentioned above, is defined as *current density*.

Once the electrons enter the body (conductor), they are dispersed through the tissue toward the pathway of least resistance to the return electrode.

Earlier electric generators used open circuits, in which electric current flowed, like water, through the patient and then out, via the "ground plate" away from the patient onto the ground. Now electric generators use closed circuits, in which the current flow is limited to a pathway between the generator and, via the ground plate, back to the generator. Some newer electric generators use return electron monitoring (REM) circuitry that monitors the returning electrons. In such systems, a safety circuit is established so that the generator continues to supply current only so long as the same amount of current is returning via the ground plate. Technically, such systems actually use a dual circuitry. Any significant loss of phasing in both systems effects a generator shutdown. Such a system prevents the abnormal effect of electrical burns secondary to increased resistance. Finally, coupled with the increased sophistication of closed circuitry with REM, electric safety is increased as a result of the newer plastic gel grounding plates, which are superior to the earlier metal grounding plates.

Electrons flow through the path of least resistance. If tissue resistance is high but the corresponding voltage pressure low, the current may cease to flow or may search out alternate pathways with lower resistance. When the voltage is increased, the electrons have more

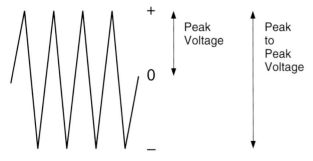

Fig. 4-5. Alternating current.

"push" to find an alternate pathway. Therefore, one should use the lowest possible voltage necessary to accomplish a given job and ensure that the dispersive electrode is in good contact with the patient and broad enough to reduce current density far below the level of tissue destruction (heat). Furthermore, this reduces the possibilities of alternate pathways of electron flow.

Another way of understanding this principle, as well as the difference between cutting and coagulation modes, is through the understanding of Ohm's law, which states

$$V = I \times R, \text{ or voltage = current} \times \text{resistance}$$

For a given resistance (such as the human body),

$$R = V/I, \text{ or resistance = voltage/current}$$

So, when one decreases the current (amperage), one must increase the voltage to achieve the same effect, and vice versa. Such an effect can be seen in the coagulation and cutting modes. The cutting mode uses high current/low voltage whereas the coagulation mode uses low current/high voltage.

Because laparoscopy is remote control surgery, it is important that unexpected movements of the electrode do not occur. By reducing peak voltage, you reduce the chance of electrons jumping or sparking to nearby structures such as the bowel. A 15,000-V pressure can push electrons more than 1 cm through room air under certain atmospheric conditions. By contrast, a modern low-voltage generator has a maximum peak voltage of 300 to 600 V.

These considerations have led the FDA to recommend that low-voltage, high-frequency electric generators for laparoscopic surgery should produce a maximum of 600 peak voltage or 1,200 peak-to-peak voltage and that the maximum power should be in the range of 100 W. Isolated ground circuitry systems are desirable, as is a fail-safe return electrode sentinel system, should ineffective or incomplete return path be present.

ELECTROSURGICAL CUTTING

The essential characteristic of CUT waveforms is that they are continuous sine waves. That is, if the voltage output of the generator is plotted over time on an oscilloscope, a pure CUT waveform will generate a continuous sine wave alternating from positive to negative at the operating frequency of the generator, 500 to 3,000 kHz (Fig. 4-6).

The COAG waveform consists of short bursts of radio-frequency sine waves with the frequency of the sine wave at 500 kHz, and the COAG bursts occur 31,250 times/sec (Fig. 4-7). An important feature of the

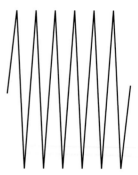

Fig. 4-6. Pure CUT waveform into a 400-Ω load.

COAG waveform is the pause between each burst, a feature that allows tissues to cool. However, less voltage is required for cut, which makes the "cut" mode safer than the "coag" mode. Using the coag to cut can be dangerous, as high voltages would be required. Using cut to coag, however, is safer and more preferable.

However, a well-processed COAG waveform can exert its effect on tissue without a significant cutting effect because the heat is more widely dispersed and because the heating effect is intermittent. The temperature of the water in the cells does not become high enough to flash into steam. In this way, the cells are dehydrated slowly. Because of the high peak voltage of a quality COAG waveform, it can drive a current through very high resistances. In this way, it is possible to fulgurate long after the water is driven out of the tissue and actually char it to carbon. Coagulation of a tubal segment during electrosurgical sterilization reveals an initial bubbling and expansion of the tissue followed by a contraction and toasting appearance.

By changing from cutting mode to coagulation or blend on an ESU, the operator changes or modulates the waveform of cutting (Fig. 4-8). For electrosurgical cutting, a nonmodulated pure sinusoidal current is selected. However, when larger surface electrodes (area of contact with tissue) or forceps are used, this same nonmodulated "cutting" current may result in nonarcing surface coagulation. Thus, one may not assume that an instrument used with current will unequivocally cut. The important factor is the PD of the current at the site of application:

$$PD = \frac{\text{volt} \times \text{ampere}}{\text{contact surface area}}$$

The electrosurgeon can obtain a cutting effect from a large electrode by increasing the applied power (which, in turn, increases the possibility of damage) or by decreasing the size of the electrode given the same voltage.

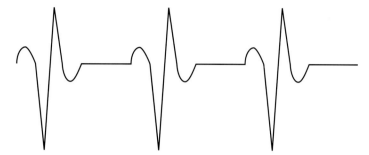

Fig. 4-7. Pure COAG waveform output at 400-Ω load.

For ultimate safety, however, I recommend the use of unipolar for cutting and bipolar for coagulation. The analogy would be to CO_2 laser for cutting and YAG for coagulation.

Potential Electrosurgical Complications

Voyles and Tucker[5] describe three types of "stray energy" that can cause inadvertent and serious tissue damage:

Type 1: insulation failure
Type 2: capacitive coupling
Type 3: direct coupling

An unrecognized defect in instrument insulation may lead to 100 percent of the electric energy being transmitted at that site. There are four zones in the pathway of an electrode through a trocar into the pelvis at which injury may occur (Fig. 4-9). Zone 1 is at the distal portion of the electrode. Zone 2 represents that portion of the electrode no longer within the trocar sleeve but not in the surgeon's view. Insulation failure at this point can lead to transmission of 100 percent of the electric current inadvertently with prolonged and sustained electric damage to vital structures. Zone 3 consists of the trocar. Although high peak voltages can cause significant umbilical skin burns in any scenario, zone 3 injuries were more common in the 1970s, presumably because of faulty grounding and higher utilized voltages. Umbilical skin injuries are less likely to occur with the current generation of REM containing ESUs. Zone 4, at the proximal end of the electrode before its entering the trocar sleeve, may cause significant and painful injury to the surgeon's hand if the electrode shielding has become defective (Fig. 4-10).

The impedance of a capacitor, or tissue that has, in essence, become a capacitor because of its dielectric properties, is inversely proportional to the capacitance times the frequency:

$$X_c = \frac{1}{2\pi Cf}$$

where X is the impedance of the capacitor, C is the capacitance, and f is the frequency. If the frequency is high, even a situation in which there is low capacitance can have low impedance. This can create an alternate current path for radio-frequency currents, which, in turn, may lead to alternate site burns (i.e., a fibroid being quadrissected by a unipolar electrode while being held by an alligator clamp is a situation in which the fibroid becomes the dielectric material forming a capacitor of the two metal objects.)

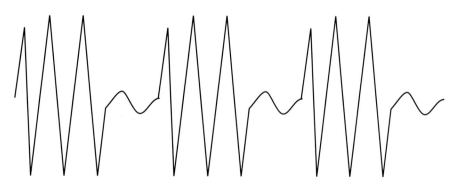

Fig. 4-8. Blend waveform into a 400-Ω load.

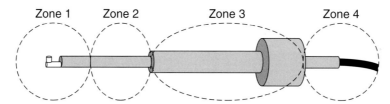

Fig. 4-9. Chance and significance of injury from insulation failure are a function of the relative location of the point of failure. (From Voyles and Tucker,[5] with permission.)

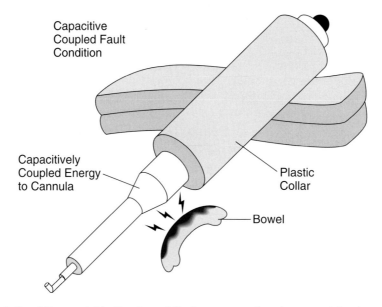

Fig. 4-10. An insulation failure outside the view of the laparoscope has the potential to burn bowel and other intra-abdominal organs. Tissue damage may go undetected and cause severe postoperative complication. (From Voyles and Tucker,[5] with permission.)

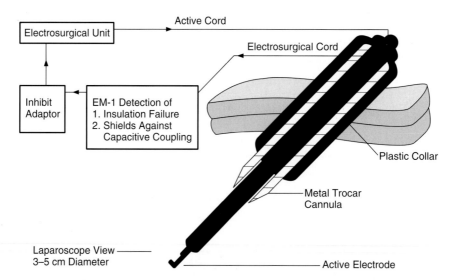

Fig. 4-11. The Electroshield EM-1 system consists of a sheath that surrounds the electrode shaft that shields against capacitance coupling. The EM-1 detects any faults in the insulation. (From Voyles and Tucker,[5] with permission.)

An advance that promises to essentially eliminate the above-mentioned injuries has been introduced by Electroscope (Electroscope, Inc., Boulder, CO) (Fig. 4-11). The system consists of a shield that fits around the electrode. The shield has a dispersive electrode through which all undesirable current is shunted to a monitor that detects the stray electrosurgical energy. The Electroshield monitor is, in turn, connected to the main ESU and will deactivate the main ESU and sound an alarm if a fault occurs. One disadvantage of the Electroshield system is that working ports need to be 7 mm, a small price to pay for this significant protection against the hazards of stray electric energy.

A BRIEF COMPARISON OF ELECTROSURGERY AND CO_2 LASERS

The performance at the end of an electrode depends on the shape of the electrode, the frequency and wave modulation, peak-to-peak voltage, current, output impedance, and PD. The tissue may be cut cleanly with a minimal zone of necrosis (with minimal hemostasis), or it can be burned and charred (with maximal hemostasis).

Electrocoagulation may be carried out in many different forms—from slow, delicate contact coagulation, especially with bipolar forceps, to the charring effects of the spray coagulation mode, at times leading to carbonization. The temperature differences may vary from 100°C to more than 500°C.

The CO_2 laser beam, with fewer variables, has a cutting effect similar to electrosurgery but can be made to mimic spray coagulation by defocusing the spot beam. Because there are fewer variables with the laser, the cut can be more uniform and perhaps made with more control and predictability.

Electrosurgical electrodes can be sculptured to perform certain tasks. A microneedle, a knife, a wire loop, or even a scissors can be shaped and sized to a specific duty. When the waveform variable is added, "cutters" can be made to coagulate and "coagulators" can be made to cut. Interwoven into these acts are the output intensity and output impedance characteristics of the different electrosurgical generators. Finally, the mechanics of a forcep compressing tissue or a scissors cutting tissue will add a dimension the laser cannot; a laser cannot manipulate tissue as can an active electrode. One electrode that deserves special mention is the suction electrode, which can coagulate a "wet" field and would be impervious to the CO_2 laser.

SUMMARY

Although electrosurgery has been with us for decades, few surgeons received formal training in the nature of electricity and how the physical laws governing electricity affected its potential clinical application. The erroneous belief that electrosurgery techniques increase scar formation or impair healing processes led surgeons to adopt other, more expensive energy sources. A more thorough understanding of electrosurgical principles, coupled with modern electric equipment, ESUs with understandable readouts, superior methods of grounding, and finer instruments with improved shielding should lead to a wider and more informed use of electrosurgery.

REFERENCES

1. Cushing H, Bovie W: Electrosurgery as an aid to the removal of intracranial tumors. 47:751, 1928
2. Clark W: Oscillatory dessication in the treatment of accessible malignant growths and minor surgical conditions. J Adv Ther 29:169, 1911
3. Kelly H, Ward G: Electrosurgery. WB Saunders, Philadelphia, 1931
4. Sebben J: Monopolar and bipolar treatment. J Dermatol Surg Oncol 15:364, 1989
5. Voyles CR, Tucker RD: Education and engineering solutions for potential problems with laparoscopic monopolar electrosurgery. Am J Surg 164:57, 1992

SUGGESTED READINGS

Association of Operating Room Nurses: Proposed recommended practices: electrosurgery. AORN J 52:370, 1990

Association of Operating Room Nurses: Recommended practices. Electrosurgery. AORN J 53:1022, 1991

Association of Operating Room Nurses: Proposed recommended practices. Electrosurgery. AORN J 58:131, 1993

Barbot J: Impact of lasers on post-operative adhesions. Prog Clin Biol Res 381:65, 1993

Bennett RG, Kraffert CA: Bacterial transference during electrodesiccation and electrocoagulation [see comments]. Arch Dermatol 126:751, 1990

Bhatta N, Isaacson K, Flotte T et al: Injury and adhesion formation following ovarian wedge resection with different thermal surgical modalities. Lasers Surg Med 13:344, 1993

Bordelon BM, Hobday KA, Hunter JG: Laser vs electrosurgery in laparoscopic cholecystectomy. A prospective randomized trial. Arch Surg 128:233, 1993

Brooks PG: Hysteroscopic surgery using the resectoscope: myomas, ablation, septae and synechiae. Does pre-operative medication help? Clin Obstet Gynecol 35:249, 1992

Brooks PG: Complications of operative hysteroscopy: how safe is it? Clin Obstet Gynecol 35:256, 1992

Brooks PG, Serden SP, Davos I: Hormonal inhibition of the endometrium for resectoscopic endometrial ablation. Am J Obstet Gynecol 164:1601, 1991

Brosens I: Prevention of adhesions in ovarian surgery. Prog Clin Biol Res 381:121, 1993

Butler PE, Barry-Walsh C, Curren B et al: Improved wound healing with a modified electrosurgical electrode. Br J Plast Surg 44:495, 1991

Daniell JF, Kurtz BR, Ke RW: Hysteroscopic endometrial ablation using the rollerball electrode [see comments]. Obstet Gynecol 80:329, 1992

Dixon AR, Watkin DF: Electrosurgical skin incision versus conventional scalpel: a prospective trial. J R Coll Surg Edinb 35:299, 1990

Dorsey JH: The role of lasers in advanced operative laparoscopy. Obstet Gynecol Clin North Am 18:545, 1991

Duffy S, Reid PC, Sharp F: In-vivo studies of uterine electrosurgery. Br J Obstet Gynaecol 99:579, 1992

Duffy S, Reid PC, Smith JH, Sharp F: In vitro studies of uterine electrosurgery. Obstet Gynecol 78:213, 1991

Ferguson CM: Electrosurgical laparoscopic cholecystectomy. Am Surg 58:96, 1992

Garry R: Hysteroscopic alternatives to hysterectomy. Br J Obstet Gynaecol 97:199, 1990

Geddes LA, Moore CR: Stimulation with electrosurgical current. Australas Phys Eng Sci Med 13:63, 1990

Gilbert TB, Shaffer M, Matthews M: Electrical shock by dislodged spark gap in bipolar electrosurgical device. Anesth Analg 73:355, 1991

Gillespie A: Endometrial ablation: a conservative alternative to hysterectomy for menorrhagia? Med J Aust 154:791, 1991

Gillespie A: Operative hysteroscopy and endometrial ablation. Aust Fam Physician 21:604, 1992

Gleich P: Transcervical resection of uterine myomas with a resectoscope. Urol Clin North Am 17:59, 1990

Hainer BL: Electrosurgery for cutaneous lesions. Am Fam Physician 44:81S, 1991

Hainer BL: Fundamentals of electrosurgery. J Am Board Fam Pract 4:419, 1991

Hulka J, Reich H (ed): Textbook of Laparoscopy. WB Saunders, Philadelphia, 1994

Hunter JG: Laser or electrocautery for laparoscopic cholecystectomy? Am J Surg 161:345, 1991

Hunter JG: Laser use in laparoscopic surgery. Surg Clin North Am 72:655, 1992

Hunter JG: Exposure, dissection, and laser versus electrosurgery in laparoscopic cholecystectomy. Am J Surg 165:492, 1993

Ke RW, Taylor PJ: Endometrial ablation to control excessive uterine bleeding. Hum Reprod 6:574, 1991

Kelly H, Ward G: Electrosurgery. WB Saunders, Philadelphia, 1931

Kim Y, Zieber HG, Wang FE: Uniformity of current density under stimulating electrodes. Crit Rev Biomed Eng 17:585, 1990

Klein SL, Leonard PF: Buzz 'em or burn 'em (letter; comment). Anesth Analg 73:358, 1991

Kramer J, Rosenthal A, Moraldo M, Muller KM: Electrosurgery in arthroscopy. Arthroscopy 8:125, 1992

Kramolowsky EV, Tucker RD: The urological application of electrosurgery. J Urol 146:669, 1991

Lane GE, Lathrop JC: Comparison of results of KTP/532 laser versus monopolar electrosurgical dissection in laparoscopic cholecystectomy. J Laparoendosc Surg 3:209, 1993

Laughlin SA, Dudley DK: Electrosurgery. Clin Dermatol 10:285, 1992

Lewis BV: Endometrial ablation. Br J Hosp Med 47:192, 1992

Louca C, Davies B: Electrosurgery in restorative dentistry: 1. Theory. Dent Update 19:319, 1992

Louca C, Davies B: Electrosurgery in restorative dentistry: 2. Clinical applications. Dent Update 19:364, 1992

Luciano A, Maier D: Electrosurgery and lasers in endoscopic pelvic surgery. Infertility Reprod Med Clin North Am 4:255, 1993

Martin DC: Carbon dioxide laser laparoscopy for endometriosis. Obstet Gynecol Clin North Am 18:575, 1991

Mausberg R, Visser H, Aschoff T et al: Histology of laser- and high-frequency-electrosurgical incisions in the palate of pigs. J Craniomaxillofac Surg 21:130, 1993

Moak E: Electrosurgical unit safety. The role of the perioperative nurse [see comments]. AORN J 53:744, 1991

Neuwirth RS: Gynecologic surgery and adhesion prevention. Asherman's syndrome. Prog Clin Biol Res 381:187, 1993

Odell R: Electrosurgery in laparoscopy. 4:289, 1933

Palmer SE, McGill LD: Thermal injury by in vitro incision of equine skin with electrosurgery, radiosurgery, and a carbon dioxide laser. Vet Surg 21:348, 1992

Pearlman NW, Stiegmann GV, Vance V et al: A prospective study of incisional time, blood loss, pain, and healing with carbon dioxide laser, scalpel, and electrosurgery (see comments). Arch Surg 126:1018, 1991

Perino A, Cittadini E, Colacurci N et al: Endometrial ablation: principles and technique. Acta Eur Fertil 21:313, 1990

Phillips E, Daykhovsky L, Carroll B et al: Laparoscopic cholecystectomy: instrumentation and technique. J Laparoendosc Surg 1:3, 1990

Pierce J: Electrosurgery. John Wiley & Sons, New York, 1986

Reagan B, Zarins B, Mankin HJ: Low conductivity irrigating solutions for arthroscopy. Arthroscopy 7:105, 1991

Reich H: Laparoscopic electrosurgical oophorectomy: risk of using "blanching" as the end point [letter; comment]. Am J Obstet Gynecol 167:1150, 1992

Richart RM, Wright T Jr: Outpatient surgery in gynecologic oncology. Curr Opin Obstet Gynecol 5:318, 1993

Riopelle VW&M (ed): Gynecologic Laser Surgery, A Practical handbook. Biomedical Communications, Houston, 1982

Rosen DJ, Margolin ML, Menashe Y, Greenspoon JS: Toxic shock syndrome after loop electrosurgical excision procedure. Am J Obstet Gynecol 169:202, 1993

Ryan C: Basic Electricity. 2nd Ed. John Wiley & Sons, New York, 1986

Sebben JE: Fire hazards and electrosurgery. J Dermatol Surg Oncol 16:421, 1990

Sebben JE: Modifications of electrosurgery electrodes. J Dermatol Surg Oncol 18:908, 1992

Shapsey S (ed): Endoscopic Laser Surgery Handbook. Marcel Dekker, New York, 1987

Slager CJ, Schuurbiers JC, Oomen JA, Bom N: Electrical nerve and muscle stimulation by radio frequency surgery: role of direct current loops around the active electrode. IEEE Trans Biomed Eng 40:182, 1993

Soderstrom RM: Electrosurgery: advantages and disadvantages. Prog Clin Biol Res 323:297, 1990

Soderstrom RM: Preventing adhesions—electrosurgery: advantages and disadvantages. Prog Clin Biol Res 358:59, 1990

Soderstrom RM: Electricity inside the uterus. Clin Obstet Gynecol 35:262, 1992

Steiner RA, Wight E, Tadir Y, Haller U: Electrical cutting device for laparoscopic removal of tissue from the abdominal cavity. Obstet Gynecol 81:471, 1993

Sullins KE: Standing endoscopic electrosurgery. Vet Clin North Am Equine Pract 7:571, 1991

Sullivan B, Kenney P, Seibel M: Hysteroscopic resection of fibroid with thermal injury to sigmoid. Obstet Gynecol 80:546, 1992

Sutton C, Diamond M (ed): Endoscopic Surgery for Gynaecologists. WB Saunders, London, 1993

Swolin K: Gynecologic surgery and adhesion prevention. Electromicrosurgery. Prog Clin Biol Res 381:45, 1993

Tucker RD, Benda JA, Mardan A, Engel T: The interaction of electrosurgical bipolar forceps and generators on an animal model of fallopian tube sterilization. Am J Obstet Gynecol 165:443, 1991

Tucker RD, Ferguson S: Do surgical gloves protect staff during electrosurgical procedures? Surgery 110:892, 1991

Tucker RD, Kramolowsky EV, Stasz P: Direct-current potentials created by arcing during monopolar radiofrequency electrosurgery. Biomed Instrum Technol 24:212, 1990

Tucker RD, Platz CE, Sievert CE et al: In vivo evaluation of monopolar versus bipolar electrosurgical polypectomy snares. Am J Gastroenterol 85:1386, 1990

Tucker RD, Sievert CE, Kramolowsky EV et al: The interaction between electrosurgical generators, endoscopic electrodes, and tissue. Gastrointest Endosc 38:118, 1992

Tucker RD, Sievert CE, Vennes JA, Silvis SE: Endoscopic radio frequency electrosurgery [editorial]. Gastrointest Endosc 36:412, 1990

Tucker RD, Voyles CR, Silvis SE: Capacitive coupled stray currents during laparoscopic and endoscopic electrosurgical procedures. Biomed Instrum Technol 26:303, 1992

Voyles CR, Tucker RD: Education and engineering solutions for potential problems with laparoscopic monopolar electrosurgery. Am J Surg 164:57, 1992

Weber PJ: The Acu-guard sterile disposable electrosurgery cover [letter]. J Dermatol Surg Oncol 19:173, 1993

Weber PJ, Weber RG: Modified electrosurgical adapters. J Dermatol Surg Oncol 18:991, 1992

Wetter LA, Payne JH, Kirshenbaum G et al: The ultrasonic dissector facilitates laparoscopic cholecystectomy. Arch Surg 127:1195, 1992

Wicker P: Electrosurgery—part I. The history of diathermy. Natnews 27:6, 1990

Wicker P: Electrosurgery—part II. The principles of electrosurgery. Natnews 27:6, 1990

Wicker P: Electrosurgery—part 3. Uses of electrosurgery. Natnews 27:13, 1990

Wicker P: Electrosurgery—part 4. The hazards of electrosurgery and principles of safe use. Natnews 27:10, 1990

Wicker P: Making sense of electrosurgery. Nurs Times 88:31, 1992

5 Laparoscopic Instrumentation

STEPHEN M. COHEN

Operative endoscopy is a technically intensive surgical procedure requiring delicate instrumentation. These instruments must be in perfect working order and readily accessible. Instrumentation can now be purchased as reusable or disposable and as a combination in which part of the instrument is replaced and part is reusable. Advantages and disadvantages of these features are discussed later in this chapter.

It is improper and risky to begin an operation without the appropriate instrumentation that may be necessary. The surgeon or his or her designee must examine all instrumentation to make sure it is functioning and that no critical parts are missing. Faulty instrumentation can cause prolonged operative time, need for more invasive procedures, injury, and even death of the patient. Equipment that is defective should be promptly replaced. Backup equipment for critical instrumentation should be available.

LAPAROSCOPE

The laparoscope, of course, is the most essential piece of instrumentation for operative procedures (Fig. 5-1). Although the laparoscope grossly appears unchanged from those manufactured 20 years ago, great improvements have occurred "under the skin." Light transmission through fiberoptic light bundles has improved dramatically. Thus, much less of the laparoscope is made up of light bundles, and more space can be devoted to the image bundles. Also because more light can be transmitted into the areas to be examined, the image is clearer and the color more accurate. The surgeon can view the operative field from more of a distance, allowing him or her to evaluate the situation more quickly and accurately. The field of view has also been widened. Distortion at the periphery of the field

has essentially been eliminated. In general, the durability of telescopes has been significantly improved, and they can tolerate more abusive handling than scopes of a few years back.

Various modifications of the standard 5- and 10-mm laparoscope have been developed in the past few years (Fig. 5-2). A rigid laparoscope with a flexible distal end (developed by WECK) is available. Also a laparoscope only 1 mm in diameter is now being manufactured by Storz, Origin, and Imagyn (Fig. 5-3). The optics of these scopes are amazingly good when the extremely small size of the system is considered. These small scopes allow the surgeon to access the pelvis safely even despite extensive adhesions. It also has the potential to make diagnostic laparoscopy an office procedure. Recently, a disposable laparoscope, manufactured by U.S. Surgical, has become available (Fig. 5-4).

TROCARS

The standard nondisposable steel trocar for laparoscopy has been available for 70 years (Fig. 5-5). This trocar is still widely and appropriately used for many procedures. These trocars come in three variations: direct insertion (sharp), direct insertion (blunt), and indirect insertion (open/Hassan). Direct insertion trocars vary little from manufacturer to manufacturer. Some have gas inlet ports; others do not. Some have trumpet valves, which allow the surgeon to open the trocar (such as for suture insertion); others have a self-sealing door, which allows instruments to be inserted without the need to open the flap but makes it difficult or impossible to pass soft supplies such as suture, bags, or adhesion barriers.

Disposable trocars come in various configurations. Some are very simple, having only a washer and no

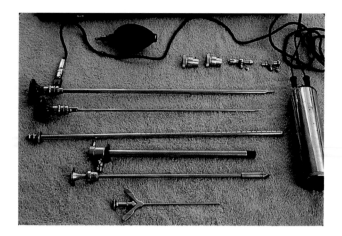

Fig. 5-1. Laparoscopy, circa 1920.

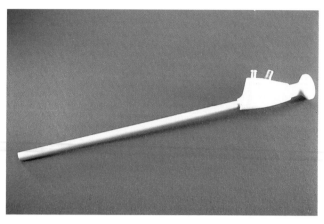

Fig. 5-4. Disposable laparoscope (U.S. Surgical).

Fig. 5-2. Standard 10-mm diagnostic laparoscope (Storz).

other controls (Fig. 5-6). Others come with one or more features including gas port, built-in or removable grip, retractable safety shields or point, changeable reducers or self-adapting reducers, and manual or automatic flapper valves (Fig. 5-7).

Gas Ports

One trocar per case must have a gas port. Usually the trocar through which the laparoscope will pass is the appropriate trocar to contain the port, as that trocar will be moved the least during the case. Secondary trocars with gas ports are unnecessary and only add to the cost of the procedure.

Grips

Grips are useful to prevent the trocar from slipping retroperitoneal as instruments are removed or from being pushed too far into the abdominal cavity as instru-

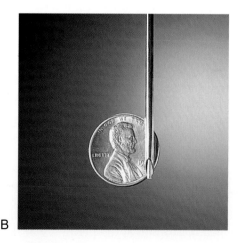

Fig. 5-3. (A&B) Micro laparoscope (Storz).

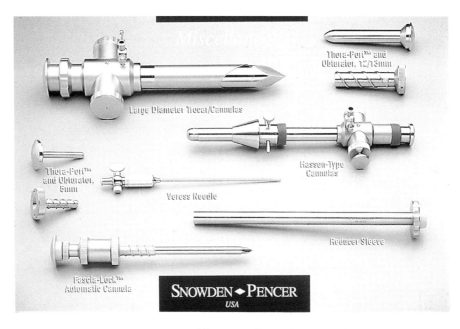

Fig. 5-5. Reusable trocars (Snowden-Pencer).

Fig. 5-6. Simple disposable trocar (Apple).

ments are inserted. The screw-type grip comes incorporated into the shaft of some trocars or as a separate device to be slipped onto the trocar shaft when necessary. The built-in grips are limited in their usefulness, because there is no way to adjust how far into the abdomen the trocar is positioned. The adjustable grips allow the operator to fix the position of the trocar just below the peritoneum, which keeps the sleeve in the proper position. Unfortunately, these grips rarely work for long periods of time, usually breaking free from the fascia as the case progresses. Also in patients who have a thick abdominal wall, the grip does not reach the fascia. Recently, new concepts in grip construction have been developed. A sticky pad (like an electrocardiogram lead) with a grip in it can be stuck to the skin, holding the trocar in place without having to screw it into the fascia (Fig. 5-8). Other trocars now have a

Fig. 5-7. Complex disposable trocars (Ethicon).

Fig. 5-8. Surgipatch (U.S. Surgical).

Fig. 5-9. Molly-bolt-design trocar (Origin).

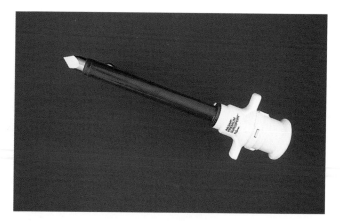

Fig. 5-11. Trocar with retractable point (U.S. Surgical).

molly-bolt-type design, so that a plastic or balloon-type end is expanded once the trocar is inserted into the abdomen, not allowing the trocar to slip back out (Fig. 5-9). Both these designs are significant improvements over the screw-type grip.

Safety Shield

The safety shield was developed as a device to help reduce damage to intra-abdominal vessels or organs (Fig. 5-10). There are no clinical data to support the theory that these devices will reduce injuries. It is unlikely that bowel injury will be reduced, in that most if not all perforations by trocars occur in bowel adhered to the anterior abdominal wall. It is possible, however, that the opposite wall of the bowel may be saved from puncture. Other problems with disposable trocars are that they are sometimes too sharp, making it difficult to control the depth of entry into the abdomen. This rapid entry may, in fact, increase the likelihood of vessel and organ damage. Another problem can occur when the safety shield that is designed to cover the point when pressure is released prematurely locks into position before perforation of the peritoneum during a slow entry into the abdomen. This distends the retroperitoneal space, making entry into the abdomen difficult. Recently, some manufacturers have introduced a retractable point trocar (Fig. 5-11). This new design shows great promise for improved safety, as the point retracts much faster than the shield-locking mechanism.

Adjustable Reducers

During operative laparoscopy, it is often necessary to place various-sized instruments into the abdomen. Also, it may be necessary to have a larger trocar (12 mm) for later tissue removal but only 5-mm instruments for the actual performance of the surgery. If this is the case, there must be a system for reducing the size of the trocar opening. Very few reusable systems accommodate this need. Many disposable trocars now have reducers attached to the trocar for ease of use. Some trocars are now equipped with reducers that self-adjust to the size of the instrument being passed through it (Fig. 5-12). This self-adjusting system saves significant operating time but, again, can sometimes make it difficult to pass sutures and other soft supplies.

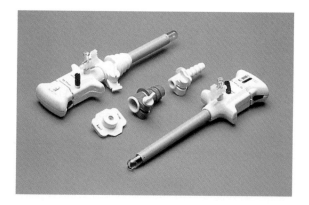

Fig. 5-10. Trocar with safety shield (Ethicon).

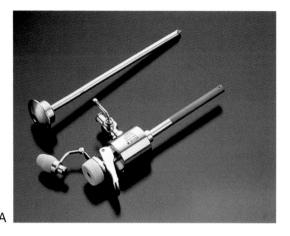 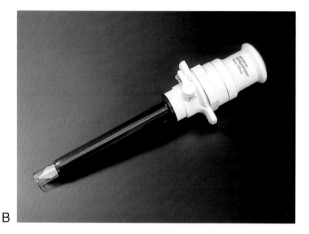

Fig. 5-12. (A) Trocar with adjustable reducer port (Storz). **(B)** Trocar with self-adjusting reducer (U.S. Surgical).

Flapper Valves

It is imperative in some cases of operative laparoscopy to have a manually operated flapper or trumpet valve trocar (Figs. 5-13, 5-14). This allows the surgeon to pass sutures, adhesion barriers, sacs, and sponges into the abdomen without these supplies becoming trapped. Also, the surgeon must be able to hold the valve open for tissue removal, so that the valve does not trap the tissue as it is removed through the trocar. Disposable or reusable trocars work equally well in this capacity.

GRASPERS

The grasper becomes the surgeon's fingers during operative laparoscopy and allows one to move tissue and organs so that the view is ideal and the operation can be accomplished safely. Unnecessary time is spent and many complications occur because the surgeon cannot position the organ in the appropriate position. Graspers come in hundreds of various configurations. However, it is important for the surgeon to have a few graspers that he or she is familiar with and feels comfortable using. There should be a plan when purchasing laparoscopic graspers; random purchases will lead to instruments that are rarely used and inappropriate for the task at hand. A list of organs and tissues that need to be grasped should be developed. That list should include ovary, tube, ligaments, uterus, fibroids, adhesions, vessels, ovarian cysts, ectopic pregnancy, serosa, peritoneum, and bowel. Then, the instrument best suited to the task should be researched by reading catalogs, examining instruments at meetings or courses, or having the manufacturer's representative

bring the instrument in for use during surgery. The various components of the instrument should be carefully examined, including handles, locks, tip design, and quality. On a list, the instrument and manufacturer best suited for each appropriate organ or tissue should be noted. This systematic approach of purchasing will allow development of a set of instruments that is cost-effective, complete, and appropriate.

Recently, graspers that more closely resemble open instrumentation have become available. The first-generation graspers had thin jaws and were quite flimsy. Second-generation graspers have been designed with more familiar configurations such as Allis, Babcock, Pennington, and Duval (Fig. 5-15). These graspers are much less traumatic and much more effective.

SCISSORS

As in open surgery, scissors are a critical part of the operative set. Nothing is more frustrating to a surgeon than dull scissors that tear tissue, or worse, do not cut at all. Scissors that are imprecise cause increased tissue damage, leading to increased bleeding, adhesion formation, and organ damage. Scissors are manufactured in disposable, reusable, and reusable with disposable tip design. Each configuration has its advantages and disadvantages. The disposable scissors are always sharp and in precise working order. No contamination or instrument breakdown has occurred from previous cases or sterilization. All components work together because there are no interchangeable parts. Also many of the disposable scissors come with electrosurgical adaption, allowing the surgeon to obtain simultaneous hemostasis with either unipolar or bipolar energy (Figs. 5-16 and 5-17). Disposable scissors may be espe-

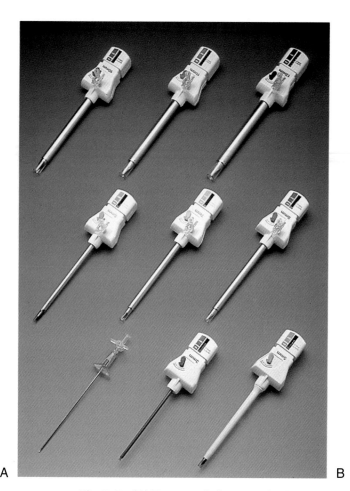

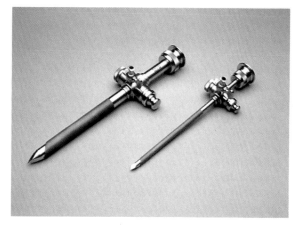

Fig. 5-13. (A) Trocar with flapper valve (U.S. Surgical). **(B)** Trocar with trumpet valve (Storz).

cially advantageous if one is having difficulty maintaining instrumentation or doing only rare cases that require the use of scissors. The disadvantages of disposable scissors are that they are costly and contribute to environmental contamination. Also, we have never found disposable scissors to be as precise as fine-crafted nondisposable scissors.

Reusable scissors are the most precise instrumentation available when supplied by a reliable manufacturer (Fig. 5-18). However, reusable scissors definitely become dull with use, and this usually becomes apparent during a case. Unless backup scissors are available, the surgeon must complete the case with dull scissors. These scissors are difficult to maintain and are often ruined by repeat sterilization procedures or handling and cleaning. There also is significant down time if scissors needs to go back for repair; and it seems as if repaired scissors never function as well as new ones.

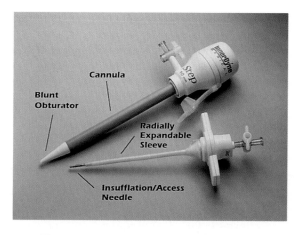

Fig. 5-14. Expandable trocar (Innerdyne).

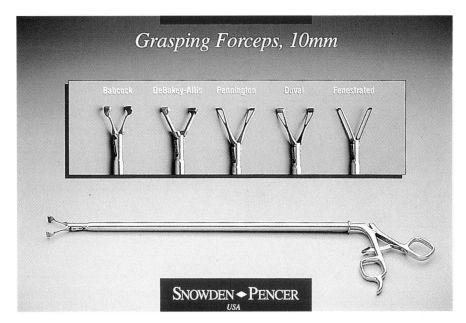

Fig. 5-15. Graspers (Snowden-Pencer).

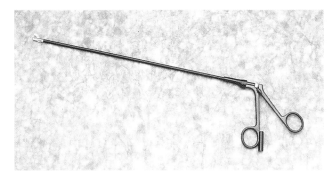

Fig. 5-16. Unipolar scissors (Storz).

Scissors with reusable handles and/or shafts but disposable blades have recently become available. Some configurations require the tips to be disposed of after each use, whereas others can be reused until dull (Fig. 5-19). This concept is good in theory, but it remains to be seen how well these systems function with sterilization and interchangeable parts. Many of the permanent and partly disposable instruments are not equipped for concurrent electrosurgical energy systems.

Various configurations of scissors should be available for use during a case. Hooked scissors and curved blunt-tipped (Metzenbaum) scissors are the most commonly needed, and both should be part of the operative set. Shafts that rotate are important from a ergonomic view, allowing the surgeon to cut tissue in the

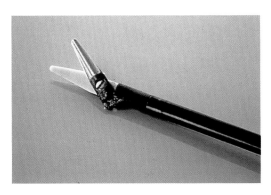

Fig. 5-17. Bipolar scissors (Evershears).

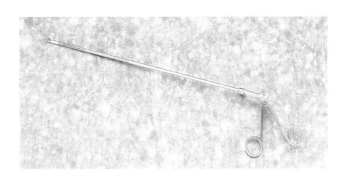

Fig. 5-18. Reusable scissors (Storz).

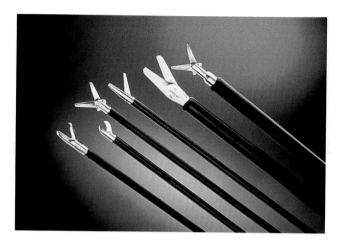

Fig. 5-19. Reusable scissors with disposable tips (Storz).

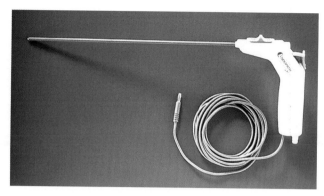

Fig. 5-20. Disposable suction/irrigators (Ethicon).

best plane while keeping his or her hand in the most re-laxed anatomic position.

IRRIGATORS-ASPIRATORS

It is essential to have a quality irrigation-aspiration system when performing operative laparoscopy. Even the simplest of cases can result in unexpected bleeding, requiring the immediate need for suction and irriga-tion to control the situation. Inadequate equipment or a staff unaccustomed to the set-up and use of this equipment can lead to the need for open laparotomy and significant morbidity. Morbidity has occurred be-cause the surgeon is either unable to visualize and con-trol bleeding or, worse, has attempted to control bleed-ing without adequate visualization, causing significant injury to adjacent organs.

Irrigation-aspiration systems can be purchased in disposable or reusable configurations (Figs. 5-20 and 5-21). Some are reusable with disposable parts (such as tubing). Some irrigation-aspiration systems allow other working elements (scissors, electrosurgical needles, etc.) to be passed through the cannula (Fig. 5-22). Re-cently, an irrigator with fluid-warming capabilities has been marketed.

During many operations, irrigation or aspiration is unnecessary, and thus any system that requires dispos-able parts should be available, but the disposable parts should not be opened until needed. This, of course, re-quires a team that can quickly assemble the equipment during the case should it become necessary. A simple nondisposable system should be available when that is all that is needed, such as aspiration of the cul-de-sac or irrigating once or twice during an ovarian cystectomy. Irrigating-aspirating systems should be available that allow suction of significant blood or blood clots and in-

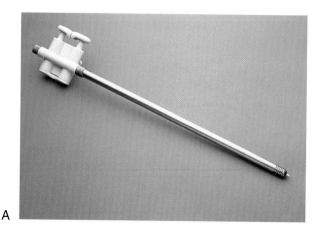

A

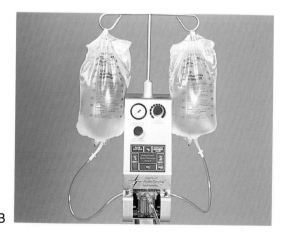

B

Fig. 5-21. (A & B) Reusable suction/irrigators (American Hydrosurgical).

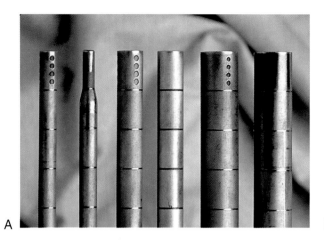

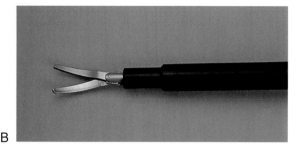

A

B

Fig. 5-22. (A & B) Irrigators with working elements (American Hydrosurgical).

fusion of large amounts of fluid. In cases of spontaneous bleeding (ectopic pregnancy, ruptured ovarian cyst), appropriate suction and irrigation often make the difference in being able to complete the operation laparoscopically or necessitating exploratory laparotomy. In these situations, a 10-mm cannula and a quality pump are usually needed. When a lengthy procedure is performed, a system that allows the use of operative instruments through the aspirator/irrigator saves significant operative time and instrument wear.

NEEDLE HOLDERS

The ability to suture is a necessary requirement for surgeons who plan to perform more advanced operative laparoscopy. The surgeon should have a pair of needle holders for curved needles (Fig. 5-23) and another pair for straight needles (Fig. 5-24). Straight needles are easier to grasp (two planes only) and place in soft flexible tissue. Curved needles are more appropriate for rigid, thick tissue, to close deep defects (myomectomy), or to place around vessels. A needle holder designed for straight needles cannot be used for curved needles. If the surgeon tries to use a straight needle holder for a curved needle, placement will be difficult, because the needle will twist as it is placed in tissue. Needle holders come with or without locks. Locks allow the operator to remove his or her hand from the handles while the needle stays secure, but releasing the needle without damaging the tissue often becomes difficult. Nonlocking handles allow easy release, but con-

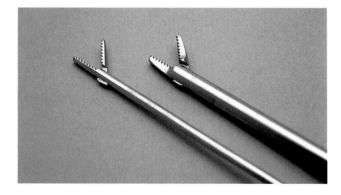

Fig. 5-23. Curved needle holders (Cook).

Fig. 5-24. Straight needle holders (Snowden-Pencer).

tinuous pressure on the handles must be maintained. Spring-loaded handles offer a compromise. Some needle holders have a spring-loaded system, in which the needle is held in the shaft of the needle holder rather than the jaws. This system holds the needle securely but requires a change to jawed instruments for intracorporeal tying.

Before purchasing a needle holder, the surgeon should use them in surgery. The choice of a needle holder is an individual decision, based on ergonomics, weight, design, and proposed usage.

MISCELLANEOUS INSTRUMENTATION

Knot-Pushers

Most knot tying after suture placement in gynecologic endoscopic surgery is performed extracorporeally. That means that the knot is tied outside the abdominal cavity and slipped down through the trocar as the tissue is secured. Endoscopically, it is necessary to replace the finger, which would traditionally be the knot-pusher in an open surgical case. The knot-pusher is a rigid rod, placed above the knot, and used to slide the knot down to tissue (Fig. 5-25). One throw is placed at a time, and each throw is pushed separately down to the tissue level. Usually, the first two throws are placed in the same direction, and the third throw is placed in the opposite direction, to square the knot.

Knot-pushers come in two basic designs: open horseshoe design and closed circle. The open horseshoe design is quicker to place on the suture but may slide off the knot as it is being pushed down through the trocar. The closed design takes longer to thread (the suture needs to be passed through the knot-pusher, like threading a sewing needle), but it cannot slide off the sutures as the knot is being pushed down through the trocar.

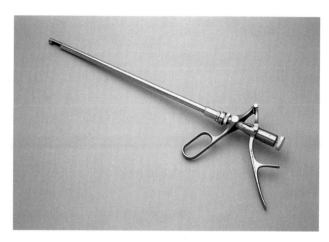

Fig. 5-26. Morcellator (WISAP).

Morcellators

Extracting large pieces of tissue out of the abdomen through small incisions is a frustrating aspect of gynecologic laparoscopic surgery. Various surgical methods have been used, such as opening the cul-de-sac, extending the abdominal incision. Instruments have been developed that allow large pieces of tissue to be divided into smaller pieces for extraction. The two most common devices are manufactured by WISAP (Figs. 5-26 and 5-27). One is a straight hollow shaft with an internal sharp jaw that takes a bite into the tissue and slides the pieces up the hollow shaft. Another is a simple hollow tube with a sharp serrated edge that bores into the tissue as it is twisted from outside the abdomen (resembling a cookie cutter). The latter is much more effective, quicker, simpler, and less expensive.

Retractors

Often during laparoscopic surgery, bowel obscures the operative field, making the surgery difficult and lengthening the operative time. Placing the patient in a steep Trendelenburg position will help mobilize the

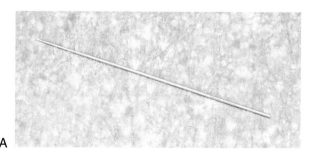

A

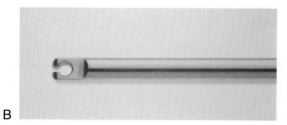

B

Fig. 5-25. (A & B) Knot-pusher (Storz).

Fig. 5-27. Morcellator (WISAP).

Fig. 5-29. Laparoscopic sacs (Advanced Surgical).

bowel out of the pelvis, but often times it becomes necessary to place a bowel retractor into the abdomen. Procedures such as presacral neurectomy and periaortic node dissection often require the use of a retractor.

Retractors come in various configurations (Fig. 5-28). However, all retractors work on the same principle, in that they have an expanded distal end that spreads to hold the bowel out of the operative field. The most common shape is a fanlike projection. Others come in a T shape. Still others have an end that can be distended with air. Retractors are available in both permanent and disposable construction.

Sacs

Plastic bags are often used in gynecologic endoscopic surgery. Most commonly, these sacs are used to remove ovarian cysts or ovaries containing cysts.

Whether benign or malignant (often undeterminable at the time of surgery), the surgeon would prefer not to spill the contents of these cysts into the pelvis. Benign cyst fluid (dermoid, mucous cyst, endometrioma) may cause an inflammatory reaction and subsequent adhesion formation. Whether spillage of malignant cyst contents increases the chance of recurrence is still unresolved and controversial at this time.

Essentially, a sac is a plastic bag at the end of a stick, into which the operator can place the ovary or cyst before withdrawal from abdomen (Fig. 5-29). The original sacs were poorly designed. They were difficult to open, which made it a task to place the ovary or cyst into the

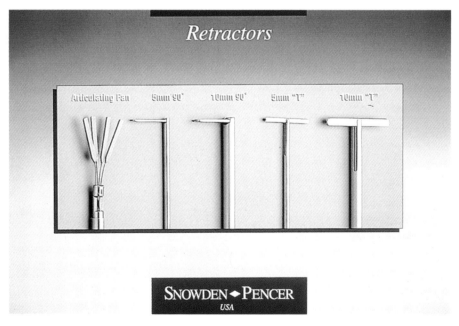

Fig. 5-28. Laparoscopic retractor (Snowden-Pencer).

sac. They had a weak drawstring. They were flimsy and often broke during extraction through the abdominal wall. They also were too narrow and short.

Improvements have been made. Most bags are much stronger now. Some have mechanisms that allow the bag to open mechanically (such as a metal ring around the rim or a bag that expands with air). It is impossible to bring an ovary or cyst through a small incision when the diameter of the ovary or cyst is much larger than the incision. The technique of using the sac is to bring the open end of the sac through the incision, out onto the abdomen. The surgeon then reaches inside with an instrument, such as a biopsy forceps, and morcellates the cyst and drains any fluid. By pulling up on the sac firmly, the surgeon can maintain the pneumoperitoneum, so that the process of removal can be clearly seen via the laparoscope.

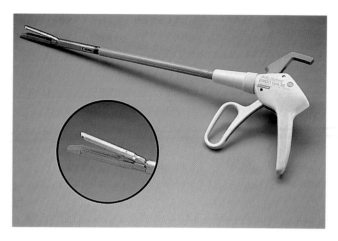

Fig. 5-31. Linear stapler (U.S. Surgical).

Staplers

Linear staplers place rows of staples into tissue to occlude the major vessels along the tissue edge to be cut. Microvascular perfusion is preserved. In addition to laying down staples, some instruments also have a knife blade that automatically cuts between these rows of staples and divides the tissue all in one motion. The two most common types of these latter instruments are made by Ethicon (Fig. 5-30) and U.S. Surgical (Fig. 5-31). Both place three rows of staples on each side of the tissue. These staples are made of metal and are permanent. These instruments come in a disposable configuration only but can be used multiple times during each case, as a new cartridge of staples can be placed into the jaws after each firing.

Recently, Cabot medical has introduced the "Tripolar" instrument into the market. This instrument is a wide bipolar forceps with a knife blade that travels down the middle of the jaws (Fig. 5-32). The results are similar to the stapler, substituting coagulation for staples.

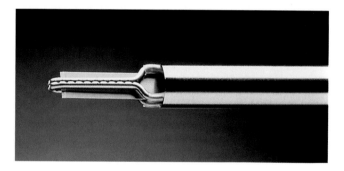

Fig. 5-32. "Tripolar" (Cabot).

Fig. 5-30. Linear stapler (Ethicon).

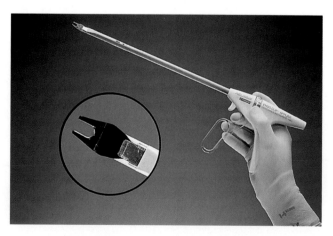

Fig. 5-33. Clip applicator (U.S. Surgical).

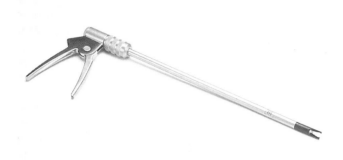

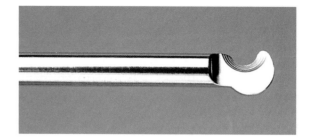

Fig. 5-36. Harmonic scalpel blade (Ultracision).

Fig. 5-34. Absorbable clip applicator (Davis & Geck).

Harmonic Scalpel

Clips

Hemostatic clips are made for endoscopic use to secure hemostasis of bleeding vessels. Often when bleeding occurs, it is safer and easier to clip than to use electrosurgery, especially near vital structures. Clipping small vessels before cutting is often easier and faster than endoscopic suturing. Clip applicators, most commonly, come as a disposable instrument loaded with multiple clips (Fig. 5-33). The clips are loaded either automatically (when one is fired the next one appears) or semiautomatically (a lever is pulled to load a clip).

Recently, Davis and Geck introduced an absorbable clip applicator for endoscopic use (Fig. 5-34). The instrument is nondisposable, and individual clips are contained in a cartridge that is placed on the end of the applicator.

The harmonic scalpel made by Ultracision is a system for endoscopic cutting (Fig. 5-35). The energy source is vibration. The power box is attached to a forceps or blade (Fig. 5-36), and the vibrational frequency of the blade approaches 55,000/sec. This causes a knifelike action of the blade through tissue, with enough heating to create coagulation of small vessels. When this vibrational energy is applied to the forceps configuration, coagulation occurs (Fig. 5-37). By rotating the bottom blade of the forceps, the instrument becomes a scissors, and the tissue can divide.

The harmonic scalpel allows the operator to cut using a tactile sense. No smoke is created, only microatomized water droplets, which are rapidly absorbed by the peritoneal surface. The instrument is extremely safe in that only tissue touched is cut; the energy source cannot travel through air, such as can happen with electrosurgery and laser.

Fig. 5-35. Harmonic scalpel (Ultracision).

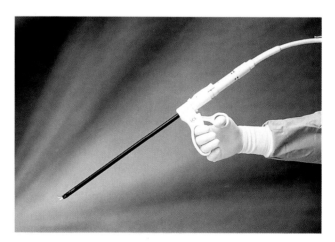

Fig. 5-37. LCS (Ultracision).

CONCLUSION

Endoscopic instruments are the key to safe and effective surgery. "Good carpenters have good tools" is an adage that can also be applied to the human carpenter, the surgeon. Instrument development by manufacturers is rapid, and new instruments are marketed on a daily basis. One needs to use common sense in evaluating new instrumentation and not be swayed by the representative. Is the new instrument a significant advance or only an expensive marketing gimmick?

6 Abdominal Entry

HOWARD T. SHARP
JAMES H. DORSEY

In most cases, laparoscopic abdominal entry is an uncomplicated process. However, previous surgery, anatomic variation, and body habitus can create difficulties if these conditions and their accompanying risks factors are not anticipated. This chapter focuses on the standard principles of laparoscopic abdominal entry, as well as techniques to avoid and manage complications.

ANATOMY

In gynecologic surgery, the most common site for primary trocar placement is umbilical. In addition to being a natural location for scar concealment, this point offers the advantage of attenuation of the layers of the anterior abdominal wall. Elsewhere, the layers of the abdominal wall include skin, subcutaneous layer (Camper's fascia and Scarpa's fascia), anterior rectus sheath, rectus muscle, posterior rectus sheath, and peritoneum. As the rectus muscles span inferiority to the pubis, the posterior rectus sheath disappears at the level of the linea semicircularis (arcuate line). Caudad to this level, the peritoneum becomes immediately deep to the rectus muscles, as the aponeurosis of the transversalis and internal oblique become superficial to the rectus abdominus (Fig. 6-1). Inferiorly, the anterior parietal peritoneum and the visceral peritoneum of the bladder meet, making the bladder a potential site for trocar injury, especially if previous surgery has fixed the bladder to a more superior location or if the bladder has not been completely emptied. A knowledge of these anatomic relationships is important for the laparoscopist. Although most laparoscopies may be initiated by "blind" insertion of needle or trochar through the umbilical incision, more sophisticated entry may be required for advanced operative procedures. For example, a preperitoneal approach to the space of Retzius requires insertion of scope or balloon on top of the posterior rectus sheath through the small "open" umbilical incision.

The inferior epigastric artery (deep epigastric) originates from the external iliac artery above the inguinal ligament, running caudad to cephalad as it approaches the rectus abdominus muscle laterally (Fig. 6-2). It has a surprisingly large mean diameter of 3.5 mm at its origin, and it branches often during its course. The distance from the insertion of the rectus tendon to the intersection of the inferior epigastric artery and the lateral border of the rectus abdominus is approximately 7 cm.[1] This artery can often be seen pulsating when the anterior parietal peritoneum is carefully viewed through the laparoscope because it lies just lateral to the obliterated umbilical artery, directly on top the peritoneum (Fig. 6-3). It consists of a single artery approximately 85 percent of the time[2] and usually enters the rectus abdominus in the middle third (78 percent) of that muscle. In the event that the vessel is difficult to identify, there are three other landmark structures that are almost always readily apparent, and these greatly aid in the location of the inferior epigastric, particularly in obese patients. These are the urachus, which is located directly in the midline, and on either side, just medial to the inferior epigastric, the obliterated umbilical arteries, which usually stand out very prominently. In our experience, the inferior epigastric artery or its pulsation can almost always be directly visualized laparoscopically, and a trocar can be safely placed well lateral to it, allowing optimum access to the adnexa.

INSUFFLATION AND VERESS NEEDLE PLACEMENT

Most laparoscopists think that the Veress needle, a relatively small-gauge instrument with a spring-loaded safety tip, is safer to use for initiation of pneumoperitoneum than is the larger trocar. However,

69

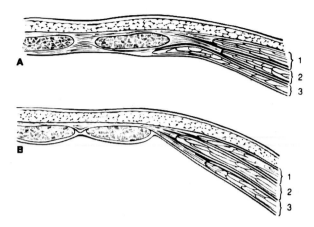

Fig. 6-1. Cross section of the anterior abdominal wall. The relationships of the anterior and posterior fascial sheaths are demonstrated above **(A)** and below **(B)** the arcuate line, noting the absence of a posterior rectus sheath below. (From DeLancey,[21] with permission.)

the subject is controversial, and some surgeons prefer to insert the umbilical trocar into a nondistended abdomen.

In any event, before the insertion of any instrument, the sacral promontory should be palpated to locate the posterior boundary of the pelvic inlet, which lies just below the bifurcation of the aorta. If there is any suggestion of gastric distention, a nasogastric tube should be inserted before the placement of a needle or trocar to avoid inadvertent injury to an overdistended stomach.[3] A subumbilical incision is made horizontally or vertically along Langer's lines, taking care to avoid full penetration of the abdominal wall by the scapel blade because the aorta and inferior vena cava may lie perilously close to the abdominal wall, particularly in thin patients. The umbilicus should be elevated and an incision made with the knife, holding the knife blade parallel to the abdominal fascia but never perpendicular,

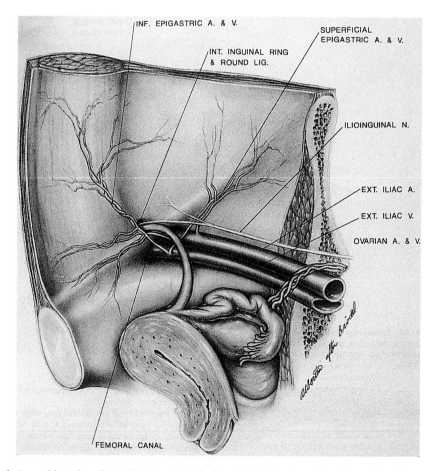

Fig. 6-2. Sagittal view of female pelvis, showing the inferior epigastric artery branching off of the external iliac artery above the inguinal ligament, running along the peritoneum to the rectus abdominus muscle. (From DeLancey,[21] with permission.)

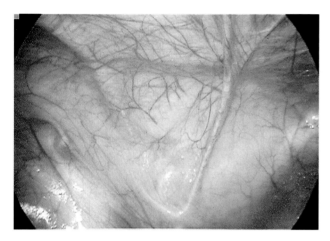

Fig. 6-3. Laparoscopic identification of the left inferior epigastric artery as seen along the left anterior abdominal wall. The obliterated umbilical artery is seen medial.

to avoid injury to the great vessels below. We have been called to the operating room on more than one occasion to repair damage to vital structures produced by a penetrating #11 scapel blade. If a reusable Veress needle is used, the spring mechanism should be checked before insertion. With the abdominal wall elevated, the tip of the needle should be used to palpate the fascia and perforation accomplished as the surgeon mentally visualizes the correct angle of entry and the relationship of the great vessels to the tip of the instrument. In obese patients, the aorta is usually above the level of the umbilicus.[4] In such cases, the Veress needle may be directed at or near 90 degrees to the fascia to avoid skimming along its surface with resulting preperitoneal insufflation. Control is the key concept in the blade insertion of any instrument into the abdominal cavity, and the "mind's eye" must concentrate on sensing the important structures below a sharp tip.

Several techniques have been described to verify proper intraperitoneal placement of the Veress needle. In 1976, Lacey[5] described a hissing sound as a clinical sign for intraperitoneal needle placement, caused by air rushing through the Veress needle from negative intra-abdominal pressure. Perhaps the most accurate method for identifying intraperitoneal entry is to use the pressure indicator of the rapid-flow insufflator. Most rapid-flow insufflators will measure negative as well as positive pressure. If the gas tubing is connected to the needle and insufflator with the electronics but not the gas turned on, elevation of the anterior abdominal wall will cause a negative pressure reading. Other tests that are useful include Veress needle aspiration test, to check for the absence of blood or gastrointesti-

nal contents, and the "hanging drop" method of placing drops of sterile saline through the Veress needle and watching as it is sucked into the needle by the negative intra-abdominal pressure when the abdominal wall is raised. "Low-flow" CO_2 insufflation is then carried out at 1 L/min. The intra-abdominal pressure should be between 5 and 8 mm Hg, depending on patient size. Tympany percussed over the liver is a clinical sign of proper intra-abdominal insufflation, which may first be present after the instillation of 1 L of intraperitoneal gas. Continued dullness to percussion over the liver or subcutaneous emphysema would suggest preperitoneal insufflation. Often, the Veress needle can be used to map out areas of intra-abdominal adhesions. If the needle is gently moved from side to side and pressure suddenly is elevated, this suggests that an adhesion or segment of bowel is interfering with outflow. If initial insertion of the Veress needle has been preperitoneal, then subsequent attempts at Veress needle placement may be increasingly difficult if the peritoneum is tented away from the abdominal wall by a pocket of CO_2. In some cases, the laparoscope may already have been inserted into the preperitoneal space. A technique has been described to advance the laparoscope to a level approximately 4 cm from the symphysis pubis, allowing the Veress needle to be inserted under direct visualization into the peritoneal cavity as it is aimed toward the pouch of Douglas.[6] Each time the Veress needle is inserted, it should be checked to ensure that tissue is not diminishing needle patency. High-flow insufflation may be carried out once intra-abdominal Veress needle placement is reassured, using flow rates of 4 to 5 L/min. Alternate sites for Veress needle placement have also been described for cases of refractory preperitoneal insufflation.

Alternate Sites for Veress Needle Placement

If placement of the Veress needle at the umbilicus is not feasible, alternate sites for placement include the posterior vaginal fornix, uterine fundus, superior edge of the umbilicus, and the left upper-quadrant midclavicular line. The transcervical uterine fundus approach was first described by Morgan[7] in 1979, who used it in 1,500 laparoscopies without complication. Contraindications to the transfundal approach include known or suspected uterine adhesions from previous pelvic inflammatory disease or myomectomy and known uterine fibroids. Also, if chromotubation is to be performed with this technique, dye may leak through the fundus rather than the fallopian tubes. More recently, this technique was recommended by Wolfe and Pasic[8] as an excellent alternate site in obese patients. Neely et al.[9] used the posterior fornix as an alternative site for insufflation. The Veress needle was inserted 1.75 cm behind the junction of the vaginal vault rugae and the smooth epithelium of the posterior cervical lip. The midclavicular line of the left upper quadrant has also been used, as this is seldom a site for adhesions. This method is contraindicated in patients with a palpable spleen or a history of previous stomach or transverse colon surgery.

UMBILICAL TROCAR INSERTION

Direct trocar insertion was evaluated by Dingfelder in 1978.[10] He elevated the abdominal wall and directly placed a trocar safely into the abdominal cavity of 301 patients. Since this report, several series of direct trocar insertion have been published.[11-14] The rationale behind direct trocar insertion is to avoid the possible complications associated with Veress needle placement, such as CO_2 embolus from inadvertent vascular insufflation, and subcutaneous insufflation with failed pneumoperitoneum, possibly leading to failed laparoscopy. Copeland et al.[15] reported only three complications occurring in more than 2,000 direct trocar insertions. Their recommendations for performing direct trocar insertion include (1) obtaining adequate lower abdominal wall relaxation, (2) making an adequate incision, and (3) ensuring that if pyramidal trocars are used, that they be sharp. Due to the low incidence of Veress needle or trocar injury, a study with enough power to show a definitive safety advantage of one method over the other is yet to be performed. Injuries to the great vessels, bowel, and stomach have been reported using either technique; hence, great caution should be used regardless of one's personal preference.

Most surgeons use their nondominant hand to elevate the abdominal wall and insert the trocar with their dominant hand. As with Veress needle placement, the trocar should be placed aiming toward the uterine fundus, away from the aorta, and away from the great vessels laterally. Intra-abdominal trocar placement is usually accompanied by hearing a rush of gas through the trocar sheath when the one-way valve is depressed but is confirmed only on direct visualization of peritoneal structures. If the trocar was not intraperitoneal, the scope can still be used to assess the situation. Frequently, a window of peritoneum will be visible if proper intraperitoneal insufflation was performed but inadequate trocar force or angle of attack was used. If

so, either a second attempt with the trocar can be made, or a probe or scissors may be passed down the operating channel of the laparoscope and the peritoneum opened under direct visualization. In the case of an extremely obese patient, the trocar used may not have been sufficiently long. If preperitoneal insufflation has occurred, an alternate site for insufflation may be used with subsequent subumbilical trocar placement, or open laparoscopy may be performed. We find the latter technique to be particularly useful in the extremely obese patient.

Open Laparoscopy

Open laparoscopy is a method of abdominal entry developed to provide an alternative to blind trocar and Veress needle insertion.[16] This technique involves making a small incision through the skin, anterior and posterior rectus sheath, and peritoneum, such that the laparoscopic port or Hasson-type port may be placed into the peritoneal cavity and tightly secured to the rectus fascia. The surgeon should be aware that the use of this method is no guarantee against bowel injury, as the incidence of bowel injury has not been reduced by using this technique.[17] Possible explanations for this fact are that this mode of entry is often reserved for the "high-risk" cases, creating a selection bias and that, just as in laparotomy, bowel is often adherent to the abdominal wall and damage is not recognized until mucosa is suddenly seen.

Secondary Trocar Sites

Whether operative or diagnostic laparoscopy is to be carried out, secondary trocar sites must be chosen for the manipulatory and operative instruments. Adequate exploration at exploratory laparoscopy cannot be achieved without proper instruments for manipulatory pelvic and intra-abdominal organs.

The placement of these trocars will depend largely on the procedure being performed and the patient's anatomy. If a midline location is chosen, care must be taken to avoid bladder injury. Foley catheter placement will give optimal bladder decompression. If the bladder is merely drained or if the patient voids before the procedure, the bladder may become rapidly distended from intravenous fluids if there is an unexpected time lapse between bladder emptying and suprapubic trocar placement. Also, if prior surgery has resulted in superior displacement of the bladder, a Foley catheter can be used to inflate the bladder to define its borders before trocar insertion.

When placing lateral trocars, great care must be taken to avoid injury to the deep inferior epigastric vessels and the retroperitoneal great vessels. As mentioned previously, before placing lateral trocars, we prefer to visually locate the deep inferior epigastric arteries. Once the vessels are appreciated, a 22-gauge needle is placed through the abdominal wall at a safe lateral location to the vessels (Fig. 6-4). The approximate "safe site" can be identified laparoscopically by depressing the skin with an index finger and looking for the corresponding location on the peritoneum in relationship to the deep epigastric vessels. Subsequent insertion of the 22-gauge needle allows the surgeon to be reasonably sure that a trocar placed along the same track as the needle will not sever the inferior epigastrics. An additional benefit of this maneuver is that it will indicate the location of the trocar, and angle of the instrumentation will be suitable for the surgery at hand. We have not found "transillumination" of the inferior epigastric vessels to be adequate for identifying the deep inferior epigastric artery, as other vessel and ligaments in the anterior abdominal wall are in the immediate vicinity. Once a needle is placed through a safe site in the abdominal wall, it can also be used to assess whether the angle of instrumentation will be suitable for the surgery at hand.

A #11 blade is used for making a skin incision, and the lateral trocar is placed using a two-step motion. The first motion is made using gentle, straight downward force until the tip of the trocar is seen just piercing the peritoneum, away from the inferior epigastric vessels. Once the deep epigastric vessels are cleared,

the angle of force is then changed and directed toward the midline, away from the great vessels that lie laterally. Again, the concept of controlled entry must be emphasized.

Trocars

Disposable trocars have the advantage of being sharp with each use and require approximately half the force to place when compared with reusable trocars.[18] This may be a consideration for laparoscopists with less upper body strength. Reusable trocars offer the advantage of lower cost but must be maintained regularly to ensure adequate sharpness. These are available with conical tips (which were initially used to "Z track" the anterior abdominal wall) or with pyramidal tips, which must be resharpened or replaced. Both disposable and reusable trocars are now manufactured with devices designed to reduce the size of the port from 12 mm to 10, 5, or 3 mm. The Surgiport "Versiport" (U.S. Surgical, Norwalk, CT) is also now available, which does not require reducers to be used. Trocar "grips" may be applied to both types of trocars and allow the surgeon to screw the sheath into the abdominal wall so that it is held in place even when instruments are passed in and out of the abdomen. Metal trocars should never be mixed with plastic grips when unipolar electricity is used. This hybrid system is prone to allow the electric current generated by capacitive coupling to pass into the abdominal cavity, causing unrecognized electric injury. Trocar size should be selected based on the instruments to be used to perform a particular operation. In general, smaller ports are used when possible. Most operative instruments including scissors, forceps, suction-irrigators, and probes will fit through 5-mm ports. If one is using an EndoGIA, Endoclip, or Endocath (U.S. Surgical Corp.), suitable larger ports must be used.

Trocar sheath removal should be performed under direct visualization to ensure that bleeding from an abdominal wall vessel has not been temporarily tampanaded by the trocar sheath. As much CO_2 as possible should be removed to minimize postoperative patient discomfort. By leaving the laparoscope in the umbilical port during removal, the surgeon can make sure that bowel is not inadvertently suctioned through the umbilical incision. To prevent incisional hernias, we close the fascia at all sites where a 10-mm trocar or greater has been used. Kadar et al.[19] reported six cases of incisional hernias among 3,560 operative laparoscopies (0.17 percent). All occurred at extraumbilical sites involving 10- and 12-mm ports.

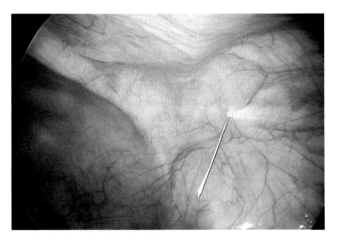

Fig. 6-4. A 22-gauge needle is seen piercing a "safe site" away from the easily identifiable right inferior epigastric artery. The obliterated umbilical artery is also seen medial to the inferior epigastric artery.

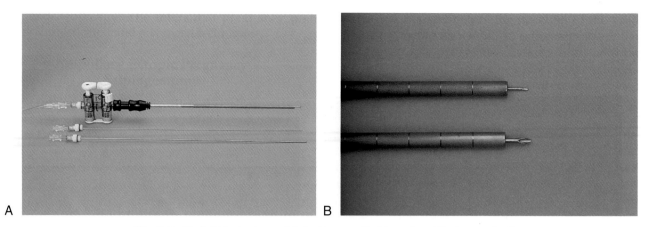

Fig. 7-3. **(A & B)** Irrigator and injection needle (American Hydrosurgical).

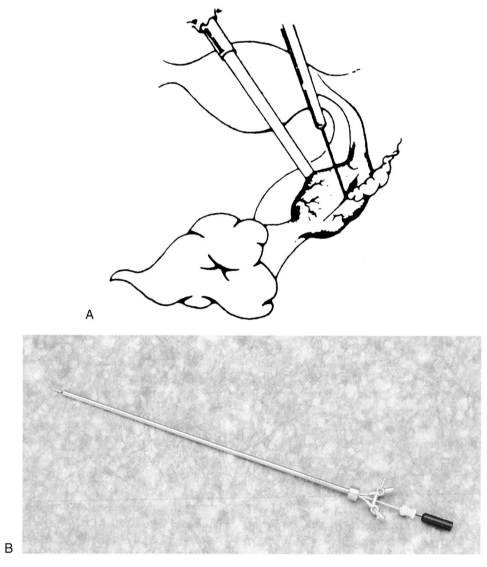

Fig. 7-4. **(A)** Ampullary ectopic pregnancy. Salpingostomy incision. **(B)** Corson needle electrode.

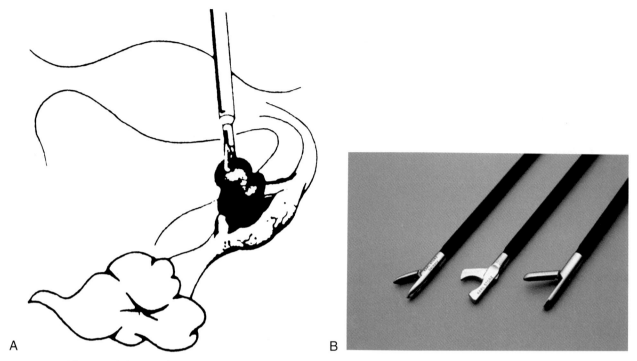

Fig. 7-5. (A) Ampullary ectopic pregnancy. Removal of products from tube. **(B)** Dulled biopsy forceps.

The incision is left open to heal by secondary intention (Figs. 7-6 and 7-7). Suturing is not performed, as it requires additional time, leaves a foreign body, creates more devitalized tissue, and is more likely to lead to stenosis at the operative site.

Whether most ectopic pregnancies occur intraluminal or extraluminal at different locations is still a mat-

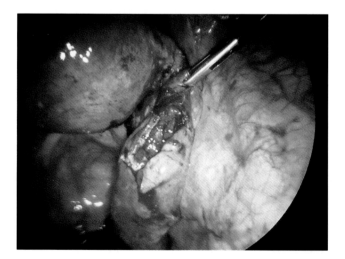

Fig. 7-6. Ampullary ectopic pregnancy. Salpingostomy completed.

ter of controversy. There is no doubt that ectopic pregnancies do occur both intra- and extraluminally.[5] What is still controversial is the relative percentages of these occurrences. Regardless, attempts at laparoscopic salpingostomy can be performed in either case. Extraluminal ectopic pregnancies can be more difficult to remove completely and may be more likely to require methotrexate therapy postoperatively for persistent trophoblastic tissue.

After the removal of the products of conception, the pelvis should be irrigated with Ringer's lactate, inspected for hemostasis, and explored for a last time. Patients are discharged the same day unless significant hemorrhage has occurred. As with all ectopic pregnancies, blood type must be determined and MICRhoGAM given if the patient is Rh-negative.

Ampullary Ectopic Pregnancy Salpingectomy

When the patient has an ampullary ectopic pregnancy and wishes sterilization or if the ectopic pregnancy has destroyed the tube beyond salvage, a salpingectomy should be performed (Fig. 7-8). This procedure can usually be performed quite rapidly and easily even in cases of active bleeding. (If blood is found on entering the abdomen, it should be removed

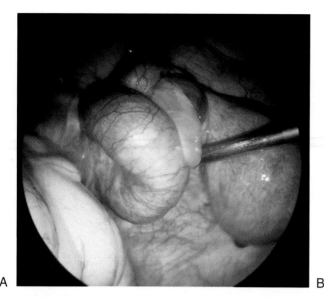
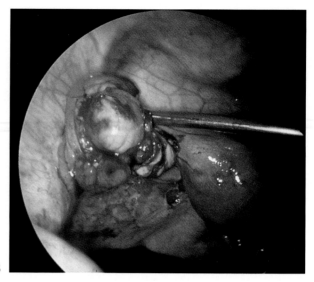

Fig. 7-7. (A) Ampullary ectopic pregnancy before salpingostomy. **(B)** Ampullary ectopic pregnancy after salpingostomy.

only if the tube cannot be located or the surgery performed.)

The tube with the ectopic pregnancy should be held with a strong grasper and examined. There are many acceptable ways to perform laparoscopic distal salpingectomy. One method is simply to place two endoloop sutures over the distal tube and secure them, occluding the entire mesosalpinx (Fig. 7-9). Scissors are then used to excise the tube. If any bleeding is noted

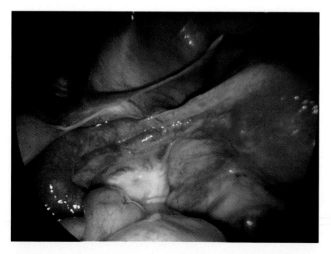

Fig. 7-8. Ampullary ectopic pregnancy. Pregnancy before salpingectomy.

from the pedicle, a third endoloop can be placed around the freed pedicle.

The tube can also be excised using only bipolar forceps and scissors (Fig. 7-10). The bipolar forceps is placed across the proximal tube and mesosalpinx. These areas are then divided with scissors. One then progressively works toward the ectopic pregnancy from both ends, alternating coagulation and cutting with scissors. An amp meter attached to the bipolar generator can visually tell the operator when the tissue is coagulated by showing that the current is no longer being passed through the tissue grasped between the forceps.

The linear stapler can also be used for performing a salpingectomy (Fig. 7-11). This device is a stapler that can be passed through a 12-mm trocar. The operator can grasp the entire mesosalpinx in one bite with the stapler. By firing the instrument, six rows of staples are released, and the tissue is divided with a knife that automatically slides between the staple lines, leaving three rows of staples on either side of the divided mesosalpinx. These stapling devices are expensive, however, increasing the cost of the procedure. Less commonly performed laparoscopic suturing and extracorporeal tying have been used, but for most surgeons, this adds significant time to the procedure.

The excised tube can then be removed by various methods (Fig. 7-12):

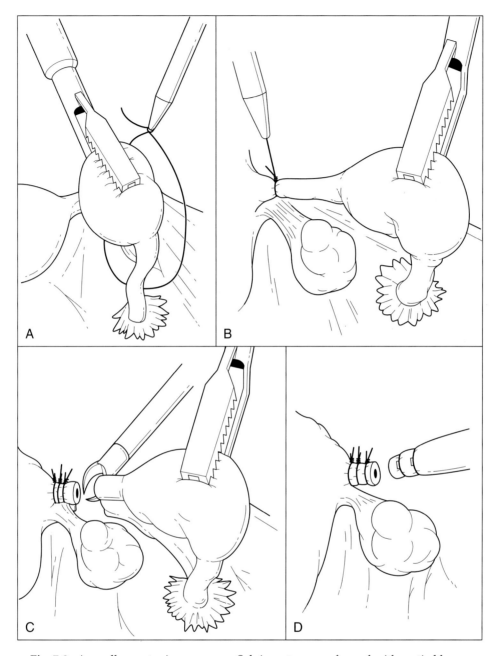

Fig. 7-9. Ampullary ectopic pregnancy. Salpingectomy performed with pretied loop.

1. The tube can be divided and removed in pieces.
2. The tube can be removed with a morcellator.
3. The tube can be removed through the umbilical incision, after a smaller scope is placed through the 5-mm lower trocar.
4. The tube can be grasped with a grasper passed down the operative channel of the laparoscope, and the entire laparoscope can then be removed holding the tube in front.

5. The tube can be removed with a Kelly clamp placed through the trocar incision site.
6. The tube can be placed in a sac and removed from the abdomen.

The other tube should then be examined for future reference. A tubal ligation can be performed at this time if requested and deemed appropriate. The pelvis

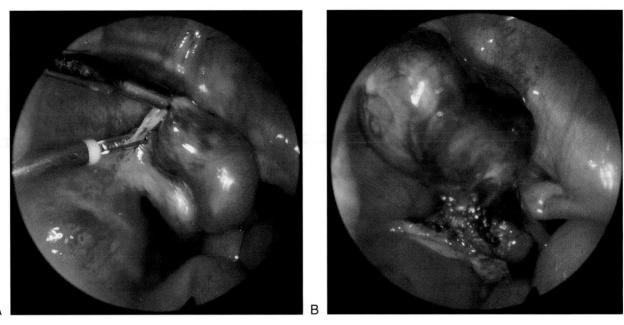

Fig. 7-10. (A & B) Ampullary ectopic pregnancy. Salpingectomy performed with bipolar forceps and scissors.

should then be irrigated and all blood removed. Rh-negative patients should be given MICRhoGAM. hCG titers should be followed postoperatively, even after salpingectomy. I and others have seen trophoblastic tissue implant and grow on pelvic organs postoperatively.[6] Methotrexate has been used to treat these patients successfully.

Isthmic Ectopic Pregnancy

The isthmic ectopic pregnancy can be treated by either linear salpingostomy or partial salpingectomy.

If the ectopic site is large, often a linear salpingos-

tomy can be performed, using the same technique previously described for ampullary ectopic pregnancy. This procedure can be more difficult with proximal ectopic pregnancies for many reasons, which include

1. The ectopic pregnancy is usually discovered early and thus is smaller and more difficult to localize. One must be

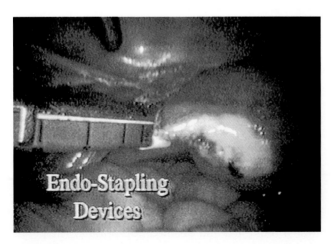

Fig. 7-11. Ampullary ectopic pregnancy. Salpingectomy performed with linear stapler.

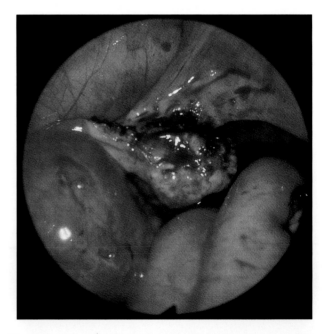

Fig. 7-12. Ampullary ectopic pregnancy. Excision complete.

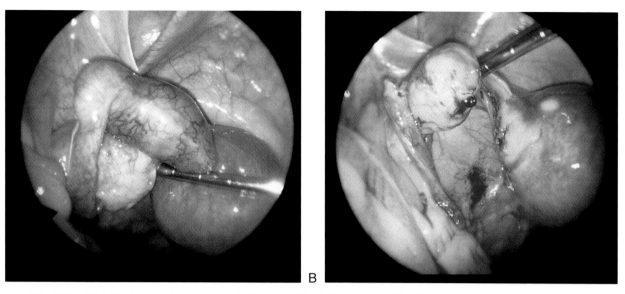

Fig. 7-13. (A) Isthmic ectopic pregnancy before partial salpingectomy. **(B)** Isthmic ectopic pregnancy after partial salpingectomy.

careful when injecting the vasoconstrictor that the site of the ectopic pregnancy is not hidden by the instilled fluid.

2. The small ectopic pregnancy and thickened tubal wall can make finding the lumen much more difficult than in the ampullary tube.
3. The thick isthmic walls of the tube make exploration and visualization of the lumen more difficult during and after the removal.
4. The isthmic ectopic pregnancy may be extraluminal.

The isthmic ectopic pregnancy can also be treated by partial salpingectomy, with the ectopic pregnancy and associated portion of tube being excised (Figs. 7-13 and 7-14). This is usually a much easier procedure and obviously the procedure of choice if the patient desires sterilization. If, however, the patient only has one functioning tube and desires her fertility, a second operation would, of course, be necessary to restore patency.

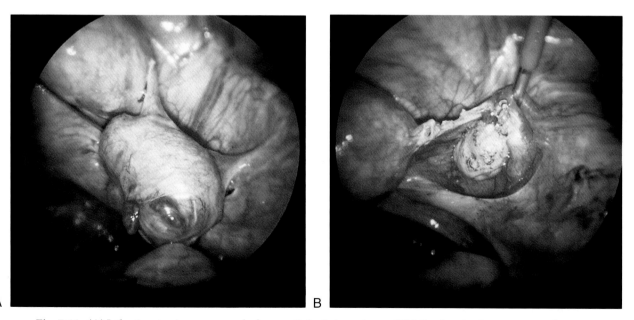

Fig. 7-14. (A) Isthmic ectopic pregnancy before partial salpingectomy. **(B)** Isthmic ectopic pregnancy after partial salpingectomy.

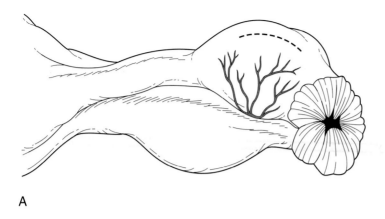

A

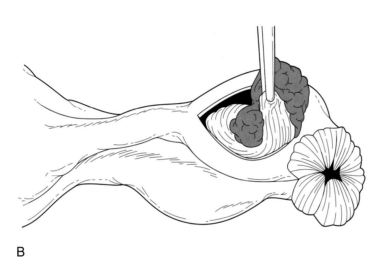

B

Fig. 7-15. Infundibular ectopic pregnancy. Salpingostomy.

Partial salpingectomy is performed using techniques similar to those described in the previous section.

Fimbrial (Infundibular) Ectopic Pregnancy

In the case of a true fimbrial ectopic pregnancy, the products of conception can often be grasped with biopsy forceps and teased away. If the ectopic pregnancy is partially in the lumen, the pregnancy may be teased, squeezed, or flushed out of the tube. I have not had great success with this method and often perform a distal linear salpingostomy to remove these products (Fig. 7-15). This allows me to better examine the tube and make sure all products are removed. This also prevents me from blindly grasping the mucosa and creating additional tubal damage.

Interstitial Ectopic Pregnancy

Interstitial ectopic pregnancies are much more difficult to treat laparoscopically than the others (Fig. 7-16). If active hemorrhage is not occurring, the surgeon should identify the ectopic site. A vasoconstrictor is placed in the area of the uterine artery (being careful to avoid intravascular injection). A bipolar forceps is then placed across the proximal tube, and it is coagulated. The tube is then divided salami style, using either laser or fine-needle cautery until normal-appearing interstitial tube is found. Bleeding is controlled using fine microbipolar forceps. The portions of tube containing the pregnancy are then removed from the abdomen using biopsy forceps.

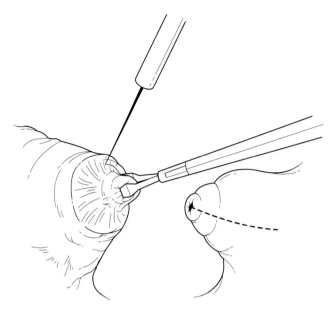

Fig. 7-16. Interstitial ectopic pregnancy. Partial salpingectomy.

CONCLUSION

Laparoscopic treatment of the ectopic pregnancy has over a very brief time become the standard of care for all but the most unstable patient. The procedure is desirable as it reduces postoperative adhesion formation, hospital stay, and short-term disability, decreases postoperative pain, is cosmetically more appealing, and reduces health care costs.[7–11]

The conservative management of the ectopic pregnancy via endoscopic means has also made it more likely that patients will still be able to become pregnant naturally with a successful intrauterine pregnancy. Many studies have now been published documenting an intrauterine pregnancy rate approaching 65 percent after tubal salpingostomy for ectopic pregnancy.[12–18]

Women who have had one ectopic pregnancy have a 6 to 13 percent likelihood of a repeat ectopic pregnancy.[18–27] That rate increases to 20 percent if they have had two prior ectopic pregnancies.[28] The chance of an intrauterine pregnancy occurring after salpingostomy in patients with only that tube remaining ranges from 32 to 60 percent.[29] Persistent ectopic pregnancy both in the fallopian tube and intraperitoneal are known risks of conservative tubal surgery, performed either laparoscopically or by laparotomy. A persistence rate of 1 to 15 percent is expected after conservative salpingostomy.[30–33] Patients must have serial

β-hCG monitoring postoperatively until titers fall to negative. Should rising titers be noted, patients should be treated with methotrexate.[34,35] A recent study by Hagstrom et al.[36] indicates that patients with preoperative progesterone levels greater than 35 nmol/L and a daily hCG change exceeding 100 IU/L had a 61 percent rate of persistence, whereas only a 2 percent persistence rate was noted if one of these criteria was not met. Lundorff et al.[37] reported that patients with preoperative hCG levels greater than 3,000 IU/L were more likely to have persistent trophoblastic tissue that required treatment.

Although conservative management of the ectopic pregnancy via laparoscopy has made a significant impact on the care of the patient with a tubal pregnancy, more research is necessary to help define the best treatment options for these women.

REFERENCES

1. Centers for Disease Control: Ectopic pregnancy—United States. MMWR 39:401, 1990
2. Young PL, Saftlas AF, Atrash HK et al: National trends in the management of tubal pregnancy, 1970–1987. Obstet Gynecol 78:749, 1991
3. Kadar N, Caldwell BV, Romero R: A method of screening for ectopic pregnancy and its indications. Obstet Gynecol 58:162, 1981
4. Lurie S, Katz Z, Weissman A: Declining beta-human chorionic gonadotropin level may provide false security that tubal pregnancy will not rupture. Eur J Obstet Gynecol Reprod Biol 53:72, 1994
5. Okaty K, Brzyski RG, Miller EB, Krugman D: Association of serum beta-hCG with myosalpingeal invasion and viable trophoblast mass in tubal pregnancy. Obstet Gynecol 85:803, 1994
6. Foulot H, Chapron C, Morice P et al: Failure of laparoscopic treatment for peritoneal trophoblastic implants. Hum Reprod 9:92, 1994
7. Manhes H, Pouly JL, Bouquet de la Joliniere J et al: Celioscopic treatment of extra-uterine pregnancy. Rev Fr Gynecol Obstet 81:27, 1986
8. Thorburn J: Advancing conservative treatment of ectopic pregnancy—laparoscopic and "non-surgical" management. Ann Med 24:43, 1992
9. Chatwani A, Yazigi R, Amin-Hanjani S: Operative laparoscopy in the management of tubal ectopic pregnancy. J Laparoendoscopic Surg 2:319, 1992
10. Lundorff P, Hahlin M, Kallfelt B et al: Adhesion formation after laparoscopic surgery in tubal pregnancy: a randomized trial versus laparotomy. Fertil Steril 55:911, 1991
11. Lundorff P, Thorburn J, Hahlin M et al: Laparoscopic surgery in ectopic pregnancy. A randomized trial versus laparotomy. Acta Obstet Gynecol Scand 70:343, 1991
12. Bruhat MA, Manhes H, Mage G et al: Treatment of ectopic pregnancy by means of laparoscopy. Fertil Steril 33:411, 1980
13. Lundorff P, Thorburn J, Lindblom B: Fertility after conservative surgical treatment of ectopic pregnancy, evaluated by a randomized trial. Ugeskr Laeger 155:3282, 1993
14. Langebrekke A, Sornes T, Urnes A: Fertility outcome after treatment of tubal pregnancy by laparoscopic laser surgery. Acta Obstet Gynecol Scand 72:547, 1993
15. Kooi S, Kock HC: Surgical treatment for tubal pregnancies. Surg Gynecol Obstet 176:519, 1993

16. Chapron C, Pouly JL, Wattiez A et al: Results of conservative laparoscopic treatment of isthmic ectopic pregnancies: a 26 case study. Hum Reprod 7:422, 1992
17. Zouves C, Urman B, Gomel V: Laparoscopic surgical treatment of tubal pregnancy. A safe, effective alternative to laparotomy. J Reprod Med 37:205, 1992
18. Chapron C, Pouly JL, Wattiez A et al: Laparoscopic management of tubal ectopic pregnancy. Eur J Obstet Gynecol Reprod Biol 49:73, 1993
19. Schoen JA, Nowak RJ: Repeat ectopic pregnancy. Obstet Gynecol 45:542, 1975
20. Sherran D, Langer R, Sadorsky G et al: Improved fertility following ectopic pregnancy. Fertil Steril 37:497, 1982
21. Langer R, Bukovsky I, Herman A et al: Conservative surgery for tubal pregnancy. Fertil Steril 38:427, 1982
22. Oelsner G, Goldenberg M, Admon D et al: Salpingectomy by operative laparoscopy and subsequent reproductive performance. Hum Reprod 9:83, 1994
23. Stoval TG, Ling FW: Single dose methotrexate: an expanded clinical trial. Am J Obstet Gynecol 168:1759, 1993
24. Chapron C, Pouly JL, Wattie ZA et al: Conservative celioscopic treatment of isthmic ectopic pregnancies. J Gynecol Obstet Biol Reprod 20:923, 1991
25. Hallatt JG: Repeat ectopic pregnancy: a study of 123 consecutive cases. Am J Obstet Gynecol 122:520, 1975
26. Kitchin JD, Wein RM, Nunley WC et al: Ectopic pregnancy: current trends. Am J Obstet Gynecol 134:870, 1979
27. DeCherney AH, Jones EE: Ectopic pregnancy. Clin Obstet Gynecol 28:365, 1985
28. DeCherney AH, Silidker JS, Mezer HC, Tarlatzis BC: Reproductive outcome following two ectopic pregnancies. Fertil Steril 43:82, 1985
29. Pouly JL, Mahres H, Mage G et al: Conservative laparoscopic treatment of 321 ectopic pregnancies. Fertil Steril 6:1093, 1986
30. Ou CS: Laparoscopic management of ectopic pregnancy. J Reprod Med 38:849, 1993
31. Seifer DB, Gutmann JN, Grant WD et al: Comparison of persistent ectopic pregnancy after laparoscopic salpingostomy versus salpingostomy at laparotomy for ectopic pregnancy. Obstet Gynecol 81:378, 1993
32. Kooi S, Kock HC: A review of the literature on nonsurgical treatment in tubal pregnancies. Obstet Gynecol 47:739, 1992
33. Stock RJ: Persistent tubal pregnancy. Obstet Gynecol 77:267, 1991
34. Rose PJ, Cohen SM: Methotrexate therapy for persistent ectopic pregnancy after conservative laparoscopic management. Obstet Gynecol 76:947, 1990
35. Bengtsson G, Bryman I, Thorburn J, Lindblom B: Low-dose oral methotrexate as second-line therapy for persistent trophoblast after conservative treatment of ectopic pregnancy. Obstet Gynecol 79:589, 1992
36. Hagstrom HG, Hahlin M, Bennegard-Eden B et al: Prediction of persistent ectopic pregnancy after laparoscopic salpingostomy. Obstet Gynecol 84:798, 1994
37. Lundorff P, Hahlin M, Sjoblom P, Lindblom B: Persistent trophoblast after conservative treatment of tubal pregnancy: prediction and detection. Obstet Gynecol 77:129, 1991

8 Pelvic Adhesions

STEPHEN M. COHEN

Pelvic adhesions secondary to salpingitis, endometriosis, or previous surgery are a common cause of infertility and pelvic pain in the female patient. Millions of dollars and thousands of hospital days are involved in the treatment of adhesions. The removal of all but the most extensive adhesions has evolved into an endoscopic procedure, reducing hospital stay and postoperative disability.

ETIOLOGY OF ADHESIONS

Intra-abdominal adhesions occur as the result of injury to the peritoneum and the body's attempt at repair. The peritoneum may be injured secondary to surgery, infection, bleeding, or endometriosis. An injury to the peritoneum results in disruption of the mesothelial surface and subsequent leakage of cells and fibrinogen from the vessels. Fibrinogen is converted to fibrin, and a matrix is laid down so that mesothelial regrowth can occur. Often this fibrin matrix causes a bridge to occur between adjacent organs. When this happens, an adhesion begins to occur. During normal healing, plasminogen is converted to plasmin. The plasmin released breaks down fibrin bridges. If the ability to make or release plasmin is decreased, adhesion formation results. The adhesion becomes more dense over time (usually 7 to 10 days), as methothial cells infiltrate the fibrin bridges. Plasmin release is decreased by surgical procedures that allow drying or dead tissue to occur, such as suturing, coagulating, and rough tissue handling.

INITIAL EVALUATION

The detailed medical history often will alert the physician to expect the possibility of pelvic adhesions. A patient who gives a previous history of pelvic surgery is always suspect for having adhesions. Certain operations, such as myomectomy, ovarian cystectomy, appendectomy, bowel resection, and lysis of adhesions, are more likely to produce adhesions than others. Cesarean section is unlikely to cause intra-abdominal adhesions. One should always obtain the previous operative report, if available, so that note can be made of previous adhesions and their locations, as well as any unusual circumstances encountered at the time of the prior surgery.

A prior history of salpingitis must lead one to suspect pelvic adhesions. Inflammation is a significant cause of adhesions. It has been documented that after one episode of salpingitis, 15 percent of distal fallopian tubes will subsequently adhere and obstruct (clubbed tube). After three episodes of salpingitis, approximately 50 percent of tubes will be distally obstructed.[1] Often, adnexal pelvic adhesions will also occur as a result of these episodes of salpingitis.

Endometriosis has been known to be a cause of pelvic adhesions. In fact, the endometriosis staging scheme of the American Fertility Society assigns staging points based more on the amount and location of adhesions than on the amount of endometriosis itself. Stage III (moderate) and stage IV (severe) endometriosis almost always have associated pelvic adhesion formation.

The pelvic examination also may alert the gynecologist that adhesions may be present. The uterus may be fixed in the cul-de-sac, or its mobility may be limited. One may also find that the adnexa is immobile or fixed to the uterus. With the exception of the hysterosalpingogram, radiologic studies rarely help to diagnose pelvic adhesions. At hysterosalpingography, one may see loculated spill on fluoroscopy during the instillation of media. This finding may correlate with the presence of adnexal adhesions, but there is a very high rate of false-positives generated by this examination.

INDICATIONS AND CONTRAINDICATIONS

Laparoscopy to diagnose pelvic adhesions, as well as other pelvic pathology, is always indicated in the infertile woman once severe male factor infertility or sterility has been excluded. There is no other way to accurately exclude this diagnosis in any patient who has been infertile for more than 1 year. Most infertile patients with pelvic adhesions relate no prior history of salpingitis.

In patients who have chronic pelvic pain, laparoscopy is necessary to exclude pelvic adhesions and endometriosis. Patients who complain of localized pelvic or abdominal pain are more likely to be found with adhesions than those who complain of diffuse symptoms. With a patient who has had previous surgery to remove adhesions and now has recurrent pain, one must decide whether the benefits of the operation outweigh the risks. Certainly, adhesions are likely to be found, but whether removing these adhesions will have any lasting benefit is a difficult question to answer. The patient must certainly be intensely involved in the decision-making process about whether to operate. She must also know that the risk of bowel perforation is significantly increased under these circumstances.

Contraindications to laparoscopic surgery for removal of adhesions are those that have previously been described as general contraindications to laparoscopy. Also, I include previous bowel resection as a relative contraindication to laparoscopic surgery. I have found adhesions to be so extensive after this type of surgery that I prefer to treat these patients with laparotomy.

PREPARATION

In patients with known or suspected adhesions, such as those who have had operations with a high likelihood of producing postoperative adhesions, I have the patient undergo a bowel preparation. An adequate bowel preparation before the operation tends to decrease bowel distention, making it easier and safer to do the extensive surgery sometimes necessary. Also, should a perforation of the bowel wall occur, primary repair rather than colostomy can often be performed. The two bowel preparations that I use are listed in Table 8-1, and patients begin the preparation the day before surgery.

Table 8-1. Bowel Preparations

Bowel Preparation 1
1. If not allergic and can tolerate, the day before surgery clear fluids (water, bouillon, ginger ale, cranberry juice, apple juice, jello, cola, plain tea, black coffee) ad lib until midnight, then nothing by mouth.
2. 8:30 A.M. Reglan 10 mg PO.
3. 9:00 A.M. to 1:00 P.M. drink one glass Golytely or Colyte every 15 minutes until gallon gone.
4. 1:30 P.M. Reglan 10 mg PO.
5. At 2:00 P.M., 3:00 P.M., and 11:00 P.M. Erythromycin *base* 1 g PO and Neomycin 1 g PO.
6. 10:30 P.M. Reglan 10 mg PO.
7. 8:00 P.M. Dulcolax suppository, one rectally.

Bowel Preparation 2
1. If not allergic and can tolerate, the day before surgery clear liquids (water, bouillon, ginger ale, cranberry juice, apple juice, jello, cola, plain tea, black coffee) ad lib until midnight, then nothing by mouth.
2. 8:30 A.M. Reglan 10 mg PO.
3. 9:00 A.M. add 1.5 fl oz Fleet Phospho-soda to ½ glass (4 fl oz) of cool water and drink; follow with one full glass (8 fl oz) of clear liquid.
4. 1:30 P.M. Reglan 10 mg PO.
5. At 2:00 P.M., 3:00 P.M., and 11:00 P.M.. Erythromycin *Base* 1 g PO and Neomycin 1 g PO.
6. 10:30 P.M. Reglan 10 mg PO.
7. 9:00 P.M. add 1.5 fl oz Fleet Phospho-soda to ½ glass (4 fl oz) of cool water and drink; follow with one full glass (8 fl oz) of clear liquid.

TROCAR PLACEMENT

In a patient who is likely to have extensive adhesions, trocar placement must be considered very carefully. In addition to the types of patients mentioned previously who more commonly have adhesions, patients who have had a previous vertical incision and those who have had an umbilical hernia repair are also likely to have adhesions in proximity to the umbilicus. Patients may not give a history of umbilical hernia repair because it may have been performed when they were a neonate, and thus the umbilicus should be carefully inspected preoperatively in all patients who are to undergo laparoscopy.

The trocar can be placed directly into the abdomen or through an open incision, using the Hassan technique. Although the open technique has been touted by some as a method to reduce the incidence of bowel perforation, the clinical data collected by the American Association of Gynecologic Laparoscopists demonstrate that the number of bowel perforations occurring ap-

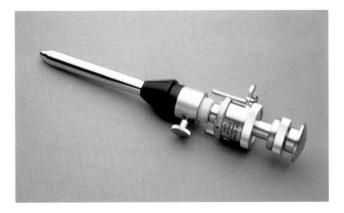

Fig. 8-1. Trocar for open laparoscopy (Storz).

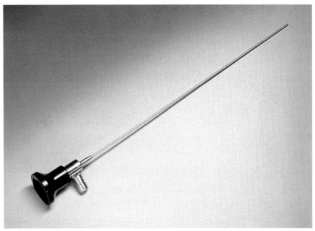

Fig. 8-2. Microlaparoscope (Imagyn).

pears to be equal with each method of insertion.[2] It is true, however, that these data are retrospective and nonrandomized. There also may be a selection bias of high-risk patients into the open technique group.

Using the open technique, the operator places a small skin incision and continues to make the incision deeper, under direct vision. Eventually, the peritoneum is identified and divided. The difficulty with this technique is that it is often impossible to identify the peritoneum at the base of this very small incision, and the bowel wall can be entered, mistaking it for a clear space. Once the abdomen is opened, an acorn-type holder is placed into the incision and secured with sutures to the fascia. The trocar and laparoscope are then passed through this device into the abdomen (Fig. 8-1).

When using the direct insertion technique for trocar placement, the trocar should be placed in an area above the most likely anticipated location of the adhesions.

Except in rare situations or cases of prior left upper-quadrant surgery, the left upper quadrant is usually devoid of adhesions. This area becomes an ideal location for insertion of the Veress needle and laparoscope. The Veress needle is inserted just above the lowest rib in the left midclavicular line. It is angled slightly caudad and placed just through the peritoneum. In this location, the peritoneum is rigidly adhered to the abdominal wall and ribs, and it is very easy to penetrate this layer. Before placement, the patient should have a gastric tube placed and drained. The operator should also percuss the liver and stomach to verify their location.

The abdomen should be tensely inflated, and the Veress needle should then be removed. A 10-mm transverse incision should then be placed approxi-

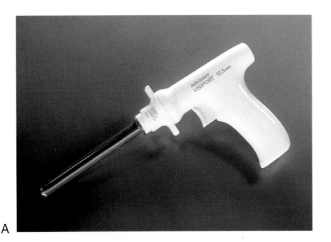

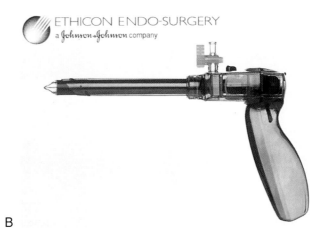

Fig. 8-3. **(A)** Visiport (U.S. Surgical). **(B)** Visual trocar (Ethicon).

mately two fingerbreaths below the last rib in the left upper quadrant in the midclavicular line. The trocar should then be slowly placed in the caudad direction, while maintaining control of the depth of penetration. Placing the laparoscope through the trocar at this time will confirm proper placement. Placing the laparoscope above the highest level of adhesions avoids the risk of bowel perforation to loops fixed to the anterior wall and gives a clear picture of the anatomy and pathology.

Recently, a new laparoscope with a diameter of only 1 mm has been introduced by Origin (Fig. 8-2). This laparoscope can be placed through a modified Veress needle before insufflation. The surgeon can place this small laparoscope into the abdomen as a first step and evaluate the abdomen for the safe and proper placement of the larger trocars. If a bowel perforation occurs with the Veress needle, repair is rarely necessary. Close observation will usually demonstrate a benign postoperative course. Recently introduced in the market are trocars with a clear tip that accommodate a laparoscope during insertion (Fig. 8-3). Insertion is accomplished by advancing a blade, either by trigger mechanism or side-to-side movement of the trocar. These trocars allow the operator to watch as the various layers of the abdominal wall are separated. In theory, as the peritoneum is contacted, it would be transparent if no adhesions exist underneath. These trocars, however, require a significant amount of pressure as they are placed, potentially limiting the anteroposterior abdominal space. Also, attention is often diverted from the abdomen to the monitor, allowing the angle of the trocar to wander. Although these trocars would seem to increase safety in theory, a review of injuries in actual practice will be necessary before a final decision regarding their usefulness can be made.

INTRAOPERATIVE ASSESSMENT

Deciding exactly what should be performed intraoperatively is the critical part of adhesion surgery. The surgeon needs a thorough understanding of the patient's specific problem, the anatomy, and the pathology. This must then be blended together with the experience gained from previous operations and results of those procedures. A good result does not simply evolve from a pelvic trainer but requires the art of medicine mixed with the science of anatomy and technology.

Adhesions may be filmy or dense, vascular or avascular, minimal or extensive. Organs may be immobilized, buried, or encased in these adhesions. The sur-

geon must always bear in mind why the surgery is being performed (infertility, pain, or both), as this will influence what operation should be performed. In general, when operating on patients with pain, all adhesions should be removed if this can be performed safely. However, when operating for infertility in a patient with no pain, the excision of adhesions should be directed to those that are interfering with the physiology of ovulation, ovum pickup, and delivery of the embryo. Excising adhesions that are not involved in this fertility process may actually worsen the situation if these adhesions reform in more critical areas of the pelvis. Filmy adhesions in the infertile patient that one can see through but that totally surround the ovaries will need to be removed even though the disease appears minimal. Dense adhesions fixing the fimbriated ends of the fallopian tube to the ovarian capsule limiting ovum pickup will need to be excised as well. On the contrary, extensive adhesions from the omentum to the uterine fundus or the anterior abdominal wall may not interfere with fertility and should be left, as otherwise the freed omentum may fall into the pelvis and adhesions that may involve the adnexa and interfere with tubal function may develop.

The American Fertility Society classification of adnexal adhesion should be recorded for each case (Fig. 8-4).

INSTRUMENTATION

In addition to the laparoscopes and trocars previously discussed, one must have an array of graspers and scissors. With well-crafted, carefully selected and maintained instrumentation, the operation for adhesions will usually flow smoothly.

Allis, Babcock, and atraumatic graspers are necessary to pick up pelvic structures such as the fallopian tube, ovary, and supporting ligaments. The surgeon must cause as little tissue trauma as possible to these organs so that function is maintained and postoperative adhesion formation remains at a minimum. The right instrument for the job is one that will remain firmly on the organ or tissue and at the same time not crush or damage the tissue.

Bowel is very commonly one of the organs involved in extensive pelvic adhesion formation. The surgeon must be able to grasp the bowel firmly yet not tear the wall. It is necessary to maintain traction on the bowel so that clean and precise cutting of the adhesions between it and other structures can occur. Standard bowel forceps (graspers) have now been modified into laparoscopic instrumentation. Laparoscopic Duval

Patient's Name _____ Date _____ Chart # _____

Age _____ G _____ P _____ Sp Ab _____ VTP _____ Ectopic _____ Infertile Yes _____ No _____

Other Significant History (i.e. surgery, infection, etc.) _____

_____

HSG _____ Sonography _____ Photography _____ Laparoscopy _____ Laparotomy _____

	ADHESIONS		<1/3 Enclosure	1/3 - 2/3 Enclosure	>2/3 Enclosure
OVARY	R	Filmy	1	2	4
		Dense	4	8	16
	L	Filmy	1	2	4
		Dense	4	8	16
TUBE	R	Filmy	1	2	4
		Dense	4*	8*	16
	L	Filmy	1	2	4
		Dense	4*	8*	16

* If the fimbriated end of the fallopian tube is completely enclosed, change the point assignment to 16.

Prognostic Classification for Adnexal Adhesions

              LEFT   RIGHT

A. Minimal   _____   0-5   _____

B. Mild   _____   6-10   _____

C. Moderate   _____   11-20   _____

D. Severe   _____   21-32   _____

Treatment (Surgical Procedures): _____

_____

_____

_____

_____

Prognosis for Conception & Subsequent Viable Infant**

_____ Excellent (> 75%)

_____ Good (50-75%)

_____ Fair (25%-50%)

_____ Poor (< 25%)

**Physician's judgment based upon adnexa with least amount of pathology.

Recommended Followup Treatment: _____

_____

Additional Findings: _____

_____

_____

_____

_____

_____

DRAWING

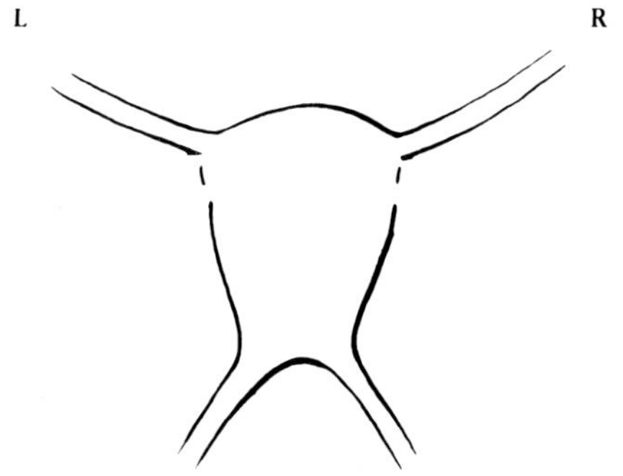

L   R

Property of
The American Fertility Society

For additional supply write to:
The American Fertility Society
2140 11th Avenue, South
Suite 200
Birmingham, Alabama 35205

Fig. 8-4. American Fertility Society classification of adnexal adhesion (From Buttram et al.,[18] with permission.)

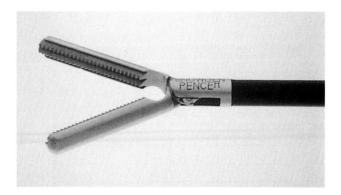

Fig. 8-5. Bowel grasper (Snowden-Pencer).

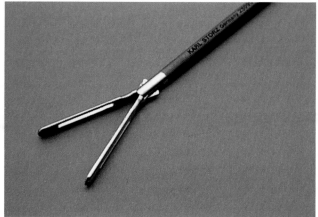

Fig. 8-6. Bowel grasper (Storz).

and Pennington graspers are now available and should be used when operating on bowel adhesions (Figs. 8-5 and 8-6).

ENERGY SOURCES

The experience of the operator, the type and location of the adhesion, and the instrumentation available usually dictate what energy source will be used to remove pelvic adhesions. In most circumstances, scissors are the safest, most inexpensive, fastest tool available. All surgeons are familiar with their use. They create no damage except at their tips. They create no smoke or plume. And what you see is what you get. The disadvantage to scissors is that unless used with electrosurgery, they do not create any hemostasis. Another disadvantage is that the surgeon must be able to touch the tissue and obtain the appropriate angle to excise the adhesions.

Unipolar electrosurgery can also be used to excise adhesions. Electrosurgery can be used alone or in combination with another instrument, such as scissors. When dividing or excising adhesions with electrosurgery, a high electron density must be maintained so that rapid vaporization occurs. Pure cutting current (undamped) should be used unless significant coagulation is necessary. Blended currents will increase the coagulation effect but at the same time create more tissue damage. The needle or fine electrode (Fig. 8-7) should be moved slowly but steadily through the tissue, so that the electrons actually are transferred to the tissue through a fine envelope of steam. There is no standard setting of watts to use when excising adhesions. The variables depend on tissue density, vascularity, and resistance. The size of the electrode tip also has a direct effect on electron density. Power settings will vary between 25 to 125 W. Unipolar electrocautery should not

usually be used in close proximity to the bowel wall, as the path of least resistance that the electrons follow may flow toward the bowel and create damage to the wall. When an adhesion is excised, the surgeon must be aware of which path the electrons will follow after one side of the adhesions is divided. For example, if an adhesion connects bowel to uterus, the side of the adhesion attached to the bowel should be divided first, so that electrons will flow toward the uterus when the proximal side of the adhesion is divided. Also, the surgeon must be conscious of capacitance, as mentioned previously, whenever using unipolar electrosurgery.

Bipolar electrosurgery should be used when the tissue to be divided is very vascular, contains large ves-

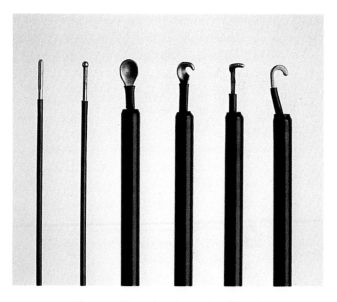

Fig. 8-7. Unipolar electrodes (Storz).

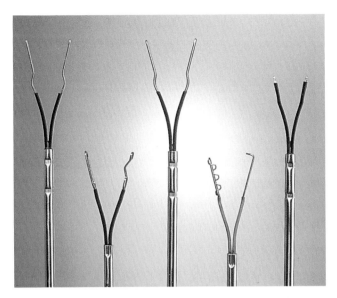

Fig. 8-8. Bipolar forceps (Storz).

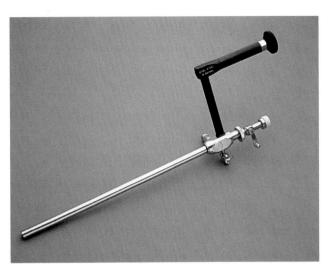

Fig. 8-9. Operating laparoscope.

sels, or is near vital structures such as a great vessel, ureter, or bowel. The bipolar forceps (Fig. 8-8) should be placed on each side of the tissue to be coagulated. The forceps should be held slightly opened so that the tissue is not crushed into the forceps as it is coagulated. This will help prevent sticking of the tissue to the forceps. If the generator being used has both a cutting and coagulation current on the bipolar circuit, cutting should usually be used, as this will also decrease sticking and give a cleaner and more precise coagulation. If sticking of tissue to the forceps does occur, the surgeon should activate the current just before separating the forceps from the tissue. Settings between 20 to 45 W of power are usually selected for most procedures.

Laser energy can also be used to separate pelvic adhesions. In general, laser is selected when adhesions are dense, extensive, difficult to reach, or associated with endometriosis. Laser energy is photons delivered to the tissue. Common medical lasers are CO_2, potassium-titanyl-phosphate (KTP), argon, and neodymium: yttrium-aluminum-garnet (Nd:YAG). The CO_2 laser energy can be delivered through the operative channel of the laparoscope (Fig. 8-9). The laparoscope is connected to the laser by a lens system. The advantages to this system is that a separate port is not needed to deliver the energy system, and the surgeon does not need to touch the tissue to divide it. Disadvantages are that significant plume is produced, a backstop is usually necessary behind the adhesion to protect normal tissue, and the field of view is limited.

The CO_2 laser beam can also be delivered through a hollow tube called a waveguide (Fig. 8-10). This allows the operator to observe the tip of the waveguide and the tissue site, so that he or she is sure that no tissue can come between the waveguide and the impact site. Waveguides also come with a backstop to protect the tissue that is behind the tissue, but usually it is much easier to use a solid anodized probe behind the adhesions. Fluids such as saline will also absorb the CO_2 laser beam and can be used to protect the areas such as the cul-de-sac.

Fiber lasers such as argon, KTP, and Nd:YAG are delivered by flexible fibers passed through small cannulas (Fig. 8-11). The laser energy is usually used to heat the fiber, and the fiber then cuts with thermal rather than laser energy. Thus, when fiber lasers are used to cut through pelvic adhesions, the actually cutting is performed with heat. More details regarding laser energy may be found in the chapter on lasers.

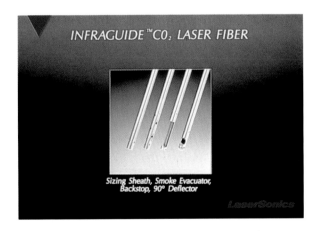

Fig. 8-10. CO_2 waveguide (Lasersonics).

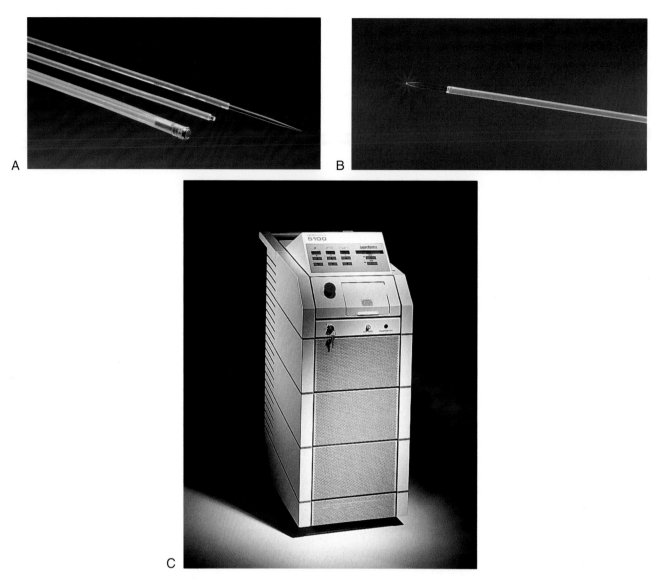

Fig. 8-11. Fiber laser system. **(A)** Quartz tip/Chamfered/free beam; **(B)** quartz tip; **(C)** Hercules 5100 Nd:YAG laser (Heraeus).

The harmonic scalpel blade cuts through tissue with a vibrating blade. The blade is powered by an energy source that connects to a hand piece. The blade is secured into the hand piece with a wrench. Blades come in both a disposable or reusable configuration. With the blade positioned against the adhesion and pressure applied, the vibrating blade will pass through the adhesion (Fig. 8-12). Minimal thermal damage is created by the vibrational energy, coagulating small vessels as the adhesion is divided. No plume is produced. Atomized water vapor generated is rapidly absorbed by the peritoneal surface. A coagulating forceps for the harmonic scalpel is also available. The adhesion is grasped, and the jaws vibrate when activated, coagulating the adhesions. The bottom jaw is rotated so that the instrument becomes a scissor, and the tissue is cut.

TIPS FOR REMOVING PELVIC ADHESIONS

1. Trocars should be placed into the pelvis as widely spaced as possible. Wider angles allow for easier manipulation of tissue.

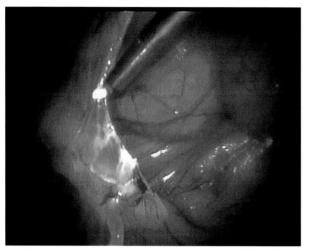

Fig. 8-12. Division of adhesion with harmonic scalpel blade.

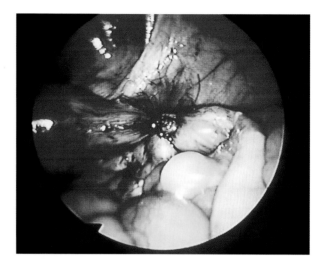

Fig. 8-13. Appendix adhered to cornua of uterus.

2. A thorough investigation of the anatomy is necessary before actually beginning the excision of the adhesions. If this is not done, vital structures such as the fallopian tubes, great vessels, bowel, or ureter may be damaged in areas of dense or confusing disease (Fig. 8-13). The pelvic side wall structures are most easily observed before beginning the excision of adhesions. After the surgery begins, bleeding and inflammation of the peritoneum make it much more difficult to recognize retroperitoneal side wall structures. If dense side wall adhesions are noted, the surgeon will need to open the retroperitoneal space away from the areas of dense adhesions. This may mean reflecting the descending colon on the left side of the pelvis (Fig. 8-14). The side wall can be opened either through the round ligament or just above the round ligament in the area between the external iliac artery and the ovarian ligament.

3. In general, adhesions should be grasped from the contralateral side of the abdomen and placed under tension (Figs. 8-15, 8-16). The instrument used to divide the adhesion should come from the ipsilateral side. This, however, is very variable and often is reversed, depending on the situation encountered.

4. One should divide adhesions that are the most superficial in the pelvis first, so that if bleeding does occur, it can be readily and safely controlled.

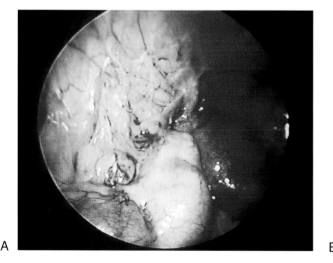

A

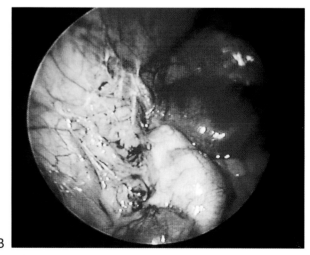

B

Fig. 8-14. (A) Descending colon adhered to pelvic side wall. **(B)** Colon after excision of adhesions.

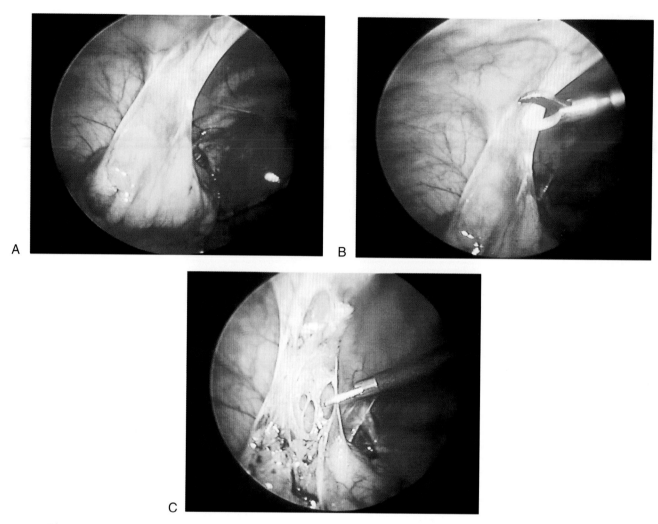

Fig. 8-15. (A) Adhesion from bowel to anterior abdominal wall. **(B)** Excision with scissors to begin. **(C)** Excision with scissors continues.

5. Large vessels should be coagulated with bipolar coagulation before dividing the adhesion so that the vessels do not retract into the normal adjacent tissue.

6. If bleeding does occur, the vessels should be grasped, and the bleeding should be temporarily controlled until the anatomy can be clearly defined.

7. If possible, adhesions should be removed from both ends rather than just divided.

8. Thrombin or other topical hemostats can be used to help control bleeding. In recent studies, it has been shown that thrombin does not increase adhesion formation.[3]

9. The pelvis should be well irrigated before finishing so that all blood and blood products are removed from the pelvis.

10. If the cul-de-sac or rectum are involved with dense adhesions, a rectal probe should be placed from below to better delineate the rectal wall (Fig. 8-17).

11. After the surgical procedure, the integrity of the rectal wall can be tested by flooding the pelvis with saline and placing air into the rectum with a rectal tube or 30-ml Foley catheter. If no bubbles are noted, the surgeon can be sure that the rectal wall is intact.

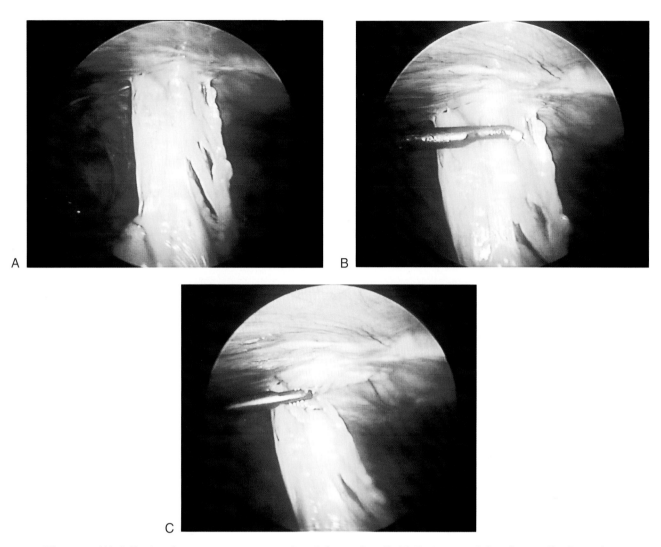

Fig. 8-16. (A) Adhesion from omentum to anterior abdominal wall. **(B)** Excision with bipolar needle electrode to begin. **(C)** Excision with bipolar electrode continues.

PREVENTION OF ADHESION REFORMATION

Adhesion reformation is a major problem after adhesiolysis surgery. Whether adhesions are excised via laparotomy or laparoscopy, reformation of adhesions occurs in approximately 75 percent of patients.[4] De novo adhesions (new adhesions not present at the time of the initial surgery) also form after surgery. Approximately 50 percent of patients undergoing pelvic surgery via laparotomy will develop de novo adhesions.[5] Half that number, approximately 25 percent, will develop de novo adhesions after laparoscopic surgery.[6–8]

Attempts at preventing postoperative adhesions have been made for decades. Various medical methods of prevention have been attempted (Table 8-2), but none have had overwhelming success.

During the past 10 years, barriers and instillates have been commonly used in an attempt at adhesion prevention. Adhesion studies performed in the 1980s

Table 8-2. Classes of Surgical Adjuvants Used in an Attempt to Minimize the Occurrence of Postoperative Adhesions

Fibrinolytic agents
    Fibrinolysin
    Papain
    Urokinase
    Hyaluronidase
    Chymotrypsin
    Trypsin
    Pepsin
Anticoagulants
    Heparin
    Citrates
    Oxalates
Anti-inflammatory agents
    Corticosteroids
    Ibuprofen
    Antihistamines
Antibiotics
    Tetracyclines
    Cephalosporins

(From Diamond and DeCherney,[17] with permission.)

Table 8-3. Materials to Block Adhesion Formation

Mechanical separation
  Intra-abdominal instillates
    Dextran
    Mineral oil
    Silicone
    Povidone
    Vaseline
    Crystalloid solutions
    Carboxymethylcellulose
  Barriers
    Endogenous tissue
      Omental grafts
      Peritoneal grafts
      Bladder strips
      Fetal membranes
    Exogenous material
      Oxidized cellulose
      Oxidized regenerated cellulose
      Gelatin
      Rubber sheets
      Metal foils
      Plastic hoods

(From Diamond and DeCherney,[17] with permission.)

did not show any efficacy when physiologic solutions were added to the abdomen before closure (hydrofloatation).[9–12] Recently, others have brought this method back and claim it to be effective. All previous studies were performed at laparotomy, and minimal amounts (less than 500 ml) of fluid were used. Currently, these procedures are performed via laparoscopy, and larger volumes of fluid (usually 2,000 ml Ringer's lactate) are being instilled. At present, no clinical studies have been published to demonstrate the effectiveness of these preventative measures.

High-molecular-weight dextran (Hyskon) in a multicenter study was effective in reducing postoperative adhesions.[13] Subsequent studies of this fluid have shown varying results. Approximately 250 ml of Hyskon is poured into the abdomen via a catheter placed through the trocar. Many adverse and allergic reactions have been reported with the use of Hyskon. Hyskon does not have Food and Drug Administration (FDA) approval for adhesion prevention and intra-abdominal use.

BARRIERS

Surgeons have attempted to block adhesion formation with barriers for many years. Various materials have been used (Table 8-3); most have been proved ineffective and have been abandoned.

Two barriers are currently approved by the FDA for the prevention of intra-abdominal adhesions. Interceed, an absorbable barrier (Johnson & Johnson), and Gortex, a nonabsorbable barrier (Gore), have been shown in clinical studies to reduce recurrent adhesion formation.

Interceed

Interceed is oxidized regenerated cellulose, similar to Surgicel in material but different in weave (Fig. 8-18).

Interceed may be placed into the abdomen using a fabric applicator through a trocar or pushed directly into the abdomen through the trocar using a solid rod.

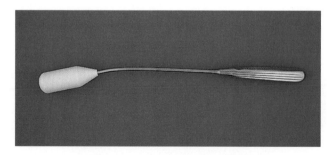

Fig. 8-17. Rectal probe (Reznik).

The material is then moved to the adhesion site with a grasper, where it is gently pressed to the organ (sidewall, ovary, tube, uterus, or cul-de-sac). The barrier is moistened slightly with saline or Ringer's lactate. The moist barrier will remain in place on the tissue. Hemostasis must be complete before placement of the barrier, as Interceed is ineffective if the fabric becomes bloodied. The fabric becomes a gel in consistency within 24 hours of application and is totally absorbed within 6 weeks of application. Many published randomized studies have shown this product to be effective in reducing pelvic adhesion formation by approximately 50 percent when compared with controls.[14,15]

Preclude/Gortex

Preclude/Gortex, the same material found in breathable clothing and artificial ligaments as well as other medical products, has been shown to be an effective barrier in preventing adhesions (Fig. 8-19). The product is delivered to the operative site through the trocar, using a grasper, and placed into the proper location. Preclude/Gortex will not stay in place without sutures or staples; thus, laparoscopic stapling or suturing must be performed to use this barrier. The material can be left in place permanently or removed at a second laparoscopy if it would interfere with fertility (such as if

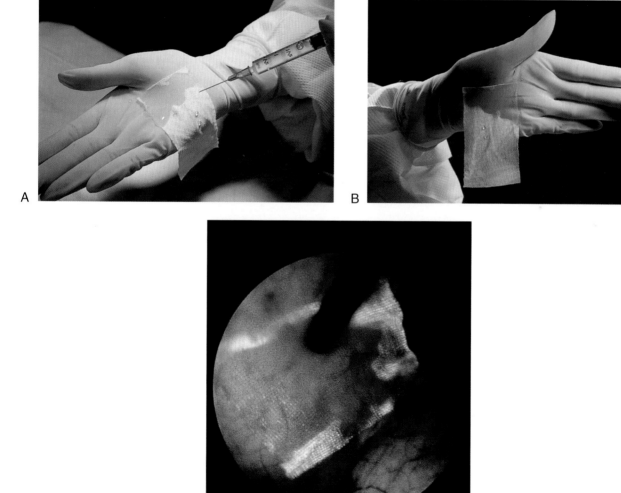

A

B

C

Fig. 8-18. (A–C) Interceed (JJMI).

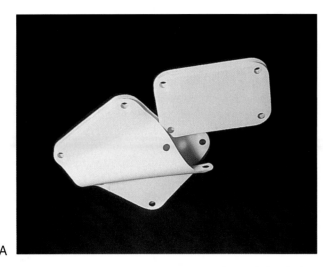
A

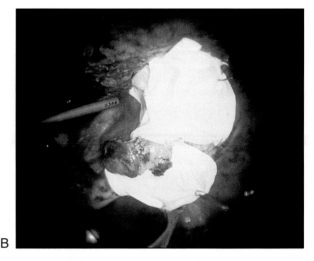
B

Fig. 8-19. (A & B) Preclude peritoneal membrane (Gore).

it were wrapped around the ovary). Published studies substantiated the effectiveness of Preclude/Gortex.[16]

CONCLUSION

Adhesions create significant problems in female patients by interfering with fertility and causing pelvic pain. Adhesions also cause major problems during surgery by lengthening the duration of surgery, increasing blood loss, and raising the risks of organ damage.

New techniques and technology to aid in the removal of adhesions have had significant impact on patient care and postoperative success. Although attempts at prevention have decreased the rate of postoperative adhesion formation, more effective products are needed.

REFERENCES

1. Westrom L: Effect of acute pelvic inflammatory disease in fertility. Am J Obstet Gynecol 121:707, 1975
2. Levy BS, Hulka JF, Peterson HB, Phillips JM: Operative laparoscopy: American Association of Gynecologic Laparoscopists, 1993 Membership Survey. J Am Assoc Gynecol Laparoscopists 1:301, 1994
3. Wiseman DM, Gottlick LE, Diamond MP: Effect of thrombin-induced hemostasis on the efficacy of an absorbable adhesion barrier. J Reprod Med 37:766, 1992
4. Diamond MP: Surgical aspects of infertility. p. 1. In Sciarra JW (ed): Gynecology and Obstetrics. Harper & Row, Philadelphia, 1988
5. Diamond MP, Daniell JF, Feste J et al: Adhesion reformation and de novo adhesion formation after reproductive pelvic surgery. Fertil Steril 47:864, 1987
6. Diamond MP, Daniell JF, Johns A et al: Postoperative adhesion development after operative laparoscopy: evaluation at early second-look procedures. Fertil Steril 55:700, 1991
7. Lundorff P, Hahlin M, Kallfelt B et al: Adhesion formation after laparoscopic surgery in tubal pregnancy: a randomized trial versus laparotomy. Fertil Steril 55:911, 1991
8. Canis M, Chapron C, Mage G et al: Second-look laparoscopy after laparoscopic cystectomy of large ovarian endometriomas. Fertil Steril 58:617, 1992
9. Rosenberg SM, Board JA: High-molecular weight dextran in human infertility surgery. Am J Obstet Gynecol 148:380, 1984
10. Larsson B, Lalos O, Marsk SE et al: Effects of intraperitoneal instillation of 32% dextran 70 on postoperative adhesion formation after tubal surgery. Acta Obstet Gynecol Scand 64:437, 1985
11. Jansen RPS: Failure of intraperitoneal adjuncts to improve the outcome of pelvic operations in young women. Am J Obstet Gynecol 153:363, 1985
12. Utian WH, Goldfarb JM, Starks GC: Role of dextran 70 in microtubal surgery. Fertil Steril 31:79, 1979
13. Adhesion Study Group: Reduction of postoperative pelvic adhesions with intraperitoneal 32% dextran 70: a prospective, randomized clinical trial. Fertil Steril 40:612, 1983
14. Interceed (TC7) Adhesion Barrier Study Group: Prevention of postsurgical adhesions by Interceed (TC7), an absorbable adhesion barrier: a prospective randomized multicenter clinical study. Fertil Steril 51:933, 1989
15. Nordic Adhesion Prevention Study Group: The efficacy of Interceed (TC7) for the prevention of reformation of postoperative adhesions on ovaries, fallopian tubes, and fimbriae in microsurgical operations for fertility: a multicenter study. Fertil Steril 63:709, 1995
16. Surgical Membrane Study Group: Prophylaxis of pelvic sidewall adhesions with Gore-Tex(R) surgical membrane: a multicenter clinical investigation. Fertil Steril 57:921, 1992
17. Diamond MP, DeCherney AH: Pathogenesis of adhesion formation/reformation: application to reproductive pelvic surgery. Microsurgery 8:103, 1987
18. Buttram VC et al: Fertil steril. American Fertility Society 49:6, 1988

9 Salpingostomy for Hydrosalpinx

ROBERT B. HUNT

It is estimated that one of four infertile women in the United States is afflicted with tubal disease. Pelvic inflammatory disease (PID), usually associated with *Neisseria gonorrhoeae* and *Chlamydia trachomatis*, is the most common cause of distal tubal obstruction.[1] Other causes are endometriosis, fimbriectomy, and peritonitis.[2] Approximately 1 million women suffer from the ravages of PID annually in the United States. Of these, 12 percent develop infertility after one episode, 25 percent after two episodes, and an astounding 50 percent after three or more episodes. It may be inferred that distal tubal obstruction will continue to be "the greatest bugbear of all infertility clinics."[2] To confound the sexually transmitted disease problem further, many *C. trachomatis* infections are silent and may be difficult to detect by culture.[3,4] Also, the patient may be treated with an antibiotic inappropriate for *C. trachomatis* or a resistant *N. gonorrhoeae* strain.

When discussing the surgical options with a woman with a hydrosalpinx, the surgeon must include in vitro fertilization and embryo transfer (IVF-ET). It is also important to counsel patients as to the chances of having a viable or an ectopic pregnancy after salpingostomy and IVF-ET. In general, the success rates are equivalent. If the severity of distal tubal disease is mild to moderate, many recommend salpingostomy as the initial therapeutic choice,[5–7] whereas others advocate IVF-ET.[8–10] If distal disease is severe, IVF-ET is desirable.

We do not live in a perfect world, and often the choice is determined by health insurance coverage and availability of technology. Fortunately, surgery and IVF-ET are not confrontational but complementary.[11]

PATHOLOGY OF HUMAN HYDROSALPINX

Hydrosalpinx simplex is characterized by a single tubal lumen, whereas hydrosalpinx follicularis contains trabeculations or septa, caused by fusion of the mucosal folds, forming compartments.[2] They are determined by histology (Figs. 9-1 and 9-2).

Chronic interstitial salpingitis is characterized by a thick-walled hydrosalpinx and is an unfavorable sign. Hydrosalpinges are often associated with destruction of the tubo-ovarian ligament.

PREOPERATIVE STUDIES

Before embarking on a surgical procedure to correct distal tubal obstruction, adequate preoperative testing must be carried out. This should include a thorough review of the patient's history; a careful physical examination including a pelvic assessment; Papanicolaou smear if appropriate; *Chlamydia* antibody and/or culture and possibly *Mycoplasma* cultures; semen analysis and/or postcoital test; and a check on ovulation, such as a midluteal phase progesterone level. It is important to review outside records pertaining to pelvic structures, particularly prior surgical procedures. If available, hysterosalpingogram (HSG) films should be reviewed. An effort should be made to determine whether adhesions are filmy or thick; fallopian tubes are small, normal, or dilated; the tubal walls are thin or thick; and the ovaries are more or less than half covered with adhesions.

HSGs are helpful in determining intrinsic tubal health. The presence of mucosal folds correlates with a

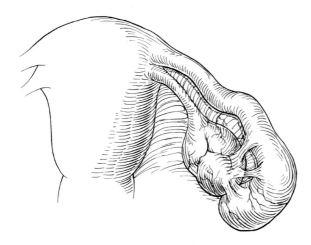

Fig. 9-1. Typical appearance of a hydrosalpinx. (From Hunt and Siegler,[34] with permission.)

greatly improved pregnancy rate.[12,13] Sometimes, salpingitis isthmica nodosa will be seen on HSG, which signifies a poor prognosis. Filling defects or strictures in the fallopian tubes are also associated with an unfavorable outcome (Fig. 9-3). One group found the pregnancy rate to be related to tubal morphologic changes such as ampullary dilation, percentage of fimbrial ciliated cells, and tubal wall thickness.[14]

Falloposcopy or tuboscopy is an excellent method for evaluating fallopian tube mucosa, although the findings do not always correlate with those seen on HSG.[15] Significant lesions were found at tuboscopy when hydrosalpinges were thought to have normal mucosal folds on HSG.[16] Conversely, 35 percent of patients thought to have abnormal mucosal folds on HSG were found to have normal mucosa at tuboscopy. The authors concluded that tuboscopy provided more accurate information on the status of tubal mucosa than did HSG (Fig. 9-4). As instrumentation improves, this modality will become increasingly important in tubal evaluation.

Tubal biopsy was heralded as a breakthrough in determining prognosis in hydrosalpinges. Elegant research from Belgium demonstrated histologic evidence of mucosal damage; however, microbiopsy results differ, depending on the precise spot from which the sample is taken.[17] Although useful as a research tool, it is impractical in determining if the woman with distal tubal obstruction should undergo salpingostomy.

Whether laparoscopy or laparotomy is recommended, the method often hinges on the skill and interest of the surgeon. I prefer operative laparoscopy in most cases of distal tubal obstruction. The procedure is performed at the time of assessment laparoscopy and includes thorough adhesiolysis, salpingostomy, and usually tuboscopy to determine the prognosis. The one exception is the small hydrosalpinx with excellent mucosa. In this situation, I believe better eversion can be achieved by laparotomy using the method of Kosasa and Hale.[18]

SALPINGOSTOMY TECHNIQUES

The most difficult aspect of performing a distal salpingostomy is the assessment of the tube and associated pathology. Often the anatomy is not what it appears to be during the initial evaluation. The entire pelvis must be carefully explored before beginning any definitive procedure. If adhesions are found, as is often the case, involving the tube, ovary, and other pelvic structures, those must be excised first, so that normal pelvic anatomy can be restored. The surgeon would not want to spend time performing a careful distal salpingostomy only to find that the ovary cannot be extracted from the deep, dense adhesions trapping it in the pelvic side wall. Occasionally, the surgeon may find that the ovary has been totally destroyed or previously removed.

After removal of all adhesions that can be safely excised, attention is drawn to the tube and ovary. Frequently, what appears to be the distal end of the fallopian tube is not. In fact, the distal end often becomes densely adhered to the ovarian capsule and curls around. If the initial incision is placed in the portion of tube farthest away from the cornua, the incision would actually be made in the midampullary region rather than in the infundibular portion of tube. It is imperative that the surgeon separate the distal tube from the ovarian capsule if adhesions have formed in that area. This not only allows the incision to be placed at the true fimbriated end but also may improve ovum pickup as the distal tube will have a greater range of motion. The separation of tube and ovary should be exaggerated, if possible, as some postoperative contraction and readhesion formation is inevitable. Scissors, lasers, harmonic scalpel, and electrosurgery all are appropriate surgical tools for this task. Hemostasis is usually secured with microbipolar forceps.

Attention should then be directed to the tube itself. At this point, perfusion into the tubes with an indigo carmine solution is usually helpful. The surgeon should perfuse slowly into the uterus, using some catheter-type system. As the progress of the fluid through the tube is observed, the location of the true

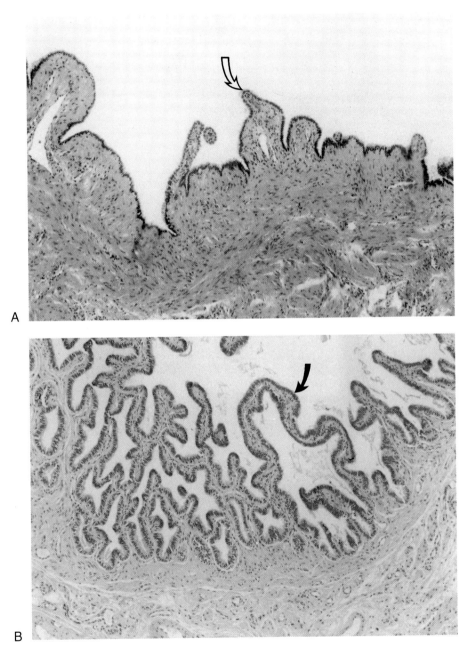

Fig. 9-2. (A) Hydrosalpinx simplex (×40). The tubal lumen is lined by a single layer of low columnar cells *(open arrow)*. **(B)** Hydrosalpinx follicularis (×40). The tubal lumen is lined by mucosa composed of follicle-like spaces of variable size that form pseudoglandular structures *(closed arrow)*.

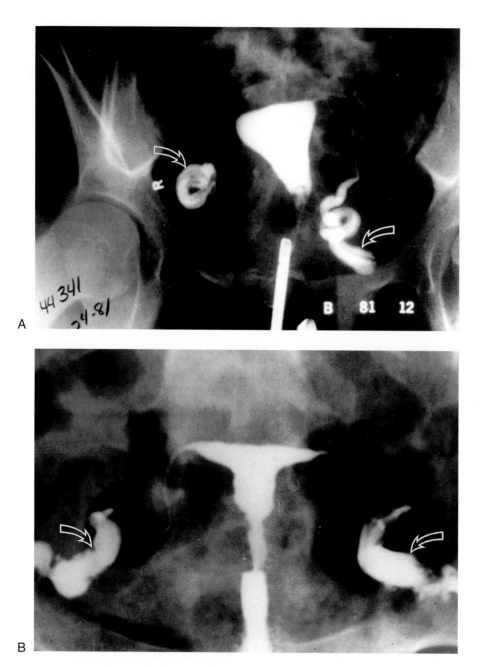

Fig. 9-3. **(A)** Bilateral hydrosalpinges with excellent mucosal patterns *(arrows)* are associated with a favorable prognosis for pregnancy after correction. **(B)** Markedly irregular mucosal surface and absent mucosal folds *(arrows)* portend a poor prognosis for pregnancy should surgical correction be undertaken.

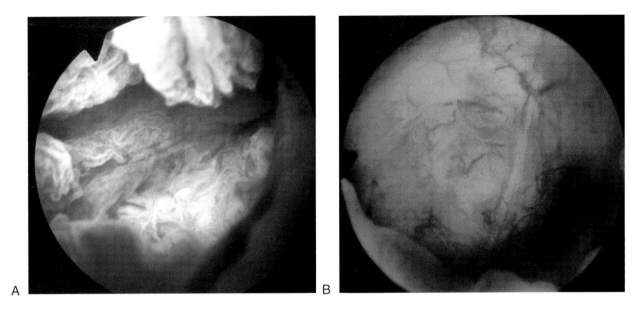

Fig. 9-4. (A) Four major mucosal folds are seen in this photograph taken during tuboscopy. The prognosis for an intrauterine pregnancy is excellent. **(B)** No mucosal folds are seen in this photograph taken during tuboscopy. The prognosis for a naturally occurring intrauterine pregnancy in this woman is poor.

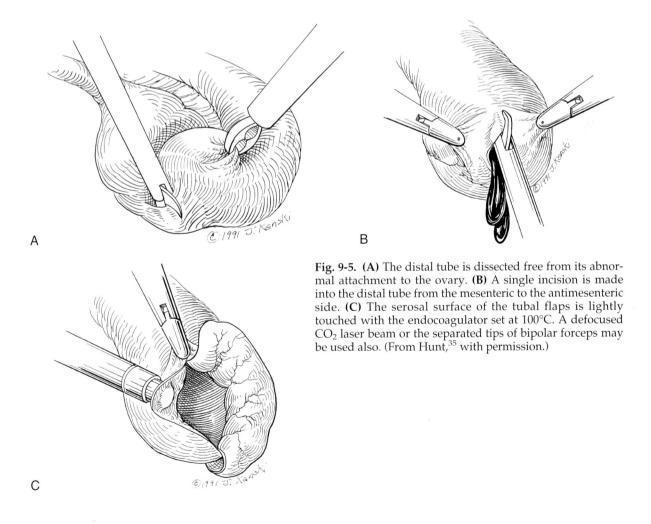

Fig. 9-5. (A) The distal tube is dissected free from its abnormal attachment to the ovary. **(B)** A single incision is made into the distal tube from the mesenteric to the antimesenteric side. **(C)** The serosal surface of the tubal flaps is lightly touched with the endocoagulator set at 100°C. A defocused CO_2 laser beam or the separated tips of bipolar forceps may be used also. (From Hunt,[35] with permission.)

distal end, often a small retracted dimple, becomes apparent.

The energy source(s) used for adhesiolysis and salpingostomy depends on the instruments available and the surgeon's preference. Whether sharp, laser, or electrosurgical dissection is chosen, the results should be the same when performed by equally skilled surgeons on women with equivalent infertility problems. I prefer bipolar forceps and scissor dissection for adhesiolysis and salpingostomy and the endocoagulator to evert serosal flaps.

One method is the modified intussusception technique.[19] A single incision is made with scissors from the mesenteric to the antimesenteric side of the distal tube (Fig. 9-5A and B).

To maintain the cuff and prevent closure, the opening must be secured. This may be accomplished using thermal energy to produce contracture of the serosal or suture to hold the cuff in place. It is important not to make the ostium too large. If a thermal technique is used, the serosa within 1 cm of the cut edge is touched lightly with an endocoagulator probe set at 100°C (Fig. 9-5C). A laser or electrosurgical generator can also be used. The contracted serosa facilitates the eversion. If eversion is not adequate, the mucosa is prolapsed through the ostium (Fig. 9-6A and B). Alternatively, an exaggerated eversion may be accomplished (Fig. 9-7) to build memory into the tissue; the tube tends to remain everted. One or two sutures may be placed at propitious points (Fig. 9-8). Typically, size 6–0 absorbable suture such as Vicryl, Dexon, or PDS is used. Some very skilled surgeons can use even finer suture. Knots are tied using intracorporeal techniques. A large, thin-walled hydrosalpinx is best managed by an exaggerated eversion, and two to four sutures will be required to maintain satisfactory eversion.

The most difficult tube to repair is the rigid, narrow, distally obstructed tube. The lumen remains small regardless of how far back the surgeon carries the incisions. These tubes are very likely to reocclude postoperatively.

After the salpingostomy is completed, tuboscopy may be performed. The tube to be examined is first stabilized with a grasping forceps. Guided by the laparoscope, the surgeon inserts a hysteroscope with attached light cord and irrigating sleeve through a secondary cannula. The tip of the hysteroscope is positioned inside the distal ampulla. The fallopian tube is distended with irrigating fluid injected through the irrigating channel of the hysteroscope, and the hysteroscope is advanced slowly to the proximal ampulla while the surgeon views through it. With tubal distention maintained, the surgeon slowly withdraws the hysteroscope, continuing to observe the mucosa; this is the time the most significant information is obtained. If present, the three or four major mucosal folds and several minor folds are easily seen, and these are favorable signs. Deciliated areas, flattened mucosa, and synechiae, also easily seen, portend an unfavorable prognosis.

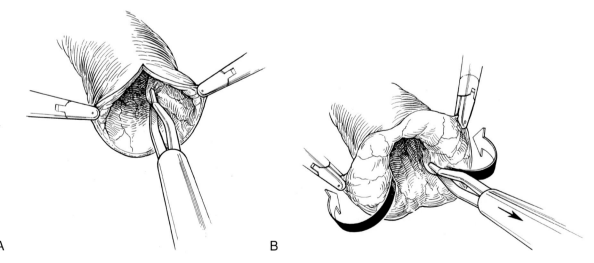

A   B

Fig. 9-6. (A) An alternative technique is the intussusception one. Either serosal flap is gripped with a biopsy instrument, and the mucosa is gently grasped with a deactivated Kleppinger forceps. **(B)** Gentle traction is applied to mucosa as the flaps are folded back. Eversion is accomplished.

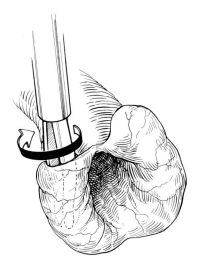

Fig. 9-7. The cut edge of the tubal wall is grasped with a deactivated Kleppinger forceps. An exaggerated eversion is accomplished. This is repeated on the opposite tubal flap. This step builds memory into tubal tissues.

At the completion of the operation, the abdomen and pelvis are carefully inspected. Two liters of Ringer's lactate warmed to body temperature is instilled into the abdomen for hydroflotation. The solution contains 20 mg bupivacaine to prevent postoperative pain as well as 20 mg dexamethasone and 25 mg promethazine to prevent adhesions. (See discussions of pain and postoperative adhesions in Chapter 18.) Abdominal incisions are infiltrated with bupivacaine and closed with size 4–0 absorbable sutures placed in a subcuticular manner. Steri-strips are applied. The indwelling Foley

Fig. 9-8. The salpingostomy is complete. Suturing is demonstrated. (From Hunt,[35] with permission.)

catheter is removed from the urinary bladder, and the cannula and tenaculum are disengaged from the cervix. The patient will have received 100 mg doxycycline containing 10 ml 4.2 percent bicarbonate preoperatively, and she is given one additional dose before discharge. Sodium bicarbonate lessens phlebitis by neutralizing the acidic doxycycline. Appropriate antibiotics are used for specific indications, such as mitral valve prolapse.

FOLLOW-UP

The woman is seen for a postoperative evaluation in 3 weeks. She is again counseled about the need to evaluate pregnancy early to confirm intrauterine implantation. If she has not conceived, an HSG is performed in 4 months under antibiotic prophylaxis. Some advocate early second-look laparoscopy.[20] No definitive study proves that second-look laparocopy after salpingostomy by laparotomy increases pregnancy rates.[9,21,22] I do not recommend it after salpingostomy by laparoscopy or laparotomy. I sometimes recommend a therapeutic laparoscopy 12 to 18 months after surgery, provided tubal mucosa appeared healthy at the time of salpingostomy, the tube(s) has remained patent by HSG, and a successful pregnancy has not occurred.[23] If the mucosa was in poor condition at the time of the initial operation, or recurrent hydrosalpinges are seen on the follow-up HSG, IVF-ET should be considered.[24] I occasionally recommend a second salpingostomy if adhesions are minimal and the mucosa are of excellent quality.

RESULTS

Intuitively, one might anticipate pregnancy rates to be similar after salpingostomy whether access is by laparoscopy or laparotomy. In general, the rates are comparable, provided patients have similar findings and the operations are performed by surgeons skilled in the techniques. Operative laparoscopy may hold an advantage in the reduction of postoperative de novo adhesions, and it is associated with a shorter hospital stay and an earlier return to a productive lifestyle.[25,26]

Four of nine patients achieved intrauterine pregnancies after laparoscopic salpingostomy.[27] Our results in an uncontrolled, retrospective study of viable pregnancy rates after salpingostomy by laparoscopy and laparotomy were 23 and 22 percent, respectively.[28] In an excellent French study of 87 patients undergoing salpingostomy by laparoscopy, the intrauterine and ectopic pregnancy rates were 33.3 and 6.9 percent, re-

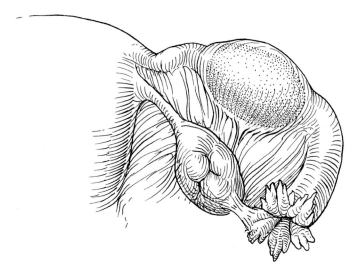

Fig. 9-9. Typical ampullary ectopic pregnancy. (From Hunt and Siegler,[34] with permission.)

spectively.[29] The women with severe tubal disease underwent salpingostomy only if they refused IVF-ET. The authors found no difference in intrauterine pregnancy rates between salpingostomies performed by laparotomy and laparoscopy, nor did they detect a difference in the laparoscopic group whether laser or mechanical methods were used. They emphasized that a high degree of skill in operative laparoscopy must be acquired by the surgeon to obtain results equivalent to those reported after laparotomy. Several other studies indicated that operative laparoscopy is ideally suited for salpingostomy.[29–32]

To resolve conclusively the question of relative effectiveness, randomized, controlled studies in patients with comparable degrees of tubal damage and with no other recognizable infertility factors have to be done. Until then, the choice of laparotomy or laparocopy will depend on availability of services and surgeon and patient preference.

CONCLUSION

Salpingostomy is an excellent operation for the patient with normal-sized, thin-walled hydrosalpinges with healthy mucosa and without extensive, dense adnexal adhesions. Operative laparoscopy appears to yield equivalent pregnancy rates as laparotomy when performed by surgeons equally skilled in the techniques and when patients with comparable tubal damage are selected.

Ectopic pregnancy continues to be a problem, and each patient who conceives after salpingostomy should be considered to have an ectopic pregnancy until proved otherwise (Fig. 9-9).[14,33] One group summed up the hydrosalpinx problem as follows: "Although we feel that optimal surgical technique is important to maximize success, we conclude that the most important prognostic factor in pregnancy outcome after neosalpingostomy for distal tubal disease is the anatomical and functional integrity of the tube."[23] I agree.

REFERENCES

1. Apuzzio JJ, Hoegsberg B: PID: hard to find, but essential to treat. Contemp Obstet Gynecol 37:23, 1992
2. Bateman BG, Nunley WC Jr, Kitchin JD III: Surgical management of distal tubal obstruction—are we making progress? Fertil Steril 48:523, 1987
3. Thejls H, Gnarpe J, Lundkvist O et al: Diagnosis and prevalence of persistent chlamydia infection in infertile women: tissue culture, direct antigen detection, and serology. Fertil Steril 55:304, 1991
4. Henry-Suchet J, Catalan F, Loffredo V et al: *Chlamydia trachomatis* associated with chronic inflammation in abdominal specimens from women selected for tuboplasty. Fertil Steril 36:599, 1981
5. Marana R, Quagliarello J: Distal tubal occlusion: microsurgery versus in vitro fertilization—a review. Int J Fertil 33:107, 1988
6. Schlaff WD, Hassiakos DK, Damewood MD, Rock JA: Neosalpingostomy for distal tubal obstruction: prognostic factors and impact of surgical technique. Fertil Steril 54:984, 1990
7. Kitchin JD III, Nunley WC Jr, Bateman BG: Surgical management of distal tubal occlusion. Am J Obstet Gynecol 155:524, 1986
8. Lilford RJ, Watson AJ: Has in-vitro fertilisation made salpingostomy obsolete? Br J Obstet Gynaecol 97:557, 1990
9. Luber K, Beeson CC, Kennedy JF et al: Results of microsurgical treatment of tubal infertility and early second-look laparoscopy in the post-inflammatory disease patient: implications for in vitro fertilization. Am J Obstet Gynecol 154:1264, 1986

10. Editorial: IVF or tubal surgery. Lancet 337:888, 1991
11. Reiss H: Management of tubal infertility in the 1990s. Br J Obstet Gynaecol 98:619, 1991
12. Young PE, Egan JE, Barlow JJ et al: Reconstructive surgery for infertility at the Boston Hospital for Women. Am J Obstet Gynecol 108:1092, 1970
13. Ozaras H: The value of plastic operations on the fallopian tubes in the treatment of female infertility. Acta Obstet Gynecol Scand 47:489, 1968
14. Donnez J, Casanas-Roux F: Prognostic factors of fimbrial microsurgery. Fertil Steril 46:200, 1986
15. Henry-Suchet J, Loffredo V, Tesuier L, Pez J: Endoscopy of the tube (= tuboscopy): its prognostic value for tuboplasties. Acta Eur Fertil 16:139, 1985
16. DeBruyne F, Puttemans P, Boeckx W, Brosens I: The clinical value of salpingoscopy in tubal infertility. Fertil Steril 51:339, 1989
17. Brosens IA, Vasquez G: Fimbrial microbiopsy. J Reprod Med 16:171, 1976
18. Kosasa TS, Hale RW: Treatment of hydrosalpinx using a single incision eversion procedure. Int J Fertil 33:319, 1988
19. McComb P, Paleologou A: The intussusception salpingostomy technique for the therapy of distal oviductal occlusion at laparoscopy. Obstet Gynecol 78:443, 1991
20. Daniell JF, Diamond MP, McLaughlin DS et al: Clinical results of terminal salpingostomy with the use of the CO_2 laser: report of the intraabdominal laser study group. Fertil Steril 45:175, 1986
21. Trimbos-Kemper TCM, Trimbos JB, van Hall EV: Adhesion formation after tubal surgery: results of the eight-day laparoscopy in 188 patients. Fertil Steril 43:395, 1985
22. Tulandi T, Falcone T, Kafka I: Second-look operative laparoscopy 1 year following reproductive surgery. Fertil Steril 52:421, 1989
23. Schlaf WD, Hassiakos DK, Damewood MD, Rock JA: Neosalpingostomy for distal tubal obstruction: prognostic factors and impact of surgical technique. Fertil Steril 54:984, 1990
24. Audibert F, Hedon B, Arnal F et al: Therapeutic strategies in tubal infertility with distal pathology. Hum Reprod 6:1439, 1991
25. Diamond MP, Daniell JF, Feste J et al: Adhesion reformation and de novo adhesion formation after reproductive pelvic surgery. Fertil Steril 47:864, 1987
26. Luciano AA, Maier DB, Koch EI et al: A comparative study of postoperative adhesions following laser surgery by laparoscopy versus laparotomy in the rabbit model. Obstet Gynecol 74:220, 1989
27. Gomel V: Salpingostomy by laparoscopy. J Reprod Med 18:265, 1977
28. Hunt RB, Cohen SM: Discussions of salpingostomy. Curr Probl Obstet Gynecol Fertil 9:130, 1986
29. Canis M, Mage G, Pouly JL et al: Laparoscopic distal tuboplasty: report of 87 cases and a 4-year experience. Fertil Steril 56:616, 1991
30. Dubuisson JB, de Joliniere JB, Aubriot FX et al: Terminal tuboplasties by laparoscopy: 65 consecutive cases. Fertil Steril 54:401, 1990
31. Mettler L, Giesel H, Semm K: Treatment of female infertility due to tubal obstruction by operative laparoscopy. Fertil Steril 32:384, 1979
32. Daniell JF, Herbert CM: Laparoscopic salpingostomy utilizing the CO_2 laser. Fertil Steril 41:558, 1984
33. Carey M, Brown S: Infertility surgery for pelvic inflammatory disease: success rates after salpingolysis and salpingostomy. Am J Obstet Gynecol 156:296, 1987
34. Hunt RB, Siegler AM (eds): Hysterosalpingography: Techniques and Principles. Mosby-Year Book, St. Louis, 1990
35. Hunt RB (ed): Atlas of Female Infertility Surgery. 2nd Ed. Mosby-Year Book, St. Louis, 1992

10 Endometriosis

DAN C. MARTIN

Endometriosis is a enigmatic disease that has become one of the most investigated gynecologic disorders. More than 4,500 articles have been published on this subject over the last quarter-century. However, despite this intense academic interest, there remain basic holes in our understanding of this disease.[1] As an example, it is frequently difficult to determine if endometriosis is coincidental or the true cause of the problems. It has been noted that endometriosis was found in 21 percent of patients with azoospermic partners as opposed to 34 percent of women with fertile partners.[2] Using these percentages as a guide, it may be that 21 percent of infertile patients with endometriosis have this as a coincidental noncontributing factor.

The clinical presentation of endometriosis is sufficiently variable that history or physical findings alone are not reliable for diagnoses. Laparoscopy enables the gynecologist to make the diagnosis of surface endometriosis with relative ease. However, microscopic endometriosis, deep infiltrating endometriosis, intraovarian endometriosis, mesenteric endometriosis, and bowel endometriosis can escape laparoscopic detection. Despite the shortcomings, the importance of laparoscopy in diagnosing and staging endometriosis is significant. Furthermore, treatment of endometriosis at the time of initial laparoscopy is a useful adjunct in select, if not all, patients. This is particularly true when superficial implants are seen on the peritoneum. For these, coagulation (desiccation), vaporization, or excision can be performed. The choice of electrosurgery, endothermy, laser, or harmonic scalpel is based on the availability of equipment and the gynecologist's familiarity with the equipment.

When patients are properly prepared for laparoscopic surgery, further medical or surgical treatment may be avoidable. However, staging the procedure based on patient preference or operative findings may be useful. A diagnostic laparoscopy with the plan to come back at a later date if needed may fit the plans of some patients and gynecologists. Furthermore, large ovarian endometriomas may be better treated by initial drainage, biopsy, and coagulation than by stripping. Stripping removes healthy ovary in addition to the pseudocapsule of the ovarian endometrioma. With large enough cysts, this may be sufficiently significant that coagulation with preparation for a second laparoscopy[3,4] will do less damage to the ovary than trying to do everything at the first surgery.

RECOGNITION

History and physical examination may guide the gynecologist to the area of endometriosis at the time of laparoscopy. Historically, severe dysmenorrhea correlates with the presence of endometriosis, although mild and moderate dysmenorrhea do not.[5] Patients may be able to point to specific areas or give a history of a specific area of tenderness. As lesions increase in volume and in depth of infiltration, the ability to predict these on palpations increases.[6]

Laparoscopy magnifies the size of lesions and facilitates identification. At the same time, visualization of the posterior cul-de-sac is improved compared with visualization at laparotomy. Despite magnification, microscopic disease may be a problem in a small group of patients.[7,8] Also, intraovarian[9] and retroperitoneal[10,11] lesions may be hidden from view. Sonography and magnetic resonance imaging (MRI) may be helpful in these situations. Recent advances in fat-saturation MRI have increased the resolution with all lesions greater than 4 mm in diameter recognized in a study of lesions from 2 to 30 mm. Fat-saturation MRI also increased the resolution of 2- to 3-mm lesions from 1 of 34 with standard MRI to 15 of 34 with fat-saturation MRI.[12]

The various colors can be subtle and confusing[13–16] (Table 10-1). Other lesions such as psammoma bodies, endosalpingiosis, and cancer may mimic or coexist with endometriosis.[17]

Table 10-1. Histologic Confirmation (%) of Lesions of Specific Descriptions

Author	Black	White	Red	Glandular	Subovarian Adhesions	Yellow-Brown Patches	Pockets
Jansen and Russell 1986[13]	ns	81	81	67	50	47	47
Martin et al. 1989[16]	94	80	75	66	39	22	39
Moen and Halvorsen 1992[15]	76	ns	57	ns	16	ns	12

Abbreviation: ns, not stated.

PROGRESSION AND REGRESSION OF LESIONS

Discussing progression and regression can be confusing, as it may apply to appearance, size, pain, dysmenorrhea, activity, or other characteristics of endometriosis (Table 10-2). Endometriosis has been described as a progressive disease during the menstruant life of a woman with regression after menopause. Regression was thought to be a function of a lack of estrogen. Also, removing the estrogen source (oophorectomy) has been said to cure endometriosis. Studies have suggested that progression in appearance requires 6 months to 20 years.[13,14,18–20] Progression of depth appears to occur over 15 to 25 years.[21] Looking at progression of symptomology, there is a 4.5-fold increase over the first 10 years after childbirth when compared with the first 5 years initially in asymptomatic patients.[22] Supporting the concept of regression of pain but opposing the concept of lesions disappearing, Kempers et al.[23] found that 93 percent of their postmenopausal patients with endometriosis were asymptomatic.[23]

However, it is suggested that at some time in their lives, almost all women may have transient endometriosis.[24] Studies demonstrating that this occurs in a spontaneous natural cycle have been published.[20,25] It is also possible that women have endometriosis that regresses secondary to hormonal suppression for contraception or due to pregnancy. Both progression and regression may be a natural part of the cycle of endometriosis in some if not most or even all women.

SURGICAL TREATMENT

Approach

The approach to treatment is based on symptoms, patient desires, physician training, and equipment available. Patients with infertility may receive more benefit from superficial coagulation than from deep excision. There is concern that deep excision may increase adhesions. Postoperative adhesions may interfere more with fertility than the endometriosis itself. As in most of endometriosis research, adequate data are lacking to draw firm conclusions.

However, pain and tenderness, particularly focal tenderness associated with nodularity, seems to respond to deep and complete excision more than to superficial coagulation or vaporization.[26,27] Staging the procedure may also be useful in pain. Some patients get sufficient relief from superficial coagulation or vaporization that deep dissection is not needed. This may be particularly important when there is involvement of the bowel, ureter, or bladder.

Tissue Techniques

Coagulation (desiccation) is generally performed using electrosurgery, endothermy, or penetrating lasers such as the argon, potassium-titanyl-phosphate, and Nd:YAG. These techniques are generally limited to 2- to 5-mm effective depth[28–31] (Table 10-3). However, deep endometriosis is found in more than 60 percent of patients.[21] In these patients, coagulation and vaporization may be inadequate. Coagulation may not reach the full depth, and vaporization to great depths creates

Table 10-2. Selected Classification Criterion

Appearance	Color (Black, dark, brown, purple, red, pink, etc.)
	Topography (raised, flat, deep infiltrating)
Size	Dimensions (diameter, depth, volume)
Pain	Character
	Intensity
	Location
Dysmenorrhea	Character
	Intensity
	Location (central, lateral)
Activity	Mitotic index
	Prostaglandins
	CA-125
	Placental protein 14
Other	

Table 10-3. Maximum Depth (mm) of Coagulative Penetration

Bipolar electorsurgery	5
Nd:Yag laser	5.2
Thermal cautery	3
CO_2 laser	2.7

(Data from Ryder and Hulka,[28] Jaffe et al.,[29] Semm,[30] and Taylor et al.[31])

significant amounts of smoke. The smoke of vaporization can obscure the view, and carbon created with these techniques can confuse the anatomic picture. Deep lesions are more accurately excised.[10,21,32]

Deep excisional techniques have been performed with bipolar coagulation and scissors, monopolar electrosurgery, CO_2 laser, fiber lasers with artificial tips, and the harmonic scalpel. All these techniques require an appreciation of the surrounding anatomy and the possibility of damage to ureters.[11,33–35] The best technique at present appears to be the technique with which a specific gynecologist has the most and best experience. There is no clear superiority for all the variable factors of any one type of equipment.

The most common technique used to excise lesions is to make an incision into the peritoneum in a normal area near the abnormal lesion. With the incision made, the peritoneum is pulled based on tension and the loose connective tissue dissected with the active instrument or a blunt probe. A blunt probe is most useful in areas near the bowel or ureter in that these will frequently push away and increase the level of safety. Blunt dissection may also help with visualization of vessels. The dissection is taken down to the level of healthy tissue.[36] Bipolar electrosurgery, ties, or sutures are available for hemostasis when needed.

Ovarian Endometriosis

Small hemorrhagic surface lesions can be handled as peritoneal lesions. However, it is kept in mind that these can be hemorrhagic sequelae of ovulation. This is a greater concern when treating larger ovarian chocolate cysts, as these may be hemorrhagic corpus luteum surface endometriosis overlying a corpus luteum, endometriosis infiltrating into a corpus luteum, or ovarian endometriomas.[37,38] An attempt is made to differentiate these various possibilities. However, there is no set of criteria that guarantees recognition at time of laparoscopy: histology is needed.[39]

In general, a biopsy of small surface lesions is sent to pathology and the remainder of the lesion coagulated or vaporized. Biopsy is needed as the presence of endometriosis does not exclude the possibility of cancer. Cancer may have presentations similar to those of endometriosis. With medium-sized chocolate cysts of 2 to 5 cm, stripping, according to the techniques of Semm,[30] is generally used.

With larger endometriomas (greater than 5 cm), the possibility of staging the surgery is considered. Initial drainage of the endometriomas followed by biopsy and coagulation of the inner surface is performed. Subsequent observation with sonography is used to determine if there is recurrence. If this occurs, then either medical suppression or surgery can be considered.[3,4]

Bowel

Laparoscopic resection of bowel endometriosis has been performed by gynecologists.[40] However, this is an operation reserved for general surgeons in most operating rooms.[41] There is an additional difficulty in bowel endometriosis in that it may often be more palpable than visual. In my patients, I have had one patient with 40 lesions found at laparotomy and only 6 at laparoscopy, whereas all three of my patients with mesenteric endometriosis have been missed at laparoscopy. A gynecologist or a general surgeon risks missing these palpable but not visualized lesions when performing this surgery at laparoscopy.

Diaphragm

Although Redwine (personal communication) has diagnosed diaphragmatic endometriosis at laparoscopy, the resection has been at laparotomy. Of note, inspection of the diaphragm may require lateral laparoscopic insertions to reach the dome and posterior diaphragm. For this approach, the patient would be in a lateral position and the laparoscope would be placed in a subcostal position in the axillary line. The insertion at this point would be visualized through the primary trocar previously placed at the umbilicus. This approach allows increased visualization of the dome of the diaphragm and the posterior diaphragm. This approach is considered in patients with cyclic shoulder pain associated with menses.

Bladder

Deep infiltrating endometriosis near the bladder is uncommon, but this is handled in a fashion similar to peritoneum and bowel. A technical advantage of operating on the bladder is that a minilaparotomy can be performed to repair a cystotomy if necessary. The patient is best informed preoperatively of the use of a Foley catheter for 10 to 14 days when this is anticipated.

Endometrioid Carcinoma

Endometrioid carcinoma of the ovary has been associated with ovarian endometriosis. This association suggests that the presence of ovarian endometriosis increases the risks of the development of endometrium ovarian carcinoma. Ovarian endometriosis, particularly in perimenopausal and postmenopausal women, may not be an innocuous lesion. Oophorectomy appears advisable in this situation.[42] A greater and more problematic question concerns the degree of risks in women of reproductive age with ovarian endometriomas. Is this risk such that they should undergo "prophylactic" oophorectomy after their reproductive years? An answer to this question is needed.[43]

MEDICAL TREATMENT

Medical treatment may be used in addition to or instead of surgical treatment in certain patients. Thirty-seven percent of patients with mild disease while approximately 74 percent with severe disease have recurrence after gonadotropin-releasing hormone agonist therapy.[44] Preoperative medical treatment may also be useful in avoiding coexistent corpus lutea and other functional cysts that interfere with surgery in patients with significant endometriosis. These appear particularly useful in cases with cystic ovaries or large masses seen on sonography.

PREGNANCY RATES

Pregnancy rates after laparoscopic coagulation have averaged 47 percent,[45] whereas after laser ablation, the rate is 54 percent.[46] Of studies in patients with and without other factors, 37 percent of patients with other factors and 74 percent with no other factors became pregnant[47–50] (Table 10-4). Recently, in patients with tubal disease, 41 percent of patients were pregnant when endometriosis and tubal disease alone were associated as opposed to 24 percent when there were multiple or other factors.[51] Life table analysis in three studies demonstrated that laparoscopic techniques are equal to medication or laparotomy in mild or moderate cases and equal or better than laparotomy in severe cases.[49,52,53]

Adamson and Pasta[54] have used meta-analysis to compare fecundity. In both their own studies and meta-analysis of the literature, either no treatment or surgery was superior to medical treatment for minimal and mild endometriosis associated with infertility. Surgery was generally used in cases with moderate and severe disease, and those patients achieved similar results at laparoscopy. This included those cases with ovarian endometriomas and complete cul-de-sac obliteration.

Furthermore, for mild endometriosis, no treatment may be as successful as medical or surgical therapy. Infertility patients with a normal hysterosalpingogram, no history of pelvic inflammatory disease, no severe dysmenorrhea,[43] and a negative chlamydia IgG[55] may be best treated with four to six cycles of supraovulation intrauterine insemination before proceeding to laparoscopy.

Pregnancy rates have not appeared to be particularly dependent on stage after laparoscopic treatment. More important than stage has been the years of infertility[56] and the coexistent of other factors. Analyzed in this fashion, success rates have varied from 82 percent with less than 2 years of infertility and no other factors to 7 percent with 8 or more years of infertility and male factor[48,57] (Table 10-5).

As an interesting finding, endometriosis can be a good prognostic finding. Patients with tubal disease and endometriosis but no other factors had higher fecundity rates than patients with tubal disease alone or with any other factors.[51]

Table 10-4. Effect of Other Factors on Pregnancy Rates

	None			Present		
	Total	Pregnant	%	Total	Pregnant	%
Feste 1985[47]	60	42	70	80	40	50
Martin 1986[48]	34	23	67	81	31	38
Adamson et al. 1988[49]	60	39	65	90	47	52
Paulson et al. 1991[50]	296	227	77	260	73	28
Total	450	331	74	511	191	37

Table 10-5. Pregnancies After Laser Laparoscopy

	≤24 Months of Infertility		>24 Months of Infertility	
	Number	Pregnant	Number	Pregnant
Martin 1986[48]	44	30 (68%)	71	26 (37%)
Keye et al. 1987[57]	8	5 (63%)	48	14 (29%)
Total	52	35 (67%)	119	40 (34%)

PAIN

Pain relief is much harder to quantitate. A clinical observation is that focal pain and tenderness, particularly when associated with nodularity, responds to removal or destruction of lesions. Diffuse pain or tenderness is much harder to predict, whereas pain associated with psammoma bodies and positive chlamydia IgG titers is the hardest to relieve.[58]

CONCLUSIONS

There still remain many holes in our basic understanding of endometriosis. At extremes are those patients who may not benefit from direct treatment of endometriosis[43] and those patients who have deep infiltrating endometriosis that responds to resection.[40,59] Care and concern are needed to individualize the treatment for various presentations.

REFERENCES

1. Olive DL: Future direction for endometriosis research. Infertil Reprod Med Clin North Am 3:763, 1992
2. Waller KG, Lindsay P, Curtis P, Shaw RW: The prevalence of endometriosis in women with infertile partners. Eur J Obstet Gynecol Reprod Biol 48:135, 1993
3. Semm K: Postoperative care after endoscopic abdominal surgery. p. 228. In Semm K, Friedrich ER (eds): Operative Manual for Endoscopic Abdominal Surgery. Year Book Medical Publishers, Chicago, 1987
4. Donnez J, Nisolle M, Karaman Y et al: CO₂ laser laparoscopy in peritoneal endometriosis and in ovarian endometrial cyst. J Gynecol Surg 5:361, 1989
5. Naish CE, Kennedy SH, Barlow DH: Correlation between pain symptoms and laparoscopic findings. (submitted for publication)
6. Ripps BA, Martin DC: Correlation of focal pelvic tenderness with implant dimension and stage of endometriosis. J Reprod Med 37:620, 1992
7. Redwine DB, Yocum LB: A serial section study of visually normal pelvic peritoneum in patients with endometriosis. Fertil Steril 54:648, 1990
8. Murphy AA, Green WR, Bobbie D et al: Unsuspected endometriosis documented by scanning electron microscopy in visually normal peritoneum. Fertil Steril 46:522, 1986
9. Russell WW: Aberrant portions of the Mullerian duct found in an ovary. Johns Hopkins Hosp Bull 94–96:8, 1899
10. Koninckx PR, Martin DC: Deep endometriosis: a consequence of infiltration or retraction or possibly adenomyosis externa? Fertil Steril 58:924, 1992
11. Moore JG, Binstock MA, Growdon WA: The clinical implications of retroperitoneal endometriosis. Am J Obstet Gynecol 158:1291, 1988
12. Takahashi K, Okada S, Ozaki T et al: Diagnosis of pelvic endometriosis by magnetic resonance imaging using "fat-saturation" technique. Fertil Steril 62:973, 1994
13. Jansen RPS, Russell P: Nonpigmented endometriosis: clinical, laparoscopic, and pathologic definition. Am J Obstet Gynecol 155:1154, 1986
14. Redwine DB: Age-related evolution in color appearance of endometriosis. Fertil Steril 48:1062, 1987
15. Moen MH, Halvorsen TB: Histologic confirmation of endometriosis in different peritoneal lesions. Acta Obstet Gynecol Scand 71:337, 1992
16. Martin DC, Hubert GD, Vander Zwaag R, El-Zeky FA: Laparoscopic appearances of peritoneal endometriosis. Fertil Steril 51:63, 1989
17. Martin DC, Khare VK, Miller BE: Association of *Chlamydia trachomatis* immunoglobulin gamma titers with dystrophic peritoneal calcification, psammoma bodies, adhesions, and hydrosalpinges. Fertil Steril 63:39, 1995
18. Sampson JA: Benign and malignant endometrial implants in the peritoneal cavity, and their relation to certain ovarian tumors. Surg Gynecol Obstet 38:287, 1924
19. Karnaky KJ: Theories and known observations about hormonal treatment of endometriosis-in-situ, and endometriosis at the enzyme level. Ariz Med January:37, 1969
20. D'Hooghe TM, Bambra CS, Isahakia M, Koninckx PR: Evolution of spontaneous endometriosis in the baboon (*Papio anubus, Papio cynocephalus*) over a 12-month period. Fertil Steril 48:409, 1992
21. Koninckx PR, Meuleman C, Demeyere S et al: Suggestive evidence that pelvic endometriosis is a progressive disease, whereas deeply infiltrating endometriosis is associated with pelvic pain. Fertil Steril 55:759, 1991
22. Moen MH: Is a long period without childbirth a risk factor for developing endometriosis. Hum Reprod 6:1404, 1991
23. Kempers RD, Dockerty MB, Hunt AB, Symmonds RE: Significant postmenopausal endometriosis. Surg Gynecol Obstet 111:348, 1960
24. Koninckx PR, Martin DC: Treatment of deeply infiltrating endometriosis. Curr Opin Obstet Gynecol 6:231, 1994
25. Hoshiai H, Ishikawa M, Sawatari Y et al: Laparoscopic evaluation of the onset and progression of endometriosis. Am J Obstet Gynecol 169:714, 1993
26. Wheeler JM, Malinak LR: Recurrent endometriosis. Contrib Gynecol Obstet 16:13, 1987
27. Redwine DB: Conservative laparoscopic excision of endometriosis by sharp dissection: life table analysis of reoperation and persistent or recurrent disease. Fertil Steril 56:628, 1991
28. Ryder RM, Hulka JF: Bladder and bowel injury after electrodesiccation with Kleppinger bipolar forceps. J Reprod Med 38:595, 1993
29. Joffe SN, Brackett KA, Sankar MY, Daikuzono N: Resection of the liver with the Nd:YAG laser. Surg Gynecol Obstet 163:437, 1986
30. Semm K: Course of endoscopic abdominal surgery. p. 130. In Semm K, Friedrick ER (eds): Operative Manual for Endoscopic Abdominal Surgery. Year Book Medical Publishers, Chicago, 1987
31. Taylor MV, Martin DC, Poston W et al: Effect of power density and carbonization on residual tissue coagulation using the continuous wave carbon dioxide laser. Colposc Gynecol Laser Surg 2:169, 1986
32. Martin DC: Laparoscopic and vaginal colpotomy for the excision of infiltrating cul-de-sac endometriosis. J Reprod Med 33:806, 1988

edematous, distended tissue on tension with loss of elasticity, making further division easy and safe using blunt dissection, scissors dissection, laser, or electrosurgery.

Aquadissectors (suction-irrigators with the ability to dissect using pressurized fluid) should have a single channel to maximize suctioning and irrigating capacity. An aquadissector with a solid (not perforated) distal tip is necessary to perform atraumatic suction-traction-retraction, irrigate directly, and develop surgical planes (aquadissection). Small holes at the tip impede these actions and spray the surgical field without purpose. The shaft should be specially treated by bead blasting to provide a dull finish to prevent CO_2 laser beam reflection, allowing it to be used as a backstop.

Scissors

Blunt- or round-tipped 5-mm scissors with one stable blade and one movable blade are used to lyse thin and thick adhesions and peritoneum sharply. Scissors that actually cut represent new laparoscopic instrumentation. Sharp dissection is the primary technique used for adhesiolysis to diminish the potential for adhesion formation; electrosurgery and laser are usually reserved for hemostatic dissection of endometriosis or adhesions where anatomic planes are not evident or vascular adherences anticipated. Blunt-tipped, sawtooth scissors cut. Hook scissors are used when the surgeon can get completely around the structure being divided but rarely maintain their sharpness.

Scissors are the best instrument to cut avascular or congenital adhesions and peritoneum. Blunt dissection can be performed with blunt-tipped scissors. This includes ovary-pelvic sidewall and tuboovarian adhesions. Loose areolar tissue is separated by inserting a closed scissors and withdrawing it in the open position. Pushing tissue with the partially open or closed blunt tip is used to develop natural planes.

Surgeons should select a scissors that feels comfortable in their hands. It should not be too long or encumbered by an electrical cord to facilitate direction changes. I prefer to make rapid instrument exchanges between scissors and bipolar forceps through the same trocar sleeve to control bleeding.

Electrosurgery

Electrosurgical knowledge and skill are essential. Monopolar cutting current is safe for laparoscopic use. At the same electrosurgical power setting, less arcing occurs at laparoscopy than at laparotomy as it takes 30 percent more power to spark or arc in CO_2 than in room air. However, electrosurgical burns may occur in areas outside the surgeon's laparoscopic view from electrode insulation defects or capacitative coupling.

Cutting current is used to both cut or coagulate (desiccate), depending on the portion or configuration of the electrode in contact with the tissue. The tip cuts while the wide body tamponades and coagulates. The voltage is too low with pure cutting current to arc or spark.

Coagulation current with conventional electrodes (80 to 120 W) can arc or spark approximately 1 mm and is used in close proximity to tissue, but not in contact, to fulgurate diffuse venous and arteriolar bleeders. It is not used in contact with tissue to coagulate, as this waveform uses voltages more than 10 times that of cutting current. Coagulation current is modulated so that it is on only 6 percent of the time. The high voltage allows it to arc or spark for 1 to 2 mm, producing very good hemostasis with venous and arteriolar bleeding, while penetrating the tissue very superficially. The Argon Beam Coagulator (argon gas at 2 L/min and high-voltage coagulation current) can be used to increase the spark or arc possible with conventional fulguration.

Bipolar desiccation for ovarian vessel hemostasis at laparoscopy was first reported in 1985 by Reich. A more uniform bipolar desiccation process is obtained using cutting current. Coagulating current is not used as it may rapidly desiccate the outer layers of the tissue, producing superficial resistance which may prevent deeper penetration and cause sparking to surrounding tissue, creating cutting instead of coagulation. Large blood vessels are compressed and bipolar cutting current passed until complete desiccation is achieved (i.e., the current depletes tissue fluid and electrolytes until it ceases to flow between the forceps as determined by an ammeter or current flow meter) (end point monitor: Electroscope EPM-1, Boulder, CO).

Suturing

Suture application is made easy by not using needles. The vessel or pedicle to be ligated is isolated by dividing and separating surrounding peritoneum and connective tissue. The suture can then be placed around the pedicle with a grasping forceps, preferably one with a curved end. Suture tying is best accomplished by making the knots with the surgeon's hands outside the body (extracorporeal) and pushing or slipping the knot down to the pedicle.

Extracorporeal tying is facilitated by using a trocar

sleeve without a trap to avoid difficulty slipping knots down to the tissue. A short trocar sleeve that does not protrude far into the peritoneal cavity, has a screw grid for retention, and has no trap is ideal.[13] Both a reusable (Richard Wolf) and a disposable version (Apple Medical) are available. The former is better for rapid instrument exchanges, but the Apple has a much tighter seal, preventing loss of pneumoperitoneum when pushing the knot down.

An excellent technique for laparoscopic extracorporeal tying was developed in 1971 by Dr. H. Courtenay Clarke using a knot-pusher (Marlow Surgical, Willoughby, OH) to tie in a manner very similar to the way one would hand-tie suture at laparotomy.[14] This device is like an extension of the surgeon's fingers. The surgeon applies the suture around the pedicle, pulls it outside, and then, while holding both strands, makes a simple half-hitch; a surgeon's knot will not slide as well. The Clarke knot-pusher is put on one strand of the suture just above the knot, the suture is held firm across the index finger, and the throw is pushed down to the tissue. The second throw is made in the same direction (i.e., a slip knot while exerting tension from above to further secure the tissue). A square knot is made with the third and fourth throws by pushing half-hitches made in opposing fashion down to the knot to secure it firmly. To suture with a straight needle, the same technique is used.

Suturing with large curved needles requires a technique to put them into the peritoneal cavity without a large incision (i.e., through a 5-mm lower-quadrant incision).[15] The lower abdominal incisions placed lateral to the rectus muscle ensure an obvious tract on removing the trocar sleeve, which is very easy to reenter. To suture with a CT-1 or CTX needle, the trocar sleeve is taken out of the abdomen and loaded by introducing a straight needle driver through the sleeve to grasp the distal end of the suture, pulling the suture through the trocar sleeve, reinserting the instrument into the sleeve, and grasping the suture 2 cm from the needle. The needle driver is inserted into the peritoneal cavity through the original tract, as visualized on the monitor; the needle follows through the soft tissue, and the trocar sleeve is reinserted over the driver. At this stage, the straight needle driver is replaced with a Cook oblique curved needle driver (Cook OB/GYN, Spencer, IN) and the needle applied around vascular pedicles or through fascia. Afterward, the needle is placed in the anterior abdominal wall parietal peritoneum for later removal after the suture is tied. The needle is cut, the cut end of the suture pulled out of the peritoneal cavity through the trocar sleeve, and the

knot tied with the Clarke knot-pusher. To retrieve the needle, the trocar sleeve is unscrewed, after which the needle driver inside it pulls the needle through the soft tissue after grasping its attached suture remnant. The trocar sleeve is replaced easily with or without another suture.

The Endoloop is a preformed knotted loop designed to fit over vascular pedicles and then be tightened. Over the past 15 years, I have used it for appendectomies and omentectomies but never for oophorectomy. Bipolar desiccation or the suture ligature method just described works better.

PREOPERATIVE MANAGEMENT

Evaluation

The patient's age, the clinical examination, and ultrasound findings provide important information that help determine the operative approach. Postmenopausal women should also have a serum CA-125 assay.

Transvaginal sonographic examination of the pelvis is a reliable and consistent method for evaluation of a pelvic mass and should be performed to determine the size and consistency of the mass.[16] Granberg et al.,[17] in a large study of 94 postmenopausal and 86 menstruating women, found that ultrasound correctly predicted benign masses in 92 percent of patients. The presence of irregular borders, papulations, solid areas, thick septa, ascites, or matted bowel should raise concern regarding the possibility of malignancy. If suspicious for malignancy, operative laparoscopic removal is usually not appropriate, and laparotomy should be performed without delay.

Dermoids, endometriomas, hemorrhagic cysts, cystadenomas, and persistent functional cysts will often have a characteristic appearance on ultrasound. Along with the clinical picture and other laboratory data, the ultrasound may help select patients that can be approached by operative laparoscopy.

Functional cysts are usually unilocular, and in premenopausal women, most purely cystic masses less than 7 cm will resolve spontaneously. Hemorrhagic cysts contain internal echoes, usually change over time, and often regress spontaneously. Dermoids have a variable appearance on ultrasound and may appear as a cystic mass with a thickened wall, echogenic material in a nondependent area, or highly echogenic areas representing bone or teeth. Endometriomas usually have regular but slightly thickened borders with low-level and diffuse internal echoes.

CA-125, a tumor-associated antigen, has been studied to determine its value in preoperative differentiation of benign and malignant pelvic masses. Vasilev et al.[18] found that 128 of 132 patients (97 percent) with pelvic masses who had a CA-125 less than 35 U/ml had benign masses. However, in patients younger than 50 years old who had an elevated CA-125 value, 34 of 40 patients (85 percent) had a benign mass. Endometriosis, leiomyomata, adenomyosis, dermoid cysts, pregnancy, and acute or chronic salpingitis may all be associated with elevated levels. Values may also be elevated with inflammatory bowel disease, colon cancer, lung cancer, breast cancer, cirrhosis, liver disease, pancreatitis, and pancreatic carcinoma.

The combination of clinical examination, sonogram, and (in postmenopausal women) CA-125 values is presently used to determine the appropriateness of laparoscopic surgery for patients with an ovarian mass.[19] Intravenous pyelograms are rarely necessary preoperatively but are ordered postoperatively if abdominal pain persists after surgery on or near the ureter. Presently, there is no indication for computed tomography scan or magnetic resonance imaging before laparoscopic ovarian surgery.

Preparation

Laparoscopy is performed before ovulation if possible. Norethindrone acetate, 10 mg daily, or depoleuprolide (Depo-Lupron), 3.75 mg intramuscularly monthly, may be administered starting before or during menses until surgery to avoid operating on ovaries containing a corpus luteum.

Patients are encouraged to drink and eat lightly for 24 hours before admission. Magnesium citrate and a Fleet's enema are routinely administered the evening before surgery to evacuate the lower bowel. When extensive cul-de-sac involvement with endometriosis is suspected, either clinically or from another physician's operative record, a mechanical bowel preparation (GoLYTELY or Colyte) is administered orally the afternoon before the surgery to induce brisk, self-limiting diarrhea to cleanse the bowel without disrupting the electrolyte balance. Patients are informed preoperatively that they are at high risk for bowel injury during laparoscopic procedures when extensive cul-de-sac involvement with endometriosis or adhesions is suspected.

Lower abdominal, pubic, and perineal hair is not shaved. Patients are encouraged to void on call to the operating room, and a Foley catheter is inserted only if the bladder is distended or a long operation anticipated. Antibiotics are administered before all cases.

The surgical treatment of endometriosis is usually not made easier by perioperative medical therapy with gonadotropin-releasing hormone agonists or danazol. Ovarian suppression is expensive, has significant side effects, and prohibits fertility during its administration. The hormonal responsiveness of deep endometriotic fibrotic lesions is unpredictable and inconsistent: "shrinkage" of fibrosis never occurs. Hormonal suppression has not been shown to improve the long-term outcome in women with extensive disease and should be abandoned.

SURGICAL MANAGEMENT

Considerations

All patients scheduled for operative laparoscopy should also consent to a possible laparotomy, and most surgeons should be prepared to proceed with staging laparotomy without delay if malignancy is found.

Under general endotracheal anesthesia, surgery is performed in the lithotomy position with an orogastric tube inserted to minimize bowel distension. The patient is flat (0 degrees) until after the umbilical trocar sleeve has been inserted and then placed in steep Trendelenburg position (20 to 30 degrees). Lithotomy position is obtained with Allen stirrups (Edgewater Medical Systems, Mayfield Heights, OH) or knee braces, which are adjusted to the individual patient by the nursing staff before she is anesthetized. Anesthesia examination is always performed before preparing the patient. A Foley catheter is inserted when the bladder becomes distended and is removed after the patient is awake.

A suction-irrigator (aquadissector), special forceps, scissors, high-flow insufflator, 30 degree tiltable operating room table, and a reliable electrosurgical generator are indispensable tools for advanced surgical procedures. Five laparoscopes are available: a 10-mm 0-degree straight viewing laparoscope, a 10-mm operating laparoscope with 5-mm operating channel, a 10-mm laser laparoscope with a 5-mm laser channel, a 10-mm 30-degree oblique laparoscope, and a 5-mm straight viewing laparoscope for introduction through a 5-mm trocar sleeve. I use my right foot to activate the CO_2 laser when used, my left foot for the bipolar electrosurgical pedal, and hand controls for monopolar electrodes. An average of 10 L of Ringer's lactate irrigant is used per case; more than 40 L has been used on occasion. Electrolyte disturbances have not been observed, and laboratory electrolyte evaluation is no longer routinely obtained.

Electrosurgical electrodes that eliminate capacitance and insulation failures (Electroshield from Electroscope) are used. Laparoscopic stapling is rarely used as gynecologic surgeons learn to suture.

The videomonitor is opposite the surgeon. This arrangement is preferred, because only one monitor is necessary. The monitor is on the patient's right, the surgeon on her left, and the assistant between the patient's legs where the monitor can be viewed. Both surgeon and assistant have access to instrument tables beside or behind them, and a scrub nurse is not necessary if a specially trained assistant is available. The circulating nurse tends the video recorder, irrigation supply, laser, etc. This arrangement requires some hand-eye adjustment for the surgeon, because the monitor is rotated 90 degrees from the plane of surgery. However, it avoids neck and back strain from twisting to see a monitor placed between the patient's legs, especially if the surgeon operates with instruments in the left hand and laparoscope in the right. Hand-eye coordination (almost mirror-image) is extremely difficult for the assistant, who often assumes a passive role of maintaining retraction or grasper positions achieved by the surgeon. Mirror-image operating skills are attainable after extensive training and will greatly increase the efficiency of the surgical team.

Initially, the upper abdomen and pelvis are inspected for obvious carcinoma, excrescences, and ascites. Pelvic and abdominal washings are performed for staging in the event that carcinoma is found. If excrescences are found, they are biopsied and sent for frozen section. If obvious carcinoma, ascites, or a positive frozen section is found, laparoscopic treatment is considered only in cases in which the surgeon can do the same operation as at open surgery without compromise.

Incisions

Three laparoscopic puncture sites including the umbilicus are used: 10-mm umbilical, 5-mm right, and 5-mm left lower quadrant. I stand on the left side of the patient and use my dominant right hand to hold, manipulate, and focus the camera. The left lower-quadrant puncture is my major portal for operative manipulation. The right trocar sleeve is used for atraumatic grasping forceps to retract tissue as needed. Specimens are removed usually intact through the cul-de-sac.

My laparoscopic puncture sites have not evolved over the past 20 years as I do not think that more and larger trocar sleeve incisions used by many surgeons today represent progress. I have, however, increased the right-sided incision from 3 mm to 5 mm. Large puncture sites or incisions bordering on minilaparotomy for tissue extraction should be replaced by an umbilical extension or a laparoscopic culdotomy approach.

The intraumbilical incision overlies the area where skin, deep fascia, and parietal peritoneum of the anterior abdominal wall meet, permitting little opportunity for the parietal peritoneum to tent away from the Veress needle and primary trocar. This vertical midline incision is made initially with a #15 blade (never a #11) on the inferior wall of the umbilical fossa extending to and just beyond its bottom. In thin patients, this incision frequently traverses the deep fascia, but intraperitoneal injury is avoided by using the thumb to pull the umbilicus onto the surgeon's forefinger, a maneuver that controls the incision's depth. Following CO_2 insufflation to an intra-abdominal pressure of 25 mmHg, the trocar is seated vertically just inside the skin in the dimple of the fascia stuck to peritoneum before a 45 degree thrust. The result is a parietal peritoneal puncture directly beneath the umbilicus.

After reducing the intra-abdominal pressure to 15 mmHg, the lower-quadrant trocar sleeves are placed just above the pubic hairline and lateral to the rectus abdominis muscle located by direct laparoscopic inspection of the anterior abdominal wall. When the anterior abdominal wall parietal peritoneum is thickened from previous surgery or obesity, the position of the muscle is judged by palpating and depressing the anterior abdominal wall with the back of the scalpel; the wall will appear thicker where rectus muscle is enclosed. The incision made with a #11 blade should be lateral to this area near the anterosuperior iliac spine.

Umbilical Extension

The 11-mm umbilical incision can be enlarged to remove benign decompressed ovaries or cysts, especially if the initial skin incision is vertical midline through the deepest part within the umbilicus. A 10-mm operating laparoscope is used with a scissors in the 5-mm operating channel. The tip of the laparoscope is placed 1 cm above the tip of the trocar sleeve, which is then carefully removed from the peritoneal cavity. Peritoneum is visualized and incised downward in the midline with the scissors in the operating channel. Next, deep fascia is identified and incised to add another 1 cm or more to the incision. Finally, the skin incision inside the umbilicus can be extended upward to incorporate the superior wall of the umbilical fossa. Compressible ovaries and cysts can be removed through this incision; this includes most benign cysts and normal ovaries removed for adhesive disease. The ovary is grasped with 5-mm biopsy forceps in the operating channel and partially delivered into the tip of the umbilical trocar sleeve. The trocar sleeve and laparoscope are popped out of the umbilicus in one motion, after which the protruding tissue is grasped with hemostats or Kocher clamps and gently teased out of the peritoneal cavity. Alternatively, a 5-mm laparoscope can be used for visualization through the 5-mm lower trocar sleeve, after which tissue to be removed is grasped with an 11-mm grasping forceps inserted through the umbilicus and extracted.

Laparoscopic Culdotomy

Solid and cystic ovaries separated intact from the pelvic sidewall are best removed through the cul-de-sac without spill into the peritoneal cavity. A posterior culdotomy incision using CO_2 laser or electrosurgery through the cul-de-sac of Douglas into the vagina is preferable to a colpotomy incision using scissors through the vagina and overlying peritoneum because complete hemostasis is obtained while making the culdotomy incision. Vaginal bleeding greater than 100 ml is usual before all cuff bleeding is stopped after scissors colpotomy.

The anatomic relationship between the rectum and the posterior vagina must be confirmed before making the laparoscopic culdotomy incision to avoid cutting the rectum. A curette is placed in the uterus for elevation and anteversion. A wet sponge in ring forceps is placed just behind the cervix to distend the posterior vaginal fornix. A rectal probe (Resnik Instruments, Skokie, IL) identifies the rectum's position and aids in the dissection required should rectum cover posterior vagina.

Alternatively, a uterine mobilizer (Valtchev, Conkin Surgical Instruments, Toronto, Canada, or Blairden, Kansas City, KS) is inserted to antevert the uterus and delineate the posterior vagina. When this device is in the anteverted position, the cervix sits on a wide acorn, making the cervico-vaginal junction readily visible between the uterosacral ligaments when the cul-de-sac is inspected laparoscopically.

Before the rectal probe is removed, it may be necessary to reflect the rectum off the posterior vagina using either scissors or the laparoscopic CO_2 laser at 10-W ultrapulse (Coherent, Palo Alto, CA). The rectal serosa at the junction of rectum with vagina, cervix, uterus, or fibrotic endometriosis is incised. The plane between rectum and attached viscera is developed using the aquadissector, and the rectum is pushed downward.

When it is clear that the rectum has been separated from the posterior vagina or vaginal apex if the uterus has been removed, the upper posterior vagina is distended with a wet sponge on ring forceps. A laparoscopic transverse culdotomy incision made with a spoon electrode at 150-W cutting current or the CO_2 laser at 50 to 100 W continuous avoids the bleeding that accompanies a vaginal colpotomy incision made with scissors. A laparoscopic CO_2 laser culdotomy incision is made at high power to obtain at large spot size (3 to 4 mm) for hemostatic cutting.[20] The sponge in the posterior vagina rapidly comes into view. A sudden loss of pneumoperitoneum and field of view may create the potential danger of grasping bowel with a sharp forceps inserted through the vagina after losing sight of the lesion to be extracted. Some difficulty may be encountered maintaining adequate pneumoperitoneum once the vagina is entered, but the sponge in contact with the incision and manual labial apposition is usually adequate for this purpose. After culdotomy, a sponge, pack, or 30-ml Foley balloon is kept in close contact with the vaginal incision to maintain pneumoperitoneum.

Laparoscopic biopsy forceps or ring forceps are inserted through the vagina to grasp the ovary or its attached tube and pull it through the culdotomy incision. Alternately, a 5-mm lower-quadrant grasping forceps can be used to push the intact mass through the culdotomy incision. On occasion, the operator's fingers can be inserted into the peritoneal cavity to grasp the ovary.

A larger cystic mass is aspirated vaginally, using a 14-gauge needle on a needle extension adapter (Crown Brothers, Decatur, GA) attached to a 50-ml syringe, until it is decompressed enough to be pulled through the culdotomy incision. If a dermoid is present, the mass can be incised so that the thick cyst contents drain into the vagina until the mass is small enough to be pulled through the incision.

Alternatively, after laparoscopic culdotomy, an impermeable sack (LapSac: Cook OB/GYN, Spencer, IN) is inserted into the peritoneal cavity through the vagina. These sacks with various sizes to 8-in. × 11-in. have a polyurethane inner coating and a nylon drawstring and are impermeable to water and dye. The free intact specimen is placed in the bag, which is closed by pulling the drawstring. The sac is delivered by the drawstring through the posterior vagina, the bag opened, and the intact specimen visually identified, decompressed, removed, and inspected.[3] Thereafter, the culdotomy incision is closed with size 2-0 Vicryl on a curved needle vaginally or laparoscopically.

Ovariolysis

Ovarian adhesions to the pelvic sidewall can be filmy or fused. The object of ovarian adhesiolysis is to preserve as much peritoneum and intact ovarian cortex as possible while freeing the ovary. If the adhesions are not obvious, dissection begins by using the aquadissector to develop potential spaces among the adhesions. Thereafter, laparoscopic scissors are used to divide the adhesions, usually taking very small bites and using traction on the ovary from the blunt scissors to elevate it. Dissection continues until the ovary is free to its hilum. On occasion, CO_2 laser is used to aid in the dissection of fused adhesions, especially if ureteral location is in doubt or the rectosigmoid is involved, as this laser causes minimal thermal damage deep to the operative site. Endometriomas usually drain spontaneously as the ovary is separated from the pelvic sidewall or uterosacral ligament.

Ovarian Cyst Aspiration

Aspiration, as an isolated procedure, is not recommended because it does not allow inspection of the cyst wall or removal of tissue for histologic evaluation. Drainage with a needle does not prevent spill and is performed for only the most benign-appearing cysts. Cytologic analysis of cyst fluid is associated with a high false-negative rate.[21] In most simple cyst cases, I favor cystectomy because this allows microscopic analysis of the cyst wall.

If a dermoid is encountered during syringe aspiration, cyst excision should be accomplished with as little spill as possible, often by placing a large impermeable sac around the ovary to collect the drainage during cyst dissection. Shelling out a dermoid from inside an ovary after drainage is usually easier than endometrioma cyst wall excision. Copious peritoneal cavity irrigation with at least 10 L of Ringer's lactate and underwater examination with direct suctioning of fatty and epidermal elements are recommended to prevent a chronic granulomatous reaction.[22]

De Wilde and colleagues[23] performed laparoscopic ovarian cystostomy with fenestration for functional cysts in 104 women with unilateral cysts of at least 6-cm diameter followed for 3 months. Histologically, the cysts were follicle cysts (58 percent) or luteal cysts (42 percent). There was an overall recurrence rate of 8 percent, although it was impossible to distinguish between a newly formed and a recurrent cyst. When pelvic adhesions were found at laparoscopy, the recurrence rate was 11 percent.[23] Others have reported aspiration to be associated with a recurrence rate approaching 30 percent.[21]

Cystectomy

Ovarian cysts are discovered during pelvic examination or vaginal ultrasound. If persistent, these cysts are surgically evaluated because of the small risk of malignancy. Laparotomy for benign cyst excision is inappropriate because of the increased risk of ovarian adhesions.[24]

Laparoscopic inspection of a suspected ovarian cyst may reveal a parovarian cyst, hydrosalpinx, inflammatory peritoneal pseudocyst, or a peritoneal pocket. Parovarian cysts are excised if large enough to disrupt ovum pickup. Pseudocysts require excision of pelvic adhesions. Hydrosalpinges are evaluated with salpingoscopy and excised or repaired. Peritoneal pockets are opened and their peritoneum excised.

The ovaries are evaluated for visual evidence of malignancy. All cysts should be smooth-walled and without excrescence. Cysts with translucent thin walls are usually functional. Most organic cysts have thick walls. All but the most benign-appearing cysts are removed intact through the cul-de-sac with or without an impermeable sac to avoid the potential risk of metastasis to the anterior abdominal wall.

All cysts opened during laparoscopic surgery, either intentionally or during mobilization of the cyst or ovary, require a careful examination of their inner walls. Cystectomy is preferable to puncture with biopsy to avoid recurrence of organic cysts.

Ovarian cystectomy for obvious functional cysts (simple cysts, follicle cysts, or corpus luteum cysts) is not a common laparoscopic procedure, and laparoscopic excision or *electrosurgical drainage* should be considered only when persistence of the cyst or pain is documented. Even an actively bleeding hemorrhagic corpus luteum cyst can be totally excised laparoscopically with minimal bleeding. Hemostasis without excision of a bleeding corpus luteum can be obtained using electrosurgical fulguration (with an electrode or the argon beam coagulator) or bipolar coagulation. Suture repair is sometimes indicated.

Simple cysts may be excised intact, drained with electrosurgery, or aspirated with a needle attached to a syringe after cul-de-sac washings have been obtained. After documentation of clear or hemosiderin-filled fluid, the ovarian cortex is opened at its most dependent portion with a knife electrode at 70-W cutting current and the cyst excised using biopsy forceps.

Enlarged ovaries containing cysts are either free in the peritoneal cavity or attached to the pelvic sidewall, uterosacral ligament, or cul-de-sac. When attached to the sidewall, the cyst frequently proves to be an endometrioma (Figs. 11-1 and 11-2). During mobilization of the cyst from the pelvic sidewall, chocolatelike hemosiderin-filled fluid will spill from the ovary (Fig. 11-3). When this occurs, the ovary is completely mobilized to its hilum using aquadissection and careful blunt dissection to avoid unnecessary pelvic sidewall peritoneal damage. The endometrioma cyst wall is then excised (Fig. 11-4). The cyst wall is usually fused to the ovarian cortex in the area of rupture during dissection or avulsion (i.e., on the portion that was adherent to the pelvic sidewall or uterosacral ligament). A knife electrode at 70-W cutting current is used at the juncture of ovarian cortex and endometrioma cyst wall to develop a dissection plane in this firmly attached area. If visible and accessible, this incision is extended through the 360 degree opening. The cutting current will destroy endometriosis at the ovarian cortex-endometrioma junction while making a divot of separation between the two structures. Thereafter, biopsy forceps are placed on ovarian cortex and endometrioma

cyst wall and traction exerted to peel the endometrioma cyst wall from the ovary[4] (Fig. 11-5). During dissection of cyst from cortex, much repositioning of the traction forceps is necessary close to the cleavage plane. Either cyst or ovarian cortex is stripped, depending on which is easier. Minimal bleeding accompanies this type of procedure and usually stops spontaneously. Hemostasis is checked by underwater examination inside the ovary, and individual bleeders are identified using irrigation and coagulated with microbipolar forceps. When the defect is large, the ovary is suture-repaired to approximate the edges of the ovary, usually with one purse-string suture, applied close to the uteroovarian ligament in one direction and the infundibulopelvic ligament in the other or with one or two interrupted sutures. In most cases, 3-0 Vicryl is used, and the knot is buried inside the ovary (Figs. 11-6 and 11-7).

If the ovary is free of the pelvic sidewall and viscera, a dermoid cyst or other benign neoplasm may be present. When a dermoid cyst is suspected, puncture drainage is avoided and an attempt is made to excise the cyst without spill.[25] A superficial incision is made in the cortex with CO_2 laser or scissors. The incision is extended with scissors and undermined with a combination of scissors and aquadissection. If it is a func-

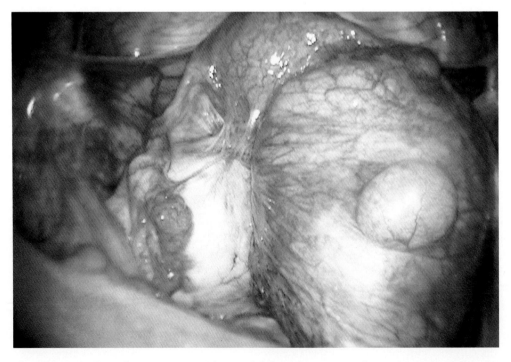

Fig. 11-1. Stage IV endometriosis is evident with bilateral ovarian endometriomas in patient desiring pelvic reconstruction.

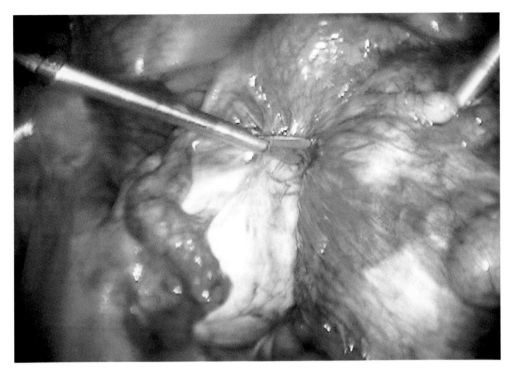

Fig. 11-2. Adhesions between ovaries, uterus, and bowel are divided with scissors.

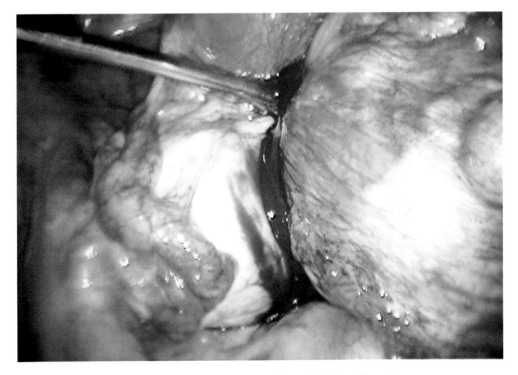

Fig. 11-3. Left endometrioma drained during dissection.

Fig. 11-4. After drainage, the left ovary was opened with a knife electrode and the endometrioma cyst wall excised.

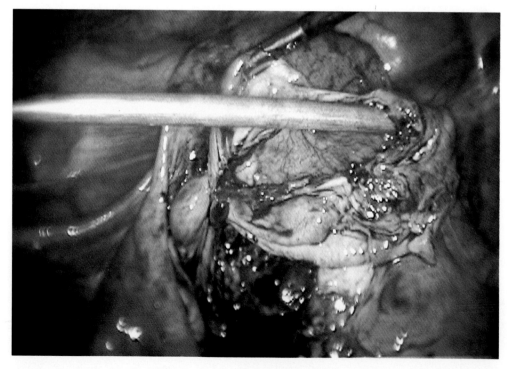

Fig. 11-5. Endometrioma cyst wall is well visualized during the end of its excision from inside the left ovary.

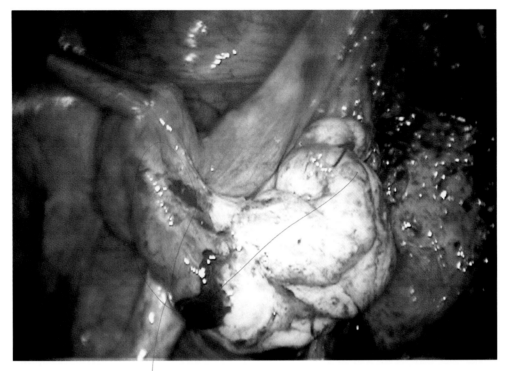

Fig. 11-6. Left ovary has been suture-repaired. Note that it is free of all surrounding structures.

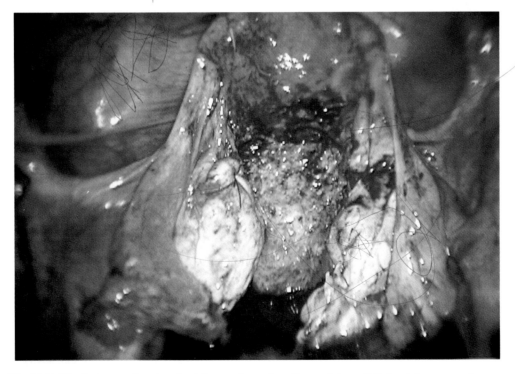

Fig. 11-7. Final picture showing the tubes and ovaries after excision of bilateral, large, ovarian endometriomas. The left ovary has been closed with a suture. Extensive endometriosis has been excised from the posterior uterus, cervix, vagina, and anterior rectum.

tional cyst (follicle cyst or corpus luteum), its thin wall will usually rupture spontaneously. If the cyst is neoplastic, it will rarely rupture, and cystectomy without spillage can be accomplished. After locating the cleavage plane between the cyst wall and the ovarian cortex, the cortex is held with a toothed forceps and an aquadissector is inserted to instill pressurized fluid to separate the dermoid cyst from surrounding ovarian tissue. Laser and scissors are used to separate fibrous adherences, and a well-defined vascular bundle is coagulated with microbipolar forceps. Caution is constantly exercised to prevent puncturing the cyst wall. After excision of the intact cyst from inside the ovary, individual bleeders are identified using irrigation and coagulated with microbipolar forceps or electrosurgical fulguration to obtain complete hemostasis. The ovarian edges usually reapproximate, and suturing is not required; large ovarian defects are suture-repaired. The cyst is removed through the cul-de-sac as previously described.[3]

Dermoid cysts involve both ovaries in 10 to 15 percent of women. In most cases, bilateral involvement, if present, will be evident on clinical examination. A normal opposite ovary with no identifiable tumor may be either left alone or cystic areas drained with the knife electrode.[26] Synchronous covert bilaterality of mature teratomas is not common, and a visually normal contralateral ovary should not be routinely bivalved or wedge-resected.

Oophorectomy

Laparoscopic oophorectomy was first reported by Semm and Mettler using a loop ligature and a tissue punch morcellator, and Reich using bipolar electrosurgical desiccation and culdotomy.[27–31] The indications for laparoscopic oophorectomy (or salpingo-oophorectomy) include pelvic pain secondary to ovarian adhesions from previous hysterectomy, pain from ovarian adhesions unresponsive to laparoscopic lysis, pelvic mass secondary to hydrosalpinx from pelvic inflammatory disease (PID) or previous surgery, and perimenopausal and postmenopausal ovarian cysts. In women not desiring future fertility, oophorectomy should be considered for pain or mass arising from ovarian endometrioma, hemorrhagic corpus luteum cyst, or dermoid cyst when the contralateral ovary is normal, especially if the cyst is on the left as this ovary frequently heals adhered to the rectosigmoid (Fig. 11-8). Postmenopausal cystic ovaries can be removed intact through a culdotomy. Women in families with two

or more first-degree relatives (mother or sister) with ovarian cancer can consider early prophylactic oophorectomy after age 35 years if childbearing has been completed. Women without a family history of ovarian cancer have a 1 in 70 risk of developing this disease. Stage I ovarian cancer may be treated by laparoscopic oophorectomy, hysterectomy, omentectomy, and lymphadenectomy in selected cases.[11,32]

Before starting oophorectomy, it is imperative that the surgeon visualize the course of the ureter. It crosses the external iliac artery near the bifurcation of the common iliac artery at the pelvic brim and is usually lower on the left, where its entrance into the pelvis is covered by the inverted V-shaped root of the sigmoid mesocolon. The peritoneum above the ureter may be opened with sharp scissors. Smooth grasping forceps are then opened parallel and perpendicular to the retroperitoneal structures until the ureter is identified. Scissors can be used to further dissect the ureter throughout its course along the pelvic sidewall.

Before removal, the ovary is released from all pelvic sidewall and bowel adhesions. Adhesions are divided and ovarian endometriomas drained, if present. The fallopian tube is grasped and pulled medially to stretch out the infundibulopelvic ligament containing the ovarian vessels. Scissors are used to incise the peritoneum on both sides of the ovarian vessels in the infundibulopelvic ligament and to spread the loose areolar tissue beneath them until a window is created through which 2-0 or 0 Vicryl sutures are applied to the skeletonized ovarian vessels with a stick tie.[12] Two ligatures are placed proximally and one distally for back-bleeding and the vessels divided with scissors. The uteroovarian ligament is similarly ligated either after skeletalization or by using a curved CT-1 needle, usually including the fallopian tube. The broad ligament is divided lateral to the vessels with a spoon electrode at 150-W cutting current (Figs. 11-9 to 11-13).

Alternatively, Kleppinger bipolar forceps are used to compress and desiccate the blood vessels in the infundibulopelvic ligament, the broad ligament, the fallopian tube isthmus, and the uteroovarian ligament with bipolar cutting current. In most cases, three contiguous areas are desiccated to coaptate or fuse the collagen fibers inside. Laparoscopic scissors divide the pedicle. In some cases, the mesovarium alone is desiccated and divided. Medial retraction with grasping forceps is helpful while the adnexa is being freed from the pelvic sidewall. The free ovary is removed through the umbilicus or cul-de-sac (Figs. 11-14 and 11-15).

Stapling devices are not used. When compared with suture and bipolar techniques, they are too expensive,

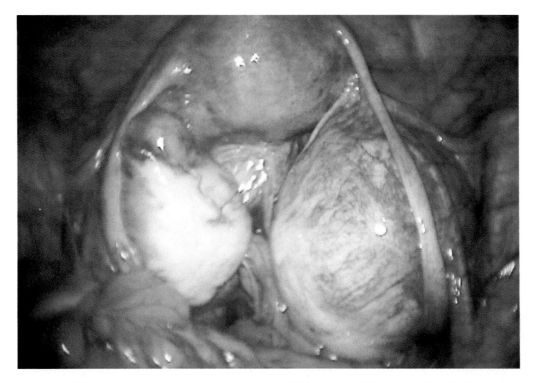

Fig. 11-8. Bilateral ovarian endometriomas are seen. Right ovary will be resected and left ovary retained after excision of endometrioma inside it.

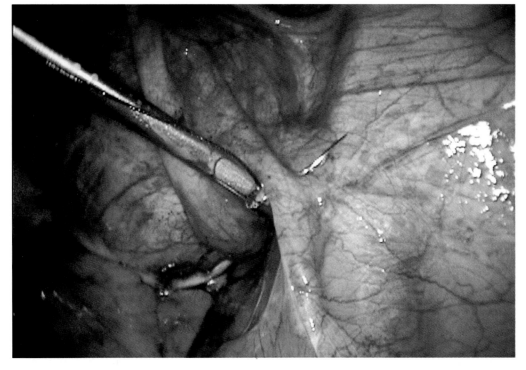

Fig. 11-9. Right infundibulopelvic ligament is suture-ligated using the Cook oblique curved needle holder and a CT-1 needle on 0 Vicryl.

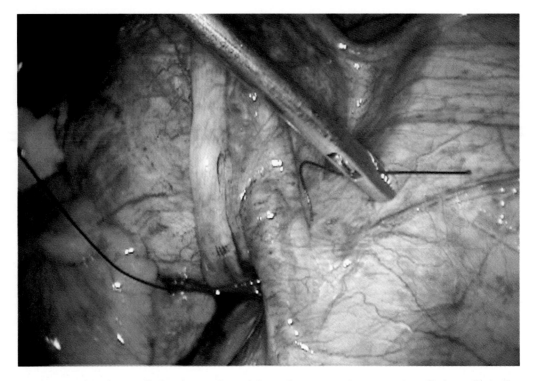

Fig. 11-10. After the needle has been released from the suture, the suture is pulled out through a trapless trocar sleeve.

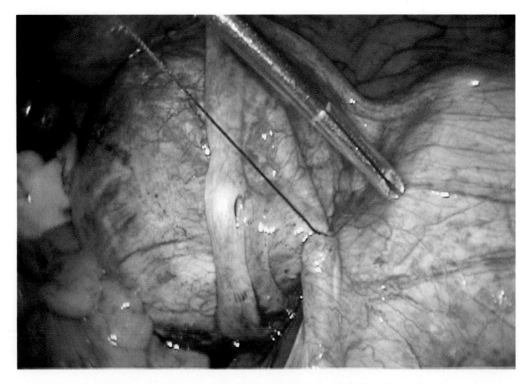

Fig. 11-11. Using the Clark knot-pusher, the pedicle is ligated.

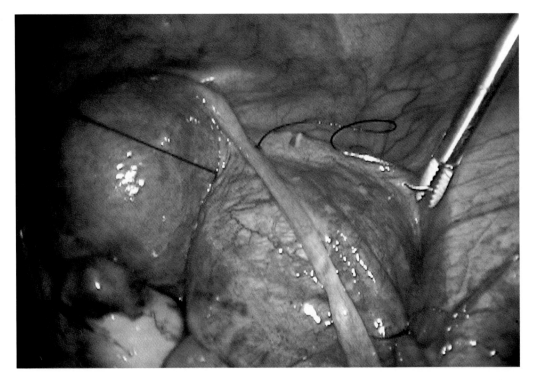

Fig. 11-12. Again suture is passed around the right uteroovarian ligament using 0 Vicryl on a CT-1 needle.

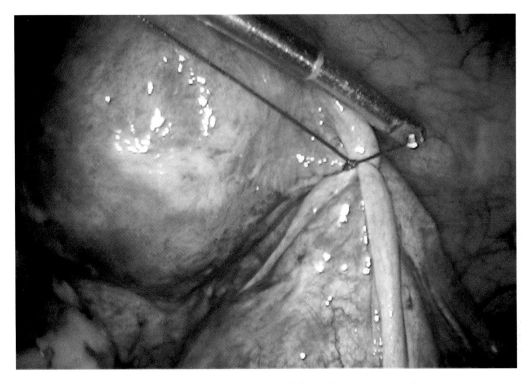

Fig. 11-13. The ligature is secured around the right uteroovarian ligament.

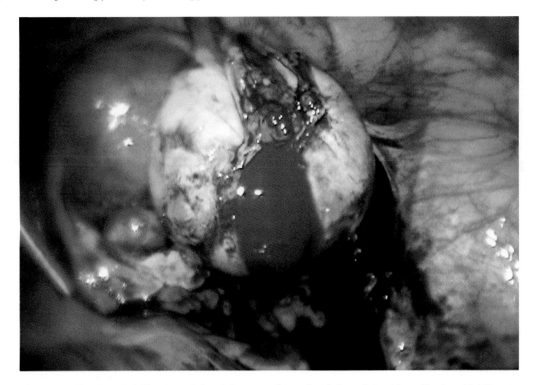

Fig. 11-14. During mobilization of the right ovary from the right pelvic sidewall, after dividing its blood supply, a small amount of hemosiderin-filled fluid drains.

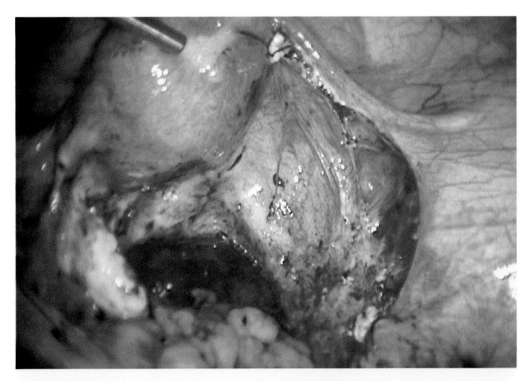

Fig. 11-15. At the end of the procedure, a clean right pelvic sidewall is seen, as is a small left ovary after removing the endometrioma that was inside it. Extensive retrocervical endometriosis was also removed during this procedure from the anterior rectum and posterior vagina.

lack precision, and may not completely seal the ovarian vessels, with resultant delayed hematoma formation.

Retroperitoneal Approach

When the ovary or ovarian remnant is fused to or within the pelvic sidewall peritoneum, a retroperitoneal approach for oophorectomy is considered. An ovarian remnant may occur after a difficult oophorectomy in cases involving extensive endometriosis or adhesions especially when the patient has undergone multiple previous surgeries. It should be considered as the cause of persistent pelvic pain after total abdominal hysterectomy with bilateral salpingo-oophorectomy, especially if the hysterectomy was performed for extensive ovarian adhesions or endometriosis.[33,34]

Scissors are used to incise the peritoneum lateral to the infundibulopelvic ligament, progressing parallel to the tube and ovary up to the uterine end of the round ligament. With medial traction on the tube, ovary, or peritoneum, the retroperitoneal space is entered and its loose areolar tissue dissected bluntly with scissors until the ureter is identified, usually attached to the sidewall peritoneum and often to the ovary if retroperitoneal. A window is made in the peritoneum medial to the ovarian vessels and a 2-0 Vicryl suture on a grasper passed through this window and around the vessel, the end pulled out through the trapless sleeve, and the knot secured using the knot-pusher. Alternatively, the ovarian vessels are desiccated just caudad to where they cross over the iliac vessels. After division of the infundibulopelvic ligament, its cut edge is placed on traction and the procedure continues caudad with division of the fibrous adhesions from the ovary to the ureter and rectosigmoid and the peritoneum just below its ovarian attachments and lateral to its rectosigmoid attachments. Finally, the utero-ovarian ligament and proximal fallopian tube are desiccated or ligated and divided, freeing the specimen. Bipolar desiccation of this ligament is performed most safely by inserting the forceps from the opposite side of the pelvis. The peritoneal sidewall defect is not closed.

In difficult cases involving the left side, dissection should start well out of the pelvis where descending colon meets sigmoid colon. The lateral attachments of this junction in the paracolic gutter are divided and the descending colon/rectosigmoid junction reflected medially. Further dissection and reflection are necessary until the external iliac artery is exposed. Going along this large vessel, the ureter is identified and in most cases the ovarian vessel pedicle can be lifted just lateral to the ureter as it crosses the external iliac artery. Both are followed into the deep pelvis with careful dissection. The rectosigmoid is carefully reflected from the deeper ureter and the ovarian vessel pedicle, which lies above until the ovarian remnant is identified. Once rectosigmoid is completely detached from the sidewall, ureteral dissection proceeds deeper into the pelvis, just beyond all attachments to the remnant. Thereafter, the ovarian vessel pedicle is ligated or desiccated with bipolar forceps, divided, and put on medial traction to further expose the lateral limits of the ovary attached to retroperitoneal structures, usually the superior vesicle and obturator vessels. Dissection continues until the ovary is completely freed from the pelvic sidewall. Bleeding from neovascularization is controlled with the microbipolar forceps, after the vessel is precisely located by irrigation. The ovarian remnant is removed from the peritoneal cavity through the umbilical incision.

In my experience with 20 patients with ovarian remnant treated laparoscopically, the ureter was contiguous with the ovarian remnant in all cases. Sixteen were left-sided and completely covered by the rectosigmoid in a retroperitoneal position. The four right-sided remnants were also retroperitoneal, with the rectosigmoid involved in two cases.[35]

Acute Adnexal Torsion

Adnexal torsion is a rare cause of acute pelvic pain. Although torsion occurs most frequently if there is an adnexal lesion, healthy organs can twist.[36] The event can occur in the gravid or nongravid woman. Classically, management has been by laparotomy, with excision of the afflicted organ without untwisting the pedicle. The rationale for this approach is to avoid the risk of embolization from the occluded ovarian venous plexus.[37]

Recently, it has been suggested that ovarian preservation can be achieved if early diagnosis is made before irreparable adnexal ischemia and the pedicle is simply untwisted.[6,38] The torsed adnexa are untwisted using a blunt probe or aquadissector and grasping forceps. After complete unraveling of the tube and ovary, often involving multiple turns, the affected adnexa is observed to ensure viability of the involved structures usually while additional surgical procedures are performed. No special precautions are taken in pregnant patients other than avoiding the placement of an intrauterine manipulator. Early recourse to laparoscopy permits accurate diagnosis and effective, safe ovarian conservation while limiting hospital stay and hence cost.

Tubo-Ovarian Abscess

The goals of managing acute tubo-ovarian abscess are prevention of infertility and the chronic sequela of infection including pelvic adhesions, hydrosalpinx, and pain, each of which may lead to further surgical intervention. The combination of laparoscopic treatment and effective intravenous antibiotics is a reasonable approach to the treatment of the total spectrum of PID, from acute salpingitis to ruptured tubo-ovarian abscess. Laparoscopic treatment is effective and economical. It offers the surgeon 100 percent accuracy of diagnosis, including the extent of tubo-ovarian involvement, while simultaneously accomplishing definitive treatment with a low complication rate. This approach allows tubo-ovarian conservation with subsequent fertility potential.

A woman presenting with lower abdominal pain and a palpable or possible pelvic mass should be laparoscoped to determine the true diagnosis. The diagnosis of tubo-ovarian abscess is suspected in a woman with a recent or prior history of PID who has persistent pain and pelvic tenderness on examination. Fever and leukocytosis may not be present. Ultrasound examination frequently documents a tubo-ovarian complex or abscess. The importance of laparoscopy cannot be overstated: even "obvious abscesses" may prove to be endometriomas, hemorrhagic corpus luteum cysts, or the result or a ruptured appendix. After presumptive diagnosis, hospitalization is arranged either on the day of diagnosis or the following morning, with laparoscopy soon thereafter.

Intravenous antibiotics are initiated on admission, usually a few hours before laparoscopy, to gain adequate blood levels to combat transperitoneal absorption during the procedure. Cefoxitin 2 g IV q4h is frequently used from admission until discharge. Oral doxycycline is started on the first postoperative day and continued for 10 days after hospital discharge on postoperative day 1 or 2. A single 1-g oral dose of azithromycin is given postoperatively, resulting in significant levels that are active against chlamydia infection persisting for 1 week or more in most tissues, including the endometrium and fallopian tubes.

At laparoscopy, either a blunt probe or an aquadissector is used to mobilize omentum, small bowel, rectosigmoid, and tubo-ovarian adhesions until the abscess cavity is entered. Purulent fluid is aspirated and inflammatory exudate excised with biopsy forceps. Afterward, aquadissection is performed by placing the tip of the aquadissector against the adhesive interface between bowel-adnexa, tube-ovary, or adnexa-pelvic sidewall to develop a dissection plane that can be extended either bluntly or with more fluid pressure. When the dissection is completed, the abscess cavity (necrotic inflammatory exudate) is excised in pieces using a 5-mm biopsy forceps.[39–41]

The importance of peritoneal lavage cannot be overemphasized. The peritoneal cavity is extensively irrigated with Ringer's lactate solution until the effluent is clear per underwater examination. The total volume of irrigant often exceeds 20 L. At the close of each procedure, at least 2 L of Ringer's lactate is left in the peritoneal cavity.

Polycystic Ovaries

Surgical treatment of polycystic ovarian disease by laparotomy (ovarian wedge resection) is no longer performed; a high incidence of ovarian adhesions resulted from these procedures as documented by second-look laparoscopy.[24,42] Recently, polycystic ovaries have been drilled laparoscopically using electrosurgery or laser.[43,44]

Polycystic/sclerocystic ovaries are usually enlarged with a smooth thickened capsule and without evidence of ovulatory stigma. Many 2- to 6-mm subcapsular follicular cysts are present with surrounding hyperplasia of the theca interna (stromal hyperthecosis). After diagnosis by endocrine studies and vaginal ultrasound, women desiring present fertility should be treated with clomiphene citrate (CC), alone or in combination with dexamethasone, and if resistant, CC-human chorionic gonadotropin. When CC does not work, the patient is given the option of treatment with menotropins (Pergonal) or laparoscopic multiple cyst puncture.

At laparoscopy, multiple symmetrically placed holes are drilled over subcapsular follicle cysts and into the stroma. Small polycystic ovarian cysts do not bleed like physiologic follicle cysts after incision. Although studies have not been performed to determine the actual depth of penetration into the stroma using the various energy sources, cutting current electrosurgery at 30 to 60 W makes a precise focal incision extending into the stroma and more than 30 such incisions can be placed in each ovary. When using CO_2 or contact tip lasers, the surface puncture is much larger, limiting the number of cysts that can be drained and increasing the surface thermal necrosis, which may result in later adhesion formation. Depth of penetration may be important in this procedure to destroy functioning theca surrounding the small ovarian follicles. Cutting current electrosurgery penetrates deeply on its way back to the large return electrode. CO_2 laser energy vaporizes very superficially and may not destroy much stroma.

Laparoscopic drilling of polycystic ovaries is, at best, a temporary solution. Normal ovulatory cycles may result for a short time. Concern remains regarding the possibility of ovarian adhesions or premature menopause from thermal damage. Care should be taken to avoid ovarian disruption close to the tubo-ovarian ligament to preserve tubal fimbrial freedom.

De novo adhesion formation after this procedure has been described. The reported relative incidence ranges from 3 to 85 percent.[45,46] The degree of adhesion formation is significantly less than that after laparotomy ovarian wedge resection. Irregardless, it is concerning that some degree of adhesion formation has been documented. These recent studies, although limited in terms of sample size, serve as an important reminder that surgical intervention of any kind can create as well as correct gynecologic pathology.

Closure

At the close of each operation, an underwater examination is used to document complete intraperitoneal hemostasis in stages; this detects bleeding from vessels and viscera tamponaded during the procedure by the increased intraperitoneal pressure of the CO_2 pneumoperitoneum. The CO_2 pneumoperitoneum is discontinued and displaced with 2 to 5 L of Ringer's lactate solution, and the peritoneal cavity is vigorously irrigated and suctioned with this solution until the effluent is clear of blood products, usually after 10 L. Underwater inspection of the pelvis is performed to detect any further bleeding, which is controlled using microbipolar forceps to coagulate through the electrolyte solution.[2]

First, complete hemostasis is established with the patient in the Trendelenburg position. Next, complete hemostasis is secured per underwater examination with the patient supine and in reverse Trendelenburg position. Finally, complete hemostasis is documented with all instruments removed, including the uterine manipulator.

To visualize the pelvis with the patient supine, the 10-mm straight laparoscope and the actively irrigating aquadissector tip are manipulated together into the deep cul-de-sac beneath floating bowel and omentum. During this copious irrigation procedure, clear fluid is deposited into the pelvis and circulates into the upper abdomen, displacing upper abdominal bloody fluid, which is suctioned after flowing back into the pelvis.

The underwater examination is then performed to observe the separated tubes and ovaries and to confirm complete hemostasis.

A final copious lavage with Ringer's lactate solution is undertaken and all clot directly aspirated; at least 2 L of Ringer's lactate solution is left in the peritoneal cavity to displace CO_2 and to prevent fibrin adherences from forming by separating raw operated-on surfaces during the initial stages of reperitonealization. Displacement of the CO_2 with Ringer's lactate diminishes the frequency and severity of shoulder pain from CO_2 insufflation. No other antiadhesive agents are used. No drains, antibiotic solutions, or heparin are used. The Ringer's lactate solution is absorbed in 2 to 3 days.[47]

A recent study found that Ringer's lactate was superior to Gore-tex and Interceed in adhesion prevention.[48] Adhesion prevention regimens that are more expensive than Ringer's lactate solution should be used only at centers doing clinical research. I believe that adhesion reduction requires minimal thermal damage to tissue, absolute hemostasis, clot evacuation, copious irrigation to dilute fibrin and prostaglandins arising from operated surfaces and bacteria, and leaving 2 to 3 L of Ringer's lactate in the peritoneal cavity at the end of each operation to physically separate normal and compromised structures. As Dr. Jaroslav Hulka said in 1988, "Reich's solution to pollution is dilution," and that opinion has not changed.

The umbilical incision is closed with a single size 4-0 Vicryl suture opposing deep fascia and skin dermis. The knot is buried beneath the fascia.

The culdotomy incision is closed from below or laparoscopically with interrupted, figure-of-eight, or running size 0 Vicryl suture. Vaginal suturing is aided by the use of a lateral vaginal retractor used to spread the lateral vagina adjacent to the culdotomy incision (Euro-Med, Redmond, WA; Simpson/Basye, Wilmington, DE). This device is self-retaining, with a thumb-ratchet release that keeps it open and in place. Vaginal suturing can be difficult as the vaginal incision frequently becomes edematous during the procedure, making exposure inadequate. Thus, the surgeon may elect to close the culdotomy incision from above, using curved needle sutures (Vicryl on a CT-2) tied extracorporeally with the Clarke knot-pusher.[15]

POSTOPERATIVE MANAGEMENT

After observation in the recovery room, the patient is transferred to the Short Stay Unit. Diet is as tolerated. Torodol or Anaprox DS is used for pain. Postoperative pelvic pain is less in desiccated pedicles; an endolooped pedicle leaves living cells distal to the loop to necrose and release lysozymes. Vistaril 50 mg intramuscularly is used for nausea and vomiting. The Foley catheter is removed when the patient is alert or aware of the catheter, and bethanechol chloride (Urecholine) 25 mg orally is then given. If no antibiotic was administered in the operating room, Septra DS is given before discharge. If spontaneous voiding of approximately 250 ml does not occur within 4 hours of catheter removal, the patient is straight cathed and administered 50 mg Urecholine. Should voiding in good quantities not occur over the next 3 hours, the patient is admitted overnight with the Foley catheter in place to be removed in the morning.

After voiding, the patient is usually discharged with Anaprox DS as the only pain medication. Because of the large amount of Ringer's lactate irrigant left in the peritoneal cavity, patients commonly ooze from their lower-quadrant 5-mm incision sites, which have been covered with Collodion without suture. This oozing of fluid ceases within 24 hours, but many patients are discharged with Chux nonwoven disposable underpads or a towel inside their undergarments.

Criteria for Patient Discharge

In most cases, the decision for discharge is made by the patient and her family. If she is awake and alert with minimal discomfort, she may leave the hospital for home or a nearby hotel on the day of the procedure. Patients undergoing laparoscopic cystectomy or oophorectomy will be discharged the same day in 85 percent of cases.

Complications Specific for This Procedure

Bipolar desiccation and suture ligation of ovarian and uteroovarian vessels have been safe methods of ligation in my experience. Postoperative pain is less after electrodesiccation than suture ligation, as electrosurgical desiccation eliminates distal ischaemic necrosis. There have been no late bleeding episodes in more than 1,000 cystectomies and 500 oophorectomies performed in this manner.

Ureteral injury occurs in approximately 0.5 to 1 percent of pelvic operations.[49] The laparoscopic surgeon must rely almost entirely on visual recognition to identify normal structures in the abdomen and pelvis. Nowhere does this create more difficulties than with identification of the ureter. When open abdominal oophorectomy is performed for benign pathology, the ureters can be palpated in the broad ligament and avoided as the infundibulopelvic ligaments or adnexa

are clamped. This option is not available to the laparoscopic surgeon, and the ureter has to be identified and often partly mobilized to make many laparoscopic operations safe. Ureteral identification and often isolation should be an integral part of laparoscopic oophorectomy procedures, and bulky staplers should rarely be used for ovarian vessel ligation. The risk of ureteral injury during laparoscopic hysterectomy using the Endo-GIA is well documented.[50,51]

Although culdotomy surgery offers an opportunity for invasion by organisms already present in the genital tract, the use of an electrosurgical or laser incision, aspiration of all blood clots, and copious irrigation with more than 2 L of irrigant left in the peritoneal cavity at the close of the procedure eliminates the environment necessary for proliferation of these organisms. Pelvic cellulitis and postoperative sepsis with laparoscopic culdotomy using these techniques have not been reported.

CONCLUSION

Most ovarian surgery can be performed using a laparoscopic approach. Anticipation of continued advances in technique, instrumentation, and video magnification and definition will further expand surgical possibilities. No longer can the surgeon or the consumer ignore the benefits of minimally invasive surgery. Although these techniques and procedures are not without risk, to deny their inherent advantages is impossible. In 1995, the onus should be on the gynecologic surgeon to prove that laparotomy results in better outcome than laparoscopy, not vice versa. Minimally invasive surgery is the future, and astute clinicians will work together to discern the most appropriate uses for this therapy.

Both laparoscopic and laparotomy surgery can be time-consuming and technically difficult and are best performed by an expert surgeon. However, most women after laparoscopic procedures avoid major abdominal incisions, are discharged on the day of the procedure on nonsteroidal anti-inflammatory medication, return to full activity within 1 week of surgery, and experience minimal complications.

REFERENCES

1. Parker W, Berek J: Management of the adnexal mass by operative laparoscopy. Clin Obstet Gynecol 36:413, 1993
2. Reich H: New techniques in advanced laparoscopic surgery. p. 655. In C Sutton (ed): Laparoscopic Surgery. Bailliere's Clinical Obstetrics and Gynaecology. WB Saunders, London, 1989

3. Reich H, McGlynn F, Sekel L, Taylor P: Laparoscopic management of ovarian dermoid cysts. J Reprod Med 37:640, 1992

4. Reich H, McGlynn F: Treatment of ovarian endometriomas using laparoscopic surgical techniques. J Reprod Med 31:577, 1986

5. The use of potassium-titanyl-phosphate laser for laparoscopic removal of ovarian endometrioma. Am J Obstet Gynecol 164:1622, 1991

6. Reich H, DeCaprio J, McGlynn F, Taylor PJ: Laparoscopic diagnosis and management of acute adnexal torsion. Gynaecol Endosc 2:37, 1992

7. Maiman M, Seltzer V, Boyce J: Laparoscopic excision of ovarian neoplasms subsequently found to be malignant. Obstet Gynecol 77:563, 1991

8. Dembo A, Davy M, Stenwig A et al: Prognostic factors in patients with stage I epithelial ovarian cancer. Obstet Gynecol 75:263, 1990

9. Parker WH, Berek JS: Management of selected cystic adnexal masses in postmenopausal women by operative laparoscopy: a pilot study. Am J Obstet Gynecol 163:1574, 1990

10. Mann W, Reich H: Laparoscopic adnexectomy in postmenopausal women. J Reprod Med 37:254, 1992

11. Reich H, McGlynn F, Wilkie W: Laparoscopic management of stage I ovarian cancer. J Reprod Med 35:601, 1990

12. Reich H: Aquadissection. p. 159. In M Baggish (ed): Laser Endoscopy. The Clinical Practice of Gynecology series. Vol. 2. Elsevier, New York, 1990

13. Reich H, McGlynn F: Short self-retaining trocar sleeves. Am J Obstet Gynecol 162:453, 1990

14. Clarke HC: Laparoscopy—new instruments for suturing and ligation. Fertil Steril 23:274, 1972

15. Reich H, Clarke HC, Sekel L: A simple method for ligating in operative laparoscopy with straight and curved needles. Obstet Gynecol 79:143, 1992

16. Neiman H, Mendelson E: Ultrasound evaluation of the ovary. p. 423. In Callen P (ed): Ultrasonography in Obstetrics and Gynecology. WB Saunders, Philadelphia, 1988

17. Granberg S, Norstrom A, Wikland M: Tumors in the lower pelvis as imaged by vaginal sonography. Gynecol Oncol 37:224, 1990

18. Vasilev S, Schlaerth J, Campeau J et al: Serum CA-125 levels in preoperative evaluation of pelvic masses. Obstet Gynecol 71:751, 1988

19. Finkler N, Benacerrat B, Lavin F et al: Comparison of serum CA 125, clinical impression, and ultrasound in the preoperative evaluation of ovarian masses. Obstet Gynecol 72:659, 1988

20. Reich H, MacGregor TS, Vancaillie TG: CO_2 laser used through the operating channel of laser laparoscopes: in vitro study of power and power density losses. Obstet Gynecol 77:40, 1991

21. Kjellgren O, Angstrom T, Bergman F et al: Fine needle aspiration biopsy in diagnosis and classification of ovarian carcinoma. Cancer 28:967, 1971

22. Kistner RW: Intraperitoneal rupture of benign cystic teratomas: review of the literature with a report of two cases. Obstet Gynecol Surv 7:603, 1952

23. De Wilde R, Bordt J, Hesseling M, Vancaillie T: Ovarian cystostomy. Acta Obstet Gynecol Scand 68:363, 1989

24. Eddy CA, Asch RH, Balmaceda JP: Pelvic adhesions following microsurgical and macrosurgical wedge resection of the ovaries. Fertil Steril 33:5,557, 1980; Fertil Steril 56:1176, 1991

25. Reich H: New techniques in advanced laparoscopic surgery. p. 655. In Sutton C (ed): Bailliere's Clinical Obstetrics and Gynecology. Vol. 3. Harcourt Brace Janovich, New York, 1989

26. Doss N, Forney P, Vellios F, Nalick R: Covert bilaterality of mature ovarian teratomas. Obstet Gynecol 50:651, 1977

27. Semm K, Mettler L: Technical progress in pelvic surgery via operative laparoscopy. Am J Obstet Gynecol 138:121, 1980

28. Reich H, McGlynn F: Laparoscopic oophorectomy and salpingo-oophorectomy in the treatment of benign tuboovarian disease. J Reprod Med 31:609, 1986

29. Reich H: Laparoscopic oophorectomy and salpingo-oophorectomy in the treatment of benign tubo-ovarian disease. Int J Fertil 32:233, 1987

30. Reich H: Laparoscopic oophorectomy without ligature or morcellation. Contemp Obstet Gynecol 9:34, 1989

31. Reich H, Johns DA, Davis G, Diamond MP: Laparoscopic oophorectomy. J Reprod Med 38:497, 1993

32. Querleu D, Leblanc E, Castelain B: Laparoscopic pelvic lymphadenectomy in the staging of early carcinoma of the cervix. Am J Obstet Gynecol 164:579, 1991

33. Price FV, Edwards R, Buchsbaum HJ: Ovarian remnant syndrome: difficulties in diagnosis and management. Obstet Gynecol Surv 45:151, 1990

34. Reich H: Pelvic sidewall dissection. p. 245. In Hulka J, Reich H, (eds): Textbook of Laparoscopy. 2nd Ed. WB Saunders, New York, 1994

35. Reich H: Pelvic sidewall dissection. p. 419. In Diamond M (ed): Clinical Obstetrics and Gynecology. Vol. 34. JB Lippincott, Philadelphia, 1991

36. Hibbard LT: Adnexal torsion. Am J Obstet Gynecol 152:456, 1985

37. Jeffcoate N: Torsion of the pelvic organs. p. 280. In: Principles of Gynecology. Butterworth, London, 1975

38. Mage G, Canis M, Mahnes H et al: Laparoscopic management of adnexal torsion. J Reprod Med 34:52, 1982

39. Henry-Suchet J, Soler A, Lofferdo V: Laparoscopic treatment of tubo-ovarian abscesses. J Reprod Med 29:579, 1984

40. Reich H, McGlynn F: Laparoscopic treatment of tubo-ovarian and pelvic abscess. J Reprod Med 32:747, 1987

41. Reich H: Endoscopic management of tuboovarian abscess and pelvic inflammatory disease. p. 118. In Sanfilippo JS, Levine RL (eds): Operative Gynecologic Endoscopy. Springer-Verlag, New York, 1989

42. Toaff R, Toaff MR, Peyser MR: Infertility following wedge resection of the ovaries. Am J Obstet Gynecol 124:92, 1976

43. Gjönnaess H: Polycystic ovarian syndrome treated by ovarian electrocautery through the laparoscope. Fertil Steril 41:20, 1984

44. Daniell JF, Miller W: Polycystic ovaries treated by laparoscopic laser vaporization. Fertil Steril 51:232, 1989

45. Gurgan T, Kisnisci H, Yarali H et al: Evaluation of adhesion formation after laparoscopic treatment of polycystic ovarian disease. Fertil Steril 56:1176, 1991

46. Dabirashrafi H, Mohamad K, Behjatnia Y, Moghadam-Tabrizi N: Adhesion formation after ovarian electrocauterization on patients with polycystic ovarian syndrome. Fertil Steril 55:1200, 1991

47. Rose BI, MacNeill C, Larrain R, Kopreski MM: Abdominal instillation of high-molecular-weight Dextran or lactated Ringer's solution after laparoscopic surgery: a randomized comparison of the effect on weight change. J Reprod Med 36:537, 1991

48. Pagidas K, Tulandi T: Effects of Ringer's lactate, Interceed (TC7) and Gore-Tex Surgical Membrane on postsurgical adhesion formation. Fertil Steril 57:199, 1992

49. Daly J, Higgins KA, Kirk A: Injury to the ureter during gynecologic surgical procedures. Surg Gynecol Obstet 167:19, 1988

50. Woodland MB: Ureter injury during laparoscopy-assisted vaginal hysterectomy with the endoscopic linear stapler. Am J Obstet Gynecol 167:756, 1992

51. Alderman B: Letter to the editor: ureteric injury. Gynaecol Endosc 2:186, 1993

12 Laparoscopic Myomectomy

HARRITH M. HASSON

Leiomyomas are the most common indication for hysterectomy in the United States. Between 1988 and 1990, 570,000 procedures were performed for leiomyomas, which accounted for one-third of all hysterectomies.[1] Another 33,000 abdominal myomectomy procedures were performed in the United States in 1988.[2] Given such a frequency, any change in the operative approach of treating leiomyoma, from standard laparotomy to operative laparoscopy, may have a significant impact on the quality of life of the patients who are treated. When compared with standard laparotomy, operative laparoscopy appears to offer several potential advantages:

1. Less trauma to the abdominal wall
   In laparotomy, a large incision is cut and retracted mechanically to permit exposure of the operative field. In laparoscopy, access is accomplished through several small incisions.
2. Less trauma to the abdominal viscera
   a. In laparotomy, the bowel is packed away by surgical sponges and pressured by metal retractors. This is not the case in laparoscopy, in which exposure is obtained through tension of the distending gas bubble, the Trendelenburg position, and occasional manipulation with probes.
   b. Because operative laparoscopy is performed with a substantially intact abdominal wall, the viscera are not dried out by exposure to room air or manipulated grossly by the human hand as is the case with laparotomy.
3. Less operative bleeding
   a. Unlike standard laparotomy, the use of operative video laparoscopy is associated with a degree of magnification that permits precise microsurgical dissection of tissue planes and accurate identification of intact blood vessels. This feature facilitates occlusion of the vessels before they are cut.
   b. Operative laparoscopy is also associated with a certain degree of intra-abdominal pressure that compresses

veins and minimizes venous bleeding if such vessels are cut before they are occluded.

Documentation of the operative procedure, which is readily available only in operative laparoscopy, is beneficial. It offers laparoscopic surgeons the opportunity to analyze and improve their technique. It helps the patients understand what was done, and it facilitates objective follow-up.

In fact, in my experience, the advantages of laparoscopic myomectomy have been reflected in reduced intra- and postoperative morbidity, shorter hospital stay and recovery time, earlier return to normal activities, fewer postoperative adhesions, better cosmetic scars, and improved documentation as compared with traditional abdominal myomectomy.[3–5] However, currently the role of laparoscopy in the management of uterine leiomyomas remains controversial. A recent technical bulletin issued by the American College of Obstetricians and Gynecologists on the subject of uterine leiomyomata mentioned laparoscopic myomectomy only briefly, expressed reservations, and stated that the procedure should be regarded as investigational.[6] This attitude underscores the following concerns:

1. Fear of intraoperative complications (especially hemorrhage) and technical difficulties
2. Apprehension concerning the ultimate status of the uterine scar (in cases of intramural tumors)
3. Uncertainty about the extent of postoperative adhesions
4. Doubt concerning the reproductive outcome and operative efficiency relative to relief of symptoms, recurrence, and re-operation

It also indicates that perhaps the technique of laparoscopic myomectomy, as practiced by others, does not follow the basic surgical principles that we adhere to to optimize safety and efficacy of the procedure.

INDICATIONS

Myomectomy by laparoscopy is indicated if the lesion is associated with one or more of the following:

1. Infertility, including recurrent abortion, with or without associated factors
2. Bleeding, pain, and pressure symptoms of significant nature and duration
   a. in patients who want to conceive
   b. in patients who want to maintain childbearing potential
   c. in patients who want to preserve their uterus for other reasons
3. Pelvic mass with
   a. a uterine size greater than 12 gestational weeks
   b. a dominant myoma greater than 7 cm
   c. a rapidly growing tumor

CONTRAINDICATIONS

Laparoscopic myomectomy is contraindicated under the following circumstances:

1. The medical condition of the patient makes it inadvisable to maintain the Trendelenburg position with the abdomen distended with gas for a long period of time.
2. The size of the uterus is greater than 18 gestational weeks, or the size of the dominant myoma is greater than 15 cm.
3. The patient has advanced disease with diffuse leiomyomatosis or more than six significant myomas 3 cm or larger.
4. The patient has a submucous myoma that protrudes more than 50 percent into the endometrial cavity.

PREOPERATIVE ASSESSMENT

The diagnosis of leiomyoma is usually made by pelvic examination and confirmed by ultrasound. Ultrasound is not accurate in patients who have marked uterine enlargement or submucous lesions,[7] congenital uterine anomalies,[8] or excessive obesity.[9] Magnetic resonance imaging (MRI) appears to be more reliable in localizing the position of lesions, predicting their number, and detecting degenerative changes within the lesions.[7] It has been used successfully to differentiate between leiomyomas and adenomyosis.[10] However, MRI is not cost-effective for most patients. The endometrial cavity has to be evaluated with hysteroscopy, ultrasound or hysterosalpingography (HSG) and sampled as indicated.

PREOPERATIVE PREPARATION

Preoperative medical therapy is usually limited to patients with leiomyomas larger than 6 cm. At this time, gonadotropic-releasing hormone agonists (GnRH-a) and their more potent analogs have effectively replaced earlier drugs including Danazol and Progestins. Medical treatment with GnRH-a is used to reduce the volume and vascularity of myomas and the host uterus, relieve associated symptoms, reduce intraoperative blood loss, and facilitate removal of the tumor masses during laparoscopic surgery. Shrinkage of the uterine volume was reported to have a mean of 36 percent at 12 weeks and 45 percent at 24 weeks[4,11] and a range of 35 to 57 percent.[12] This is accomplished primarily by inducing an anovulatory hypoestrogenic state. However, GnRH-a may have an additional inhibitory role on the growth of leiomyomas through direct action on specific GnRH binding sites in the tumors.[13]

The induced hypoestrogenic state has several unpleasant side effects including vasomotor flushes, insomnia, mood changes, headache, and vaginal dryness.[11,12] A larger concern relates to the potential of trabecular bone loss with long-term administration. Therefore, the administration of preoperative GnRH-a therapy is limited to 6 months, especially because it has been shown that near-maximal benefits are achieved by 12 weeks.[11] The primary inhibitory effect of GnRH-a on myomatous tissue as well as the reduced blood supply to the tumor that is secondary to the hypoestrogenic state may cause intense degenerative changes in larger myomas. This may lead to difficult enucleation of affected tumors during laparoscopic myomectomy.

Patients who undergo laparoscopic myomectomy receive cleansing enemas or a Golytely bowel preparation. Prophylactic antibiotics are also routinely given.

BASIC SURGICAL PRINCIPLES

1. *Work inside the pseudocapsule:* Incise the myometrium that covers the myoma with any energy source and proceed to enucleate the tumor from within its pseudocapsule. Perform all dissections inside the pseudocapsule of the myoma. Do not resect the myoma en mass with surrounding myometrium because this will invariably cause bleeding and lead to weakness of the uterine wall, which will predispose the uterus to dehiscence and fistula formation.
2. *Find the tissue planes and look for the connecting bridges:* Locate the largely avascular tissue planes that separate the tumor from its uterine bed. The arrangement is somewhat analogous to an onion; the space between two layers of an onion is similar to the avascular plane. In case of a myoma, there are bridges that connect the tumor to the compressed pesudocapsule. These bridges consist of connective tissue and blood vessels of various sizes that feed the

tumor. Larger vessels need to be coagulated before they are cut. Do not dissect haphazardly in different planes because this will lead to excessive bleeding.

3. *Coagulate larger vessels before cutting them:* Do not cut larger vessels in the connecting bridges or vascular pedicle and then attempt to control them; the vessels will retract, continue bleeding, and become difficult to control. The magnification afforded by video laparoscopy allows accurate identification of blood vessels. Coagulate medium- and large-sized vessels *prior* to cutting them.

4. *Coagulate larger vessels through compression between the blades of a bipolar instrument:* Occlude the vascular pedicle and larger feeding vessels in the connecting bridges by using bipolar electrocoagulation. Ultrasonic or thermal coagulation using a crocodile-type "bipolar" forceps is acceptable. Larger vessels need to be captured between the jaws of the instrument that carries the energy source to achieve effective hemostasis and seal the blood vessels. Coagulation of the vessel proceeds from both sides simultaneously. Using instruments that project a unidirectional spread of energy will not consistently control larger blood vessels. The vessel wall that is in contact with the energy source may be breached before complete coagulation of the contents, and the compromised vessel may retract, continue bleeding, and become difficult to find and control. Unidirectional instruments that carry energy include unipolar electrodes, CO_2 laser beam, yttrium-aluminum-garnet (YAG), potassium-titanyl-phosphate (KTP) laser fibers, and the argon spray beam. In this situation, the application of sutures or staples is effective but not practical.

5. *Close the uterine surgical defect in layers:* The cut muscles of the myometrium will tend to retract and maintain the surgical gap in the myometrium on a permanent basis unless they are connected by sutures. The sutures act as a scaffold that supports healing and remolding of the uterus. Although correct approximation and scaffolding of the myometrial edges is essential, the use of multiple layers of constricting sutures is not. In fact, excessive use of tight hemostatic sutures in the myometrial bed may be harmful. The laparoscopic placement of interrupted sutures to close the myometrial gap and a continuous suture to approximate the superficial edges and serosa is not difficult. Failure to close the myometrial defect will likely result in uterine dehiscence and fistula formation.

6. *Insist on meticulous hemostasis:* This will prevent the possibility of postoperative hematomas and mitigate against adhesion formation.

In my opinion, these principles constitute the basis of successful management of uterine leiomyomas by laparoscopic means. Over the years, we have instituted technical refinements, especially in suturing and specimen removal, that make it possible to perform laparoscopic myomectomy safely, effectively, and in a timely manner.

TECHNIQUE

Preparation, Access, Exploration, and Additional Procedures

After adequate anesthesia, the patient is placed in the lithotomy position. The legs are placed into Allen stirrups (Allen Medical Systems) with the thighs roughly parallel to the floor and the feet resting comfortably in the foot rest of the boot. The patient's toe, knee, and opposite shoulder are aligned in a straight line. Jelly pads are placed between the boot of the stirrup and the leg of the patient to prevent inappropriate pressure points.

Use of open laparoscopy is routinely recommended for primary access. Three secondary access cannulas are inserted at points drawn along the line of an imaginary Pfanensteil incision and used for operative manipulation. The level of the secondary access points varies with the size of the uterus; the larger the uterus, the higher the level. Five-millimeter stable access cannulas (Marlow Surgical Technologies) are used routinely to facilitate instrument exchanges and to prevent the trocars from slipping in or out of the abdomen during surgery.

After exploration of the pelvic organs and upper abdomen, appropriate treatment of associated conditions, such as endometriosis and adhesions, is carried out. The laparoscopic procedure is terminated in favor of an open laparotomy if this is warranted by the extent of the lesion or the severity of adhesions.

Disengaging the Leiomyoma(s)

Surgeons should usually start by injecting 10 ml of dilute vasopressin, 20 U in 50 ml of saline, subserosally along the site of incision and into the myometrium at the base of the myoma (Fig. 12-1). A vertical incision is then made into the pseudocapsule of the myoma down to the characteristically pearly white substance of the tumor (Fig. 12-2). The unipolar small surface electrodes, CO_2 laser beam, and the YAG laser (bare fiber or with sapphire tip) may be used for this purpose with equal success. More than one myoma can be removed from the same vertical incision. Pendunculated myomas are excised at the base of the pedicle.

The next step is to develop the cleavage plane between the myoma and its pseudocapsule by cutting the connecting bridges. This is accomplished, as in any other surgical procedure, by applying traction on the myoma and countertraction on the cut edge of the pseudocapsule. Once identified, the connecting bridges are severed to provide access to the cleavage

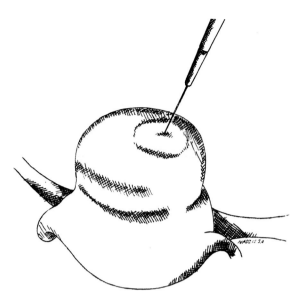

Fig. 12-1. Vasopressin injection over incision site. (From Hasson,[4] with permission.)

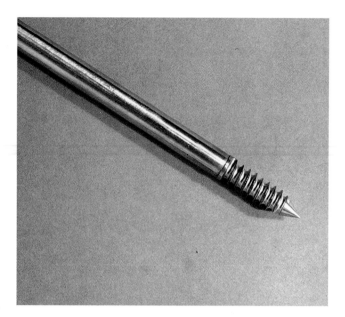

Fig. 12-3. Myoma drill (Reznik instrument).

plane. Smaller, weaker bridges are dissected bluntly, and larger vascular bridges are cut after they are coagulated. I find it helpful to turn a myoma drill (Fig. 12-3) (Resnik Instrument) into the substance of a myoma for manipulation and traction. I then use the prying method for blunt dissection and place a probe (or any instrument that functions as a probe) in the cleavage

plane to leverage the tumor against the uterine wall and pry it out of its bed (Fig. 12-4). This prying technique must be performed firmly but gently to avoid ruptured bridges and subsequent bleeding.

Once the myoma is substantially out of its bed, the myoma drill is replaced by the bulldog grasper (Fig. 12-5) (Linvatec), and strong traction is applied in vari-

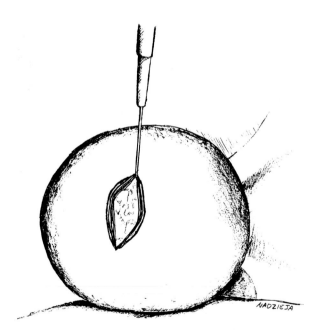

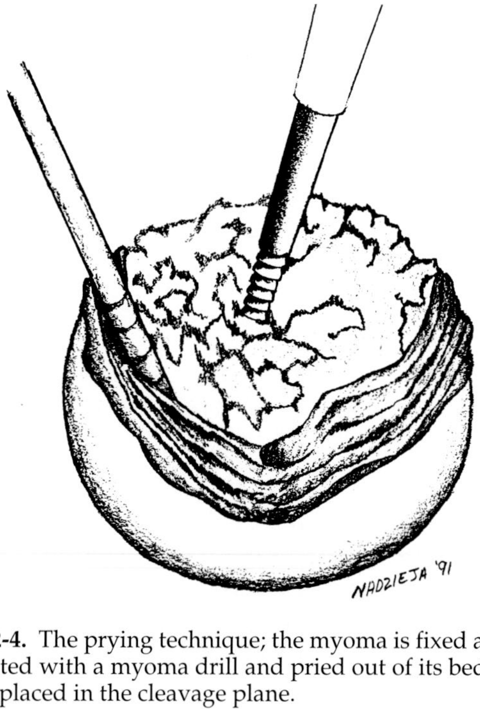

Fig. 12-2. Vertical uterine incision with unipolar electrosurgical needle.

Fig. 12-4. The prying technique; the myoma is fixed and manipulated with a myoma drill and pried out of its bed with a probe placed in the cleavage plane.

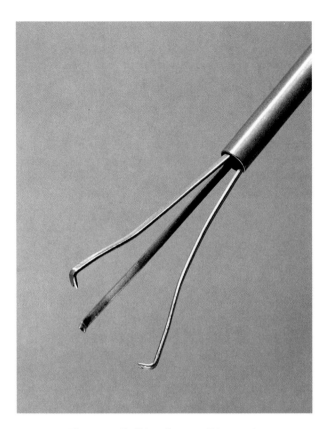

Fig. 12-5. Bulldog forceps (Linvatec).

ous directions to expose remaining bridges as well as the primary vascular pedicle (Fig. 12-6). When the proper technique is used, dissection proceeds with surprising ease and minimal or no bleeding. Once the vascular pedicle is identified, I coagulate it thoroughly with bipolar cautery and cut it with sharp scissors to free the myoma (Fig. 12-7).

At times, after incision of what appears to be the pseudocapsule, the familiar whorled appearance and rubbery consistency of a leiomyoma are replaced by a soft spongy consistency and the appearance of altered myometrium. Biopsy usually reveals adenomyosis. Management alternatives include simple biopsy and subsequent conservative medical therapy or definitive surgery, wedge resection of the lesion, and closure of the uterine defect, and at times, myolysis. At other times, the appearance is that of a homogeneous degenerating mass of tissue. This may result from benign conditions that diminish blood supply to the tumor such as use of GnRH-a or malignant transformation. Benign degeneration cannot be differentiated from sarcomatous change by gross examination. Also, intraoperative frozen sections are not always decisive.[14]

Managing the Operative Defect

For pedunculated, subserosal, and intraligamentary leiomyomas, the edges of the operative site are coagulated to achieve meticulous hemostasis. The site may be

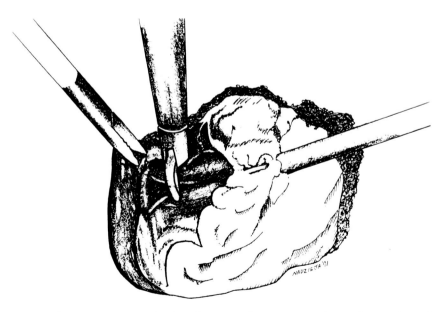

Fig. 12-6. Exposure of connective tissue bridges between the myoma and pseudocapsule with traction and countertraction and cutting of the bridges. (From Hasson et al.,[3] with permission.)

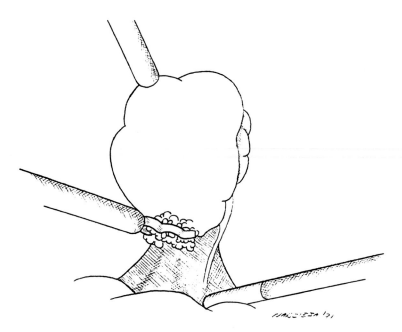

Fig. 12-7. Bipolar coagulation of the vascular pedicle. Notice the traction exerted on the myoma by the bull-dog forceps and the countertraction applied on the operative edge by an alligator forceps. (From Hasson,[4] with permission.)

covered with a tissue barrier, although this is not usually necessary. For superficial intramural tumors, hemostasis of the wound edges is achieved (Fig. 12-8) and then the uterine defect is approximated with one continuous "baseball"-type suture stitch that includes the serosa (Fig. 12-9). The needle-through-the-noose knot secures the beginning of the suture[15] (Fig. 12-10), and the half-hitch end knot secures the end[16] (Fig. 12-11).

For deep intramural myomas (with or without a submucous component), adding one or more interrupted sutures to close the myoma bed is mandatory. A 122-cm (48-in) Gore-Tex or other nonabsorbable suture, size 0, on a large straight or ski needle is used to perform what I call the "belt stitch," a vertical mattress that approximates the uterine muscles at a deep and more superficial level. The needle enters the uterus from outside in through the serosa, emerges at the surgical bed, is grasped and reapplied, and goes through the opposite uterine wall from inside out. When the needle clears the uterine wall, it is grasped and reapplied in a reverse fashion at a more superficial level to complete the vertical mattress. The needle end of the suture is brought out of the 5-mm cannula; a Roeder loop knot is tied extracorporeally and brought down into the abdomen to cinch the stitch. A staple is applied on the long suture strand over which the loop slides to secure the knot. Alternatively, the Roeder loop knot

may be secured by forming another knot between the two suture loops.

Whenever sutures are used, it is preferable to apply a tissue barrier such as expanded polytetrafluoroethylene, (Gore-Tex membrane, WL Gore and Associates) or TC7 (Interceed, Ethicon) to mitigate the development of adhesions, especially in reproductive patients. Staples may be used as markers for subsequent evaluation of the uterine scar by HSG.[17] Alternatively, the scar may be evaluated by ultrasound or MRI.

Removing the Myoma(s)

After excision, individual myomas are stored in the cul-de-sac or the left upper quadrant in preparation for removal. The stored masses are removed through a 10/12-mm cannula, a colpotomy, or a minilaparotomy incision. Generally, this is the most cumbersome and time-consuming step of the operation. I have tried morcellation according to Semm, posterior colpotomy and the orange peel technique[3] (Fig. 12-12), bisection, and minilaparotomy with externalization or morcellation outside the abdomen.[18]

Recently, my associate, Carlos Rotman, M.D., devised a simplified laparoscopic abdominal morcellation (SLAM) technique that we have found much easier and faster to perform. Essentially, the specimen is held se-

Fig. 12-8. Securing hemostasis of the wound edges using bipolar coagulation.

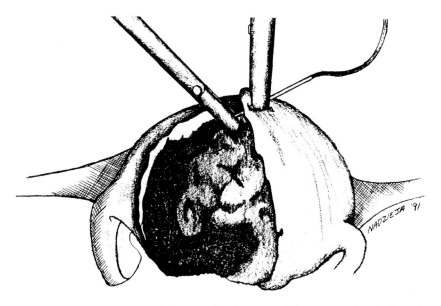

Fig. 12-9. Approximation of the superficial uterine defect using a baseball stitch.

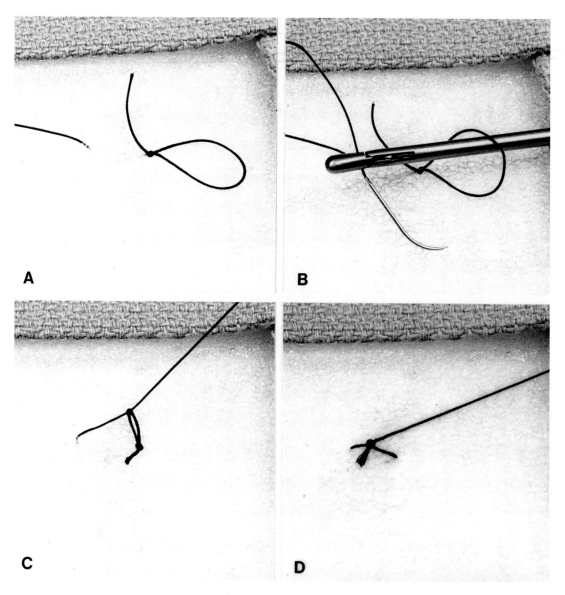

Fig. 12-10. Sequence for securing the beginning of a continuous suture using the needle through the noose knot: **(A)** noose loop resting on one side of the incision **(B)** needle pulled through the noose loop, **(C)** noose loop tightens over the enclosed suture, and **(D)** the knot is formed. (From Hasson,[16] with permission.)

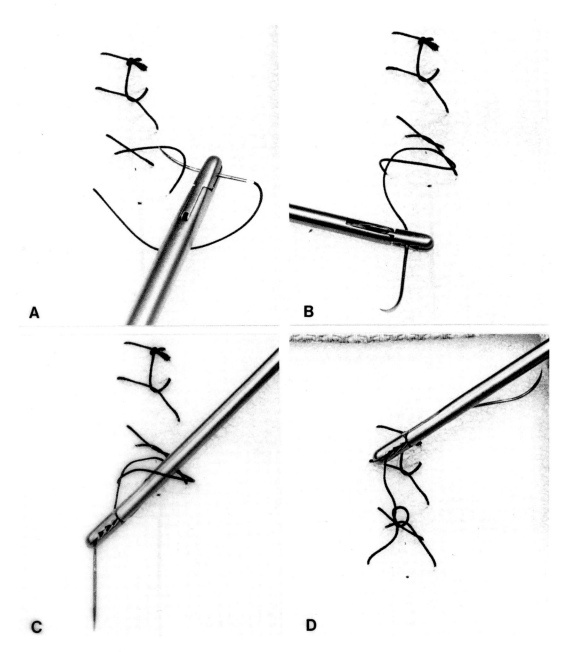

Fig. 12-11. Sequence for completing a continuous suture using the half-hitch end knot: **(A)** needle is passed under loop of the last stitch, **(B)** second loop is formed within remaining suture, **(C)** knot-forming end of suture is pulled into the loop, and **(D)** knot-forming end is pulled out of loop to tighten the sliding knot over the enclosed suture. (From Hasson,[16] with permission.)

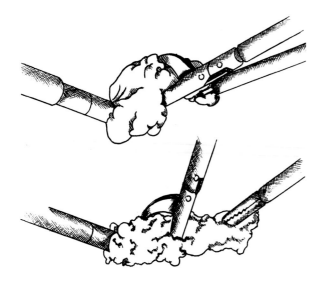

Fig. 12-12. Converting a myoma into a narrow strip of tissue with the "orange-peel technique." (From Hasson et al.,[3] with permission.)

curely from both sides and sliced longitudinally with a sharp knife. The slices are then removed through a slightly enlarged incision after the removal of the laparoscopy cannula. Instruments and methods for the SLAM technique will be reported in the near future. We use the orange peel technique with the sharp knife or scissors to complement the SLAM technique.

It is preferable to excise the myoma intact from the uterine wall and then morcellate it. However, at times the tumor can be incised after bulging out and then cut down the middle or a central portion removed to facilitate dissection of each half. At other times, portions of the myoma may be sliced transversely, when the tumor is soft and degenerated, to facilitate exposure of the vascular pedicle.

MYOLYSIS

Laparoscopic myolysis is a technique of coagulating leiomyomas to effect devascularization and subsequent shrinkage of the tumors. It is modeled after a similar hysteroscopic procedure.[19] Early experience with this technique using the Nd-YAG laser showed a 41 percent mean reduction in myoma size after 6 months and 1 year.[20] However, when second-look laparoscopy was performed 6 months after the myolysis, all the patients had dense fibrous adhesions between the treated myomas and the bowel. The authors concluded that because of this risk, further studies were required.[20]

Goldfarb[21] suggested the use of bipolar needles to accomplish the same goal and combined his procedure with endometrial ablation in most patients. The author did not report second-look procedures, and therefore the incidence of postoperative adhesions is not known. Furthermore, combining uterine coagulation from outside in (myolysis) and inside out (ablation) may potentially pose additional problems.

CLINICAL EXPERIENCE

Our experience with laparoscopic myomectomy in more than 110 cases performed during the past 6 years confirms the safety and efficacy of the procedure. When our initial experience in 56 cases[3] was compared with nine recent studies on myomectomy by laparotomy or laparoscopy,[22–30] the results were favorable (Table 12-1). Laparoscopy studies report lower estimated blood loss and shorter length of stay than laparotomy studies. With increased experience and improved technique, our operative time has diminished. Currently, it is between 1 and 2 hours, depending on the size, location, and number of leiomyomas and the extent of associated adhesions and other lesions. In our series, 34 percent of the patients had associated pelvic adhesions, 27 percent had endometriosis, and 4 percent had ovarian cysts. Others have made similar observations.[24,28,29]

Complications

There have been very few complications in our series. No blood transfusion or return to surgery was needed. One patient developed febrile morbidity associated with an upper respiratory tract infection and subcutaneous emphysema. Early in the series, five patients developed subcutaneous emphysema. However, this complication ceased after the ballooned stable access cannula was used for operative access. To date, all postmyomectomy vaginal and abdominal deliveries have been uncomplicated. At cesarean section, the

Table 12-1. Comparison Between Recent Studies on Myomectomy

Study and Approach	No. of Cases	Range Tumor Size (cm)	% Solitary	Total Removed	EBL (ml) Range/Mean	LOS (Days) Mean	% Conception	% Viable Pregnancy
Conventional laparotomy								
Babaknia et al., 1978[22]	46	—	—	—	—	—	—	
Ranney and Frederick, 1979[23]	51	1–12	76	—	—	—	—	46	42
McLaughlin, 1985[24]	9			—	—	311	—	—	—
Rosenfeld, 1986[25]	23	3–14	35	—	—	—	—	—	—
Smith and Uhlir, 1990[26]	63	—	—	—	200/400	300	4	65	56
CO$_2$ laser laparoscopy						—	—		
McLaughlin, 1985[24]	18	1–10	56	42	—	200	—	—	—
Starks, 1988[27]	32	4–18	16	—	50/400	150	—	63	53
Operative laparoscopy									
Nezhat et al., 1991[28]	154	2–15	48	347	100/600	—	1	16	11
Dubuisson et al., 1991[29]	43	1–11	—	92	—	—	2.8	—	—
Daniel and Gurley, 1991[30]	17	3–7	—	—	5/200	78	1	—	—
Hasson et al., 1992[3]	56	3–16	38	144	10/400	75	1	64	50

Abbreviations: EBL, estimated blood loss; LOS, length of stay in hospital.

uterine scar was inspected in four patients and four to be intact.

Nezhat et al.[28] reported six uterine fistulas after laparoscopic removal of deep intramural fibroids. However, the authors either did not suture the uterine defect or only approximated the uterine serosa. Harris[31] reported a case of uterine dehiscence at 34 weeks' gestation in a patient who conceived 3 months after laparoscopic excision of a 3-cm myoma that was resected from the posterior uterine wall with electrocautery after retraction with a myoma screw. The serosa of the resulting uterine defect was reapproximated with 4-0 interrupted polyglycolic sutures. I believe that appropriate layer closure of the surgical defect is essential. Excessive simultaneous use of electrocautery and the CO$_2$ laser should be avoided because it may result in serious complications such as uterine decapitation.[32]

The integrity of the uterine scar should be evaluated in reproductive patients before they are allowed to conceive. I routinely perform these evaluations at approximately 4 months postmyomectomy. Recent data developed through ultrasound assessment of uterine volume after myomectomy tend to support this concept. Beyth et al.[33] demonstrated a gradual decrease in uterine volume during the first 6 months after surgery in all patients, with the most remarkable change in size occurring during the initial 2 to 3 months. The authors suggested that the period of uterine shrinkage may represent the time of healing during which conception should be prevented.[33]

Postoperative Adhesions

As compared with abdominal myomectomy, laparoscopic myomectomy may be expected to result in fewer postoperative adhesions because of better hemostasis, diminished surgical trauma and tissue handling, and the absence of dryness that is associated with exposure of tissues to room air. In fact, all the patients who had abdominal CO$_2$ laser myomectomy followed by second-look procedures had postoperative adhesions.[27] Approximately two-thirds of patients followed by second-look procedures in our laparoscopic myomectomy series had postoperative adhesions. There appears to be an association between the site of the myomectomy incision and the occurrence of postoperative adhesions. Tulandi et al.[34] performed 26 second-look laparoscopies after abdominal myomectomy and found that incisions on the posterior uterine wall were associated with significantly more adnexal adhesions than those on the fundus or anterior uterine walls. We have observed a strong relation between the site and number of myomectomy incisions and the presence of postoperative adhesions in 28 second-look laparoscopies. Adhesions were associated with 80 percent of posterior wall incisions, 20 percent of anterior or fundal incisions, 44 percent of single incisions and 86 percent of multiple incisions. The protective value of excellent hemostasis was also demonstrated; adhesions were seen in 25 percent of patients with dry wound edges and in 80 percent of patients with wet edges.

It is generally agreed that postoperative adhesion formation is a complex, multifactorial phenomenon that involves genetic predisposition and immunologic considerations, as well as surgical technique. The laparoscopic approach will not prevent postoperative adhesions. Measures such as complete hemostasis and the use of adhesion-preventing membranes to cover exposed sutures may be of value. In reproductive patients, we strongly advocate the use of second-look laparoscopy 2 to 3 weeks after the laparoscopic myomectomy to clear potential adhesions. The beneficial effect of second-look laparoscopy adhesiolysis in improving the ultimate outcome has been confirmed in studies based on third-look laparoscopy.[35,36]

Reproductive Outcome

Despite the recognized high potential of postoperative adhesion formation, myomectomy appears to have a positive effect on fertility enhancement. Reproductive performance may not be compromised by adhesions that do not involve the adnexa. In our updated series, the conception rate in infertile patients was 71 percent and the live birth rate 59 percent.[5] These rates have remained substantially representative of subsequent experience. This may be compared with a conception rate of 40 percent after abdominal myomectomy in 1,202 infertile patients as reviewed by Buttram and Reiter in 1981.[37] In a more recent review of six studies of abdominal myomectomy in 132 infertile patients, Verkauf[38] found a conception rate of 58 percent.

The reproductive performance after myomectomy in infertile patients in individual studies is shown in Table 12-1. The low conception rate initially reported by Nezhat et al.[28] was significantly improved further follow-up (personal communication). Tulandi and associates[34] reported a pregnancy rate of 66.7 percent at 12 months after 26 abdominal myomectomy procedures in infertile women who were followed by second-look laparoscopy with adhesiolysis.

Incidence of Uterine Sarcoma

Tissue examinations of the leiomyomas in our series have revealed various benign degenerative changes in about 30 percent, adenomyosis in 7 percent, and calcification in 5 percent of the cases. These findings are similar to those reported earlier by Ranney and Frederick.[23] There were no leiomyosarcomas in either series. This diagnosis is made exclusively in the laboratory, based on the number of mitotic figures per high-power field.[39] However, authorities differ in the number of mitotic figures that justifies the diagnosis of leiomyosarcoma; from 5 per 10 high-power fields (H-PF)[14,40] to 10 per 10 H-PF[14,41] to 2 per any H-PF.[39] The degree of malignancy is directly related to the number of mitotic figures per H-PF.

Uterine leiomyosarcomas may arise within a myoma or de novo from the myometrium.[39] The incidence of sarcomatous degeneration in surgically removed leiomyomas is between 0.07[42] and 0.5 percent.[43] The incidence increases steadily from the fourth to the sixth decade of life.[14,43] The mean age at diagnosis in one recent study was 56 ± 14 years, with a range of 30 to 83 years.[44] Parker et al.[42] reported a 0.27 percent incidence of sarcoma among patients having surgery for a rapidly growing tumor. However, the authors found no cases of sarcoma among patients who met the criteria of an increase of 6 weeks' gestational size over 1 year, which was established by Buttram and Reiter.[48] Patients with lesions arising in leiomyoma have significantly better prognosis than those with primary myosarcoma.[39] Patients younger than 50 years of age have a significantly better prognosis than older patients.[39,40]

The effect of GnRH-a on sarcomatous lesions varies. The uterine mass may not change in size[45] or grow larger.[46] Also, abnormal uterine bleeding may occur during the treatment.[46,47] Therefore, lack of a shrinkage response, presence of a paradoxical growth response, or the occurrence of abnormal uterine bleeding during GnRH-a treatment of leiomyomas suggests the possibility of malignancy and mandates further evaluation and prompt surgical management. Schwartz et al.[44] reviewed a 10-year experience with 21 patients with uterine leiomyosarcomas and reported that leiomyosarcoma was either the largest or only mass in all patients except one and was limited to one mass in all the patients except one. The sarcomas had no preferential type or uterine location. The authors suggested close monitoring of the largest myoma during conservative management with GnRH-a therapy.[44]

The finding of unsuspected leiomyosarcoma in a laparoscopic myomectomy specimen poses a difficult therapeutic dilemma regarding further treatment in patients who wish to conceive. Although hysterectomy is a safer approach, preserving the uterus may be a viable option if the patient understands and accepts the risk. Only one of six patients who had myomectomy alone for leiomyosarcoma arising in a myoma developed recurrence.[39]

Recurrence and Re-operation

The rates of recurrence and re-operation after laparoscopic myomectomy are expected to be similar to those noted after abdominal myomectomy. In their 1981 review of 3,206 abdominal myomectomy cases, Buttram and Reiter[37] recorded a recurrence rate of 15 percent and a retreatment rate of 10 percent, which included re-operation and radiation therapy. In a more recent review of seven studies totaling 185 patients, Verkaur[38] reported a recurrence rate of 8 percent and a re-operation rate of 7 percent. Smith and Uhlir[26] reported on recurrence and re-operation in 62 patients who underwent abdominal myomectomy. One had recurrence at 4 years and three had recurrence after 5 years, which led to repeat myomectomy in one, hysterectomy in two, and expectant therapy in one patient. Candiani et al.[48] found the cumulative 10-year recurrence rate after abdominal myomectomy to be 27 percent by life table analysis. Clinically significant recurrences usually occurred 3 or more years after surgery.[48]

Studies that report on ultrasound recurrence of uterine myomas after abdominal myomectomy give higher rates. However, most of the recurrent myomas detected by ultrasound were not associated with clinical symptoms at the time of evaluation.[49] The recurrence rate increased with time; the cumulative 3-year ultrasound recurrence rate was 20 percent, and the 5-year value was 51 percent.[50] There was no significant relationship between the number or site of myomas removed and the risk of recurrence. The 5-year recurrence rate was 38 percent in women with one myoma, 70 percent in women with two or three tumors, and 52 percent in women in whom four or more tumors were removed.[50] However, Friedman et al.[49] reported a significantly higher ultrasound recurrence rate for surgically treated patients with more than three leiomyomas when they were followed for 27 to 38 months.

Currently, there are no published data regarding recurrence and re-operation after laparoscopic myomectomy. Although the follow-up in my series is not complete due to cases that are referred from other physicians, the rate of ultrasound-detected recurrence appears to be quite low. Two of my patients had repeat operations: one had a supracervical laparoscopic hysterectomy 3 years after laparoscopic myomectomy for recurrent menometrohaggia. The pathology report showed adenomyosis and two minute myomas. The second had another laparoscopic myomectomy for recurrent leiomyomas. I generally try to limit laparoscopic myomectomy to patients with four or fewer significant myomas (more than 3 cm).

These data confirm the benefit of myomectomy in preserving the reproductive organs of symptomatic patients.

CONCLUSION

In my experience, laparoscopic myomectomy, in selected cases, is at least as effective as laparotomy for performing myomectomy indicated for fertility enhancement or relief of symptoms associated with leiomyomas in terms of reproductive outcome, relief of symptoms, and recurrence rate. The laparoscopic approach is better than the laparotomy approach because it is associated with less blood loss, shorter length of stay and recovery time, fewer complications, less postoperative adhesions, improved cosmetic results, and better documentation for future follow-up.

To optimize safety and efficacy of the procedure, it is essential to adhere to the basic surgical principles of

Working inside the pseudocapsule of the leiomyoma
Finding the tissue planes and connecting bridges
Coagulating larger vessels with suitable means before cutting them
Closing the surgical defect in the uterus in layers
Achieving satisfactory hemostasis

The availability of a competent associate surgeon or skilled assistant is also important. However, regardless of surgical skill and experience, the laparoscopic approach is not suitable for patients with advanced disease and multiple lesions. These patients will continue to require a laparotomy.

REFERENCES

1. Wilcox LS, Koonin LM, Pokras R, et al. Hysterectomy in the United States, 1988–1990. Obstet Gynecol 83:549, 1994
2. National Center for Health Statistics: Vital Health Statistics. National Hospital Discharge Survey. Series 13, no. 108, 1989
3. Hasson HM, Rotman C, Rana N et al: Laparoscopic myomectomy. Obstet Gynecol 80:884, 1992
4. Hasson HM: Laparoscopic myomectomy. p.137. In Soderstrom RM (ed): Operative Laparoscopy, The Master's Techniques. Raven Press, New York, 1993
5. Hasson HM: Laparoscopic myomectomy. In Adamson GD, Martin D (eds): Endoscopic Management of Gynecologic Diseases. Raven Press, New York, in press
6. The American College of Obstetricians and Gynecologists (ACOG): ACOG Technical Bulletin, Uterine Leiomyomata. Publication no. 192. May 1994
7. Zawin M, McCarthy S, Scoutt LM et al: High-field MRI and US evaluation of the pelvis in women with leiomyomas. Magn Reson Imaging 4:371, 1990
8. Hricak H, Tscholakoff D, Heinrichs L et al: Uterine leiomyomas: correlation of MR, histopathologic findings and symptoms. Radiology 158:385, 1986
9. Dudiak CM, Turner DA, Patel SK et al: Uterine leiomyomas in the infertile patient: preoperative localization with MR imaging versus US and hysterosalpingography. Radiology 167:627, 1988

10. Togashi K, Ozasa H, Konishi I et al: Enlarged uterus: differentiation between adenomyosis and leiomyoma with MR imaging. Radiology 171:531, 1989

11. Freidman AJ, Hoffman DI, Comite F et al: Treatment of leiomyomata uteri with leuprolide acetate depot: a double-blind placebo-controlled multicenter study. Obstet Gynecol 77:720, 1991

12. Rock JA: Gonadotropin-releasing hormone agonist analogs in the treatment of uterine leiomyomas. J Gynecol Surg 7:147, 1991

13. Wiznitzer A, Marback M, Hazum E et al: Gonadotrophin-releasing hormone specific binding sites in uterine leiomyomata. Biochem Biophys Res Commun 152:1326, 1988

14. Leibsohn S, d'Ablaing G, Mishell RD et al: Leiomyosarcoma in a series of hysterectomies performed for presumed uterine leiomyomas. Am J Obstet Gynecol 162:968, 1990

15. Hasson HM: Suture loop techniques to facilitate microsurgical and laparoscopic procedures. J Reprod Med 32:765, 1987

16. Hasson HM: Half-hitch knot for securing the end of continuous sutures. Obstet Gynecol 80:724, 1992

17. Beyth Y, Ohel G: Postmyomectomy evaluation of uterine scar: a new hysterographic method. Fertil Steril 39:564, 1983

18. Hasson HM, Rotman C, Rana N et al: Experience with laparoscopic hysterectomy. J AAGL 1:1, 1993

19. Donnez J, Gillerot S, Bourgonjon D et al: Neodymium:YAG laser hysteroscopy in large submucous fibroids. Fertil Steril 54:999, 1990

20. Nisolle M, Smets M, Malvaux V et al: Laparoscopic myolysis with the nd:YAG laser. J Gynecol Surg 9:95, 1993

21. Goldfarb HA: Removing uterine fibroids laparoscopically. Contemp OB/GYN 39:50, 1994

22. Babaknia A, Rock JA, Jones HW: Pregnancy success following abdominal myomectomy for infertility. Fertil Steril 30:644, 1978

23. Ranney B, Frederick I: The occasional need for myomectomy. Obstet Gynecol 53:437, 1979

24. McLaughlin DS: Metroplasty and myomectomy with CO_2 laser for maximizing the preservation of normal tissue and minimizing blood loss. J Reprod Med 30:1, 1985

25. Rosenfeld DL: Abdominal myomectomy for otherwise unexplained infertility. Fertil Steril 46:328, 1986

26. Smith DC, Uhlir JK: Myomectomy as a reproductive procedure. Am J Obstet Gynecol 162:1476, 1990

27. Starks GC: CO_2 laser myomectomy in an infertile population. J Reprod Med 33:184, 1988

28. Nezhat C, Nezhat F, Silfen SL et al: Laparoscopic myomectomy. Int J Fertil 36:275, 1991

29. Dubuisson JB, Mandelbrot L, Lecuru F et al: Myomectomy by laparoscopy: a preliminary report of 43 cases. Fertil Steril 56:827, 1991

30. Daniell JF, Gurley LD: Laparoscopic treatment of clinically significant symptomatic uterine fibroids. J Gynecol Surg 7:37, 1991

31. Harris WJ: Uterine dehiscence following laparoscopic myomectomy. Obstet Gnyecol 80:545, 1992

32. Barlet E, Griffin WT: Uterine decapitation resulting from laparoscopic laser myomectomy. 48th Annual Meeting of the American Fertility Society, New Orleans, LA, November 2–5, 1992

33. Beyth Y, Jaffe R, Goldberger S: Uterine remodelling following conservative myomectomy. Ultrasonographic evaluation. Acta Obstet Gynecol Scand 71:632, 1992

34. Tulandi T, Murray C, Guralnick M: Adhesion formation and reproductive outcome after myomectomy and second-look laparoscopy. Obstet Gynecol 82:213, 1993

35. Jansen RP: Early laparoscopy after pelvic operations to prevent adhesions, safety and efficacy. Fertil Steril 49:26, 1988

36. Perez RJ: Second-look laparoscopy adhesiolysis. The procedure of choice for preventing adhesion recurrence. J Reprod Med 36:700, 1991

37. Buttram VC, Reiter RC: Uterine leiomyomata: etiology, symptomatology and management. Fertil Steril 36:433, 1991

38. Verkauf BS: Myomectomy for fertility enhancement and preservation. Fertil Steril 58:1, 1992

39. Dinh TV, Woodruff JD: Leiomyosarcoma of the uterus. Am J Obstet Gynecol 144:817, 1982

40. Kahanpaa KV, Wahlstrom T, Grohn P et al: Sarcomas of the uterus: a clinicopathological study of 199 patients. Obstet Gynecol 67:417, 1986

41. Berchuck A, Rubin S, Hoskins WJ et al: Treatment of uterine leiomyosarcoma. Obstet Gynecol 71:845, 1988

42. Parker WH, Yao SF, Berek JS: Uterine sarcoma in patients operated on for presumed leiomyoma and rapidly growing leiomyoma. Obstet Gynecol 83:414, 1994

43. Vollenhoven BJ, Lawrence AS, Healy DL: Uterine fibroids: a clinical review. Br J Obstet Gynaecol 97:285, 1990

44. Schwartz LB, Diamond MP, Schwartz PE: Leiomyosarcomas: clinical presentation. Am J Obstet Gynecol 168:180, 1993

45. Meyer WR, Mayer AR, Diamond MP et al: Unsuspected leiomyosarcoma: treatment with a gonatropin-releasing hormone analogue. Obstet Gynecol 75:529, 1990

46. Loong EPL, Wong FWS: Uterine leiomyosarcoma diagnosed during treatment with agonist of luteinizing hormone releasing hormone for presumed uterine fibroid. Fertil Steril 54:530, 1990

47. Hitti IF, Glasberg SS, McKenzie C et al: Uterine leiomyosarcoma with massive necrosis diagnosed during gonadotrophin-releasing hormone analog therapy for presumed uterine fibroid. Fertil Steril 56:778, 1991

48. Candiani GB, Fedele L, Parazzini F et al: Risk of recurrence after myomectomy. Br J Obstet Gynaecol 98:385, 1991

49. Friedman AJ, Daly M, Juneau-Norcross M et al: Recurrence of myomas after myomectomy in women pretreated with leuprolide acetate depot or placebo. Fertil Steril 58:205, 1992

50. Fedele L, Villa L, Bocciolone L et al: Risk of recurrence after myomectomy: a transvaginal ultrasonographic study. 49th Annual Meeting of the American Fertility Society, Montreal, Quebec, Canada, October 9–14, 1993

13 Gamete Intrafallopian Transfer

JOSE P. BALMACEDA
SAUL MALOUL

The development of in vitro fertilization (IVF) has accelerated in a dramatic way the understanding of the physiology of gamete interaction. Furthermore, it allowed the development of therapeutic alternatives that have proved to be as successful as the original technique. Looking for options that would improve the pregnancy rate (PR), Asch et al. reported the first pregnancy[1] and birth[2] after translaparoscopic gamete intrafallopian transfer (GIFT) in a patient with unexplained infertility. Since then, and mainly due to the reproducibility of the procedure and the consistency of results, GIFT has become widely accepted, and the large majority of the assisted reproduction programs offer it as a therapeutic alternative.

GIFT involves the direct transfer of human gametes, sperm, and preovulatory oocytes into the ampullary portion of the fallopian tube by means of laparoscopy, minilaparotomy, or transcervical intratubal gamete transfer, allowing IVF to occur at the natural site.

The application of gynecologic endoscopy is expanding continuously. Undoubtedly, one of the most interesting areas in gynecologic endoscopy is its application in assisted reproductive technologies (ART).

In this chapter, we focus our attention on the current approach of choice for GIFT, that is the laparoscopic one, but also we will mention important aspects of the other methods of transfer, as well as the current state of knowledge and the innovative and future perspectives in this therapeutic alternative.

PHYSIOLOGIC BASIS

Currently, we have a greater understanding of ovulatory events, fertilization, and cleavage processes, and corpus luteum function. Nevertheless, there are still some events in the process of conception that remain to be elucidated. The mechanisms of sperm transport through the female genitalia toward the site of fertilization in the tubes and for fimbrial oocyte pickup are still obscure. It is possible that these mechanisms, which cannot be evaluated by means of clinical or laboratory tests at present, are impaired in some of the unexplained cases of infertility. Idiopathic infertility and mild or moderate endometriosis, which anatomically do not affect the tubes or ovaries, are common diagnostic subgroups of infertility. The reason for infertility in these patients is not clear. It has been suggested that the sperm cannot reach the tubal fertilization site in these cases due to a defect in the sperm transport mechanism.[3] An alternate explanation is that there is an impairment of oocyte pickup by the fimbriated end of the tube at the time of ovulation. It has been shown that tubal pickup of the oocyte may be as low as 63 percent, even in highly fertile women, and that it appears to be extremely low in cases of unexplained infertility and endometriosis.[4] The direct placement of both gametes, oocytes and sperm, into the fallopian tubes by the GIFT technique should be able to overcome these impairments. Furthermore, the technique may work simply by quantitatively increasing the chances of oocyte and sperm encounter in the ampulla, as more than one oocyte is placed in the fallopian tube together with supraphysiologic concentrations of motile sperm.

INDICATIONS AND PREREQUISITES

The main indications for GIFT are unexplained infertility and endometriosis in patients having at least one normal fallopian tube. Other conditions in which GIFT has proved to be useful are (1) mild male factor, (2) failure of previous donor artificial insemination cycles, (3) iatrogenic pelvic adhesions, (4) cervical factor, and (5) premature ovarian failure patients using donor oocytes.

The minimal patient prerequisites should be a complete infertility evaluation demonstrating at least one normal fallopian tube and a condition not amenable to less invasive treatment, as recently outlined by the American Fertility Society.[5]

CONTRAINDICATIONS

Severe pelvic adhesions, grossly distorted tubal anatomy, and previous ectopic pregnancies are the main contraindications to the use of the GIFT technique.

TECHNIQUE

Controlled Ovarian Hyperstimulation

A controlled ovarian hyperstimulation regimen with gonadotropin derivatives is performed in every patient enrolled for a GIFT cycle. Better results in terms of number and quality of oocytes retrieved have been obtained with pituitary down-regulation with gonadotropin-releasing hormone agonists.[6] Once two or more follicles have reached a mean diameter of 20 to 22 mm measured by serial transvaginal ultrasound, and serum estradiol reaches 300 to 500 pg/ml for each mature follicle, human chorionic gonadotropin (hCG) 10,000 IU is intramuscularly administered. Cancellation of the cycle is discussed with the patients whenever less than two follicles fail to reach the above measurements.

Oocyte Retrieval

The oocyte retrieval is performed 34 to 36 hours after the administration of hCG. The follicular aspiration can be achieved either laparoscopically, as was originally described,[7] or transvaginally with sonographic guidance. The latter has become the method of choice in modern infertility practice[8] because it is easier to perform, allows better visualization of the follicles, does not require general anesthesia, and permits assessment of oocyte quality before performing laparoscopy.

Sperm Preparation

Two hours before the oocyte recovery, the male partner, whose semen analysis has previously been considered acceptable for a GIFT treatment, produces a semen sample by masturbation. The sample is allowed to liquify and is then examined for count, motility, and morphology. After doing so, the seminal plasma is removed by washing the sperm with culture medium. Finally, by a swim up[9] or percoll gradient technique,[10] the most motile fraction of the sperm is separated and used for the transfer. The standard procedure for a non-male factor case uses between 300,000 and 700,000 motile sperm. In general, the lower the count of normal forms and motility after the wash, the higher the number of sperm injected into the tube, although there are no fixed formulas.

Oocyte Preparation

Once the oocytes have been retrieved, they are graded for maturity by evaluating the expansion of the cumulus and corona radiata. Each oocyte is placed in an individual culture dish with 100 μl of modified Ham's F-10 media.

Gamete Loading

The sperm and oocytes are loaded into a special Teflon catheter that can be easily threaded into the fimbriated end of the tubes. There are several types of catheters, but none of them had proved to be superior to the rest, so surgeons should choose it according to their preferences. In our current practice, we use a 50-cm, 5-French Marrs catheter (Cook, Spencer, Indiana), which is very simple to handle, and we have achieved excellent results with it.

Transfer (Methods, Techniques, and Results)

The transfer itself can be accomplished via (1) laparoscopy, (2) minilaparotomy, or (3) transcervical catheterization of the fallopian tube.

Logically, we emphasize in this chapter the current

method of choice for transfer (i.e., the laparoscopic approach). Nevertheless, we also point out some important details of the other methods of transfer and the new developments in this matter.

Laparoscopic Gamete Intrafallopian Transfer

The laparoscopic GIFT requires general anesthesia and three abdominal punctures. The same subumbilical incision is used to insufflate the abdomen with CO_2 and to introduce the 10-mm-diameter laparoscope, which is in turn connected to a television-video camera. A second suprapubic incision allows the passage of an atraumatic grasper, used for handling the fimbriated end of the elected tube to facilitate its cannulation. Although initially oocytes/sperm were transferred to both fallopian tubes, the technique of preference today is the one using only one side. This modification shortens the operating time, reduces the amount of time the genital tract is exposed to gas, and minimizes fallopian tube manipulation. After inspecting both fallopian tubes, the surgeon chooses the one to transfer according to the anatomic findings and accessibility. If both appear to be normal, the right tube is usually preferred by a right-handed operator. Finally, a third entry is needed for introducing the Teflon catheter that will eventually cannulate the tube. This third puncture is usually performed in one of the patient's flanks, 2 to 3 cm below the umbilical incision. It is extremely important to carefully study the angle that the fimbriated ostium is offering, trying to create an ideal parallel line with the catheter, and through these means, minimize the risk of trauma during cannulation. A visible graduation at the tip of the catheter facilitates the determination of the degree of penetration. The depth of penetration of the catheter into the tube is recommended to be at least 3 cm.[11] After releasing the content, the catheter is removed and inspected by the biologist to be certain that the gametes were transferred. Then the tube is liberated from the grasper, the instruments are taken out, and the small incisions are closed with sutures. An intracervical insemination is optionally performed once the transfer has been performed.[12] The reason for the insemination is to ensure a more constant flowing of spermatozoa toward the tube. Theoretically, this should increase oocyte-sperm interaction and enhance the chances of fertilization. We have incorporated this procedure into our current practice of GIFT. After the procedure, the patient spends an average of 2 hours in the recovery room. She is then discharged, needing bed rest for the following 3 days. Sexual abstinence is recommended for at least 1 week after the transfer. Figure 13-1 shows the transfer catheter in place at the moment of the GIFT.

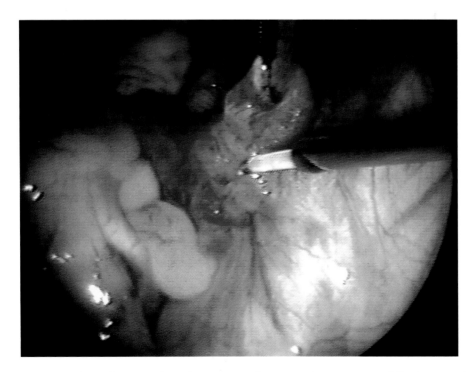

Fig. 13-1. Transfer catheter in place during a translaparoscopic gamete intrafallopian transfer.

Results

The first multinational collaborative report on GIFT involved 2,092 cases and was published in 1987.[13] Most of the participating centers achieved similar results, suggesting that this was a reproducible technique. The overall PR for GIFT was 28.7 percent, a value clearly superior to IVF-embryo transfer results published during the same period. Nevertheless, there were significant differences depending on the etiology of infertility. The lowest success rates were reported for male factor (PR=15 percent) and immunologic factor (PR=16 percent), and the highest were obtained among oocyte donation recipients and women with previous failed assisted inseminations with donor sperm (56 and 41 percent PR, respectively). Once pregnancy had been achieved, 79 percent progressed to third-trimester delivery, 17 percent had a first-trimester abortion, and 4 percent had an ectopic pregnancy. The best results were again reported for the oocyte donation group, with a 90 percent delivery rate. Since then, these results have remained stable.

Cohen[14] in 1991 reported the results obtained with GIFT during 1987 through 1989 at the four main national registries in the United States, Australia, United Kingdom, and France (Table 13-1).

The overall results of ART presented in national registries and multinational collaborative reports have consistently given better PRs for GIFT than for IVF.[14–16] Nevertheless, we must remember that they represent two different populations that cannot be directly compared. There is also a wide variation in IVF-ET results as well as in the patient selection criteria from clinic to clinic. In that sense, it is more valuable to compare results obtained by a single group of investigators as it decreases the differences between laboratories and clinicians. Unfortunately, results published in the literature appear contradictory, some clearly favoring tubal transfers[17,18] and others preferring intrauterine embryo transfer.[19,20]

The rate of congenital abnormalities associated with GIFT according the the U.S. and Canada ART registry for 1991 is 1.1 percent.[15] This rate is similar to what is published for other ART procedures and, when corrected for patient's age, does not represent a significant variation from the normal population.

Regarding oocyte quality, maturity seems to be the most important variable, even more than the number of oocytes transferred.[21] The review of Guzick et al.[22] showed a PR of 39.6 percent when one to five mature oocytes were transferred and 16.5 percent if only immature oocytes were transferred.

A frequent subject of controversy is the optimal number of oocytes to transfer. The decision needs to balance the chances of achieving pregnancy with the risk of multiple implantation. There are many publications indicating that the clinical PR is increased with the number of oocytes transferred.[11,22,23] These figures go as low as 6.3 percent for one oocyte to as high as 41 percent for four oocytes transferred. Results of the 1,601 GIFT cycles recorded through the U.S. registry during 1990 are shown in Table 13-2.[24] In this report, the PR achieved when three or fewer oocytes were transferred was significantly lower than when four or more oocytes were transferred. A very acceptable 8 percent multiple delivery rate (number of patients having multiple deliveries/total number of patients retrieved) was obtained when four oocytes were used, compared with the higher 12.7 percent rate when transferring more than six oocytes. Penzias et al.[23] reported the outcome of 399 GIFT cycles and observed a threefold increase in the PR for women receiving four or more oocytes compared with those who received three or fewer. Weckstein et al.[25] recently reported that it is beneficial to transfer four or five oocytes with GIFT but oocytes in excess of five should be inseminated in vitro and the resulting embryos cryopreserved for future transfers to avoid excessively high multiple PRs.

Table 13-1. National Registries Results Achieved With Conventional Gamete Intrafallopian Transfer

Country	Year	No. of Procedures	Clinical Pregnancy Rate (%)
United States	1988	3,080	21.0
Australia	1988	2,653	27.5
United Kingdom	1989	2,840	20.8
France	1987–1989	2,042	21.3
Total		10,615	22.6

Table 13-2. Number of Oocytes Transferred and GIFT Outcome

No. of Oocytes Transferred	Clinical Pregnancy Rate (%)	Delivery Rate (%)	Multiple Delivery Rate (%)
≤3	34/296 (11)	27/296 (9)	4/296 (1)
4	157/527 (30)	129/527 (24)	42/527 (8)
5–6	187/574 (33)	146/574 (26)	49/574 (8)
≥7	87/204 (43)	58/204 (28)	26/204 (13)
Total	465/1,601 (29)	260/1,601 (22)	121/1,061 (8)

(From the United States National IVF-ET Registry—1990.)

Alam et al.[26] have published a 52.5 percent total cumulative PR from one GIFT cycle, when all the consecutive frozen embryo transfers (FET) were considered in the same patient who had a previous failed GIFT. The authors made a mathematical calculation based on an additional 9.1 percent PR achieved with FET cycles, when using the remaining sibling embryos from the fresh GIFT procedure. These results certainly improve the PR per procedure and avoid the need of another controlled ovarian hyperstimulation cycle for the patient.

The age of the patient is probably the most important variable to consider when choosing the number of oocytes to transfer. It has been consistently demonstrated that there is a natural decline in women's fertility with increasing age.[27] This issue becomes apparent in women older than age 35 and is definitely marked in patients older than 40 years old. GIFT is the ART procedure that achieves the best results in this older group of women. Craft and Brindsen[28] reviewed 1,071 GIFT cases, finding a PR that varied between 33.5 and 40.2 percent for different age groups of patients younger than 40 years old. In the older than 40-year-old group, the PR was only 19.2 percent and the multiple PR was significantly lower than in younger patients (16.2 percent versus 29 percent). The authors reported only one case of multiple pregnancy greater than twins from a total of 193 cycles studied in women older than 40, even when all oocytes retrieved were transferred. Guzick et al.[22] concluded that the chances of pregnancy, and particularly multiple ones, are significantly reduced in patients older than 40, despite the number of oocytes transferred. Using these considerations, our actual general guidelines when choosing the number of oocytes to transfer are as follows: three oocytes in women younger than age 35, four or five between age 35 and 40, and five or six older than 40 years old.

Defective oocytes rather than poor endometrial receptivity may explain the decrease in women's fertility with aging. This hypothesis has been well documented with the oocyte donation programs, in which we have achieved a 57.9 percent PR when transferring oocytes from young donors to poor responder or premature ovarian failure recipients.[29] Cohen et al.[30] have postulated that zona pellucida hardening is the main cause of dysfunctional oocytes in older women. These authors performed IVF with assisted zonal hatching in women with poor implantation and normal fertilization rates. They observed a significant positive effect with this technique only in women older than age 38, concluding that assisted zonal hatching should be offered only to that particular age group.

Another critical point that must be evaluated before recommending GIFT to an infertile couple is the relevance of individual sperm parameters. Sperm motility and morphology seem to be the most important ones, having independent impacts on the chances of pregnancy. Guzick et al.,[22] analyzing 218 GIFT cycles performed in our center, showed a fivefold increase in PR when motility was greater than 30 percent and a threefold increase when 50 percent of the spermatozoa demonstrated normal morphology. The total sperm count did not have a significant effect when added to this analysis. The latter fact has a logical basis, as GIFT overcomes, in part, numerical problems of a semen analysis by placing a higher number of motile sperm directly into the ampulla. Nevertheless, the technique cannot overcome a major functional problem, such as very low motility or abnormal morphology.[31]

Microlaparoscopic Gamete Intrafallopian Transfer

The concept of microlaparoscopy is relatively new[32,33] and based on the possibility of minimizing the invasiveness of transabdominal endoscopy without compromising the visualization of the pelvic organs. There is only one report in the literature on the use of this approach in ART, a zygote intrafallopian transfer (ZIFT).[33] We have recently performed several cases of GIFT and ZIFT with a rigid microlaparoscope (Figure 13-2).

The GIFT with this new approach can be performed using a flexible[33] or a rigid microlaparoscope and usually only requires local anesthesia or sedation. If laparoscopic GIFT can be performed routinely under local anesthesia without compromising the results, we would overcome its major disadvantage as compared with transcervical transfers. The puncture sites are infiltrated with 3 ml of xilocaine 1 percent. A 3-mm skin incision is made in the umbilicus, and the abdomen is elevated. A Veress needle with a specially designed sleeve is advanced through the incision into the abdominal cavity. The needle is removed and the sleeve is left in place. Then the microlaparoscope is advanced through the sleeve into the abdominal cavity, and once proper intra-abdominal sleeve placement is confirmed, the CO_2 pneumoperitoneum is established. The two other 3-mm abdominal incisions, as well as cannulation of the tube and transfer of the gametes, are performed in the same manner as with conventional laparoscopy. Also, because of the small diameter of the punctures, there is no need to use suture to close them.

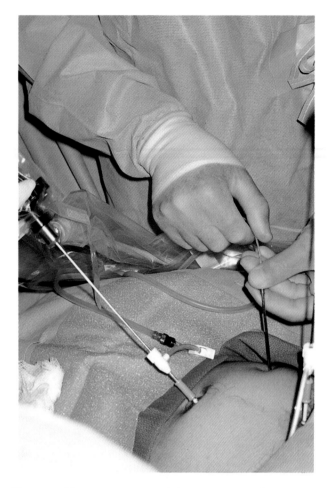

Fig. 13-2. Three punctures and the instruments during a microlaparoscopic gamete intrafallopian transfer.

At the end of the procedure, the patient is transferred to the recovery room and is observed for about 1 hour.

Transcervical Gamete Intrafallopian Transfer

The other new methods for GIFT are those that use the transcervical approach. The transcervical catheter can be placed through the tubal ostium into the ampulla under tactile sensation and by guidance with hysteroscopy or transvaginal sonography.[34] The main advantage of using hysteroscopy for transcervical GIFT is that the operator can see the tip of the catheter and the tubal ostium during the procedure, and also he or she can carefully advance it across the uterine cavity, avoiding endometrial damage.[35] Using the other two nonendoscopic methods, often more than one or two attempts to cannulate the ostium are required, and there exists a potential for producing endometrial trauma and bleeding. Moreover, using the tactile method to cannulate the tubal ostium, it is very diffi-

Table 13-3. Transcervical Gamete Intrafallopian Transfer by Tactile Sensation

Authors	Year	No. of Cycles	No. of Pregnancies	No. of Ectopics
Lisse and Sydow[36]	1990	44	10	0
Ferraiolo et al.[37]	1991	26	7	1
Total		70	17	1

cult to be completely sure where the catheter is and how deep it is into the tube. This last point is very important, because the volume required to avoid spilling the contents of the catheter through the fimbria during retrograde cannulation is directly related to the depth of the catheter in the tube.[35]

The results of the three methods used today for guidance in transcervical GIFT (tactile sensation, transvaginal sonography, and hysteroscopy) are presented in Tables 13-3, 13-4, and 13-5, respectively.

Jansen and Anderson[48] in 1987 described, for the first time, the catheterization of the fallopian tubes via a transcervical approach. These authors used a system of sliding catheters under ultrasound guidance. Since then, these and other investigators have reported a larger experience in an effort to improve the technique itself as well as to use it for intratubal inseminations and gamete and embryo tubal transfers. In general, the results are clearly inferior, in terms of PR, to those achieved by transabdominal tubal transfers, and the ectopic rate appears unacceptably high compared with classical GIFT (13.3 versus 5 percent, respectively).

Lisse and Sydow[36] reported the first GIFT series using the tactile sensation (blind) method (Table 13-3). The results are still too preliminary to draw definitive conclusions.

Hysteroscopic tubal catheterization allows a better visualization of the tubal ostium and a more precise estimation of the depth of catheter insertion into the fallopian tube. Two of the four hysteroscopic series were

Table 13-4. Ultrasound-guided Transcervical Gamete Intrafallopian Transfer

Authors	Year	No. of Cycles	No. of Pregnancies	No. of Ectopics
Jansen and Anderson[38]	1989	10	1	0
Anderson and Jansen[39]	1989	7	1	0
Bustillo et al.[40]	1989	17	1	0
Hazout et al.[41]	1989	18	1	0
Lucena et al.[42]	1989	7	3	1
Lucena et al.[43]	1990	16	4	1
Jansen and Anderson[44]	1993	20	4	0
Total		95	15	2

published by Seracchioli et al.[35,47] achieving a 28 percent PR (27 of 98). The authors proposed hysteroscopy as an alternative method for patients with pelvic adhesions, in whom translaparoscopic transfer may be difficult to perform. Whether prolonged exposure of the tubal microenvironment to CO_2 or direct endometrial trauma will limit the efficacy of this method remains to be clarified.

The noninvasive nature of the procedure, the lack of need for anesthesia, and the cost-effectiveness make these transcervical methods a very attractive alternative in ART. However, up to now results with all common transcervical alternatives have been inconsistent and significantly lower than those obtained with laparoscopy.

Post-Transfer Management and Follow-up

Because the adequacy of the luteal phase after ovarian hyperstimulation and aspiration of the follicles has been questioned, supplementation of the luteal phase with progesterone has been suggested. We recommend a daily dose of progesterone in oil, 50 mg intramuscularly, starting on the third day after the transfer, or 50 mg of vaginal progesterone suppositories every 12 hours for the succeeding 2 weeks. If a B-hCG test performed 14 days after the transfer is positive, the luteal phase support can be maintained for 4 to 6 more weeks, depending on pregnancy evaluation, and the first pelvic ultrasound is performed 3 weeks after transfer.

CONCOMITANT DIAGNOSTIC AND OPERATIVE LAPAROSCOPY AND GAMETE INTRAFALLOPIAN TRANSFER

The cost of infertility evaluation and treatment has become a major factor in the ability of the infertile couple to seek evaluation and treatment. Thus, it is important to accomplish the evaluation and treatment of the infertile couple in a cost-effective manner. A clear tendency to perform therapeutic procedures during diagnostic laparoscopy has occurred within the past few years.[49]

Combining diagnostic laparoscopy and GIFT is certainly an attractive idea for reducing cost and discomfort for the patients. However, this approach requires a significant commitment of time and considerable flexibility in surgical scheduling.[49]

Our ovarian stimulation protocol for these patients is with clomiphene citrate 100 mg given from day 3 to 7 of the cycle. We administrate hCG 5,000 IU when the leading follicle has reached a diameter of 18 to 20 mm, and the laparoscopy-GIFT is scheduled 36 hours later.

The first clinical experience was reported in 1989 by Pampiglione et al.[50] working with women who received clomiphene citrate (CC) for ovarian stimulation. Eighty-one percent of the patients responded adequately to the therapy, and 24 percent became pregnant. Gindoff et al.[51] reported similar results using human menopausal gonadotropin and hCG in 33 patients undergoing a combined laparoscopy-GIFT. Twenty-one of these patients were found to have adhesions or endometriosis, and of these, 19 received concurrent therapeutic operative endoscopy in addition to the oocyte retrieval. The authors concluded that by using laparoscopy it was possible to provide important diagnostic information, to attempt therapeutic measures, and to achieve good PRs. Johns,[49] in a larger series of 62 patients, corroborated those statements, using CC to induce ovulation in patients with combined diagnostic and operative laparoscopy and GIFT.

Table 13-6 summarizes the above findings, plus our own experience in this matter. Using CC alone, we have achieved an acceptable 35 percent clinical PR (7 of 20) with only one spontaneous abortion observed thus far.[52] Nevertheless, we had already cancelled eight patients due to premature ovulation, which is certainly an inconvenience in patients without prior pituitary down-regulation. Also, we do not advise a more aggressive protocol of ovulation induction, because a larger number of follicles can interfere with complete visualization of pelvic structures and make surgery more difficult, due to pelvic congestion and friable ovaries.

In the properly evaluated patient, CC-laparoscopy-GIFT is efficacious and cost-effective and does not significantly interfere with laparoscopic treatment of pelvic pathology.

ADVANTAGES

The GIFT technique seems to be more physiologic than IVF-ET because it mimics some of the mechanisms involved in a successful fertility cycle. Both gametes are transferred directly to the ampullary portion

Table 13-5. Hysteroscopic-Guided Gamete Intrafallopian Transfer

Authors	Year	No. of Cycles	No. of Pregnancies
Wurfel et al.[45]	1990	24	4
Possati et al.[46]	1990	27	7
Seracchioli et al.[35]	1991	50	13
Seracchioli et al.[47]	1993	48	14
Total		149	38

Table 13-6. Concomitant Diagnostic/Operative Laparoscopy and GIFT

Authors	No. of Patients	No. of Clinical Pregnancies	Clinical Pregnancy Rate (%)
Pampiglione et al.[50]	21	5	23.8
Gindoff et al.[51]	15	4	26.7
Johns[49]	62	15	24.6
Balmaceda et al.[52]	20	7	35.0
Total	118	31	26.3

of the fallopian tube, the normal site of fertilization. The fertilization and cleavage processes take place in vivo, where the natural tubal milieu is more physiologic than the standard culture media used in in vitro techniques. Early development of the very early embryo in the fallopian tube can provide a more chronologically suitable entry of the embryo into the uterine cavity, yielding a better chance of implantation.

FUTURE PERSPECTIVES

Two new endoscopic methods have recently been developed that may become predominant in the near future for gamete and embryo tubal transfers, and they are (1) microlaparoscopy and (2) falloposcopy. Technical improvements have only recently allowed significant reduction in the diameter of scopes, without significant compromise of image quality. Both methods allow the elimination of general anesthesia and subsequently may reduce the cost of the procedure. Microlaparoscopy also has the advantage of reducing the size of the abdominal incision and reducing local pain and tissue damage. Falloposcopy has the major advantage of direct access into the fallopian tube, preventing unnecessary damage to it.

The efficacy of GIFT for the treatment of infertile patients with at least one patent and normal fallopian tube is well documented. The results up to now continue to be more easily reproduced on a clinic-by-clinic basis than those for IVF. However, the continuous progress in the knowledge of embryo culture conditions is slowly improving the results of IVF-ET, which is a significantly less invasive therapeutic alternative. Efforts must be made to continue to simplify the methods of transfer of gametes to the fallopian tube for GIFT to remain a viable therapeutic alternative.

REFERENCES

1. Asch RH, Ellsworth LR, Balmaceda JP, Wong PC: Pregnancy after translaparoscopic gamete intrafallopian transfer (letter). Lancet 2:1034, 1984
2. Asch RH, Ellsworth LR, Balmaceda JP, Wong PC: Birth following gamete intrafallopian transfer (letter). Lancet 2:163, 1985
3. Cefalu E, Cittadini E, Balmaceda JP et al: Successful gamete intrafallopian transfer following failed artificial insemination by donor: evidence for a defect in gamete transport? Fertil Steril 50:279, 1988
4. Asch RH, Balmaceda JP, Cittadini E et al: Gamete intrafallopian transfer; international cooperative study of the first 800 cases. Ann NY Acad Sci 541:722, 1988
5. The American Fertility Society: Minimal standards for gamete intrafallopian transfer (GIFT). Fertil Steril 50:20, 1988
6. Hughes EG, Fedorkow DM, Daya S et al: The routine use of gonadotropin releasing hormone agonists prior to in vitro fertilization and gamete intrafallopian transfer: a meta-analysis of randomized controlled trials. Fertil Steril 58:888, 1992
7. Steptoe PC, Edwards RG: Birth after reimplantation of a human embryo. Lancet 2:366, 1978
8. Wiseman DA, Short WB, Pattinson HA et al: Oocyte retrieval in an in vitro fertilization—embryo transfer program: comparison of four methods. Radiology 173:99, 1989
9. Asch RH, Balmaceda JP, Ellsworth LR, Wong PC: Preliminary experiences with GIFT (gamete intrafallopian transfer). Fertil Steril 45:366, 1986
10. Bolton VN, Brande PR: Preparation of human spermatozoa for in vitro fertilization by isopycnic centrifugation on self generating density gradients. Arch Androl 13:167, 1984
11. Yee B, Rosen GF, Chacon RR et al: Gamete intrafallopian transfer: the effect of the number of eggs used and the depth of gamete placement on pregnancy initiation. Fertil Steril 52:639, 1989
12. Tucker MJ, Wong CJ, Chan YM et al: Post-operative artificial insemination: does it improve GIFT outcome? Hum Reprod 5:189, 1990
13. Asch RH: GIFT: indications, results, problems, and perspectives. p. 209. In Capitanio GL, Asch RH, De Cecco L, Croce S (eds): GIFT: From Basics to Clinics. Raven Press, New York, 1989
14. Cohen J: The efficiency and efficacy of IVF and GIFT (editorial). Hum Reprod 6:613, 1991
15. Society for Assisted Reproductive Technology, The American Fertility Society: Assisted reproductive technology in the United States and Canada: 1991 results from the Society for Assisted Reproductive Technology generated from The American Fertility Society Registry. Fertil Steril 59:956, 1993
16. Testart J, Plachot M, Madelbaum J et al: World collaborative report on IVF-ET and GIFT: 1989 results. Hum Reprod 7:362, 1992
17. Asch RH: Uterine versus tubal embryo transfer in the human. Comparative analysis of implantation, pregnancy and live birth rates. Ann NY Acad Sci 696:461, 1991
18. Mills MS, Eddowes HA, Cahill DJ et al: A prospective controlled study of in vitro fertilization, gamete intrafallopian transfer and intrauterine insemination combined with superovulation. Hum Reprod 7:190, 1992
19. Tanbo T, Dale PO, Abyholm T: Assisted fertilization in infertile women with patent fallopian tubes. A comparison of in vitro fertilization, gamete intrafallopian transfer and tubal embryo stage transfer. Hum Reprod 5:255, 1990
20. Hammitt DG, Syrop CH, Hahn SJ et al: Comparison of concurrent pregnancy rates for in vitro fertilization-embryo transfer, pronuclear stage embryo transfer and gamete intrafallopian transfer. Hum Reprod 5:947, 1990
21. Balmaceda JP, Heitman T, Borrero C, Asch RH: In vivo versus in vitro oocyte maturation in a primate animal model. Abstract 015, p.5, Proceedings Annual Meeting of The American Fertility Society, 1986
22. Guzick DS, Balmaceda JP, Ord T, Asch RH: The importance of egg and sperm factors in predicting the likelihood of pregnancy from gamete intrafallopian transfer. Fertil Steril 52:795, 1989
23. Penzias AS, Alper MM, Oskowitz SP et al: Gamete intrafallopian transfer: assessment of the optimal number of oocytes to transfer. Fertil Steril 55:311, 1991

24. Medical Research International, Society for Assisted Technology, The American Fertility Society: In vitro fertilization-embryo transfer (IVF-ET) in the United States: 1990 results from the IVF-ET Registry. Fertil Steril 57:15, 1992
25. Weckstein LN, Jacobson A, Galen DI: The role of cryopreservation in gamete intrafallopian transfer and zygote intrafallopian transfer. Assist Reprod Rev 2:2, 1992
26. Alam V, Weckstein L, Ord T et al: Cummulative pregnancy rate from one gamete intrafallopian transfer (GIFT) cycle with cryopreservation of embryos. Hum Reprod 8:559, 1993
27. Federation CECOS, Schwartz D, Mayaux MJ: Female fecundity as a function of age. N Engl J Med 306:404, 1982
28. Craft I, Brindsen P: Alternatives to IVF—the outcome of 1071 first GIFT procedures. Hum Reprod 4:29, 1989
29. Balmaceda JP, Alam V, Roszjtein D et al: Embryo implantation rates in oocyte donation: a prospective comparison of tubal versus uterine transfers. Fertil Steril 57:362, 1992
30. Cohen J, Alikani M, Trowbridge J, Rosenwaks Z: Implantation enhancement by selective assisted hatching using zona drilling of human embryos with poor prognosis. Hum Reprod 7:685, 1992
31. Wiedemann R, Noss U, Hepp M: Gamete intrafallopian transfer in male subfertility. Hum Reprod 4:408, 1989
32. Dorsey JM, Tabb CR: Mini-laparoscopy and fiber optic lasers. Obstet Gynecol Clin North Am 18:613, 1991
33. Risquez F, Pennehouat G, Fernandez R et al: Microlaparoscopy: a preliminary report. Hum Reprod 8:1701, 1993
34. Risquez F, Confino E: Transcervical tubal cannulation, past, present and future. Fertil Steril 60:211, 1993
35. Seracchioli R, Possati G, Bafaro G et al: Hysteroscopic gamete intrafallopian transfer: a good alternative in selected cases to laparoscopic intrafallopian transfer. Hum Reprod 6:1388, 1991
36. Lisse K, Sydow P: Transvaginal gamete intrafallopian transfer. Abstract of the II Joint ESCO-ESHRE Meeting. Hum Reprod, suppl. 5:S99, 1990
37. Ferraiolo A, Croce S, Anserini P et al: "Blind" transcervical transfer of gametes in the fallopian tube: a preliminary study. Hum Reprod 6:537, 1991
38. Jansen RPS, Anderson JC: Transvaginal gamete and embryo transfer to the fallopian tubes. p. 383. In Capitanio GL, Asch RH, de Cecco L et al. (eds): GIFT: From Basics to Clinics. Raven Press, New York, 1989
39. Anderson JC, Jansen RPS: Ultrasound guided catheterization of the fallopian tube for the non-operative transfer of gametes and embryos. p.80. Proceedings of the 6th World Congress of In Vitro Fertilization and Alternate Assisted Reproduction, Jerusalem, Israel, April 2–7, 1989
40. Bustillo M, Schulman JD: Transcervical ultrasound guided intrafallopian placement of gametes, zygotes and embryos. J In Vitro Fertil Embryo Transf 6:321, 1989
41. Hazout A, Glissant A, Frydman R: Transvaginal ultrasound-guided gamete intrafallopian transfer. p. 30. Abstract book from the 6th World Congress: In Vitro Fertilization and Alternate-Assisted Reproduction, Jerusalem, Israel, April 2–7, 1989
42. Lucena E, Ruiz JA, Mendoza JC et al: Vaginal intratubal insemination (VITI) and vaginal GIFT, endosonographic technique: early experience. Hum Reprod 658, 1989
43. Lucena E, Paulson JD, Ruiz J et al: Vaginal gamete intrafallopian transfer. Experience with 14 cases. J Reprod Med 35:645, 1990
44. Jansen RPS, Anderson JC: Transvaginal versus laparoscopic gamete intrafallopian transfer: a case-controlled retrospective comparison. Fertil Steril 59:836, 1993
45. Wurfel W, Steck T, Spingler H et al: Hysteroscopy for gamete intrafallopian transfer (GIFT). Acta Eur Fertil 21:133, 1990
46. Possati G, Seracchioli R, Melega C et al: Gamete intrafallopian transfer by hysteroscopy as an alternative treatment for infertility. Fertil Steril 56:496, 1991
47. Seracchioli R, Maccolini A, Porcu E et al: A new approach to gamete intrafallopian transfer via hysteroscopy. Hum Reprod 8:2093, 1993
48. Jansen RPS, Anderson JC: Catheterization of the fallopian tube from the vagina. Lancet 2:309, 1987
49. Johns A: Clomiphene citrate-induced gamete intrafallopian transfer with diagnostic and operative laparoscopy. Fertil Steril 56:311, 1991
50. Pampiglione JS, Bolton VN, Parsons JH, Campbell S: Gamete intrafallopian transfer combined with diagnostic and operative laparoscopy: a treatment for infertility in a district hospital. Hum Reprod 4:408, 1989
51. Gindoff PR, Hall JL, Nelson LM, Stillman RJ: Efficacy of assisted reproductive technology during diagnostic and operative infertility laparoscopy. Obstet Gynecol 75:299, 1990
52. Balmaceda JP, Gonzales J, Bernardini L: Gamete and zygote intrafallopian transfers and related techniques. Curr Opinion Obstet Gynecol 4:743, 1992

14 Combined Laparoscopic and Vaginal Repair of Pelvic Support Defects

JAMES H. DORSEY
HOWARD T. SHARP

Uterovaginal prolapse and the associated symptoms of discomfort and urinary stress incontinence have challenged gynecologic surgeons for centuries. The variety of operative procedures that have been suggested for the repair of these pelvic support defects attests to the complexity of the problem and to the dissatisfaction with relatively high long-term failure rates. Causes of these failures have been attributed to inherent connective tissue weakness, obstetric trauma, unrecognized and uncorrected fascial injury at the time of initial reparative surgery, aging, and a lack of postmenopausal estrogen replacement.[1] As noted by Shull et al.,[2,3] much of the available literature concerning pelvic support repair is confused by a lack of proper preoperative defect identification and subsequent intraoperative verification. The surgeon must not only accomplish a satisfactory repair but should also anticipate the development of future defects and perform the necessary surgery to prevent their occurrence. Repair of prolapse is seldom a single operative procedure but is comprised of a series of steps planned to correct each identifiable or predictable defect.

Currently, there has been increased interest in evaluating the laparoscopic approach to reconstructive pelvic surgery. The substitution of small puncture wounds for large abdominal incisions and the search for less traumatic surgery with faster recovery times have led laparoscopic pelvic surgeons to substitute these minimally invasive techniques for reconstructive operations traditionally performed through the open abdomen. Although these early reports are descriptional and lack long-term follow-up, preliminary evaluation of the outcomes of laparoscopic surgery for genuine stress incontinence and posthysterectomy vaginal vault prolapse are certainly very encouraging.[4–6] With the rapid development of new laparoscopic instruments and techniques, laparoscopic surgery for pelvic reconstruction is able to be performed with methods similar to those used in the open procedures. Sound surgical judgment, thorough surgical training, and meticulous attention to detail are the basic ingredients, irrespective of the operative route.

UTEROVAGINAL PROLAPSE

There continues to be controversy concerning the most effective techniques to use at the time of hysterectomy to prevent subsequent vaginal vault eversion. Morley[7] commented on the low rate of subsequent vault eversion in patients with moderate uterovaginal prolapse when proper vault suspension is carried out. However, Cruikshank and Cox[8] advocate liberal use of sacrospinous ligament suspension at the time of hysterectomy for any degree of prolapse. Elkins[9] thinks that high McCall culdeplasty is as effective as sacrospinous ligament fixation when used for the correction of uterine prolapse, whereas Porges and Smilen[10] found that sacrospinous fixation accompanying vaginal hysterectomy performed in patients with third-degree prolapse reduced the rate of reccurrence from 6.7 to 5.8 percent. Shull et al.[11] successfully manage prolapse associated with paravaginal defects by transvaginal paravaginal white line and obturator fasciae repairs accompanied by vaginal repair of any coexisting support defects. Given et al.[12] have compared vaginal length and sexual function in three possible methods of vault fixation at the time of hysterectomy (i.e., sacrospinous fixation, high uterosacral ligament fixation, and sacral colpopexy) and found the vagina slightly longer after sacral colpopexy; however, the difference was not significant. Sacral colpopexy certainly provides an anatomically correct position for the vagina, and when a properly constructed bridge of merselene or Marlex mesh is used to suspend the vault from sacral promontory periosteum, a secure and lasting support is achieved.[13] However, the operation involves major abdominal surgery through a large incision, and many gynecologists prefer the less invasive vaginal approach.

RATIONALE FOR CONCOMITANT LAPAROSCOPIC AND VAGINAL RECONSTRUCTION

In January 1991, while performing a laparoscopically assisted vaginal hysterectomy for a patient with abdominal indications for hysterectomy and a significant uterovaginal prolapse with associated genuine stress incontinence, it became very obvious to us that the anatomy of the support defects were beautifully demonstrated by the combination of vaginal and laparoscopic techniques. It also seemed logical to use a combination approach to repair these defects, because both the vaginal and laparoscopic surgeon were able to reinforce and add to the anatomic correction of defects from two different perspectives. In addition, dissection of the retropubic space was easily accomplished via laparoscopy, allowing urethropexy to be performed in a manner similar to the conventional open technique by

the laparoscopic placement of the sutures. Our initial experience yielded excellent immediate results.[14] Since then, we have continued to use a combination of vaginal and laparoscopic surgery for the correction of these problems in many patients.

Our approach has been to position the patient so that any necessary vaginal surgery such as anterior colporrhaphy, posterior colporrhaphy, perineorrhaphy, and dissection of the enterocele sac can be carried out from below. Identification and dissection of the enterocele is greatly enhanced by laparoscopy as the peritoneum bulges out of the pelvis and over the rectum due to the pressure of the pneumoperitoneum. Amputation of the enterocele sac, uterosacral ligament identification and plication, and the Moschcowitz or Halban procedure are accomplished from either below or above. In patients with marked prolapse, sacral colpopexy is performed laparoscopically. In patients with moderate degrees of prolapse, a modified high McCall procedure is carried out. Addison et al.[15] have concluded that when sacral colpopexy is performed, anterior colporrhaphy alone is inadequate to manage anterior wall relaxation and urinary stress incontinence. We also are convinced of that fact, so that since early 1991, all patients treated for total prolapse or posthysterectomy vault eversion have undergone laparoscopic retropubic urethropexy in addition to the other necessary repairs.

TECHNIQUES OF COMBINED LAPAROSCOPIC AND VAGINAL RECONSTRUCTION FOR PROLAPSE

Preoperatively, thorough evaluation of the fascial defects present are identified, graded, and recorded. Currently, urodynamic testing is performed on all patients regardless of complaints if prolapse is severe, so that unrecognized detrusor instability or minor degrees of stress incontinence are identified. Because these procedures to repair multiple defects are time-consuming, two surgeons, each with assistants, start the procedure. The surgical steps can be summarized as follows:

1. Under general anesthesia, the patient is placed in a modified lithotomy position in the gyneloop (Gyneco, Middletown, NY) so that the thighs are in the same plane as the abdomen. Elevated thighs may seriously hinder free movement of the laparoscopic instruments when directed laterally or cephalad. The use of the gyneloop stirrups allows the readjustment of the patient's legs during the operative procedure so that they may be elevated easily if vaginal surgery requires better access to the perineum.

2. After the patient is prepared and draped, a 30-cc (three-way) Foley catheter is inserted into the bladder. Often, before this step, cystoscopy is carried out and ureteral stents are placed. This step greatly aids in identification of the ureters, which in turn makes procedures such as the Moschcowitz and the Burch safer and quicker.

3. The laparoscopic surgeon then insufflates the abdominal cavity to 12 mmHg. Three trocars are inserted, one in the umbilicus and two in each lower quadrant, lateral to the inferior epigastric arteries. The trocar sheaths should be 11.5 mm in diameter so that larger diameter instruments such as curved needles, hemoclip appliers, or the Endo-stitch (USSC, Norwalk, CT) can be inserted (see Ch. 20).

4. If sacral colpopexy is to be performed for posthysterec-tomy vault prolapse, a fourth trocar is placed just to the left of the midline. This port is used primarily for retrac-tion of the sigmoid colon laterally. A fan type of laparo-scopic retractor placed through the trocar sheath does an excellent job of keeping the sacral promontory free of bowel.

5. The vaginal dissection of the rectocele and enterocele is begun at the same time as the laparoscopy. The enterocele is dramatically demonstrated as it balloons out over the rectocele (Fig. 14-1). The sac can be pushed back up high into the abdominal cavity, graphically illustrating the anatomy of the herniated peritoneum. The sac may be lig-ated from above using loop ligatures (Surgidac or Polysorb, 2–0, USSC, Norwalk, CT). At least two ligatures are applied, and the sac is amputated (Fig. 14-2).

6. The vaginal vault is then elevated with a probe (rectal sizer, USSC, Norwalk, CT) and laparoscopically denuded of peritoneum. An effort is made to identify pubocervical fascia anteriorly and rectovaginal fascia posteriorly (De-nonvilliers fascia). Whenever possible, these two layers are joined over the vaginal vault with interrupted sutures.

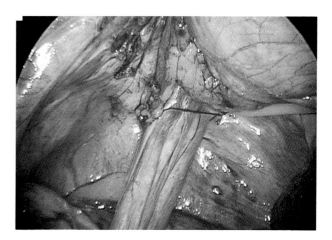

Fig. 14-2. The enterocele sac has been dissected out by the vaginal surgeon and is now pushed back up into the pelvic cavity. The sac is shown here being ligated before amputa-tion.

The uterosacral ligaments must then be identified by the laparoscopic surgeon. Often, there have been breaks in these ligaments, and the fascia has retracted posteriorly, leaving only the empty sleeve, a fold of peritoneum, at its original site of attachment to the posterior cervix and uterus. Cullen Richardson and William Saye[16] of Atlanta, Georgia, two surgeons who also use a combined vaginal and laparoscopic approach for the repair of fascial sup-port defects, have described and dramatically demon-strated this situation in laparoscopic videotapes that ex-plain the technique of identifying the empty sleeve and

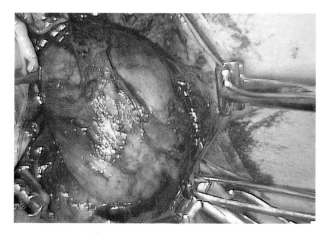

Fig. 14-1. In this patient, who is undergoing anterior and posterior colporrhaphy, an enterocele distended by the pneumoperitoneum bulges from beneath the opened mu-cosa.

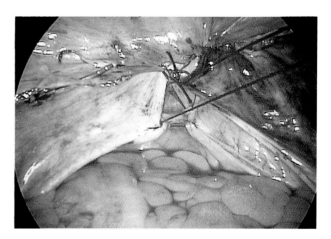

Fig. 14-3. The uterosacral ligaments have been identified la-paroscopically. This is not an "empty sleeve" of peritoneum but true, strong uterosacral ligament, which is being stitched to pubovesical fascia and vaginal vault over the closed cul-de-sac. The laparoscope provides excellent direct visualiza-tion and the opportunity for ureteral identification.

tracing it posteriorly and laterally to find the retracted uterosacral fascia. A modified laparoscopic Moschcowitz (Fig. 14-3) is then performed using permanent suture material. The uterosacral ligaments are included in the purse-string sutures and anchored in the fascia of the posterior vaginal vault. The latter is a continuation of Denonvilliers rectovaginal fascia. In suturing support fascia to vaginal fascia, whether performing uterosacral ligament plication, sacral colpopexy, retropubic urethropexy, or paravaginal defect repairs, the sutures should be placed through the full thickness of the vagina. Permanent suture material erodes through the vaginal mucosa, which then heals over the suture, and full-thickness placement helps ensure that some vaginal fascia is included in the stitch.

7. If sacral colpopexy is to be performed, the presacral space is then entered (Fig. 14-4). To accomplish this, the sacral promontory is first gently palpated and the peritoneum over the promontory elevated and incised vertically. The laparoscopic surgeon must know the anatomy of the presacral space well, and great care is used as the periosteum is cleaned. The space is bordered by the bifurcation of the aorta superiorly, the common iliac vessels laterally in its upper portion, and then in the lower regions by the right and left ureters and the mesentery of the sigmoid colon. The periosteum is gently cleaned. The middle sacral vessels are identified posteriorly on the periosteum and coagulated if necessary.

8. The peritoneum is now carefully incised down to the vaginal vault. It is easier to open the peritoneum and then close it over the vaginal support strap than it is to tunnel beneath peritoneum.

9. We prefer to use Marlex mesh as the supporting bridge between the sacral promontory and the vaginal vault, as this

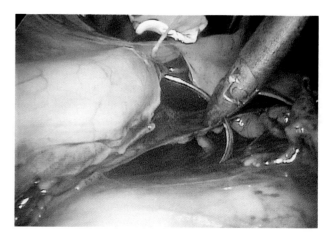

Fig. 14-5. Permanent suture material has been passed through the strap (in this case, Gortex). The suture is now placed through the periosteum of the promontory.

material serves as a lattice for fibroblasts. It is anchored both anteriorly and posteriorly to the vaginal cuff and then stitched to the periosteum of the sacral promontory (Fig. 14-5). The strap must not be pulled too tightly. The function of the strap is to support the vagina, particularly when intra-abdominal pressure is raised, and it does not need to be taut (Fig. 14-6).

Although the literature at this time is inconclusive in demonstrating the superiority of the abdominal over the vaginal route for colposuspension, one of the advantages of laparoscopic reconstructive surgery is that procedures such as uterosacral ligament plication, Moschcowitz culdeplasty, and sacral colpopexy are easily combined with anterior defect repairs such as retropubic urethropexy.

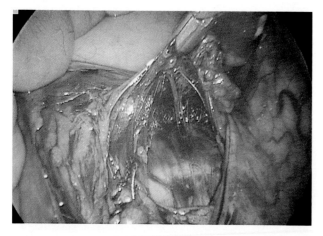

Fig. 14-4. The peritoneum over the sacral promontory has been incised and the underlying connective tissue and presacral nerves reflected or removed, bearing the periosteum of the sacrum. The bifurcation of the aorta forms the superior border of the space, and the common iliac vessels and the ureters form the lateral borders.

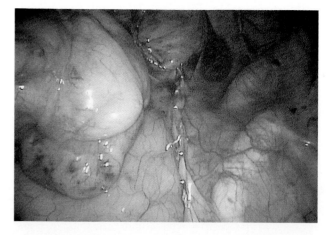

Fig. 14-6. The peritoneum has now been closed over the properly tensioned strap, eliminating the possibility of bowel sliding beneath the strap. In this case, clips afforded a very rapid and secure closure.

Retropubic Urethropexy

In our hospital, we have used two different laparoscopic techniques to perform retropubic urethropexy. Our preferred operation currently is the laparoscopic Burch procedure. This type of urethropexy does require skill in laparoscopic suturing and knot tying. Because we observed the difficulties experienced by surgeons in learning laparoscopic knotting techniques, we have also described a laparoscopic variation of needle urethropexy in which a modified Stamey needle with an eye near its point (Dorsey urethropexy needle, ETM, Butler, MD) was used to first pass through the anterior rectus sheath and then, under the direct view of the laparoscope, pierce Cooper's ligament on its way through the previously dissected space of Retzius.

The vagina is then entered with the needle at an appropriate location near the vesicle neck and suture material loaded into the eye near the point. The suture is then pulled back up through the anterior abdominal wall. Two passages of the needle provide a loop of suture, which can then be tied on the rectus fascia. Theoretically, this procedure answers most of the criticism of conventional needle retropubic urethropexy, because the technique provides the following advantages:

1. It is performed under direct vision and provides excellent accuracy in needle placement.
2. The space of Retzius may be fully dissected, and this promotes additional scarring, which is believed by some to reinforce the suturing.
3. All knots are tied on rectus fascia through a small superficial incision.
4. The suture has also passed through Cooper's ligament so that suture security is promoted by an additional sturdy structure.

Although we still occasionally use laparoscopic needle urethropexy, we now find that our laparoscopic Burch procedures can usually be accomplished in less than an hour without requiring needle threading in the vagina. If the surgeon will spend the time necessary to learn how to tie laparoscopic square knots, the Burch procedure becomes relatively easy to perform.

Entering the Space of Retzius

The retropubic space may be entered by one of two techniques: (1) the preperitoneal laparoscopic dissection, which starts on top of the posterior rectus sheath through an incision made in the umbilicus, or (2) an intra-abdominal laparoscopic incision made transversely in the parietal peritoneum of the anterior abdominal wall several centimeters above the bladder and extended laterally to the obliterated umbilical vessels.

The preperitoneal entry can be accomplished by direct dissection and development of the space between peritoneum and the rectus abdominus muscles under laparoscopic visualization or by balloon dissection. We prefer to dissect this space with the laparoscope under direct visualization because any adhesions between peritoneum and muscle, a situation common in patients who have undergone previous abdominal surgery, can be lysed without entering the peritoneal cavity. The Visiport (USSC, Norwalk, CT) may be of assistance in implementing this approach, or an operative laparoscope equipped with a laser may be used. The preperitoneal space will insufflate nicely, and the gas will assist in the development of the space.

We use the preperitoneal approach in patients who have not required intraperitoneal laparoscopy to accomplish repair of posterior pelvic support defects. Examples of these combined extraperitoneal vaginal and laparoscopic surgical repairs are afforded by patients undergoing vaginal repairs of rectocele, enterocele, and cystocele, followed by sacrospinous ligament fixation of the prolapsed vault and extraperitoneal laparoscopic retropubic urethropexy.

More commonly, our Burch procedures are performed transperitoneally because of the frequent use of combined vaginal and intraperitoneal repair of posterior support defects. Examples are patients who undergo vaginal dissection of the enterocele sac, vaginal posterior colporrhaphy, laparoscopic enterocele excision with Moschcowitz procedure, and uterosacral ligament plication. These intraperitoneal component operations are then followed when indicated by sacral colpopexy and transperitoneal dissection of the space of Retzius in preparation for Burch urethropexy or laparoscopic paravaginal repair.

When the parietal peritoneum of the anterior abdominal wall is incised, it is wise to fill the bladder with 250 to 350 ml of saline through a three-way Foley catheter. This will clearly demonstrate the limits of the bladder and help the surgeon avoid bladder damage. The weight of the fluid also assists in the entry into the space of Retzius because it pulls the inferior edge of peritoneal incision downward. The incision should be made 2 to 3 cm superior to the bladder through the urachus laterally to the obliterated umbilical vessels. The latter usually are extremely easy to see. Care should be taken to avoid the inferior epigastric vessels, which lie just on top of the peritoneum just lateral to the umbilical ligament. By gentle blunt dissection, the

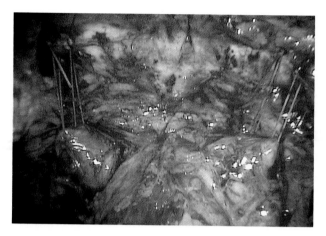

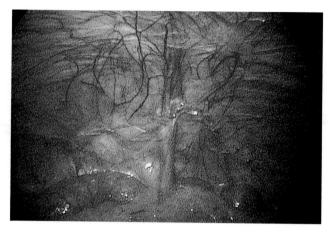

Fig. 14-7. The space of Retzius is beautifully visualized with a laparoscope. Here the pubovesical fascia and lateral vagina have been suspended from Cooper's ligament by permanent sutures.

Fig. 14-9. The peritoneum of the anterior abdominal wall, which was incised to enter the space of Retzius, is now closed with clips. The location of the incision is shown, relatively high on the anterior abdominal wall.

space of Retzius is developed, and by cleaning the fat from the symphasis and proceeding along Cooper's ligament, the anatomy is beautifully demonstrated.

With two fingers in the patient's vagina, the vesicle neck is gently moved medially by blunt dissection exactly as is done in the open procedure. When vaginal fascia is identified bilaterally, two sutures are placed first through Cooper's ligament, then through the full thickness of vaginal wall and back through the ligament (Fig. 14-7). Permanent suture material is used, usually 0 Surgidac (USSC, Norwalk, CT), and sliding square knots are tied.

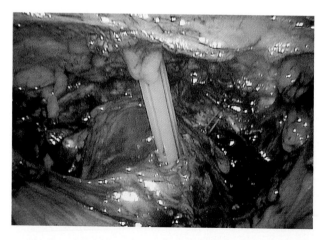

Fig. 14-8. The bladder has been distended with sterile water through a three-way Foley catheter. The suprapubic catheter is shown here being placed through the Insertacath Sheath.

We always follow these procedures with two additional steps: (1) cystoscopy and (2) placement of a suprapubic catheter. The cystoscopy is performed to ensure that no sutures have been placed in the bladder and that the ureteral orifices are spurting urine. Indigo Carmine may be given intravenously several minutes before the cystoscopy to make identification of the ureteral openings easier. If, as is often the case, ureteral stents have been placed, they are removed before the cystoscopy. Recently, we have used a #12 French Lawrence Add-A-CATH trocar, through which a cystoscope can be inserted. Under direct laparoscopic visualization, this trocar is inserted into the bladder through a small suprapubic stab wound. Cystoscopy may then be performed through the trocar sheath, and subsequent suprapubic catheter insertion is carried out through the same sheath (Fig. 14-8).

After hemostasis has been achieved, it has been our practice to close the parietal peritoneal incision made when entering the space of Retzius. This is done by using a running 3–0 suture or by approximating the peritoneum with a hernia stapling device. In either case, the closure must be tight enough to prevent herniation of small bowel into the space of Retzius (Fig. 14-9).

LAPAROSCOPIC REPAIR OF THE PARAVAGINAL FASCIAL DEFECTS

In 1981, Richardson et al.[17] published their classic description of the paravaginal fascial defect and its repair. A thorough understanding of pelvic anatomy and of the various support defects that may occur is of paramount importance to any surgeon who contemplates attempting any pelvic reconstructive procedure, and this fact has been beautifully emphasized by Richardson[18] in his reports and anatomic drawings. This author has graphically described the importance of the pubocervical fascia and its attachment to the fascia of the lateral pelvic wall at the tendinous arch of the pelvic fascia (white line or arcus tendineus fasciae pelvis). The bladder rests on this pubocervical fascia, and avulsion of the anterior portion of the fascia at the white line destroys the support to the entire anterior vagina, bladder, and urethra, thus accounting for the clinical picture of cystocele and urethrocele.

The repair of the paravaginal defect is somewhat reminiscent of the retropubic urethropexy in that first the space of Retzius is entered, the bladder and urethra are then gently moved medically away from the lateral pelvic wall, and the underlying pubocervical fascia is identified. Separation of this fascia from the lateral pelvic wall occurs about 75 percent of the time on the right side, and three distinct defects have been observed. There may be an avulsion of the arcus tendineus itself from the pelvic side wall so that it is found on the edge of the pubovesicle fascia, the white line may actually be split along its length, or the pubocervical fascia may be torn away from the white line. In any case, the repair of the defect is obvious. The pubocervical fascia must be sutured again to the white line and the lateral pelvic wall. In some cases in which the defect is severe and the remains of the white line more difficult to identify, the repair may be made a bit higher on the pelvic side wall by placing the sutures through the arcus of the levator ani muscle.

Because the paravaginal repair involves large abdominal incision and dissection, there has been great interest in developing satisfactory but less invasive techniques, and both vaginal and laparoscopic procedures for paravaginal defect repair have been described.[19]

Saye and Cullen, working in Marietta, Georgia, with Richardson, have developed a laparoscopic technique in which the repair is carried out in almost exactly the same fashion as it is performed with the abdomen open (personal communication). They have operated on more than 50 women in whom they have used the combined vaginal and laparoscopic approach to identify and repair support defects, which include the paravaginal one. They report satisfactory anatomic repair and cure of urinary stress incontinence in the 90 percent range.

Paravaginal repair has not been proved as a method that yields results comparable with retropubic urethropexy for the control of genuine stress incontinence. Laparoscopically, we have followed the procedure of Sage and Richardson for demonstrating the defect; however, we prefer to perform the Burch procedure in patients with urinary stress incontinence at this time. More data are needed before the true effect of paravaginal repair for this condition can be ascertained.

COMPLICATIONS OF THE COMBINED VAGINAL AND LAPAROSCOPIC APPROACH

In a series of 50 combined vaginal and laparoscopic operations performed for the correction of multiple pelvic support defects, there have been relatively few complications. Because these procedures usually involve the performance of several different types of repair, they tend to require several hours or more to complete. For example, a Burch procedure alone may require only 1 hour to perform laparoscopically; however, the other repairs also add significant operative time, requiring the patient to be in a modified lithotomy for the entire length of the operation. Great care must be taken to guard against peripheral nerve injury as well as phlebitis. We have had two perineal nerve injuries and one case of postoperative thrombophlebitis in this series. Fortunately, no other major complications have been encountered.

CONCLUSION

Pelvic support defects that require repair tend to be multiple in any given patient. Identification and repair of these defects involve careful and often extensive workup and relatively long operative procedures if successful outcomes are to be achieved. Knowledge of anatomy and good surgical ability are of prime importance for the gynecologist who undertakes this task, irrespective of the route chosen.

In our clinic, combined vaginal and laparoscopic surgery has yielded excellent initial results. This approach seems rational as it combines two minimally invasive techniques. The laparoscope is never used just for the sake of performing a laparoscopy but only when the advantage seems obvious. For this reason, our series consists of various combinations of vaginal or laparoscopically performed culdeplasties, colpopexies such as sacrospinous fixation and sacral colpopexy, and laparoscopic retropubic urethropexy performed either transperitoneally or preperitoneally.

The two great advantages of this combined approach are (1) a greatly increased awareness both of anatomy and of the details of the support defect, and (2) a greatly increased ability to choose and execute the most appropriate repair to secure the most desirable outcome.

This type of surgery, be it vaginal, open abdominal, or laparoscopic, must be attempted only by the surgeon who has been well trained in pelvic reconstruction. At the moment, few laparoscopic surgeons have mastered the techniques required for the successful combination approach. However, to us, the benefits seem so definite that future use of many of these laparoscopic techniques seems ensured.

REFERENCES

1. Norton PA: Pelvic floor disorders: the role of fascia and ligaments. Clin Obstet Gynecol 36:926, 1993
2. Shull BL, Capen CV, Riggs MW, Kuehl TJ: Preoperative and postoperative analysis of site-specific pelvic support defects in 81 women treated with sacrospinous ligament suspension and pelvic reconstruction. Am J Obstet Gynecol 166:1764, 1992
3. Shull BL: Clinical evaluation of women with pelvic support defects. Clin Obstet Gynecol 36:939, 1993
4. Polascik TJ, Moore RG, Rosenberg MT, Kavoussi LR: Comparison of laparoscopic and open retropubic urethropexy for treatment of stress urinary incontinence. Urology 45:647, 1994
5. Dorsey JH, Cundiff G: Laparoscopic procedures for incontinence and prolapse. Curr Opin Obstet Gynecol 6:223, 1994
6. Liu CY: Laparoscopic retropubic colposuspension (Burch procedure). J Reprod Med 38:526, 1993
7. Morley GW: Vaginal approach to treatment of vaginal vault eversion. Clin Obstet Gynecol 36:984, 1993
8. Cruikshank SH, Cox DW: Sacrospinous ligament fixation at the time of transvaginal hysterectomy. Am J Obstet Gynecol 168:469, 1993
9. Elkins TE, Hopper BJ, Goodfellow K et al: Initial report of anatomic and clinical comparison of the sacrospinous ligament fixation to the high McCall culdeplasty for vaginal cuff fixation at hysterectomy for uterine prolapse. J Pelv Surg 1:12, 1995
10. Porges RF, Smilen SW: Long-term analysis of the surgical management of pelvic support defects. Am J Obstet Gynecol 171:1518, 1994
11. Shull BL, Benn SJ, Kuehl TJ: Surgical management of prolapse of the anterior vaginal segment: an analysis of support defects, operative morbidity, and anatomic outcome. Am J Obstet Gynecol 171:1429, 1994
12. Given FT, Muhlendorf IK, Browning GM: Vaginal length and sexual function after colpopexy for complete uterovaginal eversion. Am J Obstet Gynecol 169:284, 1993
13. Podratz KC, Ferguson LK, Hoverman VR et al: Abdominal sacral colpopexy for posthysterectomy vaginal vault descensus. J Pelvic Surg 1:18, 1995
14. Dorsey JH, Green D, Johnson H et al: Laparoscopic pelvic reconstruction for vaginal and uterine prolapse and urinary stress incontinence. Obstet Gynecol Forum 6:2, 1993
15. Addison WA, Timmons MC, Wall LL, Livengood CH: Failed abdominal sacral colpopexy: observations and recommendations. Obstet Gynecol 74:480, 1989
16. Richardson C, Saye W: Pelvic Reconstruction videotape. Marietta, GA
17. Richardson AC, Edmonds PB, Williams NL: Treatment of stress urinary incontinence due to paravaginal fascial defect. Obstet Gynecol 57:57, 1981
18. Richardson AC: Pelvic support defects in women (urethrocele, cystocele, uterine prolapse, enterocele, and rectocele). p. 238. In Skandalakis J, Gray S, Mansberger A Jr et al (eds): Hernia: Surgical Anatomy and Technique. McGraw-Hill, New York, 1989
19. Shull BL, Capen CV, Riggs MW, Kuehl TJ: Preoperative and postoperative analysis of site-specific pelvic support defects in 81 women treated with sacrospinous ligament suspension and pelvic reconstruction. Am J Obstet Gynecol 166:1763, 1992

15 Hysterectomy: The Laparoscopic Procedure

JAMES H. DORSEY

Although many of the operative techniques involved in the performance of laparoscopic hysterectomy (LH) were described before 1985, the complete surgical procedure in which the laparoscope is used to accomplish a significant part of a hysterectomy with removal of the specimen through the vagina was not reported until 1989.[1] Because several studies have shown that vaginal hysterectomy is associated with shorter postoperative recovery time and lower morbidity than abdominal hysterectomy,[2,3] the rationale for using the laparoscope rests in the hope that the substitution of a minimally invasive abdominal operation, operative laparoscopy, will satisfy the indications for opening the abdomen, thus enabling the hysterectomy to be completed by the vaginal route and providing the benefits of vaginal hysterectomy to the patient. Obviously, there are two key assumptions that need to be proved: (1) operative laparoscopy is truly able to cope with the abdominal portion of the procedure just as effectively as when the abdomen is opened; and (2) the performance of a hysterectomy by operative laparoscopy plus vaginal surgery really does yield benefits similar to those of vaginal hysterectomy alone. Although these assumptions sound reasonable, they have been difficult to prove, and controversy regarding the indications, outcomes, safety, and cost of the laparoscopic procedure has arisen.[4–8] Variations in the definitions of LH as well as in the preference and abilities of gynecologic surgeons makes proper evaluation difficult. Additionally, there is a need for well-designed prospective studies to clarify many of these issues. Still, some excellent reports are now appearing that support the proposition that laparoscopic surgery provides a valuable alternative to open abdominal hysterectomy.[9,10] This has certainly been the case in my experience.

DEFINITIONS AND TYPES OF LAPAROSCOPIC HYSTERECTOMY

In early 1990, I began to use the laparoscope in hysterectomy patients who needed an abdominal operation to lyse adhesions, fulgurate endometriosis, or perform exploratory surgery. After completing these laparoscopic maneuvers, the infundibulopelvic ligaments (IPL) and other lateral uterine attachments were ligated and divided down to the level of the uterine arteries. This laparoscopic procedure allowed easy completion of the hysterectomy by a routine vaginal procedure in which the uterosacral ligaments, cardinal ligaments, and uterine vessels were taken from below and the entire specimen removed vaginally. Although the name *laparoscopically assisted vaginal hysterectomy* (LAVH) was given to the operation, this terminology is not entirely accurate. Clearly, LAVH is really a hybrid procedure in which the laparoscope is used to perform an intra-abdominal portion of the hysterectomy and a vaginal operation is used to complete the removal of the uterus. Just how much of the hysterectomy must be performed laparoscopically to justify the title of LAVH seems to be a matter decided by the surgeon, because some laparoscopists use the term for operations such as laparoscopic adhesiolysis followed by simple vaginal hysterectomy. Although this is certainly a good and legitimate use of the laparoscope, our own practice is to apply the term to a hysterectomy in which the uterus is extirpated using both laparoscopic and vaginal techniques. However, the term *laparoscopic hysterectomy* seems to imply that the hysterectomy is performed in its entirety by laparoscopic technique only. By definition, this is a very extensive laparoscopic procedure in which all vascular pedicles, the uterine ligaments, the vaginal vault incisions, and the vaginal suspension are secured or accomplished laparoscopically. Obviously, because laparoscopic surgery is carried out through relatively small trochar incisions, the uterus must be removed either through the open vaginal vault or morcellated and removed via a trochar sheath. In my opinion, there is very little use for LH in the performance of nononcologic laparoscopic surgery. Clearly, there are certain significant difficulties that may be encountered when attempting to secure the uterine artery, while avoiding ureteral or bladder damage. Hemostasis may also be difficult to achieve when working deep in the pelvis with laparoscopic instrumentation.

SELECTION OF THE PROPER LAPAROSCOPIC SURGICAL PROCEDURE FOR HYSTERECTOMY OPERATIONS

Every resident in obstetrics and gynecology is taught how to make open abdominal hysterectomy safer by the identification and careful avoidance of vital structures such as the ureters, bladder, and bowel. These organs are visualized, palpated, and occasionally, in the case of the ureters, dissected from the surrounding structures for proper identification. In both abdominal and vaginal hysterectomy, clamps are applied close to the uterus and cervix as a further measure to avoid injury. In LH (i.e., the LH procedure in which the entire operation including ligation of the uterine vessels, vaginal incision, and vaginal suspension is performed from above), the same care to avoid ureteral injury must be taken. Unfortunately, laparoscopic techniques do not allow for direct palpation of the ureter in its most dangerous location lateral to the cervix, and there are now increasing numbers of reports of ureteral injury occurring during LH.[11]

Almost always, the surgeon can visualize the right ureter as it passes into the pelvis at the bifurcation of the common iliac artery, and its course is further made obvious by gentle stroking with an instrument to elicit peristalsis. On the left pelvic wall, the sigmoid colon often covers the bifurcation of the common iliac, and it may be difficult to visualize the ureter without reflecting the sigmoid colon medially. In any case, after the ureter passes beneath the uterine artery it enters a "tunnel" in the endopelvic fascia often referred to by the gynecologic oncologist as the "web." During the rest of its course to the bladder, it is not able to be seen, although it is in close proximity to the cardinal and uterosacral ligaments.

These anatomic features produce something of a dilemma for the laparoscopist who is trying to perform a safe LH. The five most common ways in which the gynecologic surgeon avoids damaging the ureter while performing hysterectomy can be listed as follows:

1. visualization of the ureters by observing peristalsis
2. palpation of the ureters between thumb and forefinger
3. careful application of clamps close to lower uterine segment and cervix
4. dissection of the ureter from the "tunnel"
5. ureteral catherization and stent placement

It is seldom that the laparoscopic surgeon can visualize or palpate the ureter as it passes through the endopelvic fascial tunnel. The laparoscopic surgeon is also usually unable to slide a clamp, a stapling device, or bipolar forceps off of the lower uterine segment or the cervix in the safe manner that is used during abdominal hysterectomy. The angle of attack provided by the laparoscopic incisions and the trocar sheaths, the size of the uterus, the presence of pelvic pathology, and a host of other factors may preclude this important maneuver. Additionally, lateral thermal spread of heat delivered by bipolar laparoscopic forceps may extend up to 1 cm away from the application site, producing severe damage to a ureter in close proximity to the uterine artery. Thus, if a surgeon is not absolutely aware of the location of the ureter, any applications of clamps or attempts at coagulation of the paracervical tissue is an invitation to ureteral damage. The laparoscopist who wishes to take the uterine artery by laparoscopic instrumentation is therefore left with little choice but to dissect out the ureter and convincingly identify all important structures if the entire operation is to be performed safely from above. This dissection usually adds much time and often increases the morbidity associated with procedure. Most gynecologists are not skilled at the open abdominal dissection of the ureter, much less laparoscopic dissection. Even the placement of ureteral catheters that can be "wiggled" to produce motion in the ureter may not help the gynecologist avoid damaging this structure in all circumstances. When the surrounding tissue is thickened by inflammation or endometriosis, a moving catheter may give indication of the general but not the exact location of the ureter. This does not mean that ureteral stent placement is never helpful in laparoscopic surgery. Certainly, it may make ureteral identification at various locations on the lateral pelvic wall a much faster event than does dissection or induction of peristalsis by stroking the structure. However, the surgeon will often find that the most critical segment of the ureter cannot be identified by the stent. For these reasons, I believe that a relatively easy laparoscopic procedure that secures the uterine blood supply down to the uterine artery followed by a straightforward vaginal operation to complete removal is certainly the safest manner in which to accomplish this combination procedure.

Recently, I have used a ureteral catheter that emits an infrared signal that can be picked up by a special laparoscopic camera. This may be an extremely helpful tool in some difficult cases because the infrared wavelength passes through tissue.

INDICATIONS FOR LAVH

If vaginal hysterectomy can be performed for the patient, then this is certainly the route of choice and no laparoscope is needed.[12] Unfortunately, many hysterectomies are neither technically feasible nor surgically wise to perform by the vaginal route because of circumstances that require an abdominal approach. In the case of LAVH, the laparoscope provides an alternative means to satisfy the surgical indications that require the abdominal operation. Examples of the important factors that may lead the surgeon to choose an abdominal approach are

1. the necessity to perform additional surgical maneuvers in the abdominal cavity such as adhesiolysis, removal of endometriosis, or evaluation and removal of an adnexal mass
2. the presence of unexplained abdominal pain that does not seem to be uterine in origin. This problem may only be solved by abdominal exploration, and possibly further surgery such as an appendectomy or cholecystectomy may be indicated
3. excessive uterine size, which may require the abdominal route for safe removal of the uterus
4. desire to remove the ovaries in a patient with a familial history of ovarian epithelial cancer

Although I certainly agree that an adnexectomy may often be easily accomplished during vaginal hysterectomy, I also think that this particular indication and the patient's fear of cancer demands a thorough abdomi-

nal exploration at the time of surgery. To me, this is a rational surgical decision to prove that no tumor is present at the time of surgery and that the ovaries are removed in their entirety.

TECHNIQUE FOR SAFE LAVH

A thorough knowledge of laparoscopic anatomy and a compulsive desire to accurately demonstrate critical structures is a prerequisite for any surgeon who undertakes LAVH. Very often, anatomy is distorted by the disease process, and an estimation of the position of the ureter or the location of the rectosigmoid may be difficult. In my operating room, I am able to perform sigmoidoscopy and cystoscopy with placement of ureteral catheters whenever the situation demands aggressive anatomic identification. If the gynecologic surgeon anticipates a difficult laparoscopic procedure and is not able to perform cystoscopy or rigid sigmoidoscopy, it would be wise to place a probe in the rectum and request a urologist to place ureteral stents.

It follows that the position of the patient must be one that allows easy access to the perineal area. The patient is placed in the lithotomy position with the buttocks slightly over the table's edge. It is extremely important to be able to manipulate the uterus irrespective of size during the operative procedure, and it is easier to do so if the endometrial cavity contains an unbreakable instrument such as a long cervical dilator. I use a 12-inch stainless steel rod of 5-mm diameter, which is taped to a Jacob's tenaculum. The rod can be inserted to the fundus of a uterus of any size and serves to lift even the largest fundi to the anterior abdominal wall of the insufflated abdomen. This gives us easy access to the posterior and lateral pelvic walls and relieves the surgeon of the burden of using an abdominal instrument to move the uterus.

After routine preparation and draping for abdominal and vaginal surgery, the abdomen is insufflated to 14 mmHg pressure and three 12-mm Surgiports (USSC, Norwalk, CT) (or three 11.5 Premium Ports) are placed through the anterior abdominal wall, one in the umbilicus and two on either side of the lower midline. The position of these two lower ports depends on two factors: the size of the uterus and the location of the inferior epigastric vessels. I attempt to enter the abdomen lateral to the inferior epigastrics and lateral border of the rectus muscle because there is less chance of hematoma formation when the oblique abdominal muscles are penetrated. Often, it helps the surgeon to insert a 22-gauge needle through the anterior abdominal wall at the intended site of trocar puncture. This gives the surgeon a preview of the exact location of the trochars as well as an idea of the angle of attack of the instruments to be used here. The 12-mm Surgiport can also be fitted with an adapter, which allows the use of an instrument of 3 to 12 mm in diameter and, in addition, enables the surgeon to pass curved needles and suture material into the abdominal cavity (see Ch. XX).

An operative laparoscope with a zero degree lens is used through the umbilicus. I prefer the zero degree lens because it produces the least amount of distortion and the operative channel gives the surgeon an added advantage of being able to use a laser, scissors, bipolar cautery, or other instruments through the scope. The optical quality of the operative scope is equal to that of the diagnostic telescope, and often it is of great help to be able to cut and coagulate through the umbilical port. For example, in a patient with extensive adhesive disease, the anterior abdominal wall and omentum may be so involved that the surgeon is unable to find space for the secondary puncture sites. The operative scope provides a method of cleaning off the adhesions through one puncture site, the umbilicus.

If adhesions or an adnexal mass are present, adhesiolysis is carried out and the pelvic viscera freed so that uterus and adnexa are mobile. The uterus is elevated, and if the adnexa are to be removed, it is pushed from below to one side and the IPL placed under tension (Fig. 15-1). The ureter is identified on the pelvic wall (Fig. 15-2), and the EndoGIA stapling device is used to take the IPL or the uteroovarian ligament. Usually, the next application of the EndoGIA is able to include the round ligament in its grasp. Thus, the adnexa and

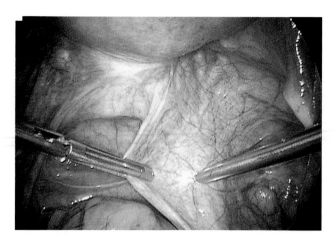

Fig. 15-2. The ureter may be close to the uterosacral ligament. Here the right uterosacral ligament is pulled medially and the right forceps points to the ureter. When the ligament is released, the ureter lies within a few millimeters of the structure.

round ligaments on both sides are divided with four applications of the stapler (Fig. 15-3).

I prefer to use the stapling device as it is fast, hemostatic, and in my estimation, safer than electricity. However, the cost of instrumentation used in laparoscopic surgery is also a factor that must be considered. Recently, a study was undertaken at the Greater Baltimore Medical Center to compare the use of the stapler with the bipolar electrode in the performance of LH. In a randomized prospective study involving 20 patients,

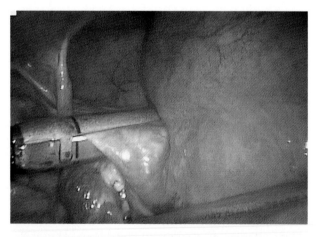

Fig. 15-1. This large uterus rises above the umbilicus. However, good elevation allows good visualization of lateral pelvic wall and deep pelvis. The stapling device is applied across the infundibulopelvic ligament.

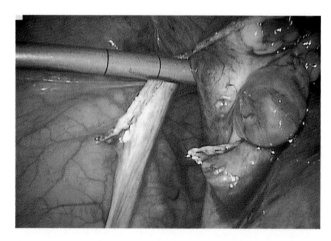

Fig. 15-3. The myomatous uterus is elevated upward and to the right so that the left pelvic side wall is easily visualized. Although the myoma is large, there is little lateral extension of the tumor, and this makes the surgical procedures relatively easy. A second EndoGIA will secure the broad ligament almost to the level of the uterine artery.

the time required for stapling the IPL or the uteroovarian pedicle and achieving hemostasis down to the uterine artery was compared with the time required to coagulate and divide these same structures with bipolar forceps and scissors. Each patient served as her own control as each device was used on randomly selected opposite sides. The stapling device averaged 13 minutes faster than bipolar electrode and scissors. The difference was even more striking when thick or inflamed pedules were encountered.[13]

After the division of the round ligament, the anterior leaf of the broad ligament is opened (Fig. 15-4). It often helps to insert the tip of the suction irrigator beneath the peritoneum when the first small opening is made and then elevate and separate the peritoneum from the underlying bladder. This same technique, when properly executed, can be used to elevate the posterior leaf of the broad ligament away from the uterine vessels and connective tissue of the cardinal ligament. Careful incision of the posterior leaf reveals this vascular structure without producing bleeding.

With the anterior peritoneum divided, the bladder is now gently freed from the lower uterus and cervix and the pubovesical fascia identified. I use a combination of blunt, sharp, and hydrodissection to accomplish this maneuver. At this point, the surgeon must decide if the uterine vessels are to be taken from above or below. Because the pathology in the pelvis and the anatomy

Fig. 15-5. A wet sponge on a sponge stick has been inserted into the vagina elevating the posterior fornix and cul-de-sac between the uterosacral ligaments. The cul-de-sac and fornix are opened between the ligament, revealing the wet sponge. The surgeon takes great care to limit the incision to the area between the ligament so that vessels and ureters are safeguarded.

varies from case to case, the relationship of ureter to the uterine artery may be very apparent and occasionally may be safe to clamp the vessel with the EndoGIA or cauterize with bipolars. However, as described earlier, usually the ureter cannot be seen, and it is extremely dangerous to try and secure the uterine artery from above.

The surgeon is now ready to open the cul-de-sac. Again, this step may be performed from above or below. I prefer to do this laparoscopically by inserting a wet sponge on a sponge stick into the vagina and elevating the posterior fornix and cul-de-sac well up into the pelvis behind the uterus. The cul-de-sac is then opened between the uterosacral ligaments over the sponge stick and into the vagina by laser or scissors (Fig. 15-5).

The surgeon now begins the vaginal operation. The laparoscopic trochar sheaths are left in the abdominal cavity so that final inspection can be made when the vaginal suspension is finished.

VAGINAL COMPONENTS OF LAVH

Two vaginal techniques have been used to complete LAVH, the Doederlein extraction and the Heaney vaginal hysterectomy method. The Doederlein technique of vaginal hysterectomy uses an anterior colpotomy incision as a window through which to deliver the fundus of the uterus so that the hysterectomy can be com-

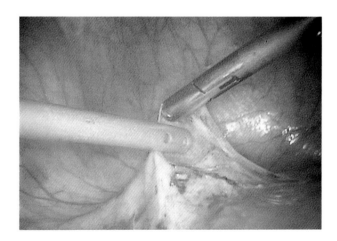

Fig. 15-4. The uterus has now been pushed upward and as close to the posterior abdomen as possible. The laparoscope is placed over the anterior surface of the uterus and now views the bladder and lower uterine segment. An incision has been made in the anterior broad ligament just below the lateral staple line. Hydrodissection will lift the peritoneum off the lower segment, and the incision is carried across the cervix to the opposite side.

pleted from below in a manner very similar to that which would be used in abdominal hysterectomy. In other words, the fundus pivots on the uterine vessels, and the surgeon applies the clamps close to the lower uterine segment and cervix coming down from above on uterine vessels, cardinal ligaments, and uterosacral ligaments. As the fundus is delivered beneath the symphysis, the cervix is pushed back into the posterior fornix.

After the anterior colpotomy incision is made, the bladder attachments are divided sharply, and then a finger is used to separate bladder from cervix. The peritoneal cavity is easily entered because the perineum has already been incised and the bladder pushed downward from above. If necessary, the colpotomy incision may be made larger by clamping and dividing the bladder pillars and the vaginal mucosa at the lateral edges of the incision. I use Leahey clamps to "walk" up the anterior fundus and pull the uterus through the incision. As the lower ligaments are taken, one blade of the clamp rests on peritoneum and vessel or ligament while the other is on the posterior vagina. As the clamp is closed, these structures are divided and sutured. The end result is the rapid completion of the hysterectomy, and the ligaments are already sutured to the lateral and posterior vaginal cuff. Thus, most of the suspension is already accomplished, and only the peritoneum and vaginal mucosa need to be closed.

The great advantage of the Doederlein hysterectomy is that it is not only simple but extremely fast. It may often be accomplished in less than 1 hour. Its greatest disadvantage is that a large uterus cannot be delivered through an anterior colpotomy incision, and morcellation may be difficult if the pubic arch is narrow or the incision small. I have not used this technique for uteri greater than 10 to 12 week size.

The Heaney technique has an advantage over the Doederlein in that it can be used to successfully remove larger uteri. It is much easier to morcellate the uterus through a fully opened vaginal cuff, and I have removed uteri that weighed more than 1,000 g by this method. This vaginal procedure simply represents the beginning of a Heaney vaginal hysterectomy. If the uterus is very large because of myomas, it will have to be morcellated for removal. After removal, the vaginal suspension sutures are placed and the peritoneum closed. I prefer to suture the uterosacral and cardinal ligaments along with the ligated ends of the uterine vessels to the vaginal cuff and close the peritoneum

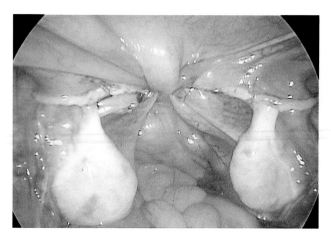

Fig. 15-6. A final laparoscopic view of a pelvis after suspension of the vaginal cuff and peritonization from below has been accomplished, which gives the surgeon a chance to check hemostasis. In this case, the ovaries have been saved and properly suspended well above the vagina.

above these structures so that if any bleeding from these stumps does occur it can be immediately identified in the vagina.

Irrespective of the method of vaginal surgery, a final look at the pelvis is taken with the laparoscope. Hemostasis can be secured laparoscopically if necessary, but in the vast majority of my cases, there is no further need for laparoscopic surgery (Fig. 15-6).

A summary of the steps involved in the two different techniques for completion of LAVH are as follows:

Doederlein Hysterectomy (uterus less than 250 g and less than 13 weeks)

anterior colpotomy
cervix pushed into posterior fornix
freed-up fundus delivered anteriorly
uterine vessels, cardinals, and uterosacrals taken from above downward
routine vaginal suspension

Heaney Hysterectomy (uterus greater than 280 g and larger than 13 weeks)

anterior colpotomy
posterior colpotomy
uterosacrals, cardinals, and uterine vessels taken from below
routine vaginal suspension

It should be emphasized that the laparoscopic operation that I have described uses a standard and very reproducible laparoscopic procedure to meet the indications for abdominal surgery and then completes the hysterectomy from below, using safe, accepted techniques for vaginal hysterectomy.

USE OF GONADOTROPIN-RELEASING HORMONE AGONISTS IN LAVH

The use of gonadotropin-releasing hormone (GnRH) agonists has become part of my LAVH protocol for patients with large myomas and endometriosis. It is my clinical impression that GnRH agonists may help in several ways. First, the size of a myoma can be somewhat reduced and certainly the vascularity of the tumor also decreases. Second, in patients with endometriosis, the dissection is often made easier by the preoperative therapy. In addition, in patients with significant anemia secondary to menorrhagia caused by the myoma, the period of amenorrhea before surgery may be used to achieve respectable hemoglobin levels.

The disadvantage of GnRH agonist therapy is, of course, the cost of the medication. Also, there are many patients who, when faced with surgery, wish to have it completed quickly and thus resist any delay. However, in some instances, it certainly seems that this delay is worthwhile.

LAVH VERSUS TOTAL VAGINAL HYSTERECTOMY AND TOTAL ABDOMINAL HYSTERECTOMY

Some gynecologists have condemned LAVH as an unnecessary and costly operation that is often used when a simple vaginal hysterectomy could have been performed.[14] Interestingly, Kovac et al.[15,16] have pointed out that "practice style," a variable determined by a host of factors such as residency training, personal experience, surgical capability, and interpretation of outcomes plays an important role in the selection of hysterectomy route. Chassin[17] has suggested that enthusiasm of the physician for a certain procedure may influence the selection of health care services. Certainly, enthusiasm for a certain type of hysterectomy plays an important role in forming practice style.

In an effort to understand how LAVH was being used in a large community hospital with a busy gynecologic surgical service, I undertook a retrospective review of 502 hysterectomies approximately equally divided between LAVH, total vaginal hysterectomy (TVH), and total abdominal hysterectomy (TAH) that were performed by experienced pelvic surgeons.[18] By applying criteria commonly accepted as justification for the performance of abdominal hysterectomy, it appeared that about 16 percent of the combined LAVH and TAH groups might have been performed vaginally by a different surgeon. Surgeon-specific preference for one hysterectomy route over another was also quite obvious. For example, in this study, there were no patients with a uterine size estimated preoperatively to be greater than 12 weeks of gestation who underwent TVH. Certainly, many excellent vaginal surgeons do not accept this size as an absolute contraindication to TVH. However, the well-known statistic that 70 percent of the approximately 650,000 hysterectomies performed in the United States are accomplished abdominally certainly indicates that a large majority of American gynecologists appear to be more comfortable with or prefer the abdominal route.[19,20] In this study, more than 30 percent of patients undergoing LAVH had uteri greater than 12 weeks size, and 16.6 percent of the LAVHs were nulliparous. Because no TVH patients had these characteristics, it would appear that these surgeons would have used TAH for these patients had LAVH not been available.

COMPLICATION RATES

Few studies have documented differences in complication rates or postoperative morbidity between these three routes of hysterectomy. In my study, intraoperative complication rates and postoperative morbidity were not statistically different with one exception. Postoperative temperature elevation was much more common in the TAH group than in either TVH or LAVH patients. Hospital length of stay was also significantly shorter in the LAVH group. In this study, no mortality occurred, and there were no ureteral or bladder injuries.

SUMMARY

LAVH, when properly performed for valid indications, is a useful operation that may help patients avoid the more invasive procedure of TAH. The advantages of LAVH include the avoidance of major abdominal scar, quicker discharge from the hospital, low morbidity rates, and a more rapid return to the patient's lifestyle.

LAVH increases the amount of vaginal surgery performed by gynecologists who have mastered the techniques of operative laparoscopy and vaginal hysterectomy. It is certainly very apparent to any surgeon who has attempted a difficult LAVH that the vaginal portion of the procedure may be the most demanding. This type of hysterectomy involves the removal of uteri in which the pelvic pathology often produces the greatest challenge to the surgeon's skill and judgment.

REFERENCES

1. Reich H, DeCaprio J, McGlynn E: Laparoscopic hysterectomy. J Gynecol Surg 5:213, 1989
2. Thompson JD, Rock JA: Hysterectomy. In Thompson JD, Rock JA (eds): Te Linde's Operative Gynecology. 7th Ed. JB Lippincott, Philadelphia, 1992
3. Dicker RC, Greenspan JR, Strauss LT et al: Complications of abdominal and vaginal hysterectomy among women of reproductive age in the United States. Am J Obstet Gynecol 144:841, 1982
4. Summit RL Jr, Stovall TG, Lipscomb GH, Ling FW: Randomized comparison of laparoscopy-assisted vaginal hysterectomy with standard vaginal hysterectomy in an outpatient setting. Obstet Gynecol 80:895, 1992
5. Grimes D: Technology follies—the uncritical acceptance of medical innovation. JAMA 269:3030, 1993
6. Pitkin RM: Operative laparoscopy: surgical advance or technical gimmick? Obstet Gynecol 79:441, 1992
7. Dorsey JH: "Technology follies": curtain call (letter). JAMA 270:2298, 1993
8. Schwartz RO: Complications of laparoscopic hysterectomy. Obstet Gynecol 81:1022, 1993
9. Boike GM, Elfstrand EP, DelPriore G et al: Laparoscopically assisted vaginal hysterectomy in a university hospital: report of 82 cases and comparison with abdominal and vaginal hysterectomy. Am J Obstet Gynecol 168:1690, 1993
10. Langbrekke A, Skar OS, Urnes A: Laparoscopic hysterectomy. Acta Obstet Gynecol Scand 71:226, 1992
11. Woodland MB: Ureter injury during laparoscopy-assisted vaginal hysterectomy with the endoscopic linear stapler. Am J Obstet Gynecol 167:756, 1992
12. Stovall TG, Summitt RL, Bran DR, Ling FW: Outpatient vaginal hysterectomy: a pilot study. Obstet Gynecol 80:145, 1992
13. Sharp JT : The effect of electrocautery vs. EndoGIA on operating room time in laparoscopically assisted vaginal hysterectomy: a randomized control study, abstracted. Submitted.
14. Nezhat C, Bess O, Admon D et al: Hospital cost comparison between abdominal, vaginal, and laparoscopy-assisted vaginal hysterectomies. Obstet Gynecol 83:713, 1994
15. Kovac RS, Pignotti BJ, Bindbeutel GA: Hysterectomy: a comparative statistical study of abdominal vs. vaginal approaches. M Med 85:312, 1988
16. Kovac RS, Christie SJ, Bindbeutel GA: Abdominal versus vaginal hysterectomy: a statistical model for determining physician decision making and patient outcome. Med Decis Making 11:19, 1991
17. Chassin MR: Practice guidelines: best hope for quality improvements in the 1990's. J Occup Med 32:1199, 1990
18. Dorsey JH, Steinberg EP, Holtz PM: Hysterectomy route: clinical indications and patient characteristics or physician preference? Am J Obstet Gynecol 173:1452, 1995
19. Dicker RC, Scally MJ, Greenspan JR et al: Hysterectomy among women of reproductive age: trends in the United States, 1970–1978. JAMA 248:323, 1982
20. Bachmann GA: Hysterectomy, a critical view. J Reprod Med 35:839, 1990

16 Burch Procedure

THOMAS L. LYONS

Urinary stress incontinence, (USI) is a problem affecting millions of women worldwide and is the source of a large economic drain, both secondary to medical treatments and lost time or effectiveness in the workplace. The source of this defect probably remains birth trauma and its the related secondary fascial defects. Correction of this problem has traditionally revolved around correction of the fascial defects via either vaginal or abdominal approaches. Retropubic culposuspension (the Burch procedure)[1,2] has been accepted as the "gold standard" for surgical treatment of genuine USI because of its higher success rate (85 to more than 90 percent) when compared with vaginal or needle procedures.[3,4] However, because of the increased morbidity associated with the abdominal approach, many patients frequently opted for the less morbid vaginal routes for correction of this problem.[5–7] Another solution to the surgical treatment of USI has now become available. This procedure combines the excellent clinical outcomes of the Burch procedure with the reduced morbidity of laparoscopic surgery. The laparoscopic Burch or minimally invasive retropubic culposuspension has been shown to be effective in correcting symptoms of USI while affording the surgeon an excellent view to the posterior compartment for correction of high rectocele and enterocele.[8–10]

This treatise does not ignore the fact that more than 70 percent of patients with USI will respond to medical therapy or that many patients with incontinence may have problems that are not surgically correctable.[11] However, in that patient who has been evaluated and judged to be a candidate for correction, a laparoscopic procedure can be considered a logical alternative.

ANATOMY

Pelvic floor abnormalities caused predominantly by birth trauma are rarely limited to the single anterior or posterior compartments. Breakdown of the endopelvic fascia and separation of the muscular supports of the pelvic diaphragm can cause malposition of the uterine corpus and herniation of rectum, bowel, vagina, or bladder. Lengthening and sagging of the levator plate may cause the genital hiatus to open, allowing a more vertical access to pelvic prolapse and enhancing the effects of gravity and straining. The lateral borders of support demarcated by the archus tendious can be torn during delivery, resulting in cystocele, whereas the anterior upper vagina depends on the cervix for support. The posterior aspect of the upper vagina has little anatomic support. This common upper defect must be addressed in any surgical procedure for pelvic relaxation. Most anatomists agree that uterine support centers around the cervix and its supportive ligaments, the cardinals and uterosacrals. The cardinal and uterosacral ligaments hold the uterus and upper vagina in their proper place and supply resistance to the descent of these organs. Anteriorly, the pubovesicocervical fascia serves a similar function to support bladder and urethra. The presence of these cervically attached ligamentous structures gives credence to the theory that supracervical hysterectomy can provide better total vault support versus total hysterectomy.[12] Also, the fact that the preponderance of neurovascular supply courses through these structures suggests that an intact cervix and ligamentous structure may improve postoperative performance both in a neuromuscular sense and with regard to the sexual function of the vagina and cervix. The pararectal fascia, with its concommitant defects, is responsible for the rectocele abnormality. Denonvillier's fascia and the fibromuscular posterior vaginal wall are confluent with the lateral insertions and are accessible for restructuring of this most common of pelvic floor problems.

It is important to emphasize again the global nature of defects within the anatomic structures described above. It is therefore equally important that any surgical approach to these defects be complete. It is simply unacceptable to "fix one side and not the other."

REPAIR RATIONALE

Surgery is a visual experience, and with the superior exposure provided at laparoscopy, this repair should be better. Also, the dissection laparoscopically begins in the avascular rectovaginal space, not the more vascular perineal body. This allows for exposure and hemostasis, which is superior. The ability to readily visualize the ureters and to expose the sacrospincious and sacrococcygeus fascia in addition to the sacrum itself for total vault prolapse repair is unparalleled. Last, the ability of the surgeon to address the anterior compartment via laparoscopy, giving the patient the known superior results of a retropubic culposuspension with the same attendant low morbidity, makes a laparoscopic approach to pelvic floor anatomically the most appropriate choice (Figs. 16-1 and 16-2). Introtial laxity must be corrected vaginally and is the only defect that is not approachable laparoscopically. This defect is repaired traditionally by a vaginal approach that is facilitated once the upper defects have been completed laparoscopically.

PATIENT SELECTION

Each patient selected for culposuspension should be carefully evaluated and noted to have genuine stress incontinence with or without associated detrusor symptomology.[13] The urethral sphincteric mechanism must be intact, and urethral support (anterior vaginal wall mobility) must be poor. After a complete gynecologic history and physical examination is completed, notation must be made of other gynecologic problems, voiding habits, neurologic symptoms, and current medication history. The *symptoms* of stress incontinence must be expressed by the patient. A voiding diary can help in this assessment. The pelvic examination should concentrate on other pelvic pathology, neurologic assessment of S2, S3, and S4, urinalysis and urine culture, demonstration of the *sign* of stress incontinence, and a Q-tip test[14] or Marshall's test. A timed void can be used to rule out decreased bladder capacity and voiding disorders. If a confusing clinical picture is presented, multichannel urodynamics or voiding cystometrics may be indicated. Patients with other

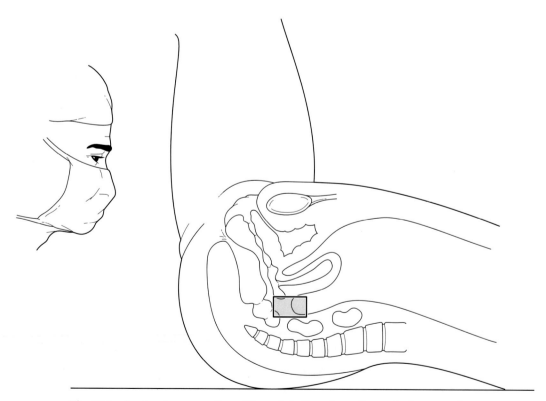

Fig. 16-1. Anatomic perspective of the pelvic floor from the vaginal approach.

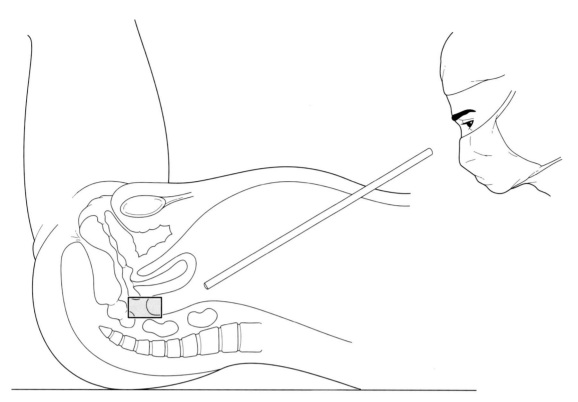

Fig. 16-2. Anatomic perspective of the pelvic floor from the laparoscopic approach.

medical conditions that would preclude surgery, patients who have not tried medical approaches, patients with voiding disorders, or patients with a shortened or scarred anterior vaginal wall should be excluded from this procedure. Detrusor instability or prior surgery is not an absolute contraindication for the procedure, but preoperative evaluation may be more extensive in these patients.[15,16]

TECHNIQUE

Consent is obtained from the patient for retropubic suspension with discussion of laparotomy as for all laparoscopic procedures. Prophylactic antibiotics are given. A 30-ml Foley balloon inflated to 20 ml is used to aid in identification of the urethrovesicle (UV) junction. Either of two approaches may be used to enter the space of Retzius. In the preperitioneal approach, an open (Hasson) trocar is inserted at the umbilicus below the anterior leaf of the rectus fascia, and the pneumoperitoneal is created in the preperitoneal space. The space is dissected via blunt dissection through the operating channel of the laparoscope. Alternatively, this dissection may be accomplished by insertion of a balloon dissector into the subumbilical trochar. These devices are currently available from several companies. Once the space is opened, a second 10/12 trochar is placed midline at 2 to 3 fingerbreadths above the symphysis under direct visualization. A 5-mm trochar is then placed lateral to the rectus musculature, avoiding the epigastric vasculature (Fig. 16-3A).

In the transperitoneal approach (usually dictated by other procedures involved or prior lower abdominal surgeries), the trochar placement is the traditional four puncture placed with a 10/12 trochar at the subumbilical site, a 10/12 trochar at the midline superpubic site, and a 5-mm trochar lateral to the rectus muscles bilaterally (Fig. 16-3B). The entry to the retroperitoneal space is made by incising the peritoneum 1 in. above the symphysis pubis in a transverse cut extending to the obliterated umbilical ligaments bilaterally. Blunt dissection is then carried out using an endoscopic Kitner (Ethicon Endosurgery, Cincinatti, OH). The operator's fingers are placed in the vaginal vault to identify the fascia lateral to the UV junction. A 20-ml Foley balloon also aids in identification of the junction. Cooper's ligaments are readily identified bilaterally. All these structures must be cleaned of excessive fat or areloa tis-

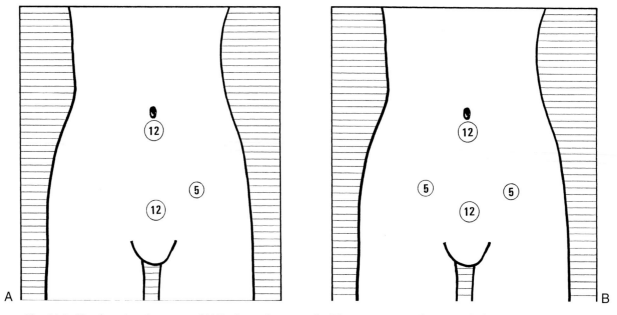

Fig. 16-3. Trochar site placement. **(A)** Peritoneal approach; **(B)** transperitoneal approach. (From Lyons and Winer,[36] with permission.)

sue (Fig. 16-4). 0-Vicryl or 0-Ethibond suture on CT-3 needle is then placed 1 to 2 cm lateral to the UV junction bilaterally in a figure-of-eight technique (Fig. 16-5). The suture is placed full thickness into the vault, with the operator's fingers in the vagina identifying the UV junction. One of two techniques may be used. In the classic Burch technique, the suture is then placed through Cooper's ligament, and each suture is tied in

turn using extracorporeal knot methods (Fig. 16-6). The suture should not be tied flush to Cooper's ligament but rather 0.5-cm spacing left in an effort to elevate the UV junction to 1 cm posterior to the symphysis (Fig. 16-7).

The second method is a modification that I developed. In this alternative, an end-knot loop can be created after the vaginal suture and the loop stapled into

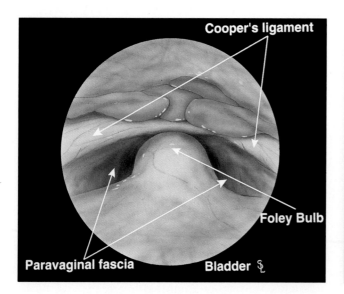

Fig. 16-4. Space of Retzius.

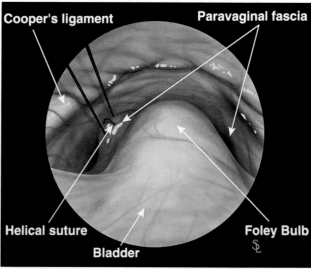

Fig. 16-5. Suture placement in the paravaginal fascia.

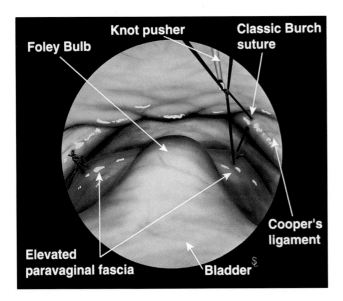

Fig. 16-6. Classic Burch technique knot-pusher being used to tie extracorporeal knots.

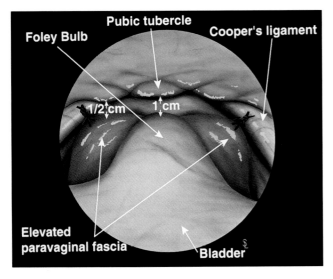

Fig. 16-7. Completed suspension (one suture per side) classic Burch technique.

Cooper's ligament with the endoscopic stapler. As the loop is shortened, the UV angle is increased with elevation (Nolan/Lyons modification)[10] (Fig. 16-7). Alternatively, the figure-of-eight suture can be placed at the UV angle, and then one arm of the suture is stapled to Cooper's ligament with the EMS stapler (Ethicon) and then tied in an extracorporeal technique (Nolan/Lyons modification). The Cooper's ligament suture pass is

deemed most difficult early in the learning curve and spawned the Nolan/Lyons technique. Secondary sutures can then be placed to further lengthen the urethra and adequately elevate the UV angle if the operator deems this is indicated (Fig. 16-8). With hemostasis ensured, the laparoscope and trochars are removed, and incisional sites are closed. In the transperitoneal approach, the peritoneum is closed with a pursestring suture of size 2-0 Vicryl. A posterior culdoplasty (Moschcowitz or Halban) is also performed to prevent enterocele in appropriate patients. (A drain may be left in the space of Retzius if the operator desires.)

The Foley catheter is removed after the operation, and the patient is allowed to void. If difficulty in voiding is noted, a leg bag is fitted with a Foley in place and the patient is discharged. The catheter can be removed 24 to 48 hours later. Postoperative instructions limit vigorous activity, intercourse, or straining for 4 weeks. The patient is allowed to resume other normal activities immediately.

DISCUSSION

USI is an endemic problem that has a significant effect on the patient's lifestyle and long-term psychological and physical health. Medical therapy is and should remain the mainstay of therapy, as these modes are successful in up to 70 percent of patients with USI. However, in severe stress incontinence problems, surgery may be mandated or best considered because of other associated gynecologic pathology. In the past, needle procedures (Raz,[10] Pereyra,[11] Stamey,[12] Gittes[5]) and anterior culporrhaphy[2] offered the lowest morbidity procedures but with the highest failure rates (40 to 50 percent in some studies) (Table 16-1). Retropubic approaches (Marshall et al., Burch) have become the "gold standard," with long-term success rates of 80 to 90 percent.[3,4] Unfortunately, these highly effective procedures were the most morbid of the USI correction procedures, secondary to the large abdominal incision necessary to accomplish them. Therefore, these procedures were usually reserved for patients who had failed vaginal approaches or were having other indicated abdominal surgery.

Since 1991 when the first retropubic culpopexy via laparoscopy was reported,[8] significant interest in a minimally invasive approach to the space of Retzius has arisen. Case reports of laparoscopic Burch procedures have demonstrated comparable success rates to open procedures.[8–10] Morbidity from the classic Burch procedure is usually isolated around hospital recovery

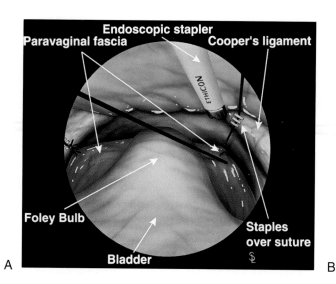
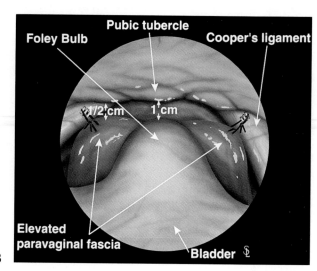

Fig. 16-8. (A) Nolan/Lyons modification using endoscopic stapler to fix suture to Cooper's ligament. **(B)** Finished results; note staples in Cooper's ligament.

Table 16-1. Traditional USI Procedures

Author	No.	Procedure	Clinical Outcomes(%)[a]			
			3 mo	6 mo	1 yr	2 yr
Stanton and Cardoza (1986)[23]	50	Anterior culporrhaphy	36			
Well et al. (1984)[24]	44	Anterior culporrhaphy	57			
Dukno et al. (1986)	54	Anterior culporrhaphy		50		
Van Geelan et al. (1988)[25]	90	Anterior culporrhaphy		45		
Bergman et al. (1991)	289	Anterior culporrhaphy		69		
Bergman et al. (1989)	107	Anterior culporrhaphy	82	65		
Bosman et al. (1993)[26]	42	Raz	93		55	
Hilton and Mayne (1991)[27]	100	Stamey	83		53–76	
Ashken (1990)[28]	100	Stamey		72		
Richardson et al. (1991)[33]	5	Stamey		40		
Bergman et al. (1989)	107	Pereyra	84	72		
Bergman et al. (1989)	289	Pereyra		70		
Nitti et al. (1993)[29]	92	Raz		88		
Raz et al. (1992)	206	Raz		90.3		
Walker and Texter (1992)[30]	284	Stamey		82		
Golomb et al. (1994)[31]	88	Raz		85		
Ramon et al. (1991)[32]	36	Raz		78		
Well et al. (1994)	42	Needle		50		
Richardson et al. (1991)[33]	29	Burch		85		
Gilton et al. (1992)[34]	40	Burch		85		
Bergman (1994)	66	Ball-Burch		90		
Bergman et al. (1989)	289	Burch		87		
Bergman et al. (1989)	107	Burch		91		
Stanton and Cardoza (1986)[23]	50	Burch		84		
Weil et al. (1984)[24]	86	Burch		91		
Van Geelan et al. (1988)[25]	90	Burch		91		
Fegereisl et al. (1994)[35]	87	Burch				81.7

[a] Patient reports no loss of urine with Valsalva.

Table 16-2. Laparoscopic USI Procedures

Author	No.	Procedure	Clinical Outcomes(%)[a]			
			3 mo	6 mo	1 yr	2 yr
Van Caillie and Schuessler (1991)[8]	9	MMK	100			
Liu (1993)[9]	58	Burch	94.8			
Ou et al. (1993)	40	Mesh/Burch	100			
Hill et al. (1994)	9	Burch (mod.)	100			
Nezhat et al. (1994)[17]	62	Burch/MMK		92		
Liu (1993)[9]	107	Burch		97.2		
Lyons (1994)	38	Burch/Staple Mod.			92	
Lyons (1995)	100	Burch		90		
Underwood[20] (in press)		Burch				
Smith (1994, personal communication)	65	Burch		91		
Van Caillie (1994, personal communication)	42	Burch		81		

[a] Patient reports no loss of urine with Valsalva.

time, catheterization length, and other surgical parameters. Significant changes in these areas are conclusively demonstrated when laparoscopic procedures are compared with open procedures.[1] The Nolan/Lyons/Burch (NLB) technique alleviates the need of placing the most difficult Cooper's ligament suture pass by using existing endoscopic equipment. Other authors have demonstrated excellent clinical outcomes as well, using a variety of techniques (Table 16-2). It is not surprising that these patients have performed as well as traditional open Burch procedures because the procedure is performed in the same or similar fashion but with the superior visualization afforded by laparoscopy. It is also not unexpected that surgical morbidity is reduced. Of particular interest is the decreased need for lengthy catheterization and decreased incidence of long-term (more than 2 weeks) detrusor symptomology in some reports.[14] The economic benefits of these procedures are readily evident when noting decreased hospital stay and more rapid return to work. This fact alone could have a multimillion dollar effect on our presently stressed medical economic picture. The importance of a posterior supportive procedure has not been emphasized in the chapter but should be noted. Each patient should undergo a posterior supportive procedure (Moschcowitz, Halban, Rectocele, or Enterocele repair), dependent on the surgical indications at the time of the repair. A global approach to pubic floor dysfunction is the only logical approach, and this type of approach is facilitated by the excellent visibility in the posterior pelvis made possible by the laparoscope. Unfortunately, the surgical skills to accomplish these procedures remains a barrier to many physicians wishing to attempt the repairs, and there-

fore many patients may not be afforded the option of these lower morbidity procedures. Laparoscopic suturing is difficult, and despite innovations such as the NLB and other modifications the ability to successfully complete these procedures may be slow to penetrate the gynecologic community. It is incumbent, however, for those physicians who serve women to take the steps necessary to provide the best and lowest morbidity procedures, both medically and economically, to our patients. Minimally invasive retropubic culposuspension (laparoscopic Burch) will surely be such a procedure.

REFERENCES

1. Marshal VF, Marchetti AA, Krantz KE: The correction of stress incontinence by simple vesicourethral suspension. Surg Gynecol Obstet 88:590, 1949
2. Burch JC: Urethrovaginal fixation to Cooper's ligament for correction of stress incontinence, cystocele and prolapse. Am J Obstet Gynecol 81:281, 1961
3. Bergman A, Ballard C, Koonings P: Primary stress urinary incontinence and pelvic relaxation: prospective randomized comparison of three different operations. Am J Obstet Gynecol 161:97, 1989
4. Bergman A, Ballard C, Koonings P: Comparison of three different surgical procedures for genuine stress incontinence: prospective randomized study. Am J Obstet Gynecol 160:1102, 1989
5. Gittes RF, Loughlin KR: No incision pubovaginal suspension for stress incontinence. J Urol 138:568, 1987
6. Karram MM, Bhatia NN: Transvaginal needle bladder neck suspension procedures for stress urinary incontinence: a comprehensive review. Obstet Gynecol 73:906, 1989
7. Horbach NS, Genuine SUI: Best surgical approach. Contemp OB/GYN (Special issue: Urogynecology) 37, 1992
8. VanCaillie TG, Schuessler W: Laparoscopic bladder neck suspension. J LapEndosc 2:169, 1991
9. Liu CY: Laparoscopic retropubic colposuspension (Burch procedure). Gynecol Endosc 2, 1993
10. Lyons TL: Minimally invasive retropubic urethropexy, the Nolan/Lyons modification of the Burch procedure. 22nd annual meeting of AAGL, 1993

11. Norton PA: Nonsurgical management of stress urinary incontinence. Contemp OB/GYN (Special issue: Urogynecology) 37:63, 1992
12. Lyons TL: Laparoscopic supracervical hysterectomy: a comparison of morbidity results with laparoscopically assisted vaginal hysterectomy. J Reprod Med 38:763, 1993
13. Walter MD, Realini JP: The evaluation and treatment of urinary incontinence in women: a primary care approach. JABFP 5, 1992
14. Walters M, Shields L: The diagnostic value of history, physical examination and the Q-tip cotton swab test in women with urinary incontinence. Am J Obstet Gynecol 159:145, 1988
15. Varner RE, Sparks JM: Surgery for stress urinary incontinence. Surg Clin North Am 1:1111, 1991
16. Lam TC, Hadley HR: Surgical procedures for uncomplicated (routine) female stress incontinence. Uro Clin North Am 18:327, 1991
17. Nezhat CH, Nezhat F, Nezhat CR, Rottenberg H: Laparoscopic cystourethropexy. JAAGL 1:339, 1994
18. Liu CY, Park W: Laparoscopic retropubic culposuspension (Burch procedure). JAAGL 1:31, 1993
19. Lyons TL, Winer WK: Minimally invasive retropubic culposuspension. Gynecol Endosc (in press)
20. Underwood L: Laparoscopic Burch procedure. J Am Assoc Gynecol Laparosc (in press)
21. Davis GD, Lobel RW: Laparoscopic retropubic culposuspension: the evolution of a new needle procedure. Proceedings of the World Congress of Gynecologic Endoscopy, 22nd Annual Meeting, AAGL, 1993
22. Carter J: Laparoscopic culposuspension: the Carter modification of the Burch procedure. Proceedings of the World Congress of Gynecologic Endoscopy, 22nd Annual Meeting, AAGL, 1993
23. Stanton SL, Cardoza LD: A comparison of vaginal and suprapubic surgery in the correction of incontinence due to urethral incompetence. Br J Urol 51:497, 1989
24. Weil A, Reyes H, Bischoff P: Modifications of the urethral rest and stress profiles after different types of surgery for urinary stress incontinence. Br J Obstet Gynecol 91:46, 1984
25. Van Geelan JM, Theeuves AGM, Eskes TKAB, Martin CB: The clinical and urodynamic effects of anterior repair and Burch culposuspension. Am J Obstet Gynecol 159:137, 1988
26. Bosman G, Vierhout ME, Huikeshoven FJ: A modified Raz bladder neck suspension operation. results of a one to three year follow-up investigation. Acta Obstet Gynecol Scand 72:47, 1993
27. Hilton P, Mayne CJ: The Stamey endoscopic bladder neck suspension: a clinical and urodynamic investigation, including actuorial follow-up over four years. Br J Obstet Gynaecol 98:1141, 1991
28. Ashken MH: Follow-up results with Stamey operation for stress incontinence of urine. Br J Urol 65:168, 1990
29. Nitti VW, Bugg KJ, Sussman EM, Raz S: The Raz bladder neck suspension in patients 65 years old and older. Br J Urol 149:802, 1993
30. Walker GT, Texter JH: Success and patient satisfaction following the Stamey procedure for stress urinary incontinence. Br J Urol 147:1521, 1992
31. Golumb J, Galdwasser B, Mashiach S: Raz bladder neck suspension in women younger than sixty-five years compared with elderly women three years experience. Urology 43:40, 1994
32. Ramon J, Mekras J, Webster GD: Transvaginal needle suspension procedures for recurrent stress incontinence. Urology 38:519, 1991
33. Richardson DA, Ramahi A, Chalas E: Surgical management of stress incontinence in patients with low urethral pressure. Gynecol Obstet Invest 31:106, 1991
34. Gilton G, Englestern D, Servadin C: Risk factors and their effect on the results of Burch culposuspension for urinary stress incontinence. Israel J Med Sci 28:354, 1992
35. Fegereisl J, Drecher E, Haenggi W et al: Long term results after Burch culposuspension. Am J Obstet Gynecol 171:647, 1994
36. Lyons TL, Winer WK: Clinical outcomes with laparoscopic approaches and open Burch procedures for urinary stress incontinence. J Am Assoc Gynecol Laparosc 2:193, 1991

17 Pelvic/Aortic Node Dissection

THOMAS SEDLACEK

HISTORY

Although operative laparoscopy has been in existence for nearly a quarter century, applications in the field of gynecologic oncology and, more broadly, surgical oncology have much more recent vintage. Dargent[1] published the first description of laparoscopic node dissection in 1987. Reports in the literature remain scant. The first laparoscopic periaortic node dissection was presented by Nezhat[2] in 1989. The concept of laparoscopic pelvic and aortic node dissection is, however, expanding, and prospective randomized trials are currently underway. These trials will provide important information regarding morbidity, safety, and hospital length of stay.

INDICATIONS

Pelvic and aortic node dissection is almost exclusively a gynecologic oncology area of special interest. Virtually all patients considered for pelvic and aortic node dissection will have a gynecologic malignancy. Some controversy exists regarding specific indications, and until prospective trials are completed, we must view all discussions of laparoscopic node dissection as developmental. Positions of advocacy promote scientific discussion and encourage innovative clinical ideas and application but should not be confused with scientific fact or standard practice.

Laparoscopic pelvic/aortic node dissection appears very attractive in patients with cancer of the cervix, ovary, and endometrium. There will be little indication in patients with carcinoma of the vulva, and because fallopian tube carcinoma is rarely if ever diagnosed preoperatively, those patients will generally be considered as patients with ovarian cancer. The gynecologic oncologist/endoscopist may occasionally be called on to facilitate staging of prostate cancer, testicular cancer, or lymphoma, and in that context, pelvic and aortic node dissection is useful outside the field of gynecology.

Clinical trials are currently underway evaluating the role of endoscopic surgery in patients with cervix cancer. For the past 10 to 15 years, patients with advanced-stage cervical cancer (stages 2B to 3B) often undergo pretreatment staging with extrafacial para-aortic node sampling and laparoscopic assessment of intraperitoneal disease.[3] Knowledge gained from this procedure allows for more precise selection of radiation therapy fields and permits rational choice regarding concomitant chemotherapy. Patients undergoing this procedure are hospitalized for 5 to 7 days and, because of the extent of retroperitoneal dissection and blood loss, frequently experience significant ileus and occasional bowel obstruction. This extraperitoneal approach has been associated with diminished radiation side effects and complications. This salutary effect is thought to be due to the lack of an incision on the posterior peritoneum and consequent decrease in adhesions that immobilize especially the small bowel. Theoretically, this same subset of patients could be managed entirely endoscopically. All the data currently derived from the laparoscopic and open components could be obtained endoscopically. Patients undergoing laparoscopic aortic node sampling are generally hospitalized for only 2 days, and in my experience, blood loss is minimal and no patients have required transfusion. It will, of course, be critical to determine whether patients who undergo laparoscopic aortic node sampling with consequent posterior peritoneal incision experience a greater risk of radiation complications than patients who have undergone an extraperitoneal procedure.

Pelvic and aortic node dissection may be performed in the course of an endoscopic radical hysterectomy as definitive management for patients with stage IA2 or IB carcinoma of the cervix. Several centers throughout the world are examining these options. The node dissection may be approached by an umbilical[7-11] laparoscopic trocar with right and left lower-quadrant portals or by incisions in the groins.[12] After completion of the node dissection, a radical hysterectomy may be performed by the umbilical laparoscope/lower abdominal portal method or using the radical vaginal hysterectomy technique of "Shauta." The Shauta radical vaginal hysterectomy fell into disfavor in large measure because of the inability to conduct a lymph node dissection, which was of primary diagnostic importance and possible therapeutic importance. Laparoscopic pelvic and aortic node dissection will, I am sure, cause a rebirth of interest in radical vaginal surgery techniques.

In the United States, probably the most common indication for pelvic and aortic node dissection will lie with patients with adenocarcinoma of the endometrium. Because adenocarcinoma of the endometrium requires surgical staging[13] and because the overwhelming majority of patients with endometrial carcinoma require a lymph node dissection and because endometrial carcinoma is now the most common gynecologic malignancy, node dissection may even expand into the community hospital. Based on observations of the Gynecologic Oncology Group (GOG), full-fledged lymph node dissection is not required to properly stage patients with endometrial cancer.[14,15] Suspicious lymph nodes should be moved, and if none are found, random sampling of each of the relevant lymph node areas should be undertaken. Endometrial cancer tends to spread by lymphatic routes in an anatomic fashion very similar to cervical carcinoma. In fact, the same parametrial lymphatic channels are used. Thus, nodes that lie in the obturator fossa, nodes that lie between the external iliac artery and vein, and nodes that lie anteriorly lateral to the external iliac artery as well as common iliac nodes must be sampled on each side of the pelvis to be sure of proper staging. Because para-aortic nodal spread may also occur, both para-aortic groups must be sampled. Thus, satisfactory node sampling for patients with endometrial cancer would include at least one node from each of these end nodal groups (five on each side of the abdomen). Before sampling the node, cytologic washings are taken to rule out intraperitoneal spread of endometrial cancer. The GOG experience clearly documents that the morbidity of lymph node sampling is significantly less than the morbidity of lymph node dissection, and therefore, for all patients with endometrial cancer except stage IA, grade I, lymph node sampling has become standard. The requirement for lymph node sampling in stage IAI patients remains controversial. At a recent Society of Gynecologic Oncologists informal poll, the audience was split approximately 50/50 on the need to sample lymph nodes in patients with well-differentiated cancers. Arguments in favor of sampling focused on the fact that the histologic grade as determined by dilatation and curettage is frequently found to be in error, and depth of myometrial penetration assessed at the operative table may also be erroneous. Furthermore, if the uterine specimen is sent to the laboratory to assess hysterectomy specimen grade and depth of penetration, a node sampling can usually be completed before the frozen section material is available for intraoperative decision making. Because endometrial cancer is frequently treated at the community hospital level rather than the tertiary care level, postoperative laparoscopic pelvic and aortic node sampling with a tertiary care physician may become common. Ideally, patients should not be forced to undergo two surgical procedures when one will suffice, and so, careful preoperative evaluation should be undertaken so that the node sampling may be conducted at the time of the hysterectomy. This, of course, can all be performed laparoscopically.

Laparoscopic pelvic and aortic node dissection for ovarian carcinoma is technically possible.[16] It has been performed as a component of primary definitive management, primarily for patients with early-stage ovarian carcinoma and appears to be of great benefit. The technique is of special benefit to patients who have undergone an ovarian cystectomy or oophorectomy and after discharge from the hospital have been found to have carcinoma of the ovary. These patients in the past have been forced to undergo a second open operation to properly stage the patients and to determine the need for adjunctive chemotherapy. In properly selected patients, all the required components of adequate staging for ovarian carcinoma can be completed laparoscopically. This includes pelvic and aortic node sampling, peritoneal washes and biopsy, diaphragmatic washes and biopsies, infracolic omentectomy, biopsies of nodules, or adhesions on the small and large intestine. Advantages of this procedure are, of course, the diminished hospital stay, the diminished morbidity from blood loss, and the almost certain diminished psychological trauma. These patients are already experiencing great psychological trauma because of the diagnosis of ovarian carcinoma. The laparoscopic staging potential should ease their burden considerably.

All the above-referenced indications may be performed by the well-trained endoscopic surgeon. As with any surgical procedure, patient selection plays a critical role in patient outcome. In modern endoscopic surgery, there are practically no absolute contraindications to surgery, but there are relative contraindications of increasing magnitude that must be taken into consideration in choosing those patients to undergo a laparoscopic node dissection as opposed to an open node dissection. The patient's body weight is certainly a consideration. Although we have conducted modified radical hysterectomy and lymph node dissections for endometrial carcinoma in patients weighing as much as 287 lb, we have also found patients weighing as little as 80 lb to be technically difficult and occasionally impossible. Body weight in and of itself is not as great a negative determinate as body habitat (thickness of the interior abdominal wall and proportion of weight distributed across the chest and breast). Because these patients are in very steep Trendelenberg position, the amount of tissue on the chest wall may lead to significant hypercapnia and may limit the ability to complete a good node dissection. Patients with a history of stroke or Berry aneurysm should probably not undergo laparoscopic node dissection because of the need for steep Trendelenberg position. Similarly, patients with compromised pulmonary function and chronic obstructed pulmonary disease and long-term smokers are at increased risk because of the steep Trendelenberg position and fluid accumulation from a relatively long surgical procedure. Patients who have undergone pelvic surgery can generally undergo pelvic and aortic node dissection. Selective use of an intracostal trocar site and adhesiolysis or supraumbilical trocar site with adhesiolysis will allow safer visualization of the pelvic viscera in the previously operated patient.

Patients who have undergone small bowel resection or retroperitoneal surgery or pelvic and periaortic radiation therapy may be at extreme risk for bleeding or trauma to the veins of the retroperitoneum, and extreme caution should be exercised if a node dissection is undertaken in these patients. As with any other surgical technique, good clinical judgment, thorough discussion of the risks and benefits with patients, and thorough informed consent will select patients who should not undergo laparoscopic pelvic and aortic node dissection.

ANATOMY

A clear understanding of the retroperitoneal anatomy, boundaries of spaces, and location of structures is essential to the conduct of laparoscopic pelvic and aortic node dissection. Because the aorta may bifurcate as much as 10 cm above the sacral promontory, any nodes lying more than 5 cm above the promontory may be considered para-aortic nodes. In general, the inferior mesenteric artery is the upper boundary of lymph node sampling for endometrial cancer and dissection for cervix cancer. However, for patients with ovarian carcinoma, the renal vessels should be considered the upper boundary of node dissection. Care must be taken to identify both the right and left ureters and to ensure that they are not compromised during the lymph node sampling. This may be done by retraction of the ureter or simply ensuring that the ureter is not in the surgical field as the nodes are removed. Tilting the operating table from one side to another will sometimes facilitate exposure or retraction of the ureter. The lymph nodes of the right para-aortic chain lie between the aorta and vena cava and lateral to the vena cava. Bifurcating veins to the vena cava are frequently encountered. These veins must be identified before they are transected and either cauterized or clipped. I prefer cautery. The lymph nodes of the left para-aortic group lie posterior and lateral to the left side of the aorta and posterior to the sigmoid colon mesentery. Care must be taken not to inadvertently dissect into the sigmoid mesentery and to be sufficiently posterior to ensure para-aortic node sampling. Posterior and medial to the left para-aortic node, delicate and fragile venous complexes will be encountered that can be the source of considerable bleeding.

The presacral nodes lie between the right and left common iliac arteries and overlie the sacral promontory. They lie at the confluence of the left and right common iliac veins. They lie anterior to the presacral nerve complex. The nodes should be removed in the course of a radical hysterectomy or for staging of cervical carcinoma. If these nodes are gently and delicately dissected free from the posterior veins, perforating veins can easily be recognized. Care must be taken not to damage the midsacral veins, which lie deep and posterior between the left and right common iliac vein. The pelvic lymph nodes are bounded laterally by the psoas muscle and by the lateral femoral cutaneous nerve and genital femoral nerve, which lie on the psoas approximately 1 cm lateral to the external iliac artery. These nerves may be easily traumatized or transected in the course of node sampling or dissection, because the nerves are roughly the same caliber as the lymphatics connecting a series of lymph nodes. The ureter crosses the vessels at the bifurcation of the common iliac artery and serves as the apex of a triangle that represents the nodes to be sampled along the pelvic sidewall. The inguinal ligament and pelvic floor will roughly occupy the base of that triangle. So the triangle is composed of psoas muscle, ureter, and inquinal ligament with pelvic floor. When sampling the lymph nodes that lie between the external iliac artery and vein, at the cephalic limit, care must be taken not to traumatize the confluence of external iliac and internal iliac vein. This is a particularly dangerous area that should generally be avoided. The obturator fossa is bounded anteriorly by the external iliac vein, laterally by the bony pelvic sidewall, and posteriorly by the obturator nerve. This is a critical group of nodes and is usually the sentinel group for both cervical and endometrial cancer, so great care should be taken to properly evaluate these nodes and not traumatize the adjacent normal tissue or the obturator nerve.

INSTRUMENTATION

A wide variety of instruments is available, and selection of specific instruments will clearly vary from surgeon to surgeon. I have tended to use a 10-mm umbilical trocar, a 5-mm left lower-quadrant trocar, and a 12-mm right lower-quadrant trocar. On occasion, a 5-mm suprapubic trocar site will be developed though which the suction irrigator is used to suck, irrigate, and retract. Bipolar and monopolar electrosurgical scissors and forceps will be required. Microbipolar forceps are infrequently used and probably should not clutter up the instrument set. Equipment for laparoscopic staples

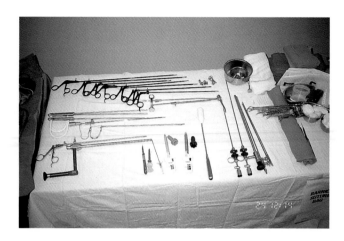

Fig. 17-1. Instrumentation for pelvic/aortic node dissection.

and vascular clips as well as suturing equipment must be available on the set. It is also useful if not necessary to have an endoscopic babcock and retractor device available. The CO_2 laser is of little value in facilitating node sampling. I have found that a very high-flow insufflator, which delivers 15 L/min significantly aids the procedure because there is a need to withdraw lymph nodes frequently through the trocar, and this causes a loss of pneumoperitoneum. It is annoying to use an old-fashioned insufflator that only slowly renews the pneumoperitoneum. Also, because operating time is frightfully expensive, every minute saved in the conduct of the surgery diminishes the patient's bill and health care cost. The ability to instill Gelfoam, Surgicel, or Avatine may be very useful, especially in the para-aortic node sampling. Because this is a procedure that requires two experienced endoscopic surgeons, at least two high-quality monitors are required. Figure 17-1

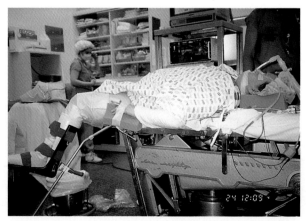

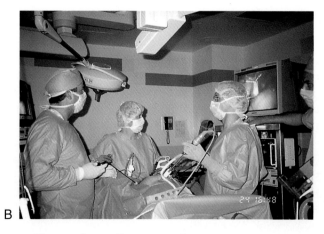

Fig. 17-2. (A) and **(B)** Patient and surgeon positions and operating room setup.

demonstrates the standard equipment table setup used in my institution for endoscopic node dissection, and Figure 17-2 demonstrates the typical location of monitors and equipment in my institution.

TECHNIQUE

In general, all endoscopic surgical procedures should mimic their open counterparts as closely as possible. This, I believe, is especially true in the case of laparoscopic pelvic and aortic node dissection. Pneumoperitoneum is first induced with the Veres needle. An infraumbilical trocar is inserted, and a 5-mm trocar is inserted in the left lower quadrant and a 12-mm trocar in the right lower quadrant. Because both of these trocars will require extensive manipulation, it is important to use trocars that will not be inadvertently withdrawn from the abdominal cavity and cause subcutaneous emphysema or traumatic reinsertion of the trocar sheath. Ideally, the trocars will also permit endoscopic suturing. Once the trocars are properly situated, the abdomen is explored visually, and careful notice is taken of any evidence of intraperitoneal spread or extension of the primary disease process. Cytologic washings are taken from the pelvic peritoneum, from the pericolic gutters, and when appropriate from the hemidiaphragm. If the uterus is in place, the round ligament is transected. I find it quickest and most cost-effective to cauterize the round ligament and then transect the round ligament, using a bipolar cautery forcep from the assistant's side and a bipolar scissors from the surgeon's side. The paravesicle and pararectal spaces are then developed. Pelvic node dissection may proceed. I believe it is useful to start with the nodes lateral to the external iliac artery, as this facilitates visualization and dissection of the other nodes. Because the arteries are more resistant to trauma and veins, it is safer to start by dissecting the nodes off the artery rather than off the vein. The assistant elevates the lymph nodes with an atraumatic grasping forceps. The nodes are gently dissected free from the lymphatic channels. The channels are coagulated with a bipolar scissors or forceps and then transected. Countertraction by the assistant is critical to distinguish the lymphatic vessels from adjacent nerves and to visualize any penetrating veins or vasa. This dissection is carried caudal toward the inguinal ligament and is generally stopped at the circumflex iliac vein. The magnification that is provided by the laparoscope allows a tremendous amount of safety, and one can easily identify the small veins and venules under the nerves that may be damaged in the course of a node dissection. The suction irrigator is used as needed to help visualize and to aspirate away blood. Hydrodissection (i.e., the insertion of fluid under pressure) is rarely used as this may cause confusion and confound the anatomy.

After the external iliac nodes have been removed, the nodes lying between the external iliac artery and vein are gently elevated medially to distinguish the boundary between the artery and vein. These nodes are then retracted medially and caudally to demonstrate the lymphatic attachments, which are sequentially severed with the bipolar scissors. This is a small group of nodes and generally does not require a great deal of time to complete the dissection. We have found that the nodes can generally be brought out through a trocar individually or as a group, taking advantage of the 12-mm trocar size. It is essential that the trocar not have a membrane or flap that will fragment the nodes and destroy the nodal architecture and slow down the procedure. An alternative technique is to lump the nodes in one area in the pelvis and then insert a series of bags, placing each nodal group in a separate bag and withdrawing it for analysis by the laboratory. I have chosen not to use bags, primarily as a cost-effective measure but also because it did not improve my ability to remove all the lymph nodes that I had dissected. The lymph nodes in the obturator fossa are next grasped and retracted initially medially so that the lateral boundary can be identified and detached and then retracted caudally so that the superior margin can be identified and detached and then retracted cephalically so that that margin can be identified and detached. I have found it to be useful on many occasions to gently mobilize the external iliac artery and vein medially and approach the lateral attachments of the obturator nodes from that direction. Great care must be taken to identify the obturator nerve and to ensure that it is not transected or traumatized during the node dissection. The obturator artery and vein will generally lie posterior to the nerve, and so if the dissection is maintained anterior to the obturator nerve, trauma to those vessels can be prevented.

After the nodes have been removed, each area is inspected. Bipolar cautery is applied to any area of bleeding. In the obturator fossa, because it is a partially closed space, tiny but irritating oozes may be controlled by applying pleggets of Avatine, Gelfoam, or Surgicel. I make no attempt to reconstruct the peritoneum. In patients who have previously undergone a hysterectomy and the round ligament is not available as an anatomic landmark, the peritoneum is opened lateral to the external iliac artery, approximately halfway between the origin of the external iliac artery and the inguinal ligament. The peritoneum is then dissected medially with the ureter attached on the medial flap, the paravesicle and pararectal spaces are developed, and the dissection occurs as mentioned above.

The para-aortic nodal groups in my experience always require very steep Trendelenberg positioning for access, and the small intestine should be elevated into the upper abdomen to provide adequate exposure of the posterior peritoneum overlying the aorta. On occasion, patients with an abnormal sigmoid mesentery or a shortened or tethered small bowel mesentery will be encountered, and this approach may be extremely difficult or impossible. The sigmoid mesentery is retracted by a fan-shaped retractor or by the suction irrigator, and an incision is made over the aorta. The peritoneum is gently retracted laterally and dissected. The ureter is identified and visualized. I try to extend the peritoneal incision on the right side down to the bifurcation of the common iliac artery, at which point the ureter can be easily identified. The lymph nodes lateral to the common iliac artery are then elevated, first anteriorly and then laterally, and the dissection precedes on the artery using the artery as a pressure point. There is nearly always a confluence of vessels at the bifurcation of the common iliac artery, and these should be either avoided or cauterized before transecting the nodes. The node dissection then proceeds cephalad, the appropriate counterattraction being placed on the nodes to facilitate vision and safe dissection. Occasionally, it is possible to continue the dissection up the right para-aortic group, but in most cases, these nodes fragment easily, and for purposes of nodal identification, I generally stop the common iliac dissection just superior to the sacral promontory.

The dissection of the left common iliac lymph nodes may be difficult or impossible from that same incision. I therefore generally extend my left pelvic retroperitoneal incision on the course of the left common iliac artery. Rotating the table to a right lateral position will help deviate the sigmoid colon toward the right and will facilitate both exposure and dissection of the left common iliac nodal groups.

The para-aortic node dissection begins with the right para-aortic lymph nodes. The dissection begins on the anterior wall of the aorta. The right para-aortic nodes are elevated and deviated laterally, and the lymphatic vessels and attachments to the artery are gently dissected and cauterized with the bipolar scissors. As the dissection gravitates over the vena cava, great care must be taken to avoid transecting or traumatizing the small perforating veins that nearly always are found 1 to 2 cm cephalad, the bifurcation of the aorta. The right

para-aortic nodes are dissected laterally to the psoas muscle, which provides a margin of approximately 5 to 10 mm medial to the ureter. A skilled assistant accomplished in the art of countertraction will be of invaluable assistance at this stage of the dissection.

The left para-aortic nodes are technically the most difficult to reach because of the sigmoid mesentery and because the nodes lie posterior and lateral to the aorta. The suction irrigator may be used to deviate the aorta toward the right side, which will expose the right margin of the left para-aortic lymph nodes. These nodes can then be grasped by the first assistant and elevated slightly anteriorly. The second assistant then releases the aorta with the suction irrigator and retracts the sigmoid mesentery and left ureter laterally so that the left para-aortic node bundle can be visualized more completely. I generally mobilize the right side of this nodal group first so that I can visualize the venus complex posterior to the nodes and then transect the cephalic margin, first cauterizing and then transecting with bipolar cautery. The nodal group is then retracted toward the right, and the margin between the ureter and the lymph node packet can be defined and dissected. The caudal margin of the lymph node packet is then the last component of the dissection. It is cauterized with the bipolar forceps and transected.

As with any advanced endoscopic surgical technique, the surgeon is fully dependent on the operating room support staff, the anesthesia department, and the physician who assists the surgeon. A weakness in any of these component parts jeopardizes the conduct of the procedure and may make it unsafe for the patient. The surgeon must honestly evaluate his or her institutional capacities for the conduct of such procedures. I have modified my approach somewhat over the past 2 years, and the technique described above represents the current state of the art, in my hands, in my institution. The reader will note that I avoid hemoclips. This is primarily so that my patients may undergo magnetic resonance imaging (MRI) postoperatively. The radiographic community has considerable concern about MRI dislodging metallic clips and, in my area, will often refuse to perform an MRI on a patient who has had metallic clips as demonstrated by scout film. Also, hemoclips are relatively expensive, and in my hands, bipolar cautery or CO_2 laser has worked as well for hemostatis for small lymphatics as hemoclips. The surgeon must always have in mind the intent of the procedure (i.e., full-bore lymph node dissection in which meticulous care will be taken to remove every visible node versus lymph node sampling). There is a direct relationship of morbidity to the number of nodes removed. Because one of the prime theoretical benefits of the endoscopic node dissection technique is diminished hospital stay, clearly increased morbidity will diminish the potential impact of the procedure.

Maintenance of pneumoperitoneum is very important in the conduct of this procedure. My insufflator is normally set at 18 to 22 lb of pressure. This, I think, facilitates hemostatis and clearly facilitates exposure. It may create problems for the anesthesiologist and for the patient, and so I work in concert with my anesthesiologist to use the least possible Trendelenberg position that will provide satisfactory exposure and the least possible intraperitoneal pressure that will provide adequate exposure. On occasion, significant hypercapnia has developed, and I have stopped operating and placed the patient in reverse Trendelenberg position until satisfactory serum CO_2 levels could be obtained.[17]

RISKS AND COMPLICATIONS

The risks and complications of endoscopic pelvic and aortic node dissection are exactly the same as the risks and complications of an open pelvic and aortic dissection. These include primarily damage to the blood vessels, lymphatics, ureter, bladder, or intestine. I am experienced in handling these complications in open surgical procedures and take advantage of the greater exposure a large abdominal incision provides. To the neophyte retroperitoneal endoscopist, it can be very anxiety-provoking to suffer a significant bleed from the external iliac vein or artery. Pressure may be applied by an assistant, and electrocautery may be used in such an event. Sutures, or hemoclips may be placed to correct that sort of bleeding. The techniques used to correct complications are identical to open procedures, but the lack of exposure and new surgical techniques that are required to implement them require repeated practice. When in doubt, if endoscopic techniques cannot be used to resolve a complication, the patient must undergo a laparotomy, and the complication must be resolved in a more traditional fashion.

There are complications of endoscopic node dissection that are additional and different from the traditional open approach, and these relate to the use of the laparoscope and the endoscopic method. I have experienced herniation in 5-, 10- and 12-mm trocar sites. I make every effort to close the fascia in the 10 and 12-mm sites. I do not close the fascia in 5-mm sites as it seems to be anatomically difficult, if not impossible. Also, potential damage with the Veress needle to the

omentum, bowel, or even retroperitoneal structures may occur. Because the trocar insertion is still a blind procedure even with the newer trocars that provide safety shields, occasional inadvertent trauma may occur. Puncture wounds in the stomach have been reported. In general, these will not occur if proper anesthetic techniques have been used and the stomach has not been hyperinflated. A preoperative bowel preparation with a gallon of Colyte and a nasogastric tube at surgery significantly diminishes these risks. Care must be taken when inserting the lateral ports to visualize the inferior epigastric artery and vein and to place the trocars in a safe position so as not to traumatize these vessels. In my experience, these vessels are usually traumatized when the trocar is inadvertently withdrawn during the procedure and is somewhat blindly reinserted or when a trocar site needs to be enlarged to remove a larger specimen and either the enlargement of the incision or the withdrawal of the specimen traumatizes the vessel. If the trocar site is still relatively small, a Foley catheter may be inserted through the trocar site, and traction may be applied. This will stop bleeding from minor inferior epigastric artery and vein trauma. If more major trauma is seen, these vessels may be sutured laparoscopically or the trocar site incision may be enlarged and the vessels visualized and sutured or clipped through the skin incision. Very rarely, a laparotomy is required to identify such bleeders and to secure hemostatis.

As with any procedure involving stirrups and relatively long operative time, care must be taken not to unnecessarily traumatize the calf, feet, or ankle. Damage to the common peroneal nerve has been reported from calf compression. Pressure sores and necrosis have occurred from heel compression. These sorts of injuries are associated with prolonged operative times and poor patient positioning.

TRAINING AND CREDENTIALING

No formal guidelines exist defining the training of endoscopic surgeons. Several organizations and groups have proposed training programs, and a multidisciplinary committee of the American Medical Association is working to develop general curricular guidelines and training guidelines. Training of an endoscopic surgeon may be categorized as follows: (1) cognitive information, (2) acquisition of technical skills, (3) refinement of technical skills, and (4) maintenance of technical skills. A formal didactic course is required to familiarize the surgeon with the cognitive skills required to perform endoscopic surgery. Such a

Fig. 18-1. Note the defective insulation *(arrow)*.

cumventing difficulties presented by an overinflated bladder.

An orogastric tube is positioned after the patient is anesthetized; this keeps the stomach away from the operative field and prevents displacement of the bowel into the pelvis. It also may lessen postoperative nausea and reduce the risk of regurgitation. The tube is removed at the conclusion of the operation.

I ask the anesthesiologist to avoid nitrous oxide if the operation is to last more than 2 hours. The gas may be associated with increased bowel distention in prolonged operations.

Mechanical bowel preparation reduces large bowel contents and places the bowel into a contracted configuration, thus making it easier to mobilize out of the pelvis. Adequate Trendelenburg position also facilitates displacing bowel out of the pelvis.

If poor visibility is a problem after these steps have been taken, the surgeon should check with the anesthesiologist to determine the level of anesthesia. If the patient's abdominal muscles are not relaxed, the bowel falls into the pelvic cavity, and there is a concomitant

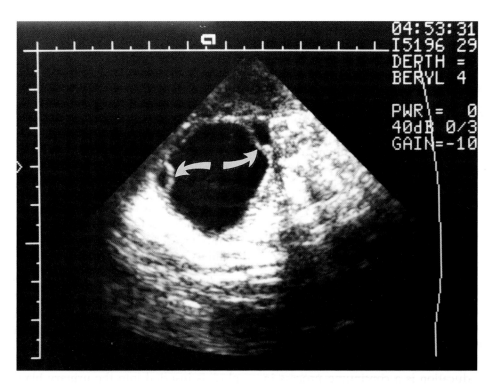

Fig. 18-2. Ultrasound image of a benign ovarian cyst. Note the thin septa *(arrows)*. (Courtesy of Beryl Benaceraf, M.D., Boston, MA.)

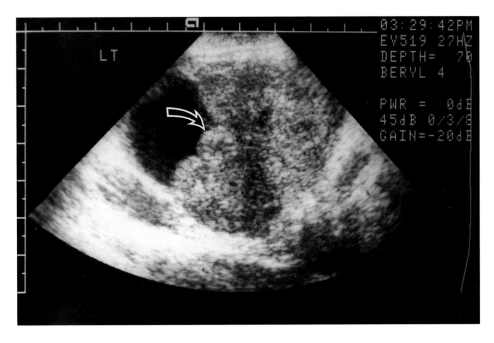

Fig. 18-3. Ultrasound image of a malignant ovarian cyst. Note the solid components *(arrow).* (Courtesy of Beryl Benaceraf, M.D., Boston, MA.)

reduction in the volume of the pneumoperitoneum due to increased intra-abdominal pressure.

Fogging

One hindrance is inability to see clearly due to fogging of the laparoscope lens. It usually occurs because of a relatively cold laparoscope being placed into the warm, moisture-rich environment of the abdominal cavity.[2] Insufflated gas in contact with the laparoscope lens is cooled below the dew point, and condensation forms on the lens. Once this temperature differential is overcome, fogging should cease.

Briskly rubbing the laparoscope barrel with a dry sponge before it is inserted into the abdomen warms the laparoscope and shortens the condensation period. Also, dipping the laparoscope tip into a nearby cup containing a small amount of pHisoHex and thoroughly wiping the lens clean with a dry sponge often eliminates the problem. Connecting the tubing through which the insufflated gas flows to the sideport of a secondary cannula directs the cold gas away from the laparoscope lens and may reduce fogging. Commercial laparoscope warmers and defogging solutions are also available.

Viewing the Operative Field

Bifocal glasses should be avoided when the surgeon views directly through the laparoscope. Their focal length does not match the length of the laparoscope, and a blurred image results.

The surgeon should keep the laparoscope lens clean at all times. Often blood or other fluids accumulate on the distal lens and must be removed continually with the irrigator, by brushing the lens against peritoneal surfaces or by cleaning it with pHisoHex and a dry sponge.

Hemostasis

The most careful laparoscopic surgeon will encounter troublesome bleeding from time to time. When confronted with this situation, the surgeon should consider several questions. Is exposure adequate? This may mean placing additional secondary cannulas for retraction or requesting steeper Trendelenburg position. Are irrigation and suction sufficient? It may be necessary to place irrigation in one secondary port, suction in another, and the coagulation instrument in a third. Have contiguous structures been located? Identification of abutting structures is essential.

Time often can be gained by closing the paddles of a Kleppinger forceps, disconnected from its power source, around the bleeding site. Ancillary measures, such as application of Avitene, can be taken. If all reasonable steps fail, laparotomy should be considered; it is preferable to coagulating blindly at laparoscopy. One caveat is to never have two energy sources in the abdomen at the same time (Fig. 18-4).

Many surgeons advocate injecting vasopressin into operative sites to reduce bleeding. This intense vasoconstrictor may decrease bleeding in patients undergoing such procedures as salpingotomy for tubal pregnancy and myomectomy (Fig. 18-5). A dilute solution, such as 20 U vasopressin in 200 ml Ringer's lactate, should be used. The amount should be limited, if feasible, to 2 U during an operation. The anesthetist must be alerted and permission granted for its use, as hypertension can result.

The operative field is inspected for hemostasis by instilling irrigation fluid into the abdomen and releasing the pneumoperitoneum. This "underwater" examination will reveal bleeding sites.[3] Alternatively, the surgeon may inspect the sites by reducing intraperitoneal pressure to approximately 5 mm Hg.

Glycine

Glycine is an excellent medium for operative laparoscopy.[4] It allows one to visualize a bleeding vessel easily as blood streams through it. Also this electrolyte-free fluid allows the surgeon to coagulate a submerged bleeding vessel. It has a pH of 6.1, which is approximately that of Ringer's lactate. I remove glycine from the abdomen at the end of the operation.

Choice of Laparotomy Incision

If laparotomy is required to repair an injury, a low transverse incision should be chosen if possible, even if it is not optimal. If a vertical incision is required, the least disfiguring one should be chosen. If surgery is performed by a consultant, the gynecologic surgeon should be present in the operating room and should follow the patient postoperatively. Not only will the patient and family be appreciative, but litigation may be avoided.

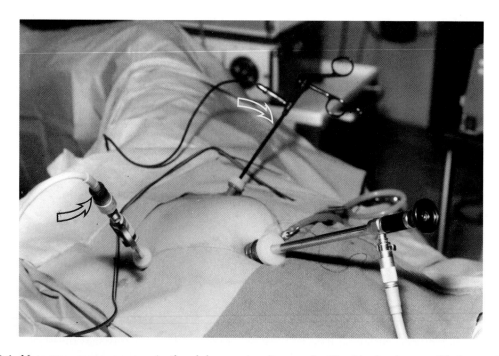

Fig. 18-4. Note two energy sources in the abdomen simultaneously. The bipolar forceps *(black arrow)* and unipolar scissors *(white arrow)* are both connected to power sources. This is potentially a dangerous situation as the wrong activation pedal may be depressed.

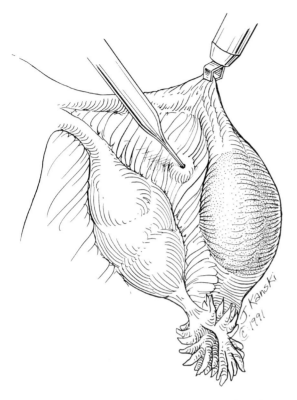

Fig. 18-5. Dilute vasopressin is being injected in the serosa beneath an ampullary ectopic pregnancy. (From Hunt,[84] with permission.)

"I Think It's OK" Syndrome

Beware of the words, "I think it's OK." The surgeon must determine whether the organ in question is or is not injured. If the conclusion is that it is injured, proper steps are taken to deal with it. The matter should not be put aside for a period of observation.

The "Weekend" Syndrome

Patients recovering from laparoscopic surgery should only improve. If a patient does not improve or worsens, she must be evaluated forthwith. Viscus injury must be considered until that possibility has been ruled out. Often, the diagnosis of a complication is delayed when the patient has had surgery on Friday, and the surgeon has assigned her to the care of a colleague for the weekend. Not knowing the circumstances, the covering physician may order analgesics instead of evaluating the patient when contacted. Disaster is the rule in these cases. If the surgeon needs to be away the day after these operations, the patient should be as-signed to a physician whose medical judgment is absolutely trustworthy. It is also essential to inform the covering physician about all such postoperative patients.

NEUROLOGIC COMPLICATIONS

Patient positioning should be supervised by the surgeon.[5] Low-profile lower-extremity supports such as Allen stirrups are desirable. Pressure points can be avoided by padding the supports and positioning the legs properly. Weight should be borne by the heels and not the legs. Undue stress on muscles and joints should be avoided. These steps lessen the possibility of such postoperative sequelae as peroneal nerve injury or simply painful muscles and joints.[6] One problem associated with Allen-type stirrups is that the foot of a stirrup can project beneath a nearby table. When the patient is placed into the Trendelenburg position, the stirrup can turn the table over, possibly injuring the patient's foot and likely damaging equipment.

The upper extremities must be positioned carefully. Arms should never be abducted more than 90 degrees, preferably less, as brachial plexus injury can occur easily in the anesthetized patient.[7] One colleague observed five brachial nerve palsies over a 6-month period. They occurred from a combination of abduction of the arms to at least 90 degrees, improperly positioning shoulder braces, and deep Trendelenburg position. Preferably, the arm on the same side as the surgeon should be tucked at the patient's side. The contralateral arm should be placed on an armboard close to the patient's side if there is no assistant or by the patient's side if there is.

The ilioinguinal nerve can be entrapped at the time of a laparoscopic uterine suspension or severed by a secondary cannula. The surgeon should review the course of the nerve, and plan abdominal incisions accordingly.

The femoral nerve can be injured if the surgeon is unaware of its course. In the pelvis, it is located just lateral to the femoral artery; damage to the nerve can result in weakness or paralysis of the quadriceps femoris muscles, loss of thigh and leg sensation, and absence of the patellar reflex.[5] The surgeon also must be aware of the course of the obturator nerve when resecting endometriosis implants on the pelvic sidewall or when performing pelvic lymphadenectomy. Injury to the obturator nerve may cause permanent motor and sensory loss to skin and muscles in the thigh.

HEART

Fortunately, cardiac disease is infrequent in the healthy patient. If the history or physical examination reveals a significant cardiac problem, antibiotics should be administered when appropriate and consultation obtained when indicated.

Healthy patients tolerate large volumes of irrigating fluids without sequelae. Although rare, cardiomyopathy has been associated with laparoscopy and may result in congestive heart failure and pulmonary edema.[8]

Cardiac arrhythmias, including bradycardia and asystole, have occurred with laparoscopy, usually at the time of insufflation or when traction is applied to pelvic structures. One author attributes the problem in part to newer, shorter-acting muscle relaxants such as atracurium and vecuronimum.[9] Another group implicated succinylcholine as one cause of arrhythmias and cardiac collapse.[10] Several contributory mechanisms were suggested in the case report of cardiac arrest in a healthy 29-year-old woman when the pneumoperitoneum was being established.[11] In addition to cardiovascular support, treatment consisted of rapid release of the pneumoperitoneum, which was immediately followed by normal cardiac activity. There was no evidence of intra-abdominal injury.

TROCAR AND INSUFFLATION COMPLICATIONS

Scope of the Problem

A survey among Canadian obstetricians and gynecologists revealed one-fourth of them had experienced at least one case of sharp trocar or needle injury. One-half of the injuries required laparotomy to rectify.[12] A survey from France reviewed 17,521 laparoscopic operations performed over a 4-year period.[13] Complications were defined as either death or an event necessitating unintended laparotomy. The rate of complications among diagnostic or minor laparoscopic procedures was 1.1 per 1,000 operations, and the rate for major or advanced procedures was 5.2 per 1,000. Injuries included hemorrhage (17), stomach perforation (1), small bowel perforation (10), large bowel perforation (16), urinary bladder (6), ureter (1), and peritonitis or obstruction without perforation (6). One death was secondary to trocar injury.

Vascular Injuries

Injuries to the great vessels (aorta, inferior vena cava, iliac arteries and veins) of the abdomen do occur and can be lethal.[14] A study from France reported 31 major vessel injuries, 20 with the Veress needle and 11 with the trocar.[15] Another study reported five cases of major vessel injury.[16] One resulted in laparotomy with repair of the right iliac artery; one in laparotomy, repair of the aorta, and several units of blood; one in a second laparotomy, 22 U of blood, and a half-million-dollar lawsuit; one in permanent brain damage; and one in death. The authors suggested open laparoscopy to reduce the frequency of vascular complications.

A survey by the Royal College of Obstetricians and Gynaecologists revealed nine major vessel injuries in 10,000 laparoscopies.[17] In 1975, 12 laparoscopist from the United States, Great Britain, and Holland reported 19 such events.[18] The Centers for Disease Control monitored deaths from sterilization procedures from 1977 to 1981. Of the three deaths caused by vascular injuries, one each resulted from the Veress needle and trocar and one from inappropriate use of a scalpel to open the skin.[19] One author collected more than 100 injuries to the great vessels caused by either the Veress needle or trocar.[20] The American Association of Gynecologic Laparoscopists reported a frequency of 1.8 injuries per 1,000 sterilizations and 2.6 per 1,000 diagnostic procedures.[21]

Injuries to the great vessels are most likely to occur in the thin patient. Because bleeding is frequently retroperitoneal, it may not be apparent. The injury often causes sudden vascular collapse and requires immediate diagnosis and repair. Of 16 vascular injuries, 11 were inflicted at the time of needle insertion for the pneumoperitoneum, 3 were trocar injuries, and the misdirected instrument was not named in 2.[14] Two deaths were reported in that survey.

Inferior epigastric and deep circumflex iliac vessels may be damaged when the secondary cannula is inserted. Troublesome bleeding also can occur from injury to the superficial circumflex and superficial epigastric. To avoid these injuries, I recommend viewing the deep vessels from the peritoneal side through the laparoscope and identifying the superficial ones by transillumination before placement of the secondary cannula (Figs. 18-6 and 18-7). The inferior egigastric vessels course just lateral to the obliterated umbilical artery and, even if not visible, can usually be avoided by knowing their location. Should an injury to these arteries occur, various methods to control the bleeding may be attempted.

Often direct pressure applied by a solid probe through another port will stop the bleeding, especially if the vessel is not transected entirely or only a small

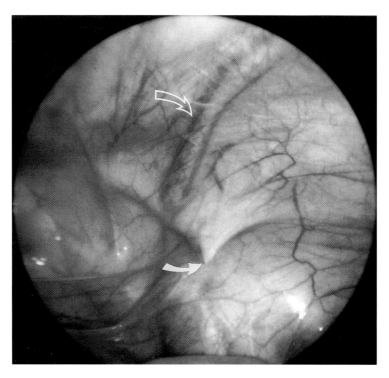

Fig. 18-6. Inferior epigastric vessels consist of an artery blanketed by two veins *(open arrow)*. The tip of the secondary cannula is tenting the peritoneum *(closed arrow)* just lateral to the vessels.

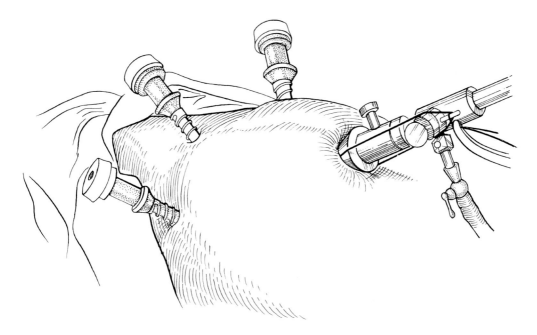

Fig. 18-7. The primary and three secondary cannulas are positioned. (From Hunt,[84] with permission.)

branch of the vessel is torn. Pressure should be applied for 5 minutes, once the bleeding has stopped.

Bipolar coagulation is also effective in some cases, in particular, if the exact bleeding point can be seen. The vessel should be grasped approximately 0.5 cm behind the bleeding point. If bleeding stops when the forceps is applied, then the vessel should be coagulated. If the forceps does not stop the bleeding after it is applied, coagulation should not be used, as it is unlikely to control the bleeding, and may disrupt the anatomy.

Should these methods not work, temporary control of the bleeding can usually be accomplished by passing a Foley catheter through the trocar, inflating the balloon, and pulling the trocar out of the incision. Traction is then placed on the catheter, so that the balloon tamponades the bleeding vessel.

Suturing the vessel is the best method to control a significant bleed. The suture can be passed using various techniques. A large stay or veterinarian needle and suture can usually be passed around the vessel all externally, using laparoscopic control. This method works well in the thin patient, but is difficult to do in the obese patient. Another method of tying the vessel is to pass a long straight needle into the abdomen, grasp it with a laparoscopic needle holder, and pass it back out of the abdomen on the other side of the bleeding vessel. We have found the easiest and quickest method of suturing a bleeding vessel is to use one of the many laparoscopic suture passers that are sold for fascial closures. The simplest devices are the best. The suture is placed through the abdominal wall directly on one side of the vessel. The suture is released, the instrument withdrawn and then passed back empty into the abdomen on the other side of the vessel. The end of the suture is regrasped and brought out of the abdomen on the other side of the vessel.

Regardless of which method of suturing is used, the suture is tied externally. Prior to tying the suture, intraabdominal pressure should be released and the Foley balloon deflated. The suture should be placed under traction until bleeding stops, and then tied in that position. A small sponge can be placed between the abdominal wall and the knot.

If these methods are tried, it is quite rare to have to make an abdominal incision to expose the epigastric vessels for control of bleeding.

Gastrointestinal Injuries

If the surgeon performs a large number of operative laparoscopies, bowel injury is almost inevitable, and the surgeon should be prepared to deal with it. The important thing is to make the diagnosis at the time of the injury and to repair it appropriately.

When the operation is complete, the surgeon should withdraw the primary cannula from the abdomen, then slowly withdraw the laparoscope while viewing the abdominal wall structures (Fig. 18-8). If the bowel has been punctured near the entry site of the primary cannula, the injury will most likely be detected at the time of this final check.

If the surgeon encounters periumbilical adhesions, another site of entry should be considered, such as the left upper quadrant 3 cm inferior to the left rib cage and 3 cm to the left of midline.[22] Alternatively, a site between the ninth and tenth ribs in the anterior axillary line may be chosen for inserting the Veress needle.[23] After the pneumoperitoneum has been established, a 5-mm trocar and cannula may then be inserted 1 cm beneath the tenth rib and medial to the anterior axillary line, followed by insertion of a 5-mm laparoscope. Adhesions can be cleared away from the periumbilical site and a standard subumbilical entry effected. An orogastric tube should be in place to lessen the chance of stomach injury.

The surgeon must be aware that unipolar bowel burns may be much more extensive than apparent. A bowel resection should include several centimeters on either side of the injury before anastomosis.[24] In a classic study on thermal injury, a histologic difference was detected in the the appearance of bowel at the injured site after electrosurgical injury compared with mechanical injury.[25] When stained with Mallory trichrome stain, the former has a very clean, almost ghostlike appearance; the mechanical injury site shows an intense inflammatory reaction. The authors strongly recommended submitting the resected segment of bowel to pathology for Mallory trichrome stain and study. The surgeon should personally deliver the specimen to the pathologist with an explanation of what is to be determined. This histologic documentation is essential.

Shielded Trocars

Shielded trocars are designed to prevent gastrointestinal and vascular injuries; however, many anecdotal reports of injuries by the instrument have been circulated. One group reported one bowel perforation in 40 cases using a shielded trocar-cannula system.[26] The authors stressed that disposable shielded systems are not cost-effective and do not provide the margin of safety that had been hoped. Some believe this trocar instills a false sense of security in the surgeon, who might

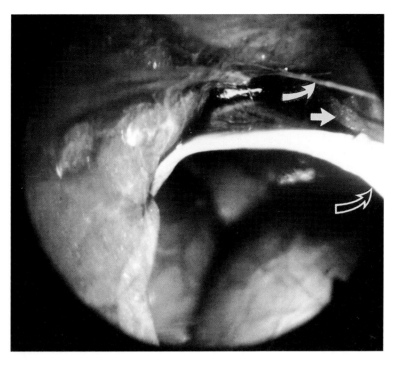

Fig. 18-8. The peritoneum and transversalis fascia *(curved open arrow)*, rectus muscle *(straight arrow)*, and peritoneum *(curved closed arrow)* are easily seen as the laparoscope is withdrawn.

not always adhere to sound laparoscopic principles of insertion.

Gas Emboli

A case of circulatory collapse was reported from air emboli.[27] The patient was 8 weeks pregnant and wished to have a termination of pregnancy and a tubal interruption. After evacuating the uterus, the surgeon elected to insufflate the peritoneal cavity through a Veress needle inserted through the vagina toward the posterior cul-de-sac. After 1.5 L carbon dioxide had been placed at a pressure of 10 to 20 mmHg, the patient had no blood pressure, and a mill-wheel murmur was heard. She was resuscitated and recovered without sequelae. The authors postulated that external cardiac massage during resuscitation broke up some of the large bubbles obstructing outflow from the right atrium and ventricles. These smaller bubbles were then rapidly absorbed to the point at which efficient cardiac work was restored, and the patient recovered. The patient underwent tubal interruption 1 week later by minilaparotomy. At that time, the uterus was noted to be in fixed retroversion.

I am aware of a medicolegal case of an obese woman who underwent a dilation and curettage just before laparoscopy. A cannula was then inserted into the cervix for mobilization, and the patient was placed in the Trendelenburg position for laparoscopy. The combination of obesity and Trendelenburg position created a negative intraperitoneal pressure. Room air was sucked through the uncapped cervical cannula into the endometrial cavity and freshly curetted uterine veins. Massive air emboli ensued. The lesson to be learned is to cap the cervical cannula with a syringe if the uterus has been recently traumatized.

Insufflated Gas in Unintended Sites

At the time of insufflation, gas may extend into subcutaneous, retroperitoneal, or omental spaces, producing subcutaneous and omental emphysema, pneumomediastinum, pneumopericardium, pneumothorax, or gas emboli.[28–30] An intra-abdominal pressure of 25 mmHg is estimated to produce pressure on intra-abdominal structures of 30 g/cm^2 or 0.5 lb/in^2 (Fig. 18-9).[31] The total force on the diaphragm could exceed 50 kg at these pressures. Hiatal hernia, a congenital diaphrag-

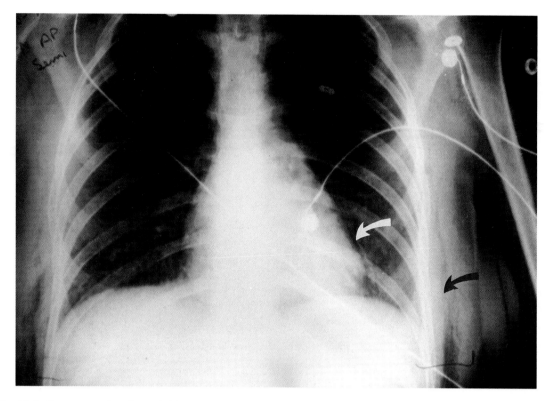

Fig. 18-9. Pneumopericardium *(white arrow)* and subcutaneous emphysema *(black arrow)* resulted from intra-abdominal insufflation of gas at too high pressure.

matic defect, or a tear in the visceral peritoneum can result in retroperitoneal extension of insufflated gas into the mediastinum. Rupture of the mediastinal pleura or along the pulmonary vessels into the pleural space would result in a pneumothorax or pneumopericardium.[30–32] If unrecognized, either event could result in a catastrophy.

Newer insufflation units are equipped to deliver in excess of 6 L gas/min. The quantity of gas used is irrelevant, but intra-abdominal pressure is exceedingly important. I usually set the insufflator at 10 to 12 mmHg pressure, and I do not exceed 15 mmHg.

The importance of preventive maintenance cannot be overstated. To illustrate, instead of the preset value of 15 to 25 mmHg, a faulty insufflator delivered pressure in excess of 50 mmHg, resulting in extensive subcutaneous emphysema.[33]

Steps should be taken to avoid insufflation into the extraperitoneal space or the omentum. Safety checks, such as the hanging drop technique, and irrigation and aspiration of the Veress needle are helpful. Open laparoscopy should avoid this problem. One group advocates direct insertion of a shielded trocar without first creating a pneumoperitoneum.[34] The authors cited two reasons for favoring this policy: it reduces the number of blind entries by eliminating Veress needle insertion, and more vascular injuries have been caused by the Veress needle than by the trocar.

Acute Compartment Syndrome

One potentially disastrous complication is the acute compartment syndrome.[35–37] This rarely encountered condition involving extremities has been associated with trauma, pneumatic stockings, and being in stirrups for a long period of time. Muscle in the fascial compartments of the leg(s) undergoes swelling, which obstructs venous outflow. Arteries continue to perfuse these compartments, and muscle necrosis occurs. The conscious patient will complain of unilateral or bilateral leg pain. The involved extremity(ies) may be swollen, with arterial pulses intact. Myoglobin levels are enormously elevated. Immediate fasciotomy is mandatory or the extremity(ies) may be lost.

ADHESIONS, CAPACITANCE, AND THERMAL INJURY

Adhesiolysis is an operation of tissue tensions. Often adhesions are stronger than the tissues of the organ to which they are attached, and too much traction can avulse a portion of the organ. Great care must be taken to apply enough traction for safe dissection but not so much that injury occurs (Fig. 18-10).

Capacitance is also associated with injury. This has been particularly problematic in the hybrid cannula, which has a metal barrel with a nonconductive component fixed in the abdominal wall.[38,39] When a unipolar electrosurgical instrument is inserted through the barrel and activated, an electric charge can develop on the barrel surface. This is capacitance. The electrically charged cannula can inflict thermal injury to any structure it touches. The Food and Drug Administration has agreed with the concept that only conductive cannulas larger than 7 mm in diameter should be used in conjunction with monopolar electrosurgery.[40]

Although the physics of capacitance are somewhat arcane, a few general principles seem clear. Bipolar instruments do not appear to be a problem. Hybrid cannulas should not be used as secondary cannulas in conjunction with activated unipolar instruments. Only all-metal primary cannulas should be used if the surgeon plans to apply unipolar electrosurgical energy through an operating laparoscope. If a nonconductive primary cannula is used in this situation, the laparoscope may become a capacitor, whereas a metal cannula allows electric charges created by capacitance to flow harmlessly into the abdominal wall. Recently, a sleeve that slips just inside the trocar and removes the charge so that a capacitor is not created has been manufactured by Electroscope.

Another area of concern is heat conduction from an energy source to adjacent structures. For example, if a uterosacral ligament is coagulated for too long, enough heat may be transferred to nearby rectum or ureter through intervening tissue to cause significant tissue necrosis. One must always keep this bridging concept in mind when delivering energy to tissue.

URINARY TRACT COMPLICATIONS

Urinary Bladder

The urinary bladder may be perforated when inserting a secondary cannula, particularly when the entry is in the midline.[41] The surgeon should be particularly careful in a patient who has had a previous pelvic laparotomy. Secondary cannulas should be inserted in or superior to a lower abdominal transverse incision, as the bladder may be retracted to the incision. If the bladder cannot be visualized from the peritoneal side or if a bladder perforation is suspected, the bladder should be distended with dilute indigo carmine. This will define better the limits of the bladder, and it will quickly demonstrate the site of a perforation. The perforation may treated by catheter drainage for 7 to 10 days or by suturing, depending on its site, size, and cause. The location of the ureteral orifices relative to the site of injury must be considered before plans for correction are made.

One author reported a cystotomy that occurred when a Rubin's cannula became detached from the stabilizing tenaculum.[42] Manipulation of pelvic structures with the cannula resulted in a transvaginal bladder perforation with the cannula tip. Cystoscopy revealed a 2- to 3-mm laceration lateral to the trigone, 1 cm from the left ureteral orifice. A ureteral stent was placed and the defect repaired successfully.

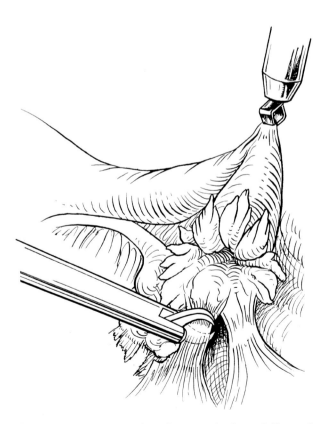

Fig. 18-10. Traction on the tube is applied carefully so that fimbria are not avulsed. (From Hunt,[84] with permission.)

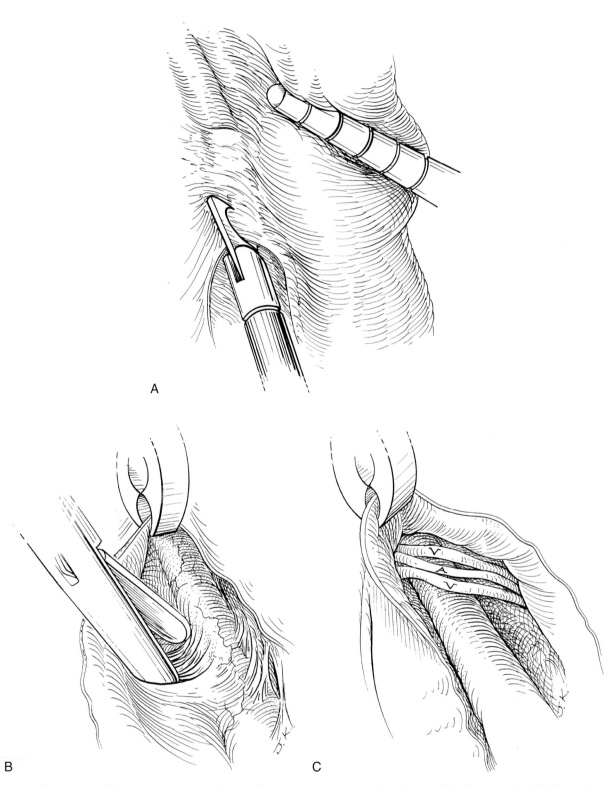

Fig. 18-11. **(A)** Peritoneum is incised near the right ureter as the right adnexa is lifted anteriorly. **(B)** The right ureter is dissected free from surrounding tissue. **(C)** The right ureter has been dissected to the site that it disappears into the tunnel beneath the uterine artery *(A)* and veins *(V)*. (From Hunt,[84] with permission.)

Ureter

"The venial sin is injury to the ureter; the mortal sin is failure of recognition"[43] (attributed to the late Thomas H. Green, Boston, MA). The ureter is much less forgiving than the urinary bladder.[43-47] The best way to avoid injuring it, as with the bladder, is to identify it.[48] The ureter may follow an aberrant course. Peristalsis must be noted before positive identification can be made. If the surgeon has difficulty identifying the ureter, it should be located at the pelvic brim. It is usually best to open the peritoneum lateral to the ureter to keep the ureter on the medial peritoneal leaf. The ureter can then be dissected caudally to the so-called tunnel (Fig. 18-11). If the surgeon still has difficulty locating or tracing the ureter, an illuminated ureteral stent may be positioned. One caveat is that the ureter may remain on the pelvic sidewall rather than with the medial peritoneal leaf during dissection.

Most likely, ureteral injuries occur due to application of energy to inappropriate sites rather than to a faulty instrument. Three common sites of injury are adjacent to the infundibulopelvic ligament (salpingo-oophorectomy), at the level of the uterosacral ligament (laparoscopic uterosacral nerve ablation), and near the uterine artery (laparoscopic-assisted vaginal hysterectomy).[49-51] When laceration of the ureter is suspected, the surgeon should inject 5 to 10 ml undiluted indigo carmine intravenously. If a perforation is present, the dye will appear at the injured site within minutes; appropriate urologic consultation should be obtained and corrective action instituted. Sometimes, an indwelling ureteral stent with or without suturing the defect is all that is necessary.

If the infundibulopelvic ligament is to be divided, the peritoneum should be opened between it and the ureter and the latter reflected away from the ligament. The ligament may then be operated on with complete safety as far as the ureter is concerned (Fig. 18-12). At the time of laparoscopic uterosacral nerve ablation, the uterus should be acutely anteflexed and an incision made parallel and lateral to the respective uterosacral ligament. The ureter can then be reflected away. The ligament is coagulated and divided or ablated near the insertion of the ligament into the cervix. If a laparoscopic-assisted vaginal hysterectomy is being performed and the surgeon plans to divide the uterine arteries laparoscopically, the respective ureter must be identified and kept out of the way before ligation or coagulation and subsequent division of the uterine artery and vein.

The obliterated umbilical artery may be easily confused with the ureter. It courses through the retroperitoneal space very close to the ureter and is similar in appearance to it (Fig. 18-13). The difference is that only the ureter peristalses. The surgeon must also remember that a double ureter may be present; conversely, the contralateral ureter may not be present, as in the patient with a unicornuate uterus.

Urachal Sinus

An unusual complication is laceration of a patent urachal sinus during trocar insertion.[52,53] It can be diagnosed by voiding cystourethrogram. Treatment varies from catheter drainage for 2 weeks to laparotomy for acute pertitonitis developing several hours after laparoscopy. If a patient complains of long-standing umbilical drainage, preoperative evaluation to rule out a patent urachal sinus is prudent. A patent omphalomesenteric duct or Meckel diverticulum can also cause chronic umbilical discharge.

FOREIGN BODIES, ENDOMETRIAL CELLS, AND BACTERIAL CONTAMINATION

Instruments sometimes detach, and needles may be lost (Fig. 18-14). An alert scrub nurse and a thoughtful surgeon can often circumvent a potential problem by carefully checking instruments for defects. Flushing solid particles and bacteria into the abdomen from supply tanks also is possible.[54,55] Some insufflation units provide a filter to prevent this.

Endometrial cells were present in peritoneal fluid when chromotubation was performed after hysteroscopy.[56] This is of concern should there be endometrial malignancy.

Although one may classify laparoscopic surgery as a clean rather than a sterile procedure, postoperative infections are unusual in the absence of injury to peritoneal structures. A study of peritoneal fluids before and after tubal lavage at laparoscopy yielded a 90 percent frequency of vaginal bacteria being displaced into the abdominal cavity.[57] The concentrations of bacteria were low, not exceeding 105 organisms per milliliter. Nevertheless, copious rinsing of the peritoneal cavity should be accomplished and administration of prophylactic antibiotics considered.

HYPOTHERMIA

Often the core temperature of an anesthetized patient may drop markedly during prolonged laparoscopic operations. This can be detrimental to recovery

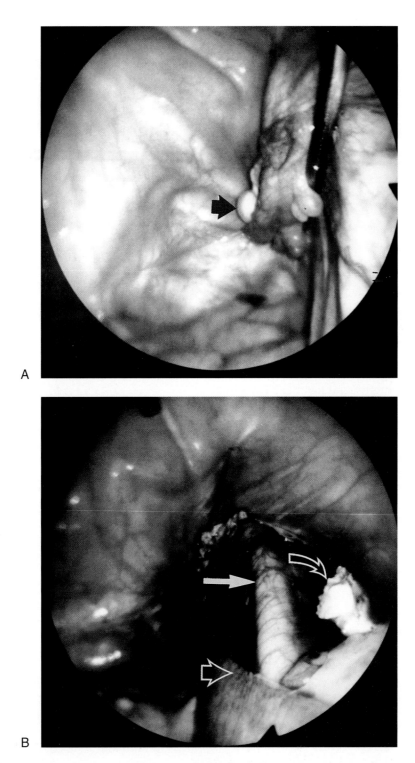

Fig. 18-12. (A) The right adnexa *(arrow)* is seen in this woman who experienced significant right-sided pelvic pain after a hysterectomy. **(B)** The right adnexa has been removed. One notes that the right ureter *(open straight arrow)* has been reflected medially, the adnexa has been dissected from the right external iliac artery *(white arrow)*, and the right infundibulopelvic ligament *(open curved arrow)* has been coagulated and divided.

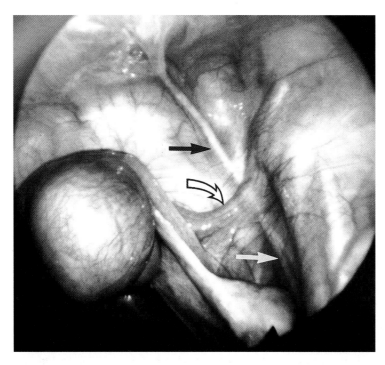

Fig. 18-13. The right obliterated umbilical artery is seen *(straight arrows)* as it courses beneath the right round ligament *(curved arrow)* onto the right pelvic sidewall.

and may delay discharge in patients undergoing ambulatory surgery.[58–61] Several steps may be taken to lessen this. Operating room temperature up to about 70°F can be tolerated by operating room personnel, provided relative humidity is kept low. The Bair Hugger and other devices are designed to maintain the patient's core temperature by keeping skin temperature warm. Irrigating fluids should be kept warm but not hot. At least one company designed a laparoscopic insufflator that warms gas before its being insufflated into the abdomen. Anesthetic gases can also be warmed and kept moist. These are some of the techniques being used to avoid hypothermia with its associated unhealthful metabolic changes.

NAUSEA, POSTOPERATIVE PAIN, AND URINARY RETENTION

Nausea

A scopolamine patch placed behind the ear the evening before surgery and removed 3 days postoperatively is often beneficial in preventing nausea. Nitrous oxide as an inhalation agent has been implicated

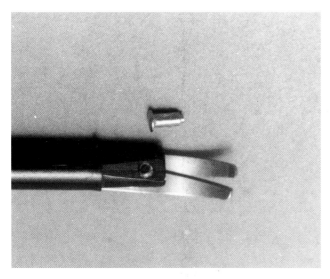

Fig. 18-14. The loose screw was seen falling out of the scissor into the pelvis. It was retrieved laparoscopically.

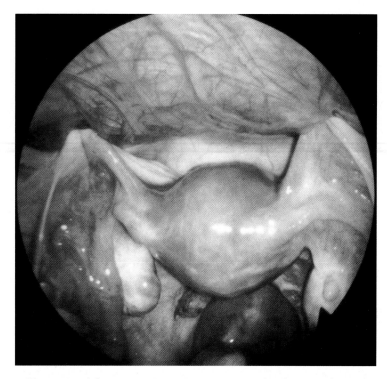

Fig. 18-15. A laparoscopic uterine suspension has been performed.

as a cause of postoperative nausea and vomiting, although one center reported no such association in a prospective, controlled study.[62] The frequency of postoperative nausea and vomiting in women undergoing laparoscopy was correlated with the time it is performed in the menstrual cycle.[63] Patients undergoing surgery on days 1 through 8 had more problems, with day 5 being the worst. Better timing was days 18 through 20.

Pain

It has been postulated that pain after laparoscopy is caused by peritoneal and phrenic nerve irritation resulting from carbonic acid. One group placed a drain in the peritoneal cavity through the navel incision at the completion of sterilization or diagnostic procedures, taking advantage of peristaltic and voluntary muscle activity to expel residual gas for a few hours. Postoperative pain attributed to retained intra-abdominal gas was one-half as frequent in the treated group; furthermore, the severity of pain was significantly reduced.[64] Another group kept patients in a head-down position on a stretcher for the first half hour postoperatively.[65]

Some believe that pain is reduced if nitrous oxide is used instead of carbon dioxide as the insufflation medium. One study attempted to elucidate the mecha-

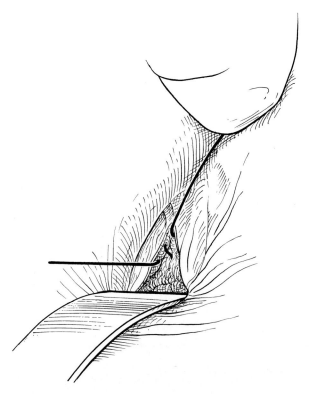

Fig. 18-16. A fascial defect is being repaired with 2–0 absorbable suture. (From Hunt,[84] with permission.)

nism for this, and concluded that if there is benefit, it most likely occurs on a local level and not a systemic one. Absorption of nitrous oxide from the peritoneal cavity was insignificant during diagnostic laparoscopy.[66]

Intraperitoneal placement of local anesthetics at the conclusion of laparoscopic procedures might be a useful technique to reduce postoperative pain.[67,68] I leave 2 L Ringer's lactate containing 20 mg dexamethasone, 20 mg bupivacaine, and 25 mg promethazine intraperitoneally at the time of wound closure and while the patient is still in Trendelenburg position. The fluid displaces retained intraperitoneal gas and allows it to escape through the cannulas. The drugs diminish peritoneal and referred pain and may reduce postoperative adhesion formation. An additional 20 mg bupivacaine is infiltrated into the fascia at the primary cannula site and into the skin of all incisions. This eliminates most shoulder and incisional pain.

Shivering is both uncomfortable for the patient and greatly increases oxygen consumption. It can be managed effectively by intravenous administration of 12.5 to 25 mg meperidine. Patient warming devices, such as the Bair Hugger, also does much to eliminate shivering.

Urinary Retention

Urinary retention is a common problem. To help prevent it, an indwelling catheter with a catheter plug is in place throughout the operation. At the conclusion of the operation, the bladder is drained, the urine is inspected for color and amount, and the catheter is removed. After performing uterine suspensions, I leave the catheter in until the next morning, as many of these patients have difficulty voiding postoperatively (Fig. 18-15).

ADVERSE REACTIONS

Allergic reactions are relatively common, due in part to the polypharmacy to which our patients are subjected. A careful allergy history will avoid some of them. High-molecular-weight dextran for adhesion prophylaxis may cause an allergic reaction.[69] The anesthesiologist, surgeon, and nursing staff should always be alert to these problems and be prepared to deal with them.

HERNIA

A hernia can occur postoperatively and may produce bowel obstruction and other major sequelae.[70–74] The surgeon is advised to suture all secondary sites accommodating cannulas 10 mm or greater in diameter (Fig. 18-16). Skin hooks greatly facilitate locating the fascia, and the defect is closed with size 2-0 absorbable material. Fascial defects at secondary cannula sites should be closed while the laparoscope is still in place to avoid bowel entrapment. A chance still exists that the bowel can become incarcerated between the peritoneum and muscle.

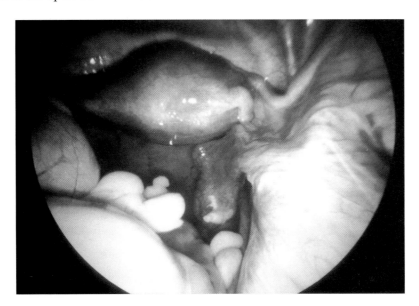

Fig. 18-17. After adhesiolysis, the surgeon has instilled 2 L of Ringer's lactate intra-abdominally. Note how the fatty epiploica floats the rectosigmoid colon away from pelvic structures.

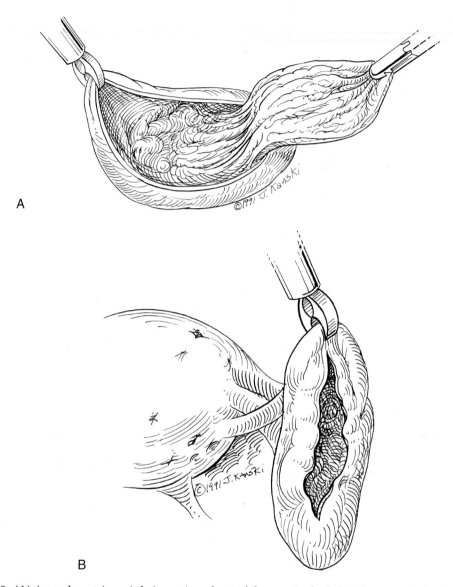

A

B

Fig. 18-18. **(A)** An endometrioma is being stripped out of the ovarian bed. **(B)** The ovary is depicted after the endometrioma has been resected. (*Figure continues.*)

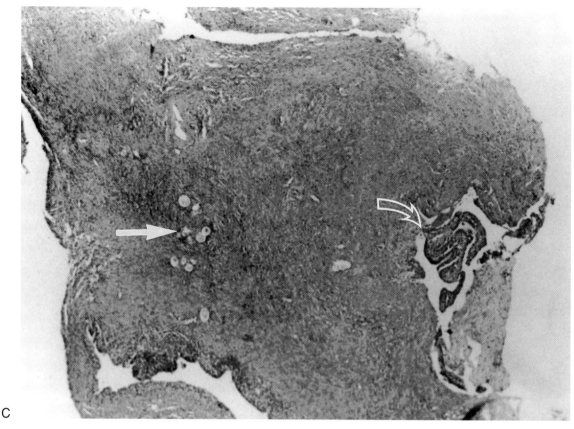

Fig. 18-18 *(Continued).* **(C)** An endometrioma cyst wall is shown (×20). Note endometrial glands *(curved arrow)* and follicles *(straight arrow).* (From Hunt,[84] with permission.)

POSTOPERATIVE ADHESIONS

Postoperative adhesions are the bane of the infertility surgeon. De novo adhesions are reduced with laparoscopy but have been reported to occur in 51 percent of patients undergoing laparotomy.[75] An excellent study conducted in rabbits compared application of laser energy by laparoscopy to that applied by laparotomy.[76] No de novo adhesions were seen in the laparoscopic group, but many developed in the laparotomy group. No adhesions were present at operated sites in those undergoing laparoscopy, but they did occur in all those undergoing laparotomy. A second arm of the study addressed the question of adhesion reformation in animals undergoing lysis of pre-existing adhesions. The laparoscopic group had a substantial reduction in postoperative adhesions compared with minimal reduction in the laparotomy group. In recent human studies, laparoscopy did not impact readhesion formation, but did reduce de novo adhesions by 50 percent.[77–79]

I favor hydroflotation, as described in the discussion of pain. The reasons to leave 2 L Ringer's lactate intraperitoneally at the conclusion of the operation are to separate operated surfaces and to dilute any transudate or blood for the first several hours postoperatively (Fig. 18-17). Also, the fluid displaces intra-abdominal gas out of the abdomen, thus reducing postoperative shoulder pain. Prophylactic antibiotics are administered routinely to avoid infection. I add 20 mg dexamethasone and 25 mg promethazine to the Ringer's lactate, but their benefit in preventing adhesions remains unproved.[80] Some advocate applying oxidized regenerated cellulose (Interceed) to hemostatic, operative surfaces.[81] This would preclude hydroflotation.

OVARIAN FAILURE

If a patient is experiencing oligomenorrhea, hot flushes, or other manifestations of ovarian failure, it is prudent to measure the follicle-stimulating hormone

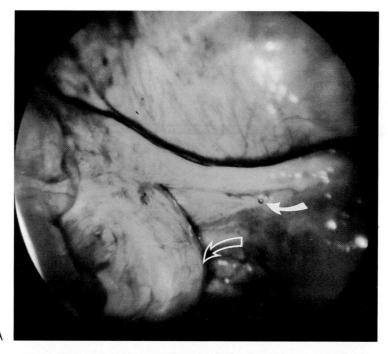

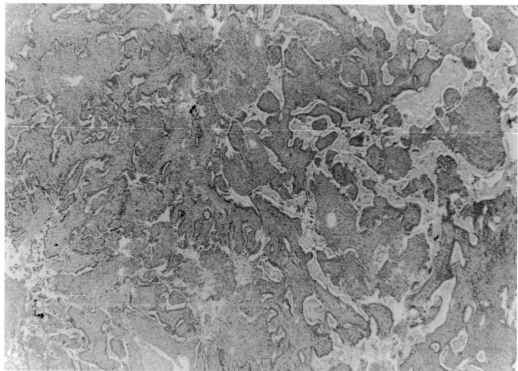

Fig. 18-19. **(A)** An adhesed left ovary of normal size is shown *(open arrow)*. A 1.5-cm cyst was resected from its lateral surface. Note the implant of endometriosis *(solid arrow)*. **(B)** Histologic examination of the cyst (×40) revealed endometrioid carcinoma.

level preoperatively, as she may have impending ovarian failure.

When an endometrioma is removed, ova are removed with the cyst wall.[82] If enough ova are removed, as in the case of bilateral ovarian cystectomies for endometriomata, ovarian failure may result (Fig. 18-18). Also, tissue from an ovarian cyst should be removed and sent for pathologic analysis when possible (Fig. 18-19).

ECTOPIC PREGNANCY

Ectopic pregnancy is the nemesis of the infertility surgeon. The patient at increased risk should be counseled to notify her physician as soon as she thinks she has conceived. I assume each pregnant patient who has undergone tubal surgery for infertility to have an ectopic gestation until proved otherwise.

RECURRENT PELVIC PAIN

Patients operated on to correct a chronic pelvic pain syndrome must be followed actively and aggressively.[83] These women often have multiple system involvement, and to maximize results, the surgeon has to address these systems as well, including the psychological ones.

FAILED INFERTILITY SURGERY

Should the operation fail to achieve its intended result of a successful pregnancy, the surgeon must determine if further surgery or fertility testing is required or if other avenues should be chosen, such as assisted reproductive technologies or adoption. These options are best explored during a face-to-face consultation with the couple and the physician.

POSTOPERATIVE FOLLOW-UP

The patient who undergoes operative laparoscopy, as with any surgery, must be followed carefully postoperatively. A summary letter and other pertinent records should be sent to her and her referring physician. At the time of the postoperative visit, incisions are checked, a pelvic examination is performed, operative and pathology reports are reviewed, and appropriate follow-up is planned. The postoperative visit is the culmination of the surgical experience. It should end with a satisfied patient.

REFERENCES

1. Parker WH: Management of adnexal masses by operative laparoscopy. p. 51. In Hunt RB (ed): Endoscopy in Gynecology: AAGL 20th Annual Meeting Proceedings. Port City Press, Baltimore, 1993
2. Ott DE: Laparoscopy and the dew point—why a lens fogs. p. 360. In Hunt RB (ed): Endoscopy in Gynecology: AAGL 20th Annual Meeting Proceedings. Port City Press, Baltimore, 1993
3. Reich H, Hunt RB: Advanced laparoscopic surgery. p. 276. In Hunt RB (ed): Atlas of Female Infertility Surgery. 2nd Ed. Mosby-Year Book, St. Louis, 1992
4. Soderstrom RM: Applied electrophysics in laparoscopy. p. 45. In Soderstrom RM (ed): Operative Laparoscopy: The Masters' Techniques. Raven Press, New York, 1993
5. Hershlag A, Loy RA, Lavy G, DeCherney AH: Femoral neuropathy after laparoscopy. J Reprod Med 35:575, 1990
6. Cohn GM, Rosenweig BA, Adelson MD, Sze EHM: A complication associated with pneumatic compression stockings used for gynecologic surgery. J Gynecol Surg 5:389, 1989
7. Reich H: Laparoscopic treatment of extensive pelvic adhesions, including hydrosalpinx. J Reprod Med 32:736, 1987
8. Hill GA, Perry SM, Herbert CM III, Wentz AC: Cardiomyopathy in a patient undergoing laparoscopy for oocyte retrieval during in vitro fertilization/embryo transfer. J Reprod Med 35:741, 1990
9. Myles PS: Bradyarrhythmias and laparoscopy: a prospective study of heart rate changes with laparoscopy. Aust NZ Obstet Gynaecol 31:171, 1991
10. Lip H, Delhaas E: Cardiovascular collapse during laparoscopy. Am J Obstet Gynecol 162:873, 1990
11. Shifren JL, Adlestein L, Finkler NJ: Asystolic cardiac arrest: a rare complication of laparoscopy. Obstet Gynecol 79:840, 1992
12. Yuzpe AA: Pneumoperitoneum needle and trocar injuries in laparoscopy. J Reprod Med 35:485, 1990
13. Querleu D, Chapron C, Chevallier L, Bruhat MA: Complications of gynecologic laparoscopic surgery—a French multicenter collaborative study. N Engl J Med 328:1355, 1993
14. Baadsgaard SE, Bille S, Egeblad K: Major vascular injury during gynecologic laparoscopy. Acta Obstet Gynecol Scand 68:283, 1989
15. Mintz M: Risks and prophylaxis in laparoscopy: a survey of 100,000 cases. J Reprod Med 18:26, 1977
16. Penfield AJ: Vascular injuries and their management. p. 299. In Phillips JM (ed): Endoscopy in Gynecology. American Association of Gynecologic Laparoscopists, Downey, CA, 1978
17. Chamberlain G, Brown JC (eds): Gynaecological Laparoscopy: The Report of the Confidential Enquiry into Gynaecological Laparoscopy. Royal College of Obstetricians and Gynaecologists, London, 1978
18. Penfield AJ: How to prevent complications of open laparoscopy. J Reprod Med 30:660, 1985
19. Peterson HB, DeStefano F, Rubin GL et al: Deaths attributable to tubal sterilization in the US 1977–1981. Am J Obstet Gynecol 146:131, 1983
20. Penfield AJ: Open laparoscopy, surgical equipment and training in reproductive health. p. 17. In Burkman RT, Magarick RH, Waife RS (eds): Johns Hopkins Program for International Gynecology and Obstetrics. Johns Hopkins University Press, Baltimore, 1979
21. Phillips JM, Hulka JF, Hulka B, Corson SL: 1979 AAGL membership survey. J Reprod Med 26:529, 1981
22. Soderstrom RM: Basic operative technique. p. 25. In Soderstrom RM (ed): Operative Laparoscopy: The Masters' Techniques. Raven Press, New York, 1993
23. Reich H, DeCaprio J, Polin M et al: Intercostal Veress needle insertion. p. 335. In Hunt RB (ed): Endoscopy in Gynecology:

AAGL 20th Annual Meeting Proceedings. Port City Press, Baltimore, 1993

24. Soderstrom RM, Levinson C, Levy B: Complications of operative laparoscopy. p. 194. In Soderstrom RM (ed): Operative Laparoscopy: The Masters' Techniques. Raven Press, New York, 1993

25. Levy BS, Soderstrom RM, Dail DH: Bowel injuries during laparoscopy: gross anatomy and histology. J Reprod Med 30:168, 1985

26. Voyles CR, Haick AJ, Koury AM et al: Trocar/cannula systems in laparoscopic surgery. Surg Rounds 15:799, 1992

27. Ostman PL, Pantle-Fisher FH, Faure EA, Glosten B: Circulatory collapse during laparoscopy. J Clin Anesth 2:129, 1990

28. Herrerias J, Ariza A, Garrido M: An unusual complication of laparoscopy: pneumopericardium. Endoscopy 12:254, 1980

29. Shak P, Ramakantan R: Pneumoperitoneum and pneumomediastinum: unusual complications of laparoscopy. J Postgrad Med 36:31, 1990

30. Knos GB, Sung Y-F, Toledo A: Pneumopericardium associated with laparoscopy. J Clin Anesth 3:56, 1991

31. Seed R, Shakespeare T, Muldoon M: Carbon dioxide homeostasis during anesthesia for laparoscopy. Anesthesia 25:223, 1970

32. Whiston RJ, Eggers KA, Morris RW, Stamatakis JD: Tension pneumothorax during laparoscopic cholecystectomy. Br J Surg 78:1325, 1991

33. Bard PA, Chen L: Subcutaneous emphysema associated with laparoscopy. Anesth Analg 71:101, 1990

34. Nezhat FR, Silfen SL, Evans D, Nezhat C: Comparison of direct insertion of disposable and standard reusable laparoscopic trocars and previous pneumperitoneum with Veress needle. Obstet Gynecol 78:148, 1991

35. Schwartz LB, Stahl RS, DeCherney AH: Unilateral compartment syndrome after prolonged gynecologic surgery in the dorsal lithotomy position. J Reprod Med 38:469, 1993

36. Werbel GB, Shybut GT: Acute compartment syndrome caused by a malfunctioning pneumatic compression boot. J Bone Joint Surg 68A:1445, 1986

37. Green TL, Louis DS: Compartment syndrome of the arm; a complication of the pneumatic tourniquet. J Bone Joint Surg 65A:270, 1983

38. Voyles CR, Tucker RD: Education and engineering solutions for potential problems with laparoscopic monopolar electrosurgery. Am J Surg 164:57, 1992

39. Tucker RD, Voyles CR, Silvis SE: Capacitive coupled stray currents during laparoscopic and endoscopic electrosurgical procedures. Biomed Instrum Technol 26:303, 1992

40. Soderstrom RM: Laparoscopic sterilization. p. 164. In Soderstrom RM (ed): Operative Laparoscopy: The Masters' Techniques. Raven Press, New York, 1993

41. Georgy FM, Fetterman HH, Chefetz MD: Complication of laparoscopy: two cases of perforated urinary bladder. Am J Obstet Gynecol 120:1121, 1974

42. Sherer DM: Inadvertent transvaginal cystotomy during laparoscopy. Int J Gynaecol Obstet 32:77, 1990

43. Thompson JD: Transvaginal ureteral transection with vaginal hysterectomy and anterior colporraphy. p. 181. In Nichols DH (ed): Clinical Problems, Injuries, and Complications of Gynecological Surgery. 2nd Ed. Williams & Wilkins, Baltimore, 1988

44. Cheng YS: Ureteral injury resulting from laparoscopic fulguration of endometriotic implant. Am J Obstet Gynecol 126:1045, 1976

45. Irwin TT, Goligher JC, Scott JS: Injury to the ureter during laparoscopic tubal sterilization. Arch Surg 110:1501, 1975

46. Stengel JN, Felderman ES, Zamora D: Ureteral injury, complication of laparoscopic sterilization. Urology 4:341, 1974

47. Winslow PH, Kreger R, Ebbeersson B et al: Conservative management of electrical burn injury of ureter secondary to laparoscopy. Urology 27:60, 1986

48. Nezhat C, Nezhat FR: Ureteral injuries at laparoscopy: insights into diagnosis, management, and prevention. Obstet Gynecol 76:889, 1990

49. Hurt WG, Jones CM III: Intraoperative ureteral injuries and urinary diversion. p. 901. In Nichols DH (ed): Gynecologic and Obstetric Surgery. Mosby-Year Book, St. Louis, 1993

50. Grainger DA, Soderstrom RM, Schiff SF et al: Ureteral injuries at laparoscopy: insights into diagnosis, management, and prevention. Obstet Gynecol 75:839, 1990

51. Gomel V, James C: Intraoperative management of ureteral injury during operative laparoscopy. Fertil Steril 55:416, 1991

52. McLucas B, March C: Urachal sinus perforation during laparoscopy. J Reprod Med 35:573, 1990

53. Yong EL, Prabhakaran K, Lee YS, Ratnam SS: Peritonitis following diagnostic laparoscopy due to injury to a vesicourachal diverticulum. Br J Obstet Gynaecol 96:365, 1989

54. Anonymous: Contaminated CO_2 gas could injure laparoscopy patients. Biomed Safety Standards Bull 20:49, 1990

55. Ott DE: Bacterial contamination in carbon dioxide gas cylinders used for pneumoperitoneum insufflation. p. 177. In Hunt RB (ed): Endoscopy in Gynecology: AAGL 20th Annual Meeting Proceedings. Port City Press, Baltimore, 1993

56. Ranta H, Aine R, Oksanen H, Heinonen PK: Dissemination of endometrial cells during carbon dioxide hysteroscopy and chromotubation among infertile patients. Fertil Steril 53:751, 1990

57. Pyper RJD, Ahmet Z, Houang ET: Bacteriological contamination during laparoscopy with dye injection. Br J Obstet Gynaecol 95:367, 1988

58. Slotman GJ, Jed EH, Burchard KW: Adverse effects of hypothermia in postoperative patients. Am J Surg 149:495, 1985

59. Lennon RL, Hosking MP, Conover MA, Perkins WJ: Evaluation of a forced-air system for warming hypothermic postoperative patients. Anesth Analg 70:424, 1990

60. Hines R, Barash PG, Watrous G, O'Connor T: Complications occurring in the postanesthesia care unit: a survey. Anesth Analg 74:503, 1992

61. Giuffre M, Finnie J, Lynam DA, Smith D: Rewarming postoperative patients: lights, blankets, or forced warm air. J Post Anesth Nurs 6:387, 1991

62. Hovorka J, Korttila K, Erkola O: Nitrous oxide does not increase nausea and vomiting following gynaecological laparoscopy. Can J Anaesth 36:145, 1989

63. Beattie WS, Lindblad T, Buckley DN, Forrest JB: The incidence of postoperative nausea and vomiting in women undergoing laparoscopy is influenced by the day of menstrual cycle. Can J Anaesth 38:298, 1991

64. Alexander JI, Hull MGR: Abdominal pain after laparoscopy: the value of a gas drain. Br J Obstet Gynaecol 94:267, 1987

65. Dobbs FF, Kumar V, Alexander JI, Hull MGR: Pain after laparoscopy related to posture and ring versus clip sterilization. Br J Obstet Gynaecol 94:262, 1987

66. Phillips RS, Goldberg RI, Watson PW et al: Mechanism of improved patient tolerance to nitrous oxide in diagnostic laparoscopy. Am J Gastroenterol 82:143, 1987

67. Narchi P, Benhamou D, Fernandez H: Intraperitoneal local anaesthetic for shoulder pain after day-case laparoscopy. Lancet 338:1569, 1991

68. Goodman NW: Local anaesthesia to prevent post-laparoscopic shoulder pain. Lancet 339:868, 1992

69. Borten M, Seibert CP, Taymor ML: Recurrent anaphylactic reaction to intraperitoneal dextran 70 used for prevention of postsurgical adhesions. Obstet Gynecol 61:755, 1983

70. Schiff I, Naftolin F: Small bowel incarceration after uncomplicated laparoscopy. Obstet Gynecol 43:674, 1974

71. Rajapaksa DS: Asymptomatic omental herniation following laparoscopic sterilization. Ceylon Med J 28:35, 1983

72. Bourke JB: Small intestinal obstruction from a Richter's hernia at the site of insertion of a laparoscope. BMJ 2:1393, 1977

73. Thomas AG, McLymont F, Moshipur J: Incarcerated hernia after laparoscopic sterilization. J Reprod Med 35:639, 1990

74. Maio A, Ruchman RB: CT diagnosis of postlaparoscopic hernia. J Comput Assist Tomogr 15:1054, 1991
75. Diamond MP, Daniell JF, Feste J et al: Adhesion reformation and de novo adhesion formation after reproductive pelvic surgery. Fertil Steril 47:864, 1987
76. Luciano AA, Maier DB, Koch EI et al: A comparative study of postoperative adhesions following laser surgery by laparoscopy versus laparotomy in the rabbit model. Obstet Gynecol 74:220, 1989
77. Diamond MP: Surgical aspects of infertility. Ch. 61:1. In Sciarra JW (ed): Gynecology and Obstetrics. Harper and Row, Philadelphia, 1988
78. Lundorff P, Hahlin M, Kallfelt B et al: Adhesion formation after laparoscopic surgery in tubal pregnancy: a randomized trial versus laparotomy. Fertil Steril 55:911, 1991
79. Canis M, Chapron C, Mage G et al: Second-look laparoscopy after laparoscopic cystectomy of large ovarian endometriomas. Fertil Steril 58:617, 1992
80. Holtz G: Prevention and management of peritoneal adhesions. Fertil Steril 41:497; 1984
81. Azziz R, Murphy AA, Rosenberg SM, Partton GW Jr: Use of an oxidized, regenerated cellulose absorbable adhesion barrier at laparoscopy. J Reprod Med 36:479, 1991
82. Hunt RB: Complications of infertility surgery. p. 494. In Hunt RB (ed): Atlas of Female Infertility Surgery. 2nd Ed. Mosby-Year Book, St. Louis, 1992
83. Hulka JF, Sanfilippo JA, Steege JF: Pelvic pain. p. 21. In Hunt RB (ed): Endoscopy in Gynecology: AAGL 20th Annual Meeting Proceedings. Port City Press, Baltimore, 1993
84. Hunt RB (ed): Atlas of Female Infertility Surgery. 2nd Ed. Mosby-Year Book, St. Louis, 1992

Appendix 18-1
Bowel Preparation I

1. Purchase one Fleet enema and one bottle of magnesium citrate from your pharmacy.
2. The day before surgery:
   a. Drink one-half bottle of magnesium citrate in the morning and one-half in the afternoon.
   b. Administer a Fleet enema to yourself 1 hour before bedtime.
   c. Follow diet

Breakfast—light breakfast (cereal, cream of wheat, juice, coffee, etc.). Avoid milk products all day
Lunch—just liquids (such as custards, jello, soups, cream of wheat, oat meal)
Dinner—just clear liquids (such as apple juice, bouillon tea)

   d. Take nothing by mouth after midnight.

Call if any questions!

Bowel Preparation II

1. Purchase one Fleet enema, two bottles of magnesium citrate, and two 8-ounce cans of Ensure Plus from your pharmacy.
2. Two days before surgery:
   a. Drink one-half bottle of magnesium citrate in the morning
   b. Follow diet

Breakfast—light breakfast (cereal, cream of wheat, juice, coffee, etc.)
Lunch—full liquids (such as custards, jello, soups, cream of wheat, oatmeal)
Dinner—just clear liquids (for example, bouillon, tea, ginger ale, apple juice, coffee)

3. The day before surgery:
   a. Drink one-half bottle of magnesium citrate in the morning and one-half bottle in the afternoon.
   b. Administer yourself a Fleet enema an hour before bedtime.
   c. Have clear liquids for each meal. Avoid milk products.
   d. Take one can of Ensure Plus with lunch and another with dinner.
   e. Take nothing by mouth after midnight.

Call if any questions!

Appendix 18-2
Informed Consent for Diagnostic and Operative Laparoscopy*

PURPOSE

Laparoscopy is an extremely valuable procedure in gynecology and infertility. It may be performed to establish a diagnosis, such as determining the cause of infertility or pelvic pain. It is often used as therapy, such as removing adhesions (scar tissue) or destroying endometriosis. Pregnancy must be avoided during the menstrual cycle when the operation is to be performed.

PROCEDURE

The operation is usually performed with the patient asleep (general anesthesia). In certain instances, it may be performed under local anesthesia. With the patient appropriately anesthestized, an instrument (cannula) is placed in the cervix and secured with a tenaculum. These instruments enable the surgeon to position the uterus and aid in the pelvic assessment. A catheter is placed in the urinary bladder to drain it.

The abdomen is inflated with a gas (usually carbon dioxide or nitrous oxide) to allow adequate intra-abdominal visualization. An incision is then made at the navel, through which a telescope (laparoscope) is inserted. One to four incisions are then placed in the lower abdomen. These incisions leave scars 0.25- to 0.5-in. in length. Through these incisions, the surgeon inspects the pelvic structures and performs indicated procedures. Among these are removal of some pain nerves behind the uterus to alleviate menstrual cramps and suspension of the uterus forward to enhance fertility and reduce pelvic discomfort. A photograph of the pelvic structures is often taken to document the findings. This also helps the patient to understand what was found and done.

After the operation has been completed, the gas is allowed to escape from the abdomen, all instruments removed, and the abdominal incisions are closed with sutures. Often fluid and medications are placed in the abdomen to prevent adhesion (scar tissue) formation. Sometimes a dilation and curettage (D&C) is required.

FOLLOW-UP

The patient will frequently experience pain in her shoulder, chest, and upper abdominal areas caused by the gas. She will also experience tenderness at the incision sites. These discomforts usually diminish markedly after 2 days. Because fluids are often left in the abdomen to prevent adhesion formation, the patient will frequently leak fluid from the incisions and observe swelling in these areas. This fluid leakage and swelling should disappear within 2 days. There is usually some bruising at the incision sites. This disappears in approximately 2 weeks. Many patients go home the day of surgery but must be transported by a responsible adult.

COMPLICATIONS

1. *Anesthesia:* anesthesiologists have made significant advances in improving patient safety; however, anesthetic accidents still happen. If anesthesia is required, the anesthesiologist should discuss these complications with the patient before surgery. If the patient has had prior anesthesia, she should acquire those records and show them to the anesthesiologist at the time of the preoperative consultation.
2. *Hemorrhage:* excessive bleeding can occur when developing the portals of entry in the abdominal wall, as well as during pelvic dissection. Both events are infrequent and can usually be dealt with laparoscopically, but laparotomy is sometimes required. Although the necessity for blood transfusions in laparoscopy is uncommon, the patient should inquire as to the advisability of donating her own blood before the procedure to avoid receiving blood from donors, thus lessening the chance of such sequelae as hepatitis and AIDS.

---

*(From Hunt,[84] with permission.)

3. *Gastrointestinal injuries:* injuries to the intestinal tract occur approximately 1 per 500 operations. This may happen when establishing the portals of entry for the instruments, as well as during pelvic dissection. This is a serious complication and must be rectified. The repair usually requires major surgery. Although a colostomy is a possibility, it is a remote one.

4. *Urologic injury:* because much dissection is performed around the drainage tubes from the kidney (ureters) or the urinary bladder, there is always the possibility of injury to one of these structures. These may be minor or serious, resulting in major surgery and even, rarely, loss of a kidney.

5. *Gas emboli:* a serious complication is passage of gas used to inflate the abdomen into a major blood vessel, from which it may travel to the patient's heart and lungs. The surgeon uses several checks to lessen this possibility.

6. *Phlebitis:* the patient may experience tenderness along the vein used for intravenous administration of fluids and medications. This responds to warm compresses and is usually temporary. Occasionally, a small lump at the intravenous site will persist.

7. *Incisions:* infrequently an incision will become infected, requiring warm compresses, antibiotics, and drainage.

8. *Pelvic infections:* the patient will sometimes develop a pelvic infection after surgery. She usually receives an antibiotic during surgery to lessen this prospect. When infection develops, she must notify the physician immediately.

9. *Allergic reactions:* several medications are used during surgery, and there is always a possibility of a reaction to one or more of them. Appropriate steps are taken to counteract it.

10. *Ovarian failure:* the ovary(ies) may go into permanent failure after surgery. This is usually associated with extensive ovarian surgery, such as removal of cysts.

11. *Neurologic injuries:* pelvic nerve injuries may occur when extensive pelvic dissection is required. These are most often characterized by temporary numbness or tingling in the abdomen or lower extremities, but muscle weakness may occur rarely and be permanent. Similarly, weakness of the upper extremity has been reported but, fortunately, is very infrequent.

12. *Failed procedure:* occasionally, the surgeon will have to terminate the operation due to a technical problem or because the procedure is inappropriate for the disease, as in the discovery of a pelvic malignancy. Major surgery would be performed at that time only for an urgent problem and, if appropriate, after consultation with the family.

13. *Death:* catastrophic complications resulting in death of the patient are rare.

FOLLOW-UP

The patient should call the office the first postoperative day to advise us as to any problems she is having and to make her return appointment for 3 weeks. She should remain out of work for 1 week and should report any unusual signs or symptoms such as unusual vaginal discharge, fever, or increasing pain.

CONCLUSION

We have an advanced operative team. Our equipment is modern. We are constantly reviewing our techniques and instrumentation to maximize patient safety. The patient is encouraged to ask as many questions as necessary to clear up doubts.

Hysteroscopy

19 History of Hysteroscopy

JACQUES E. RIOUX

Hysteroscopy is the oldest gynecologic endoscopic procedure. Why then did it take so long to find its place in the daily armamentarium of the gynecologist? The reasons are many: our ancestors had to find a way to distend the uterus and keep it distended, send the light in and bring the images out, learn what they meant, and finally, develop a therapeutic application through smaller and smaller instruments.

Who among these pioneers contributed the most to the development of hysteroscopy? In the following pages we review the work of the most outstanding contributors to hysteroscopic instrumentation and technique.

P. Bozzini is credited by everybody to have carried out the first endoscopic procedure in 1805.[1] He had built a "light conductor," which was a lantern made of tin with a system of mirrors and tubes through which candlelight could be reflected into the body via a tube-shaped speculum. He used his device to inspect the nasal cavity, the urethra, the vagina, and the rectum. For doing so, he was reprimanded by the Medical Faculty of Vienna for "undue curiosity."[2] He died a few years later at age 35 before he could further develop his light conductor and was unrecognized for his great achievement because of professional jealousy.

The next name in endoscopy is *A.J. Désormeaux,* who in 1853 invented the first cystoscope. It was a straight tube, 12 mm in diameter, at the end of which the light from a candle was reflected by a mirror. Désormeaux was the first urologist, and in 1865 he published a book devoted entirely to the diagnosis and treatment of the diseases of the urethra and bladder.[3]

In 1863, *E.J. Aubinais,* using a similar instrument inserted in the vagina of a delivering woman, was able to watch the baby's head emerging from the cervix and, for this reason, might have performed the first vaginoscopy.[4]

D.C. Pantaleoni was, without a doubt, the first hysteroscopist. In 1869, he performed a bona fide hysteroscopy on a 60-year-old patient complaining of postmenopausal bleeding. Using a cystoscope like the one devised by Désormeaux, he introduced the straight hollow tube, via the predilated cervical canal, into the uterine cavity. He then observed a "polypous vegetation at the bottom of the cavity towards the posterior part of the fundus uterin." Using silver nitrate, he cauterized the lesion by local application and, according to his publication, cured the patient.[5] None of his contemporaries was able to reproduce this feat, and he himself published nothing more on the subject. Many years passed before any other meaningful contribution was published on the subject.

In 1879, *M. Nitze* developed a beautiful cystoscope, the optical lenses and illuminator of which were introduced directly into the bladder.[6] This instrument markedly increased both illumination and field of vision. But, unfortunately, it was not readily adopted by gynecologists. Indeed, in 1893, *R.T. Morris* was still using a straight silver and brass tube, 9 mm in diameter and 22 cm long, to observe the endometrium and the tubal ostia.[7] The only new feature of his gadget was an interior obturator, which could be withdrawn once the instrument had been introduced into the uterine cavity.

The first complete book devoted to the subject of hysteroscopy was written in 1898 by two Frenchmen, *S. Duplay and S. Clado.* This illustrated book provided detailed descriptions of instruments, techniques, and clinical studies.[8] Their hysteroscope was an open-ended tube with a battery-powered light source.

The next book, also from France, was written as a thesis on hysteroscopy in 1908 by *C. David*.[9] His instrument was the first hysteroscope. Like Nitze's cystoscope 30 years earlier, David's hysteroscope had its own lens system incorporated into the endoscope, although unlike Nitze's instrument, its light source was mounted externally. However, his technique of methodically exploring the entire uterine cavity is well described, and he presents color illustrations of many intrauterine pathologies. Over the following 50 years, small but steady progress was made both in the technique of uterine distention and in the hyteroscope itself.

A. Heineberg, in 1914, annoyed by the fact that the hysteroscopic image was constantly obscured by the presence of blood over the distal lens, developed a system to rinse off the blood but was not intended to distend the uterine cavity.[10] That was *I.C. Rubin's* idea,[11] in 1925, using CO_2 instead of water. He had gained much experience with CO_2 for tubal pertubation and this time applied it to hysteroscopy using a modified McCarthy cystourethroscope.

The next interesting innovation to the hysteroscope was made by *H.F. Seymour* in 1926.[12] He added two channels to the scope so that water could be circulated and mucus and blood aspirated, with a third channel for instrumentation. This hysteroscope is, "in its design," the ancestor of the present operative hysteroscope.

Moreover, with this instrument, the idea of continuous-flow irrigation is adopted, but the water pressure is weak and sufficient only to spread the walls of the uterus slightly. The main reason for this was the concern that by raising the pressure too much, fluid would pass into the peritoneal cavity via the tubes.

To prevent fluid egress, *R. Segond* devised a new instrument in which the caliber of the intake of fluid was smaller than the one for the output, making it impossible to overdistend the uterus and inundate the peritoneal cavity.[13] Also, the optic was, for the first time, oblique and was mounted with the light source on a rod that slid inside the sleeve. This design made it possible to see the biopsy forceps or a coagulating catheter very clearly. He was so proud of his instrument he predicted that, someday, hysteroscopies will be performed as easily as cystoscopies!

W.B. Norment should be considered the father of American hysteroscopy. Between 1943 and 1957, he wrote many papers dealing with all aspects of hysteroscopy.[14,15] First, he compared the diagnostic value of hysterography, hysteroscopy, and dilation and curettage (D&C) and concluded that they were com-

plementary to each other and should all be used in difficult cases. No one procedure by itself could replace them all, but he thought that hysteroscopy was consistently yielding the most accurate results. Indeed, he was the first to point out that the D&C "often failed to detect" many pathologies and that this blind procedure should therefore always be complemented by a hysteroscopy. At the beginning, his main problem was to obtain an adequate uterine distention. He experimented on a new technique using a transparent rubber balloon mounted on the tip of the hysteroscope. Illumination was provided by an external light transmitted through a glass fiber conductor. The balloon was filled with air after the instrument had been inserted into the uterine cavity.

The purpose of the balloon was to distend the cavity and prevent bleeding, but it also precluded any form of biopsy and therapy and, thus, was self-defeating. Norment then reverted to the use of circulating water, thereby obtaining the desired intrauterine pressure by raising the column of water. He was worried about the passage of liquid through the tubes but thought that it would be no worse than CO_2 used for insufflation. He did take great care to avoid doing hysteroscopy in the presence of active infection to prevent transmission to the abdominal cavity.

His main interest was the diagnosis and treatment of metrorrhigia and the proper identification of the filling defects that could be seen in the hysterography. Finally, he went so far as to coagulate the intramural portion of the tube to achieve sterilization. He performed too few procedures to be able to report on the efficacy of the method.

In 1952, a giant step was taken by *M. Fourestier, A. Gladu,* and *J. Vulmière* from France when they used quartz rods to transmit light within the scope from an external light source.[16] Finally, the intensity of the light, which could remain cold, was sufficient, and good visualization was possible.

H.H. Hopkins and *N.S. Kapany* went one step farther 2 years later by introducing a new rod lens system in which the lenses were longer, leaving much smaller air spaces between them than the traditional bead optical system.[17] The innovation provided a wider viewing angle and a brighter image. Later, he also developed the flexible bundle, which transmitted light for illumination by means of glass fibers.

R. Palmer,[18] who had been working with a modified version of *Segond's* hysteroscope since 1937, finally developed a modern version of it in 1957. It was reduced to 5 mm and fitted with a more powerful light bulb. The biggest advantage was that no cervical dilation was necessary, although only observation was possible.

Now that abundant illumination and good visualization were possible, the next goal was to achieve and sustain an adequate distention of the uterine cavity.

K. Edström and *I. Fernström*[19] did just that by introducing the high-molecular dextran 70 (Hyskon) in 1970. This highly viscous material is crystal clear and transmits light with little loss. It does not mix easily with blood and mucus, thus preserving its clarity. It is very easy to use, requiring only a syringe and tubing. The introduction of this new medium of distention gave hysteroscopy the impetus it needed because it made possible the execution of many surgical procedures that could not previously be performed.

In 1972, the use of CO_2 was brought back as a medium of distention. First, *H.J. Lindemann* demonstrated that its use was quite safe as long as the flow rate was kept below 100 cc/min,[20] and *R. Porto* and *J. Gaujoux* helped popularize it by adding a suction cup to the cervix to improve the seal and prevent escape of gas at that level.[21] *R.G. Quinones*, the following year, introduced the use of dextrose 5 percent solution with selective catheterization of the fallopian tubes.[22]

The last major improvement of the hysteroscope itself was made by *J. Hamou*, who, in 1980, introduced the microcolpohysteroscope.[23] This most ingenious little optical marvel starts out as a regular 4-mm panoramic hysteroscope with a 30 degree fore-oblique vision. To that are added three possible magnifications: 20× shows a mucosa not unlike the view delivered by a colposcope; 60× shows the architecture of the mucosa, its glandular structure, and capillary vascularization; and 150×, which allows observation at the cellular level, showing a layer of cells and the detail of their cytoplasm and nuclei. The latter two magnifications are at the contact mode, no adjustments are necessary, and the blood and mucus do not interfere, acting as the oil for immersion microscopy. Finally, a sleeve can be added, allowing for the use of flexible instruments and the possibility of minor interventions.

With all these distending media available, together with their specific systems to sustain an adequate distention of the uterine cavity and with very good hysteroscopes affording perfect and reproducible visualization, the field was wide open to pioneers with wild imagination. These pioneers then searched for indications for this "new" endoscopic procedure, which was no longer the preserve of only a few exceptional individuals but had finally become available to all.

The first modern surgical hysteroscopist is *R.S. Neuwirth*, who as early as 1976 had the idea of using a urologic resectoscope to excise submucous fibroids under hysteroscopic control to avoid laparotomy.[24]

The most frequent and puzzling problem facing a gynecologist is dysfunctional uterine bleeding in a patient for whom traditional medical treatment has failed and who presents compelling contraindications to hysterectomy.

Blind destruction of the endometrium by various agents, chemical, physical (hot or cold), radiation, etc., had been tried without success because the endometrium regenerates unless the basal layer is destroyed. With the advent of reliable hysteroscopy, controlled destruction under direct vision could be attempted, and *M.H. Goldrath*, in 1981, did so using an neodymiun: yttrium-aluminum-garnet (nd:YAG) laser.[25] By direct contact with a 0.6-mm quartz fiber, the laser energy was delivered to the endometrium using the dragging technique, and complete destruction was achieved in most cases.

The technique was used only by a few because, despite its great efficacy, it was quite onerous and not everybody could buy a laser for the sole purpose of endometrial ablation.

A.H. Decherney alleviated that problem by using electric energy. In 1987, he published his technique, which used the wire loop attachment of a resectoscope to literally resect a full-thickness endometrium.[26] In his hands, the technique was described as rapid and safe, but to make it even safer, *T.G. Vancaillie*, in 1989, devised a new electrode that had a ball at its end.[27] With this technique, the endometrium is not removed but destroyed. The broader contact is facilitated by the rotation of the ball, which fits better in the cornua and is less likely to perforate the uterus.

Many publications have appeared describing these three techniques and their variations. It is impossible to mention them all in this short historical notice. Other accounts, however, deserve a mention . . . and more. The list of honorable mentions will be incomplete and short. In chronologic order, let us pay tribute to those who have contributed to the literature on our subject in the past decade: First, *R.F. Valle*,[28] who since 1975 and often with *J.J. Sciarra*,[29] has published on diagnostic and operative hysteroscopy including infertility, synechiae, and uterine septa; *F.D. Loffer*, who, in 1984, described the use of formed-in-place silicone plugs to obstruct the tubes for female sterilization[30] then went on to resectoscopic excision of myomas and, later, laser ablation of the endometrium, *J. Daniell*,[31] *J. Lomano*,[32] and *A.L. Magos*,[33] with large series of ablation with the use of the nd:YAG laser; *L. Mencaglia*,[34] who proposed the use of hysteroscopy for chorionic villi sampling, and *M.S. Baggish*,[35] who, having published on lasers, developed his own instruments and went on to write a text and an atlas.

Finally, one cannot write on the history of hysteroscopy without making a bow to the great nobleman of endoscopy, *A.M. Siegler*. In his quiet way, this man has written more (two books,[36,37] innumerable papers), given more scientific presentations, and taught more people on the subject of hysteroscopy than anyone alive today. He is an inspiration for us all.

REFERENCES

1. Bozzini P: Der Lichtleiter oder Beschreibung einer einfachen Vorrichtung und ihrer Anwendung zur Erleuchtung innerer Höhlen une Zwischenräume des lebenden animalischen Köpers. Weimar Landes-Industries-Comptoir, 1807
2. Gomel V, Taylor PJ, Yuzpe AA, Rioux JE: Laparoscopy and hysteroscopy in gynecologic practice. Year Book Medical Publishers, Chicago, 1986
3. Désormeaux AJ: De l'endoscope et de ses Applications au Diagnostic et au Traitement des Affections de l'Urèthre et de la Vessie. Balliere, Paris, 1865
4. Aubinais EJ: De l'uteroscopie. J Sect Med Soc Acad Dept Loire Infertil 39:71, 1863
5. Pantaleoni D: On endoscopic examination of the cavity of the womb. Med Press Circ 8:26, 1869
6. Nitze M: Über eine neue Beleuchtungsmethode der Höhlen des menschlichen Körpers. Wien Med Presse 20:851, 1879
7. Morris RT: Endoscopic tubes for direct inspection of the interior of the bladder and uterus. Trans Am Assoc Obstet Gynecol 6:275, 1893
8. Duplay S, Clado S: Traite d'hysteroscopie. Rennes, Simon, 1898
9. David C: L'Endoscopie utérine (hystéroscopie). Applications au diagnostic et au traitement des affections intrautérines. Master's thesis, University of Paris, G Jacques, Paris, 1908
10. Heineberg A: Uterine endoscopy, an aid to precision in the diagnosis of intra-uterine disease. Surg Gynecol Obstet 18:513, 1914
11. Rubin IC: Uterine endoscopy, endometroscopy with the aid of uterine insufflation. Am J Obstet Gynecol 10:313, 1925
12. Seymour HF: Endoscopy of the uterus with a description of a hysteroscope. J Obstet Gynaecol Br Emp 33:52, 1926
13. Segond R: Hystéroscope. Bull Fed Soc Obstet Gynecol 23:709, 1934
14. Norment WB: A study of the uterine canal by direct observation and uterogram. Am J Surg 60:56, 1943
15. Norment WB: Hysteroscopic examination in older women. Geriatrics 11:13, 1956
16. Fourestier M, Gladu A, Vulmière J: Perfectionnements de l'endoscope médicale. Presse Med 60:1292, 1954
17. Hopkins HH, Kapany NS: Flexible fiberscope, using static scanning. Nature 173:39, 1954
18. Palmer R: Un nouvel hystéroscope. Bull Fed Soc Gynecol Obstet Franc 9:300, 1957
19. Edström K, Fernström I: The diagnostic possibilities of a modified hysteroscopic technique. Acta Obstet Gynecol Scand 49:327, 1970
20. Lindemann HJ: The use of CO_2 in the uterine cavity for hysteroscopy. Int J Fertil 17:221, 1972
21. Porto R, Gaujoux J: Une nouvelle méthode d'hystéroscopie: instrumentation et technique. J Gynecol Obstet Biol Reprod 1:691, 1972
22. Quinones RG, Alvarado DA, Aznar RR: Tubal catheterization: applications of a new technique. Am J Obstet Gynecol 114:674, 1972
23. Hamou J: Microhysteroscopy: a new procedure and its original applications in gynecology. J Reprod Med 26:375, 1981
24. Neuwirth RS, Amin HK: Excision of submucous fibroids with hysteroscopic control. Am J Obstet Gynecol 126:95, 1976
25. Goldrath MH, Fuller TA, Segal S: Laser photovaporization of the endometrium for the treatment of menorrhagia. Am J Gynecol 140:12, 1981
26. DeCherney AH, Diamont MP, Lavy G et al: Endometrial ablation for intractable uterine bleeding; hysteroscopic resection. Obstet Gynecol 70:668, 1987
27. Vancaillie TG: Electrocoagulation of the endometrium with the ball-end resectoscope. Obstet Gynecol 74:425, 1989
28. Valle RF, Freeman DW: Hysteroscopy in the management of the "lost" intrauterine device. Adv Plan Parent 10:164, 1975
29. Valle RF, Sciarra JJ: Current status of hysteroscopy in gynecologic practice. Fertil Steril 32:619, 1979
30. Loffer FD: Hysteroscopic sterilization with the use of formed-in-place silicone plugs. Am J Obstet Gynecol 149:261, 1984
31. Daniell J, Tosh Meisels S: Photodynamic ablation of the endometrium with the nd:YAG laser hysteroscopically as a treatment of menorrhagia. Colposc Gynecol Laser Surg 2:43, 1986
32. Lomano JM: Dragging technique versus blanching technique for endometrial ablation with the nd:YAG laser in the treatment of chronic menorrhagia. Am J Obstet Gynecol 159:152, 1988
33. Magos AL, Baumann R, Lockwood GM, Turnbull AC: Experience with the first 250 endometrial resections for menorrhagia. Lancet 337:1074, 1991
34. Mencaglia L, Ricci G, Perino A et al: Hysteroscopic chorionic villi sampling: a new approach. Acta Eur Fertil 17:491, 1986
35. Baggish MS, Barbot J, Valle RD (eds): Diagnostic and Operative Hysteroscopy: A Text and Atlas. Year Book Medical Publishers, Chicago, 1989
36. Siegler AM, Lindeman HJ: Hysteroscopy principles and practice. JB Lippincott, Philadelphia, 1984
37. Siegler AM, Valle RF, Lindemann HJ, Mencaglia L: Therapeutic Hysteroscopy Indications and Techniques. C.V. Mosby, St. Louis, 1990

20 Hysteroscopic Instrumentation

STEPHEN M. COHEN

Hysteroscopy has become an essential procedure in the field of gynecology. Although described almost 150 years ago, hysteroscopy has only recently become popular. Both diagnostic and operative hysteroscopic procedures have become increasingly common in the past few years as reported in the most recent American Association of Gynecologic Laparoscopists survey.[1] As more advanced surgeries are attempted, more sophisticated instrumentation has to be developed.

HYSTEROSCOPIC TELESCOPE

The hysteroscopic telescope is manufactured in both a rigid and flexible design. The rigid design is used more often and is very similar to the laparoscope (Fig. 20-1). It contains light bundles and fiberoptic viewing bundles. The diameter of rigid scopes varies in size from 1 to 4 mm. Most can be gas or cold-soak sterilized.

The distal viewing end of the telescope can be set straight (0 degrees) or at an angle varying between 15 to 30 degrees. The 0-degree telescope is easiest to use as the telescope is directly aimed at the object in view. However, an angled telescope is useful for both diagnostic and operative procedures. The 30-degree telescope allows the operator to look at the cornual openings of the fallopian tubes with minimal lateral deflection of the telescope. In cases of congenital deformities, fibroids, and DES-deformed uteri, the 30-degree scope may be the only way to view the cornual areas. During operative procedures when a resectoscope is being used, a telescope with a viewing angle of 12 to 15 degrees is optimal, as this allows the operator an unobstructed field of view, and the operative element, such as the ball or loop, never extends beyond the field.

Flexible hysteroscopes are telescopes that have a flexible body and a tip that can be deflected through an arc of 120 degrees in two directions (Figs. 20-2 and 20-3). They are available in two models: one with a 3.6-mm outside diameter, and a larger scope with a 5-mm outside diameter. These telescopes are advantageous in uteri that are severely deformed by large submucous fibroid or prior DES exposure. A flexible hysteroscope with an operative channel also may have some advantages over rigid telescopes in some operative procedures, such as hysteroscopic tubal catheterization or gamete intrafallopian transfer procedures.

SHEATHS

For all rigid hysteroscopic procedures, a sheath that covers the telescope and allows instillation of distending media is necessary. Diagnostic and operative sheaths are available. The diagnostic sheath (Fig. 20-4) is a simple metal tube that covers the telescope. A channel is provided for insufflation of media through a side port. The media is discharged at the distal tip of the telescope. Most sheaths available for diagnostic work are not continuous flow, and thus the media leaves the uterus between the sheath and the cervix, through the cervical canal.

Operative sheaths are wider sheaths that allow for the passage of instrumentation inside the sheath alongside the telescope (Fig. 20-5). Scissors, graspers, and biopsy forceps are available to be used in this fashion (Fig. 20-6). The shafts of these instruments are flexible, and the working elements of these instruments are small and fragile, requiring delicate use and care. Other devices such as small suction tubes (pediatric feeding tubes), tubal catheters for tuboplasty, and laser fibers also can be placed through these channels. Most operative scopes have one channel, but some scopes are available with two.

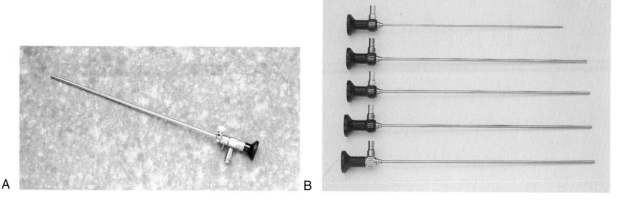

A B

Fig. 20-1. (A & B) Rigid hysteroscope.

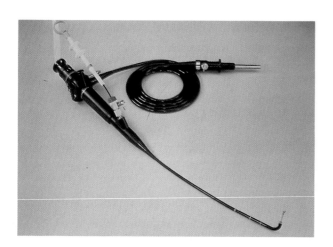

Fig. 20-2. Flexible hysteroscope.

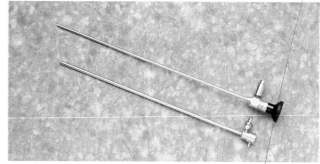

Fig. 20-4. Diagnostic sheath.

Fig. 20-3. A 120 degree arc of flexible hysteroscope.

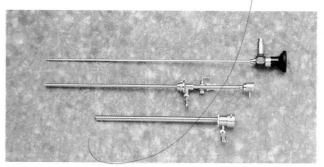

Fig. 20-5. Operating sheath.

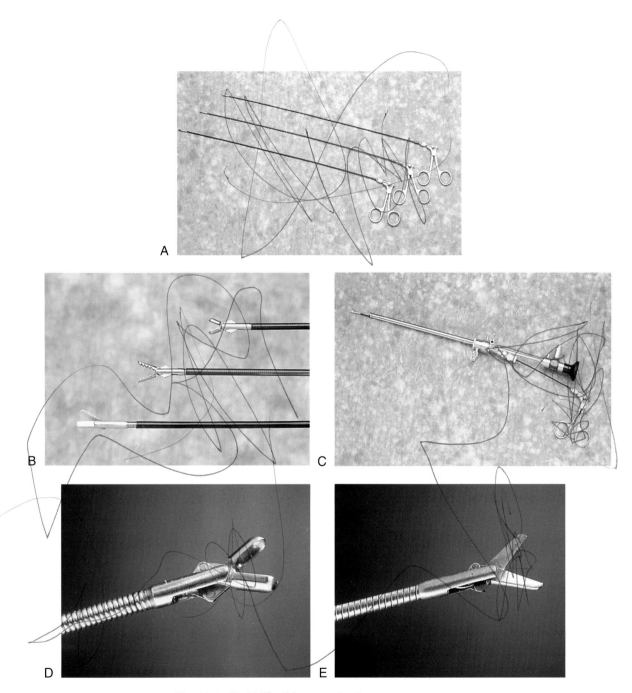

Fig. 20-6. (A–E) Flexible operating instruments.

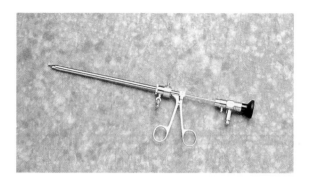

Fig. 20-7. Optical scissors.

The optical scissors and biopsy forceps are rigid instruments through which a telescope is passed (Fig. 20-7). These instruments are much stronger and larger than the flexible ones. However, they are not as easy to manipulate, and the working elements must remain at a fixed distance from the distal end of the telescope.

The resectoscope developed for gynecologic use is a modification of the urologic resectoscope (Fig. 20-8). The telescope passes through a rigid sheath that contains a working element. This element can be moved forward and back in front of the distal end of the telescope by means of a trigger-type mechanism controlled at the near end. The excursion of the working element is approximately 2 cm. These elements come in various configurations, including loops for resection, balls, and barrels for coagulation and blades for cutting (Fig. 20-9). These elements are all easily interchangeable. They come both in a reusable and disposable design and are connected to the generator by means of a post on the sheath.

The original resectoscopes had only one channel for fluid input. There was no exit channel. The fluid containing blood, debris, and bubbles needed to be cleared between the telescope/sheath and cervical canal. If the cervical canal was tight or narrow, the fluid egress was slow or nonexistent. This created a clouded field of view, as clean fluid could no longer flow into the endometrial cavity. Often, procedures were prolonged as the resectoscope needed to be constantly removed and replaced into the uterus.

To alleviate this problem, a continuous-flow resectoscope was developed. This telescope has two channels, one for infusion and another for removal of the fluid. Fluid coming into the resectoscope flows down the in-

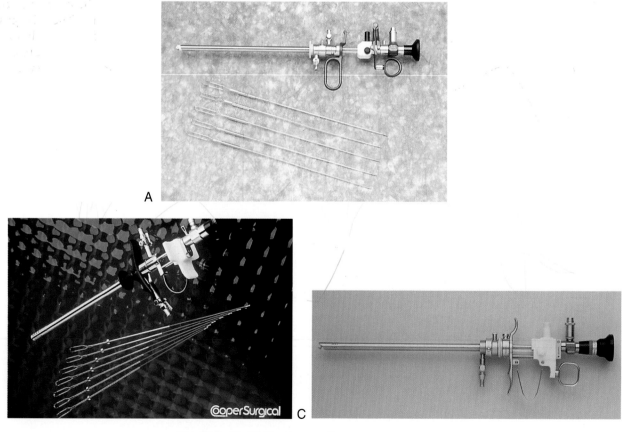

Fig. 20-8. (A–C) Continuous-flow resectoscopes.

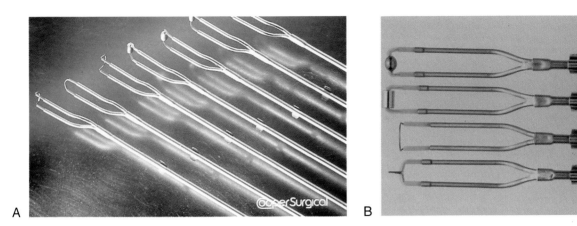

Fig. 20-9. **(A)** Operating electrodes; **(B)** close-up operating electrodes.

ner channel, entering into the endometrial cavity at the distal end of the telescope. Media leaving the uterus flows into small holes placed at the distal end of the sheath and out the exit port (Fig. 20-10). This system provides a constant flow path for used media, and dependence on the potential space between the cervix and sheath is eliminated. The field stays clear, increasing efficiency and safety.

DISTENDING MEDIA

The endometrial cavity is a potential space and must be distended to observe or operate in this area. Both fluid and gas distending media are used for hysteroscopic procedures.

CO$_2$ Gas

CO$_2$ gas media is a simple, clean, and clear media for distending the endometrial cavity during diagnostic procedures. The insufflator resembles the laparoscopic insufflator but limits flow and intrauterine pressures significantly below those that a laparoscopic insufflator can produce (Fig. 20-11). The insufflator is connected to the sheath via soft tubing. The CO$_2$ gas is stored in a small tank or CO$_2$ cartridge. Flow should be limited to 100 cc/min, and intrauterine pressures should be held to less than 100 mmHg. Pressures and flows greater than these values significantly increase the risk of gas emboli.

The refractive index of CO$_2$ gas is 1, and thus this

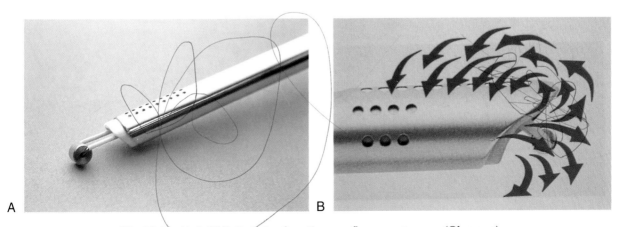

Fig. 20-10. **(A & B)** Exit ports of continuous-flow resectoscope (Olympus).

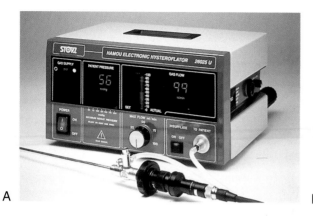
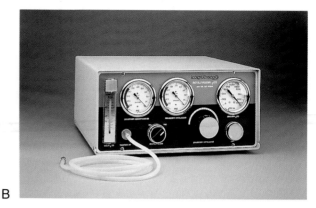

Fig. 20-11. (A & B) Hysteroflater.

media gives the clearest picture. If there is blood present in the endometrial cavity, however, the CO_2 gas bubbles through the blood, which is very distracting, limiting viewing. CO_2 gas media cannot be used in operative procedures, as once bleeding occurs, the lens of the scope becomes blood-covered and the view severely restricted.

Fluid Media

Fluid media are necessary for all operative procedures to keep the field clear. The most common fluid media used are saline, glycine, sorbitol, and dextran 70. The fluid can be administered by pump, syringe, infusion cuff, or gravity. Saline, glycine, and sorbitol are packaged in bags of 1 and 3 L. Most new continuous-flow resectoscopes will have acceptable flow rates using gravity alone as the delivery system. The bags are hung approximately 4 feet above the operating table and connected to the sheath with large bore tubing, such as arthroscopic or cystoscopic tubing. A height of 42 inches above the patient will generate a pressure of approximately 80 mmHg. Flow can be controlled by using either the lever on the sheath connector or the slide on the tubing itself. The endometrial cavity should be distended and then the flow progressively limited to just the rate necessary to keep the cavity distended. The limitation of this method is that the exact pressure in the endometrial cavity cannot be determined but only estimated by height of the bag above the patient.

On occasion, flow cannot be generated by gravity alone. A simple method of generating flow is placing the bag of infusion media inside a blood infusion cuff (Fig. 20-12). These cuffs are available to fit both 1- and 3-L bags. A button located at the bottom of the cuff measures the pressure placed against the infusion media bag. The advantage of this method is that it is low cost, readily available, and easy to use. The problems that exist with this method are

1. The pressure gauge tends to be inaccurate.
2. The cuff needs to be constantly reinflated, because as the bag empties, the cuff pressure on the bag continually falls.
3. It is very difficult to estimate the amount of fluid delivered while the bag is compressed inside the cuff.

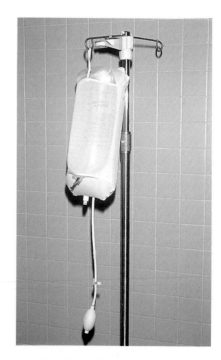

Fig. 20-12. Bag in infusion cuff.

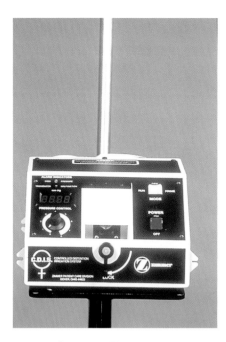

Fig. 20-13. Zimmer pump.

Currently, only one pump is available for delivery of a fluid media. This pump is manufactured by Zimmer (Fig. 20-13). The pump is the most accurate method of delivering fluid, as pressure is actually monitored electronically and the volume delivered can be easily observed. The Zimmer pump, however, can only deliver 80 mmHg pressure. Although this is often enough, there are times when more pressure is necessary to dis-

tend the endometrial cavity. The cost of the disposable tubing for this pump is also significantly more expensive than cystoscopy tubing.

For simple diagnostic procedures or whenever dextran 70 is being used, a syringe and intravenous extension tubing set provide a simple and inexpensive method of fluid delivery. This method does not lend itself to long cases with the need for large fluid volume.

Saline, sorbitol, and glycine are relatively interchangeable as distending media. All three are clear and easily deliverable. Because saline conducts electricity, it cannot be used with electrosurgery, as the current will be conducted away by the fluid, and no effect will occur at the electrode–tissue interface.

When dextran 70 is used, it must be delivered by syringe, as the product is supplied in bottles and cannot be delivered by gravity or pump. However, dextran 70 is immiscible with blood, and thus this fluid is of great benefit in keeping a clear field when blood is present. I mix dextran 70 with saline at a 50:50 concentration and find that this concentration retains most of the properties of immiscibility and yet is much easier to deliver.

Complications associated with various fluids and volume overload are discussed in Chapter 28.

REFERENCES

1. Hulka JF, Peterson HA, Phillips JM, Surrey MW: Operative hysteroscopy: American Association of Gynecologic Laparoscopists' 1993 membership survey. J Am Assoc Gynecol Laparoscopists 2:131, 1995

21 Indications and Contraindications of Hysteroscopy

KENNETH L. NOLLER

Indicate *4. to point to as the required treatment*
Webster's New World Dictionary, 1994

Despite many years of attempts, there is as yet no clear universal meaning for the word *indication* when applied to a medical procedure. Although all practicing physicians seem to understand when a given procedure is "indicated," it is very difficult to reduce this to the printed page in a way that allows for the myriad of conditions for which a procedure might be appropriate. Quality assessment committees have struggled with this concept for decades. Also, many conditions represent a disease spectrum for which a given procedure may not always be indicated. A good example is uterine fibroids. Although few would argue with the use of hysterectomy to treat a woman with a 16-week-size uterus due to uterine leiomyomata who is having menorrhagia that is unresponsive to medical therapy and causes anemia, hysterectomy is not indicated for small asymptomatic fibroids.

Thus, there is no good way to present the topic "Indications for Hysteroscopy." Although this chapter suggests several conditions for which hysteroscopy is clearly the best treatment alternative, there will be other conditions for which the procedure is sometimes used. Just because something *can* be done does not mean that it *should* be done.

Finally, the skill of the operator is an extremely important factor.[1,2] For example, some gynecologists are trained to perform radical hysterectomy, whereas most are not. Likewise, some physicians do not have the necessary skills to perform all the procedures that can be completed through the hysteroscope.

This chapter is arranged by anatomic site and disease entity. Also, only transcervical procedures are considered. Although it is certainly possible to introduce a hysteroscope through the uterine wall or by passing one of the new extremely fine flexible scopes retrograde through the tube, these procedures are not discussed in this chapter.

UTERINE CERVIX

Cervical Intraepithelial Neoplasia

The extent of intraepithelial neoplasia in the endocervical canal is a concern of all who regularly deal with this disease. If it were possible to document accurately the upward extent of cervical intraepithelial neoplasia (CIN), it would then be possible to perform cold-knife conization, loop electrosurgery, or ablative procedures more accurately and with less chance of disease persistence.

The microcolpohysteroscope was developed in an attempt to evaluate the epithelium of the endocervix.[3] A hysteroscope usually used for evaluation of the endometrial cavity is not adequate for this procedure. Most microcolpohysteroscopes have variable magnification that allow for the examination of the individual cells of the endocervix. With the aid of dyes that stain nuclear material, very expert technicians can reliably determine the extent of CIN and, to some extent, the presence or absence of adenocarcinoma in situ. Unfortunately, this skill is very difficult to acquire and is best performed only by those individuals who have extensive experience.

Invasive Cervical Cancer

Hysteroscopy is not indicated for evaluation of invasive squamous cell cancer of the uterine cervix. The information that could potentially be added would not change the treatment plan. Also, very heavy bleeding could occur.

Cervical Incompetence

At the present time, it does not appear that hysteroscopy is useful for the determination of the competence of the internal cervical os. Although this area is easily seen during routine hysteroscopy, there is no method of evaluation for cervical competence that has been proved to be effective.

ENDOMETRIAL CAVITY

Menorrhagia/Menometrorrhagia (Younger Than 35 Years)

Most women younger than 35 years of age do not experience significant menorrhagia or menometrorrhagia that is unresponsive to hormonal therapy. Indeed, few clinicians believe that it is necessary to perform endometrial biopsy in this age group before initiating therapy. However, in those women for which cyclic hormonal therapy does not result in the abatement of symptoms, further investigation is warranted. Submucous leiomyomata and endometrial polyps are common causes for such bleeding. Hysteroscopy is perhaps the best method of diagnosing both of these entities.[4] Although ultrasound can identify uterine leiomyomata, very often it is not possible to determine whether these lie immediately adjacent to the endometrium or deeper in the myometrium. Likewise, dilatation and curettage (D&C) often fails to remove or identify all uterine polyps.

Menorrhagia/Menometrorrhagia (35 Years or Older)

In the 35-and-older age group, the clinician must be aware of the ever-increasing possibility that noncyclic or heavy cyclic uterine bleeding may be due to neoplasia. Although the most common cause between ages 35 and 50 is simply those hormonal changes associated with the perimenopausal state, some of these women will be found, on biopsy, to have endometrial hyperplasia or adenocarcinoma as an explanation for their bleeding. However, uterine leiomyomata and endometrial polyps remain the most common causes of such bleeding until the perimenopause. As mentioned above, hysteroscopy provides an excellent method of identifying both endometrial polyps and submucous leiomyomata and of treating endometrial polyps.[5–7]

Unfortunately, there has been as yet no published study that documents the accuracy of hysteroscopy in the detection of endometrial neoplasia. Large series of consecutive cases have been reported in which both adenocarcinoma and endometrial hyperplasia have been identified, but no study has been performed in a manner adequate to prove that hysteroscopy is more accurate (or for that matter as accurate) as D&C.[8]

Endometrial cancer can be identified and biopsied by means of hysteroscopy. However, the average clinician has seen so few cases of endometrial adenocarcinoma through the hysteroscope that it does not seem reasonable to suggest that this technique supplant D&C for the detection of this most common genital malignancy.

If neoplasia has been ruled out, hysteroscopy can be used for the treatment of perimenopausal menometrorrhagia by combining its diagnostic capability with the treatment possibilities afforded by use of a roller ball or resectoscope.[9,10] In the past, this has been touted as a nearly magical treatment for all women with such bleeding. However, it is now recognized that the technique has limitations. Thus, although the technique may be indicated for some patients, it is certainly not a universally indicated procedure for heavy perimenopausal bleeding.

Infertility

Hysteroscopic evaluation of the endometrial cavity for women with infertility has become a common procedure. In most cases, the procedure is performed either to investigate a filling defect demonstrated by hysterosalpingography or in women in whom all tests have been normal.[11] There is little doubt that hysteroscopy can correctly evaluate filling defects. However, there are few data to suggest its usefulness in unexplained infertility.[12,13]

Submucosal Leiomyomata (Fibroids)

It is relatively easy to identify distortion of the uterine cavity caused by submucous fibroids with the hysteroscope. Also, many times considerable bleeding will be seen from these areas, or large vessels overlying the fibroid can be identified. Excision of such fibroids is sometimes possible.[14,15] However, large fibroids often result in incomplete excision, rapid resumption of symptoms after therapy, and need for repeat hysteroscopic resection.[16]

Uterine Synechaie

The presence of uterine synechaie (Asherman syndrome) is a clear-cut indication for hysteroscopy. The technique can be used to take down virtually all intrauterine adhesions caused by postpartum or postoperative infection. Perhaps the only exception are those synechaie caused by intentional endometrial ablation.

Uterine Septum

Hysteroscopy is the method of choice for the treatment of most uterine septae.[17–20] A variety of techniques has been developed to manage these congenital abnormalities. Although laparotomy and various reunification procedures are still performed occasionally, most septae are now corrected with hysteroscopy.

Uterine Scars

Some authors have suggested that hysteroscopy provides an accurate method of evaluating the competence of uterine scars that have resulted from myomectomy, cesarean section, or other similar procedures.[21] Again, the correct studies have not been performed to determine whether the information obtained from evaluation of these scars represents useful clinical information. Indeed, hysteroscopy can almost always identify the site of a previous cesarean section scar, for example, but it is not clear whether the competency of such a scar can be adequately determined by the technique.

Removal of Intrauterine Devices

Although intrauterine contraceptive devices (IUCDs) are no longer used in large numbers, occasional women are still seen who are known to have a device in place with no visible string. In some of these women, it is important to remove this foreign body. Hysteroscopy is probably the ideal method of removing the device if office techniques (colposcopy and IUCD hooks) are unsuccessful.[22]

FALLOPIAN TUBE

Tubal Patency

It is possible to identify the openings to the fallopian tubes in virtually every hysteroscopy unless dense synechaie occlude the area. Once the ostia have been identified, it is relatively easy to determine whether the distending medium is flowing out the tube unless a very viscus medium is being used. Very fine, flexible hysteroscopes have been developed to examine the interior of the fallopian tube.[23,24] At the present time, they should still be considered experimental as it is not clear that the information obtained from such examination is more useful than that obtained from hysterosalpingography alone.

Multiparity/Sterilization

For many years, attempts have been made to develop techniques that allow for occlusion of the fallopian tubes by means of the hysteroscope.[1,25] Although it is possible to accomplish tubal occlusion in many women by using one of several techniques, at the present time all these techniques have higher failure rates than more standard means of tubal occlusion using laparoscopy.

CONTRAINDICATIONS

There are a few contraindications to hysteroscopy. An active endometritis or recent transmural uterine incision probably represent the full spectrum.

For many years, there was a concern that hysteroscopy might be responsible for spreading endometrial adenocarcinoma because of the free flow of fluid from the tubes during the procedure.[26–28] Although it has been shown that, in cases of endometrial adenocarcinoma, tumor cells do flow from the tubes into the peritoneal cavity, they do not seem to be able to implant.

It is certainly possible during hysteroscopy to accidentally perform a hysterotomy.[7] In these cases, it is contraindicated to repeat the procedure until the defect has healed.

SUMMARY

Hysteroscopy has become a widely used and useful clinical tool. For some disease processes, it is clearly the treatment method of choice (Table 21-1). For other diseases, it represents a technique that can be helpful in

Table 21-1. Indications for Hysteroscopy

Best technique available
Division/ablation of uterine septum
Treatment of uterine synechaie
Removal of IUCD when blind methods fail
Evaluation of intrauterine filling defects
Removal of endometrial polyps
Useful in some cases
Evaluation of CIN
Removal of submucosal leiomyomata
Evaluation of unexplained uterine bleeding
Evaluation of uterine scars
Evaluation of unexplained infertility
Investigational
Diagnosis and staging of endometrial neoplasia
Endosalpinx evaluation
Tubal occlusion for sterilization

selected cases, and for other problems, it remains investigational.

REFERENCES

1. Hysteroscopy. ACOG Technical Bulletin No. 191. April 1994
2. Cararach M, Penella J, Ubeda A, Labastida R: Hysteroscopic incision of the septate uterus: scissors versus resectoscope. Hum Reprod 9:87, 1994
3. Hamou J: Hysteroscopy and microhysteroscopy with a new instrument: the microhysteroscope. Acta Eur Fertil 12:29, 1981
4. Cicinelli E, Romano F, Anastasio PS et al: Sonohysterography versus hysteroscopy in the diagnosis of endouterine polyps. Gynecol Obstet Invest 38:266, 1994
5. Coeman D, Van Belle Y, Vanderick G et al: Hysteroscopic findings in patients with a cervical polyp. Am J Obstet Gynecol 169:1563, 1993
6. Loffer FD: Removal of large symptomatic intrauterine growths by the hysteroscopic resectoscope. Obstet Gynecol 76:836, 1990
7. Grainger DA, DeCherney AH: Hysteroscopic management of uterine bleeding [review]. Baillieres Clin Obstet Gynaecol 3:403, 1989
8. Taddei GL, Moncini D, Scarselli G et al: Can hysteroscopic evaluation of endometrial carcinoma influence therapeutic treatment? Ann NY Acad Sci 734:482, 1994
9. Daniell JF, Kurtz BR, Ke RW: Hysteroscopic endometrial ablation using the rollerball electrode. Obstet Gynecol 80:329, 1992
10. Boto TC, Fowler CG: Surgical alternatives to hysterectomy for intractable menorrhagia [review]. Br J Hosp Med 44:93, 1990
11. Valle RF: Hysteroscopy in the evaluation of female infertility. Am J Obstet Gynecol 137:425, 1980
12. Golan A, Ron-El R, Herman A et al: Diagnostic hysteroscopy: its value in an in-vitro fertilization/embryo transfer unit. Hum Reprod 7:1433, 1992
13. Wang Y, Han M, Li C et al: The value of hysteroscopy in the diagnosis of infertility and habitual abortion. Chin Med Sci J 7:226, 1992
14. Donnez J, Gillerot S, Bourgonjon D et al: Neodymium: YAG laser hysteroscopy in large submucous fibroids. Fertil Steril 54:999, 1990
15. Neuwirth RS, Amin HK: Excision of submucous fibroids with hysteroscopic control. Am J Obstet Gynecol 126:95, 1976
16. Wamsteker K, Emanuel MH, deKruif JH: Transcervical hysteroscopic resection of submucous fibroids for abnormal uterine bleeding: results regarding the degree of intramural extension. Obstet Gynecol 82:736, 1993
17. Assaf A, Serour G, Elkady A: Endoscopic management of the intrauterine septum. Int J Gynaecol Obstet 32:43, 1990
18. Candiani GB, Vercellini P, Fedele L et al: Repair of the uterine cavity after hysteroscopic septal incision. Fertil Steril 54:991, 1990
19. Marabini A, Gubbini G, Stagnozzi R et al: Hysteroscopic metroplasty. Ann NY Acad Sci 734:488, 1994
20. Elchalal U, Schenker JG: Hysteroscopic resection of uterus septus versus abdominal metroplasty [review]. J Am Coll Surg 178:637, 1994
21. Petrikovsky BM: Endoscopic assessment of the integrity of the postcesarean uterine wall before a trial of labor. Transcervical Endoscopy Registry. J Reprod Med 39:464, 1994
22. Valle RF, Sciarra JJ, Freeman DW: Hysteroscopic removal of intrauterine devices with missing filaments. Obstet Gynecol 49:55, 1977
23. Daykhovsky K, Segalowitz J, Surrey E et al: Falloposcopy: a microendoscopic technique for visual exploration of the human fallopian tube from the uterotubal ostium to the fimbria using a transvaginal approach. Fertil Steril 54:390, 1990
24. Venezia R, Zangara C, Knight C, Cittadini E: Initial experience of a new linear everting falloposcopy system in comparison with hysterosalpingography. Fertil Steril 60:771, 1993
25. Darabi KF, Richart RM: Collaborative study on hysteroscopic sterilization procedures. Preliminary report. Obstet Gynecol 49:48, 1977
26. Sagawa T, Yamada H, Fujimoto S: A comparison between the preoperative and operative findings of peritoneal cytology in patients with endometrial cancer. Asia Oceania J Obstet Gynaecol 20:39, 1994
27. Schmitz MJ, Nahhas WA: Hysteroscopy may transport malignant cells into the peritoneal cavity. Case report. Eur J Gynaecol Oncol 15:121, 1994
28. Romano S, Shimoni Y, Muralee D, Shalev E: Retrograde seeding of endometrial carcinoma during hysteroscopy. Gynecol Oncol 44:116, 1992

22 Office Hysteroscopy

PAUL D. INDMAN

Office hysteroscopy provides a simple, safe, and effective means of diagnosing intrauterine abnormalities. Surprisingly little equipment is necessary to get started in office hysteroscopy: a telescope with sheath, a light source, and a means to distend the uterus. The technique of office hysteroscopy should be mastered by every gynecologist.

INDICATIONS AND CONTRAINDICATIONS

Dilation and curettage and suction curettage have been shown to be significantly less reliable in detecting intrauterine pathology than hysteroscopy.[1,2] Hysteroscopy is thus indicated as the primary procedure for the evaluation of the endometrial cavity whenever an intrauterine abnormality is suspected. Although thorough suction curettage has a low risk of missing endometrial cancer, the combination of hysteroscopy plus suction curettage has a diagnostic accuracy approaching 100 percent.[3]

The most common indication for hysteroscopy is the evaluation of abnormal bleeding. This is best done in the follicular phase of the cycle if the patient is premenopausal. Other indications include the evaluation of the endometrial cavity before abdominal myomectomy, evaluation of recurrent pregnancy loss, and infertility of endometrial pathology is suspected.

Hysteroscopy is contraindicated in the presence of active infection, or in the presence of a continuing pregnancy in the absence of specific indications such as removal of a lost intrauterine device (IUD). Active bleeding is a relative contraindication to office hysteroscopy only because blood interferes with vision when CO_2 is used as a distending medium. It is prudent to do hysteroscopy in patients who have severe medical problems in an outpatient setting where full monitoring and resuscitation facilities are available.

DISTENDING MEDIA

Because the choice of distending medium influences the choice of equipment, this is discussed first. The requirements for a distending medium for office hysteroscopy differ from those for operative hysteroscopy. The time required and the ease of setting up for and cleaning up after a procedure is important if a procedure is to be accepted by the physician and staff.

Hyskon provides good visualization of the endometrial cavity and does not require special equipment. The high viscosity of Hyskon requires quite a bit of pressure to overcome the resistance of the narrow space between a standard 5-mm sheath and a 4-mm telescope. A larger 7-mm operative sheath provides less resistance to flow, and Hyskon can be diluted to reduce viscosity. Although blood does not mix with Hyskon, it forms a suspension that can interfere with visualization. It is helpful to have a suction cannula available to aspirate any blood or debris that may impair vision. The catheter is passed through the operative port of the hysteroscope sheath. A major disadvantage to using Hyskon in an office setting is its propensity to act like glue when it dries. If instruments and stopcocks are not completely disassembled and thoroughly cleaned immediately after use, they can be very difficult to unfreeze.

Low-viscosity media do not cause the problems with instrument maintenance found with Hyskon. Blood in the endometrial cavity will mix with these solutions and cloud view. Flow-through hysteroscope systems allow a rapid turnover of fluid to rinse away any cloudy fluid. Alternately, the cervix can be dilated to allow egress of fluid around the scope. Like Hyskon, no special equipment is needed to supply low-viscosity fluids. They can be delivered by a large syringe or by gravity. A mechanism is necessary to collect the liquid that is recovered via an outflow port of the hysteroscope or that leaks around the cervix. Unfortunately, much of this fluid often winds up on the floor. It is easy to understand how the enthusiasm of the staff could be tempered by the need to clean up after each procedure. Although low-viscosity media are rarely used in an office setting, the recent introduction of a 5.5-mm-diameter flow-through hysteroscope may kindle an interest in these fluids.

Because of the drawbacks of liquid media in an office setting, CO_2 is the most widely used distending medium for office hysteroscopy. Absolutely no preparation time or clean-up is necessary with CO_2, making it well accepted by the office staff. As with any medium, experience is necessary to obtain optimal visualization. CO_2 provides an exceptionally clear view when it is unhampered by blood in the endometrial cavity. Blood will interfere with visualization and at times make vision impossible. A tight seal of the cervix around the hysteroscope is needed to avoid loss of distension. Techniques for the effective use of CO_2 are discussed later in this chapter. A minor disadvantage to the use of CO_2 is the necessity of a device to deliver the gas at a controlled rate and pressure.

EQUIPMENT

Hysteroscopes

Hysteroscopes are available in two categories: rigid and flexible. Each type of hysteroscope has its own advantages and disadvantages. Rigid lens systems have been standard for many years and are most widely used (Plate 22-1A). The heart of the system is the telescope. Telescopes are available in several diameters, but the 4-mm telescope is generally accepted as providing the best compromise between ease of insertion and image quality. Smaller-diameter telescopes provide a narrower and dimmer view. Also, the smaller telescopes are often used with smaller sheaths that may not provide a good seal at the cervix. Some telescopes provide vision that is directly in line with the telescope, whereas others look off to the side (foreoblique). A 30 degree fore-oblique telescope is most widely used for diagnostic hysteroscopy as it allows visualization of the tubal ostia without requiring excess torque on the cervix to see into the cornual areas.

The sheath used for diagnostic hysteroscopy with CO_2 only needs to contain a single channel to pass the distention medium. The outer diameter of a sheath for a 4-mm telescope is 5 mm. To do procedures with ancillary instruments, such as directed biopsy, it is necessary to use a sheath with an instrument channel. These are typically 7 or 8 mm in diameter. Most manufactures provide flexible or "semirigid" biopsy forceps, scissors, and graspers that fit through the operative sheath. It should be remembered that these instruments are extremely fragile. It is easy to bend the shaft of the instrument while the operator's attention and vision are concentrated on the view through the hysteroscope. A disadvantage to the rigid system of instrumentation is the need to switch to a larger operative sheath to use ancillary instruments.

Although office hysteroscopy instruments have traditionally been designed for use with CO_2 for distension, I have recently used a newly introduced hysteroscope that is 5.5 mm in diameter (ACMI-Circon, Santa Barbara, CA) with a flow-through design (Fig. 22-1B & C). Low-viscosity fluids enter through a small channel adjacent to the telescope and are allowed to egress through the outer sheath through side holes in the distal sheath. This allows excellent visualization even in the presence of blood in the endometrial cavity. Other manufacturers have also introduced narrow diameter flow-through systems.

Flexible instruments transmit the image through a bundle of fine discreet fiberoptic light cables rather than a lens system, as used by rigid instruments (Fig. 22-2). The amount of light transmitted and the resolution of the image are proportional to the number and diameter of the fibers. Smaller-diameter scopes have a limited number of fibers and provide a small grainy image that lacks detail, whereas larger-diameter scopes provide an image almost as clear as the rigid scopes (Fig. 22-3). A lever near the eyepiece of the hysteroscope steers the tip up or down approximately 90 degrees. Rotating the entire instrument allows the tip to be directed to the right or left. Flexible hysteroscopes provide a 0 degree (looking straight ahead) wide-angle view. Just as with conventional photography, a wide-angle lens tends to accentuate perspective. This makes far away objects appear very small and close-up objects appear very large. This effect should be kept in mind when attempting to judge the size of intracavitary lesions when using a hysteroscope with a wide-angle view.

Whereas rigid hysteroscopes rely on an external sheath to provide insufflation and instrument channels, these functions are built in to the flexible scope. A close-up view of the distal end of a flexible hysteroscope shows the light carrying and optical viewing channels, as well as a channel for insufflation and in-

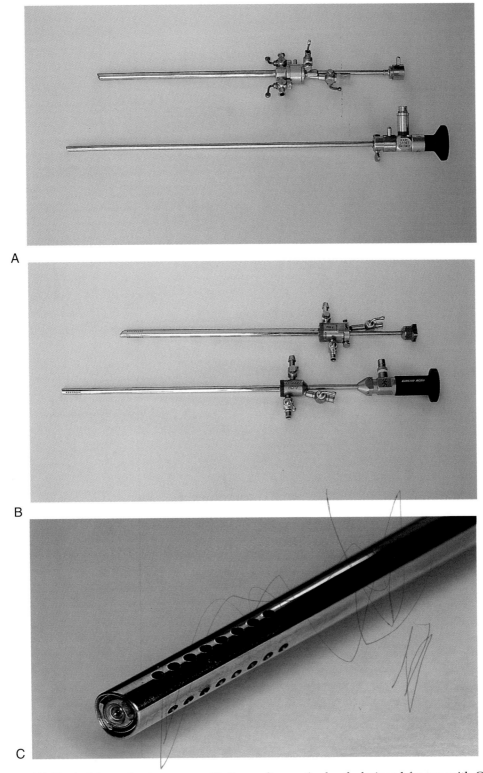

Fig. 22-1. (**A**) Typical 4-mm hysteroscope with 5-mm diagnostic sheath designed for use with CO_2 as distending medium. A 7-mm sheath with operating channel is above. (**B**) Flow-through hysteroscope with 5.5-mm sheath. A 7-mm operative sheath is above. (**C**) Close-up of distal end of flow-through sheath. Fluid enters uterus through small channel below telescope and egresses through side holes.

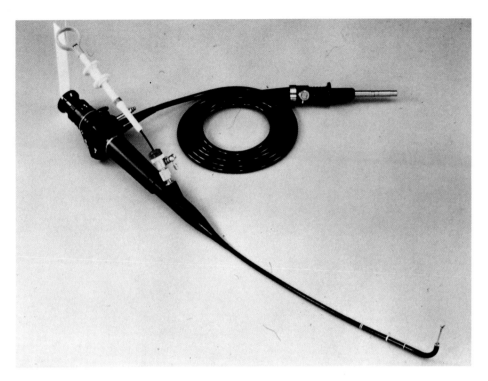

Fig. 22-2. A 4.9-mm flexible hysteroscope. (Courtesy of Olympus Corporation).

struments. A trade-off for eliminating the outer sheath is that size of the optical channel is decreased to allow room for the instrument channel.

The decision of whether to use a flexible or rigid instrument is often one of operator preference. Although increased patient comfort is claimed with flexible instruments, with experience a rigid instrument can be inserted with little discomfort. Also, it is often necessary to dilate the cervix for all but the smallest flexible instruments, as they lack the rigidity to overcome the resistance of the internal cervical os. If a video camera is not used, however, a flexible hysteroscope provides better comfort for the operator as he or she does not need to change position to see an acutely anteflexed or retroflexed uterus. The care of the flexible instrument requires more time from the staff, as the channels need to be cleaned and disinfected. Flexible hysteroscopes are more expensive than their rigid counterparts, are far more fragile, and require more maintenance.

Light Source

An inexpensive halogen light source is sufficient to provide illumination for direct viewing. It is a good idea to have a spare bulb available. Although modern video cameras are becoming more light-sensitive, it is often necessary to use a high-power xenon or osram light source. Some video cameras have a "low light" setting, which increases the gain of the system. Unfortunately, this also increases video "noise," resulting in a grainy picture. It is important to evaluate any light source in conjunction with the hysteroscope and video camera that will be used.

Insufflator

Hysteroscopy requires a flow of CO_2 at a maximum rate of 100 ml/min. Lower rates are preferred at times to prevent bubble formation, but higher rates of flow can produce a gas embolus and should not be used. Fatalities have been caused by the use of insufflators designed for laparoscopy; *insufflators designed for applications other than hysteroscopy should never be used!* Hysteroscopy insufflators have gauges that display pressure and flow rate; these are extremely useful in diagnosing any difficulty with vision. Although some operators have successfully used other CO_2 sources designed for urethroscopy or tubal insufflation, I believe that the critical importance of this instrument and the information provided by the flow and pressure gauges more than offsets the cost of an insufflator designed for hysteroscopy.

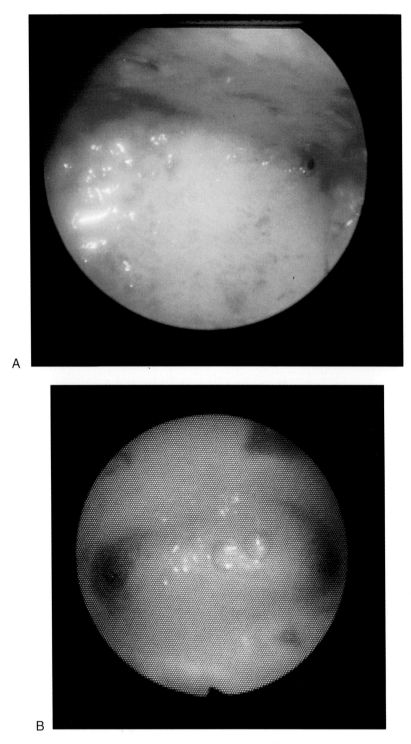

Fig. 22-3. (**A**) Normal uterus as seen through rigid hysteroscope (Karl Storz Endoscopy) using CO_2 as distending medium. (**B**) Normal uterus seen through 4.9-mm Olympus hysteroscope. Currently available smaller-diameter flexible scopes give smaller picture with much less detail.

Video Camera

A perfectly satisfactory hysteroscopic examination can be performed without the aid of a video camera. Although a video camera offers many advantages, the cost of a video system should not dissuade one from initiating office hysteroscopy as video equipment can be added at a later time. When performing rigid hysteroscopy, it is often necessary to raise or lower the position of the eyepiece to allow the hysteroscope to negotiate an anteverted or retroverted uterus. The operator's position is not dictated by the angle of the uterus when a video camera is used. The biggest advantage of using video is that the patient is allowed to see the examination in progress. The degree to which this helps her understand her problem cannot be overstated. Also, the ability to videotape the examination allows one to review the findings or obtain consultation without the need for repeating the procedure.

The requirements for video in hysteroscopy are not as stringent as required for laparoscopy, which demands ultra-high resolution. Virtually all endoscopic cameras use a solid-state chip to form the image. Single-chip designs are quite acceptable for hysteroscopy and are less expensive than three-chip designs needed for laparoscopy. Much of the expense in constructing an endoscopic camera is in waterproofing to allow sterilization. Because this is not necessary for office use, a number of relatively inexpensive models have recently been introduced. There is a tremendous variation in the quality of these units that cannot be detected by examining specification sheets. Furthermore, a camera may look good in a laboratory setting but may be unsatisfactory in actual use. It is essential to evaluate a camera under consideration during actual hysteroscopy with the light source, cable, and hysteroscope that it will be used with.

A video camera must be used with a monitor. It is essential that the monitor be located in an area that provides comfortable viewing for both the patient and surgeon. I learned this first-hand when severe muscle strain was traced to a monitor placed off to the side. The solution was to place a monitor to the side for the patient to watch and a monitor mounted on the ceiling for the surgeon. The size of monitor required is directly related to the viewing distance. A 9-inch monitor placed close to the surgeon provides the same clarity as a larger monitor placed at a greater distance. The resolution of the monitor should be at least equal to that of the video camera.

Newer videotape formats are higher quality and record more information than was possible with conventional formats but may not be compatible with home recorders. Hi-8 is the most compact of the newer formats, but players are not currently as readily available as the VHS format. Super-VHS (S-VHS) has a resolution of 400 lines compared with 240 lines of conventional VHS (broadcast television is 330 lines). An S-VHS recorder can record conventional VHS, but a tape recorded in S-VHS must be played on an S-VHS deck.

Supplies

A simple pack can be made up with the necessary instruments. An open-sided speculum is often preferred for hysteroscopy, as it can be removed with the hysteroscope in place if it interferes with the examination. The pack also includes a tenaculum, 13-15 and 17-19F Pratt dilators, packing forceps, a medicine cup, 4×4's, and cotton balls. Instruments that are immediately available include polyp forceps and, optionally, an operative sheath for the hysteroscope with hysteroscopic scissors, graspers, and biopsy instruments. Several varieties of suction curettes are kept available.

In addition to supplies specific to hysteroscopy, local anesthetics, analgesics, and adequate resuscitation equipment should be available wherever procedures are performed.

TECHNIQUE

Psychology of Office Surgery

Patients naturally have concerns about undergoing any medical procedure. Perhaps the greatest area of apprehension is the fear of pain. The approach that the physician and the office staff takes to handle this fear has a major impact on how the patient will perceive her experience.

Patients need to have realistic exceptions about what to expect. If this trust is violated, then any further assurances will be met with disbelief. In describing the procedure, certain words trigger more anxiety and stimulate more fear than others. When scheduling a procedure, a women will often ask "will it hurt?" An answer of "it won't be too painful" implies that it is still a painful procedure. However, a reply of "you will probably feel some cramping, but most women do not find it too bothersome" is a truthful statement but is not telling the patient that the procedure is painful.

An anxious patient will be apprehensive long before the procedure starts. A build-up of anxiety starts when the patients drives to the office and increases with each step that brings her closer to the procedure, such as being called into the room, undressing, and getting onto the table. If a medication to combat anxiety is to be given, therefore, the ideal time is before the anxiety cycle starts rather than in the examination room where it has reached its peak. It is often helpful to give a particularly anxious patient 10 mg of diazepam to take at home an hour before the time of her appointment. (She should not drive a car after taking this.)

I have clear memories as a child of visiting a doctor's office where a long needle, obviously bent and straightened numerous times, was prominently displayed in a glass case. The only thing I could think about at every visit was "I hope he does not use that on me!" Many instruments that appear innocuous to us can be extremely frightening to the patient. Instruments and objects such a syringes and needles in the examination room should be placed out of sight.

Most patients want to know what to expect rather than what is actually being done. Telling a patient "you may feel some pinching" creates far less anxiety than telling her "we're going to give you a little shot in your cervix."

The medical assistant or nurse should also to avoid words that suggest pain and should focus the patient's attention away from the procedure. Asking the patient "does that hurt?" "tell me when it hurts," or "tell me what you are feeling" will focus attention to and intensify any discomfort. If a patient appears to be uncomfortable, asking "is that bothering you?" is a way of asking the same question without suggesting pain.

Analgesia

Although office hysteroscopy can be performed without anesthesia or analgesia, there is no reason why the procedure should not be made as comfortable as possible. Once the patient experiences pain, the remainder of the procedure will be more difficult and stimuli that would not have been perceived as uncomfortable may be interpreted as painful. The use of a prostaglandin inhibitor, such as naproxen sodium 550 mg, taken an hour before the procedure will decrease cramping. Paracervical or intracervical block anesthesia will also decrease cramping and will make application of the tenaculum painless. In selecting a local anesthetic agent for a short procedure, rapid onset and low

toxicity are important criteria. Nesacaine (chlorprocaine) has a more rapid onset than other local anesthetics. Nesacaine also has the most rapid half-life of available agents as it is hydrolyzed by pseudocholinesterase. My preference is to inject a total of 2.5 ml of 2 percent Nesacaine submucosally in four quadrants at the vaginal fornices. A 25-gauge needle with a needle extender, coupled with slow injection, allows the procedure to be virtually painless. It may be necessary to use an iris hook to manipulate the cervix to allow injection, but a tenaculum is never placed until the cervix is anesthetized.

Paracervical anesthesia, with distraction provided by a well-trained medical assistant, is adequate analgesia for most procedures. Occasionally, however, a woman may find this insufficient. In this case, it is helpful to have a short-acting narcotic available. Fentanyl is a potent analgesic that has a rapid onset and short duration of action. Although respiratory depression or "stiff chest syndrome" can occur, side effects are unusual when small doses are injected slowly. Intravenous injection of 0.1 mg of fentanyl provides excellent analgesia with little drowsiness. Although the risk of an adverse reaction is low, a narcotic antagonist and resuscitation equipment should be available whenever such agents are used.

Technique of Hysteroscopy

After administration of the paracervical block, a tenaculum is applied to the cervix. I prefer to pass a 13-French Pratt dilator just to the internal os to allow easier passage of the hysteroscope, although some hysteroscopists insert the hysteroscope without prior dilation of the cervix. Care must be taken not to overdilate the cervix, as CO_2 will leak out around the sheath, preventing adequate distention of the uterus. The hysteroscope is inserted through the cervix under direct vision, keeping in mind that the cervical canal will appear off-center when a 30 degree fore-oblique hysteroscope is directed through the cervix.

The endometrial cavity is thoroughly inspected, taking care to see the lower uterine segment and cervix—areas in which pathology is often overlooked—as the hysteroscope is being withdrawn. It is possible to press the hysteroscope against the endometrium and use the depth of the groove created to judge the thickness of the endometrium.

After the endometrial cavity is completely visualized, directed biopsies may be taken or a suction curet-

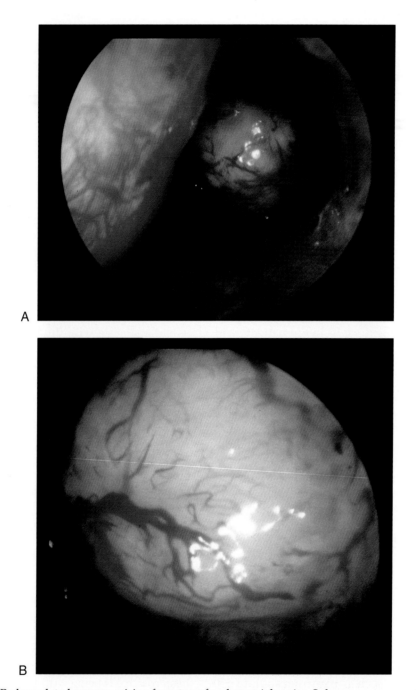

Fig. 22-4. (**A**) Pedunculated myoma arising from top of endometrial cavity. Submucous myoma in lower uterine segment partially blocks view. (**B**) Close-up of pedunculated myoma. Note large but regularly branching vessels.

tage can be performed. If a flexible hysteroscope with an instrument channel is used, it is a simple matter to pass a biopsy forceps through the instrument channel to obtain one or more biopsies. If a rigid system is being used, then it is necessary to remove the hysteroscope and exchange the diagnostic sheath for the larger operative sheath. In addition to directed biopsies, it may be possible to remove small polyps or retrieve a "lost" IUD string with these instruments.

As an alternative to directed biopsy, a suction curettage will thoroughly sample the endometrial cavity as well as remove many small polyps. If a small syringe is used as a source of suction, it is helpful to insert the curette into the uterus to allow the escape of residual CO_2 before attaching the syringe. If this is not done, residual CO_2 in the uterus will fill the syringe and prevent adequate suction. This is not a problem if a 50- to 60-ml syringe is used. The larger syringe is also recommended, in conjunction with a 6-mm canula, when multiple or large polyps are present.

Antibiotics are not routinely administered, as infections are uncommon after office hysteroscopy. Patients with a history of pelvic infection or in whom extensive or prolonged manipulation has been carried out are given a 5-day course of an oral antibiotic, such as doxycycline.

FINDINGS

Normal endometrium is variable in thickness. Often the tip of the hysteroscope will lift up an area of endometrium. The groove created can be used to judge the thickness of the endometrium. The lifted endometrium, however, can easily be mistaken for a polyp.

Uterine myomas vary being pedunculated and contained entirely in the endometrial cavity to residing almost entirely in the myometrium, with only a small portion protruding into the cavity. Myomas may be covered by relatively normal-appearing endometrium or by thin endometrium underlying large blood vessels (Fig. 22-4). Although these vessels can be quite large, the regular branching pattern is a clue to their benign nature. It is often necessary to estimate the proportion of myoma that is in the cavity to decide whether hysteroscopic resection is feasible. This can be determined by noting the angle between the myoma and surrounding endometrium. It is often difficult to judge the size of the myoma if there is not a structure of known size for comparison. Correlation of vaginal probe ultrasound with hysteroscopic findings can be extremely helpful in assessing the size and location of myomas and can be rapidly carried out at the time of hysteroscopy.

Endometrial polyps can vary in size from several millimeters to filling the entire endometrial cavity. Atypical vessels should make one suspicious of malignant change. Small polyps can be removed under direct vision with a biopsy forceps. This is especially convenient if a flexible hysteroscope is being used, as it is not necessary to change to an operative sheath. Many polyps, however, can be removed by simple suction curettage with a 6-mm curette or, once located, grasped with a polyp forceps (Fig. 22-5).

It is not uncommon to find minor synechiae. These are usually clinically insignificant unless they cover a large area. Dense or extensive adhesions can interfere with fertility. Occasionally, adhesions may be associated with retained placental tissue, as seen in Fig. 22-6.

The uterus often has an arcuate shape. A true septum will be seen as a definite division of the endometrial cavity into two horns. Alternate methods, such as ultrasound or laparoscopy, are necessary to distinguish a septate uterus from a bicornuate uterus, as both will present an identical picture on hysteroscopy.

Hyperplasia and cancer present a spectrum of overgrowth from a simple thickened endometrium to a complex growth pattern. Many colposcopic characteristics of cervical malignancy may also be seen in the endometrium, such as atypical vessels and necrosis (Fig. 22-7).

SOLVING PROBLEMS

Most problems in office hysteroscopy can be traced to difficulty with uterine distension. The intrauterine pressure and flow gauges on the insufflator are extremely helpful in diagnosing problems with distension. If the uterus is not distending and the intrauterine pressure is zero, the flow meter will indicate either no flow, indicating that the unit is out of CO_2, or high flow, indicating a leak in the system. The leak can be through a patulous cervix or through a loose connection in the tubing or hysteroscope. If pressure is high, then be sure that all stopcocks are open to allow the CO_2 to reach the uterus. If all stopcocks are open, high pressure indicates adequate pressure in the uterus.

Bubbles are a common annoyance. Bubbles can usually be avoided by starting with a low flow rate, such as 50 ml/min of CO_2, and increasing only if necessary

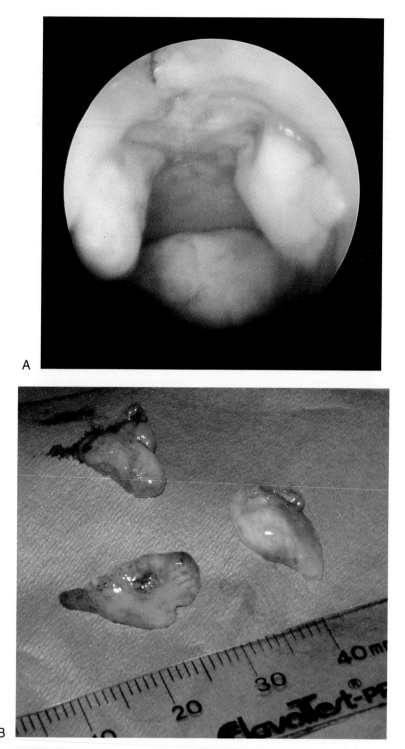

Fig. 22-5. (**A**) Endometrial polyps in a menopausal women presenting with bleeding. (**B**) Polyps removed by suction curettage. (*Figure continues.*)

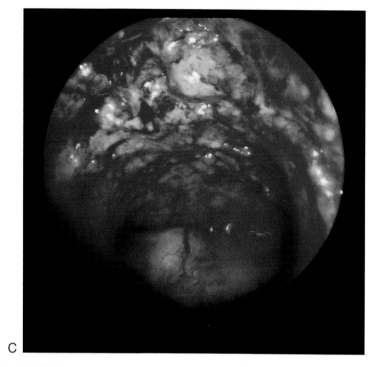

Fig. 22-5. (*Continued*). (**C**) Hysteroscopy immediately after removal of polyps. Small submucous myoma remains.

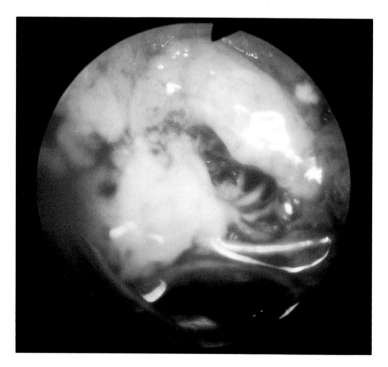

Fig. 22-6. Endometrial cavity obliterated with adhesions and retained placental tissue.

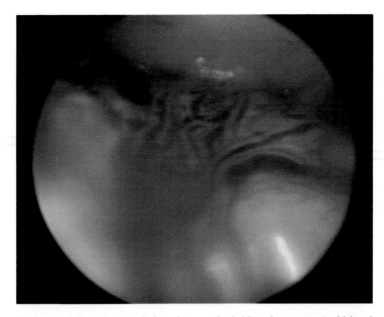

Fig. 22-7. Endometrial carcinoma (taken from video). Note large atypical blood vessels.

to a maximum of 100 ml/min. Rapid to-and-fro movement of the hysteroscope will act as a piston and increase bubbling. It may be possible to slowly bring the scope through the bubbles to contact the endometrium at the top of the fundus and then slowly withdraw it.

Blood in the endometrial cavity can be a problem when CO_2 is used for distension. It is often possible to control bleeding by hormonal methods or suction curettage and do hysteroscopy at a later date. If blood interferes with vision, it can be helpful to thread a 8F pediatric feeding tube through the cervix to the top of the fundus (without the hysteroscope in place) and irrigate the endometrial cavity with saline. Alternately, a suction curettage may remove enough debris to allow

some visualization but is less than ideal. If a liquid distending medium is available, it is preferred in the presence of bleeding.

REFERENCES

1. Gimpelson RJ, Rappold, HO: A comparative study between panoramic hysteroscopy with directed biopsies and dilation and curettage. Am J Obstet Gynecol 158:489, 1988
2. Loffer FD: Hysteroscopy with selective endometrial sampling compared with D&C for abnormal uterine bleeding: the value of a negative hysteroscopic view. Obstet Gynecol 73:1620, 1989
3. Goldrath MH: Office hysteroscopy and suction curettage: can we eliminate the hospital diagnostic dilatation and curettage? Am J Obstet Gynecol 152:220, 1985

23 Endometrial Ablation: Electrosurgery

RAYMOND LUI
ALAN DECHERNEY

Abnormal uterine bleeding that has not responded to hormonal methods and dilation and curettage (D&C) has been treated by hysterectomy in the past. The use of the hysteroscope diagnostically has enabled the gynecologist to better evaluate this problem.[1,2] As technology and equipment have improved, it is not surprising that operative endoscopy and, in particular, endometrial ablation of the uterine cavity have become an increasingly accepted alternative method of treatment for abnormal uterine bleeding that is satisfactory to both the patient and physician. Endometrial ablation can be accomplished with either the neodymium:yttrium-aluminum-garnet (Nd:YAG) laser or electrosurgery. The latter surgical approach is the focus of this chapter.

ENDOMETRIAL ABLATION VERSUS HYSTERECTOMY

Approximately 25 percent of hysterectomies are performed for abnormal uterine bleeding. Hysteroscopic management of abnormal uterine bleeding by endometrial ablation has been initially described in those individuals who also have a contraindication to hysterectomy due to major medical diseases or who are unwilling to undergo hysterectomy.[3–5] As experience increases, endometrial ablation appears to offer several advantages over hysterectomy due to the less invasive nature of the procedure. These advantages include reductions in several areas: operating time, amount of anesthetic agents, patient recuperation time, hospital length of stay, and immediate costs. It remains to be

seen, however, whether ablation will provide a lasting alternative to hysterectomy in those individuals who are otherwise able to undergo traditional hysterectomy.

ELECTROSURGERY VERSUS LASER

The Nd:YAG laser is an effective way of accomplishing endometrial ablation but does have several disadvantages in comparison to electrosurgery. Cost alone may make access to the laser prohibitive. Not only is the laser expensive but frequently a dedicated operating room must be used due to the special plumbing needed for the water cooling requirements of the machine. Also, significant training is required of the operating room personnel to conduct the procedure in a safe and efficient manner. However, electrosurgery is available in all operating suites, and its use is not new to the surgeon or operating room staff. The electrosurgical technique is generally easier to perform and appears to be equally effective in achieving the goals of amenorrhea or hypomenorrhea when compared with the laser.[6]

INDICATIONS

Women with disabling uterine bleeding who have failed standard therapy, including hormonal therapy, may be candidates for endometrial ablation. Ideally, the endometrial cavity should be free of other pathology such as fibroids, polyps, endometrial hyperplasia, or premalignant conditions that may be the source of abnormal bleeding. Success with expanded indications for endometrial resection in the management of intractable uterine bleeding has been reported by many authors.[7–10]

PREOPERATIVE CONSIDERATIONS

Diagnostic Hysteroscopy and Endometrial Sampling

In addition to a thorough history and physical examination, diagnostic hysteroscopy and endometrial sampling should be performed during the preoperative period. Hysteroscopy is likely to be more valuable than blind curettage in evaluating patients with abnormal uterine bleeding.[1,2,11] By performing hysteroscopy, one is frequently able to identify polyps and submucous myomas that were missed by blind D&C. Also, diagnostic hysteroscopy yields information regarding the size and contour of the uterine cavity. Endometrial sampling can be performed at the time of hysteroscopy to rule out a hyperplastic, malignant, or premalignant condition.

Laboratory Evaluation

Before surgery, one should obtain a baseline complete blood count. All other laboratory tests that are obtained should be based on the patient's underlying medical condition. Relevant laboratory tests may include electrocardiogram, chest radiograph, coagulation profile, and electrolyte status, which can be altered if an excessive amount of distending medium is absorbed.

Patient Counseling

As with all surgical procedures, appropriate preoperative counseling and discussion about the risks, benefits, alternatives, and complications of the procedure must take place. The patient must understand and have realistic expectations of the procedure. Amenorrhea has been reported to range from 30 to 67 percent.[12–14] In general, it appears that 40 to 50 percent of patients will develop amenorrhea and that 40 to 50 percent of patients will have a significant reduction in their menstrual flow. Overall, success of the procedure is approximately 90 percent.[6] Realistically, if the patient's priority and expectation are that of complete amenorrhea, she may be better served with hysterectomy. Similarly, if pain is a significant component of

the overall clinical picture, it is unlikely to improve if it is secondary to adenomyosis or uterine fibroids. Nevertheless, pelvic discomfort and other related premenstrual symptoms may improve.[15,16] The patient must also accept that sterilization will likely occur as a result of the procedure, although it is by no means ensured. Pregnancy has been reported after ablation.[17] Concomitant laparoscopic sterilization can be offered to those individuals at risk for pregnancy. Finally, one must acknowledge that the procedure is relatively new and that long-term data regarding the success of the procedure are lacking.

Endometrial Preparation

Successful ablation involves irreversible destruction of the entire basal layer of the endometrium. Operating in the early proliferative phase or preparing the uterus either chemically or mechanically to create a thin atrophic lining can help to improve the likelihood of a successful ablation. The most common chemical agents used have been the progestins, danazol, or gonadotropin-releasing hormone (GnRH) agonists. In comparing the agents, GnRH agonist appears to offer advantages in terms of effectiveness and acceptable drug side effects.[18,19] With the administration of the long-acting GnRH agonist, compliance is not an issue. After a single intramuscular injection, one can schedule surgery to follow in 4 to 6 weeks. Also, the drug-induced amenorrhea that frequently occurs can improve a preoperative anemia that has developed secondary to the abnormal bleeding. Alternatively, mechanical preparation of the endometrium has also been shown to be equally effective in thinning the endometrial lining immediately before surgery and avoids the costs and timing issues associated with medical suppression. A 6- or 7-mm suction curette rapidly denudes the lining after 3 to 5 minutes.[20,21]

Distention Media

Electrosurgical endometrial ablation requires the use of nonelectrolyte distending media to achieve panoramic visualization and appropriate current conduction. Liquid media consists of two types: low viscosity and high viscosity.

The most frequently used low-viscosity media include sorbitol, dextrose 5 percent, or glycine 1.5 percent. These media can be simply administered via a gravity-fed system, raising a 5-L bag of solution above the patient's head. Additional distending pressure can be provided by insufflating a blood administration bag to produce 100 mmHg pressure around the bag. The availability, low cost, and low maintenance of these media make them attractive to use. Unfortunately, the low-viscosity media are easily miscible with water, and if significant bleeding occurs, visualization becomes markedly impaired. Technical advances have helped to overcome the visibility problems that occur with bleeding. Fluid can now be more rapidly instilled and removed from the endometrial cavity with the combined use of a hysteroscopic pump and a two-channel continuous-flow hysteroscope. These operative hysteroscopes have separate inflow and outflow ports that allow the uterine cavity to be extensively flushed with fluid so that blood and small debris are cleared from the operative field (Fig. 23-1 and 23-2). Also, the outflow channel allows one to more easily keep accurate assessment of fluid balance; otherwise, problems with excessive absorption of fluid media can develop. Most surgeons now prefer to use low-viscous media for their operative procedures.

For those surgeons who prefer the high-viscosity media, 32 percent dextran-70 (Hyskon) is a clear non-conductive medium that provides excellent visualization throughout the surgery because it does not mix easily with blood. Hyskon can be simply administered

via a hand-held 50-ml syringe. Unfortunately, the highly viscous nature of the Hyskon requires that the instruments be thoroughly cleaned immediately after the procedure to prevent crystallization from occurring. High temperatures can also result in carmelization of the medium.

TECHNIQUE

A typical operating room set up is illustrated in Figure 23-3. A good light source, video camera, and gynecologic continuous-flow hysteroscope are necessary. If a nonelectrolyte low-viscous medium is used, a perineal drape or buttock drape is placed beneath the patient so that the distending media escaping around the cervical os can be retrieved. Allowing the outflow port of the hysteroscope to drain into a calibrated container is also helpful in obtaining a complete collection of fluid return. Accurate assessment of the net amount of fluid absorbed is crucial to avoiding fluid-related complications. If Hyskon is used, volumes greater than 300 ml should generally not be used.

The procedure was initially described using the 90-degree wire loop electrode to resect the endometrial lining.[3] Although this technique remains the preferred

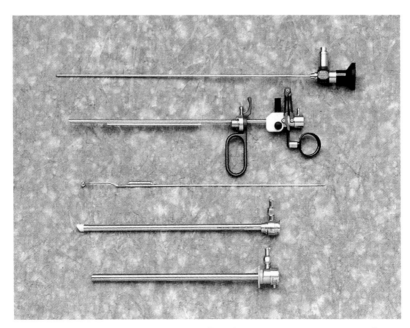

Fig. 23-1. Components of a two-channel continuous-flow hysteroscope. From top to bottom: hysteroscope, working component, ball electrode, inner sheath, outer sheath.

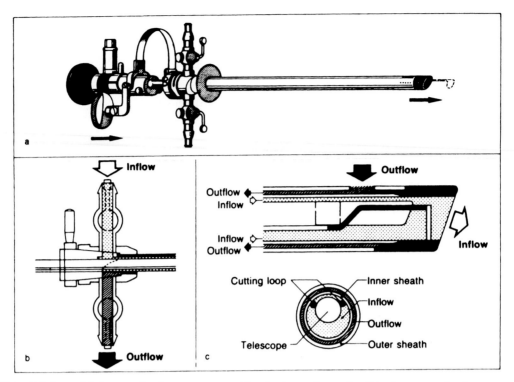

Fig. 23-2. (A) Assembled operative hysteroscope with wire loop electrode; **(B)** schematic of inflow and outflow ports; **(C)** longitudinal and cross-sectional views of operative hysteroscope. The inner sheath contains the scope, electrode, and lumen for the inflow of distending media. Fluid outflow occurs between the inner and outer sheath. (From Indman,[42] with permission.)

method in Great Britain, it generally requires a higher level of technical skill; otherwise, irregular troughs and ridges will result. Also, there is an increased risk of uterine perforation because the electrode can deeply invade the myometrium with an aggressive resection. In the United States, the electrode most commonly used is the 2-mm "rollerball" (Fig. 23-4). The ball has a much larger surface area than the wire loop electrode, and technically, it is easier to use. The electrosurgical unit is set at 50 to 100 W cutting or coagulating current. With the tip of the hysteroscope placed in center of the endometrial cavity, the rollerball is slowly extended. One should not extend the electrode when it is at the fundus because it can lead to inadvertent perforation. The ball is initially pressed into the posterior uterine wall and the electrode slowly retracted as the current is applied. The surgeon should keep the ball in view at all times as the ablation is proceeding. As the ball rolls along the endometrial surface, it may be necessary at times to sharply angle the hysteroscope upward or downward to maintain contact with the endometrial surface. Continuous contact is crucial to achieving effective thermal injury. One can expect to see bubbling

of the media as the lining is ablated. A shallow crater will develop, and it should be inspected. Thermal injury is considered adequate when the borders of the crater have been carbonized and the crater itself has a yellow-brownish hue (Fig. 23-5). The wattage should be adjusted until the desired results are achieved.

Having established the appropriate energy level, the uterine cavity is "painted" in a systematic fashion. The uterus is ablated in thirds: upper fundal, midportion, and lower uterus. Beginning at the right tubal ostium, work across the fundus to the left ostium. Diligence is necessary when cauterizing the ostial region because the uterus is relatively thin at this level. It can also be technically difficult to gain access to this area to achieve an effective ablation at times. Inadequate ablation will leave islands of residual tissue that can lead to significant bleeding and resulting treatment failure. The midportion of the uterus should be ablated at its anterior, posterior, and lateral regions followed by a similar systematic ablation of the lower portion of the uterus down to the level of the internal cervical os. Carbon deposits or tissue debris that develop on the ball surface should be wiped away because they have an

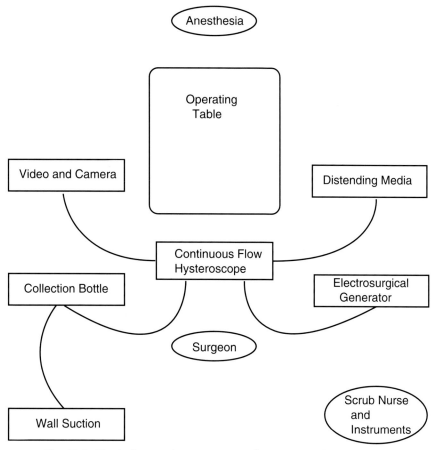

Fig. 23-3. Typical operating room setup for operative hysteroscopy.

adverse impact on the transmission of energy. Once the entire endometrium has been covered, the cavity should be closely inspected, and any area appearing inadequately treated should have the electrode reapplied.

A "rollerbar" has also been used that has even greater surface contact with the uterus than the 2-mm rollerball. Increasing the surface contact area can result in an even more rapid rate of ablation, but it may be necessary to increase the energy level. Close inspection

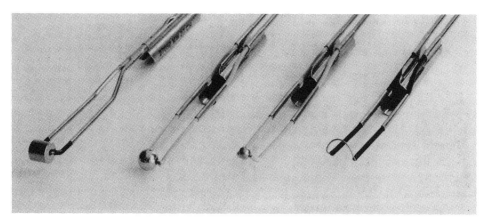

Fig. 23-4. Frequently used electrode tips: "roller" bar, large ball, small ball, and 90 degree wire loop. (From Indman,[42] with permission.)

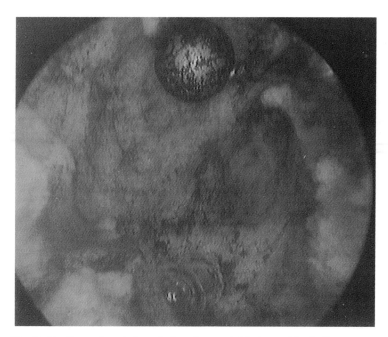

Fig. 23-5. Charred and denuded endometrial lining with shallow crater.

of the crater will again determine the appropriate power setting.

RESULTS

Generally, treatment has been considered successful if the patient has become amenorrheic or has had a significant reduction in abnormal uterine bleeding. The overall success of the procedure as previously mentioned is approximately 90 percent. Although these results are encouraging, long-term studies are lacking. Success with the procedure also appears to be age-related. Abnormal uterine bleeding is more likely to persist in the younger premenopausal patient. As one might expect, amenorrhea rates are highest among patients older than age 50.[22,23] One may also theorize that delayed bleeding, occurring several years after the procedure, would also be more likely to develop in the younger patients than in those women who are peri- or postmenopausal at the time of their ablation procedure.

Randomized trials comparing endometrial resection and abdominal hysterectomy for the treatment of menorrhagia have demonstrated shorter operating time and hospital stay and decreased initial cost. Overall recovery time has been decreased, as suggested by reduced time taken to return to work, to return to normal daily activities, and to return to sexual intercourse.[24–26] Interestingly, endometrial ablation has not necessarily resulted in higher patient satisfaction rates when compared with abdominal hysterectomy in patients evaluated 4 months after their respective surgery. There was a 10 percent immediate failure rate, and symptoms of dysmenorrhea, bloating, and breast tenderness seemed greater in the ablation group.[24] Additional randomized long-term trials are needed to better evaluate the role of endometrial ablation as an alternative to abdominal or vaginal hysterectomy.

COMPLICATIONS

Operative hysteroscopy is generally a safe procedure. In a survey of operative hysteroscopy involving more than 170,000 cases, the overall complication rate was approximately 2.5 percent.[26] Nevertheless, acute and late complications can occur involving distending media, hemorrhage, infection, internal organ injury, recurrent bleeding, or the development of endometrial cancer. Diligence and knowledge on the part of the surgeon are necessary to appropriately treat or perhaps to avoid them altogether.

Distending Media

Use of Hyskon has been associated with significant complications including anaphylaxis, disseminated intravascular coagulation, adult respiratory distress syndrome, and noncardiogenic pulmonary edema.[27–29] With the use of Hyskon, one is most likely to have difficulty related to its ability to act as a volume expander. Hyskon is highly viscous, and when it enters the venous system through intrauterine vascular channels, this medium can pull in up to 10 times its volume into the intravascular space. The surgeon and anesthesiologist must be fully aware of this fact and monitor the patient for the signs and symptoms of pulmonary congestion. These symptoms may develop either intraoperatively or in a delayed fashion in the recovery room area. Accurate monitoring of the amount of Hyskon used and limiting instillations so that less than 300 ml of the medium is absorbed appears to diminish the risk of complications.[30] Although anaphylaxis is rare, intravenous injection of dextran 15 percent 2 minutes before using Hyskon can possibly prevent its occurrence.[31] Realistically, the risk of this complications is so uncommon that this precaution is not routine. If there are significant concerns regarding a possible reaction to Hyskon, it would be more prudent to use the low-viscous media.

Excess absorption of the low-viscous media can result in cardiopulmonary complications developing from volume overload. Also, absorption of large volumes of fluid can also lead to water intoxication, with resultant hyperglycemia or hyponatremia.[32] Early treatment of severe hyponatremia is recommended to prevent acute seizures or respiratory arrest. Should hyponatremia be recognized relatively late (24 to 48 hours postoperatively), correction should be performed gradually. Too rapid correction can result in a demyelinating brain injury. Central pontine myelinolysis occurs as a result of the brain's response to changes in serum osmolarity. Several neurologic findings can develop, including paresis, mutism, pseudobulbar palsy, behavioral changes, and movement disorders.[33] To avoid this problem, as mentioned above, use of a perineal or buttock drape to capture the outflow volume is crucial. The amount of fluid recovered can then be subtracted from the amount of fluid instilled every 15 to 20 minutes to determine the amount of fluid being absorbed. Absorption of more than 1,000 ml of fluid should generally be avoided. Even lesser amounts may be poorly tolerated if the patient's underlying medical status is poor. Discrepancies of more than 1 L of fluid should prompt assessment of the patient's electrolyte status. Appropriate diuretic use or fluid restriction is instituted if evidence of excess fluid absorption is noted. Use of lower intrauterine distending pressures may also help to prevent significant fluid absorption.[34]

Uterine Perforation

Perforation of the uterus is the most common complication resulting from operative hysteroscopy, occurring at a rate of 11.1 per 1,000 cases.[26] Fortunately, most perforations do not result in serious injury but generally require that the surgery be discontinued and may necessitate laparoscopy to rule out traumatic injury to internal organs. Perforation during dilation of the cervix frequently does not result in significant bleeding. If necessary, bleeding at the uterine perforation site can often be controlled with laparoscopic bipolar coagulation. Expanding broad-ligament hematomas require control either by laparoscopy or by laparotomy, with careful identification of the ureter before ligation of uterine vessels. Use of cervical laminaria preoperatively will help to decrease the likelihood of perforation. Usually, not more than one laminaria tent is necessary; otherwise, excess dilation results in difficulty with uterine distention as fluid is rapidly loss around the os. If difficulty is encountered with uterine distention, the possibility of uterine perforation should also be considered. Other techniques that may help to reduce the risk of perforation include advancing the resectoscope only with the tip under direct visualization and ablating the endometrium only as the resectoscope tip is being retracted. Finally, the surgeon should have a low threshold for performing concomitant laparoscopy if there is any question of uterine perforation with active bleeding or organ injury. On occasion, concomitant laparoscopic guidance during the ablation may be helpful in avoiding inadvertent perforation.

Bleeding

With the use of the ball-end electrodes, bleeding complications have been uncommon. If a specific site of bleeding is visualized, coagulation can be attempted; otherwise, intrauterine tamponade with a balloon catheter has generally been successful. After the catheter is placed in the uterine cavity, it is inflated with 10 to 30 ml of fluid and can be left overnight if necessary.

Bowel Injury

Unrecognized uterine perforation followed by the use of electrosurgery can cause thermal bowel injury. Overall, the risk of bowel injury with rollerball ablation is small because the relative thickness of the myometrium provides a safe barrier to the transmission of heat. Thermocouples applied to the uterine serosa during ablation procedures have shown only a modest rise in the uterine serosa temperature even with a relatively prolonged and high energy current.[35] Nevertheless, even in the absence of uterine perforation, care must be taken to evaluate symptoms suggestive of bowel injury that have occurred after an uneventful ablation.[36]

Endometrial Cancer

There has always been concern that endometrial ablation may delay the diagnosis of endometrial cancer until the disease has become advanced. Theoretically, the ablation procedure could cause intrauterine synechiae that would prevent the outflow of blood that heralds the onset of hyperplasia or malignancy. Furthermore, the patient who is obese, hypertensive, and diabetic with a compromised cardiovascular status may, in fact, be the best candidate for the less invasive surgery that endometrial ablation provides to treat her abnormal uterine bleeding. At the same time, this is the patient profile for an individual who is also at increased risk for the development of endometrial cancer. Also, despite preablation endometrial biopsies that have revealed "benign" or "inactive endometrium," tissue obtained at that time of mechanical preparation of the endometrium has revealed hyperplasia with atypia.[37] Similarly, an incidental finding of endometrial carcinoma after endometrial ablation performed by the resection technique has been reported despite preoperative hysteroscopy and D&C showing a normal cavity with normal secretory endometrium.[38] It is not surprising then that endometrial cancer has been reported occurring 5 years after the initial endometrial ablation procedure.[39] Given the very real possibility of malignancy developing after the ablation procedure, emphasis must be placed on the persistent evaluation and surveillance of bleeding that occurs after the procedure, whether it be immediate or delayed. Also, women who are placed on hormone replacement therapy after a successful ablation procedure should not be assumed to have complete destruction of the endometrial glands even if they are amenorrheic. They should be treated with both an estrogen and progestin because islands of endometrium may have escaped ablation. Residual endometrial tissue can also exist deep within the myometrium as pockets of adenomyosis out of the reach of the resectoscope.

Treatment Failures

As mentioned previously, approximately 10 percent of patients undergoing endometrial ablation fail to have significant improvement of their bleeding. Failure rates may even be greater as more patients are fol-

lowed over time. These patients should have appropriate re-evaluation of their bleeding that could include hysteroscopic and pathologic investigation as well as review of their symptoms and expectations of surgery. After the appropriate information has been gathered, the surgeon can then discuss additional treatment options, which could include hormonal therapy, a second ablation procedure, or hysterectomy. Experience with repeat ablation procedures has generally been favorable.[8,12,40]

Infection

Infectious complications of operative hysteroscopy are generally rare. If endometritis develops, it can generally be treated on an outpatient basis. It is unclear whether routine antibiotic prophylaxis is necessary. Individuals with a previous history of pelvic inflammatory disease, however, are likely to benefit from prophylactic therapy as tubo-ovarian abscesses have occurred in this setting. Doxycycline appears to be effective in reducing the risk of infection in those individuals who have a history of pelvic inflammatory disease.[41]

CONCLUSIONS

In those individuals with persistent abnormal uterine bleeding, endometrial ablation may offer both surgeons and patients a favorable alternative to hysterectomy. Patients who have a relative contraindication to major abdominal surgery perhaps are most suited to the procedure because it is less invasive, requires less anesthesia and operating time, and provides a relatively rapid recovery. However, it is less clear whether ablation offers a clear-cut advantage to those patients who would otherwise have no significant contraindications to hysterectomy. Preliminary results would suggest a relatively high rate of patient satisfaction with ablation, but not necessarily greater than compared with patients undergoing abdominal hysterectomy. Clearly, the failure rates are higher in younger patients in terms of bleeding and control of dysmenorrhea. Also, the rare but real risk of developing endometrial cancer remains that would otherwise be eliminated. Long-term studies are needed to document the real efficacy, safety, and cost-effectiveness of the procedure. Nevertheless, the procedure will always have its appeal to those individuals wishing to avoid hysterectomy for those reasons cited above or simply because the procedure preserves the uterus. Therefore, it is important that an effective dialogue takes place between the patient and physician so that a realistic expectation and understanding of the procedure occurs when endometrial ablation is the procedure elected over traditional hysterectomy.

REFERENCES

1. Loffer FD: Hysteroscopy with selective endometrial sampling compared with D&C for abnormal uterine bleeding: the value of a negative view. Obstet Gynecol 73:16, 1989
2. Gimpleson RJ: Panoramic hysteroscopy with directed biopsies vs. dilatation and curettage for accurate diagnosis. J Reprod Med 29:575, 1984
3. DeCherney AH, Polan ML: Hysteroscopic management of intrauterine lesions and intractable uterine bleeding. Obstet Gynecol 61:392, 1983
4. DeCherney AH, Diamond MP, Lavy G et al: Endometrial ablation for intractable uterine bleeding: hysteroscopic resection. Obstet Gynecol 70:668, 1987
5. Goldrath MH, Fuller TA, Segal S: Laser photovaporization of the endometrium for the treatment of menorrhagia. Am J Obstet Gynecol 140:14, 1981
6. Taylor PJ: Hysteroscopy: where have we been, where are we going? J Reprod Med 38:757, 1993
7. Serden SP, Brooks PG: Treatment of abnormal uterine bleeding with the gynecologic resectoscope. J Reprod Med 36:697, 1991
8. Wortman M, Daggett A: Hysteroscopic management of intractable uterine bleeding: a review of 103 cases. J Reprod Med 38:505, 1993
9. Wood C: Indications for endometrial resection. Med J Aust 156:157, 1992
10. Indman PD: Hysteroscopic treatment of menorrhagia associated with uterine leiyomyomas. Obstet Gynecol 81:716, 1993
11. Valle RF: Hysteroscopic evaluation of patients with abnormal uterine bleeding. Surg Gynecol Obstet 153:521, 1981
12. Daniell JF, Kurtz BR, Ke RW: Hysteroscopic ablation using the rollerball electrode. Obstet Gynecol 80:329, 1992
13. Vancaille TG: Electrocoagulation of the endometrium with the ball-end resectoscope. Obstet Gynecol 74:425, 1989
14. McLucas B: Endometrial ablation with the roller ball electrode. J Reprod Med 35:1055, 1990
15. Lefler HT, Lefler CF: Ablation of the endometrium: three year follow up for perimenstrual symptoms. J Reprod Med 37:147, 1992
16. Lefler HT, Lefler CF: Endometrial ablation: improvement in PMS related to the decrease in bleeding. J Reprod Med 37:596, 1992
17. Mongelli JM, Evans AJ: Pregnancy after transcervical endometrial resection. Lancet 338:578, 1991
18. Brooks PG, Serden SP, Davos I: Hormonal inhibition of the endometrium for resectoscopic endometrial ablation. Am J Obstet Gynecol 164:1601, 1991
19. Serden SP, Brooks PG: Preoperative therapy in preparation for endometrial ablation. J Reprod Med 37:679, 1992
20. Gimpelson RJ, Kaigh J: Mechanical preparation of the endometrium prior to endometrial ablation. J Reprod Med 37:691, 1992
21. Lefler HT, Sullivan GH, Hulka JF: Modified endometrial ablation: electrocoagulation with vasopressin and suction curettage preparation. Obstet Gynecol 77:949, 1991
22. Daniell JF: Endometrial ablation. p. 173. In Azziz R, Murphy AA (eds): Practical Manual of Operative Laparoscopy and Hysteroscopy. Springer-Verlag, New York, 1992
23. Brooks PG, Serden SP: Endometrial ablation in women with abnormal uterine bleeding aged fifty and over. J Reprod Med 37:682, 1992
24. Dwyer N, Hutton J, Strirrat G: Randomised controlled trial comparing endometrial resection with abdominal hysterectomy for the surgical treatment of menorrhagia. Br J Obstet Gynaecol 100:237, 1993
25. Gannon M, Holt EM, Fairbank J et al: A randomised trial comparing endometrial resection and abdominal hysterectomy for treatment of menorrhagia. BMJ 303:1362, 1991
26. Sculpher MJ, Bryan S, Dwyer N et al: An economic evaluation of transcervical endometrial resection versus abdominal hysterectomy for the treatment of menorrhagia. Br J Obstet Gynaecol 100:244, 1993
26. Hulka JF, Peterson HB, Phillips JM et al: Operative hysteroscopy. American Association of Gynecologic Laparoscopists 1991 membership survey. J Reprod Med 38:572, 1993
27. Ahmed N, Falcone T, Tulandi T et al: Anaphylactic reaction because of intrauterine 32% dextran–70 installation. Fertil Steril 55:1014, 1991
28. Jedeikin R, Olsfanger D: Disseminated intravascular coagulation and adult respiratory distress syndrome: life threatening complications of hysteroscopy. Am J Obstet Gynecol 162:44, 1990
29. Zbella EA, Moise J, Carson SA: Noncardiogenic pulmonary edema secondary to intrauterine instillation of 32% dextran 70. Fertil Steril 43:479, 1985
30. McLucas B: Intrauterine applications of the resectoscope. Surg Gynecol Obstet 172:425, 1991
31. Brooks PG: Complications of operative hysteroscopy. Clin Obstet Gynecol 35:256, 1992
32. Carson SA, Hubert GD, Schriock ED et al: Hyperglycemia and hyponatremia during operative hysteroscopy with 5% dextrose in water distention. Fertil Steril 51:341, 1989
33. Witz CA, Silverberg KM, Burns WN et al: Complications associated with the absorption of hysteroscopic fluid media. Fertil Steril 60:745, 1993
34. Hasham F, Garry R, Kokri MS et al: Fluid absorption, during laser ablation of the endometrium in the treatment of menorrhagia. Br J Anaesth 68:154, 1992
35. Indman PD, Brown WW III: Uterine surface changes caused by electrosurgical endometrial coagulation. J Reprod Med 37:667, 1992
36. Kivnik S, Kanter MH: Bowel injury from rollerball ablation of the endometrium. Obstet Gynecol 79:833, 1992
37. Gimpelson RJ, Lentz RD: Endometrial ablation. A report of four cases. J Reprod Med 38:592, 1993
38. Dwyer NA, Stirrat GM: Early endometrial carcinoma: an incidental finding after endometrial resection. Case report. Br J Obstet Gynaecol 98:733, 1991
39. Cooperman AB, DeCherney AD, Olive DL: A case of endometrial cancer following endometrial ablation for dysfunctional uterine bleeding. Obstet Gynecol 82:640, 1993
40. Gimpelson RJ, Kaigh J: Endometrial ablation repeat procedures. Case studies. J Reprod Med 37:629, 1992
41. McCausland VM, Fields GA, McCausland AM et al: Tuboovarian abscesses after operative hysteroscopy. J Reprod Med 38:198, 1993
42. Indman PD: Instruments and video cameras for operative hysteroscopy. Clin Obstet Gynecol 35:211, 1992

24 Laser Endometrial Ablation

J. M. LOMANO

ASHERMAN SYNDROME

Asherman syndrome was first described in 1948.[1] The syndrome most commonly involves traumatic uterine synechia causing amenorrhea, hypomenorrhea, and secondary infertility. Histologic evaluation of the affected uteri shows a destruction of the mucosal lining, as well as fibrous adhesions between the myometrial walls. Hysterectomy is one of the most commonly performed major operations in the United States, and many hysterectomies are performed for indications of excessive uterine bleeding. There is a need for a conservative method to control chronic menorrhagia.

The procedure of endometrial ablation with neodymium:yttrium-aluminum-garnet (Nd:YAG) laser was first described by Dr. Milton Goldrath in 1981.[2] Many investigators had tried various chemical and physical methods of destroying the endometrium. The Nd:YAG laser is the most appropriate method of creating destruction of the uterine lining cells because of the inherent forward scatter of the Nd:YAG laser energy as it interacts with the surface of the endometrium. Two components to Asherman syndrome are necessary to produce intrauterine synechia. There must be some form of trauma to the endometrial lining cells in combination with the hypoestrogen state. Asherman syndrome is most commonly seen after abortion or pregnancy when the genital tissues are atrophic. The source of tissue trauma in naturally occurring Asherman syndrome is very often a vigorous postpartum dilation and curettage (D&C) or a significant endometritis.

Many investigators have attempted to create an Asherman syndrome with various chemical and physical means. Iatrogenic tissue trauma has failed in the past to create Asherman syndrome for two reasons. One, there were significant complications with reflux of materials into the fallopian tubes, resulting in significant salpingitis and peritonitis. The second reason is the tremendous capacity of the endometrium to regenerate itself. There must be a *complete* destruction of the basalis layer of the endometrium to have an Asherman syndrome. An incomplete Asherman syndrome results in hypomenorrhea and scant menstrual cycles because of cyclic bleeding of small tufts of regenerated endometrial tissue.

Approximately 750,000 hysterectomies are performed annually in the United States. It is estimated that 20 to 30 percent of these hysterectomies result in some type of morbidity. This morbidity is most often minor febrile morbidity treated successfully with modern antibiotic therapy. However, 600 women die annually as a complication of hysterectomy. Because of the large number of hysterectomies, the procedure consumes vast amounts of health care dollars. It is estimated that 30 to 40 percent of all hysterectomies are performed due to some type of abnormal uterine bleeding. Certainly, if a minor, less complex procedure to treat refractory menorrhagia could be found, a considerable amount of morbidity, mortality, and health care dollars would be saved. The procedure of laser endometrial ablation has been developed as an alternative to hysterectomy in patients with chronic refractory menorrhagia.

MEDICAL LASERS

When energy is applied to an atom, the electrons orbiting that atom jump to a higher energy level. This unstable condition lasts a very short time and when the electron returns to the ground state, a photon packet of energy is emitted. If the photons hit other unstable atoms, additional photons will be emitted.

Laser energy light amplified by stimulated emission of radiation is collimated and parallel, which minimizes divergence of the transmitted light. Moreover, it is coherent (all waves are in phase) and monochromatic (one color only is emitted from the tube).

Four major medical lasers are on the market today. The CO_2 laser is an infrared wavelength of 10,600 nm. Its effect on biologic tissue is independent of color, and it is instantly absorbed by water with minimal scattering into body tissues. The argon laser produces a visible blue-green light at a wavelength of 488 to 515 nm. It is easily transmitted through clear liquid, as well as fiberoptic systems. Argon laser energy is absorbed by water. The potassium titanyl-phosphate (KTP) crystal emits a wavelength of 532 nm in the blue-green range. Like the argon laser, it can be transmitted fiberoptically and is absorbed by water. However, the Nd:YAG laser is a solid crystal of yttrium, aluminum, and garnet, surrounded by neodymium. The Nd:YAG laser light is in the near infrared region with a wavelength of 1,064 nm. This laser can be transmitted through clear liquids as well as fiberoptic systems and is an excellent coagulator because of its forward scatter. As it strikes human tissue, it is selectively absorbed by any tissue with color. Because of this forward scatter, the Nd:YAG laser is the most valuable laser in creating destruction of the endometrium when compared with the other medical lasers.

PATIENT SELECTION

Patients with chronic refractory menometrorrhagia that have not responded to surgical D&C and hysteroscopy or hormone manipulation with progesterone and androgenic medical therapy become candidates for laser endometrial ablation. It is a conservative procedure designed to benefit the 30 to 40 percent of women who would otherwise undergo hysterectomy for chronic menorrhagia. The goal is to sufficiently reduce the amount of menstrual flow to eliminate the need for a major surgical procedure. Candidates usually have a long history of dysfunctional uterine bleeding. Many will have already undergone multiple D&C procedures, as well as variations of hormone regimens, to control their heavy flow.

Other women who may benefit from laser ablation are those classified as "high-risk" surgical patients because of major medical problems (i.e., cardiac and pulmonary disorders, severe pelvic adhesive disease coagulopathies, or obesity). These medically handicapped patients may be considered poor surgical candidates for a major operative procedure. This often requires bed rest and decreased ambulation, which can result in postoperative complications.

Laser ablation is not appropriate for premalignant or neoplastic lesions of the endometrium because patients with chronic menometrorrhagia are at high risk for endometrial cancer. It is necessary that candidates for this procedure have a benign endometrial sampling within 6 months before the procedure. It is also important that these patients be closely monitored for the potential development of endometrial carcinoma or endometrial hyperplasia after the ablation. Because the cervix remains open after the procedure, patients with endometrial neoplasia will most likely present with menometrorrhagia, which would signal the physician to do an endometrial sampling to rule out neoplastic disease.

Also, patients with a recent pregnancy or active pelvic inflammatory disease should be excluded as candidates for endometrial ablation. Because of the postoperative intrauterine scarring and subsequent Asherman syndrome created by the laser, patients must be willing to accept sterility after the procedure. Postoperative sampling of the endometrial cavity will show low cuboidal epithelium with surrounding fibrosis and rare endometrial glands. Even though this is not compatible with normal implantation, patients must be counseled in regard to postoperative birth control measures, as pregnancies have been reported.

The preoperative evaluation should begin with a pelvic examination to confirm relatively normal anatomy. Patients with large myomata (greater than 16 weeks' size), and patients with adnexal enlargement are not considered to be candidates for endometrial ablation. An office hysteroscopy and endometrial biopsy should be performed to rule out the presence of significant submucous myomas, endometrial hyperplasia, and other pathologic conditions that would preclude ablation. If a submucous fibroid occupies more than one-half of the uterine cavity, it is best approached with an abdominal incision. Submucous fibroids occupying less than one-half of the volume of the uterine cavity can be approached hysteroscopically with the Nd:YAG laser. The myomas are transected with the YAG laser using a contact method until the entire myoma is removed down to the level of its attachment to the uterine myometrium. Patients with myomas that occupy more than one-half the volume of the uterine cavity can be given a trial of leuprolide acetate (depo-Lupron) for 3 months to shrink the size of the fibroid. Many depo-Lupron-treated patients will become candidates for a hysteroscopic myomectomy after treatment.

ENDOMETRIAL PREPARATION

Because one of the components of Asherman syndrome is an atrophic endometrium, most surgeons prefer to prepare the endometrium before proceeding with YAG laser treatment. Goldrath and colleagues have recommended Danazol 400 mg twice daily for 4 weeks before the proposed surgery. This creates a thin atrophic endometrium, exposing the basal regenerative layer of the endometrium 4 to 5 mm below the surface. This is the layer that the YAG laser energy must penetrate to ensure a complete Asherman syndrome. YAG laser energy dispersed at 40 to 60 W of power will result in a penetration of the endometrium from 4 to 6 mm in depth. It therefore becomes imperative that the endometrium be less than 6 mm in thickness.

Other investigators have elected to use one of the gonadotropin-releasing hormone (GnRH) agonists to create the atrophic state of Asherman syndrome. These drugs operate at the level of the pituitary gland to suppress follicle-stimulating hormone and luteinizing hormone activity. This results in a hypoestrogen state with regression of the endometrium and atrophy consistent with Asherman syndrome. It has been found that GnRH agonists require an additional 2 weeks of therapy to obtain an equivalent suppression to Danocrine therapy. Intramuscular (depo-Lupron), leuprolide acetate given at a dosage of 3.75 mg 6 weeks before surgery and a second equivalent dosage 2 weeks before surgery provides sufficient atrophy of the endometrium to complete a laser ablation of the endometrium. It is helpful to give the depo-Lupron on day 21 of the cycle to prevent the surge of gonadotropin from the pituitary gland.

Although most patients on GnRH agonist therapy will complain of mild hot flashes, these complaints are usually not sufficient to discontinue therapy. Patients on Danocrine have very few side effects because the drug is only used for a 4-week period. Most of the androgenic side effects of Danocrine commence 6 to 8 weeks after initiation of therapy. Both of these drugs are relatively well tolerated by patients. Expense can be a significant factor for those who have limited financial resources. There is no scientific evidence that other drugs may be equally effective in producing en-

dometrial atrophy. There are sporadic reports of use of intramuscular medroxyprogesterone (Depoprovera), as well as progestin-dominated birth control pills for endometrial preparation. Also, it is possible that the atrophic component of Asherman syndrome might not be an absolute prerequisite to destruction of the endometrium. It is possible that YAG laser energy could be applied to the endometrium during the early proliferative stage of the cycle. This could result in significant penetration of the endometrium in the basalis layer. There is a definite need for ongoing prospective studies to determine the degree of uterine synechia as it relates to various types of preparation of the endometrium.

PROCEDURE

The prerequisites to the performance of endometrial ablation are basic understanding of the mechanics and physics of the Nd:YAG laser, along with the surgical skills of an accomplished hysteroscopist. Proper operative equipment is vital to the success of the procedure. The system must allow for adequate uterine distention, irrigation, and drainage of the operative site. The irrigation system should create optimal visualization during the surgery that will enhance the safety of the procedure. Hysteroscopy can be accomplished through a video camera or by direct vision through the lens of the operating telescope. The surgeon may select a beam splitter, which will allow for direct visualization by the surgeon, while a portion of the light is transferred to a television video monitor, allowing other members of the operating team to view the procedure.

Endometrial ablation is an outpatient surgical procedure. After induction with general anesthesia, the patient is prepared for hysteroscopy. Regional anesthetics can be used for those patients who do not tolerate general anesthesia. Paracervical anesthesia has been found to be unacceptable to most patients. The cervix is grasped with a double-tooth tenaculum and dilated significantly to allow the hysteroscope to advance through the cervical canal. A system of "overdilation" (Fig. 24-1) of the cervix is preferred to allow the egress of the distending media to flow around the hysteroscope, over the posterior weighted retractor, and finally into a plastic collecting drapery. The fluid flows to standard suction canisters, which are used to continuously record the amount of fluid that is returned from the patient. Simple subtraction of the amount of fluid recovered in these canisters from the amount of fluid used to distend the uterine cavity reflects the amount of fluid the patient has absorbed intravascu-

Fig. 24-1. Overdilation of the cervix allows for the flow of the distending media to pass around the hysteroscope and into a plastic collecting drapery.

larly. A gravity flow system that results in 75 to 100 mmHg pressure to distend the uterine cavity is preferred. It is important that the surgeon select the larger arthroscopic tubing to obtain these pressures. Irrigation pumps add a significant expense to the procedure with no measurable improvement in visualization of the uterine cavity.

The distending media for endometrial ablation should be a balanced electrolyte solution such as normal saline or Ringer's lactate. Hypotonic solutions such as 5 percent dextrose and water can be absorbed intravenously, resulting in electrolyte disturbance in the patient. High-viscosity dextran solutions should not be used in operative hysteroscopy because of the potential for intravenous absorption and secondary allergic reaction or fluid overload.

After inspection of the uterine cavity, a 600- to 1,000-μg fiberoptic strand is passed through the operating channel of the hysteroscope and attached to a Nd:YAG laser with a power setting of 50 to 60 W in a continuous pattern. The laser energy is discharged as the fiber is directed at the endometrial lining. An Alberran's bridge is helpful in stabilizing the fiber tip (Fig. 24-2). Protective goggles must be worn by all personnel in the operating room to prevent retinal eye injury.

Endometrial ablation is performed under direct vision or through the video monitor. There is a slight loss of depth perception when using the video system compared with direct visualization through the telescope. The operating surgeon must be able to see the fiberoptic tip as well as the helium neon beam reflection onto the endometrium before firing the laser. Firing the laser while the fiberoptic tip is still in the distal end of the hysteroscope can result in significant damage to the lens system. The fiberoptic tip must never pass through the endometrium to avoid damage of the uterus and intra-abdominal organs. The endometrial surface is destroyed by systematically and continuously moving the hysteroscope in a triangular pattern so the endometrium is ablated down to the level of the internal cervical os. The ablation should begin at each cornual opening of the fallopian tubes. As the laser energy is discharged, the cornual openings will close as a direct result of tissue edema and muscular spasm. This closure is only temporary but does prevent the reflux of the distending media through the fallopian tubes into the peritoneal cavity. Once the cornual areas are

Fig. 24-2. Alberran's bridge supporting the laser fiber.

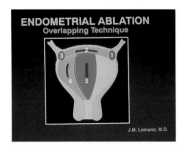

Fig. 24-3. Pattern of endometrial ablation.

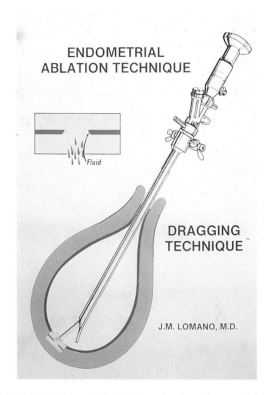

Fig. 24-4. Endometrial ablation: the dragging technique.

ablated, the surgeon should make a path connecting the two cornual areas and then continue the ablation along the sidewalls of the endometrial cavity (Fig. 24-3). The success of the procedure depends on the completeness of the ablative process. It is important that the surgeon proceed in a systematic fashion with slight overlapping of the paths of destruction as the lateral walls are ablated. Laser energy should not be discharged into the endocervical canal to avoid a cervical stenosis with subsequent hematometrium.

If significant bleeding is encountered during the procedure, the YAG laser energy can be discharged in a noncontact fashion to coagulate the bleeding vessel. If the YAG laser energy is insufficient to adequately control the uterine bleeding, the surgeon can place an intrauterine Foley catheter with a 50-ml balloon. Once the balloon is inserted into the uterine cavity and filled with normal saline, a downward traction should be placed to occlude the cervical os. The pressure of the bleeding vessel will eventually be surpassed by the distention pressure within the uterine cavity with resultant hemostasis. If the balloon becomes necessary for uncontrollable bleeding, the patient should be admitted overnight with removal of the catheter balloon the morning after surgery. She will have to return at a later date for the completion of the endometrial ablation.

DRAGGING VERSUS BLANCHING

The procedure of endometrial ablation originally reported by Dr. Milton Goldrath in 1981 and further documented by Lomano in 1986 and Dr. Frank Loffer in 1987 describes the dragging technique (Fig. 24-4). In the dragging technique, the Nd:YAG laser fiber is brought into direct contact with the endometrium while the laser energy is discharged in a continuous wave using 50 to 60 W power. The surgeon moves the hysteroscope in a back-and-forth motion as the instru-

ment is advanced from the fundus to the internal cervical os. The end point is a charred endometrium from thermal conduction of the YAG laser energy to the proteins of the endometrium. Using this technique, as the fiber cuts through endometrial blood vessels, bleeding into the endometrial cavity can be sufficient enough to obscure the visual field. Also, the open veins and arteries can conduct the distending fluid into the vascular system of the patient with a potential for fluid overload. Significant fluid overload in patients with a compromised cardiovascular system can lead to pulmonary edema and congestive heart failure.

The blanching technique (Fig. 24-5) described by Lomano and Loffer involves withdrawing the fiber 1 to 5 mm from the endometrial surface before firing the YAG laser energy. Using this technique, the surgeon uses an additional 10 W power and proceeds with a symmetric endometrial ablation down to the level of the internal cervical os. The end point of the blanching technique is a change in color from the normal tan to pink endometrium to that of a snow-white endometrium. As the YAG energy passes through the endometrial tissue, there is coaptation of the blood ves-

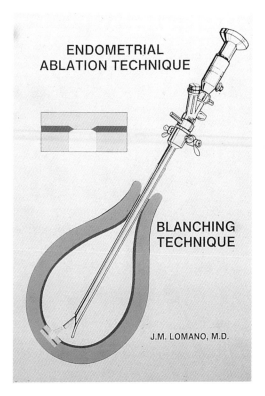

ENDOMETRIAL
ABLATION TECHNIQUE

BLANCHING
TECHNIQUE

J.M. LOMANO, M.D.

Fig. 24-5. Endometrial ablation: the blanching technique.

sels within the endometrium. This prevents bleeding into the distending media and prevents the distending media from entering into the patient's vascular system. Using the end point of charring in the dragging technique and the snow-white effect with the blanching technique, the surgeon maintains a consistent 4 to 6 mm of thermal necrosis of the endometrium.

The blanching technique avoids the problems of visual field clouding as well as fluid overload. It is, however, difficult to develop a right-angle approach in the lower uterine segment to accomplish the blanching technique. For that reason, the surgeon should proceed with endometrial ablation using the blanching technique in all areas of the endometrium that are accessible. In the lower uterine segment, a tangential approach to the endometrium is usual. The surgeon must use the side of the fiber in contact with the endometrium to cover this area. Very often, it is necessary to complete the endometrial ablation in the lower uterine segment using the dragging technique originally described by Dr. Goldrath.

When using the dragging technique, the fiber is in direct contact with the endometrium. This results in an extremely small spot size compared with the larger

spot size when the fiber is withdrawn in the blanching technique. Because of the larger spot size, an endometrial ablation is accomplished in a shorter time when compared with the dragging technique. When using the dragging technique, the fiber comes in direct contact with carbon particles, resulting in overheating of the fiber and fracture of the terminal portion of the fiber. These fractures can result in an extremely large spot size, significantly diminishing the power density. Therefore, the laser must be held in contact with the tissue for a longer time. This problem adds to the time necessary to accomplish the dragging technique. The problem can be solved by removing the fractured fiber and replacing it with a new fiberoptic bundle.

RESULTS

Patients are discharged on the day of their surgery with instructions to avoid strenuous activities for 2 to 3 days. There is often a watery, bloody discharge for up to 6 weeks after endometrial ablation. Delayed hemorrhage is an extremely rare complication. Postoperative endometritis, also a rare complication, is easily treated with second-generation cephalosporin drugs. Compared with hysterectomy, most patients are able to resume normal activities after 3 days and return to work in a shorter period of time, thus adding to the financial benefits of this procedure. Premenstrual syndrome also has been shown to improve after laser ablation as described by Dr. Lefler.[3]

Our results demonstrate a dramatic decrease in menstrual flow in patients with normal uteri, enlarged uteri, and fibroid uteri (less than 16 weeks' gestational size.[4] Table 24-1 demonstrates the pattern of flow before endometrial ablation in each of the three categories described above. Table 24-2 demonstrates a marked reduction in menstrual flow after Nd:YAG laser ablation. Approximately 50 percent of patients undergoing laser ablation of the endometrium will be-

Table 24-1. Menses Before Ablation

	Normal Uterus	Enlarged Uterus	Uterine Fibroids
Amenorrhea	0	0	0
Light flow	1 (1%)	0	2 (6%)
Normal flow	2 (3%)	6 (9%)	1 (3%)
Heavy flow	33 (53%)	51 (79%)	11 (33%)
Severe flow	27 (43%)	8 (12%)	19 (58%)
Total	63	65	33

Table 24-2. Menses After Ablation

	Normal Uterus	Enlarged Uterus	Uterine Fibroids
Amenorrhea	34 (54%)	32 (49%)	16 (49%)
Light flow	9 (14%)	27 (42%)	13 (39%)
Normal flow	15 (24%)	5 (7%)	4 (12%)
Heavy flow	5 (8%)	1 (2%)	0
Severe flow	0	0	0
Total	63	65	33

come totally amenorrheic, whereas an additional 30 to 35 percent will have light cyclic flows, very often requiring only one or two tampons per month. Approximately 95 percent of the patients are satisfied with the results. Only 2 of 161 patients had to undergo hysterectomy because of ongoing menometrorrhagia. Other reports have supported our conclusions in the hysteroscopic treatment of menorrhagia associated with uterine leiomyomas.[3]

There have been scattered reports of gas embolization during endometrial ablation when the surgeon has incorrectly selected a "gas fiber" versus a "bare" urologic fiber. The use of a gas-cooled sapphire tip is totally inappropriate for ablation of the endometrium.

CONCLUSIONS

Endometrial ablation is a safe and effective alternative to hysterectomy in patients with chronic menorrhagia refractory to surgical and medical therapy. It reduces bleeding sufficiently to avoid major surgery in most patients. Endometrial ablation may decrease the symptoms of the menstrual syndrome. The enlarged or fibroid uterus is not necessarily a contraindication to endometrial ablation and may be effective in at least temporarily controlling bleeding. The blanching technique minimizes the problems of visual field clouding and potential fluid overload. Certainly, ongoing perspective, randomized studies will be required to determine the long-term effectiveness of the procedure.

REFERENCES

1. Asherman JG: Amenorrhea traumatica (atretica). J Obstet Gynaecol Br Emp 55:23, 1948
2. Goldrath MH, Fuller TA, Segal S: Laser photovaporization of the endometrium for the treatment of menorrhagia. Am J Obstet Gynecol 140:14, 1981
3. Lefler H: Premenstrual syndrome improvement after laser ablation for menorrhea. J Reprod Med 34:905, 1989
4. Loffer FD: Hysteroscopic endometrial ablation with the Nd:YAG laser using a non-touch technique. Obstet Gynecol 69:4, 1987

25 Septi and Intrauterine Adhesions

STEPHEN M. COHEN

SEPTUM

Congenital uterine deformities are commonly found in the population. Although most animal species normally have nonunified uteri and reproduce without difficulty, a divided human uterus often results in premature delivery, abortion, or infertility.

The diagnosis of a congenital uterine deformity is usually made by hysterosalpingogram, pelvic ultrasound, or D&C. These studies may have been performed as part of an infertility or pregnancy loss workup or for many various other indications.

Before the development of modern operative hysteroscopic techniques, uteri with deformities were reconstructed via major surgery, necessitating an exploratory laparotomy. The Jones and Tompkins metroplasties for septate uteri were commonly performed and highly successful. However, because these were major surgical procedures, carrying with them the potential for mortality and morbidity (infection, bleeding, organ damage, and adhesion formation) and prolonged disability (6 to 8 weeks), these operations were usually reserved for women who had already had a late first-trimester or second-trimester pregnancy loss. Because it was well known that not all women with uterine defects would have these problems, the reasoning was accurate and appropriate.[1] Waiting, however, created much anxiety in women who were diagnosed with this problem and had to test their ability to carry a pregnancy to viability. Women who were not successful and delivered prematurely had to deal with the emotional trauma of fetal death or neonatal intensive care units.

With advanced operative hysteroscopic techniques, both patients with previous loss and those who have not been pregnant can be offered surgical treatment that is less morbid and disabling. Of course, during the informed consent process before surgery, it is explained to patients that even with an unrepaired deformity, some women will carry a pregnancy to term.

PREOPERATIVE PREPARATION

The surgeon needs to be as sure as possible of the exact nature of the uterine deformity. Not uncommonly, variations of the basic deformities (arcuate, septate, bicornuate, unicornuate, didelphys) are found (Fig. 25-1). Unilateral, unbalanced, and noncommunicating deformities often make the surgical procedure more complicated. A pelvic ultrasound, although not infallible, often will allow the surgeon to anticipate the likely deformity. Additional studies must still be performed to discover the contour of the endometrial cavity. Hysterosalpingography, office hysteroscopy, fluid-enhanced sonography, and magnetic resonance imaging are complementary and can help predict the deformity. It is certainly not necessary to perform all these studies before surgery. However, the surgeon should not hesitate to obtain whatever tests are needed when the anatomy appears confusing. At times it is very difficult to define the congenital deformity during surgery, unless some preoperative studies have been performed. Regardless of the preoperative information available, laparoscopy needs to be performed to determine precisely the external shape of the uterus. Occa-

THE AMERICAN FERTILITY SOCIETY CLASSIFICATION OF MULLERIAN ANOMALIES

Patient's Name ______________________ Date __________ Chart # __________

Age _____ G _____ P _____ Sp Ab _____ VTP _____ Ectopic _____ Infertile Yes _____ No _____

Other Significant History (i.e. surgery, infection, etc.) ______________________

____

HSG ________ Sonography ________ Photography ________ Laparoscopy ________ Laparotomy ________

EXAMPLES

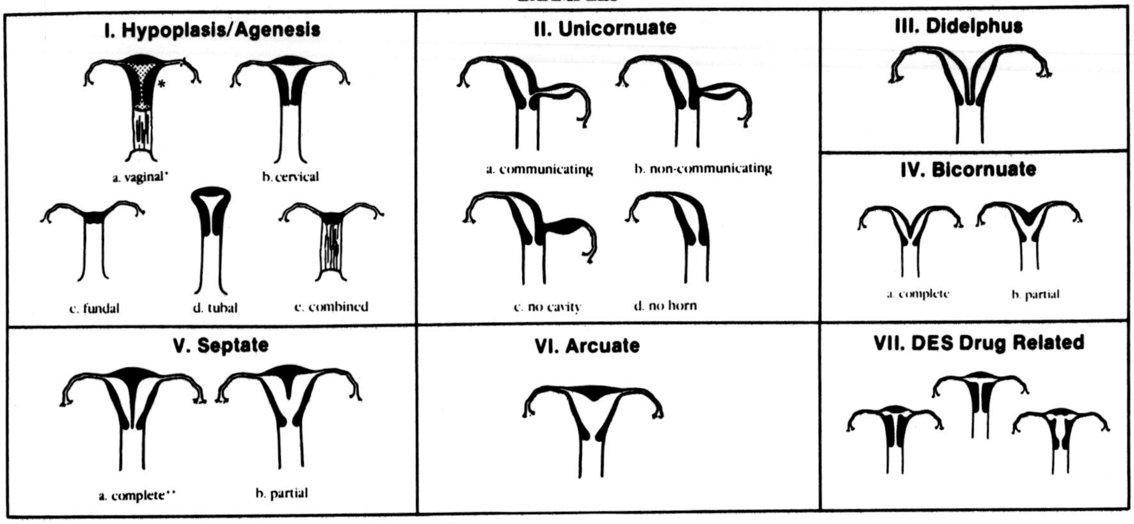

I. Hypoplasia/Agenesis
a. vaginal*
b. cervical
c. fundal
d. tubal
e. combined
II. Unicornuate
a. communicating
b. non-communicating
c. no cavity
d. no horn
III. Didelphus
IV. Bicornuate
a. complete
b. partial
V. Septate
a. complete**
b. partial
VI. Arcuate
VII. DES Drug Related

* Uterus may be normal or take a variety of abnormal forms.

** May have two distinct cervices

Type of Anomaly

Class I ________ Class V ________

Class II ________ Class VI ________

Class III ________ Class VII ________

Class IV ________

Treatment (Surgical Procedures): ______________________

____

____

Prognosis for Conception & Subsequent Viable Infant*

_____ Excellent (> 75%)

_____ Good (50-75%)

_____ Fair (25%-50%)

_____ Poor (< 25%)

*Based upon physician's judgment.

Recommended Followup Treatment: ______________________

____

____

Additional Findings: ______________________

____

____

Vagina: ______________________

Cervix: ______________________

Tubes: Right ____________ Left ____________

Kidneys: Right ____________ Left ____________

DRAWING

L R

Property of
The American Fertility Society

For additional supply write to:
The American Fertility Society
2140 11th Avenue, South
Suite 200
Birmingham, Alabama 35205

Fig. 25-1. American Fertility Society classification of Mullerian anolmalies.

sionally, still photos or video tapes of a prior laparoscopy can be obtained that will suffice. The finding of a bicornuate uterus eliminates the possibility of a hysteroscopic metroplasty.

I treat all patients preoperatively with DepoLupron 3.75 mg IM 4 to 5 weeks before surgery, so that the cyclic endometrium is atrophic. This allows a clearer view of the septum and the tubal ostia. By shrinking the endometrium before surgery, the surgeon is able to better locate the cornual openings as the base of a broad-based septum is approached. As these procedures are exclusively performed to improve fertility, it is imperative to spare the tubal ostia from damage, especially when laser or electrosurgery is the method chosen to excise the septum. When the septum is long and approaches the internal os of the cervix, the opening between the two cavities may be very small and, if covered with endometrium, difficult to find. In cases in which the uterine septum continues into the cervical canal, having the septum devoid of endometrium makes placing the initial incision between the two cavities much easier and safer.

Dilating the cervix wide enough to accommodate a 26 to 28F resectoscope or slightly smaller operative hysteroscope can be the most difficult and time-consuming part of the procedure. Many cervices will dilate easily, but some are stenotic or soft and become lacerated during this phase of the procedure. Also, perforation of the lower uterine segment and cervix is more likely to occur, as false passages are often created. A cervical dilator, such as Laminaria, eliminates

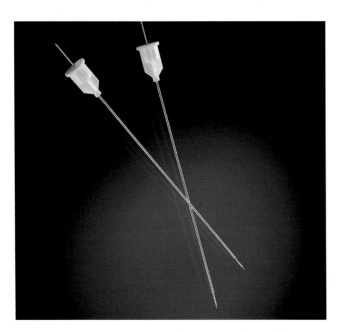

Fig. 25-2. Potocky needle. (Cooper Surgical).

this sometimes difficult step. I place a 4-mm Laminaria into the cervical canal the afternoon before surgery. Two tampons are placed into the vagina to hold the Laminaria in place. Before placement of the Laminaria, the cervix is injected with Lidocaine 1 percent with 1:200,000 epinephrine intrastromally (using a Potocky needle distributed by Cooper Surgical) (Fig. 25-2). Approximately 4 ml of this solution is used. Others have used Marcaine as the anesthetic of choice because of the longer-acting effect. Patients are given analgesic medication to take at home after the insertion. They should be informed that use of a mechanical dilator is off-label and only approved for use in the *pregnant* patient. In the operating room, after the patient is anesthetized, the surgeon needs to gently remove the dilator, as improper extraction can cause the material to tear, leaving pieces in the endometrial cavity and cervical canal.

The anesthesiologist should be informed that this patient may absorb a significant amount of fluid during the procedure and thus should keep the intravenous fluid volume to a minimum. Some operators also obtain a serum sodium preoperatively to compare with a postoperative value.

THE PROCEDURE

The patient is anesthetized and placed in the lithotomy position. Laparoscopy is not necessary if there is an accurate recording of the uterine deformity, either by photo, video, or personal prior observation. If the operator feels more comfortable performing the metroplasty with a laparoscope in the abdomen for control, it certainly should be performed.

The cervix is grasped with a single-tooth tenaculum. The dilator is removed. A large Hank dilator is passed to ensure that the internal os has been dilated. All equipment is set up and examined to confirm that it is in working order, including scissors, lasers, electrosurgical generators, cords, and electrodes. Once the equipment is assembled, the hysteroscope is placed through the cervical canal and into the endometrial cavity under direct vision, observing the process on the video monitor. The septum is located; the width and length are noted. The tubal ostia must be carefully observed, and a mental note needs to be made of their location and distance from the lateral margins of the septum.

Regardless of the method chosen to excise the septum, the surgeon must carefully divide it in the plane midway between the anterior and posterior uterine walls (Fig. 25-3). Deviation from the midplane increases the likelihood of bleeding and perforation. Be-

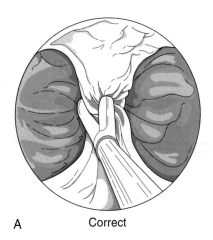
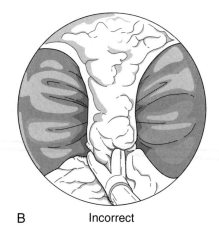

A   Correct   B   Incorrect

Fig. 25-3. (A) Correct. Incision midposition between interior and posterior uterine walls. **(B)** Incorrect. Deviation anteriorly or posteriorly may cause bleeding or uterine perforation.

fore beginning the division, careful note should be made of the uterine cavity direction, with attention to the direction of the top of the fundus (anteverted, midposition, retroverted). During the procedure, the surgeon must frequently back out the hysteroscope to get a panoramic view of the septum and endometrial cavity, so that the incision does not begin to wander away from the midline.

During any operative hysteroscopic procedure, inflow and outflow need to be constantly and accurately reported. I have the circulating nurse report these figures to the operator at 10-minute intervals. If the deficit is greater than 1,000 ml of sorbitol, glycine, or saline, the surgeon should consider terminating the procedure or using other methods to control fluid overload and hyponatremia (see Chapter 28).

Many studies have shown that regardless of the method used to remove the septum, similar results are obtained. A description of a few of the most common techniques follows.

EXCISION WITH SCISSORS

Dividing the septum with scissors is the simplest method of metroplasty. No knowledge of laser or electrosurgery is needed to use this method. And although perforations can occur, they are unlikely to cause significant delayed damage.

A standard operative hysteroscope is placed into the endometrial cavity under direct vision. This endoscope may have one or two operative channels (Fig. 25-4). One channel is used for introduction of the scissors. The second, if available, may be used for accessory instruments such as a probe or small catheter. Any of the

available distending media can be used during this procedure, including Hyskon, sorbitol, glycine, saline, or sorbitol-mannitol, because no electrosurgical energy source will be used. Most modern operative hysteroscopes are continuous-flow type, having both an entry and exit port. If an operative scope that is not continuous flow is to be used, the cervix must be dilated significantly more than the diameter of the endoscope to allow unrestricted egress of the infused media. Gravity is usually satisfactory to obtain adequate flow, although a Zimmer pump or infusion cuff may be necessary on occasion.

Once the hysteroscope has been placed into the endometrial cavity under direct vision and the anatomy has been assessed, scissors are introduced down the operative port, until it comes into view (Figs. 26-5 to 26-7). Various techniques have been described in the literature, but in general, the surgeon begins the incision into the septum at the lowest point and continues the dissection toward the top of the fundus, taking small

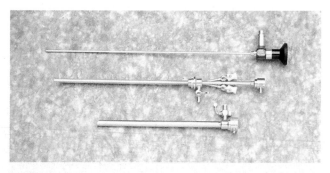

Fig. 25-4. Operative hysteroscope with two operating channels (Storz).

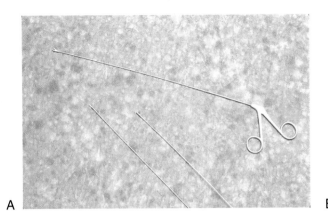 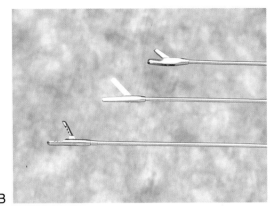

Fig. 25-5. (A & B) Hysteroscopic scissors (Storz).

Fig. 25-6. Hysteroscopic scissors (Cooper Surgical).

bites and constantly reassessing the incisional plane. If the septum is broad, alternating cutting from one side and then the other allows the operator to continue the incision (Figs. 25-8 to 25-11). The surgeon should again locate the tubal ostia as the incision nears the top of the fundus, both to help decide when to stop and also to prevent perforation through the thin cornual area. The surgeon should not try to flatten the top of the endometrial cavity to the level of the ostia, as perforation may occur through the top of the fundus. As the myometrium is approached at the top of the septum, the texture of the septum changes, appearing less fibrous and more vascular. Often, bleeding is seen to occur, and this signals that the septum has been satisfactorily removed. Once the procedure has been completed, the

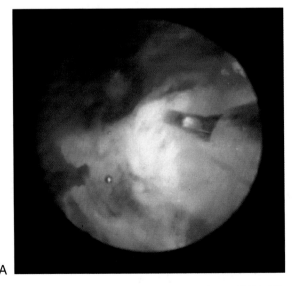 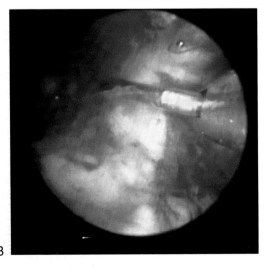

Fig. 25-7. (A & B) Dividing the septum with scissors.

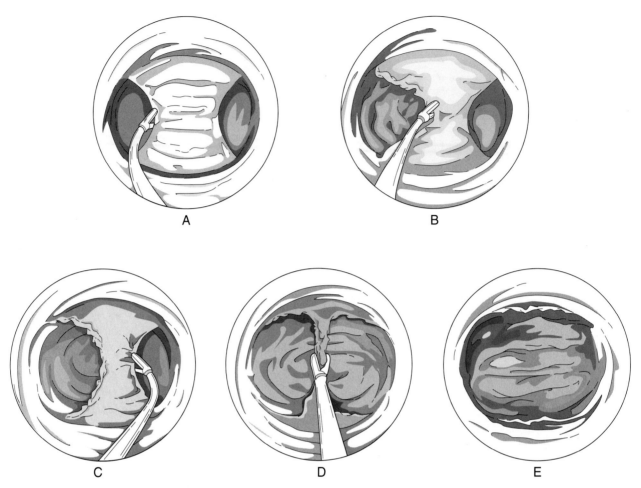

Fig. 25-8. (A–E) Incisions made alternatively from each side, reducing the width of the septum until it is removed.

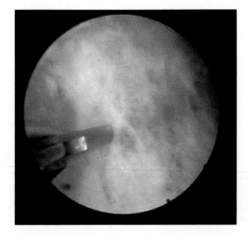

Fig. 25-9. Septum almost completely divided.

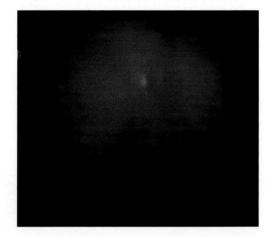

Fig. 25-10. Hysteroscopic view with light turned down.

Fig. 25-11. Laparoscopic view with light turned down.

endometrial cavity should be observed again panoramically. The distending pressure should be reduced, allowing the endometrial cavity to slowly collapse, and the cavity should be observed for any significant bleeding.

EXCISION WITH LASER

The laser may be used to excise the septum in a fashion very similar to the scissors. The operative hysteroscope is placed into the endometrial cavity, and a laser fiber is passed down the operative channel. All liquid distending media are acceptable for use during this procedure. Usually a sculptured-tip yttrium-aluminum-garnet fiber is used for the incision, as that improves the cutting obtainable from this laser. However, potassium-titanyl-phosphate and argon laser fibers have also been used with reported success as well (Fig. 25-12). The fiber is dragged back and forth in a transverse plane beginning at the distal edge nearest to the internal os. As always, the surgeon must be aware of the plane of the incision and the location of the tubal ostia. Because bleeding will not occur as the top of the septum is reached, the level of the ostia and texture change must be used as an indicator that the entire sep-

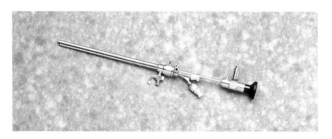

Fig. 25-12. Operative hysteroscope with three channels and laser bridge (Storz).

tum has been incised. The procedure is ended in a similar fashion as that described above using scissors.

EXCISION WITH RESECTOSCOPE

The uterine septum may be rapidly and safely excised using the resectoscope that has been designed for gynecologic procedures. The urologic resectoscope has been modified for gynecology by adding an exit channel, so that it is a continuous-flow system (Fig. 25-13).

When electrosurgery has been selected to incise the septum, the distending media is restricted to a nonconductive fluid such as sorbitol, glycine, or dextran 70 (Hyskon). Saline cannot be used because it conducts electrons away from the incisional site, and division of the septum will not occur.

The cutting element for incision is chosen and placed into the resectoscope before placing the resectoscope into the endometrial cavity. The most common elements used are the loop, blade, or Collins blade. These elements are manufactured in both a disposable and reusable configuration. All currently available resectoscopes allow easy placement and exchange of the elements.

The resectoscope is placed into the endometrial cavity in a similar fashion to the operative hysteroscope. The anatomy of the cavity is assessed. If a straight blade is used, it is moved in a similar fashion to that of a laser fiber, beginning at the level closest to the internal os and progressing upward toward the top of the fundus in a back-and-forth motion. If a Collins blade is used, the resectoscope must be turned at a 90-degree angle, so that the blade is transverse across the septum (Fig. 25-14). The blade is then pressed against the septum, and by using short bursts of power controlled by

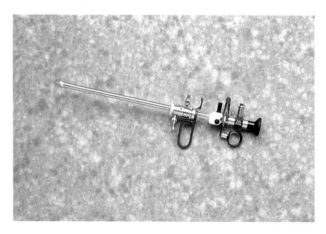

Fig. 25-13. Continuous flow resectoscope (Storz).

Fig. 25-14. Continuous flow resectoscope with knife electrode (Storz).

the foot pedal, the septum can be divided quickly and bloodlessly. Unlike most operative hysteroscopic procedures, during this procedure the electrode is activated as it is being moved away from the scope. This must be done carefully and with short bursts rather than a continuous motion. It is also important that the uterus is well distended, as tension on the septum will make for more rapid division with less need for excessive pressure. As with laser, bleeding will not occur as the fundus is reached, and thus, texture and ostia must be used as landmarks signifying that the septum has been completely removed.

If a loop is used, the surgeon again turns the resectoscope at a 90-degree angle and resects the midportion of the septum by placing the loop approximately 1 to 1.5 cm back from the near end of the septum. The loop is then brought toward the resectoscope, excising a strip of septum in the midplane (Fig. 25-15). As the septum broadens, the surgeon alternates resecting from each side. Care must be taken to remain in the midplane of the endometrial cavity and avoid damaging the ostia.

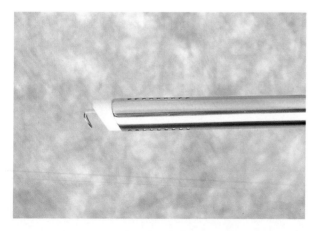

Fig. 25-15. Continuous flow resectoscope with loop electrode (Storz).

A cutting or a blend setting (cutting and coagulation mixed) is usually selected on the electrosurgical generator for this procedure. A blend setting adds some extra hemostatic properties, although the septum itself is mostly avascular. Blend 1 on most generators (15 percent coagulation) is usually adequate coagulation current for this procedure. I select power settings in the higher ranges (100 to 125 W). At this level, cutting is smooth and fast with minimal sticking of the electrode or thermal damage to surrounding endometrium. The procedure is ended in a similar fashion to those performed with scissors or laser.

POSTOPERATIVE CARE

Patients are instructed to expect some bloody discharge for up to 6 weeks after surgery. I do not prescribe antibiotics postoperatively. Mild analgesics, such as nonsteroidal anti-inflammatories, Tylenol, or aspirin, are given for pain management. No intrauterine device placement or uterine sounding is performed, although others have reported the use of these procedures. If medical suppression of the endometrium has been selected preoperatively, conjugated estrogen 1.25 mg daily is given for 25 days. Medroxyprogesterone 10 mg daily is added on day 21 and continued for 5 days. Attempts at pregnancy are allowed after 8 weeks. Patients are told to report any heavy bleeding, increasing pain, or temperature elevation.

RESULTS

Successful surgical removal of the uterine septum is most often the case after hysteroscopic metroplasty.[2] Only a small percentage of patients will need a repeat procedure for a residual septum.

If the hysteroscopic metroplasty was performed to correct late spontaneous abortions or second-trimester loss, almost all studies report outstanding success rates. Daly et al.[3] reported the first series of hysteroscopic metroplasty with follow-up pregnancy rates. Twenty-five patients had a metroplasty after a previous loss. During the study follow-up period, 10 patients became pregnant. Seven term pregnancies, one spontaneous abortion, and two ongoing pregnancies resulted. No preterm deliveries occurred in this high-risk group. Other studies demonstrate successful delivery rates at viability varying between 87 to 100 percent.[4–6]

In regard to correcting spontaneous abortion or infertility, the data are difficult to interpret. Although successes have been reported in both these conditions, it is impossible at this time to know if these successes are the result of the procedure or just the natural course of events. However, because of the ease of septum removal via hysteroscopy, most gynecologists now advise prophylactic removal to prevent the relatively high probability of pregnancy loss in this group of patients.

INTRAUTERINE ADHESIONS

Intrauterine adhesions can cause infertility, spontaneous abortions, preterm delivery, placenta accreta, hypomenorrhea, and amenorrhea. Most patients diagnosed as having intrauterine adhesions have had a D&C after either a spontaneous or therapeutic abortion. Occasionally, other events such as nonpregnancy-related D&C, metroplasty, or myomectomy can precede the development of adhesions. The diagnosis is usually made by hysterosalpingogram after a pregnancy loss or during an investigation for infertility. A history of hypomenorrhea or amenorrhea after a D&C should alert the physician to the possibility of this diagnosis.

The hysterogram will demonstrate areas of nonfilling, which are usually consistant with the location of the adhesions. In some instances, the entire endometrial cavity is not able to be visualized, either representing severe adhesion formation of the entire endometrial cavity or a complete scar across the lower uterine segment. Office hysteroscopy provides complementary information to that obtained by hysterosalpingogram, and both should usually be performed before the definitive operative procedure (Fig. 25-16). The hysterosalpingogram may show open areas of the endometrial cavity that cannot be visualized with the hysteroscope but the knowledge of which would be extremely helpful during the operative procedure. The hysteroscopic examination can demonstrate adhesions along the periphery of the endometrial cavity, which are not clearly demonstrated by the hysterosalpingogram. The correlation between the hysterosalpingogram and the hysteroscopic examination is often very close, but in the small percentage of cases in which they differ, the hysterosalpingogram usually predicts more extensive adhesions than are found at surgery.[7]

Removal of intrauterine adhesions via operative hysteroscopy is very similar to removal of the uterine septum just described; however, the scarring can make it very difficult to determine exactly where to place the incision in an attempt to restore the normal cavity. Some adhesions are completely avascular, whereas others may have a rich blood supply.

Medically suppressing the endometrium preoperatively with Danocrine or gonadotropin-releasing hormone agonist has both advantages and disadvantages. By removing the endometrium, the adhesions can be more clearly defined, and the spaces between the adhesions are more obvious. However, there are occasions when being able to distinguish the endometrial tissue from scar is hampered by this preoperative suppression.

If possible, a Laminaria is placed into the endocervical canal to dilate the cervix the afternoon before surgery. If extensive scarring of the lower uterine segment has occurred, the surgeon will not be able to place the Laminaria. Persistent attempts at placement may lead to lower uterine segment perforation. Although this surgical procedure can be performed under local paracervical block and sedation, I recommend regional or general anesthesia in most patients with moderate or severe adhesions. I do not routinely perform a concomitant laparoscopy but do not hesitate to add it if the scarring has made the anatomy confusing.

In most instances of intrauterine scarring, the operative hysteroscope and scissors are the preferred instruments for division of these adhesions. The operative hysteroscope is smaller and more maneuverable than the resectoscope in tight quarters. The surgeon can also control the amount of scar removed in areas such as the cornua, where the ostia may not be apparent. However, if the scar in more midline and thickened, the resectoscope can be used in a manner similar to that described for the removal of a septum (Figs. 26-17 and 26-18). A fiber laser can also be used for this procedure. Mild, filmy adhesions can be removed with the hysteroscope itself by pushing or swinging the sheath through the adhesion. Some operators have placed a secondary instrument, such as scissors or a probe, through the cervix alongside the hysteroscope. However, manipulating both instruments in the canal is often difficult.

Most patients can be treated during one operative procedure, with 90 percent of patients having complete removal of adhesions. Occasionally, patients will need a second procedure, either because the procedure was not able to be completed in one operation (bleeding or fluid absorption) or because of recurrent adhesions on the postoperative hysterosalpingogram.

Success rates for re-establishing menses and improving fertility are significantly better when directed excision of adhesions via hysteroscopy is compared with the blind techniques that have been used to treat this problem in the past. Term pregnancy rates have been reported between 38 to 89 percent after hysteroscopic resection.[8-14]

THE AMERICAN FERTILITY SOCIETY CLASSIFICATION OF INTRAUTERINE ADHESIONS

Patient's Name _____ Date _____ Chart # _____

Age _____ G _____ P _____ Sp Ab _____ VTP _____ Ectopic _____ Infertile Yes _ __ No _____

Other Significant History (i.e. surgery, infection, etc.) _____ _____

_____

HSG _____ Sonography _____ Photography _____ Laparoscopy _____ Laparotomy _____

Extent of Cavity Involved	<1/3	1/3 - 2/3	>2/3
	1	2	4
Type of Adhesions	Filmy	Filmy & Dense	Dense
	1	2	4
Menstrual Pattern	Normal	Hypomenorrhea	Amenorrhea
	0	2	4

Prognostic Classification

		HSG* Score	Hysteroscopy Score
Stage I	(Mild)	1-4	_____	_____
Stage II	(Moderate)	5-8	_____	_____
Stage III	(Severe)	9-12	_____	_____

*All adhesions should be considered dense

Treatment (Surgical Procedures): _____

_____

_____

_____

_____

Prognosis for Conception & Subsequent Viable Infant*

_____ Excellent (> 75%)

_____ Good (50-75%)

_____ Fair (25%-50%)

_____ Poor (< 25%)

*Physician's judgment based upon tubal patency.

Recommended Followup Treatment: _____

_____

_____

Additional Findings: _____

_____

_____

_____

_____

_____

DRAWING

HSG Findings

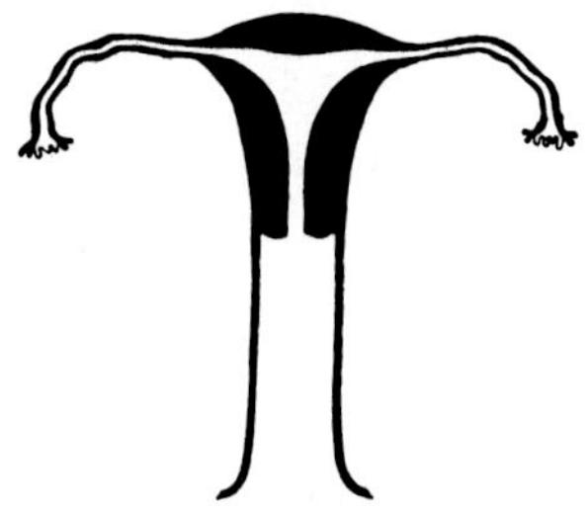

Hysteroscopy Findings

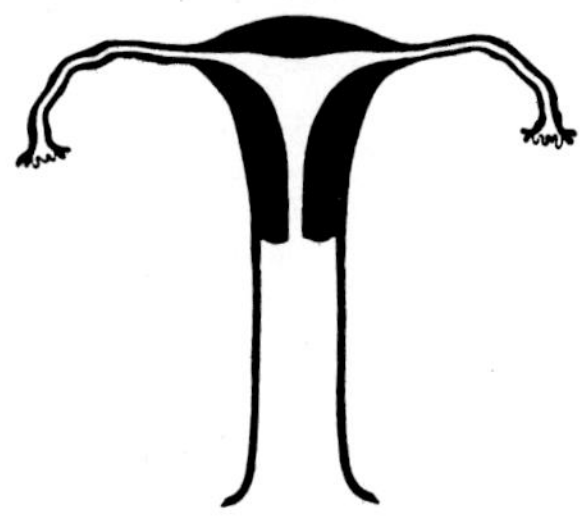

Property of
The American Fertility Society

For additional supply write to:
The American Fertility Society
2140 11th Avenue, South
Suite 200
Birmingham, Alabama 35205

Fig. 25-16. American Fertility Society classification of intrauterine adhesions.

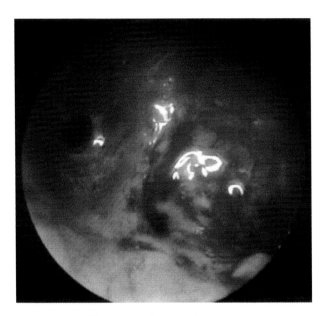

Fig. 25-17. Intrauterine scar.

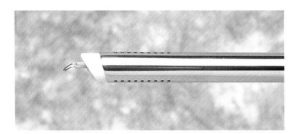

Fig. 25-18. Resectoscope with horizontal loop electrode (Storz).

REFERENCES

1. Buttram VC, Gibbons WB: Mullerian anomalies: a proposed classification (an analysis of 144 cases). Fertil Steril 32:40, 1979
2. Marabini A, Gubbini G, Stagnozzi R et al: Hysteroscopic metroplasty. Ann NY Acad Sci 734:488, 1994
3. Daly DC, Walters CA, Soto-Albors CE et al: Hysteroscopic metroplasty: surgical technique and obstetrical outcome. Fertil Steril 39:623, 1983
4. Valle RF, Sciarra JJ: Hysteroscopic treatment of the septate uterus. Obstet Gynecol 67:253, 1986
5. March CM, Israel R: Hysteroscopic management of recurrent abortion caused by septate uterus. Am J Obstet Gynecol 156:834, 1987
6. DeCherney AH, Russell JB, Graebe RA, Polan ML: Rectoscopic management of mullerian fusion defects. Fertil Steril 45:726, 1986
7. March CM: Hysteroscopy and the uterine factor in infertility. p. 661. In Mishell DR Jr, Davajan V, Lobo RA (eds): Infertility, Contraception, and Reproductive Endocrinology. Blackwell Scientific Publications, Boston, 1991
8. Lancet M, Kessler I: A review of Asherman's syndrome and results of modern treatment. Int J Fertil 33:14, 1988
9. Valle RD, Sciarra JJ: Intrauterine adhesions: hysteroscopic diagnosis, classification, treatment, and reproductive outcome. Am J Obstet Gynecol 158:1459, 1988
10. March CM, Israel R: Gestational outcome following hysteroscopic lysis of adhesions. Fertil Steril 36:455, 1981
11. Taylor PJ, Cumming DC, Hill PJ: Significance of intrauterine adhesions detected hysteroscopically in eumenorrheic fertile women and role of antecedent curettage in their formation. Am J Obstet Gynecol 139:239, 1981
12. Neuwirth RS, Hussein AR, Schiffman BM et al: Hysteroscopic resection of intrauterine scars using a new technique. Obstet Gynecol 60:111, 1982
13. Hamon J, Salat-Baroux J, Seigler AM: Diagnosis and treatment of intrauterine adhesions by microhysterecopy. Fertil Steril 39:321, 1983
14. Schenker JG, Margalioth EJ: Intrauterine adhesions: an updated appraisal. Fertil Steril 37:169, 1982

26 Hysteroscopic Myomectomy

DUANE TOWNSEND

In this chapter, I review the management of the major organic causes of abnormal uterine bleeding (i.e., submucous myomas and intrauterine polyps). Polyps are included in this chapter because they are frequently the cause of abnormal uterine bleeding, particularly in the postmenopausal woman and are managed virtually the same as submucous myomas. My experience in dealing with these organic causes encompasses more than 800 patients.

An historical perspective is followed by methods for evaluating and managing these lesions. Lastly, the complications of hysteroscopic myomectomy are reviewed in depth, and the parameters that will reduce these complications are emphasized.

HISTORY

The first reported use of ``operative hysteroscopy'' was by Panteloni in 1869.[1] He cauterized and removed several large polyps in a postmenopausal woman who was complaining of heavy vaginal bleeding. Although his instrumentation was crude when compared with modern instruments, his results were satisfactory.

Hineberg[2] in 1914 used a wire loop to resect myomas that were within the uterus. Although he likened his technique to resecting the prostate, he did not think that the urologic resectoscope could be applied to the uterine cavity. However, Neuwirth and Amin,[3] some 60 years later, pointed out the usefulness of the resectoscope to manage submucous myomas. After their pioneering work, several authors[4-13] have reported similar success resecting submucous myomas and polyps both in pre- and postmenopausal women. In addition to using the urologic resectoscope, the neodymium:yttrium aluminum-garnet (Nd:YAG) laser has also been used to treat such lesions.[14,15]

SYMPTOMS

Bleeding is the primary symptom that a woman will note when she has either a submucous myoma or a polyp. The type of bleeding from these two lesions, however, is significantly different. Bleeding from submucous myomas is usually quite heavy and profuse, often with large clots, and occurs primarily at the time of menstruation. Polyps usually cause bleeding throughout a menstrual cycle, and this bleeding is generally light but can be heavy if the polyps are quite large. In the postmenopausal woman, the bleeding can occur at any time with either lesion.

Submucous myomas generally cause heavy bleeding for the first several days of a menstrual flow, and several sanitary napkins or tampons are often changed hourly to absorb the bleeding. Profound anemia (i.e., hemoglobins of 4 to 5 g) have been noted in some cases. Surprisingly, many women believe that it is normal to have a ``heavy period'' and will often ignore their symptoms. Other women will not seek medical assistance because they have been mistakenly told that the only way to treat their problem is by hysterectomy. Women in the reproductive years may also experience pregnancy wastage along with heavy bleeding. Unfortunately, unless there is pregnancy wastage in these individuals, the lesions are not diagnosed for several years. In postmenopausal women, bleeding from these lesions may occur at any time but is usually heaviest when they are on cyclic hormone replacement therapy.

Why a woman bleeds from these lesions has not been completely resolved. The large vessels that often traverse the surface of the myomas are probably a contributing factor. However, if these vessels were the major cause of bleeding, the patient should have a bleeding problem throughout the menstrual cycle and not primarily with menstruation. Because bleeding of my-

281

omas usually occurs during menstruation, other factors must be important.

One of the major mechanisms by which a woman stops bleeding during a menstrual period is contraction of the uterine muscles. Anything that interferes with this contraction may cause heavy bleeding. Adenomyosis that invades the uterine wall probably causes heavy menstrual flow because of interference with normal uterine contractility. Likewise, women with submucous myomas may also have bleeding because of interference with uterine contractility. However, in addition to delayed muscle activity, many submucous myomas are surrounded by large venous sinuses and lakes from which blood literally pours out during menses.

The large vessels over polyps probably are the reason polyps bleed throughout a menstrual cycle. When these lesions are quite large, however, they may interfere with uterine contractility and cause a heavy menstrual flow.

DIAGNOSIS

The diagnosis of a submucous myoma should be entertained in any woman who complains of unusually heavy bleeding during her menstrual cycle. Women are usually subjected to dilation and curettage (D&C) to control their bleeding. This method has been shown to be consistently inaccurate to pick up these lesions.;s8 Hysterosalpingography is performed by many physicians, particularly when there is pregnancy wastage. This technique may pick up intrauterine lesions, but there are also a large number of false-positives due to bubbles within the radio-opaque media.

Pelvic ultrasound is becoming more and more important in the diagnosis of intrauterine disease. The ultrasound may miss small lesions, and it is often difficult to differentiate between submucous myomas and polyps. However, the ultrasound should be strongly considered in evaluating the patient with heavy abnormal bleeding, leading up to the most accurate method to diagnosis their problem (i.e., hysteroscopy).

Hysteroscopy without question is the sine-qua-non that permits evaluation of the endometrial cavity. Unfortunately, some women bleed heavily during most of the menstrual cycle, and it is impossible to examine these individuals hysteroscopically when CO_2 is the distending media. I have found that using dilute Hyskon (a 50:50 dilution with saline) is an ideal distending media. By diluting the Hyskon, the fluid flows very easily but still retains the nonmiscibility of this media.

In addition to visualizing the uterine cavity for proper diagnosis, tissue samples should be obtained in any woman who has heavy bleeding, particularly if she is older than the age of 35. The sample should not be taken during heavy bleeding because the blood may mix with the tiny fragments of endometrium, particularly if the aspiration method is used.

MANAGEMENT OF SUBMUCOUS MYOMAS AND POLYPS

Once the diagnosis has been established, therapy can take place. Unless the patient is bleeding actively or has profound anemia, there is seldom a rush for treatment. In the postmenopausal patient, once malignancy has been excluded, there is never a rush to therapy.

Preoperative Preparation

Whenever possible, the endometrium should be made flat or atrophic before therapy. The primary reason for this is safety. I have evaluated both the mechanical as well as the chemical means to achieve an atrophic endometrium. A suction or sharp curettage can be used if the patient is just ending her menstrual cycle or is in the early proliferative phase. If the mechanical means are attempted in the secretory phase, there will be a considerable amount of endometrial tissue left behind, which will interfere with visualization of the cavity.

I have used a variety of progestins, and in at least 20 percent of the patients, a significant degree of endometrial tissue is present, even after 6 weeks of medication. Both the injectable and oral preparations gave a similar result. A variety of birth control pills have also been used, and unless the medication is given for at least three cycles, a thick endometrium will be encountered.

Several years ago, I began to use the gonadotropin-releasing hormone (GNRH) agonists and have been impressed with their ability to consistently make the endometrium atrophic. I prefer the injectable type because of the unpredictable absorption by the other agonists. The dose that I use is Depo Lipron 3.75 mg. It has been suggested that the injection be given in the luteal phase,[16] but I have found that the injection can be given any time of the menstrual cycle and achieve an adequate atrophic endometrium. After the single injection, surgery is performed within 3 to 5 weeks. However, some physicians prefer a two-injection method. If this regimen is followed, surgery is performed 2 to 3 weeks after the last injection but never longer than 5 weeks. When two injections are used, many patients will begin to experience hot flashes and some type of adback regimen can be used. The adback regimen must include progesterone, otherwise the estrogen will thicken the endometrium. If the uterine cavity sounds to greater than 11 cm, then at least three injections of the agonist should be used to reduce the uterine cavity volume. This is important, particularly in endometrial ablations, because a larger cavity will result in a higher failure rate.[17] If a patient has a submucous myoma greater than 5 cm, then three injections should also be used.

In the postmenopausal women, no preoperative preparation is required because the patient already has an atrophic endometrium. If the patient is on hormone replacement therapy, it is not necessary to stop this medication. In evaluating and treating more than 250 women with postmenopausal bleeding while on hormone replacement therapy, I never encountered a thick endometrium. The only sequela of stopping hormone replacement therapy is to reintroduce the problem of hormone withdrawal.

After the injection of the GNRH agonist, some patients will continue to have bleeding, sometimes heavy. Surgery can be conducted even if the patient is bleeding heavily. The patient should be receiving adequate amounts of iron to restore her depleted iron stores and to maintain her hemoglobin. Rarely will one have to perform surgery before the planned date because of bleeding.

Immediate Preoperative Preparation

I believe all women undergoing any type of operative hysteroscopic procedure should have a laminaria tent placed up to and through the internal cervical os on the day before the planned procedure.[18] The laminaria will soften the cervix, thereby reducing the chance of cervical lacerations, but more significantly it hastens the dilation process and reduces the chance of perforation. Overdilation is particularly advantageous because it makes it virtually impossible to build up high intrauterine pressures. Overdilation is particularly helpful in the woman who has large submucous myomas. In resecting myomas, chips from the resection are left within the cavity until it is no longer possible to operate because of the diminished view from the chips. The chips are then removed, and the resectoscope will be reinserted. This may happen several times during the course of the operation. If the internal os is barely dilated, so that the resectoscope can just barely pass into the cavity, there will be difficulty

when the scope is removed and reinserted during the course of the procedure.

To insert a laminaria, a bimanual examination is first performed to determine the position of the uterus. The cervix is cleansed with iodine and then grasped with a tenaculum. The uterus should be sounded to confirm its position and to overcome any internal os resistance. Next, a 2- to 3-cm laminaria tent is placed into the uterus and if possible through the internal os. If the uterus is markedly ante- or retroverted, it may be impossible to place the laminaria through the internal os. In these cases, the laminaria should not be forced but merely placed up to the internal os. The beneficial effects of the laminaria will still be realized (i.e., cervical softening) even if the internal os is not traversed. A sterile 4×4 gauze sponge is used to secure the laminaria in place. The patient is given two prescriptions, one for pain control and one for antibiotics (doxycycline). Synthetic dilators should be avoided. I have had to abandon several operative procedures because of fracturing and even disintegration of the synthetic dilators.

Intraoperative Preparation and Performance

Patients are administered a general anesthetic unless there is a major contraindication. Local anesthetics as well as conduction anesthetics have less effect on uterine relaxation. Uterine relaxation is most important, particularly when resecting submucous fibroids or polyps. Once the patient has been anesthetized, her legs are placed in a hanging-type stirrup (i.e., candy cane). Knee stirrups should be avoided because they may not adequately separate the thighs, which will interfere with the lateral movement of the resectoscope. Once positioned, the patient is prepared and draped after the laminaria and 4×4 gauze dressings have been removed. It is critical that all fluid be collected during the course of the operative procedure. A Mayo stand cover with its closed end cut is an ideal and inexpensive collecting system. One edge of the Mayo stand cover is placed beneath the buttocks and then folded out in a funnel-like fashion. The other open end is placed into a 15-L transparent plastic bucket onto which 1,000-ml lines have been drawn. This will make it extremely easy for the nurse or operating room personnel to watch the meniscus rise in the collecting bucket during the course of the operative procedure. An alternative method of sucking up fluid into the canisters is vastly inferior and has unfortunately lead to confusion, inaccuracy, and severe hyponatremia.

Draping is completed as if for a D&C. The cervix is grasped with a tenaculum, and the internal os is dilated to at least 13 mm or 39F. The stubby dilators (i.e., Hegars) are ideal. The Hanks and Pratts should be avoided because they may perforate the small uterus. Once maximum dilation has been achieved, the largest dilator is left in the cavity.

After dilation has been completed, all the various wires and tubes are attached to the resectoscope. There must be a drainage tube connected to the output port of the outer sheath, which is directed into the collecting bucket. A wire loop electrode is placed in the resectoscope. When resecting polyps and myomas, there is little role for the rollerball unless it is to be used for coagulating the base of these lesions or when an ablation is performed along with the resection.

Equipment

A gynecologic resectoscope is preferable to the urologic devices. Unfortunately, virtually all resectoscopes that have been used to date were designed for bladders and prostates. Many companies have mislead physicians to believe that they have a gynecologic resectoscope, which in reality is nothing more than a urologic device. The true gynecologic resectoscopes have better flows and have custom-made balls and loops that can be interchanged without disassembling the equipment. Moreover, they are designed in such a fashion to improve the output flow, which is particularly important in operative hysteroscopy. The ideal instrument does not contain valves on the input and output ports because valves merely impede flows. I have compared flow rates in resectoscopes with and without valves, and I note that the valves reduce flows by at least 20 percent.

The key to a safe and speedy operative procedure is an excellent view of the cavity. This is achieved by high-volume, low-pressure flows. Some resectoscopes have such poor flows that they require the use of pumps to maintain adequate flow rates.

Pumps, in my opinion, merely add to the confusion of the operation. Also, many operating room personnel mistakenly believe that any tubing can be used when performing operative hysteroscopy. The ideal tubing is the large two-lead arthroscopy tubing (irrigation set #2C4030, Baxter Health Care Corp., Glenville, Illinois).

The irrigating fluid used is isotonic and nonelectrolytic and is either sorbitol, glycine, or Resectisol. With the large two-lead arthroscopy tubing, two bags are hung at one time, but only one bag is allowed to flow through the tubing. After the proper attachment of the tubing to the irrigating bags, excess air must be removed from the tubing to prevent air locks that reduce flows. Next the tubing is attached to the input port of the resectoscope. Fluid control is by the clip lock that is attached to the tubing and not by the valves that frequently come with resectoscopes. The irrigating bags are placed approximately 1 m above the anterior abdominal wall for proper pressures and fluid flows.

Procedure

All procedures are performed on video. A good single-chip system is all that is necessary for operative hysteroscopy. Unfortunately, there has been a great degree of misinformation, primarily from manufacturers, as to the importance of the so-called triple-chip camera. My experience in performing more than 2,000 operative cases using both triple-chip and single-chip systems reveals little visual advantage with the highly expensive triple-chip system. When using a video system, it is important that a proper coupler (i.e., the interface between the camera and resectoscope) be of appropriate degree. When viewing the video screen, the entire hysteroscopic picture must be visible. If part of the circle spills off the screen, there is invariably a wrong coupler. It is important for safety reasons that the entire picture be viewed on the screen.

Once everything has been properly assembled, the operation begins. The tenaculum is grasped by the scrub nurse or the assistant, and the dilator, which has been left in the cervix, is removed. Irrigating fluid is permitted to flow through the resectoscope as it is placed into the uterine cavity. The resectoscope is placed into the uterus until it touches the top of the fundus and then is completely withdrawn out of the cervix. The maneuver of inserting the scope in the uterus and removing it is continued until the cavity is cleared of debris. Next, the cornua are identified along with the contour of the cavity. Once the cavity and the anatomic features have been identified, the location and size of the myoma or myomas are noted (Figs. 26-1 and 26-2). Polyps are examined in the same fashion. If the myoma is on a small stalk, it is best to remove most of the myoma before transecting the stalk. If the stalk is resected early, the myoma will merely spin within the flowing fluid, making its removal quite difficult. Polyps, being fleshy, do not present this same kind of problem.

When removing myomas, it is important to realize that it may not be possible to take out the entire lesion. If only one-half or less of a myoma is visualized within the cavity, it is usually impossible to resect this lesion completely unless it is quite small. If, for some inexpli-

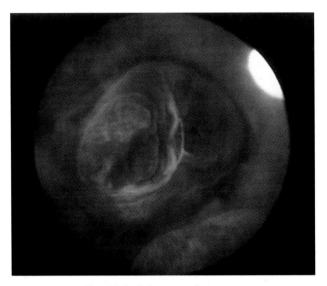

Fig. 26-1. Submucosal myoma.

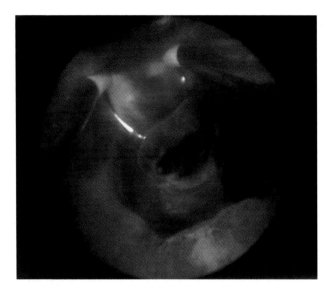

Fig. 26-3. Resection with loop electrode about to begin.

cable reason, a perforation occurs at this time, the operation is terminated. A laparoscopy should be performed. Dealing with perforations is discussed in detail later in this chapter.

Laparoscopy is not routinely performed in women undergoing myomectomy because it is not usually necessary. Laparoscopy will not prevent a perforation. Laparoscopy merely contributes to the cost and length of the procedure. The only time laparoscopy should be performed is in repeat ablations and when resecting uterine septa.

The loop electrode is used for resecting myomas and polyps. A standard operating room electrocautery unit

is usually placed at 110 W pure cut. The resectoscope is positioned so that when the loop is extended it reaches just beyond the myoma (Fig. 26-3). With the resectoscope held in position, the loop is withdrawn into the resectoscope when current is activated. Never activate current with any electrode going forward. Activating the electrode only when it is traveling toward the scope will reduce the chance of perforation with the loop or ball electrode.

When resecting the myoma or polyp, the chips or pieces should be left within the cavity until it is difficult to safely view the cavity (Fig. 26-4). At this point, the resectoscope is taken out, and the chips are re-

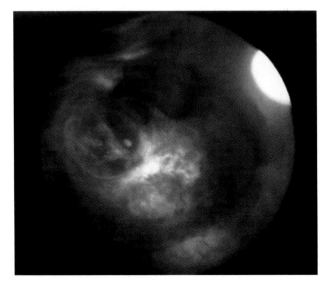

Fig. 26-2. Submucosal myoma: panoramic view.

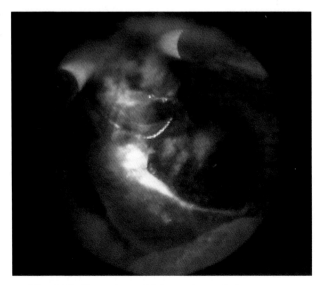

Fig. 26-4. Resection with loop electrode in progress.

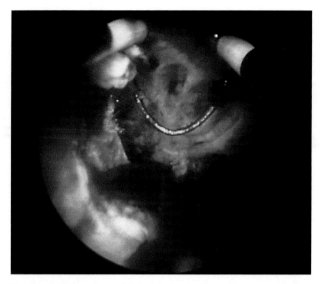

Fig. 26-5. Resection with loop electrode nearing completion.

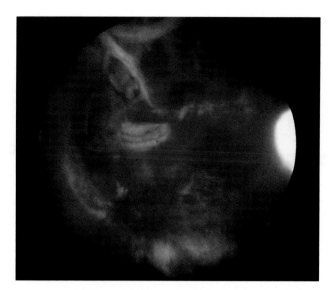

Fig. 26-7. Resection completed.

moved with an ovum forceps. Bleeding can be brisk at this time so this should be performed with efficiency. Once as many chips as possible have been removed, the uterus is cleared of the blood, debris, and clots that have accumulated during the removal of the chips (Figs. 26-5 and 26-6). The myoma is resected farther until the contour of the cavity has been re-established (Figs. 26-7 and 26-8). The resectoscope is removed along with any remaining chips, and several minutes are allowed to pass. The uterus will contract down and often extrude the myoma farther into the cavity. The myoma can be additionally resected again down to the

contour of the cavity. This method of resecting, waiting, and irrigating and re-resecting is continued until the entire myoma has been removed or until it no longer extrudes into the cavity.

Control of Bleeding

Often, when resecting myomas, there will be brisk bleeding from the arterioles that supply the nutrients to the lesion. This bleeding can usually be controlled by passing the loop electrode with coagulation current flowing (110 W). Venous bleeding will not be con-

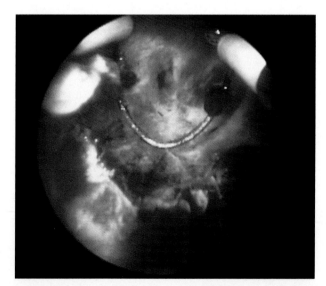

Fig. 26-6. Close-up of resection with loop electrode nearing completion.

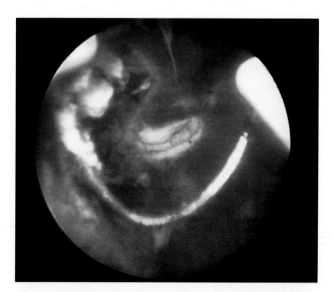

Fig. 26-8. Close-up of resection completed.

trolled with coagulation but generally is controlled with the pressures within the uterine cavity.

If, during resecting of the myoma, large venous channels are exposed, there is a strong likelihood the patient will absorb a considerable amount of fluid during the procedure. Consequently, the operating room personnel must be vigilant in measuring fluid balance. If a fluid discrepancy begins to develop (i.e., fluid in is greater than fluid out by 1,000 ml), hyponatremia may occur, which is discussed later.

Because of the potential danger of the urologic loops that are provided with most instruments, I have redesigned the resecting loops to conform more closely to the uterine cavity. A 3-mm loop is used for resecting shallow lesions, and a 5-mm deep loop is used for resecting larger lesions. These loops have straight sides and a slightly beveled horizontal bar to more anatomically "fit" the uterine cavity.

When encountering polyps, as much of the polyp as possible should be removed with ovum forceps and even by suction or sharp curettage. Most of the polyp can be removed in this manner, but the base has to be resected and cauterized.

In an occasional instance, there will be bleeding from the myoma that cannot be controlled with cauterization. If this occurs, a dilute Pitressin solution should be used that is 20 U of Pitressin diluted in 50 ml of saline, and 5 ml of this solution should be injected transvaginally at the site of the uterine artery bilaterally. Intramuscular injection must be avoided. The cervix should not be injected directly, for this will have little effect on the bleeding from the myoma. After the injection, the uterus will markedly contract for about 5 to 10 minutes, and surgery will be delayed. The uterus will relax, but the vasoconstrictive effect of the Pitressin will continue for 45 minutes more.

If there is excessive bleeding at the end of the operation and it is impossible to control the bleeding with the coagulation current, a dilute Pitressin pack is suggested.[19] A 1-in. Nu Gauze dressing 60 in. in length is placed into the dilute Pitressin solution. The soaked gauze pack is snugly packed in place with packing forceps. It is left in situ for about 2 hours and then removed by the recovery room nurse. In more than 200 cases, I have not encountered any significant postoperative bleeding in these patients after removal of the pack.

I have tried the large Foley's to control bleeding and have concluded that these methods do not work well when compared with the Pitressin pack.

In women who are having only a fibroid or polyp resected, all that is necessary is to resect the lesion and wait and see the success of the operation.

A significant number of woman who were complaining of heavy bleeding before the resection will still have heavy bleeding after surgery. In these patients, ablation will probably be necessary. In women who are having a pregnancy wastage problem, it is best to hysteroscope the woman about 6 to 8 weeks after surgery to confirm the fact that the endometrium has grown over the raw surface.

Ablation With Resection

Women who are having an ablation along with a resection are managed differently. Originally, I would resect first and then perform the ablation. However, I have had several instances of fluid absorption during this time and think that the absorption was probably due to the large sinuses that were being opened up during the fibroid resection. Because I was unable to perform the ablation, many patients complained about the unsatisfactory results of the procedure. I now perform the ablation first, destroying as much of the endometrium as possible, and then resect the myomas. My technique of ablation is similar to that described previously[19] except I am often unable to completely ablate the entire cavity. However, I ablate as much as possible, resect the myoma, and then finish ablating those areas that were not properly ablated because of interference of the myoma. Fluid balance again must be watched carefully in these patients, as these are the ones who are likely to have a problem with fluid absorption.

After completion of the resection or ablation, a paracervical block using 0.5 percent Sensorcaine is given in both uterosacral areas. Patients are usually discharged within 2 hours after surgery, and most are fully recovered in 24 hours. Vaginal bleeding or spotting is not uncommon for up to 6 to 8 weeks. Patients are examined in the office approximately 6 weeks after surgery and every 6 months for 1 year and then annually. Patients are advised to refrain from any physical activity for at least 2 to 3 weeks to avoid heavy postoperative bleeding.

Success of these operations varies significantly. In many patients, the resection of the myoma or polyp will be sufficient to control their bleeding. However, a significant number of patients will still have heavy bleeding. These patients will require additional procedures to satisfy their needs.

COMPLICATIONS

The complications of hysteroscopic myomectomy include perforation, fluid absorption and hyponatremia, bleeding, infection, and post-tubal ligation pain. Perforation and fluid absorption are a bit more common when resecting myomas and polyps.

Perforation

Perforation of the uterus is a very common event with a variety of procedures that involve the uterus (e.g., D&C, intrauterine device insertion, endometrial biopsies). It is seldom a problem, except when perforation occurs at the time of operative hysteroscopy, particularly when it is caused by the loop or ball electrode. The tragedy occurs when the perforation is not recognized in a timely fashion.

The most common cause of perforation in operative hysteroscopy is with the uterine sound or uterine dilators. There is rarely a perforation with a laminaria tent insertion, although in the markedly retroverted and anteverted uterus, the laminaria may be placed into the myometrium. Then when the patient is anesthetized and the uterine position not appreciated, the uterus is dilated and the dilator will take the same track of the laminaria, and perforation will occur. In addition, using the wrong dilator, as mentioned previously, may result in perforation, particularly in the small uterus.

If a perforation occurs during the time of dilation, the operation must be stopped. It is not necessary to laparoscope the patient. The individual should be observed for 3 to 4 hours in the recovery room, with blood counts taken during this time. If the blood count is stable, the patient is discharged home on antibiotics and is to return for an office examination in 3 to 4 weeks. If a repeat operation is planned, it should not be attempted until the perforation site heals, which takes approximately 3 months.

If perforation occurs with a resectoscope, it is usually as a consequence of a weakened portion of the uterus during dilation. Again, laparoscopy is not necessary. The operation is terminated, and the same plan is followed for postoperative observation. Operative hysteroscopy should never be continued if there is a perforation because of the high chance of fluid absorption with the passage of fluid into the abdominal cavity. If excessive fluid is permitted to pass into the abdominal cavity, it is vital that the patient be laparoscoped and as much fluid as possible be removed to avoid the development of hyponatremia.

A more serious perforation occurs with a loop or ball electrode. There have been several deaths due to perforation with a loop or ball electrode. Invariably, the perforation has taken place near the cornua, and the loop or ball electrode has injured a major pelvic vessel. This complication must be dealt with rapidly or the patient may expire.

A sign of perforation is a sudden change in fluid balance. If there is a sudden change in fluid balance (i.e.,

2,000 to 3,000 ml), the patient must be laparoscoped to note if there is a perforation, and if there is a perforation, whether there is a burn ring or burn area at the perforation site. If there is a burn ring at the perforation site, the patient must have a laparotomy, and the bowel and other vital organs must be carefully evaluated.

Fluid Absorption and Hyponatremia

Hyponatremia is also a potentially lethal complication of this operation.[20] Once again, there have been several deaths from fluid absorption because operating room personnel were not keeping track of the fluid differentials. It is vital that the collecting system be one that is simple and highly accurate. A simple system has been described previously. Generally, I check fluid balance every 3,000 ml. When resecting fibroids or polyps, it is not unusual to note a gradual widening of the fluid discrepancy. If this is occurring, the physician must be aware that there is some fluid absorption taking place, and the operation may have to be terminated before the entire lesion has been treated. It is possible to return to the operating room at a later date. In fact, some physicians will elect to use a two-stage plan (i.e., resections 2 months apart) with particularly large lesions.

If the fluid differential is 1,000 ml, then the operation must be terminated within 5 to 10 minutes. Usually, another 250 ml will be absorbed during this time, but this will not result in hyponatremia (i.e., serum sodium less than 120 mEq/L). However, if the fluid absorption is greater than 2,000 ml, the patient will definitely have hyponatremia, and measures to correct this problem must be undertaken. Blood should be immediately drawn for sodium and potassium values, 10 mg of intravenous furosemide given, and a Foley catheter inserted. Then there is a waiting period as diuresis takes place. It is not necessary to use hypertonic saline. However, a sodium level of less than 120 mg should never occur if operating room personnel and physicians are paying proper attention to fluid balance. Most patients will require a brief hospital stay. More than 10 mg of furosemide should not be used for a higher dose may result in hypokalemia.

Bleeding

Bleeding problems can be controlled with Pitressin and Pitressin pack, which have been detailed previously. Late bleeding (i.e., 3 to 4 weeks after surgery) is usually controlled by having the patient rest for 1 or 2 days. I had to use the Pitressin pack in one patient who bled 1 week postoperative from the large submucous myoma bed. This was left in situ for 24 hours. The patient had no subsequent problems.

Infection

Infection is a very rare complication. I have had three infections in 450 patients[21] who were not started on antibiotics at the time of the laminaria insertion. However, the control group of 1,000 patients in whom the antibiotics were started with the laminaria insertion did not have any evidence of an infectious process.

Post-tubal Ligation Pain

There is a late complication noted primarily in women who have had a tubal ligation followed by an endometrial ablation.[22] It is not noted in women who have had only a fibroid resection but is noted in those women who have a fibroid or polyp resected followed by an ablation. Women who have had a previous tubal ligation in which the midportion of the tube has been occluded will develop, in the rare case, pain approximately 6 to 9 months after the resection and ablation. What happens in these patients is a retrograde bleeding from the cornua into the fallopian tube. Because the tube has been ligated, the tube swells, causing significant pain. The pain is usually accompanied by light bleeding, so it occurs at the time of expected menstruation. This probably occurs in less than 1 percent of women who have had a tubal ligation followed by an ablation or resection and ablation. Therapy is a laparoscopic cauterization or removal of the fallopian tube.

CONCLUSION

In summary, the diagnosis management of submucous myomas and polyps has been briefly reviewed. Parameters for a safe and effective operation have been presented. The physician and operating room personnel must be thoroughly instructed as to the technique of the operation. A high-flow gynecologic resectoscope along with proper irrigating fluid and tubing is important. Meticulous attention must be paid to fluid intake and output, which is the single most important parameter that will signal that there is trouble developing. Success rates will vary from patient to patient, but most patients will experience gratifying results with

the operation. If an ablation is to be performed along with resection of the polyp or myoma, the ablatation should be first and the resection next to reduce the chance of complications.

REFERENCES

1. Taylor PJ: Diagnostic and operative hysteroscopy. p. 363. In Seibel MN (ed): Infertility: A Comprehensive Check. Norwalk, CT, Appleton & Lange, 1990
2. Heinberg A: Uterine endoscopy; an aid to precision in the diagnosis of intrauterine disease. Surg Gynecol Obstet 18:515, 1914
3. Neuwirth RS, Amin HG: Excision of submucous fibroids with hysteroscopic control. Am J Obstet Gyncol 126:95, 1976
4. Neuwirth RS: A new technique for and additional experience with hysteroscopic resection of submucous fibroids. Am J Obstet Gynecol 131:91, 1978
5. Haning RV et al: Preservation of fertility by transcervical resection of a benign mesodermal uterine tumor with a resectoscope and glycine distending media. Fertil Steril 33:209, 1980
6. DeCherney AH, Polos ML: Hysteroscopic management of intrauterine lesions and intractable uterine bleeding. Obstet Gynecol 61:392, 1983
7. Hallez J et al: Methodical intrauterine resection. Am J Obstet Gynecol 156:1080, 1987
8. Brooks PC et al: Resectoscopic removal of symptomatic intrauterine lesions. J Reprod Med 34:435, 1989
9. Laufer FD: Removal of large symptomatic intrauterine growths by hysteroscopic resectoscope. Obstet Gynecol 75:836, 1990
10. Valle RF: Hysteroscopic removal of submucous leiomyomas. J Gynecol Surg 6:89, 1990
11. Corsol SL, Brooks PG: Resectoscopic myomectomy. Fertil Steril 55:1040, 1991
12. Enman PH: Hysteroscopic treatment of menorrhagia associated with uterine leiomyomas. Obstet Gynecol 81:716, 1993
13. Townsend DE, Fields G, McCausland A, Kauffman K: Diagnostic and operative hysteroscopy in the management of persistent postmenopausal bleeding. Obstet Gynecol 82:419, 1993
14. Baggish MF et al: Hysteroscopic treatment of symptomatic submucous myoma uteri with an Nd:YAG laser. J Gynecol Surg 5:27, 1989
15. Donez J et al: Neodymium:YAG laser and enlarged submucous fibroids. Fertil Steril 54:999, 1990
16. Brooks PJ et al: Hormonal inhibition of the endometrium for resectoscopic endometrial ablation. Am J Obstet Gynecol 164:1601, 1991
17. Townsend DE, Melkonia NR: Laminaria tent for diagnostic and operative hysteroscopy. J Gynecol Surg 6:271, 1990
18. Townsend DE: Vasopressin packs for post myoma resection bleeding. Am J Obstet Gynecol 165:1405, 1991
19. Townsend DE et al: Rollerball coagulation of the endometrium. Obstet Gynecol 76:310, 1990
20. Arieff AI, Ayus JC: Endometrial ablation complicated by fatal hyponatremic encephalopathy. JAMA 270:1230, 1993
21. McCausland V et al: Tubo-ovarian abscess after operative hysteroscopy. J Reprod Med 38:198, 1993
22. Townsend DE et al: Post ablation tubal sterilization syndrome. Obstet Gynecol 82:422, 1993

27 Catheterization of the Proximal Fallopian Tube

ELI RESHEF
JOSEPH S. SANFILIPPO

PATHOPHYSIOLOGY OF PROXIMAL TUBAL DISEASE

Proximal (interstitial) tubal obstruction is found in 10 to 20 percent of patients evaluated radiographically for infertility.[1] The causes of proximal tubal occlusion may be inflammatory, mechanical, congenital, or intraluminal debris. Most cases of proximal tubal occlusion are the consequence of an inflammatory process such as infection or endometriosis. Pathologic changes consistent with chronic salpingitis have been identified in more than half of the cases in which the occluded proximal tube was resected.[2] Obliterative fibrosis, chronic salpingitis, and salpingitis isthmica nodosa (SIN) have been noted in more than 90 percent of excised proximal tubes after unsuccessful transcervical cannulation.[3] Endometriosis constitutes a less common etiology for proximal occlusion. Congenital atresia of the isthmus has been reported, albeit rarely. Mechanical obstruction can be caused by intra- or extrauterine lesions, most commonly leiomyomas or polyps. Mechanical obstruction may also be associated with proximal tubal spasm, which accounts for 15 to 40 percent of false-positive results of hysterosalpingography (HSG).[4] Spasm may also be precipitated by surgical manipulation of this region. The presence of intraluminal debris or inspissated secretions may lead to proximal occlusion, which can be readily dislodged.[5]

Ascending infection after cervical colonization by pathogens such as *Chlamydia trachomatis* and *Neisseria gonorrhoeae* is thought to initiate most cases of pelvic inflammatory disease (PID). Progression from cervical infection to inflammation of the endometrium (endometritis), the fallopian tube mucosa (endosalpingitis), and ultimately the intraperitoneal structures characterizes the course of acute PID. Secondary infection with vaginal and gastrointestinal pathogens such as aerobic and anaerobic gram-negative bacteria contributes to further tissue destruction and subsequent scarring and fibrosis. However, "silent," asymptomatic infection leading to extensive endosalpingeal and intra-abdominal scarring of the reproductive tract has been described and attributed to *Chlamydia* colonization.[6]

DIAGNOSIS OF PROXIMAL TUBAL OCCLUSION

Transcervical injection of radiographic dye (HSG) or instillation of dye during laparoscopy (chromopertubation) are the two most common methods to diagnose tubal obstruction. Pelvic ultrasound aided by instillation of fluid into the uterus has been suggested for diagnosis, but experience with this method is limited. HSG is preferred over chromopertubation as the initial diagnostic method because it does not involve general anesthesia and it also provides useful information about the contour of the uterine cavity and the tubal mucosa. A false-positive rate of 15 to 40 percent regarding proximal tubal occlusion[4] is one of the pitfalls of HSG. This is thought to be due to either proximal tubal spasm or to the "path of least resistance" phenomenon. Medical agents to prevent spasm have not

291

been consistently effective. In the presence of the characteristic radiographic SIN changes in the cornual region (proximal microdiverticuli), however, one may be confident that the proximal occlusion is indeed real. Often, a repeat HSG will show patency even if a previous HSG showed occlusion. In the face of unexpected bilateral proximal occlusion that does not correlate with the patient's clinical history, one may therefore either repeat the HSG or perform chromopertubation at laparoscopy for confirmation. Even laparoscopic chromopertubation may result in false-positive results. Proximal spasm may occur, as well as equipment failure or occlusion of the distal injection port by improper positioning.

Proximal occlusion may be confirmed by selective HSG, during which cannulation may be attempted, or by trancervical cannulation during laparoscopy with selective chromopertubation. During selective HSG, which may be performed under fluoroscopic or sonographic guidance, the operator attempts to direct a catheter into the tubal ostium and selectively injects contrast material into each tube. The diagnosis of proximal unilateral or bilateral occlusion can then be confirmed, and relief of the obstruction can be attempted at the same time. Hysteroscopic confirmation of proximal occlusion can be performed at the time of laparoscopy, immediately followed by an attempt at cannulation. Falloposcopy, which allows visualization of the tubal lumen, may help in determining the extent of luminal fibrosis, if present.

PROXIMAL TUBAL CANNULATION

Cannulation of the proximal fallopian tube is most commonly performed to relieve obstruction. The earliest report of proximal tubal cannulation for this purpose appeared in 1849 when Smith[7] attempted to recanalize the proximal tube by tactile sensation using a whale bone sound. Corfman and Taylor[8] described selective salpingography using a curved metal cannula in 1966, but it was not until the mid-1980s when first reports of trancervical tubal cannulation by wire and by balloon were published.[1, 9, 10] This followed the advent of catheter technology for angiography of small blood vessels. Platia and Krudy[9] performed trancervical fluoroscopic recanalization of the proximal tube in 1985 with a 0.018-inch pediatric guidewire in one patient with bilateral proximal occlusion. This patient conceived but spontaneously aborted at 5 weeks. Confino et al.[10] first described transcervical balloon tuboplasty (TBT) in 1986. The procedure was performed through a rigid hysteroscope and used a modified coronary an-

gioplasty 4-French catheter that accommodated a 0.018-inch guidewire.

Entry into the proximal fallopian tube can be accomplished under fluoroscopic guidance, ultrasound guidance, or at hysteroscopy. The advantage of fluoroscopic and sonographic guidance is the avoidance of general anesthesia and probable reduction in cost. The advantage of the hysteroscopic approach under general anesthesia is that concommitant laparoscopy can detect additional tubal and peritoneal pathology, such as bipolar tubal disease, which may profoundly affect the prognosis for conception. Hysteroscopic proximal cannulation, however, may be attempted in an office setting, allowing direct visualization of the uterine cavity.

Fluoroscopic Proximal Tubal Cannulation

Fluoroscopic proximal tubal cannulation is performed in the radiology suite and requires little or no anesthesia or analgesia. A paracervical block with 1 percent xylocaine and oral or intravenous benzodiazepines (e.g., diazepam 5 to 10 mg PO or midazolam 1 to 2 mg IV) may be administered if indicated. The radiation exposure during fluoroscopy is usually less than 1 rad if the fluoroscope is operated under 10 minutes.[11] One should first inject radiographic contrast material (e.g., Sinographin or Renographin [Squibb, Princeton, New Jersey] or Conray [Mallinckrodt, St. Louis, Missouri]) through the cervical canal to verify unilateral or bilateral blockage. Once the proximally occluded side is identified, a semirigid catheter (e.g., a 5.5-French curved introducing Teflon catheter, Novy cornual cannulation set [Figure 27-1], or Jansen-Anderson insemination set [Fig. 27-2] [Cook OB/GYN, Spencer, Indiana]) is advanced toward the tubal ostium under fluoroscopic guidance. Contrast material may then be injected through the catheter into the ostium to verify occlusion. Occasionally, this side may prove patent by either dislodging debris under pressure or by bypassing the "path of least resistance." If the proximal tube is still occluded, cannulation should be attempted with a coaxial cannulation set (e.g., Novy cornual cannulation set; Fig. 27-1). The patient will often experience a short-term mild-to-moderate discomfort during proximal cannulation, especially if successful. A guidewire with a flexible tip (e.g., 0.018-inch stainless steel or a 0.015-inch Cope Mandril stainless steel wire) is coaxially passed through the outer rigid catheter and through the tubal ostium into the isthmic portion of the tube. One must not apply excessive force to the wire, as perforation may readily occur in that

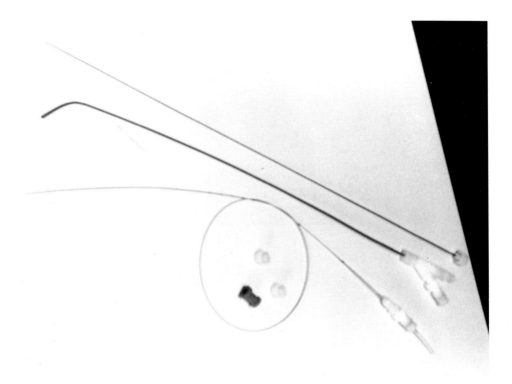

Fig. 27-1. Novy cornual cannulation set (Cook OB/GYN, Spencer, Indiana). *(Top to bottom)*: Stainless steel obturator; a 5.5-French curved introducing catheter; a 0.018-in. guidewire within a 3.0-French catheter. This set can be used for proximal cannulation during hysterosalpingography under fluoroscopic guidance or via the operating channel of a hysteroscope.

area. Although uncommon, perforation may produce bleeding and peritoneal infection. Coiling or excessive resistance may signify substantial proximal scarring (as in the case of SIN) or misapplication of the tip to the opening. The wire should be withdrawn slightly, the rigid outer catheter redirected, and the procedure attempted again. If cannulation with wire is successful, a flexible inner catheter (3-French) is slipped over the guidewire and advanced into the isthmic portion. The wire is then withdrawn, and contrast material is injected through the inner catheter to prove patency. If part or the entire tubal lumen is highlighted, successful cannulation should be assumed. Dispersion of contrast material in an irregular pattern may signify perforation. If balloon tuboplasty is desired, the balloon is slipped over the guidewire and proximal dilatation can then be performed.

Cannulation Under Ultrasound Guidance

Ultrasound-directed cannulation was described by Jansen and Anderson in 1987.[12] A new catheter system was used (Cook Australia Pty, Melbourne, Australia;

Fig. 27-2). Vaginal sonography was used concommitantly to confirm placement. Despite superior visualization of the uterus and its landmarks by vaginal sonography, manipulating a vaginal probe and a transcervical device may be difficult. Hurst et al.[13] described trancervical cannulation under abdominal ultrasound guidance. The bladder must be full to improve visualization and displace the anteverted uterus to midposition. Using this approach, transfer of gametes (gamete intrafallopian transfer [GIFT] or zygotes (zygote intrafallopian transfer [ZIFT]) have been described.

Hysteroscopic Cannulation

Novy et al.[14] used a coaxial set of catheters and a guidewire (Cook OB/GYN, Spencer, Indiana; Fig. 28-1) through the operating channel of a hysteroscope to directly visualize and cannulate the cornua. Carbon dioxide was used as distention medium. The system included a 5.5-French Teflon outer cannula fitted with a Y-adapter with a Luer-lok hub. A Cope-type stainless steel guidewire (0.018-in. diameter) fitted inside a 3-

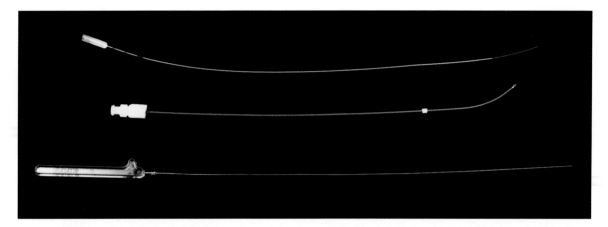

Fig. 27-2. Jansen-Anderson insemination set (Cook OB/GYN, Spencer, Indiana). *(Top to bottom)*: A 3.0-French delivery inner catheter with a 2.0-French tip; a 5.7-French echogenic silicone guiding catheter; a Malleable stainless steel obturator. This set may be used for intratubal insemination, selective hysterosalpingography, or transcervical transfer of gametes or zygotes.

French Teflon inner catheter was inserted through this port into the tubal ostium. The flexible blunt-tip guidewire was advanced beyond the uterotubal junction into the isthmic portion. Confirmation of patency was accomplished by advancing the inner catheter over the wire, withdrawing the wire, and injecting dye while watching the distal tube for spill via the laparoscope. Using this system in 10 patients with unilateral or bilateral proximal occlusion, 11 of 12 fallopian tubes were successfully cannulated. This procedure, when performed under general anesthesia, has the advantage of reduced patient discomfort and allows the operator to verify successful cannulation and to detect pelvic pathology via a concommitant laparoscopy. In theory, proximal spasm during manipulation may be reduced under general anesthesia, even though support for this observation is scant. Hysteroscopy may be performed in the office using paracervical block and mild oral or intravenous sedation. A small rigid or flexible hysteroscope (e.g., a Storz 4-mm chorionhysteroscope [Storz, Culver City, California]; or an Olympus 3.5-mm or 4.5-mm flexible Hystero-fiberscope [Olympus, Lake Success, New York; Fig. 27-3] should be used to minimize discomfort. Both cannulation and falloposcopy can then be performed, thus reducing the morbidity of general anesthesia and the cost of hospitalization. To date, there are no controlled, prospective studies comparing hysteroscopic with fluoroscopic or sonographic proximal cannulation. However, in an era in which surgical procedures are increasingly performed on an outpatient basis and in the office, one should consider the latter two approaches first if feasible.

In analyzing the results of studies of transcervical proximal recanalization, the different techniques and methodologies used prevent a valid comparison. Successful relief of proximal occlusion may be attained by simply injecting dye under pressure into the tubal ostium without actual cannulation. Not all studies used selective salpingography before cannulation and therefore may overreport success in achieving patency be cannulation. Successful recanalization has ranged from 31 to 96 percent of treated fallopian tubes,[11,15–17] resulting in an intrauterine pregnancy rate (short term) of 23 to 44 percent[11,15–17] ectopic pregnancy rate of 0 to 66 percent of all pregnancies[11,15–17]; and estimated long-term (>6 months) patency of 35 to 82 percent.[11,15–17]

Complications

Complications of transcervical tubal catheterization are uncommon. Potential complications include bleeding due to perforation, creation of sinus tracts due to perforation, intratubal or intraperitoneal infection, hypotension due to vagal reaction, and complications due to anesthesia. Tubal perforation with guidewires has been reported in 5 percent or less of all patients.[11] Severe sequellae of perforation have not been reported. Perforation can be avoided by visualization of the wire combined with tactile sensation. If resistance is encountered or coiling or distortion of the distal tip is visualized, the procedure should be abandoned or attempts at redirection of the wire should be made. Isolated cases of infection have been reported. Flare-up of pre-existing endometrial or endosalpingeal disease

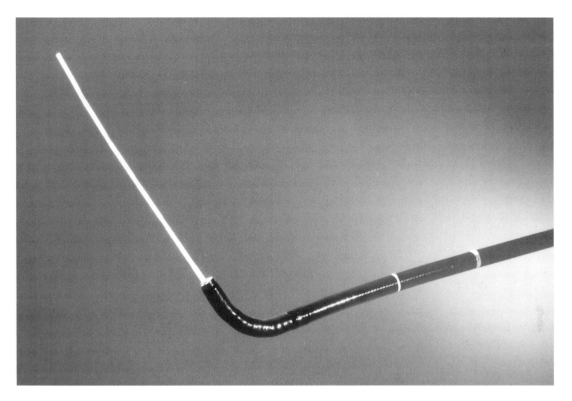

Fig. 27-3. The tip of a flexible Hystero-Fiberscope (Olympus, Lake Success, New York) with an outer diameter of 3.6 mm and a 1.2-mm inner channel. The latter can accommodate a 3.0-French or smaller catheter for transcervical transfer of gametes or zygotes.

or transmission of cervical or vaginal pathogens into the tube is possible. Antibiotic prophylaxis should probably be instituted in most patients undergoing transcervical cannulation, even though this has not been thoroughly studied.

TRANSCERVICAL GAMETE OR ZYGOTE TRANSFER

Trancervical cannulation to deposit gametes or zygotes in the fallopian tube (GIFT or ZIFT) has been described.[18–20] This procedure is less invasive and theoretically less expensive than laparoscopic GIFT or ZIFT. Jansen et al.[18] first reported successful ultrasound-guided transcervical ZIFT in 1988. One of five patients conceived after cannulation with a new catheter system (Cook Australia Pty, Melbourne, Australia; Fig. 27-2), which contained a firm, precurved 5.5-French outer catheter, a metal obturator, and a soft, flexible 3-French inner catheter. The outer catheter was positioned in the cornual region, and the inner catheter was advanced into the isthmic portion under vaginal ultrasonic guidance. The use of abdominal ultrasound

guidance to overcome the technical difficulties of concommitant vaginal probe placement and transcervical manipulation has been suggested.[13] Review of the literature of ultrasound-guided transcervical ZIFT in 248 patients[21–23] revealed a pregnancy rate of 9 to 32 percent (interestingly, these two figures were reported by the same investigator, with the lower figure published 4 years after the initial higher figure[22]) and a delivery rate of 9 to 29 percent. For comparison, the delivery rate per retrieval in the United States after conventional ZIFT was 19.7 percent in 1991.[24] The only recent randomized study comparing trancervical ZIFT to intrauterine transfer of embryos in conventional in vitro fertilization (IVF)[22] reported a statistically significant inferior result with transcervical ZIFT (4 versus 12 percent implantation rate). Ultrasound-guided transcervical GIFT results in 66 patients[21] revealed a pregnancy rate of 20 to 31 percent and a delivery rate of 10 to 25 percent. For comparison, conventional GIFT results (livebirths per retrieval) for 1991 were 26.5 percent.[24]

Transcervical GIFT via hysteroscopy has been reported by Possati et al. in 1991.[20] Unilateral transfer of gametes in a 3-French Teflon catheter via the operating channel of a rigid 4-mm 30 degree hysteroscope with CO_2 insufflation was performed in 26 patients, achieving a 27 percent pregnancy rate and 19 percent delivery rate. Seracchioli[25] performed a hysteroscopic GIFT on 48 patients using a 3.6-mm flexible hysteroscope and CO_2 as distension medium. The Jansen-Anderson intratubal transfer set (Fig. 28-2) was placed transcervically near the hysteroscope and advanced under direct vision. Fourteen pregnancies (29 percent) were achieved, of which 3 spontaneously aborted. No ectopic pregnancies resulted. Hysteroscopic GIFT or ZIFT can be performed in the office with intravenous or oral sedation using a flexible hysteroscope (e.g., Olympus 3.6-mm fiberscope with a 1.2-mm irrigation channel; Fig. 27-3) and a coaxial catheter-guidewire system (e.g., Katayama catheter set [Cook OB/GYN, Spencer, Indiana]; Fig. 27-4). In theory, hysteroscopic GIFT offers no advantage over the ultrasound-guided approach. It may potentially create greater disruption of the endometrial cavity and introduce a gametotoxic factor by the distension medium (e.g., changing the pH of the intratubal fluid by CO_2). Studies comparing hys-

teroscopic with the ultrasound-guided technique have not been performed. The results in terms of conception rates have been equal or inferior to the more traditional approach with GIFT. It remains to be seen whether further refinements of techniques and advances in the reproductive laboratory will popularize the transcervical approach in assisted reproductive technology practice.

Transcervical intratubal insemination, by either ultrasonic guidance[18,26] or by tactile sensation,[27] has been reported. A pregnancy rate of 12 to 24 percent has been achieved. One case of acute salpingitis was reported.[27] To date, no randomized prospective studies comparing intratubal to intrauterine inseminations have been performed, and the use of this technique is therefore debatable.

FALLOPOSCOPY

Endotubal pathology can be directly visualized by fiberoptic instruments, either abdominally during laparoscopy or via the transcervical route. Recent tech-

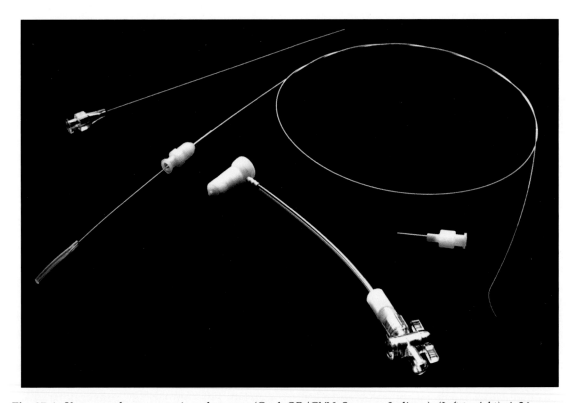

Fig. 27-4. Katayama hysteroscopic catheter set (Cook OB/GYN, Spencer, Indiana). *(Left to right)*: A 26-gauge stainless steel delivery cannula; a 0.015-in. Cope Mandril stainless steel guidewire with a flexible platinum tip within a transluscent 2.5- or 3.0-French catheter; an adapter assembly with stopcock; a polyethylene introducing sleeve. This set can be used via a flexible hysteroscope (see Fig. 28-3) for transcervical transfer of gametes or zygotes

nologic advances have allowed reduction in the diameter of falloposcopes and increase in flexibility, making it possible to reduce luminal trauma and patient discomfort. Direct visualization of tubal luminal pathology by this technique has some promising applications, even though currently its practical contribution to treatment of tubal disease is still under debate. Rigid falloposcopy during laparoscopy was first reported by Henry-Suchet et al.[28] Using this technique, distal endotubal pathology such as stenosis, polyps, adhesions, and mucinous plugs could be identified and may provide additional clues as to prognosis of surgical repair. Kerin et al.[29] first explored the proximal tube transcervically using a flexible 0.5-mm falloposcope containing 1,800 to 2,200 imaging fibers. This fiber was passed through the operating channel of a 3.3-mm flexible hysteroscope. Intraluminal fibrosis, partial or total obstruction, and adhesions were readily identified. Kerin et al.[30] subsequently proposed a falloposcopic classification of luminal tubal disease. A linear everting falloposcopy system was described by Pearlstone et al.[31] and Scudemore et al.[32] in 1992 (Imagyn, Laguna Miguel, California). With this unique system, falloposcopy is possible without a hysteroscope. A linear everting system uses an inflatable 1.25-mm catheter, which advances atraumatically by eversion into the tubal lumen. A 0.5-mm falloposcopic fiber is then introduced through the inner lumen. Office falloposcopic assessment using this system was recently described by Dunphy.[33] The advantage of this system is in eliminating the shear forces between the catheter and the tubal lumen, thus reducing epithelial damage. Although not extensively studied, falloposcopy offers a promising future to a less invasive approach to the diagnosis and perhaps the treatment of tubal disease.

TREATMENT OF ECTOPIC PREGNANCY

With the advent of medical treatment for ectopic pregnancy,[34] other less invasive alternatives to surgical treatment have been proposed. Transvaginal injection of methotrexate (MTX) or prostaglandin has been reported.[35] Risquez et al.[36] reported the transcervical administration of MTX into the tubal lumen in four patients with ectopic pregnancies. A prospective multicenter study involving 31 patients treated in a similar fashion resulted in complete resolution of the ectopic pregnancy in 87 percent.[37] Seven of seven patients who subsequently had an HSG had patency of the involved side. These results are similar to results of outpatient

treatment with intramuscular MTX,[38] which, unlike high-dose intravenous administration of this agent, is associated with minimal side effects. Local administration of chemotherapeutic agents to treat ectopic pregnancy may theoretically reduce the dose and hence the side effects. However, this approach is more invasive than intramuscular administration, and its effectiveness has not been directly compared with this mode of administration.

STERILIZATION

Various methods have been tested to occlude the proximal fallopian tube for sterilization by using a less invasive transcervical approach. These included electrocoagulation, cryocoagulation, caustic chemicals, and permanent or temporary plugs. None of these methods is comparable with surgical sterilization in terms of efficacy of sterilization. Hysteroscopic electrocoagulation has essentially been abandoned after an unacceptable failure and complication rate.[11] Application of luminal plugs such as silicon or chemical agents to scarify the proximal tube (quinacrine, phenolatabrine, methylcyanoacrylate) requires repeated applications to ensure sterility.[11] At present, then, transcervical sterilization does not provide a substitute to sterilization by a transabdominal approach.

CONCLUSIONS

Transcervical approach to the fallopian tube has been gaining momentum in the past 10 years, especially for relief of proximal obstruction and transfer of gametes or zygotes. Technologic advances in this field offer improved optics, reduced diameter of fiberoptic instruments, improved catheter characteristics, and improved imaging techniques. The probability, then, of replacing some of the more invasive reproductive procedures (such as cornual resection and tubal reimplantation or even laparoscopic GIFT or ZIFT with less invasive transcervical procedures is quickly becoming a reality. Transcervical cannulation procedures are compatible with the recent trend to reduce invasiveness and move procedures from the inpatient setting to the outpatient and even in-office environment and even with the cost-cutting trend. Less promising at present is the prospect of transcervical sterilization replacing the traditional approach. Transcervical falloposcopy is a promising technique whose applicability to clinical practice must be further investigated.

REFERENCES

1. Thurmond AS, Novy M, Uchida BT, Rosch J: Fallopian tube obstruction: selective salpingography and recanalization. Radiology 163:511, 1987
2. Grant A: Infertility surgery of the oviduct. Fertil Steril 22:496, 1971
3. Letterie GS, Sakas EL: Histology of proximal tubal obstruction in cases of unsuccessful tubal canalization. Fertil Steril 56:831, 1991
4. World Health Organization: Comparative trial of tubal insufflation, hysterosalpingogram and laparoscopy with dye hydrotubation for assessment of tubal patency. Fertil Steril 46:1101, 1986
5. Sulak PJ, Letterie GS, Coddington CC et al: Histology of proximal tubal occlusion. Fertil Steril 48:437, 1987
6. Hager DW: Acute salpingitis. p. 191. In Siegler AM (ed): The Fallopian Tube. Futura, Mount Kisco, NY, 1986
7. Smith WT: New method of treating sterility by removal of obstructions of the fallopian tubes. Lancet 1:529, 1849
8. Corfman PA, Taylor HC: An instrument for transcervical treatment of the oviducts and uterine cornua. Obstet Gynecol 27:880, 1966
9. Platia MP, Krudy AG: Transvaginal fluoroscopic recanalization of the proximally occluded oviduct. Fertil Steril 44:704, 1985
10. Confino E, Friberg J, Gleicher N: Transcervical balloon tuboplasty (TBT). Fertil Steril 46:963, 1986
11. Risquez F, Confino E: Transcervical tubal cannulation, past, present, and future. Fertil Steril 60:211, 1993
12. Jansen RPS, Anderson JC: Catheterisation of the fallopian tubes from the vagina. Lancet 2:309, 1987
13. Hurst BS, Persutte WH, Awoniyi CA et al: Ultrasound guided transcervical tubal catheterization for assisted reproduction: a learning program using laparoscopy for confirmation. Fertil Steril 59:236, 1993
14. Novy MJ, Thurmond AS, Patton P et al: Diagnosis of cornual obstruction by transvaginal fallopian tube cannulation. Fertil Steril 50:434, 1988
15. Isaacson KB, Amendola M, Banner M et al: Transcervical fallopian tube recanalization: a safe and effective therapy for patients with proximal tubal obstruction. Int J Fertil 37:106, 1992
16. Thurmond AS: Pregnancies after selective salpingography and tubal recanalization. Radiology 190:11, 1994
17. Thompson KA, Kiltz RJ, Koci T et al: Transcervical fallopian tube catheterization and recanalization for proximal tubal obstruction. Fertil Steril 61:243, 1994
18. Jansen RPS, Anderson JC, Sutherland PD: Nonoperative embryo transfer to the fallopian tube. N Engl J Med 319:288, 1988
19. Seracchioli R, Possati G, Bafaro G: Hysteroscopic gamete intra-fallopian transfer: a good alternative, in selected cases, to laparoscopic intra-fallopian transfer. Hum Reprod 6:1388, 1991
20. Possati G, Seracchioli R, Melega C et al: Gamete intrafallopian transfer by hysteroscopy as an alternative treatment for infertility. Fertil Steril 56:496, 1991
21. Hurst BS, Schlaff WD: Assisted reproduction: what role for ZIFT? Contemp OB/GYN 39:9, 1994
22. Scholtes MCV, Roozenburg BJ, Verhoeff A et al: A randomized study of transcervical intrafallopian transfer of pronucleate embryos controlled by ultrasound versus intrauterine transfer of four- to eight-cell embryos. Fertil Steril 61:102, 1994
23. Hercz P, Vine SJ, Walker SM: Experience with transcervical fallopian tube catheterization. Fertil Steril 61:551, 1994
24. Society for Assisted Reproductive Technology: Assisted reproductive technology in the United States and Canada: 1991 results. Fertil Steril 59:956, 1993
25. Seracchioli R, Maccolini A, Porcu E et al: A new approach to gamete intra-fallopian transfer via hysteroscopy. Hum Reprod 8: 2093, 1993
26. Lucena E, Ruiz JA, Mendoza JC et al: Vaginal intratubal insemination (VITI) and vaginal GIFT, endosonographic technique: early experience. Hum Reprod 4:658, 1989
27. Pratt DE, Bieber E, Barnes R et al: Transvaginal intratubal insemination by tactile sensation: a preliminary report. Fertil Steril 56:984, 1991
28. Henry-Suchet J, Loffredo V, Tesquier L et al: Endoscopy of the tube (tuboscopy): its prognostic value for tuboplasties. Acta Eur Fertil 16:139, 1985
29. Kerin JF, Daykhovsky L, Segalowitz J et al: Falloposcopy: a microendoscopic technique for visual exploration of the human fallopian tube from the uterotubal ostium to the fimbria using a transvaginal approach. Fertil Steril 54:390, 1990
30. Kerin JF, Williams DB, San Roman GA et al: Falloposcopic classification and treatment of fallopian tube lumen disease. Fertil Steril 57:731, 1992
31. Pearlstone AC, Surrey E, Kerin JF: The linear everting catheter: a nonhysteroscopic, transvaginal technique for access and microendoscopy of the fallopian tube. Fertil Steril 58:854, 1992
32. Scudmore I, Dunphy BC, Cooke ID: Outpatient falloposcopy: intra-luminal imaging of the fallopian tube by transuterine fibre-optic endoscopy as an outpatient procedure. Br J Obstet Gynaecol 99:829, 1992
33. Dunphy BC: Office falloposcopic assessment in proximal tubal occlusive disease. Fertil Steril 61:168, 1994
34. Tanaka T, Hayashi H, Kutsuzawa S et al: Treatment of interstitial ectopic pregnancy with methotrexate: report of a successful case. Fertil Steril 37:851, 1982
35. Feichtinger W, Kemeter P: Conservative treatment of ectopic pregnancy by transvaginal aspiration under sonographic control and methotrexate injection. Lancet 1:381, 1987
36. Risquez, F, Mathieson J, Pariente D et al: Diagnosis and treatment of ectopic pregnancy by retrograde selective salpingography and intraluminal methotrexate injection: work in progress. Hum Reprod 5:759, 1990
37. Risquez F, Forman R, Maleika F et al: Transcervical cannulation of the fallopian tube for the management of ectopic pregnancy: prospective multicenter study. Fertil Steril 58:1131, 1992
38. Pansky M, Golan A, Bukovsky I et al: Nonsurgical management of tubal pregnancy. Necessity in view of the changing clinical appearance. Am J Obstet Gynecol 164:888, 1991

28 Complications of Hysteroscopy

JACQUES E. RIOUX

As with all operative procedures, complications will occur both during the procedure and throughout the postoperative period (Table 28-1). As more gynecologists perform operative hysteroscopy and more difficult procedures are performed, the rate of complications will increase. History predicts that the rate of complications will be higher at first, as operators begin the learning curve, and then settle at a lower percentage once experience has been gained. In general, most complications are minor, but serious life-threatening complications have been reported. Most complications in operative hysteroscopy can be prevented by obtaining a thorough knowledge of the procedure and equipment, and then applying simple precautions and prudence.

INTRAOPERATIVE COMPLICATIONS

Complications Secondary To Uterine Distention

CO_2 Embolization

CO_2 is the distending medium of choice for diagnostic hysteroscopy.[1] With a refractive index of 1.00, the image transmission is perfect, and an adequate uterine distention can be obtained. A special insufflator dedicated to hysteroscopy must be used to avoid complication. Indeed, the flow rate of the CO_2 must never exceed 100 ml/min, and these hysteroflators have a built-in safety feature, a reducing valve, that ensures just that. The intrauterine pressure can reach 200 mm Hg without untoward effect in the intact uterus. However, the theoretical rupture of a thin hydrosalpinx is possible at that pressure. The total volume of gas used during a procedure is unimportant because CO_2 has a long history of safety. Therefore, it is ideal for office hysteroscopy; it is clean, cheap, and easy to obtain.

However, CO_2 is far from ideal for operative hysteroscopy. Indeed, mixed with blood, it forms bubbles and soon the view becomes obscured. Moreover, during any kind of surgical procedure, blood channels are open, and it is easy to understand that when the intrauterine pressure of CO_2 is greater than the blood pressure of the patient, CO_2 is forcefully injected into the blood stream. Fortunately, as noted earlier, when the flow rate is less than 100 ml/min and pressures are less than 100 mm Hg, the CO_2 is absorbed and the mechanism for clearing the insufflated CO_2 from the body is sufficient.[2]

This was not the case for five women on whom the neodymium:yttrium-aluminium-garnet (Nd:YAG) laser with sapphire tips or coaxial air-cooled fibers was used for intrauterine surgery. Four of them died in a sequence of sudden cardiovascular collapse followed by irreversible cardiac arrest. The other became critically ill and, after prolonged hospitalization, survived with neurologic deficits. The use of high-pressure, gas-cooled Nd:YAG fibers for intrauterine laser surgery is associated with mortal danger for the patient and hence should be avoided. The instillation of air, nitrogen, or CO_2 at a flow rate between 100 and 1000 ml/min. may result in gaseous embolism with resultant cardiovascular collapse.[3]

Anaphylactic Reaction to Dextran 70

Dextran 70 (Hyskon) is a clear, high-viscosity polysaccharide composed of glucose units. Its molecular weight is 70,000, and it is presented in a sterile solution of dextrose 10 percent. It has excellent optical properties and is very viscous and sticky. Because of this, the instruments must be washed in hot water immediately

Table 28-1. Complications of Operative Hysteroscopy: A Classification

---

Early complications (during procedure)
    Secondary to uterine distention
        CO_2 embolization
        Anaphylactic reaction to dextran
        Fluid overload
        Dilutional hyponatremia syndrome
        Noncardiogenic (hypervolemic) pulmonary edema
    Secondary to the interventions
        Cervical tear
        Uterine perforation
        Bleeding
        Thermal injury: electrical-laser with and without uterine perforation
Late complications (after the procedure has been terminated)
    Infection
    Bleeding
    Synechiae
    Pregnancy
    Cancer

---

after use to avoid caramelization and bonding of the components and valves. It does not mix readily with blood, and a clear field can be maintained despite the bleeding that results from surgical interventions. Electrosurgery can be performed with Hyskon because it is nonconductive. For these reasons, it became a first choice for diagnostic hysteroscopy for most of the earlier interventions performed either with scissors and biopsy forceps and, later, with laser and the resectoscope. Hyskon was usually delivered in small amounts in a 50-ml hand-held syringe. The "strong" assistant would instill the fluid on the instructions of the gynecologist; rarely was more than 300 ml of Hyskon used for a single procedure. Later, a pump using CO_2 from an external high-pressure supply was introduced, making insufflation easier. The pump was equipped with a safety-check ball to prevent inadvertent pumping of gas into the patient's uterus.[4] It was discovered that the pump could fail, allowing gas to mix with the Hyskon itself. Currently, no Hyskon pump is marketed.

Severe allergic reactions to Hyskon have been reported. The incidence of life-threatening anaphylaxis to dextran is estimated to be between 3 and 8 per 10,000 cases.[5] This reaction is not dependent on the amount given and often occurs early in the infusion process. Prior exposure to dextran may not be necessary because the body may have produced antibodies by prior exposure to native dextran in dental deposits, dextran-producing organisms in the gastrointestinal tract, dietary sugars, or food additives containing polysaccha-

rides.[6] Because of the risk and despite the fact that large quantities are not mandatory to initiate the reaction, it is recommended that, to minimize risk, only 300 ml be allowed to be absorbed during operative use of the resectoscope. Some reactions reported as anaphylactic may, in fact, have been due to fluid overload and hyponatremia. Indeed, because of the colloid osmotic property of dextran, each gram of dextran 70 will hold about 27 ml of water. Therefore, each 100 ml of 32 percent dextran 70 solution that is absorbed intravascularly would expand the circulating volume by about 860 ml. Also, dextran causes hemodilution as a direct result of the plasma volume expansion and, when administered intravenously in excess of 1.5 g/kg body weight, interferes with coagulation by inhibiting factor VIII. This explains the hemodilution and the coagulopathy found in some patients that may have been attributed to allergic reaction.[7]

Fluid Overload, Dilutional Hyponatremia Syndrome, and Noncardiogenic (Hypervolemic) Pulmonary Edema

Three complications are reported separately in the literature but are, in fact, different manifestations of the same phenomenon: *fluid overload* leads to hemodilution expressed by *hyponatremia*, possibly leading to *pulmonary edema* and even cerebral edema if not treated in time.

The low-viscosity fluids most often used for operative hysteroscopy are dextrose 5 percent, sorbitol, and glycine. Normal saline should never be used in the presence of electric current but is safe with the use of laser and, being isotonic, is theoretically less dangerous (Urologists have been using them for many years during transurethral resection of the prostate and they have described a syndrome similar to what we now see in identical circumstances.) The hemodilution is the result of fluid overload and is translated biologically by a diminution of the protidemia, hematocrit, and natremia. The first clinical sign is pulmonary edema and cardiovasculatory failure. If the patient is under a general anesthetic, the first sign will therefore be the appearance of bibasilar rales, which can be objectified by radiograph showing pulmonary edema and congestion of the upper chest with facial edema. If the procedure is being performed under regional anesthesia, she will express some confusion, restlessness, and even convulsions.

When detected early, the situation is reversible and responds very well to diuretics. Moreover, it is preventable by careful fluid-balance monitoring.

Most overhydration with irrigation fluid is a result of a miscalculation of fluid administration and collection. Indeed, it is easy to forget a 3000 ml bag if it was added while the circulating nurse was out to lunch! By the same token, a lot of fluid is lost every time the hysteroscope is removed from its sheaths, around the scope via a dilated cervix, ending up on the floor where it is very difficult to quantify. Therefore, concern should be directed at the fluid absorbed rather than the total fluid used for irrigation. Careful monitoring is essential; input and output should be reported to the surgeon by the circulating nurse every 10 minutes.

Secondary Complications

Cervical Tear

A cervical tear is a benign complication that occurs when cervical dilation is necessary to introduce the operative hysteroscope. Cervical stenosis may be present, but even with a normal cervix, acute dilation up to 1 cm, using a Pozzi tenaculum and forceful counteraction with the dilator, can tear the pericervical fascia. To prevent this, the use of laminaria, placed the night before is recommended. Patients need to be informed that use of this product in a nonpregnant woman is off-label, and not approved by the Food and Drug Administration (FDA). Cervical laceration rarely needs treatment, but should bleeding occur, a single stitch will stop it and repair the tear at the same time.

Uterine Perforation

Uterine perforation is the most common complication of hysteroscopy, occurring in 14 per 1,000 cases;[8] it is also underreported and, fortunately, not usually significant if performed with nonelectric and nonlaser equipment. Indeed, as soon as the perforation is detected, the procedure should be abandoned to avoid fluid overload and damage to adjacent tissues. Very rarely is a laparotomy necessary to control bleeding secondary to perforation. However, if the perforation was not recognized and electric instruments or lasers were used after its occurrence, the patient must be monitored during the early postoperative hours and instructed to consult if any symptoms should occur after her discharge. To prevent perforation, the hysteroscope should be advanced under direct vision only, no undue pressure should be made against the fundus, and when visibility is inadequate, the operator should stop and start again only when good visibility has been re-established.

Bleeding

Bleeding is an infrequent complication of operative hysteroscopy; when it does occur, it is more a nuisance than a real complication. Vessels should be coagulated as the surgery progresses. Bleeding may obscure the field of vision during hysteroscopic surgery. Active circulation of the distending medium will restore visibility, and increasing the intrauterine pressure will stop active bleeding. After the procedure has been completed and the uterus deflated, active bleeding may recur, and some corrective measure must be undertaken to stop it. Bimanual compression should be attempted first. Should that fail, the use of a Foley catheter with a 30-ml balloon or a specially designed intrauterine balloon to tamponade the endometrial cavity. These balloons can be removed after a few hours or left overnight.

The use of diluted vasopressin either by injection into the cervical stroma or by packing the uterus with a soaked sponge has been advocated, but the mechanism of action is obscure and cardiac complications, have been reported including arrhythmias, myocardial injury, and death, with the use of vasopressin.

Thermal Injury

Thermal injury to the bowel after hysteroscopic female sterilization using an electric tubal probe to electrocoagulate the isthmic portion of the tube was reported more than 15 years ago. Once the electrode is introduced via the ostium, the procedure becomes a blind one, and it is impossible to know if the probe is within the tubal lumen or in the peritoneal cavity. Activating the current was therefore guesswork and after a few serious accidents occurred,[10] the FDA forbade the use of that technique as a means of female sterilization.

Some time lapsed before somebody dared to use electric current within the uterine cavity. This time, however, the procedure was under direct vision and in a controlled situation—so it was thought! Indeed everyone understands that after a uterine perforation, the use of electric instruments or laser fibers blindly within the abdominal cavity could result in a serious thermal injury of the adjacent tissues followed by major complications. But what few operators know was that thermal injury to the bowel has been reported after hysteroscopic surgery using the Nd:YAG laser or the rollerball electrode *without uterine perforation.*[11]

In those cases, the pathologic examination of the uterus revealed no perforation, and the histologic sections through the serosal lesion showed transmural coagulative necrosis. These lesions are still part of the

Appendix
Informed Consent; A Process

GANSON PURCELL, JR.

As the decade of the 1980s dawned, Congress mandated in Public Law 95-622 a study of "The Ethical and Legal Implications of the Requirements for Informed Consent." The resultant President's Commission for the Study of Ethical Problems in Medicine and Biomedical and Behavioral Research submitted its report in October 1982. A key conclusion of that report was as follows: "Ethically valid consent is a process of shared decision making based upon mutual respect and participation, not a ritual to be equated with reciting the contents of a form that details the risks of particular treatments."[1]

The commission noted that the ethical foundation of informed consent is rooted in the promotion of two values: personal well-being and self-determination.[1] Indeed, in thoughtful expositions of the process of informed consent, the following key words are evident: *freedom, trust, understanding, self-determination.* Although the purpose of this essay is to provide a framework for the practical application of informed consent when using operative endoscopy, it is nonetheless instructive to consider briefly the historical evolution.

HISTORICAL DEVELOPMENT OF INFORMED CONSENT

Grodin[2] traces the initial stirrings of the concept of informed consent to the time of Hippocrates. The Hippocratic tradition sought to focus on concern for the patient's welfare as an underlying goal for therapeutic practice. In this dawning of the age of beneficence, it was the physician who determined what was good and what was harmful for the patient. In this time of antiquity, there was no consideration given to the need for self-determination on the part of the patient. Indeed, as the President's commission notes, Hippocrates decreed quite the opposite in *Decorum*:

Perform (these duties) calmly and adroitly, concealing most things from the patient while you are attending to him. Give necessary orders with cheerfulness and sincerity, turning his attention away from what is being done to him; sometimes reprove sharply and emphatically, and sometimes comfort with solicitude and attention, revealing nothing of the patient's future or present condition.[1]

It was in the early part of this century (1914) that Judge Cardozo firmly established the patient's right of determination in the *Schloendorff* case: "Every human being of adult years and sound mind has a right to determine what shall be done with his own body; and a surgeon who performs an operation without his patient's consent commits an assault for which he is liable in damages." The President's commission makes special note of two aspects of this landmark decision. First, there was no consideration of the information a patient would need to exercise his right of self-determination. Second, even though the patient's right to consent was emphatically stated, recovery of damages was denied.

Although the post-World War II Nuremberg trials uncovered revelations of horrific human experimentation in concentration camps and the resultant Nurenberg codes, laying the groundwork for rules of conduct in human medical experimentation, are generally considered the roots of the modern concept of informed consent,[3-5] it was not until the right's movement of the 1960s and 1970s with its antipaternalism revolt, and further evolution into the 1980s, which firmly established the concept of shared decision making in medical therapeutics.[2,3,4,6]

INFORMED CONSENT: LEGAL DOCTRINE OR ETHICAL IMPERATIVE?

As one peruses the literature dealing with informed consent, one is quickly struck by the tension that exists as to whether informed consent is fundamentally a legal doctrine or an ethical imperative. The Ethics Committee of the American College of Obstricians and Gynecologists (ACOG) initiates its Committee Opinion on informed consent with the statement: "Informed consent is an ethical concept that has become integral to contemporary medical ethics and medical practice."[4] Although acknowledging that the precursors of the modern doctrine of informed consent are found in English common law regarding battery, the President's commission declared that "although the informed consent doctrine has substantial foundations in law, it is essentially an ethical imperative."[1] However, in a commentary critical of the ACOG Ethics Committee opinion, Annas and Elias declare that informed consent is "primarily a legal doctrine, articulated not only by the American judges sitting at Nuremberg, but also by judges in almost all the 50 states, by more than half of the state legislatures, and by federal research regulations."[5]

In an accompanying commentary, Kenneth Heland,[6] a lawyer who sat with ACOG's Ethics Committee during the crafting of the Committee Opinion, acknowledges the tension between the legal and ethical aspects of the doctrine and attempts to provide a "legal road map" to guide the physician in practice. Heland focuses on the degree of disclosure needed for a legally valid informed consent. He indicates the courts and state jurisdictions have adopted three different degrees of disclosure: (1) the professional or reasonable physician standard; (2) the materiality or reasonable patient viewpoint standard; and (3) the subjective patient viewpoint standard. We revisit these concepts in the next section of our discussion. Suffice it to say here, Heland avers that physicians who comprehend the section of ACOG's Committee Opinion entitled "Ethical Applications of Informed Consent" and who understand the degree of disclosure required in their particular jurisdiction (and any other specific laws on informed consent that apply in their state) will have essentially fulfilled their legal obligation for informed consent.

Although acknowledging that there is inevitably and appropriately a legal aspect to informed consent, the President's commission expressed a commonly held concern "that efforts to draw the law further into regulating the subtler aspects of relationships between patients and healthcare professionals may prove ineffective, burdensome, and ultimately counterproductive."[1] In a wonderfully lucid discussion entitled "The Meaning and Justification of Informed Consent," Beauchamp and Childress[3] strip away the polarizing rigidity of the legal-versus-ethical terminology and provide the functional essence of the concept underlying informed consent. These authors, speak of the "two senses" of informed consent. The first sense is that of an "autonomous authorization." In this sense, an informed consent can be viewed to have occurred if the patient has a substantial understanding of what is to be done and, in the absence of control by others, intentionally authorizes the practitioner to carry out a procedure.

The second sense of informed consent considers "the social rules of informed consent." In this sense, the authorization must take place in a context that conforms to the institutional rules of consent—these rules having been adopted in conformance with local legal requirements. Hence, an authorization is effective if it is obtained through procedures that conform with the rules of institutional practice. These two senses of informed consent stress authorization (i.e., an individual's autonomous authorization carried out in a manner that reflects the local rules of governance). Such authorization is valid if it is given by a patient who is competent to make such authorization and who does so with a sufficient understanding of the implications of the procedure proposed. When all these factors are in place, we have the functional construct of valid informed consent. Let us now look at the total construct.

ELEMENTS OF INFORMED CONSENT

In defining five elements, or components, of the informed consent process, Beauchamp and Childress provide a clear and utilitarian guideline (Table A-1). The five components are broken down into three elements: a threshold element, information elements, and consent elements.

The threshold element consists of one component—establishment of the patient's competence to make a decision. Beauchamp and Childress describe the essential meaning of competence as "the ability to perform a task." The authors point out that to exercise autonomy or self-governance (a precept central to the modern-

Table A-1. Elements of Informed Consent

Threshold element
    Competence
Information elements
    Disclosure of information
    Understanding of information
Consent elements
    Voluntariness
    Authorization

(From Beauchamp and Childress,[3] with permission.)

day concept of exercising informed consent), one must first establish the individual's competence to make that autonomous decision.

The authors emphasize that the context in which the competence is assessed is circumstantial and continuous. They note that a knowledgeable, calm individual is in a much better position to make a decision than a stressed, fearful person. Responsible physicians will recall their own discomforture at having patients make treatment decisions in the emotionally laden context of an office visit during which they have just been told they have a condition that might require surgical intervention. Not infrequently it is better to have the patient return, perhaps with a supportive loved one, to discuss options at a later date. In any event, it is incumbent on the physician to make an assessment of the patient's competence for decision making and, in doing so, the physician must make a judgment regarding the patient's experience, maturity, responsibility, state of welfare, and state of mind.

Once having established the patient's competence for decision making, the process can then proceed to a consideration of information transfer. Information must be conveyed in a manner that the patient will understand. Beauchamp and Childress stress that the key to information transfer is that a dialogue, not a monologue, take place, and hence, the emphasis is less one of disclosure than of "discovering what information is relevant and how to frame and use it." Nonetheless, the issue of what is to be disclosed is extremely important and accordingly, certain standards of disclosure have arisen. As noted above, these standards are generally categorized into those of professional practice standards; reasonable persons standards; and subjective standards. The time-honored professional practice standard holds that disclosure is adequate when the patient is apprised of what is the traditional or common practice within a medical community. The obvious limitation of such a standard is that the common practice in a locale may, in fact, be substandard in the broader medical community. However, it stands to reason that, at the very least, patients must be apprised of what is/are the accepted practice(s) for the condition present.

More and more, states have adopted the reasonable persons standard as the foundation for appropriate disclosure. By this standard, jurisdictions have decreed that a patient needs such information that a reasonable person in the patient's circumstances would find relevant and be able to assimilate to make an appropriate treatment decision.

The authors are quick to point out the difficulties

with such a concept. Who is the hypothetical reasonable person? In such a hypothetical situation, it is difficult for physicians to project just what a reasonable patient would need to know. Beauchamp and Childress also point out that there are investigational studies that indicate that, whereas patients surveyed believe they benefit from information disclosed, the fact is that relatively few patients actually use the information in coming to their decision. Nonetheless, all would agree that patients do need an information basis on which to make their decision and, in fact, that information basis should suit their particular situation, hence the subjective standard. In this concept, the information that a reasonable person would need to arrive at a decision must be tailored to the individual patient and the patient's circumstances (i.e., made subjective).

Having provided a framework in which information is disclosed, we must now define the criteria by which the patient can be determined to comprehend. Beauchamp and Childress state that "one understands if one has justified beliefs about the nature and consequences of one's actions." The authors observe that the information need not be full or complete because a substantial grasp of central facts may be sufficient. They note that some facts are vital, some are irrelevant. They point out that the test is not that the patient need be fully informed but that the patient be adequately informed. In summing up their discussion of information exchange, the authors cite some of the problems that compromise information processing: information overload; limited time to inform/understand; selective perception on the part of the patient; inappropriate processing of risk (perhaps inappropriately influenced by how information is presented). The authors also stress the milieu in which information processing takes place. As noted above, time, place and circumstance are extraordinarily important to rational decision making, and on balance, decisions should not be rushed. Other difficulties in the process of information transfer are those of nonacceptance by the patient in which the patient may hold some firm false beliefs and situations in which the patient may attempt to waive informed consent, in essence delegating the decision-making authority to the physician or requesting not to be informed. The authors suggest that in situations in which the patient appears to want to waive consent, a third neutral party, such as a hospital ethics committee, could play a useful role.

The final component of the informed consent process consists of the consent elements. The authors note that consent must be given in a climate of voluntariness. The authors define voluntariness as a situation in which a person wills an action without being under the control of another agent's influence. Beauchamp and Childress describe three types of influence: coercion, manipulation, and persuasion. In coercion, one uses credible and severe threats of harm or force to control another individual. Through persuasion, an individual is convinced to believe in something through the merit of reasons advanced by another. In this construct, manipulation is viewed as a middle ground (i.e., the process of getting people to do what one wants by means other than coercion or persuasion). Devices used might be lying, withholding information, true assertions omitting vital qualifications, misleading exaggerations to cause a person to believe what is false. Although the authors note that manipulation and coercion may infrequently be justified, they state that the primary challenge to the professional is "to restrict influence attempts to explanation and persuasion, in order to secure a non-manipulated consent from the patient." It is in this environment of disclosure that the patient will be best able to respond.

INFORMED CONSENT AND OPERATIVE ENDOSCOPY

Many situations in medicine require that the process of informed consent be undertaken. Among them are

when a procedure is proposed, the purpose of the procedure needs to be known
when the procedure is invasive or intrusive
when there are risks to the procedure
when there are alternatives to the procedure

Procedures of operative endoscopy qualify under all counts. Hence, there needs to be a thorough discussion in each of these areas.

In describing the purpose of the procedure, practitioners will review the process by which they came to their proposal or proposals. They must state the objectives. These are diagnostic, therapeutic, or both. Physicians must be very clear about the limits of the procedure so that undue expectations are not raised. Endoscopic procedures usually require some form of anesthesia or sedation. By their very nature, these procedures involve instrumentation of a body cavity. Hence, they are invasive or intrusive, and these aspects of the procedure must be made thoroughly known to the patient.

Discussion of risks and alternatives is especially relevant when operative endoscopy is being considered. The risks of anesthesia or sedation must be reviewed. The possible complications attendant on probing a body cavity or part—infection, bleeding, perforation—must be made known, as well as the complications attendant to using insufflation agents, be they gas or liquid. The possibility that a complication might be incurred or that lack of ability to accomplish the mission by endoscopic means may require that a "bigger" operation be necessitated at this sitting, or later, must be made known.

Whereas complications can occur with any level experience of the operator, it is well known that there is a broad spectrum of capability even among the most competent practitioners. The patient has the right and need to know the depth of the physician's skill and experience. Whereas there has been a virtual explosion of endoscopic techniques and technology in the past 30 years and most obstetricians/gynecologists have had the opportunity to become trained and proficient in the basics of endoscopic armamentarium and application, most practitioners have not had the time, opportunity, and inclination to become proficient in all endoscopic procedures.

Indeed, the very breadth of diagnostic and therapeutic possibilities with the endoscope suggest that some of these applications should realistically be considered in the investigative developmental stage even in the most capable hands. The combination of this circumstance and the fact that many endoscopic applications have proven alternatives mandate that these alternatives be adequately discussed with the patient before a final choice of approach is made. The operative experience of the surgeon is extraordinarily important, and in any one operator's hands, a more "conventional" approach may be the more prudent. "Tried and proven" modalities may be the procedure of choice, even when considerations of cost/benefit and patient convenience are taken into account. For the ultimate comfort of both practitioner and patient, a thorough and honest discussion of alternative approaches must take place. When the technique, purpose, risks/benefits, and alternatives have been thoroughly and relevantly reviewed, a process of collaborative decision making is significantly enhanced.

Although the essential process of informed consent is the verbal dialogue(s) that takes place between the physician and patient, there must, in addition, be written documentation, at least in summary form, of the key points of this dialogue. The documentation will consist of an established consent form and should be supplemented by a narrative elsewhere in the patient record. There are several requisite elements of the consent form. The form will contain the name(s) of the physician(s) who will perform the operation, as well as the name of the patient on whom the procedure will be performed.

The name of the specific procedure must be detailed with complex medical terminology supplemented by conventionally understood terms. Significant possible preoperative, intraoperative, and postoperative complications should be listed, particularly those that might require additional interventions. If not contained elsewhere in the record, a consent to administration of anesthestics should be included on the form. Any anesthetic or operative exclusions arrived at during the physician/patient dialogue should be specified on the form. Finally, there should be a summary statement that the nature of the patient's condition, the type and purpose of the procedure, possible alternative methods of treatments, potential risks, and possible consequences and complications have been explained to the patient and by whom explained. It is probably also wise to include a statement that medicine is not an exact science and that no guarantees have been made by anyone concerning the results of the proposed procedure. Such a form and any accompanying narrative simply document that a complete and meaningful collaborative decision-making process has taken place between patient and physician—and does not replace that process.

SUMMARY

Although there is a legal framework underlying the process of informed consent, the meaningful substance of the process is an ethical imperative. The imperative is for a decision-making process engaged in by patient and physician—a process that assumes a patient competent to arrive at a decision for self, in a voluntary manner, based on information supplied by the physician and clarified by a verbal interaction to enhance understanding. When applied in the context of a proposed procedure to be performed in an institutional environment, there is formal documentation of the process, which ensures that the legal imperative of the local jurisdiction, relevant to informed consent, has been followed.

It was in ancient times that certain medical sages established the mandate that, as a basic precept of medicine, physicians must act out of concern for the patient's welfare. In the early age of beneficience, it was the physician who determined what was good for the patient, and not infrequently the physician acted without the patient's acquiescence or awareness. In the United States, the early 1900s saw the dawning of the concept of self-determination. However, it was not until the post-World War II era, catalyzed by the rights movement born of the 1960s and advanced during the 1970s and 1980s, that the concept of informed consent as a process of shared decision making evolved into its present-day form. Among the benefits of this patient-physician collaboration are the consequent building of mutual trust and respect and ensuring of self-determination and patient autonomy.

The circumstances of operative endoscopy virtually epitomize situations in which the process of informed consent must be engaged. Because the procedure will involve invasion of a body cavity and, hence, an intrusion into the patient's physical being, she must be made fully aware of just what is going to be done. Because the purpose for using operative endoscopy may be diagnostic, therapeutic, or both, the patient must be fully cognizant of the objectives so that inappropriate or unrealistic expectations are not engendered. Because there are recognized complications to be incurred with a certain frequency, the patient must be so informed to weigh the risks and benefits. Because there are not infrequently acceptable alternatives to endoscopic application, the patient must be made aware of these so that she can exercise choice and arrive at a plan of action most advantageous to her. Operative endoscopy is a marvelous and still-evolving technology that has significantly advanced the two principal goals of modern-day medical therapeutics: improved patient outcomes and cost-effectiveness. A patient who has the opportunity to elect such technology after a process of informed choice has been availed of the best that contemporary medicine has to offer.

REFERENCES

1. The President's Commission for the Study of Ethical Problems in Medicine and Biomedical Research: Making Health Care Decisions: The Ethical and Legal Implications of Informed Consent in the Patient-Practitioner Relationship. Vol. 1. (Stock No. 040-000-00468-8.) U.S. Government Printing Office, Washington, DC, 1982
2. Grodin MA: The Evolution of Informed Consent: Beyond an Ethics of Care. Women's Health Issues 3:11, 1993
3. Beauchamp TL, Childress JF: Principles of Biomedical Ethics, 3rd Ed. Oxford University Press, Oxford, 1989
4. American College of Obstetricians and Gynecologists: Ethical Dimension of Informed Consent. ACOG Committee Opinion 1008. ACOG, Washington, DC, 1992
5. Annas G, Elias S: Confusion law and ethics: why the committee report and informed consent should be reconsidered. Women's Health Issues 3:25, 1993
6. Heland K: Ethics versus law: a lawyer's roadmap to the ethics committee opinion on informed consent. Women's Health Issues 3:22, 1993

Index

Page numbers followed by f indicate figures; those followed by t indicate tables.